The ABOMINABLE

The

ABOMINABLE

A Novel

DAN SIMMONS

LITTLE, BROWN AND COMPANY

NEW YORK BOSTON LONDON

Little, Brown and Company
Hachette Book Group
237 Park Avenue, New York, NY 10017
littlebrown.com

First Edition: October 2013

Little, Brown and Company is a division of Hachette Book Group, Inc. The Little, Brown name and logo are trademarks of Hachette Book Group, Inc.

The publisher is not responsible for websites (or their content) that are not owned by the publisher.

The Hachette Speakers Bureau provides a wide range of authors for speaking events. To find out more, go to hachettespeakersbureau.com or call (866) 376-6591.

Library of Congress Cataloging-in-Publication Data
Simmons, Dan, 1948-
  The abominable : a novel / Dan Simmons.
    pages cm
  ISBN 978-0-316-19883-7 (hc) / 978-0-316-23991-2 (large print)
1. Racers (Persons)—Fiction. 2. Everest, Mount (China and Nepal)—Fiction. I. Title.
PS3569.I47292A26 2013
  813'.54—dc23   2013017754

10 9 8 7 6 5 4 3 2 1

RRD-C

Book design by Sean Ford
Printed in the United States of America

This book is dedicated, with respect,
to the memory of
Jacob "Jake" William Perry
April 2, 1902 — May 28, 1992

Great things are done when men and mountains meet.
— William Blake

INTRODUCTION

I met Jake Perry in the summer of 1991.

I'd had a longtime interest—in Antarctic exploration and explorers—actually since the International Geophysical Year in 1957–58, when the U.S. established permanent bases down there, which really grabbed my 10-year-old's imagination—and around 1990 I had a vague hunch that there might be an idea for a novel set in Antarctica. It was to be another fifteen years before I actually wrote and published a book about a doomed Arctic (not Antarctic) expedition—my 2007 novel *The Terror*—but in the summer of 1991 it was that time again when I had to suggest a package of three new books to my publisher. My interest was in Antarctica, not the North Polar expeditions, which never interested me very much (but which I eventually ended up writing about), and that interest was fueled by many more years of reading about the adventures of Ernest Shackleton, Robert Falcon Scott, Apsley Cherry-Garrard, and other heroes and martyrs of the Antarctic.

Then, during that summer of 1991, a friend of my wife's said that she knew an actual Antarctic explorer. This old guy—who had moved into an assisted living home for the elderly in the little town of Delta on the Western Slope of Colorado—had actually been with Rear Admiral Richard Byrd during American expeditions to Antarctica in the 1930s.

At least Karen said that this is what Mary had told her. Personally, I suspected Alzheimer's, lying, an inveterate teller of tall tales, or all three.

But according to Mary, this eighty-nine-year-old gentleman named Jacob Perry had been on the 1934 U.S. Antarctic expedition. That was the clusterboink expedition in which Admiral Byrd, always eager for a bit more solo fame, had spent five winter months alone in a hole in the ice at an advanced meteorological station where he almost died from carbon monoxide poisoning due to a poorly ventilated stove. (Byrd was to write his best-selling book about this experience, a book titled, obviously enough, *Alone.*)

According to what Mary said to my wife, Karen, this elderly Jacob Perry had been one of four men who'd crossed a hundred miles of Antarctica in the total darkness and howling storms of the 1934 South Polar winter to rescue Admiral Byrd. Then the whole group had to wait until October and the advent of the Antarctic summer to be rescued themselves. "It sounds like he'd be perfect to give you information about the South Pole," said Karen. "You might write the whole book about this Mr. Perry. Maybe he's the Admiral Perry who also was the first to reach the *North Pole*!"

"Perry," I said. "Perry of the Antarctic. But he's not the Rear Admiral Robert Peary who claimed to be the first man to reach the North Pole in nineteen oh-nine."

"Why not?" said Karen. "It could be."

"Well, first of all, there's the difference in spelling of their names," I said, mildly irritated at being poked into action, or perhaps irritated in the way I always am when someone else, anyone else, suggests what I should be writing about. I spelled the difference between "Admiral Peary" and Mary's little old man in Delta, Mr. "Perry."

"Also," I said, "Rear Admiral Peary would be about a hundred and thirty–some years old now..."

"All right, all right," said Karen, holding up her hands in a signal we've worked out over decades of marriage—a signal that theoretically keeps either party from going for the jugular. "I stand corrected. But this Mr. Perry might still have a wonderful story to tell and..."

"Also," I interrupted, being somewhat of a jerk, "Admiral Robert Peary died in nineteen twenty."

"Well, this Jacob *Perry* is still alive in Delta," said Karen. "Barely."

"Barely? You mean because of his age?" To me, anyone who's eighty-nine or ninety falls into the category of "barely alive." Hell, to me in 1991, anyone over *sixty* was circling the drain. (In the interests of full disclosure, I admit that I'm now sixty-three years old as I write this preface in 2011.)

"No, not just his age," said Karen. "In the e-mail, Mary also mentioned that he has cancer. He still gets around evidently, but..."

I'd been at my computer, just fiddling around with ideas for books—typing in possible titles—when Karen had come in. Now I turned the computer off.

"Mary really says he was with Byrd in Antarctica in 'thirty-four?" I said.

"Yeah, *really*," said Karen. "I knew you'd be interested in him." Somehow my wife manages not to sound smug even when she's correct. "It'd be good for you to get out of the office for a few days. That'd be a five- or six-hour ride, even staying on the interstate all the way to Grand Junction. You can stay overnight with Guy and Mary in Delta."

I shook my head. "I'll take the Miata. And get off I-seventy to go through Carbondale and then up and over McClure Pass."

"Can the Miata get over McClure Pass?"

"You just watch it," I said. I was thinking of what clothes I'd throw in my duffel for the two-day trip, assuming I'd talk to Mr. Perry the morning of the second day and then head home. I had a little North Face soft duffel that fit perfectly in the Miata's tiny trunk. I made a mental note to bring my Nikon camera. (These were pre-digital days for me, at least when it came to photography.)

And so, because of my urge to drive my new 1991 Mazda Miata in the mountains, I met Mr. Jacob Perry.

Delta, Colorado, was a town of about six thousand people. Coming at it the way I did—turning south off I-70 from Glenwood Springs, then turning onto Highway 65 at Carbondale, following that narrow two-lane road over the high passes and past the remote outposts of Marble and Paonia—one gets a sense of how surrounded by mountains the little town really is. Delta is in a wide river basin south of the Grand Mesa, which locals describe as "one of the largest flat-top mountains in the world."

The place where Jake Perry lived in Delta certainly didn't *look* like an old folks' home, much less one where nursing help was available twenty-four hours a day. With the assistance of several federal grants, Mary had renovated a once grand but now run-down hotel and merged it with an empty store next door. The result was a space that felt more like a four-star hotel from, say, 1900 than an assisted living facility.

I found that Jacob Perry had his own room on the third floor. (Part of Mary's renovation was putting in elevators.) After Mary's introductions and explanations again of why I wanted to talk to him—Dan was a novelist doing research on a possible book set at the South Pole and he'd heard of Jake, she said—Mr. Perry invited me in.

The room and the man seemed to complement each other. I was surprised how large Perry's room was—a double bed, neatly made, near one of three windows that looked out and over the roofs of the lower downtown stores toward the mountains and Grand Mesa to the north. Floor-to-ceiling bookcases filled with hardcover books—many of them, I noticed, about mountain ranges around the world—and mementos: coils of old-style climbing rope, Crooke's glass goggles such as Arctic explorers used to wear, a worn leather motorcycle helmet, an ancient Kodak camera, an old ice axe with a wooden staff much longer than modern ice axes would have.

As for Jacob Perry—I couldn't believe the man was eighty-nine years old.

Age and gravity had taken their toll: some curvature and compression of the spine over nine decades had robbed the man of an inch or two of height, but he was still over 6 feet tall; he was wearing a short-sleeved denim shirt, and I could see where his biceps had withered some with age, but his muscles were still sculpted, his forearms especially formidable; the upper part of his body was, even after time's robberies, triangular with power and shaped from a lifetime of exertion.

It was several minutes before I noticed that two fingers of his left hand, the smallest finger and the one next to it, were missing. It seemed to be an old wound—the flesh over the stubs of bone just above the knuckles was brown and as weathered as the rest of the skin on his hands and forearms. And the missing fingers didn't seem to bother his dexterity. Later, while we were talking, Mr. Perry fiddled with two thin pieces of leather shoestring, each about eighteen inches long, and I was amazed to see that he could tie complicated knots, one with each hand, using both hands to tie the knots at the same time. The knots must have been nautical or technical climbing knots, because I couldn't have tied any of them using both of my hands and the assistance of a Boy Scout troop. Mr. Perry, without looking, idly tied such knots, each hand working individually, and then absentmindedly untied them, with only the two fingers and thumb of his left hand. It seemed to be an old habit—perhaps one to calm him—and he paid little attention to either the finished knots or the process.

When we shook hands I felt my fingers disappear in his larger and still more powerful grip. But he was making no small-town-bully effort to squeeze; the strength was simply still there. Mr. Perry's face showed too many years in the sunlight—in high-altitude and thin-air sunlight, where UV had had its way with his epidermal cells—and between the permanent brown patches there were scars where he'd had small surgeries for possible melanomas.

The old man still had hair and kept it cut quite short. I could see browned scalp through the thinning gray. When he smiled, he showed his own teeth save perhaps for two or three missing on the lower sides and back.

It was Mr. Perry's blue eyes which I've remembered the most clearly. They were startlingly blue and, it seemed to me, ageless. These were not the rheumy, distracted eyes of a man in his late eighties. Perry's bright blue gaze was curious, attentive, bold, almost...childlike. When I work with beginning writers of any age, I warn them against describing their characters by comparing them with movie stars or famous people; it's lazy, it's time-bound, and it's a cliché. Still, fifteen years later my wife Karen and I were watching the movie *Casino Royale,* the first of the new James Bond films with Daniel Craig as James Bond, and I whispered excitedly, "There! Those are the kind of bluer-than-blue blue eyes that Mr. Perry had. In fact, Daniel Craig looks a lot like a young version of my late Mr. Perry."

Karen looked at me a moment in the darkened theater and then said, "Shush."

Back in 1991 at the assisted living home in Delta and somewhat at a loss for words, I'd spent a few minutes admiring the handful of artifacts on Perry's shelves and desk top—the tall, wooden-staffed ice axe propped in a corner, some examples of stone which he later told me were taken from the summits of various peaks, and black-and-white photographs gone sepia with age. The small camera on the shelf—a Kodak of the kind one unfolded before snapping a picture—was ancient but unrusted, and it looked well maintained.

"It has film in it from . . . quite a few years ago," said Mr. Perry. "Never developed."

I touched the small camera and turned toward the older man. "Aren't you curious to see how your snaps turned out?"

Mr. Perry shook his head. "I didn't take the pictures. In fact, the camera's not mine. But the druggist here in Delta told me that the film would probably still develop. Someday I'll see if the pictures turned out." He waved me to a chair next to the built-in desk. Scattered around the desk I could see careful drawings of plants, rocks, trees.

"It's been a long, long time since I've been interviewed," said Mr. Perry with what might have been an ironic smile. "And even then, many decades ago, I had almost nothing to say to the press."

I assumed that he was talking about the 1934 Byrd Expedition. I was stupidly wrong on that and also too stupid to clarify it at the time. My life, and this book, would have been quite different if I'd had even the most basic journalist's instinct to follow up on such an answer.

Instead, I brought the conversation back to myself and said modestly (for an egoist), "I've rarely interviewed anyone. Most of the research I do for my books is in libraries, including research libraries. Do you mind if I take notes?"

"Not at all," said Mr. Perry. "So it's just my time with Byrd's 'thirty-three to 'thirty-five Antarctic expeditions that you're interested in?"

"I think so," I said. "You see, I have a kernel of an idea of writing a suspense thriller set in Antarctica. Anything you tell me about South Polar expeditions would be helpful. Especially if it's scary."

"Scary?" Perry smiled again. "A thriller? Would there be some evil entity other than the cold and dark and isolation trying to do in your characters?"

I returned his smile but realized I was a little embarrassed. Book plots often sound silly when removed from their wordy context. Let's face it; sometimes they're silly *in* context. And, indeed, I *had* been thinking of some giant scary thing to chase and kill and eat my characters. I just had no idea at the time what it might be.

"Sort of," I admitted. "Something really big and threatening trying to get at our heroes—something out in the dark and cold. Something clawing to get in their Antarctic hut or frozen-in ship or whatever. Something not human and very hungry."

"A killer penguin?" suggested Mr. Perry.

I managed to laugh with him even though my wife, agent, and editor had asked the same thing each and every time I'd suggested an Antarctic thriller—*So, what, Dan? Is this monster of yours going to be some sort of giant mutant killer penguin?* Wry minds work alike. (And I've never admitted until now that I *had* considered a giant mutant killer penguin as my Antarctic threat.)

"Actually," said Perry, probably seeing my blush, "penguins can kill just from the guano stench of their rookeries."

"So you've actually visited some rookeries?" I asked, pen poised over the skinny notebook I used for my research notes. I felt like Jimmy Olsen.

Mr. Perry nodded and smiled again, but this time that bright blue gaze seemed to be turned inward to some memory. "I spent my third and last winter and spring there at the Cape Royds hut...supposedly to be studying the nearby rookery and penguin behavior there."

"Cape Royds hut...," I said, amazed. "Shackleton's hut?"

"Yes."

"I thought that Ernest Shackleton's hut was a museum—closed to all visitors," I said. My voice was tentative. I'd been too surprised to write anything down.

"It is...," said Mr. Perry. *"Now."*

I felt like an idiot and hid my new blush by bending my head to write.

Jacob Perry spoke quickly, as if to relieve me of any embarrassment I might be feeling. "Shackleton was such a national hero to the Brits that the hut was already a museum of sorts when Admiral Byrd sent me there to observe the rookeries in the Antarctic winter of nineteen thirty-five. The British used the hut from time to time, occasionally sending ornithologists there to observe the rookery, and there were provisions stored there all the time so that Americans from the nearby base or others in trouble could use the hut in an emergency. But at the time I was ordered there, no one had wintered over in the hut for many years."

"I'm surprised that the British granted permission for an American to spend months in Shackleton's hut," I said.

Mr. Perry grinned. "They didn't. They almost certainly wouldn't have. Admiral Byrd never asked permission of the Brits. He just sent me there with seven months of my own supplies on two sledges—the guys took the sledges and their dogs back to Byrd's base the day after they dropped me off—oh, and a crowbar to pry the door and shuttered windows open. I could really have used some of those dogs as company that winter. Truth was, the admiral didn't want me in his sight. So Byrd sent me as far away as he could where I might still have a chance of surviving the winter. The admiral liked to play at doing science, but in truth he didn't give a single penguin turd about observing or studying penguins."

I wrote all this down, not really understanding it but sensing that this might be important for some reason. I had no idea how I could use Shackleton's hut in my vaguely conceived suspense novel with no title.

"Shackleton and his men built the hut in nineteen oh-six," continued Mr. Perry. His voice was soft and slightly husky, the rasp due—I learned from him later in the conversation—to the loss of part of his left lung in surgery the previous winter. But even with the rasp his voice was still a pleasant tenor. Before the surgery, I guessed, Mr. Perry would have had an almost perfect voice for storytelling.

"Shackleton's people abandoned it in nineteen oh-eight...there was still the hulk of a motorcar they'd left behind when I got there," he was saying. "It's probably still there, the way things rust and decay so slowly down there. I doubt if the darned thing ever traveled ten feet in the deep snow Shackleton kept encountering, but the Brits did like their gadgets. So did Admiral Byrd, for that matter. Anyway, I was dropped off at the old hut early in the Antarctic autumn. That was March of nineteen thirty-five. I was picked up at the beginning of the Antarctic spring—early October—of the same year. My job was to report on the Adélie penguins in the large rookery at Cape Royds."

"But that's the Antarctic winter," I said, pausing, sure that I was going to say something unutterably stupid. "I thought that the Adélie penguins didn't...I mean, you know...didn't winter over. I thought that they arrived sometime in October and left with their chicks—those little ones that survived—in early March. Am I wrong? I must be wrong."

Jacob Perry was smiling again. "You're exactly right, Mr. Simmons. I was dropped off there just in time to see the last two or three penguins waddle and then paddle out to sea—the water was just preparing to freeze over again there at Cape Royds in early March, so that open water would soon be dozens of miles from the hut—and I was picked up in spring, October, before any of the Adélie penguins returned again to mate and raise their young there at the rookery. I didn't get to see any penguin action."

I shook my head. "I don't get it. You were ordered there for...my God, more than seven months, almost eight months...to observe the rookeries on the Cape when there were no penguins. And no sunlight much of the time. Are you a biologist or some sort of scientist, Mr. Perry?"

"Nope," said Mr. Perry with that lopsided smile again. "I'd been an English major at Harvard—eighteenth- and nineteenth-century American literature with a lot of English Lit thrown in. Henry James was hot stuff when I graduated in nineteen twenty-three. James Joyce had published *Ulysses* just the year before—'twenty-two—and his *Portrait of the Artist as a Young Man* six years earlier. Already in Europe for a year of skiing and mountain scrambling—I had a small inheritance that came due when I turned twenty-one—in nineteen twenty-four I read a story in Ford Madox Ford's *transatlantic review* and decided I immediately had to leave Switzerland and travel to Paris to meet the young man named Hemingway who'd written such a story and show him some of my own writing."

"Did you?" I asked.

"Yep," said Mr. Perry, smiling. "Hemingway was working from time to time as the French-based European correspondent for the *Toronto Star* then and he had this neat trick to get rid of pains in the ass like me. I met him in his office—a grubby little place—and he immediately asked me downstairs to a café for some coffee. Then after a few minutes, with me and so many others, he'd glance at his watch, say he had to get back to work, and leave the would-be writer sitting there alone in the café."

"Did you show him your stories?"

"Sure. He glanced at the first pages of three of them and said that I should stick with my day job. But that's all a different story, isn't it? We old men tend to maunder and meander."

"It's interesting" was all I murmured, but I was thinking—*Jesus, to meet Ernest Hemingway and be told by him that you weren't a writer. What would that feel like? Or is Perry just bullshitting me?*

"So to return to what you're interested in, Mr. Simmons—Antarctica in 'thirty-three to 'thirty-five—I was hired by Admiral Byrd as a roustabout and because I had experience as a mountain climber. You see, the scientists in the group had plans to do some research on various peaks during that expedition. I didn't know a damned thing about science or about penguins then and not much more now, despite all the nature documentary channels our cable TV gets here at the home. But it didn't really matter in nineteen thirty-five because the point was to get me out of Admiral Byrd's sight until the Antarctic spring, when we'd all be leaving the continent."

"So you were alone there in the dark and cold for seven months," I said stupidly. "What did you do that made him dislike you so much?"

Mr. Perry was cutting an apple with a short but very sharp folding knife, and now he offered me a slice. I took it.

"I rescued him," he said softly, speaking around his own chunk of apple.

"Yeah, Mary said that you were part of the small group that rescued Admiral Byrd from his solo Advance Base in nineteen thirty-four," I said.

"Correct," said Mr. Perry.

"So because he was embarrassed having one of his rescuers around, he exiled you to Shackleton's hut on Cape Royds to experience the same solitude he had?" It made no sense to me.

"Something like that," said Perry. "Except that I didn't poison myself with carbon monoxide like the admiral did...or require rescue the way he did. And he had a radio to contact with our base, Little America, every day. I didn't have a radio. Or any contact with the base."

"When you were part of the group that rescued Byrd that previous August," I said, looking at the notes I'd taken from talking to Mary and looking things up in reference books (1991 being pre-Google), "you and three others drove a hundred miles through the South Polar winter—with the few warning flags for the maze of crevasses blown away or covered by snow—a hundred miles in near-absolute darkness on a snow tractor that wasn't much more than a Model T with a metal roof. Just you and three others from the Little America Base."

Mr. Perry nodded. "Dr. Poulter and Mr. Waite and my direct boss in charge of the snow tractors, E. J. Demas. It was Demas who insisted that I come along to drive the tractor."

"That was your job in the expedition? Thanks." Perry had given me another delicious slice of apple.

"As roustabout, I did a lot of work on those damned tractors and ended up driving them in the summer for the various scientists who had to do things away from Little America," said the older man. "I guess Mr. Demas thought I had the best chance of keeping us all out of a crevasse, even in the dark. We had to turn back once after we learned that most of the crevasse warning flags were gone, but tried again right away—even though the weather had grown worse."

"It still sounds as if Admiral Byrd was punishing you," I said, the taste of apple clean and fresh in my mouth. "Sending you into solitary confinement for seven months."

Jake Perry shrugged. "The admiral's 'rescue'—he hated anyone using that word to describe it—embarrassed him. He couldn't do anything about Dr. Poulter or Mr. Waite—they were bigwigs in the expedition—but he assigned Demas to jobs where he, Admiral Byrd, would rarely see him. And he sent me out on the summer's expeditions and then assigned me to Cape Royds for the entire Antarctic winter. In the end, Admiral Byrd didn't even mention me in the report about his . . . rescue. My name's not in most of the history books about Antarctica."

I was astounded at the meanness and pettiness of such an action on Admiral Byrd's part. "Being sent to spend the winter alone at Cape Royds was the equivalent of you being put in solitary confinement," I said, letting my anger come through in my tone. "And no radio? Admiral Byrd went nuts after three months of being alone—and he had daily radio contact with Little America."

Mr. Perry grinned. "No radio."

I tried to understand this but could not. "Was there any purpose—any reason at all—for you to spend seven months of isolation and five months of absolute darkness in Shackleton's hut on Cape Royds?"

Mr. Perry shook his head, but neither his expression nor his voice showed any anger or resentment. "As I said, I was hired on the expedition to climb mountains. After we'd rescued Byrd—which required the four of us staying with him in that little underground cell he'd created at Advance Base from August eleven, when we arrived, to October twelve, when Byrd and Dr. Poulter were flown out in the *Pilgrim*—I finally did get to go on some summer expeditions where I could help the scientists with my climbing skills."

"The *Pilgrim* was a plane?" I said.

Mr. Perry had every right to say something like *What else could it be if they* flew *out in it? An oversized albatross?* but he only nodded politely and said, "They started the expedition there with three planes—the big Fokker..." He paused and smiled. "That's 'Fokker,' Mr. Simmons. F-o-k..." He spelled it for me.

I grinned. "Got it. But call me Dan."

"If you'll call me Jake," he said.

I was surprised that I couldn't—easily call him Jake, that is. I'm rarely impressed when I find myself with people known for their fame or title or supposed authority, but I found that I was *deeply* impressed in the presence of Mr. Jacob Perry. To me, even after I'd managed to say "Jake" a few times, he stayed "Mr. Perry" in my mind.

"Anyway," he continued, "they had the big Fokker, named *Blue Blade*...but it crashed the first time they tried to get it off the ground—or ice, really—after we arrived in Antarctica. And they had an even bigger seaplane, named the *William Horlick,* but it always seemed down for maintenance. So the little monoplane, *Pilgrim,* was sent to fetch Admiral Byrd and Dr. Poulter as soon as the weather stabilized in October after we'd reached him and fixed the ventilation in his little subterranean hidey-hole in the ice. I remember that during the weeks we were waiting, Dr. Poulter did a lot of the star sightings, meteor watching, and barometric work that Byrd was too ill and befuddled to carry out. The carbon monoxide buildup hadn't exactly sharpened the admiral's brain cells. Then, after the *Pilgrim* flew Admiral Byrd and Dr.

Poulter out in August, Waite, Demas, and I took the tractor back to Little America...just in time for me to join some of the expeditions heading out to the Haines Mountains."

"Had you joined the expedition in order to climb mountains in Antarctica?" Mary had knocked and come in with lemonade for both of us, but it was a brief interruption. And the lemonade was homemade and excellent.

Mr. Perry nodded. "That was my one real skill. My one real reason for being on that expedition. Climbing. Oh, I could handle motors and fiddle with equipment well enough...that's how I ended up working with the snow tractors for Demas during the winter, when there was no climbing...but I went to Antarctica for its mountains."

"Did you get to climb many?" I asked.

Perry grinned and again his blue gaze grew ruminative. "McKinley Peak that summer of 'thirty-four...not *the* Mount McKinley, of course, but the peak near the South Pole with the same name. Several of the unnamed peaks in the Haines range...the scientists were looking for moss and lichens there, and after I got them safely situated on their ledges, I'd just bag the summit before coming back down to help them with their equipment. I summited Mount Woodward in the Ford range during that summer of 'thirty-four, then Mount Rea, Mount Cooper, then Saunders Mountain. None of them very interesting from a technical perspective. Lots of snow and ice work. Lots of crevasses, ice cliffs, and avalanches. Jean-Claude would have enjoyed it."

"Who's Jean-Claude?" I asked. "Someone else on the Byrd Expedition?"

Mr. Perry's eyes had been at their most ruminative, but now they came back into focus and he looked at me and smiled. "No, no. Just a climber I knew a long time ago. Someone who loved any problem involving snow, ice, glaciers, or crevasses. Oh, I climbed Mount Erebus and Terror."

"Those last two are volcanoes," I said, trying to show that I wasn't totally ignorant of all things relating to the South Pole. "Named after British ships, weren't they?"

Mr. Perry nodded. "They were named in eighteen forty-one by James Clark Ross—he was credited for actually finding Antarctica, although they never really set foot on the continent—and the HMS *Erebus* was his flagship, while the HMS *Terror* was captained by Ross's second-in-command, a certain Francis Crozier."

I scribbled all this down, not knowing what use it might be for my possible book about giant mutant killer penguins attacking Shackleton's hut in Antarctica.

"Crozier was second-in-command a few years later on Sir John Franklin's expedition, where both *Erebus* and *Terror* were lost in the northern ice fields," Mr. Perry said almost absently, as if finishing a thought. "The British icebreaker ships, that is," he said with a smile. "Not the volcanoes. *They're* still there."

I looked up. "They sank? The two ships the volcanoes were named after, *Erebus* and *Terror*... they sank a few years later?"

"Worse than that, Dan. They totally *disappeared.* Sir John Franklin, Francis Moira Crozier, and a hundred and twenty-seven men. They were trying to force the Northwest Passage, and somewhere north of Canada the two ships and all the men just...disappeared. Some graves and a few bones of the men have been found here and there on empty islands up there, but there's been no sign of the ships or the majority of the crew's remains to this day."

I scribbled madly. I'd had no interest in writing about the North Pole and its expeditions, but more than a hundred men and two ships just...gone? I asked for this Captain Crozier's full name and the spelling of it and Mr. Perry gave it to me, spelling it out as patiently as if I were a child.

"Anyway," concluded Mr. Perry, "since Admiral Byrd wasn't all that happy seeing me around—I guess I reminded him of his near-criminal negligence for gassing himself up at his much-ballyhooed 'Advanced Base' and making other men risk their lives to save his behind—for my next and last winter there, instead of my wintering on the main base with the other men, Admiral Byrd ordered me to 'observe the penguins' while staying alone in Shackleton's hut on Cape Royds. March to October nineteen thirty-five."

"Observe the penguins that had already left," I said.

"Yes." Mr. Perry folded his arms as he chuckled, and again I could see how powerful his forearms still were. They also showed several livid scars. Old scars. "But in the autumn, before it got too ungodly cold, I could smell the overpowering guano stench of their rookeries every day. But one gets used to bad smells."

"It must have felt like real punishment," I said to him again, still feeling the horror of such isolation and moved to real anger at Admiral Byrd's pettiness. "Not the guano, I mean. The sense of solitary confinement."

Perry only smiled at me. "I loved it," he said. "Those winter months at Shackleton's hut were some of the most wonderful days I've ever spent. Dark and cold, yes...very cold at times, since the Cape Royds hut wasn't really designed to heat for just one person, and the wind found its way in through a thousand cracks and crevices every dark day there...but wonderful. I used canvas and Shackleton's old crates to create a little cubby near the door where I could stay a little warm, although some mornings the wolverine fur around the opening of my sleeping bag was almost covered with frost. But the experience itself...wonderful. Absolutely wonderful."

"Did you climb any mountains that winter?" I asked. I realized it was a stupid question as soon as I asked it. Who can climb mountains in the dark when it's sixty or seventy degrees below zero?

Amazingly, he nodded again. "Shackleton's men climbed Mount Erebus — at least to the rim of the volcano — in nineteen oh-eight," he said. "But I climbed it solo three times, by different routes. Once at night. Oh, and although they credit the first winter climb of Erebus to a British climber, Roger Mear, just six years ago in nineteen eighty-five, I climbed Erebus twice in the winter of 'thirty-five. I don't think that's in any record book. I guess I just never bothered to mention it to anyone who might have written it down."

He fell silent and I also stayed silent, wondering again if this nice old man was bullshitting me. Then he stood, lifted his old wooden-staff ice axe, and said, "Just a few months ago...this past January...an iron-worker at McMurdo Station, a guy named Charles Blackmer, did a solo ascent of Mount Erebus in seventeen hours. It was in various alpine journals because it set an official record. Beating the older recorded times by hours and hours."

"Did you pay attention to your time climbing the mountain fifty-six years earlier?" I asked.

Mr. Perry grinned. "Thirteen hours, ten minutes. But then, I'd done it before." He laughed and shook his head. "But this doesn't help you with your research, Dan. What do you want to hear about South Polar exploration?"

I sighed, realizing how unprepared I was as an interviewer. (And, in some ways, as a man.) "What can you tell me?" I said. "I mean something that I might not get from books."

Perry rubbed his chin. Some white bristles there scraped audibly. "Well," he said softly, "when you look at the stars near the horizon...especially when it's really cold...they tend to jitter around. Jumping left, then right...all while they jiggle up and down at the same time. I think it has something to do with masses of super-cold air lying over the land or frozen sea acting like a lens that's being moved..."

I was scribbling madly.

Mr. Perry chuckled. "Can this trivia possibly be of help in writing a novel?"

"You never know," I said, still writing.

As it turned out, the jiggling stars near the horizon appeared in a sentence that spanned the bottom of the first page and top of the second page of my novel *The Terror*, which came out sixteen years later and which was about Sir John Franklin's Northwest Passage debacle, not about Antarctica at all.

But Mr. Perry had died of his cancer long before *The Terror* was published.

I found out later that Mr. Perry had been on several famous climbing expeditions, and various Alaskan and South American expeditions, and to K2 as well as the three-year South Polar expedition with Admiral Byrd we discussed that summer day in 1991. Our "interview" — mostly wonderful conversation about travel, courage, friendship, life, death, and fate — lasted about four hours. And I never asked one right question the whole time: a question that could have told me about his amazing Himalayan experience in 1925.

I could tell that Mr. Perry was tiring by the end of our long talk. He was also speaking with more of a wheeze in his voice.

Noticing me noticing, he said, "They removed a chunk of one of my lungs last winter. Cancer. The other's probably packing up, too, but the can-cer's metastasizing elsewhere so probably the lung won't be what gets me."

"I'm sorry," I said, feeling the absolute inadequacy of the words.

Mr. Perry shrugged. "Hey, if I reach ninety, I'll have beaten a lot of odds, Dan. More than you know." He chuckled. "The pisser is that I have lung cancer but I never smoked. Never. Not once."

I didn't know what to say to that.

"The added irony is that I moved to Delta so that I would be just minutes away from the mountains," added Mr. Perry. "But now I end up wheezing and gasping if I climb a low hill. Just climbing a few hundred feet of pasture at the edge of town now reminds me of trying to climb and breathe above twenty-eight thousand feet."

I still didn't know what to say—the loss of a lung to cancer must be a terrible thing—and I was too dull-witted to ask him where and when he might have climbed above 28,000 feet. The region above 8,000 meters, around 25,000 feet, is called the Death Zone for good reason: every minute a climber is at such altitude, his body is becoming weaker, he is cough-ing, gasping, always short of breath; and the climber is unable to recharge energy even by sleeping (which is all but impossible at such altitude any-way). I later wondered if Mr. Perry was just using that altitude—28,000 feet—as an example of how hard it was for him to breathe now or if he'd actually ever ventured that high. I knew that Mount Vinson, the tallest mountain in Antarctica, was just a little over 16,000 feet high.

Before I got around to asking an intelligent question, Mr. Perry clapped my shoulder. "I'm not complaining. I just love irony. If there is a God of this poor, sad mess of a universe it's got to be Bitch Irony. Say . . . you're a published writer."

"Yes," I said. My voice may have sounded wary. The most common thing that published writers are approached for by new acquaintances is to be invited to help that would-be writer either (a) find an agent, (b) get published, or (c) both of the above.

"You have a literary agent and all that?" said Perry.

"Yes?" I was even more tentative now. After just four hours I admired the man greatly, but amateur writing is amateur writing. Almost impos-sible to get published.

"I've been thinking of writing something . . ."

There it was. In a way, I regretted hearing those familiar words. They were the punch line of too many conversations with new acquaintances. But I also felt a sense of relief. If he hadn't already written his book or whatever, what were the chances that he could do so now, almost ninety years old and dying of cancer?

Mr. Perry saw my face, read my thoughts, and laughed loudly. "Don't worry, Dan. I'm not going to ask you to get something of mine published. I'm not sure I'd want it published."

"What then?" I asked.

He rubbed his cheek and chin again. "I want to write something and I want someone to read it. Does that make sense?"

"I think so. It's why I write."

He shook his head, almost impatiently I thought. "No, you write for thousands or tens of thousands of people to read your thoughts. I'm hunting for just one reader. One person who might understand it. One person who might believe it."

"Family, maybe?" I suggested.

Again he shook his head. I sensed that it was hard for him to make this request.

"The only family I know about is a grandniece or great-grandniece or whatever the hell she is in Baltimore or somewhere," he said softly. "I've never met her. But Mary and the home here have her address written down somewhere...as a place to send my things when I check out. No, Dan, if I manage to write this thing, I want someone to read it who would understand it."

"Is it fiction?"

He grinned. "No, but I'm sure it'll read like fiction. Bad fiction, probably."

"Have you started writing it?"

He shook his head again. "No, I've been waiting all these decades...hell, I don't know *what* I've been waiting for. For Death to bang on my door, I guess, to give me some motivation. Well, he's banging."

"I'd be honored to read anything you'd choose to share with me, Mr. Perry," I said. I surprised myself with the emotion and sincerity of my offer. Usually I approached reading amateurs' efforts as if their manuscripts were coated with the plague bacillus. But I realized I'd be excited to read anything this man wanted to write, although I assumed at the time it would probably be about Byrd's South Polar expedition in the thirties.

Jacob Perry sat motionless and looked at me for a long moment. Those blue eyes seemed to touch me somehow—as though the eight blunt, scarred fingers of his were pressing hard against my forehead. It was not altogether a pleasant sensation. But it *was* intimate.

"All right," he said at last. "If I ever get the thing written, I'll send it your way."

I'd already given him my card with my address and other information on it.

"One problem, though," he said.

"What?"

He held up his two hands, so dexterous, even with the left hand missing most of the last two fingers. "I can't type worth a damn," he said.

I laughed. "If you were submitting a manuscript to a publisher," I said, "we'd find a typist who could type things up for you. Or I'd do it myself. But in the meantime..."

From my battered briefcase, I produced a Moleskine blank book journal—its 240 creamy blank pages never touched. The blank journal was wrapped in a soft leather "skin" that had a leather double loop to hold a pen or pencil. I'd already slipped a sharpened pencil into the loop.

Mr. Perry touched the leather. "This is too dear...," he began, moving to hand it back.

I loved hearing the archaic use of the word "dear," but I shook my head and pressed the leather-wrapped blank journal back into his hands.

"This is mere token payment for the hours you spent talking to me," I said. I'd wanted to add "Jake," but still couldn't manage calling him by his first name. "Seriously, I want you to have it. And when you write something you want to share with me, I look forward to reading it. And I promise you that I'll give you my honest assessment of it."

Still turning the leather journal over and over in his gnarled hands, Mr. Perry flashed a grin. "I'll probably be dead when you get the book...or books...Dan, so be as honest as you want in your critique. It won't hurt my feelings a bit."

I didn't know what to say to that.

* * *

I talked to Jacob Perry in July 1991, twenty years ago as I write this foreword to his manuscript in the late summer of 2011.

In late May 1992, Mary phoned to tell us that Mr. Perry had passed away in the Delta hospital. The cancer had won.

When I asked Mary if Mr. Perry had left anything for me, she seemed surprised. Everything he'd left behind—and it wasn't much, his books and artifacts—had been packed up and shipped to his grandniece in Baltimore. Mary hadn't been at the hospice at the time—she'd been in a hospital in Denver. Her assistant had mailed the packages.

Then, nine weeks ago, in the late spring of 2011, almost twenty years after my trip to Delta, I received a UPS package from someone named Richard A. Durbage (Jr.) in Lutherville-Timonium, Maryland. Assuming that it was a batch of my old books that someone wanted signed—something that really irritates me when the reader hasn't asked permission of me to send the books—I was tempted to return the package to the sender, unopened. Instead, I used a box cutter to slash the package open with more than necessary energy. Karen looked at the shipping information and made me laugh by saying that we'd never had books for signing sent from Lutherville-Timonium and she immediately went to look it up online. (Karen does love her geography.)

But they weren't old books of mine to be signed.

In the package were twelve Moleskine notebooks. I flipped through and saw that each page, front and back, was filled with small, precise cursive handwriting in a man's strong hand.

Even then I stupidly didn't think of Mr. Perry until I got to the last journal at the bottom.

The leather cover was wrapped around it, still holding the stub of a #2 pencil, but the leather was now weathered and worn and darkened by the oils transmitted through the repeated touch of Mr. Perry's hands. He'd obviously transferred the leather cover to each volume during his ten months of effort at writing this single, long tale.

There was a typed note.

Dear Mr. Simmons:

My mother, Lydia Durbage, passed away this April. She was 71 years old. In going through her things, I found this box. It had been sent to her in 1992 by the nursing home where a distant relative of hers, a Mr. Jacob Perry, had lived his last years and where he died. Not really knowing and never having met her grand-uncle, it seems that my mother only glanced at the contents of the box, chose one or two items for sale at her weekly garage sale, and left the rest untouched. I don't believe she ever opened the notebooks I have included in this package.

On page one of the top notebook there was a note, not to my mother but evidently to a certain "Mary" who ran the assisted living facility in Delta, that asked that these notebooks and a certain Vest Pocket Kodak camera be sent to you. Your address was given, which was how I knew where to send this much-belated package.

If these items were something you anticipated receiving twenty years ago, I apologize for the delay. My mother was absent-minded, even in her middle years.

Since the notebooks were meant to be sent to you, I've decided not to read them. I did skim through and noticed that my mother's relative was an accomplished artist: the maps, drawings of mountains, and other sketches seem to be of professional quality.

Again, I apologize for the inadvertent and accidental delay that kept you from receiving this package in the timely manner that I'm sure Mr. Jacob Perry had hoped for.

Sincerely yours,
Richard A. Durbage, Jr.

I carried the box to my study and lifted out the stack of notebooks and began reading that afternoon and read straight through the night, finishing about nine the next morning.

After pondering his wishes for months, I've decided to publish two versions of Jacob Perry's final (and only) manuscript. In the end, I've decided that publication is what he would have wanted after spending the last ten months of his life laboring over the effort. I also believe it's why he chose me as his primary reader. He knew that I could judge whether a manuscript deserved publication or not. I believe with all my heart that Jacob Perry's manuscript—this book—does deserve that publication.

A second and very limited edition will show Mr. Perry's own handwriting and will include the scores of sketches, portrait drawings, carefully done maps, mountain landscapes, old photographs, and other elements that Mr. Perry had added to the text. This version will be of text alone. I think it succeeds in telling the story that Jacob Perry, 1902–1992, wanted me to hear. Wanted *us* to hear. As his editor, I've made only a few spelling corrections and added a very few explanatory notes to his text. I can only trust and hope that, in allowing me to be his first reader and editor, Mr. Perry understands my own hunger to allow others to read this strange and oddly beautiful testament.

I *do* think this is what he wanted.

I can only hope to God that it was.

PART I

THE CLIMBERS

The summit of the Matterhorn offers very clear choices: a misstep to the left and you die in Italy; a wrong step to the right and you die in Switzerland.

⎯⎯⎯⎯∞⎯⎯⎯⎯

he three of us learn about Mallory and Irvine's disappearance on Mount Everest while we are eating lunch on the summit of the Matterhorn.

It is a perfect day in late June of 1924, and the news lies folded in a three-day-old British newspaper that someone in the kitchen at the small inn at Breuil in Italy has wrapped around our cold beef and horseradish sandwiches on thick fresh bread. I've unwittingly carried this still-weightless news—soon to be a heavy stone in each of our chests—to the summit of the Matterhorn in my rucksack, tucked along-side a goatskin of wine, two water bottles, three oranges, 100 feet of climbing rope, and a bulky salami. We do not immediately notice the paper or read the news that will change the day for us. We are too full of the summit and its views.

For six days we have done nothing but climb and re-climb the Matter-horn, always avoiding the summit for reasons known only to the Deacon.

On the first day up from Zermatt we explored the Hornli Ridge—Whymper's route in 1865—while avoiding the fixed ropes and cables that ran across the mountain's skin like so many scars. The next day we traversed to do the same on the Zmutt Ridge. On the third day, a long day, we traversed the mountain, again climbing from the Swiss side via the Hornli Ridge, crossing the friable north face just below the summit that the Deacon had forbidden to us, and then descending along the Italian Ridge, at twilight reaching our tents on the high green fields facing south toward Breuil.

I realized after the fifth day that we were following in the footsteps of those who'd made the Matterhorn so famed—the determined artist-climber 25-year-old Edward Whymper and his ad hoc party of three Englishmen: the Reverend Charles Hudson ("the clergyman from the Crimea"); Reverend Hudson's 19-year-old protégé and novice climber Douglas Hadow; and the confident 18-year-old Lord Francis Douglas (who had just passed at the top of the British Army's examination list, some 500 marks ahead of the next closest of his 118 competitors), the son of the eighth Marquess of Queensberry and a neophyte climber who'd been coming to the Alps for two years. Along with Whymper's motley assortment of young British climbers with such wildly different levels of experience and ability were the three guides Whymper had hired: "Old Peter" Taugwalder (only 45, but considered an oldster), "Young Peter" Taugwalder (age 21), and the highly skilled Chamonix Guide, 35-year-old Michel Croz. In truth, they would have needed only Croz as a guide, but Whymper had earlier promised employment to the Taugwalders, and the English climber was always as good as his word, even when it made his climbing party unwieldy and two of the guides essentially redundant.

It was on the Italian Ridge that I realized the Deacon was introducing us to the courage and efforts of Whymper's friend, competitor, and for-mer climbing partner Jean-Antoine Carrel. The difficult routes we were enjoying had been Carrel's.

We had our mountain tents—Whymper tents, they were still called, since the famous Golden Age climber had designed them for use on this very mountain—pitched on the grassy fields above the lower glaciers on both sides of the mountain, and we arrived on one side or the other just before dusk every evening, often after dark, there to eat lightly, to talk softly by the small fire, and to sleep soundly for a few hours before rising to climb again.

We climbed the Matterhorn's Furggen Ridge but bypassed the im-pressive overhangs near the top. This was not a defeat. For one full day we explored approaches to that never-climbed overhang, but we decided that we had neither the equipment nor the skill to climb it direct. (The overhang would eventually be climbed by Alfredo Perino and Louis Car-rel, known as "the little Carrel" in honor of his famous predecessor, and by Giacomo Chiara eighteen years later, in 1942.) Our modesty in not killing ourselves in an impossible—given the equipment and techniques of 1924—attempt on the Furggen Ridge overhang reminded me at the time of how I had first met the 37-year-old Englishman Richard Davis Deacon and the 25-year-old Frenchman Jean-Claude Clairoux at the base of the unclimbed north face of the Eiger—the deadly Eigerwand. But that is a tale for another time.

The essence is that both Deacon—known as "the Deacon" to many of his friends and climbing partners—and Jean-Claude, just become a fully accredited Chamonix Guide, perhaps the most exclusive climbing fraternity in the world, had agreed to take me along for months of their winter, spring, and early summer climbing in the Alps. It was a greater gift than I had ever dreamed of. I'd enjoyed going to Harvard, but my education with the Deacon and Jean-Claude—whom I eventually came to call "J.C." since he did not seem to mind the nickname—for those months was by far the most demanding and exhilarating educational experience of my life.

At least until the nightmare of Mount Everest. But I get far ahead of my tale.

On our last two days on the Matterhorn we made a partial ascent of the mountain by its treacherous west face, then rappelled down to work out routes and strategies on the truly treacherous north face, one of the Alps' final and most formidable unsolved problems. (Franz and Toni Schmid will climb it seven years later, after bivouacking one night on the face itself. They will ride their bicycles all the way from Munich to the mountain and, after their surprise ascent via the north face, will ride them home again.) For the three of us, it was a reconnaissance only.

This final day we had teased out routes on the seemingly unassailable "Zmutt Nose" overhanging the right part of the north face, then retreated, traversed to the Italian Ridge, and—when the Deacon nodded his permission to climb the final 100 feet—finally found ourselves here on the narrow summit on a perfect day in late June.

During our week on the Matterhorn we endured and climbed through downpours, sudden snowstorms, sleet, ice that turned rock to verglas, and high winds. On this final day, the weather on the summit is clear, calm, warm, and quiet. The winds are so docile that the Deacon is able to light his pipe after striking only a single match.

The top of the Matterhorn is a narrow ridge about a hundred yards long, if you wish to walk the distance between its lower, slightly broader "Italian summit" and its higher and narrowest point at the "Swiss summit." In the past nine months or so, the Deacon and Jean-Claude have taught me that all good mountains give you clear choices. The summit of the Matterhorn offers very clear choices: a misstep to the left and you die in Italy; a wrong step to the right and you die in Switzerland.

The Italian side is a sheer rock face falling 4,000 feet to rocks and ridges that would stop a fall about halfway down the face, and the Swiss side falls away to a steep snow slope and rocky ridges hundreds of feet lower than the halfway mark, boulders and ridges that might or might not stop a body's fall. There is enough snow here on the ridgeline itself for us to leave clear prints of our hobnailed boots.

The Matterhorn's summit ridge is not quite what excited journalists like to call "a knife-edge ridge." Our boot prints in the snow along the actual ridge prove this. Had it been a knife-edge ridge, with snow, our boot prints would have been on *both sides,* since the smart way to traverse a true knife edge is to hobble slowly along like a ruptured duck, one leg on the west side of the narrow summit ridge, one on the east. A slip then will lead to bruised testicles but not—God and fate willing—a 4,000-foot fall.

A slightly wider "knife-edge ridge" of snow, a vertical snow cornice, as it were, would have readied us for what Jean-Claude liked to call "a game of jump rope." We'd probably be tied together on such a snowy knife edge, and if the climber directly ahead of or immediately behind you slips off one side, your immediate reaction (since there's little hope of belay from such a snowy knife edge)—an "immediate reaction" made instinctive only by many drills—must be to jump off the *opposite side* of the ridgeline, both of you now dangling over 4,000-foot or greater emptiness, in the desperate hope that (a) the rope does not break, dooming both of you, and (b) *your* weight will counter *his* weight in the fall.

It *does* work. We practiced it numerous times on a snowy knife-edge ridge on Mont Blanc. But it was a ridge where the punishment for failure—or a rope break—was a 50-foot slide to level snowfields, not a 4,000-foot drop.

I was 6 feet 2 inches tall and 220 pounds, so when I played "jump the rope" with poor Jean-Claude (5 feet 6 inches tall, 135 pounds), logic would dictate that he'd come flying up over the top of the snowy ridgeline like a hooked fish, sending both of us sliding out of control. But because Jean-Claude had the habit of carrying the heaviest pack of any of us (and was also the quickest and most skilled with his long ice axe), the balancing act usually worked, the heavily stressed hemp rope digging into the vertical snow cornice until it found either rock or solid ice.

But as I say, this long summit ridgeline of the Matterhorn is a wide French boulevard compared to knife-edge ridges: wide enough to walk upon, at least single file in some places, and—if you're very brave, supremely skilled, or totally stupid—to do so with your hands in your pockets and other things on your mind. The Deacon has been doing precisely this, pacing back and forth along the narrow line, pulling his old pipe from his jacket pocket and lighting it as he paces.

The Deacon, who could be taciturn to the point of silence for days, evidently feels expansive this late morning. Puffing on his pipe, he gestures for Jean-Claude and me to follow him in single file to the far side of the summit ridge, where we can look down on the Italian Ridge that saw the majority of the early attempts on the mountain—even by Whymper, until he decided to use the seemingly more difficult (but in truth somewhat easier due to the angle of the huge slabs) Swiss Ridge.

"Carrel and his team were there," says the Deacon and points to a line a third of the way down the narrow, rock-steepled ridge. "All those years of effort and Whymper ends up making the summit two or three hours ahead of his old friend and guide from Italy."

He's talking, of course, about Whymper and his six fellow climbers' first summit ascent of the Matterhorn on July 14, 1865.

"Did not Whymper and Croz throw rocks down upon them?" asks Jean-Claude.

The Deacon looks at our French friend to see if he is joking. Both men smile.

The Deacon points to the sheer face on our left. "Whymper was mad to get Carrel's attention. He and Croz shouted and dropped rocks down the north face—nowhere near the ridge where the Italians were climbing, of course. But it must have sounded like cannon fire to Carrel and his team."

All three of us gaze down as if we could see the heartbroken Italian guide and his companions staring up in shock and defeat.

"Carrel recognized his old client Whymper's white slop trousers," says the Deacon. "Carrel thought he was an hour or less from the summit—he'd already led his party past the worst obstacles of the ridge—but after he identified Whymper on the summit, he just turned around and led his party back down." The Deacon sighs, inhales deeply from his pipe, and looks out over the mountains, valleys, meadows, and glaciers below us. "Carrel climbed the Matterhorn two or three days later, still from the Italian Ridge," he says softly, almost speaking to himself now. "Establishing Italy's secondary provenance to the mountain. Even after the British chaps' clear victory."

"Clear victory, *oui*... but so tragic," says Jean-Claude.

We walk back to where we've stowed our rucksacks against some boulders along the north end of the narrow summit ridge. Jean-Claude and I begin unpacking our lunch. This is to be our last day on the Matterhorn, and it may be our last day climbing together for some time... perhaps forever, although I desperately hope not. I want nothing more than to spend the rest of my European *Wanderjahr* climbing in the Alps with these new friends, but the Deacon has some business in England soon, and J.C. has to return to his Chamonix Guide duties and an annual assembly of Chamonix Guides in that tradition-haunted Chamonix Valley, with its sacred brotherhood of the rope.

Shaking away any sad thoughts of endings or farewells, I pause in my unpacking to take in the view yet again. My eyes are hungrier than my belly.

There is not a single cloud in the sky. The Maritime Alps, 130 miles away, are clearly visible. The Écrins, first climbed by Whymper and the guide Croz, bulk blankly against the sky like the sides of some great white sow. Turning slightly to look north, I see the high peaks of the Oberland on the far side of the Rhône. To the west, Mont Blanc rules over all lesser peaks, its summit snows blazing with reflected sunlight so blinding that I have to squint. Swiveling slightly to face the east, I can see peak after peak—some climbed by me during the last nine months with my new friends here, some waiting to be climbed, some never to be climbed—the stuttered and irregular array of white pinnacles diminishing to a mere bumpy horizon wreathed in the haze of distance.

The Deacon and Jean-Claude are eating their sandwiches and sipping water. I snap myself out of my sightseeing and romantic reverie and begin to eat. The cold roast beef is delicious, the bread rich with a crust that makes me work at chewing. The horseradish makes my eyes water until Mont Blanc becomes even more of a white blur.

Looking south, I celebrate the view that Whymper wrote about in his classic book *Scrambles Amongst the Alps in the Years 1860–1869*. I can clearly recall the words I read only the evening before, read by candle-light in my tent above Breuil, the words describing Edward Whymper's first view from the summit of the Matterhorn on July 14, 1865, *this* view that I'm devouring in late June of 1924:

> There were forests black and gloomy and meadows bright and lively, bounding waterfalls and tranquil lakes, fertile lands and savage wastes; sunny plains and frigid *plateaux*. There were the most rugged forms, and the most graceful outlines—bold, perpendicular cliffs, and gentle, undulating slopes; rocky mountains and snowy mountains, sombre and solemn, or glittering and white with walls—turrets—pinnacles—pyramids—domes—cones—and spires! There was every combination that the world can give, and every contrast that the heart could desire.

Yes, you can tell that Edward Whymper was an absolute romantic, as were so many of the Golden Age climbers in the mid- and late 1800s. And his writing is flowery and old-fashioned by the lean, modern standards of 1924.

But as to the charge of being a hopeless romantic, I confess that I am as well. It's part of my nature. Perhaps it *is* my nature. And although I'd graduated from Harvard as an English major ready to write my own great travelogues and novels—all in the lean modern style, of course—I'm surprised to find that Edward Whymper's nineteenth-century wording—flowery prose and all—has once again moved me to tears.

So on this June day in 1924, my heart responds to the words written more than fifty years earlier, and my soul responds even more hopelessly to the view that prompted those words from the sentimental Edward

Whymper. The great mountain climber was twenty-five years old when he first climbed the Matterhorn and saw this view; I've just celebrated my twenty-second birthday, two months before earning this view for myself. I feel very close to Whymper and to all the climbers—some of them hard-bitten cynics, but others romantics like myself—who have looked south at Italy from this very ridge, from this very throne of a low boulder.

During the autumn, winter, and spring months that I've been climbing in the Alps with Jean-Claude and the Deacon, there has been a question-and-answer session after each summiting, a catechism, as it were, for each mountain. The tone of the questioning has never been condescending, and I've actually enjoyed the process, since I've learned so much from the two alpinists. I'd been a good climber when I came to Europe from the United States; under Jean-Claude's and the Deacon's gentle, sometimes bantering, but never pedantic guidance, I know that I'm becoming an excellent climber. A *world-class* climber. Part of a very small fraternity indeed. More than that, the Deacon's and Jean-Claude's tutelage—including these summiting catechisms—have helped me learn how to *love* the mountain I've just climbed. Love it even though she may have been a treacherous bitch during my intimate time with her: rotten rock, avalanches, traverses without so much as a fingerhold, deadly rockfall, forced bivouacs on ledges too narrow to hold a book upright yet we were forced to cling there in freezing weather, hailstorms or thunderstorms, nights when the metal pick in my ice axe glowed blue with its anticipatory electrical discharge, hot days without so much as a sip of water and more bivouac nights when, without pitons to tie oneself in, you held a lit candle under your chin to keep from falling asleep and tumbling off into the void. Yet through all that, the Deacon and especially Jean-Claude were teaching me how to love the mountain, love her for what she truly was, while loving even the hardest times spent engaged with her.

The catechism for the Matterhorn is led by Jean-Claude and is briefer than most.

You must love something about every good mountain. Matterhorn is a good mountain. Did you love the faces of this mountain?

Non. The faces of the Matterhorn, especially the north face upon which we spent the most time, were not worth loving. They were rubble. They were constant rockfall and avalanche.

But you love the rock itself?

Non. The rock is treacherous. Friable. It lies. Drive in a piton with a hammer and you never hear the proper ring of steel against iron, of iron against rock, and a minute later you can easily pull the useless piton out with two fingers. The rock on the faces of the Matterhorn is terrible. Mountaineers know that *all* mountains are in a constant state of collapse — their verticality being inescapably and inevitably worn down every moment by wind, water, weather, and gravity — but the Matterhorn is more of an unstable pile of constantly crumbling rubble than most peaks. Love the rock here? Nowhere. Never.

But you love the ridges?

Non. The famous ridges of the Matterhorn — the Italian and the Swiss, the Furggen and the Zmutt — are either too dangerous, raked with rockfall and snow avalanche, or too tame, pocked with cables and fixed ropes for the lady climber and the seventy-year-old English gentleman. Love for this mountain's ridges? There is none. At least not since Edward Whymper's day, when all was new.

But you love the mountain. You know you do. What do you love?

Oui. The Matterhorn is a mountain that gives the climber numerous problems to solve, but — unlike the unclimbed north face of the Eiger and certain other peaks I've seen or heard about — the Matterhorn also gives a good climber a clean, clear solution to each problem.

The Matterhorn is a heap of tumbling rubble, but the faces and ridges are beautiful to look upon from a distance. She is like an aging actress who, beneath the sadly obvious and peeling makeup, still boasts the cheeks and bone structure of her younger self, and there are frequent glimpses of a once near-perfect beauty. The shape of the peak itself — standing alone, unconnected to other mountains — is perhaps the cleanest and most memorable in all the Alps. Ask a young child who has never seen mountains to draw a mountain, and she will use her crayon to draw the Matterhorn. It is that iconic. And with its upper north face actually bending out beyond the vertical, like a wave breaking, the mountain appears to be constantly in motion. And that sheer, overhanging face breeds its own weather, gives rise to its own masses of clouds. It is that serious a mountain.

And you love the ghosts.

Oui. The ghosts are there to love and cannot be avoided. Edward Whymper's loyal guide Jean-Antoine Carrel's patriotic betrayal in choosing to lead Felice Giordano up the Italian Ridge for the glory of an all-Italian first summit on July 14 of 1865. The ghosts of 25-year-old Whymper's desperate dash to Zermatt—to try the opposing ridge—with his hastily assembled party of young Lord Francis Douglas, Reverend Charles Hudson, 19-year-old Douglas Hadow, the Chamonix Guide Michel Croz, and the two local guides, "Young Peter" and "Old Peter" Taugwalder.

The ghosts of the four dead men from that day speak the loudest from the stone to me, and any climber must learn to hear them and to love and respect climbing on the same stones they trod, sleeping on the same slabs where they slept, triumphing on the same narrow summit where Whymper's seven shouted in triumph, and focusing hard on descending safely down the still treacherous section where four of them fell thousands of feet to their deaths.

And, mon ami, *you love the view from the top.*

Oui. I do love the view. It makes the aching muscles and bleeding hands all worthwhile. Better than worthwhile—forgotten. The view is all.

While I'm chewing and staring out at this view, Jean-Claude, catechism lesson for me completed, straightens out the newspaper that had been wrapped around the cheesecloth covering our sandwiches.

"Mallory and Irvine killed in attempt to conquer Everest," he reads aloud in his soft French accent.

I quit chewing. The Deacon is in the process of tamping the embers or ashes out of his pipe before eating, batting the pipe against the side of his hobnailed boot, but he also freezes in place, boot on his knee and now empty pipe against the boot, and stares at Jean-Claude.

Our friend continues: *"London, June twenty, nineteen twenty-four—The Mount Everest Committee has received with profound regret the following cablegram from . . ."* He stops and thrusts the crumpled newspaper toward me. "Jake, it is your language. You should read it."

Surprised, not understanding Jean-Claude's reticence—as far as I know he's as completely fluent in reading English as he is in speaking it—I take the paper, smooth it out some more on my knee, and read aloud.

London, June twenty, nineteen twenty-four—The Mount Everest Committee has received with profound regret the following cablegram from Colonel Norton, dispatched from Phari Dzong, June nineteen, at four fifty p.m.

"Mallory and Irvine killed on last attempt. Rest of party arrived at base camp all well that day. Two climbers who were not members of the expedition die in Everest avalanche on last day after others have left."

The committee has telegraphed to Colonel Norton, expressing deep sympathy with the expedition. In the loss of their two gallant comrades, which must have been due to most unfavourable conditions of weather and snow, which from the first arrival at the scene of operations impeded climbing this year...

I continue reading the columns, part sorrowful report, part hagiography:

The tragic death of these two men—George Leigh Mallory, who alone of all those engaged in the present attempt had also taken part in the two previous expeditions, and A. C. Irvine, one of his band of recruits—is a terribly sad ending to the story of the assaults of the mountain that began three years ago. It is only a few days since we published Mallory's own account of the second reverse suffered by the present expedition...

That reverse had been wind and snow, which had driven the men from their highest camps—"discomfited but very far from being defeated" was Mallory's message to the *Times.* There followed several more paragraphs, summarizing Mallory's refusal to surrender despite the cold weather, high winds, avalanches, and imminent onset of the monsoon that would end this year's climbing season.

I pause and look at my two friends, seeking any signal that I should quit reading and hand the newspaper around, but Jean-Claude and the Deacon simply stare at me. Waiting for more.

A slight breeze has come up, so I grip the crumpled paper tightly now as I continue reading the long second column of prose.

Mallory wrote his whole dispatch in this spirit of one who was about to en-gage in a desperate battle. "The action," he said, "is only suspended before the more intense action of the climax. The issue will shortly be decided. The third time we walk up East Rongbuk Glacier will be the last, for better or worse." He had counted the odds and was ready to face them. "We expect," he said in a later passage of his dispatch, "no mercy from Everest": and Everest, alas! has taken him at his word.

I pause. The Deacon and Jean-Claude sit waiting. Far beyond the Dea-con's shoulder, a large raven hovers motionless on the slight breeze, its body poised above almost 5,000 feet of empty air.

I skip any criticism of the prose style and continue reading: Mallory's history as a "distinguished mountaineer" and his absolute determination to summit Mount Everest ("Alas!" I think, but do not say), the contribu-tions of General C. G. Bruce, Major E. F. Norton, and others in the past, surpassing the Duke of Abruzzi's height record of 22,000 feet, set on a distant and irrelevant mountain named K2.

The story focuses on 37-year-old George Leigh Mallory, the deter-mined and tested veteran of Everest, and young Andrew Irvine, only 22 years old — my age exactly! — leaving their high camp on the morning of June 8, presumably carrying oxygen apparatus, the two heroes being seen again only once more, hours later, by fellow climber Noel Odell, who glimpsed them "going strong for the top," and then the clouds closing in, the snowstorm intervening, and neither Mallory nor Irvine seen again.

I read aloud that, according to the *Times* report, on the evening of their disappearance, Odell had gone all the way up to the precarious Camp VI, shouting out in the roaring high-altitude night in case Mal-lory and Irvine were trying to descend in darkness. Mallory had left his flare and lantern behind in the tent at Camp VI. He would have had no means to signal others below, even if he were alive in the terrible night.

After fifty hours had passed, said the *Times* tale, even the ever hopeful Noel Odell gave up hope and placed two sleeping bags in the shape of a T for observers with telescopes at the lower camps to see. The prearranged signal meant that no further search should be attempted — the two climbers were lost forever.

Finally I lower the paper. The rising breeze tugs at it. The raven no

longer marks the blue sky, and the sky itself is darkening now with afternoon. I shake my head, feeling the strong emotion from my two friends
but not really understanding the depth and complexity of it. "There's
just a little more of the same," I say, my voice hoarse.

The Deacon moves at last. He puts his cold pipe in the chest pocket
of his tweed jacket. "They said there were two more," he says softly.

"What?"

"The first paragraph said that two men died. Who? How?"

"Oh." I fumble with the paper, running my finger down the last column to the final paragraphs. Everything is Mallory and Irvine, Irvine and
Mallory, and then Mallory again. But there at the end. I read:

*After the main party had left Everest Base Camp, according to German
explorer Bruno Sigl, who was on a reconnaissance mission for a possible future German attempt on Everest, Sigl witnessed thirty-two-year-old Lord
Percival Bromley, brother of the fifth Marquess of Lexeter, and a German
or Austrian climber whom Sigl identified as Kurt Meyer, being swept away
by an avalanche between Camp V and Camp VI. Young Bromley—Lord
Percival—while not a formal member of the Mallory Expedition led by
Colonel Norton, had followed the expedition from Darjeeling to the Everest
Base Camp. Although the monsoon season had arrived and Colonel Norton's expedition had retreated from the mountain, it is thought that perhaps
Lord Percival and Meyer were making one final attempt to locate Mallory and Irvine. The bodies of Lord Percival and the German or Austrian
climber were not recovered.*

I lower the paper again.

"Lord Bromley, a peer of your realm, dies on Mount Everest and it
barely makes the newspaper," mutters Jean-Claude. "It is all Mallory.
Mallory and Irvine."

" 'Lord Percival' or 'Lord Percy' is how we say it in England," the Deacon says very softly. " 'Lord Bromley' is his older brother, the marquess.
And Percy Bromley would have been a poor excuse for a peer even if he
had been next in line. George Mallory, although from a humble background, was the royalty on that expedition." The Deacon stands, puts his
hands in his trouser pockets, and strolls away down the narrow ridge, his

head lowered. He looks like nothing so much as an absent-minded professor walking on campus, pondering some esoteric problem in his field.

When the Deacon is out of hearing range, I whisper to Jean-Claude, "Did he know Mallory or Irvine?"

Jean-Claude looks at me and then leans closer, speaking so softly that it is almost a whisper even though the Deacon is many yards away. "Irvine? I do not know, Jake. But Mallory...yes, the Deacon knew him for many years. Before the War they were students in the same small college in Cambridge. During the War they crossed paths on the battlefields many times. The Deacon was invited by Mallory to go on the nineteen twenty-one reconnaissance and nineteen twenty-two Everest climbing expeditions, and did so. But there was no invitation from Mallory or the Alpine Club for this year's attempt on Everest."

"Good heavens!" Before today I thought I'd really begun to know my two new friends and climbing partners. Now it seems that I know—and knew—almost nothing. "It could have been Mallory and the Deacon, rather than young Sandy Irvine, missing on Everest," I whisper to J.C.

Jean-Claude bites his chapped lip, looks to make sure that the Deacon is still far away on the Italian-side summit, seeming to be staring out at nothing.

"No, no," whispers Jean-Claude. "During the first two expeditions, Mallory and the Deacon had several...how do you say it in English?... falling-downs."

For a moment I imagine the two climbers falling while roped together but then understand. "Falling-out," I say.

"*Oui, oui.* Serious outfallings, I am afraid. I am sure that Mallory had not spoken to the Deacon since they returned from the 'twenty-two expedition."

"Falling-outs over what?" I whisper. The wind has risen again and is blowing icy pellets of summit snow into our faces.

"The first expedition...it was officially called a reconnaissance expedition, but the actual goal for Mallory and the others was to find the fastest route to the mountain through all the icefalls and glaciers at its base, and then begin climbing as soon as possible. I know that both Deacon and Mallory believed they might summit during that first effort in nineteen twenty-one."

"Ambitious," I murmur. The Deacon is still at his remote perch on the Italian end of the summit ridge. With the wind now blowing even more strongly from his direction, I doubt he could hear us even if we shouted. Still, Jean-Claude and I continue our conversation in little more than a hurried whisper.

"So Mallory insisted that the best way to the North Col—the most obvious route from the north side of Everest—was from the east, up the Kharta Valley. It was a...how do you say *cul-de-sac?*"

"Dead end."

Jean-Claude grins. Sometimes I think he enjoys the rough-edged quality of English. "*Oui*—a very dead end. And Mallory kept leading them all around the mountain, pursuing one dead end after the other. He even had Guy Bullock go so far up the West Rongbuk that they almost crossed the border into Nepal, looking over to the south approaches to Everest and deciding that the glaciers and icefalls approaching the South Face and ridges were totally impassable. The solution had to be on this North Face side."

"I wonder...," I whisper, but more to myself than to J.C.

"At any rate, months were wasted," says Jean-Claude. "Wasted at least as far as the Deacon was concerned—exploring ever eastward and westward, measuring everything, photographing everything. Never finding a workable approach to the North Col."

"I've seen some of the photographs," I say, glancing to make sure that the Deacon is still at the far end of the summit. He doesn't appear to have moved a muscle. "They're beautiful."

"Yes," says J.C. "But the first series of photographs for which Mallory climbed a serious peak to gain the perfect vantage point, he put the plates in the camera the wrong way around. Nothing came out on the print, of course. Bullock and the others did most of the real photography."

"What's this got to do with Mallory and the Deacon falling out?" I ask. "Almost becoming enemies after so many years of association and...I presume...mutual respect?"

Jean-Claude sighs. "Their first base camp near the mountain was pitched at the head of a small valley where a river runs down onto the plain. They must have walked by that valley a hundred times but never explored it. The Deacon wanted to look into it as a possible approach to the North Col right from the beginning, but Mallory always over-ruled him, insisting that it just ran to the East Rongbuk Glacier and stopped. They could see the entrance to a side valley—easy walking with gravel and just pinnacles of old snow as all that was left of the former glacier—and the Deacon suggested that this valley might curve west again—which it does—and would give them a safe and easy path to the North Col and the beginning of their climb. Mallory said no to that...what is the word?...that opportunity, and the weeks of useless reconnoitering to both the east and west dragged on. Also, Mallory and the Alpine Club had decided the summer monsoon season was the best time to try to climb Mount Everest, but by June, even Monsieur Mallory had to agree that the summer monsoon season, with its endless snow-fall, was bad, bad...a bad time to reconnoiter the mountain, much less to attempt a climb—since the storms were much...how do you say it?...more fiercer higher up."

"So that was their nineteen twenty-two falling-out," I whisper.

Jean-Claude smiles almost sadly. "The last brick...no...what do you say? The last something that breaks the back of the camel?"

"Straw."

"The last straw was the Deacon's constant urging that they climb Lhakpa La to get a view from there. For many weeks Mallory thought such an effort would be useless and said no to the Deacon's request."

"What's Lhakpa La?" I ask. My knowledge of Mount Everest's im-mediate geography in this late June of 1924 is just about nonexistent. Essentially I know that the tallest peak in the world shares a border with Nepal and Tibet, that Tibet is the only way one could get to it—given the politics of the era—and that this meant the climb, should it ever happen, will have to be up the North Face. Up the North East Ridge above the North Ridge and the North Face, to be specific, if all of the expeditions' photographs are to be believed.

"Lhakpa La is a high pass to the west that separates the Kharta Glacier from the East Rongbuk Glacier," says J.C. "They climbed to it in an ab-solute blinding blizzard, holeposting...is that the word, Jake?"

"Postholing."

"Postholing up to their waists in the deepening snow, able to see nothing even when they reached the flat area they assumed was the summit. Even setting up their tents was a nightmare in the blizzard, and Mallory was furious at the waste of time. But then, in the morning, the weather completely cleared, and from their snow-covered camp on Lhakpa La they could see the perfect route to the North Col—directly up the valley and side valley which Deacon had argued so many times they explore, and then across snow and ice up onto the other side of the cwm and then, without any apparent difficulty, up onto the North Col itself. And from there, directly to the North Ridge all the way up to the high North East Ridge. But the monsoon snows kept burying them, the winds were terrible, and even though they reconnoitered the correct route all the way to a thousand-foot ice wall that led up onto the North Col, it was too late in the year to attempt the summit. They withdrew from the mountain on the twenty-fourth of September—without ever actually setting foot on the bare rock of Mount Everest."

The Deacon has been smoking his pipe again, but now he is batting out the ashes. He'll be returning any minute now.

"So that's what caused their falling-out," I whisper. "And it kept the Deacon from going with Mallory on this year's Everest expedition."

"No," says Jean-Claude. His whisper now is fast and harsh. "It was an incident at the end of the second expedition—the men had barely been in England a few weeks after the nineteen twenty-two expedition before they began mounting their return in 'twenty-four. The Deacon was invited, but grudgingly. A part of a letter from Mallory to his wife was somehow copied and distributed among climbers in nineteen twenty-three, and I mostly remembered—but later looked up—exactly what Mallory wrote: *'Despite the years that I've known Mr. Deacon—and we were quite good friends at Cambridge, especially during the climbing in Wales after those school days were over, I don't find myself greatly liking him. He is too much the don, too much the landlord, too much the coddled poet, and one with not only Tory prejudices that come into the open from time to time, but with a highly developed sense of contempt, sometimes bordering on actual hatred, for other sorts of people than his own. Our friend Mr. Richard Davis Deacon loves being called by his common nickname, given to him by the other men, and there were only fifty of us total, in his first year at our little Magdalene College, Cambridge—"the Deacon"—I am sure it flatters his inflated ego. At any rate, Ruth, after the last expedition I felt I should never be at ease with him—and in a sense I never shall be. He is well informed and opinionated and doesn't at all like anyone else to know things he doesn't know. And when he is lucky in his random guesses, as he was about finding our route from the summit of the pass called Lhakpa La, he takes his good fortune as his due—as if he were the leader rather than I.'"*

"You have a hell of a memory, my friend."

Jean-Claude looks surprised. "But of course! Are not young students in America required to memorize hundreds of pages of verse and fine literature and other materials? Word for word? And punished severely if they fail? In France, memory is learning and learning is memory."

The Deacon is looking back this way, his expression still vacant, obviously still thinking hard about something. But I am sure he will rejoin us in a minute.

"Quickly," I say to Jean-Claude, "tell me what happened on the nineteen twenty-two expedition which was the last straw that broke the back of the camel that was their friendship."

I admit it is not the finest sentence I've ever constructed, but Jean-Claude looks at me as if I've suddenly begun babbling in Aramaic.

"In 'twenty-two they all felt that they had a strong chance for the summit," begins Jean-Claude, as the Deacon starts to stroll back in our direction. "They climbed the imposing ice wall onto the North Col, traversed it to the North Ridge, climbed that ridge to the North East Ridge, and headed for the summit—but terrible winds drove them off the ridge onto the North Face itself, and there progress was slow and dangerous. They had to retreat to base camp. But on the seventh of June, Mallory insisted on another effort up the North Col—still imagining, despite day after day of deep monsoon snow, that they might still make the summit.

"The Deacon argued against taking porters and climbers up the North Col again. He pointed out that the weather had turned and the summit was lost to them this year. More importantly, the Deacon knew much more about snow and ice conditions than Mallory—whose expedition time on glaciers and in the Alps was very limited—and the Deacon said that the conditions were perfect for avalanches. Just the day before, returning from a reconnoiter of the North Col, some of the climbers, upon descending toward the rope ladder they'd left on the ice wall, found a fifty-meter-wide area where a slide had wiped out their tracks during the past two hours. The Deacon refused to go."

That same Deacon is less than 50 feet away now, and we would have to cease the conversation if not for the wind howling and certainly drowning our words. But still Jean-Claude hurries with the last sentences.

"Mallory called the Deacon a coward. That morning, seven June, Mallory led a party of seventeen men up to the North Col, all the Sherpas roped together. The avalanche hit them about two hundred meters below the North Col on exactly the type of slope the Deacon had warned them about. Nine of the porters were swept away together. Mallory missed being carried away by only a few meters, but even he was caught up in the tidal wave. Two of the porters were later dug out, but seven died and their remains were buried in the crevasse to which they had almost been carried by the avalanche. It had been, as the Deacon had tried to explain, madness to attempt to cross those loose snow-slab slopes under such conditions."

"My God," I whisper.

"Exactly," Jean-Claude agrees. "The two old friends have not spoken since that June day two years ago. And the Deacon was *not* invited on this year's expedition."

I say nothing. I'm stunned that the Deacon *might*—had it not been for this "falling-down" between Mallory and him—have been invited on such an important adventure. Perhaps the adventure of the century. Certainly the heroic tragedy of the century, if the newspapers are to be believed. I think about immortality, such as it is, how it seems to come for Brits only after a hard death, and how it is being crafted for George Leigh Mallory now by words in the *London Times,* the *New York Times,* and a thousand other newspapers.

We've missed all this the past four days—concentrating only on our climbing, our descending, our sleeping, and our climbing again.

"How did...," I begin, but immediately fall silent. The Deacon has almost reached us. The rising wind tugs at his wool jacket and tie. I can hear his hobnailed boots—almost certainly nearly identical to the ones worn this past week by Mallory and Irvine—crunching and see them leaving new prints in the shallow snow of the Matterhorn's summit ridge.

His hands still in the pockets of his woolen trousers, his pipe cold in his upper-right pocket, the Deacon gives Jean-Claude an intense look and says softly, *"Mon ami,* if you had a chance to try to climb Mount Everest, would you take it?"

I expect Jean-Claude to make some joke—it would be in his nature to do so despite the sad news in the newspaper—but instead he looks up at our de facto leader for a long, silent moment. The Deacon's disturbingly clear gray eyes look up from J.C. and seem so focused on a distant point that I actually check behind me to see if the high-flying raven has returned.

"Oui," Jean-Claude says at last. "Mount Everest is very large and very far away, far from my valley of Chamonix where I have duties as a guide and patrons waiting for me—and it is more a British mountain, I think, than one yet open to the world—and I think it is now and shall continue to be a cold killer of men, my friend Richard Deacon. But, *oui, mon ami,* if I were to get the chance to go climb the beast, I would go. Yes. *Absolutely."*

I'm waiting for the Deacon to ask me the same question and am not sure exactly how I'll respond—but there is no question for me.

Instead the Deacon says loudly over the wind, "Let's go down the face and then take the Swiss Ridge toward Zermatt."

This is a small surprise. Our better tents and sleeping bags and the bulk of our supplies are on the Italian side, on the high slopes above Breuil. Ah, well. It will just mean another long hike over Théodule Pass and back. As junior member of the trio, I'll probably get the duty. I only hope I can find a mule to rent in Zermatt.

We start down the suddenly steep ridge toward the shaded, near-vertical roof of the mountain—"the bad bit," Edward Whymper had called it when they ascended, and so it fatally proved itself when they descended—and the Deacon surprises me as well as Jean-Claude (I can tell by Jean-Claude's almost infinitesimal hesitation) by saying, "What do you say we rope up for this part?"

We had done the bulk of our climbing on face and ridge unroped. If one falls—well, he falls. Most of the ridge and large slab work here requires no ropes for belay, and the downward-tilting north face slabs such as we are going out on now are too treacherous for any real belay. There are almost no outcroppings or projections over which the highest climber can toss a safety loop, as is the alpine mountaineer's habit in 1924.

Uncoiling the different strands of rope over my shoulder, I now play out the shortest one. We all tie on at the waist, only about 20 feet separating us. There is no discussion of order. Jean-Claude goes first—he is strongest on snow and ice but also brilliant on sheer rock slabs such as we're going to encounter in a minute—then I go second, the least experienced climber here but very strong with my arms, and finally the Deacon. The Deacon as sheet anchor. The Deacon as third man on the rope, responsible for belaying both Jean-Claude and me if we fall...a belay on this treacherous rock that would be beyond the abilities of almost any man on earth, as well as almost certainly far beyond the snapping point of our thin hemp rope.

But the brotherhood of the rope gives a strong sense of security even when the rope is thin to the point of being little more than a metaphor. And so does the fact of Richard Davis Deacon as our anchorman on the rope. We go over the Swiss edge of the summit and begin our descent.

When not placing my feet most carefully on the wet and downward-sloping narrow slabs, I notice that there are old fixed ropes and one metal cable hanging or pitoned in further away from the edge of the face: a few of the ropes strung by solicitous guides this summer; most of the others many years old and quickly turning to powder due to age, winter weather, and high-altitude sunlight hastening the chemical and physical processes of their own slow, certain disintegration. "Clients"—tourists to these high peaks, strangers to the way of rock, ice, rope, and sky—tie on to these fixed ropes, some using them for a quick rappel down this almost vertical and disturbingly exposed "bad bit" of the mountain, but while one rope might hold you in such a rappel, the one next to it might snap immediately and send you hurtling thousands of feet to the boulders and crevasses of the glacier below.

It's almost impossible to tell, just by looking, which hemp ropes are new and reliable and which are ancient, rotten, and certain death to clip on to. That's what guides are for.

The three of us stay clear of all the ropes as we descend, Jean-Claude angling us closer to the edge of the face, where rockfalls and small snow avalanches are more frequent, even in June. He is trading the slight chance of rockfall or avalanche during the minutes we're on this part of the face for the definite advantage of more solid footing closer to the ridge.

But why come this way? Why reproduce the last steps of doomed Lord Francis Douglas and the other members of Edward Whymper's summit party from July 14, 1865?

Most people even mildly interested in mountain climbing know that there are more serious accidents during the *de*scent stages of a climb than during the *a*scent, but what they might not know is that a climber has a different relationship to the mountain, especially while climbing on rock, during each of the ascent/descent stages. Climbing up the mountain, the climber is leaning into the rock face, body intimately spread out against the rock, cheek touching rock, fingers groping for any ledge or handhold in the rock, the climber's entire body seeking out even the smallest ledges, fissures, wedges, overhangs, slabs — it's like making love to the mountain. During the descent stage, it's usually more common for the climber to be facing *out*ward, thus making it easier for the climber to *see* the tiny ledges and footholds in the yards and meters beneath and beside him; that way the climber's back is against the rock, his face turned toward (and attention now on) the drop beneath him, much of the view now being the empty sky and beckoning void rather than the very solid and reassuring rock or snow mass.

So descending a mountain is almost always more frightening for the novice climber and more demanding of full attention for even the most experienced climber. Descents claim more lives than the mere *climbing* of a mountain. But even as I'm taking care to set my feet and hands and following J.C., even as I'm wondering why the Deacon seems to have suggested this particular death route that claimed more than half of Whymper's party, much of my mind keeps turning over the question *Why didn't the Deacon ask me if I'd be willing to climb Mount Everest?*

Of course, it would have been a silly and useless question: I have no money to join one of the Alpine Club's Himalayan expeditions. (In a real sense, it is a sporting club for men of means, and I've already spent most of the modest inheritance I received when I turned twenty-one so that I could come to Europe to climb.) And it is the British Alpine Club — they don't invite Americans along. British climbers and their Old Boy establishment consider Mount Everest — named for a British cartographer by a British surveyor—an English hill. They'd never invite an American, no matter how skilled he might be.

What's more, I simply didn't have the experience required for those heroes who attempt Everest. I had done a good deal of climbing during my years at Harvard—more climbing than studying, to be honest, including three small summer expeditions to Alaska—but that and my months here with Jean-Claude and the Deacon weren't enough experience or training in advanced techniques to take on the tallest and perhaps fiercest unclimbed mountain in the world. I mean, *George Leigh Mallory* had just died on Everest, for God's sake, and it might well have been his wonderfully physically fit but young and relatively novice high-climbing partner, Andrew "Sandy" Irvine, who'd fallen and pulled Mallory with him to his death.

And finally, I admit to myself as we edge another few meters lower, the rope connecting the three of us always properly a little slack, I don't believe, when push comes to shove, that I have the nerve to go try Everest, even if the Alpine Club should suddenly decide to invite an underskilled and anxious impoverished Yank to accompany their next Everest expedition. (And I know there will be another expedition. Once the Brits get their teeth into some huge heroic expedition challenge, they simply don't give up, even when their heroes—Robert Falcon Scott, George Mallory—die in the attempt. Stubborn people, those Englishmen.)

But suddenly Jean-Claude and I are at the precise point where four members of Whymper's first successful summit party fell to their terrible deaths.

I have to interrupt my own narrative here to say that I know it seems strange that I am suddenly going to describe an accident that happened in July of 1865, 60 years previous to the adventure I hope to tell you of that took place in 1925. But as you'll see, at least one of the seemingly irrelevant details of that tragedy of the Whymper party's first successful ascent of the Matterhorn became the improbable element which allowed the *very* unofficial and almost totally unreported Deacon-Clairoux-Perry Himalayan Expedition of 1925.

The Whymper party had climbed the mountain roped together—all seven of them—but for some reason, they began the descent in two roped groups. Perhaps Edward Whymper's group and the excellent guide Michel Croz's were impeded by their giddiness and fatigue. On the first rope of four men, Croz—the best climber of them all—went first, followed by the true amateur, Douglas's friend Hadow, then the fairly experienced mountaineer Hudson, and finally the 18-year-old gifted amateur climber, Lord Francis Douglas.

The three remaining men—still standing at the extreme Swiss edge of the summit as their fellows began to descend—then roped up together: first "Old Peter" Taugwalder, then "Young Peter" Taugwalder, and finally Edward Whymper. Two mediocre guides and one excellent climber. Thus the descending victorious summit party consisted of four British climbers—one a professional, one a gifted amateur, and two pure amateurs—two only moderately competent Valaisans (the Taugwalders), and one truly gifted Savoyard, Michel Croz. By all logic, the supremely experienced guide Croz should have led the expedition—making decisions as well as leading the way—but although he was in the lead of the descent through the "treacherous bit" above the sheer overhang, it was still Whymper who commanded the expedition. And Croz had his hands full; although Hudson was a great help, occasionally steadying or even physically setting the following Lord Francis Douglas's feet on the proper niches and holds, Croz was doing the same to the more anxious and infinitely less physically capable Hadow for every step of this difficult descent. And Croz had to do this while finding the best and safest route down and then right to the easier summit ridge.

And so the seven descended the "treacherous bit" between the summit and the curving overhang which Jean-Claude, Deacon, and I had just come down.

But just above the spot where we now stood—the fatal spot, as it were—Lord Francis Douglas, the youngest among them, had the courage and brains to suggest that they all rope up and descend together, one team, just as they'd successfully ascended the mountain. I don't know why Whymper or Croz had not suggested it earlier.

In point of fact, it offered almost no additional safety. This "treacherous bit" of the Matterhorn descent below the summit and above the wave-cresting overhang is difficult now in 1924 with fixed ropes, clear routes established, and a majority of the loose rock long since kicked free of the mountain by climbers. In Whymper's day, the "treacherous bit" was even more treacherous, especially in terms of "objective danger" such as rockfall, but the greatest danger here—then and now—is that while the niches, fingerholds, and footholds are tiny and hard to find, the projecting boulders and flat areas where a man can brace himself for a belay are all but nonexistent.

So while the seven climbers, especially the amateurs, felt much more confident now that Whymper and the two Taugwalder guides were tied to their rope—by a totally inadequate rope connecting Old Peter and Lord Francis Douglas, it was discovered later—the new arrangement really didn't offer much, if any, additional safety.

And then it all happened at once. Despite a legal inquest in Zermatt which questioned all the principals just days after the event, despite later articles and newspaper stories and books by Whymper and all the other survivors, and despite a thousand newspaper stories about the event, no one is completely sure what happened and in which sequence.

It seems most probable that the rankest amateur, the 19-year-old Douglas Hadow, missed his step—even with Croz's guiding hands—and fell, hitting Croz hard and pulling the guide off his own perch. The combined weight of the suddenly plummeting Croz and Hadow must have plucked the more experienced Reverend Charles Hudson and the amazed Lord Francis Douglas off their tiny footholds in less than a second. In almost an instant, four of the seven roped men were bouncing and sliding toward their deaths.

The remaining three on the rope—"Old Peter" Taugwalder, still connected to Lord Francis Douglas and the other falling men by a cheap piece of rope, then "Young Peter," then Edward Whymper himself—acted immediately out of instinct and years of experience.

Old Peter was the only one who had any real chance of stopping the fall by a strong belay. He had a good, comparatively broad foothold. More than that, he was standing below one of the very few rock outcroppings on this entire "treacherous bit" of descent, and he'd looped the climbing rope around it without even thinking about it. Above him, Young Peter and Whymper grabbed what rock they could with one hand and braced themselves for a desperate belay with their other hands on the rope.

The rope went as taut as an arrow in flight. The physical shock of impact from four falling and constantly accelerating human bodies on the three braced men—especially on Old Peter—was terrible. The rope whipped through Old Peter's hands, leaving a terrible sear that remained for many weeks. (In his guilt and dismay, Old Peter would show anyone who would look his scarred hand.)

But despite the loop around the small outcropping above Old Peter—or perhaps because of it—the rope snapped in midair. Much later, Edward Whymper told a reporter that he had perfectly remembered the terrible sound of that snapping for twenty-five years and would until the moment of his own death.

In his book Whymper wrote:

For a few seconds, we saw our unfortunate companions sliding downwards on their backs, and spreading out their hands, endeavouring to save themselves. They passed from our sight uninjured, disappeared one by one, and fell from precipice to precipice on the Matterhorngletscher below, a distance of nearly 4,000 feet in height.

It takes a while for men to fall almost a mile. Luckily—if that's the word—they are almost always dead and largely dismembered long before they reach the bottom. Many was the time that I'd heard climbers—both in the States and in Europe—describe the horrors of slowly descending for hours after a comrade or comrades had fallen. It was not pristine. Each described following intermittent trails, on rock and snow and ice, of blood—so very much blood—and shattered ice axes and shredded, bloody clothing and boots, and, always, fragments of rended body parts.

Whymper and the Taugwalders' route—when they finally worked up the nerve to begin moving again, which was up to half an hour after their friends' fall, according to Whymper (who blamed the blubbering, terrified Taugwalders for the delay)—was on the slab-stepped ridge itself. From that angle they had a clear view of the bloody path of their friends' violent descent—bodies bouncing from boulder to boulder, ricocheting from precipice to precipice—down the sheer north face of the Matterhorn onto the unyielding ice of the Matterhorn Glacier.

In the end, it took Whymper more than two days to urge, cajole, threaten, bribe, and shame the Zermatt guides to climb back up to that glacier to "retrieve the bodies." The local guides—members all of a strong guides' trade union—obviously knew better than the gifted amateur British climber what "bodies" would consist of after such a fall. The guides also had a much better appreciation of what Whymper was calling "a simple climb to the base of the mountain." The climb to the glacier at the base of the north face of the Matterhorn was a dangerous proposition—in some ways as dangerous as climbing the mountain—with hidden crevasses, seracs that could collapse at any time, unstable pinnacles and leaning towers of old ice, and a maze of ice boulders in which men could, and usually did, get lost for hours or days.

But eventually Whymper got his volunteers—paid "volunteers" in the case of most of the guides who grudgingly agreed to go on Monday (on Sunday they all had to stay in Zermatt for Mass)—and eventually they found the bodies.

Whymper later admitted that he'd fully hoped, through some miracle of soft snow and lucky sliding for almost a vertical mile, that he would find one or more of his climbing partners alive.

Not even close.

What was left of the three corpses was scattered on the ice and rock at the base of the north face. Rocks were falling all around the "rescuers" almost the entire time they were there, but when the guides fled for cover, Whymper and other Englishmen who'd joined him held their ground. Or, to be specific, the Brits stupidly and stubbornly held their spot on the glacier, with rocks and boulders slamming down all around like cold meteors.

At first no one, not even Whymper, could distinguish the bits of one corpse from another. But then the Englishman was able to identify his guide and friend Michel Croz by a bit of his beard. Croz's arms and legs had been torn off, as well as most of his skull, but a fragment of his lower jaw remained, and the beard there was the color of Croz's beard. One of the guides who returned when the rockfall let up, an old friend of Michel Croz's, identified scars on a shattered forearm lying many yards away and a hand atop an ice boulder with more scars that Croz's friend well remembered.

Oddly enough, there were slight tatters of trousers left around Croz's dismembered trunk, and six gold coins had stayed in the pocket during his entire descent. .

Someone noticed that Croz's crucifix—without which he never climbed—had dug itself deep into the surviving fragment of the guide's lower jaw, embedding itself as deep and solidly as a cross-shaped bullet. One of the men, Robertson, clicked open his penknife and dug it out, thinking that Croz's family might want it.

Hudson's remains were identified only by his wallet, and by a letter from his wife that had completed the descent with him when his arms, legs, and head had not. Whymper found one of Hudson's gloves and, wandering wider on the bloodied glacier, picked up a broad-brimmed English sunhat that he, Whymper, had only recently given Croz.

The majority of Hadow's remains were scattered between those of Croz and Hudson.

As the guides ran for shelter during another rock avalanche, Whymper stood by the bodies and noticed for the first time that the rope was still attached between what was left of the torsos of Croz and Hadow, and also between Hadow and Hudson.

There was no body of Lord Francis Douglas. Some records say that the men that day found one of Douglas's boots—no human foot inside—while others say that it was a belt that Whymper had noticed Douglas wearing during the ascent. Another story says that it was a single glove.

Whymper's realization at that moment was that the first three men had been secured by one of the thicker, more solid ropes, while Old Peter Taugwalder had tied Douglas to himself by a much thinner, lighter rope, not often used for roping the actual climbers. There was no doubt in Whymper's mind at that moment that Old Peter had deliberately used a less secure rope in case the first four men should fall. In later years, the famous British climber came close to accusing the old guide of this in plain words and print.

In truth, though, *all* the ropes—even the thinner one Old Peter Taugwalder had around his shoulder when it came time to tie Lord Francis Douglas on to the common rope connecting all seven of them—had been used without any thought or undue concern as connecting ropes between the climbers during the descent that day and on many others. Edward Whymper simply didn't concern himself with relative rope thicknesses, tensile strengths, and the mathematics of breaking points in different diameters and makes of rope until *after* the tragedy on his day of triumph on the Matterhorn.

No one ever did find the remains of 18-year-old Francis Douglas, and this fact gave rise to an odd little footnote to the tragedy.

Lord Francis Douglas's somewhat elderly mother, Lady Queensberry, as Whymper wrote, "suffered much from the idea of her son not having been found."

In truth, it was worse than that. Lady Queensberry soon became obsessed with the morbid conviction that her young son was still alive somewhere on the Matterhorn—trapped high in an ice cave, perhaps, while surviving by eating lichens and bits of mountain goats, drinking the water that tumbled over his prison from the snows above. Perhaps—most probably Lady Queensberry thought—her beloved son Francis was injured, unable to descend on his own and even unable to find a way to signal to those so far below. Or perhaps, she told one old friend during a visit, Francis had survived the fall to the glacier—after all, he wasn't attached by rope to those who had died so horribly—and was even now eking out a cold survival in a crevasse somewhere.

Men of honor such as Professor John Tyndall—who had almost joined Whymper on the famous first ascent—then returned to the Matterhorn to carry out systematic searches for Douglas's remains. He wrote to Lady Queensberry and promised "to exert to the full extent of my abilities in the difficult and dangerous—but necessary for your piece of mind—task of finding and returning your brave son's body to his native land and ancestral home."

But Douglas's mother wasn't interested in someone returning her darling son Francis's body. She knew he was alive and she wanted him found.

She went to her grave believing that Lord Francis Douglas still lived, stranded high on the north face of the Matterhorn or wandering the cold blue caverns beneath the glacier at the mountain's foot.

So the Deacon calls a halt to our descent through the "treacherous bit," and Jean-Claude and I stand there a few meters lower than him, both of us getting colder by the minute (the north face is in full shadow now and the wind has grown colder as it increases its howling), and—at least on my part—wondering what the hell old Richard Davis Deacon is up to. Perhaps, I think, he's getting senile. After all, the Deacon, although physically more fit than I am at 22, is entering his dotage at age 37 (the precise age of George Mallory when he disappeared on Everest this same month).

"This is the place," the Deacon says softly. "Precisely the place where Croz, Hadow, Hudson, and Lord Francis Douglas fell and went over that edge..." He points only 40 or 50 feet below, where the arching crest of the Matterhorn's picturesque overhang becomes an invariably fatal drop.

"Merde," says Jean-Claude, speaking for both of us. "Jake and I know that. You *know* that we know all that. Don't tell us, Richard Davis Deacon, former schoolteacher that you are, that you brought us down this miserable route with no fixed ropes—we have a dozen or more to choose from just thirty steps to your right, and I'd be delighted to drive in a piton and clip in a fresh rope if you like—don't tell us you brought us this way just so you could show and tell us a piece of history that everyone who loves the Alps and this mountain has known since we were in short pants. Let us quit talking and get off this fucking face."

We do so, moving easily and confidently to our right, always aware of the emptiness below us here, until we move out onto the relatively safe slabs—a series of upturned steps was the way Whymper once described the ridge after giving up on the Italian side (downturned slabs) and trying this Swiss Ridge—and from there we unrope, and the descent becomes, despite the continued danger of rockfall or slipping on ice, "easy as eating your piece of pie," as Jean-Claude would sometimes say.

We knew now that, barring any nasty surprise, we'd reach the Hornli Hut at 3,260 meters, almost 11,000 feet—a comfortable enough hut for one perched on a narrow ledge and wedged into the mountain itself—before full darkness fell. Two-thirds of the way down we reached an old cache of ours. (Our cache—mostly just some extra food, water, and blankets for the hut—was set almost exactly where Whymper's people had left their rucksacks during their ascent. What must the three survivors have felt and thought on their silent descent as they lifted their dead friends' four rucksacks and carried them down the mountain with them?)

I realize that I'm feeling morbid and depressed as hell—plus my week of climbing the Matterhorn, not to mention the many previous months with these two men, is now over. What am I going to do now? Go back to Boston and try to get a job? Literature majors tend to end up teaching literature they love to bored freshmen who couldn't give the slightest bucket of warm spit about the material, and this thought of making my future living in the Fifth Bolgia of the Eighth Circle of Academic Hell depresses me even more. Jean-Claude looks pretty miserable as well, but he has a *great* job to return to as a Chamonix Guide. He's very close friends with the Deacon and obviously sorry to see the long climbing vacation—and relationship—end for now.

The Deacon is grinning like an idiot. I'm not certain that I've ever seen Richard Davis Deacon fully grin before—smile ironically, sure, but *grin* like a normal human being? Much less grin like an idiot? Uh-oh. Something is very wrong with that grin. His voice, although audibly excited, is slow, almost formal in its Cambridge cadences. The Deacon is taking turns making serious eye contact with each of us as he speaks—something else he rarely does.

"Jean-Claude Clairoux," he says softly. "Jacob William Perry. Would you care to accompany me on a fully funded expedition to climb Mount Everest in the next spring and early summer of nineteen twenty-five? It will just be the three of us as climbers and some necessary porters—including a few high-climbing Sherpas to help establish the high camps, but still just porters. We will be the three climbers—the three men attempting the summit. Only us."

This is where Jean-Claude and I, knowing that this must be pure fantasy or mean-spirited bullshit, should be shouting, "You can't be serious" and "Go tell it to someone who just got off the boat, Limey," but this is the Deacon speaking, so the young French Chamonix Guide and I look at each other intently for a long few seconds, turn back to the Deacon, and say in total solemnity and almost perfect unison...

"Yes. We'll go."

And so it begins.

*So there at the center of the most beautiful 9,400 acres in
the world resides a permanently broken heart and an
eternally damaged mind.*

The car ride from London to the Bromley estate in Lincolnshire takes us about two hours, including a lunch stop in Sandy since we are running ahead of schedule and don't want to arrive early, but by mid-afternoon, still a few minutes ahead of schedule, we've reached Stamford Junction. We are only a couple of miles from our destination, and I admit to feeling nervous almost to the point of nausea, although I've never been carsick before—especially not in an open touring car on a beautiful summer day with pleasant breezes smelling of farm fields and forest, astounding scenery on all sides, and a perfectly cloudless blue sky above.

A sign names Stamford Junction "Carpenter's Lodge" in the usual British way of obfuscating everything, and we turn left down a narrow lane. A ten-foot-high solid masonry wall blocks the view on our left for all of these last two miles.

"What's the wall for?" I ask the Deacon, who is driving.

"It encloses a small part of the Bromley estate," says the older climber around his pipe stem. "That's the famous Bromley Deer Park on the other side of the wall, and Lady Bromley doesn't want her deer—tame as they are—jumping out and getting hurt."

"Or allow the poachers to get in all that easily, I imagine," says Jean-Claude.

The Deacon nods.

"How big is the Bromley estate?" I ask from the backseat.

"Well, let me think," says the Deacon. "I seem to remember that the previous marquess, the late Lord Bromley, set aside about eight thousand acres for farmland—most of it usually fallow and used for hunting—about nine hundred acres of woodland, pristine forest going back to Queen Elizabeth. And I think only about five hundred acres for the deer park, gardens, and grounds, all tended year-round by a small army of foresters and gardeners."

"Almost ten thousand acres of estate," I say stupidly, turning to stare at the high wall as if I might suddenly be able to see through it.

"Almost," agrees the Deacon. "In truth, it's much larger than the ninety-four hundred acres here. The village of Stamford we passed through back there officially belongs to the Bromley estate—as did all the people living in it and in the other hundred and forty–some residences around Stamford and edges of the estate—and there are several dozen commercial properties, in and beyond Stamford, that Lady Bromley still owns and administers as part of the estate. When they said lord of the manor in the old days, they meant it."

I try to imagine this. I've seen huge patches of privately owned land, of course. On my summer climbing trips during my years at Harvard, I'd headed out west to climb in the Rockies, and some of the ranches the train passed through probably approached or surpassed half a million acres—perhaps a million. Someone out there told me that while a cow needed a little less than an acre to graze on happily back in my home state of Massachusetts, the same cow would require more than forty acres just to stay alive in the high plains of eastern Colorado or Wyoming. Most of the huge ranches out there grew sagebrush, rabbit brush, and a few old cottonwood trees along the creeks—if the land *had* any creeks. Most of it did not. The Bromley estate, according to the Deacon, has 900 acres of ancient woodland used for . . . what? Hunting, probably. Strolling in. Shade for the tame deer when they get tired of hanging around the sunny parts of their dedicated park area.

The wall curves away to the south, we drive a bit further and turn left down a narrow and rather rutted road, and then suddenly we are passing under an ancient archway into the estate. There is a large gravel approach here—no estate house or gardens or anything of interest visible all the way to the green, hilly horizon—and the Deacon parks our touring car in the shade and leads us to a carriage, complete with mustachioed driver and two white horses, waiting near a narrow asphalted road winding away into the green depths of the estate. The carriage is so ornately bedecked with badges and doodads along the sides and back that it looks as if it might have been designed for Queen Victoria's coronation parade.

The driver hops down and opens the topless carriage's door for us. He looks old enough that he, too, might have taken part in Queen Victoria's parade. I admire his long, pure-white twin mustaches, which make him look a bit like a very tall, very thin walrus.

"Welcome back, Master Richard," the old man says to the Deacon as he shuts the door. "If I may be allowed to say so, sir, you look very fit indeed."

"Thank you, Benson," says the Deacon. "You do as well. I'm delighted that you're still livery master."

"Oh, only in charge of the entrance carriage now, Master Richard." The old man spryly hops up to his place in front and takes the reins and whip in hand.

As we roll out onto the lane, the sound of the carriage wheels—iron, not rubber—on the asphalt surface and the clop-clop of the huge horses' hooves make it probable that anything we say in a normal tone of voice won't be heard by Mr. Benson. Still, we speak with heads leaning close and just above a whisper.

Jean-Claude: "*Master* Richard? You've been here before, *mon ami*."

"I was ten years old the last time I was here," says the Deacon. "And spanked by one of the butlers for punching young Lord Percival on his prominent snout. He cheated in some game we were playing."

I keep turning my head, trying to take in as much as I can of the perfectly mowed and manicured hills, trees, bushes—a lake of some acres sends light flashes toward us as the wind ruffles it into low waves—while far off to the south I believe I can see the beginning of formal gardens and the hint of a tall building on the horizon. But it's far too broad and expansive to be a single building—even for Bromley House—so it must be a village of sorts.

"You were—are—a social equal to the Bromleys?" I whisper. It's a rude question, but I ask it out of surprise and slight shock. The Deacon had insisted that I go to his tailor at Savile Row to get a bespoke suit for this meeting—I've never owned one that fit so well or felt so good on me—and he insisted on paying for it, but I had been certain from the months together in Europe that the Deacon had no great reservoir of funds to fall back on. Now I'm wondering if the next 9,000-acre estate beyond Stamford is called Deacon House.

The Deacon shakes his head, puts away his pipe, and smiles ruefully. "My family has an old name and no money left for its final disappointment of a scion...me. It's not legal now to surrender one's hereditary title, but if it were, I would do so in a heartbeat. As it is, I have attempted to avoid all use of and reference to it since I returned from the War. But way back in another century, I occasionally came here to play with Charles Bromley, who was about my age, and his younger brother Percy—who had no real friends or playmates for reasons you'll discover soon enough. That all ended on the day I punched Percival in the nose. After that, Charles came to visit me instead."

I knew that the Deacon had been born in the same year as George Leigh Mallory—1886—but because of his still-dark hair and superb physical condition, surpassing (as I believe I've mentioned) both Jean-Claude's and mine in most aspects of climbing, ice and snow work, and stamina, I never really thought of Richard Davis Deacon having lived fourteen years of his life in the previous century... fifteen years under Queen Victoria!

We clop onward.

"Do all visitors park their cars at the gate and take carriages to the house?" J.C. loudly asks Benson, the driver.

"Oh, no, sir," replies the old man without turning his head in our direction. "When there is a party or reception at Bromley House or Bromley Park—although there are precious few of those these days, the Lord knows—chauffeured guests may ride in their motorcars directly to the house. The same applies to our most esteemed visitors, including the former queens and His current Majesty."

"King George the Fifth has visited Bromley House?" I say, hearing the awestruck provincial quality and American twang in my own voice.

"Oh, yes, sir," Benson says brightly, tapping the slower of the two white horses on the rump with a light touch of the whip.

All I knew about the current British king was that he'd changed his family name from the House of Saxe-Coburg and Gotha to the more

English-sounding House of Windsor during the Great War, in an effort to renounce all his close connections to Germany. Still, the Kaiser had been George V's cousin, and it was said that they'd been affectionate. They certainly looked very much alike. If they had swapped medals and uniforms on one of their many visits to see each other, I almost believe each could have ruled the other's kingdom without anyone noticing.

I'd once asked the Deacon about the current king and all he said was, "I'm afraid he divides his time between shooting animals and sticking stamps in albums, Jacob old boy. If George—His Majesty—has a third passion or ability, we, his loyal and loving subjects, have yet to learn about it."

"Has other British royalty visited Bromley House?" asks Jean-Claude in a voice loud enough for Benson, our driver, to hear.

"Oh, my, yes," says the driver, glancing back over his black-liveried shoulder this time. "Almost every royal has visited and stayed at Bromley House since construction of the home began in fifteen fifty-seven, the year before Elizabeth came to the throne. Queen Elizabeth had apartments here which have never been used by guests other than royal. The so-called George Rooms were used as a vacation suite by Queen Victoria for several months in eighteen forty-four—and she returned to them many times. It is said that Her Majesty especially enjoyed the ceilings painted by Antonio Verrio."

We clop along in relative silence for another minute.

"Yes, many of our kings and queens and Princes of Wales and other royals have enjoyed parties, overnight stays, and long vacations at Bromley House," adds Benson. "But in recent years the royal visits have dropped off. Lord Bromley—the fourth marquess, you know—died ten years ago, and His current Majesty may have more pressing things to do than visit widows... if you don't mind me saying so, sir."

"Isn't there an older son still living, big brother to the Percy Bromley who disappeared on Everest?" I whisper to the Deacon. "The fifth Marquess of Lexeter?"

"Yes. Charles. I know him well. He was gassed during the War, was invalided out but never really recovered. He's been virtually a prisoner in his room and attended to by nurses for some years now. Everyone had been suspecting that the end was near for Charles and that Percy would take up the mantle as the sixth Marquess of Lexeter sometime later this year."

"How, gassed?" whispers Jean-Claude. "Where in the British Army does one put a Lord?"

"Charles was an army major and had survived much of the worst fighting, but in the last year of the War, he and other important personages from government and the army were part of a Red Cross delegation, visiting forward positions to make a report to the agency," the Deacon says quietly. "A three-hour cease-fire had been arranged between the British section of the Front there and the Germans, but something went wrong and there was an artillery barrage almost on their positions...mustard gas. And most of the delegation's members had forgone carrying gas masks with them. It did not matter for Charles, since his worst wounds weren't in his lungs but were the result of actual mustard powder from the shells spilling onto his flesh. Some wounds, you see—especially being exposed to mustard gas powder—literally never heal. They must be dressed anew every day and the pain never ceases."

"Damned *boches,*" hisses Jean-Claude. "Never to be trusted."

The Deacon smiles grimly. "They were British artillery firing. English mustard gas that fell a bit short. Someone didn't get the cease-fire notice." Then, after a short interval filled only by the sound of the carriage wheels and the clop of the huge horses' hooves, the Deacon adds, "Actually, it was the artillery unit that George Leigh Mallory was in charge of that killed half a dozen Red Cross important personages and turned poor Charles Bromley into an invalid, but I've heard that Mallory wasn't there at the time...was back in Blighty nursing his own wound or illness of some sort."

The Deacon, more loudly: "Benson, could you tell us about the door for the royals on the west side?"

Ahead of us I catch a glimpse of formal gardens, perfectly manicured fields and low hills, and many spires and steeples rising above the horizon. Far too many spires and steeples for a *house;* too many for a mere village. It is as if we're approaching a city amidst all this perfect greenery.

"Certainly, Master Richard," says the driver. The long white mustaches are twitching slightly—I can see that even from the rear as he drives—perhaps because he's smiling.

"Arrivals for Queen Elizabeth since the sixteenth century, Queen Victoria, King George the Fifth, and others were always arranged for late afternoon or very early evening—if convenient for the royals, of course, sirs—since, you see, the hundreds of windows there on the west side were specifically designed to capture the sunset. The glass was actually treated in some way, I believe. They would all glow gold, as if there were a bright fire behind every one of those many windows, you might say, sirs. Very warm and welcoming to His or Her Majesty, even on a winter's eve. And in the center of the west wall of the House, used by no one else but royals, is the gold door—or, rather, gold carved portal might be more accurate, since it is only the outer layer of several beautiful doors, designed and constructed specifically for Elizabeth's first visit. This was sometime before the death of the first Lord Bromley. I believe Queen Elizabeth and her court retinue came to stay with us for several weeks in fifteen ninety-eight. There is a beautiful courtyard at the center of the residential wings, sirs—totally private, although you may catch a glimpse of it when you have tea with Lady Bromley—where it's said that Shakespeare's troupe of players performed several times. The courtyard was actually designed—in terms of perfect natural amplification of the human voice and every other aspect—specifically for theatrical events with audiences of hundreds."

I interrupt with a banality: "Jean-Claude, Deacon, look at that ancient ruin on the hill. It looks like a small medieval castle—or a keep—that's gone to ruin. Tower all overgrown with ivy and stones tumbling down, an old tree growing out of that tall Gothic window on that broken wall standing alone. Amazing. I wonder how old it is?"

"Almost certainly less than fifty years old," says the Deacon. "It's a folly, Jake."

"A what?"

"A folly. They were all the rage in the seventeenth through the nineteenth century—going in and out of style. I think it was the last-but-one Lady Bromley in the late eighteen hundreds who demanded her medieval folly on that hill, where she could see it when she went riding. Most of the landscaping, though, was redesigned earlier—in the late seventeen hundreds, I believe—by Capability Brown."

"By whom?" asks Jean-Claude. "That would be a good name for a good climber—'Capability.'"

"His real first name was Lancelot," says the Deacon. "But everyone called him Capability Brown. He was considered England's greatest gardener in the eighteenth century and designed the gardens and grounds for, I think—I'm not sure of the exact number—almost two hundred of England's top country houses and estates, and for such noble piles as Blenheim Palace. I do remember my mother telling me about what Capability Brown said to Hannah More in the seventeen sixties, when they were both famous."

"Who or what was Hannah More?" I ask, no longer embarrassed by my ignorance. England is a stranger land than I'd bargained for.

"She was a religious writer—*very* widely read—and a very generous philanthropist up until her death sometime in the eighteen thirties. Anyway, Capability Brown called his complicated gardens and grounds *grammatical landscapes,* and when he was showing Hannah More around some completed estate grounds—perhaps her own, although I have no idea if she hired him to do her country place—he put his landscaping in Hannah More's own terms, and I remember most of what my mother, who was an avid gardener right up until her death twenty years ago, quoted from Brown's soliloquy."

I think even Benson up on the driver's seat is listening, since he is leaning back further than before without reining in the horses in any way.

"*Now there,* Capability Brown would say, pointing his finger at some landscape figure which looked as if it had always been there but which he'd designed," says the Deacon. "*There I make a comma, and there*—pointing to some boulder or fallen oak or other seeming natural element, perhaps a hundred yards away or in the gardens—*where a decided turn is proper, I make a colon; at another part, where an interruption is desirable to break the view, a parenthesis; now a full stop, and then I begin another subject.*" The Deacon pauses. "Or something fairly close to that. It's been a lot of years since my mother talked to me about Capability Brown."

I can see by the inward direction of his gaze that he's been hearing his mother's voice.

"Maybe that castle folly on the hill is a semicolon," I say stupidly. "No, wait, you said Capability Brown didn't do the folly."

"He would not have constructed a folly for a million pounds," says the Deacon with a smile. "His specialty was doing elaborate gardens where even the trained eye doesn't realize there's a garden there." The Deacon points to a partially wooded hillside with an amazing variety of shrubbery, fallen trunks, and wildflowers.

But then the carriage tops a low rise, we make a slight right turn with hooves still clopping on asphalt, and all of our babble ceases.

The formal gardens are clearly visible now, surrounded and sometimes intersected by straight and circular driveways of pure white gravel—or perhaps crushed oyster shells, or maybe pearls for all I know. The gardens and fountains are breathtaking, but it's the first full sight of Bromley House beyond the gardens that has me immediately standing in the carriage, looking over Benson's shoulder, and muttering loudly, "My God. Dear God."

Not exactly the most sophisticated entrance I've ever made. But quite probably the most American-fundamentalist-religion-sounding (though my family in Boston were Unitarian freethinkers).

Bromley House is officially a Tudor mansion, designed—as I mentioned earlier—by the first Lord Bromley, who was chief clerk and assistant to Queen Elizabeth's Lord High Treasurer, Lord Burghley, when he began work on the house in the 1550s. The Deacon later told me that Bromley House was one of several *prodigy houses* built by rising young men in England around that time, but I've forgotten what the term really means. He also told me that although the first Lord Bromley and his family moved into the livable parts of the estate in 1557, the actual building period of Bromley House extended over thirty-five years.

Thirty-five years plus another three and a half centuries, since it is obvious even to my architecturally untutored eyes that generations of lords and ladies have added on to, subtracted from, fiddled with, experimented with, and altered this estate a thousand times.

"The House..."—I can hear the capital letters in Benson's soft but proud old voice—"was damaged some during the Civil War—Cromwell's men were beasts, absolute uncaring beasts, uncaring and careless about even the finest works of art—but the fifth earl enclosed the damaged south side with windows to create a great gallery. Filled with light, I've been told, and charming in all except the cold winter months.

That gallery was enclosed and turned into a Great Hall — much easier to heat — sometime later in the seventeenth century by the eighth earl."

"Earl?" I whisper to the Deacon. "I thought we were dealing with lords and ladies and marquesses with Percival's family."

The Deacon shrugs. "Titles change and shift a little over time, old boy. The fellow who designed this pile in the fifteen hundreds was William Basil, the first Lord Bromley. His son Charles Basil, also Lord Bromley, was anointed the first Earl of Lexeter in sixteen oh-four, the year after Queen Elizabeth died."

I understand nothing of this except the part about Elizabeth dying. Our carriage is rolling around the south face of the huge structure toward a distant entrance on the east side.

"You might find this blank corner a bit interesting," the Deacon says, pointing to a corner of the house we're passing. On the west side, two vertical rows of beautiful windows rise sixty or eighty feet, but the corners of the building look less elegant, as if they had been covered almost hastily with heavy masonry.

"A few hundred years ago, whatever Lord Bromley it was at the time realized that while the elevation of his Great Hall looking out onto the Orangery Court was beautiful and light-filled, almost all glass across this entire exposure, there were just too damned many beautiful windows and not enough load-bearing walls. The incredible weight of the English oak roof, combined with the weight of the thousands of Collywestons..."

"What is a Collyweston?" asks Jean-Claude. "It sounds like the name of an English hunting or herding dog."

"A Collyweston is a slab of a particularly heavy sort of gray slate used for the roof tiles in many of the larger old estates in England. It was first found and produced right here, on this property, by the Romans. Actually, that Collyweston slate is almost impossible to find in England today except here on the grounds of Bromley House and a couple of other remote sites. At any rate, you can see where the alarmed earl a few centuries ago covered over more beautiful vertical lines of windows and added more load-bearing stone. Those little windows you see up around where the fourth story would be as we came in from the north — they have glass panes but just more masonry behind them. That roof is one heavy bugger."

The totality of Bromley House is staggering—larger within its myriad walls and interior courtyards than many Massachusetts villages I've visited—but it is the rooftop and above that pulls my gaze upward at the moment. (I suspect that my mouth is hanging open, but I'm too carried away by this sight to worry about that. I'm sure the Deacon will close it for me if I look too much the village idiot.) Benson spryly hops down from his perch and comes around to the side of the carriage to open the half-door for us.

Just the rooftop of the endless manor—so far above us—is an almost impossible mass of vertical (and some horizontal) protrusions: obelisks with no seeming purpose, a magnificent clock tower with the face of the clock turned toward the apparently unused-for-guests south face of the house, row upon row of high, ancient-Greek-looking columns that are actually smokestacks for the countless fireplaces in the city-sized house below, arches arching over nothing to speak of, crenellated towers with high, thin windows on their erect shafts and tiny little round windows under their priapic muffinheads, more windows on horizontal Old London Bridge–style hanging upper floors that connected some of these thicker and more windowed erections, and finally a series of taller, thinner, more sexually provocative towers scattered at apparent random around and between and above the other projections on the tower-cluttered rooftop. These last are graceful towers which look like nothing so much as Moslem minarets pilfered from some Middle Eastern mosque.

Another butler in very formal and old-fashioned livery—this gentleman apparently even older than our carriage driver but clean-shaven, bald as a proverbial billiard ball, and with a much more stooped posture caused by curvature of the spine—bows toward us at the open east entrance door and says, "Welcome, gentlemen. Lady Bromley is expecting you and will join you shortly. Master Deacon, you must forgive me if I comment that you look extremely well and tanned and fit."

"Thank you, Harrison," says the Deacon.

"Pardon me, sir?" says Harrison, cupping his left ear. He seems to be almost deaf as well as terminally stooped over and evidently not very good at reading lips. The Deacon repeats his three words in a low shout. Harrison smiles—showing perfect dentures—and rasping out, "Please follow me, gentlemen," turns to lead us inside.

As we follow this ancient butler's slow shuffle through anterooms and then into a series of Great Rooms on our march to God Knows Where, the Deacon whispers to us, "Harrison is the butler who paddled my arse when I punched young Lord Percival thirty years ago."

"I would like to see him try it today," whispers Jean-Claude with an evil smile that I've seen before and which somehow manages to look attractively roguish to the ladies.

We follow the shuffling old butler through a series of art-hung, Persian-carpeted, and red-drapery-laden foyers, then out into and through at least three "public rooms," where the art and color and size and quality of the antiques alone take one's breath away.

But it's not the gilded antique furniture that almost makes me stop in amazement.

Harrison manages a feeble wave of his left arm toward the ceiling and room in general and announces in his old man's croak, "The Heaven Room, gentlemen. Quite..."

I don't catch the last word, but it might have been "famous."

To me it seems more like "the Football Room," since the ceilings are at least forty feet high and the room looks to be as long and almost as wide as an American football field. My thought is that you could set rows of bleachers up against these gilded, picture-addled walls and hold the Harvard-Yale game in here.

But it is the endless and elaborately painted ceiling that makes my jaw drop open again.

I'm sure that the hundreds (*hundreds!*) of naked or mostly naked male and female grappling forms up there are supposed to be gods and goddesses gamboling in some innocent pagan god way, but it just looks like the world's largest orgy to my barbarian's eye. Amazingly, the artist has many of the figures spilling off the ceiling itself and grappling and tumbling and evidently fornicating their way down the actual walls, stacking up in the corners in fleshy masses of thighs, breasts, and biceps, with more intertwined bodies painted onto side doors and mirrors, as if they're trying to stop their tangled mass from falling to the Persian-carpeted parquet floor. The three-dimensional effect is dizzying and disturbing.

"Antonio Verrio did most of these murals in sixteen ninety-five and ninety-six," the Deacon says softly, obviously assuming that our aged guide won't hear him. "If you think this is something, you ought to see his Mouth of Hell murals on the ceiling at the head of the grand staircase—according to Verrio, the Mouth of Hell is the maw of a giant cat gobbling up naked lost souls like so many mangled mice."

"*Magnifique*," whispers Jean-Claude, also looking at the Heaven Room ceiling. And in an even lower whisper, "Although—what is your word?—ostentatious. *Very* ostentatious."

The Deacon smiles. "Word is that during the year or so Verrio was here painting, he had his way with every female servant on the estate—including the peasant girls who worked in the fields. Actually the walls weren't completely finished when they brought in a children's book illustrator—I think his name was Stothard—to finish off this hell of a heaven."

I stare at the scores upon scores of entangled, thrusting, intertwined naked male and female forms, many—as I mentioned—falling off the ceiling and writhing down the walls in their physical grapplings, and think, *A children's book illustrator painted some of this?*

As I follow the shuffling, silent butler through the Heaven Room, I'm grateful that the Deacon insisted on my going to his tailor on Savile Row for a proper dark suit. Since J.C. had once mentioned to me that the Deacon, the last of his once well-to-do family, had little money these days, I protested strongly, but the Deacon said that he simply couldn't allow me to meet Lady Bromley in that "dusty, dung-colored, misshapen *tweedy* thing that you wear when a suit is called for." I huffily explained to the Deacon that this "dung-colored thing"—my best tweed suit—had seen me through all of the formal demands of Harvard (at least where evening dress wasn't necessary), but my British climbing friend was not impressed with my argument.

So as we leave the Heaven Room to enter a smaller, much more intimate side room, I once again appreciate the tailored smoothness of my new Deacon-chosen and Deacon-paid-for Savile Row suit. Jean-Claude, on the other hand, has enough personal confidence that he's wearing an old suit in which he's probably guided climbs—it looks as if it would go well with mountain boots, and I'm sure it has.

* * *

Old Harrison the butler finally parks us in a side room only two absurdly imposing hallways and a breathtaking library away from the Heaven Room. After the great expanses we've covered getting here, this cozy little side room seems like a dollhouse miniature, even though it's probably half again the size of most middle-class Americans' front parlors.

"Please have a seat, gentlemen. Tea and Lady Bromley will be with you promptly," says old Harrison and shuffles out. The way he announces it makes the tea and the lady of one of England's greatest estates somehow sound like conjoined equals. Perhaps one never travels anywhere without the other.

For a moment the small size and sense of intimacy of this little room—only a few pieces of furniture centered atop a gorgeous Persian rug surrounded by gleaming parquet floors, one high-backed chair upholstered in a fabric that looks to be from the nineteenth century, a low round table presumably for the imminent tea service, two delicate chairs on either side looking too flimsy for an adult male to sit in, and a red settee directly across from the upholstered chair—make me think that this is one of the *private* rooms in Bromley House, but then I immediately realize I'm wrong. The small paintings and photographs on the delicately wallpapered wall are all of women. The few bookshelves, unlike the impossibly huge library we glimpsed earlier, hold only a few volumes, and they look homemade, perhaps scrapbooks or photo albums or collections of recipes or family genealogy.

But, no, however much it looks like one, this room is not a private room for the house. I realize that Lady Bromley must use it to meet people of lesser social stature in an informal setting. Perhaps she'd talk to her landscaper or head gamekeeper or very distant visiting relatives here—ones that were *not* going to be offered a room for the night.

Jean-Claude, the Deacon, and I are squished thigh to thigh as we sit upright and waiting on the red settee. It's an uncomfortable piece of furniture—perhaps another invitation not to stay too long. I nervously run my thumb and finger down the sharp crease in my new suit trousers.

Suddenly a door hidden in the library wall opens and Lady Elizabeth Marion Bromley comes through. The three of us almost stumble over one another in our hurry to stand.

Lady Bromley is tall, and her height is emphasized by the fact that she's dressed all in black, a lacy sort of dress with a high frilly black collar that might have been from the nineteenth century but which looks strangely modern. Her erect posture and poised but seemingly unself-conscious way of walking add to the sense of height and importance. I'd expected to meet an old lady—Lord Percival Bromley was in his thirties when he disappeared on Everest this summer—but Lady Bromley's hair, swept up in a complicated fashion I'd seen only in magazines, is mostly dark with only the slightest traces of gray at the temples. Her dark eyes are bright and alert and—to my deeper surprise—she comes toward us walking quickly, coming around the table to be closer to us, smiling kindly and evidently sincerely, and with both her hands—elegant, pale, with long pianist's fingers, not an old woman's hands in any way—outstretched in greeting.

"Oh, Dickie...Dickie...," says Lady Bromley, taking the Deacon's large, calloused hand in both of hers. "It's so wonderful to see you back here. It seems like just yesterday that your mother was dropping you off here to play with Charles...and, oh, how irritated both of you older boys became at little Percy's attempts to keep up with you!"

Jean-Claude and I risk a look and silent query to each other. *Dickie?!*

"It is wonderful to see you, Lady Bromley, but I am so deeply sorry about the circumstances which bring us together again," says the Deacon.

Lady Bromley nods and looks down for a second as her eyes fill, but she smiles and lifts her head again. "Charles greatly regrets that he cannot greet you himself today—his health is very poor, as you know."

The Deacon nods sympathetically.

"But you were also wounded during the War," says Lady Bromley, still holding the Deacon's hand with one of her hands above his, the other below.

"Mild wounds, long healed," says the Deacon. "Nothing like the terrible gassing that Charles experienced. My thoughts have gone out to him a thousand times."

"And your letter of condolence about Percival was beautiful, just beautiful," Lady Bromley says very softly. "But I am being rude—please, Dickie, introduce me to your friends."

The introductions and short conversations go smoothly. Lady Bromley speaks in fluent French to J.C., and I pick up enough of it to understand that she is expressing how impressed she is that such a young man should be known as such a fine Chamonix Guide, and Jean-Claude replies with his biggest, brightest grin.

"And Mr. Perry," she says when it is time to turn to me, taking my clumsily outstretched hand gracefully in hers. A brief touch but somehow electrifying. "Even in my rural isolation, I've heard of the Perrys of Boston—a fine family."

I stammer my thanks. I am from a well-known and fine old family, Boston Brahmins all down to the next-to-last generation, a family history traceable back to the 1630s, family members famous as merchants and Harvard professors, and a few brave ones who distinguished themselves in places like Bunker Hill and Gettysburg.

But alas, the Brahmin Perrys of Boston were now almost broke. Declining wealth had not kept my parents from calling the Harvard-Yale football game only "the Game," or from doing their modest Christmas shopping downtown at the seven-story S. S. Pierce Company, which had been serving families like ours since 1831. Nor, initially, did our advancing poverty prevent me from experiencing the best private schools, the tennis courts and greens and formal dining areas of the Brookline Country Club (which, of course, we referred to only as "the Country Club," as if no others existed in the world), and of having my parents pay my way through Harvard—which finally drained the last resources of the family. All so that I could spend every spare minute and all my college summers climbing rocks and mountains with friends, never worrying about the expenses. Even with the inheritance of my aunt's $1,000 when I turned twenty-one, I never considered giving it to my parents to help them with some of their bills—or mine—but subsidized this year in Europe, climbing in the Alps.

"Please, sit down," Lady Bromley is saying to us all. She's moved to the other side of the low table and taken her place in the comfortable-looking high-backed chair. As if on cue, three maids—or servants of some kind—come in through another door with trays carrying a teapot, ancient porcelain cups and saucers, silver spoons, silver containers of sugar and cream, and a five-tiered silver serving dish with small pastries and biscuits on each layer.

One of the servants offers to pour the tea, but Lady Bromley says that she will do it, and she does, inquiring of each of us—except for "Dickie," who, she remembers, takes his tea with a bit of cream, a bit of lemon, and two sugars—how we take our tea. I answer, idiotically, "Straight, ma'am," and receive a smile and my saucer and a cup of tea only. I hate tea.

There are a few minutes of small talk, mostly between the Deacon and Lady Bromley, but then she leans forward and says briskly, "Let us discuss your other letter, Dickie. The one I received three weeks after the beautiful condolence card. The one about the three of you going to Everest to look for my Percival."

The Deacon clears his throat. "Perhaps it was presumptuous, Lady Bromley, but there seem to be so many unanswered questions about Lord Percival's disappearance that I thought I might offer my services in an attempt to clear up the mystery surrounding that accident or fall or avalanche...or whatever happened."

"Whatever happened, indeed," says Lady Bromley, her voice almost harsh. "Do you know, that German gentleman who was the only witness to that so-called 'avalanche' that he says carried away Percy and a German porter—that Herr Bruno Sigl—will not even answer my cables and letters? He sent one brutish note stating that he had no more to say on the matter, and he's maintained that silence, despite the Alpine Club and Mount Everest Committee demanding more details from him."

"That is not right," Jean-Claude says quietly. "Families need to know the truth."

"I am not fully convinced that Percival is dead," says Lady Bromley. "He might be injured and lost on the mountain, barely surviving, or in some nearby Tibetan village awaiting help."

Here it is, I think. *The insane part of all this that the Deacon wants us to cash in on.* I feel a little nauseated and set down my cup and saucer.

"I understand that the chances of that—of my Percy still being alive on the mountain—are very low, gentlemen. I still retain all my faculties. I live in the real world. But without a rescue or retrieval mission to the mountain, how will I ever be able to know for sure? Percival's young life was so...so private...so complex...I have understood so little about him over the past years. I feel that I should, at the very least, understand the details of his death . . . or disappearance. Why was he in Tibet at all? Why on Mount Everest? And why with that Austrian man . . . Mr. Meyer . . . when he died?"

She stops, and I think of all the reports I've heard of young Lord Percival Bromley being a rake, a high-stakes gambler, someone who spent years in Germany and Austria, an endless rambler who rarely came home to England to visit and who stayed in the best suites in the best of Europe's hotels, and, it was often whispered (although I'd not had the courage to ask the Deacon about it), was a sodomite specializing in German and Austrian brothels for men who like such things. Private, complex—yes, a life filled with such preferences and activities would be private and complex, wouldn't it?

"Percy was such a wonderful athlete . . . you must remember that, Dickie."

"I do," says the Deacon. "Is it true that Percival was going to row for England in the nineteen twenty-eight Olympics?"

Lady Bromley smiles. "At his advanced age—out of his twenties—it sounds ridiculous, does it not? But that was precisely Percy's plan, to go to the Ninth Olympiad in Amsterdam in four years and row with the British crew. You remember how he excelled at rowing when he was at Oxford. He has—had—kept in superb physical shape and trained with Olympic-class English rowing teams whenever he was here for a visit. He practiced in Holland, France, and Germany as well. But rowing was only one of the sports in which Percy excels . . . or excelled."

"What was his climbing experience before going to Everest?" the Deacon asks. "I'd been out of touch with Percival for a long time."

Lady Bromley smiles and pours more tea for each of us. "More than fifteen years of climbing in the Alps with the best guides and with his cousin," she says proudly. "Since he was a young boy. All five summits of the Grandes Jurasses, including the highest and true summit—Point Walker, I believe it's called—from the south side, by the time he was twenty. The Matterhorn, of course. The Piz Badille . . ."

"From the south?" interrupts the Deacon.

"I'm not sure, Dickie, but I believe so. Also Percy and his guide made a—what is it called—a long sideways travel during a climb?"

"A traverse?" offers Jean-Claude.

"Oui. Merci," says Lady Bromley. "Percy and his guide had made a traverse of Mont Blanc from the Dôme hut to the Grands Mulets in what he called a summer blizzard. I remember his writing about doing the Grand Combin, whatever it is, in a very short time—he wrote mostly about the view from the summit. I have postcards from him talking about his...traverse, yes, that is the word...of the Finsteraarhorn and successful ascent of the Nesthorn." She smiles sadly at us. "Through all the years of Percy's risky sports, including these climbs, I spent many an anxious mother's hours looking up these hills and peaks on maps in our library."

"But he never joined the Alpine Club," says the Deacon. "And he wasn't an official member of last spring's Everest expedition with Norton, Mallory, and the others?"

Lady Bromley shakes her head, and once again I admire the complex simplicity of her hair. It makes the tall, perfectly upright woman seem even taller.

"Percival was never much of a joiner of groups," she says, and there's a sudden shadow of sadness passing over her face and eyes as she realizes that she's already speaking of her son in the past tense. "I received a brief note from him in March, posted from his cousin Reggie's tea plantation near Darjeeling, saying that he might follow along after or with Mr. Mallory's expedition and walk into Tibet, and then nothing...silence...until the terrible news reports in June."

"Can you remember the names of any of his alpine guides?" asks the Deacon.

"Oh, yes," says Lady Bromley, brightening some. "There were three favorites of his who were from Chamonix..."

She gives the names, and Jean-Claude makes a silent whistle with his lips. "Three of the best we have," he says. "Geniuses on rock, snow, and ice. Great guides and brilliant climbers in their own right."

"Percival loved them," says his mother. "Another British man he climbed with frequently in the Alps was also named Percy...Ferrou, Ferray?"

"Percy Farrar?" asks the Deacon.

"Yes, that's it," says Lady Bromley, smiling again. "Isn't it odd how I can remember the names of all of his French and German guides, but not a fellow British subject?"

The Deacon turns to look at J.C. and me. "Percy Farrar would have had sixteen or seventeen years of extreme alpine experience when he was climbing with Percy...with young Lord Percival." Looking directly at me, he adds, "Farrar later became president of the Alpine Club and was the one who first proposed that George Leigh Mallory be included in that first nineteen twenty-one expedition to Everest."

"So your son climbed with the best," Jean-Claude says to Lady Bromley. "Even though he wasn't invited on the Everest expedition, his climbing abilities could have been formidable."

"But Percy wasn't on any of the official rosters of either the Alpine Club or the Everest Committee," says the Deacon. "Do you happen to know, Lady Bromley, how it was that your son came to be on Everest at almost the same time as Mallory's climbers?"

Lady Bromley sips the last of her tea and sets the cup on its saucer with a delicate touch. "As I say, I received only that brief note from Percival, written from the Darjeeling plantation in March," she says patiently. "Evidently Percy met Mallory and the other members of this year's expedition at his cousin Reggie's plantation near Darjeeling in the third week of March. My son had just trekked through parts of Asia and arrived unannounced at our tea plantation very near to Darjeeling...the plantation that's been owned and managed for years now by Percy's cousin Reggie.

"Cousin Reggie was very helpful in finding Nepalese porters for Mallory's expedition—Sherpas, they are called—many who have relatives who've worked at our plantation for years. The actual leader of the expedition at that time, as you must know, was Brigadier General Charles Bruce...but from what Colonel Norton told me when the others returned to England, General Bruce was in poor health and had to turn back only two weeks after the expedition had left Darjeeling to pass through the Serpo La to Kampa Dzong and Tibet. I understand that Colonel Norton, who was already part of the group, was chosen to replace General Bruce as expedition leader, and then, according to Colonel Norton himself—who was very kind in visiting me—he appointed George Mallory as climbing leader. That's really all I know of the details of Percival's last days. He did not camp with the British expedition, nor attempt to climb with them."

"Did Lord Percival travel alone or with manservants?" asks the Deacon.

"Oh, Percy always preferred to travel alone," says Lady Bromley. "It made no sense—all that fussing by oneself over wardrobe choices and luggage—but it was his preference, and Colonel Norton says that he camped alone during the five-week trek in to Mount Everest."

"Never staying with the official party?" asks Jean-Claude with some slight wonderment in his voice. Why would a British lord travel separately from a British expedition?

Lady Bromley shakes her head ever so slightly. "Not according to Colonel Norton's and the Alpine Club's report to me. Nor did his cousin Reggie know why Percy was going to Tibet or choosing to travel near the expedition but not with it."

"What about these Germans?" asks the Deacon. "This Meyer person who is said to have been caught in the same avalanche with Lord Percival. Bruno Sigl, who says he witnessed it from lower down on the mountain. Do you happen to know if Percival knew these gentlemen?"

"Oh, heavens no!" cries Lady Bromley. "I am quite sure he did not. This Meyer seems to be very much a nonperson as far as the Alpine Club and my friends in His Majesty's Government can make out, and Herr Sigl...well, let us say that he was not the sort of man with whom Percival would have social intercourse."

The Deacon rubs his brow as if he has a headache. "If Lord Percival was not with the British expedition when Mallory and Irvine were lost, how is it, according to this Bruno Sigl, that he and some unknown German were supposed to have been carried away by an avalanche between Camp Five and Camp Six? Mallory's Camp Five was a few hundred feet above seven thousand six hundred and twenty-five meters—that's twenty-five thousand feet, Lady Percival, very high—but Camp Six, their jumping-off point for the summit, was over *eight thousand* meters—around twenty-six thousand eight hundred feet. Less than three thousand feet below the summit of Everest. The newspapers speculate that Lord Percival was attempting a search for Mallory and Irvine, days after they were declared lost by Norton and the others on the expedition. No one on the expedition saw either Lord Percival or Meyer or this Sigl person during their retreat from the mountain. Can you think of any other explanation for Percival to have been so high on the mountain after Colonel Norton and the others had left the area?"

"I'm sure I have no idea," Lady Bromley says. "Unless Percival... my Percy... was making an attempt to climb to the summit of Mount Everest on his own, or with this Austrian climber. It is not an impossibility. Percy was... is... was *very* ambitious, you know."

The Deacon only nods at that and glances at me. Norton and the others, after giving up Mallory and Irvine for dead, ended all further summit attempts, not merely out of respect for their lost fellows, but because of fears that the monsoon season had begun in earnest. They retreated from Everest Base Camp in strangely clear weather but feared that the monsoon would catch them any day en route. Certainly even an amateur such as Bromley would not attempt to summit the mountain—or even climb high to hunt for the missing Mallory and Irvine—under the imminent threat of monsoon weather. Being caught high on Everest when the monsoon struck would have been a particularly stupid and useless form of suicide.

The silence stretches until it feels almost uncomfortable. There's no more tea to drink to distract us, and only Jean-Claude and I have eaten anything. Finally the Deacon speaks.

"Lady Bromley, do you wish the three of us to carry out this... a year after Lord Percival's disappearance is too late to call it a rescue mission, but it certainly can be a search and *recovery* mission... this coming spring when climbing becomes possible again at Mount Everest?"

She looks down, and I see white teeth softly biting her full lower lip. "The Everest Committee and the Alpine Club are not planning a nineteen twenty-five expedition, are they, Dickie?"

"No, ma'am," says the Deacon. "The loss of Mallory and Irvine—and, of course, of your son—has so shaken the Club and Committee that it may be several years before another formal expedition is launched toward Everest. Also, the Tibetan authorities seem angered at the Alpine Club and the Everest Committee for reasons I don't fully understand. Word is that the Tibetan prime minister and local chieftains might not allow another expedition soon. Yet, of course, both the Alpine Club and Everest Committee consider Mount Everest a British hill and can't even dream of some other nation climbing it first, but there are rumors in the Alps that the Germans are considering such a bid. Although not, I think, for next summer. Not for nineteen twenty-five. But the three of us could do it."

"But Mallory's expedition which Percy joined had dozens of men with them," says Lady Bromley. "More than a score of white men, I believe, and hundreds of porters and more hundreds of pack animals. I remember Percy writing and complaining from the plantation about their plan to use Tibetan army mules, which he said were all but impossible to manage. And Colonel Norton described to me how slow the process was of establishing one camp after the other, first on the glacier, then up onto that icy ridge between Everest and its neighboring summit—I studied my geography of the mountain, gentlemen, oh, how I studied it—with the white climbers cutting steps for the porters every few feet of the way up the initial ice wall of that ridge, the North Col. It takes that many men *weeks upon weeks* of slow ascent. How on earth could the three of you succeed—not in summiting the mountain, which is not my interest in this expedition, but in getting high enough to Camps Five and Six to look for my son?"

It's Jean-Claude who answers. "Lady Bromley, we shall climb very quickly, alpine style rather than this military assault style that all of the Mallory expeditions used. We shall hire only a few Sherpas to act as porters, including high-climbing porters—perhaps finding these good men at your tea plantation with the help of Percy's cousin Reggie—but from the time we reach the actual mountain, speed and efficiency will be our constant goals. We shall climb, sleep, and eat alpine style—often taking our bivouac gear with us in our rucksacks, not worrying about a series of established camps—and we should be able to carry out a comprehensive search from Camp Four on the North Col all the way to and above Camp Six within a week or two...rather than the five to ten weeks it takes to get that far with a huge expedition such as General Bruce's."

Lady Bromley looks at the three of us, and then steadily at the Deacon. Her gaze has suddenly gone...not cold, exactly, but distant, businesslike. "How much will this rescue...recovery...expedition cost, gentlemen?"

The Deacon answers, and his voice is as businesslike as Lady Bromley's. "The Alpine Club set aside ten thousand pounds for the entirety of the first two attempts—the nineteen twenty-one reconnaissance and the nineteen twenty-two serious attempt on the mountain. Their estimate was that the reconnaissance would cost only three thousand pounds, the actual climbing attempt in 'twenty-two using up the rest of the ten thousand pounds. But they went over budget on both. And this year's climb—the nineteen twenty-four climb on which your son, Mallory, and Irvine were lost—cost them almost twelve thousand pounds."

Lady Bromley's no-nonsense gaze never leaves the Deacon's face now.

"So you are asking me for twelve thousand pounds to attempt this...recovery...expedition to seek out my son?"

"No, ma'am," says the Deacon. "With just the three of us and perhaps two dozen good Sherpa climbing porters, everything—including steamship transportation to Calcutta, tents, climbing gear, including oxygen rigs such as Finch designed and Sandy Irvine refined for the last expedition, plus the rental of some horses and pack mules to get us and the gear to Everest Base Camp—I estimate the total cost of this recovery expedition at being no more than twenty-five hundred pounds."

Lady Bromley blinks her surprise at the low figure. I confess that it does not sound low to me.

"We're professional alpine climbers, ma'am," the Deacon says, leaning closer to the woman in black. "We climb fast and through all weather, we eat light, we sleep in canvas bags tied to the mountainside by a rope or—failing that—sit out the night on a narrow ledge with a lit candle under our chins to keep us from nodding off."

Lady Bromley looks at all three of us and returns her gaze to the Deacon. She remains silent.

"Lady Bromley," says the Deacon, "as you mentioned, Norton and Mallory's expedition which your son followed to Everest carried tons upon tons of supplies. The Army and Navy Co-operative Society alone added sixty tins of quail *foie gras,* three hundred one-pound Hunter hams, and four dozen bottles of Montebello champagne. You must understand that this will not be our kind of expedition—three expert alpine climbers, moving quickly, knowing in which places to look for your son, and capable of getting high up on the mountain quickly, doing that job, and getting out."

It is a long speech for the Deacon, and I'm not sure if it has convinced Lady Bromley until she finally speaks.

"I will provide three thousand pounds for your expedition," she says softly. "But there will be one condition."

We wait.

"I want a member of the family along," says Lady Bromley in a tone I haven't heard from her before. It's almost royal in its there-will-be-no-argument-about-this, soft but infinitely certain finality. "Percy's cousin Reggie has climbed in the Alps—with Percy and many of the excellent guides I mentioned earlier—and is fully capable of going with you at least to the lower reaches of Mount Everest, perhaps all the way to Camp Three or whatever high camp you number up on that icy ridge between the mountains. You will, of course, make all climbing decisions, Dickie, but Reggie will be in charge of the overall expedition, of disbursing funds—to the Sherpas, to the yak sellers at Kampa Dzong—whatever is required. And Cousin Reggie will keep track of every receipt, every pound spent, every farthing. Agreed?"

The Deacon turns to look at Jean-Claude and me and I can read his mind. Having another Percy-type amateur along... it will probably slow us down, possibly put us in dangerous situations if we have to rescue him on the glacier or North Col ice face. But Lady Bromley's tone has been clear enough: no Cousin Reggie, no expedition. And this "Cousin Reggie" obviously won't be doing any of the truly high climbing with us.

"Yes, ma'am, we agree," says the Deacon. "We will be delighted to travel with Percy's cousin Reggie. It frees me from keeping track of expenses, a task at which I confess to be terrible."

Lady Bromley stands suddenly, and the three of us quickly get to our feet. She shakes the Deacon's hand, then Jean-Claude's, and finally mine. I see tears filling her dark eyes, but she does not allow them to fall.

"How long...," she begins.

"We should have the expedition completed and our complete report back to you by midsummer of next year," says the Deacon. "I'm bringing a small camera, but I promise that we'll retrieve anything that we can... Lord Percival's personal possessions, clothing, letters..."

"If he is dead," Lady Bromley interrupts in a totally flat tone, "I believe he would have preferred to be buried there on the mountain. But I would so much appreciate a few of the tokens of remembrance you've mentioned and... as hard as it will be to look at them... photographs."

We all nod. I feel absurdly close to weeping myself. I also feel very guilty. And exhilarated.

"If my Percy is alive," says Lady Bromley, standing straighter and taller than ever, "I want you to bring him home to me."

And without another word, she turns and leaves the room through the secret door in the library wall.

It takes a few seconds to realize that we've been dismissed and also that the Deacon got us exactly what he'd promised—a funded three-man (and one accountant now) alpine-style expedition to climb Mount Everest. If we find poor Percy's body, all the better. If not, the tallest mountain on Planet Earth may well be ours to summit.

There's a quiet cough, and we turn to find old Harrison, the butler, standing near the far door, ready to lead us back through the hallways and then the impossibly huge library and then more hallways and the Heaven Room and the foyers and God knows what else to the front door and freedom.

The carriage ride to the entrance of the estate seems endless. Benson, the walrus-mustachioed driver, says nothing, and we three in the carriage do not speak. But our emotions surge around us.

Benson drops us off at the white gravel chauffeured-car park, empty except for our coupe parked under nearby trees, and still we do not speak.

Suddenly Jean-Claude runs at the endless expanse of trimmed grass beyond the gravel, whoops loudly, and does a perfect four-circle cartwheel. The Deacon and I laugh and grin at each other like the pleased idiots we are at this moment.

But as we drive away, one thought keeps seeping through my joy and anticipation of this impossible expedition: *there at the center of perhaps the most beautiful 9,400 acres in the world resides a permanently broken heart and an eternally damaged mind.*

Can we bring some peace to her? It is the first time in all our planning—our "conniving," as I've thought of it—that this question has entered my mind. I realize it should have been the first thing I'd thought of when we started discussing this impossible-to-believe-in three-man Everest expedition.

Can we bring Lady Bromley some peace of mind?

Riding in the open air in a beautiful English summer afternoon, with the shadows just beginning to lengthen across the fields and empty highway, I decide that perhaps we can—can do this climb the right way, can find the remains of Percy Bromley, and can bring back something, anything, from that mountain of death that will ... will what? Not heal Lady Bromley's broken heart, for she's soon to lose her older son to the endless effects of mustard gas dropped on him eight years ago by British shells, and her younger son is lost forever on Mount Everest, but perhaps we can quiet her mind about the details, the reality, of Lord Percival Bromley's senseless death on this particular mountain.

Perhaps.

The Deacon is grinning as he drives, and Jean-Claude is grinning as he rides in the front passenger seat, his head cocked to one side to catch the wind like a dog, and I decide to join them both in grinning.

We have absolutely no concept of what lies ahead for us.

If we can find the remains of Lord Percival, we can cer-
tainly find Mallory or Irvine... or both of them.

here are many memorial services for Mallory and Irvine in that late summer and autumn of 1924, but perhaps the most important one is held at Saint Paul's Cathedral on October 17. It is essentially an invitation-only memorial service, and from our group, only the Deacon is invited to attend. He does so and says little about it to us afterward, but the London newspapers are filled with the eulogy by the Bishop of Chester. The bishop ends with an adaptation of King David's lament from the Bible—"Delightful and very pleasant were George Mallory and Andrew Irvine; in life, in death, they were not parted."

Jean-Claude points out to me the next day that if—as was probably the case—one of them fell first on their way up or down the mountain, they were certainly parted in their last minutes or hours.

The deaths of Lord Percival Bromley and Kurt Meyer are mentioned only in the abstract during the bishop's eulogy for Mallory and Irvine—"as we remember others who also perished on the mountain that month"—and Lady Bromley holds no memorial service for her son that summer or autumn (perhaps because she still believes he is alive somewhere on Mount Everest or the Rongbuk Glacier below and truly does believe that the three of us will find and rescue him a year after he disappeared). Lady Bromley has urged the Deacon to start the expedition this very autumn of 1924 and to attempt the Everest "rescue" in winter, but he assured her that both the mountain and access routes to the mountain are impassable and unclimbable in the Himalayan winter. Deep within her, Lady Bromley—even through her shock and temporary mental instability—knows that our expedition the next spring and summer of 1925 will be, at best, a *recovery* attempt, *not* a rescue effort.

That same evening of October 17 there is held an assembly related to Mallory and Irvine which the Deacon *does* get J.C. and me into, despite its being so crowded that the group has to rent the Royal Albert Hall for the occasion. The Royal Geographical Society and its Alpine Club are holding their joint meeting "to Receive the Reports from the Mount Everest Expedition of 1924." To say that the crowd—mostly of climbers and a mob of reporters—is enthusiastically interested would be an understatement.

The finale of the program is the reading of the report from the photographer-climber-geologist Noel Odell—who many believe should have been Mallory's partner in that final summit attempt rather than young Andrew Irvine—and it tells of Odell's efforts to wait for the missing climbers at their high camp and his final sighting of them from his point between Camps IV and V when the clouds parted briefly, although Odell seems confused at times as to whether he saw the "two, moving black dots" on a snowfield above the First Step along the North East Ridge, above the Second Step, or even possibly above the lesser Third Step and on the "pyramid of snowfields" approaching the summit itself.

"The question remains," Odell wrote in his report, "has Mount Everest been climbed? It must be left Unanswered, for there is no direct evidence. But bearing in mind all the circumstances...and considering their position when last seen, I think there is a strong probability that Mallory and Irvine succeeded. At that I must leave it."

This causes a low murmuring and susurration in the crowd of England's best climbers. Many of the men—even some of Mallory's and Irvine's other climbing partners on the expedition—do *not* believe the evidence suggests that the two men had summited. Even if Odell's sighting was real and Mallory and Irvine had somehow climbed the ominous Second Step, it was too late in the day for a successful summit attempt—they would have had to descend in the dark—and their oxygen canisters must have been on or near empty at such a late hour. So it is the opinion of most of the world-class climbers in the Albert Hall this night that Mallory and Irvine had pressed on too far, too late, had attempted to descend in the dark—probably well before getting anywhere near the summit—and both had fallen to their deaths on the North Face in the dark and windy lunar-cold night somewhere there above 27,000 feet, and possibly in the unbreathable Martian-thin air around 28,000 feet.

But I remember that Odell's report caused a powerful wave of opposition when he ended his communiqué with his belief that the two men had died of exposure.

"Exposure" simply wasn't a noble enough death for these two national heroes, these mere men who were quickly turning into an English legend, but even foreign climbers who'd known and climbed with Mallory—men immune from the patriotic fervor filling the Albert Hall this mid-October night—don't believe that he, or even Sandy Irvine, for that matter, was so foolish as to die of exposure. Most of the climbers we listen to after the meeting guess that one of the two missing men—almost certainly Irvine—fell, probably on the return from the summit or their high point that evening before the sun set, perhaps in the darkness, possibly on the North Face itself in their effort to get out of the howling winds, and, in falling, pulled the other climber off his perch to his death.

Even the official leader of the fatal 1924 expedition, Edward "Teddy" Norton, had written from Base Camp, "I am very sorry Odell put that bit about their dying of exposure in his communiqué." And he'd added, to the Mount Everest Committee, "All the rest of us are agreed it is any odds on a fall-off."

On our walk back to the hotel late that October night after the Alpine Club meeting, Jean-Claude asks the Deacon, "*Ree-shard*, do you think Mallory and Irvine reached the summit?"

"I have no idea," says the Deacon around the stem of his pipe. The fragrance of his tobacco leaves a scent trail in the cold, damp air as we hurry along.

"Do you believe they died of exposure?" persists J.C. "Or fell?"

The Deacon removes the pipe and looks at us, his gray eyes bright in the light from the corner streetlamp. "There simply isn't enough public or *Alpine Journal* information from Odell or anyone else who was there to make a judgment about how or where they died. The three of us need to talk to Norton, John Noel, Odell, Dr. Somervell, and other friends of mine who were on last spring's expedition. Then we'll have to go to Germany—to Munich—to talk to this climber Bruno Sigl, who says he was high enough on the lower parts of Everest to see the avalanche he says carried Bromley and the mysterious Austrian or German, Meyer, away. Don't you agree?"

Jean-Claude and I look at each other. I can see in his eyes that J.C. will never travel to Germany with the Deacon and me. The Germans killed three of his brothers, and he swore long ago never to cross that border into Deutschland.

"I know, Jean-Claude," says the Deacon even though J.C. hasn't said a word. "I understand. Jake and I can go to Munich next month—November—and report to you later what this Sigl person says about the death of Lord Percival and that other man, Meyer, as well as give us any details he has about the disappearance of Mallory and Irvine. But do stay in London long enough to visit Norton and the others with us."

"What if this Sigl fellow doesn't have any details about anything?" I say almost plaintively. "What if you and I waste time going to Munich next month and learn nothing new about Mallory and Irvine or—more important to *our* mission—about what happened to Percival Bromley?"

"Well," says the Deacon with a smile that looks almost hungry, "then we'll just have to go to Everest next March through June and find out for ourselves what happened to them. If we can find the remains of Lord Percival, we can certainly find Mallory or Irvine...or both of them. The dry winds of Mount Everest desiccate and mummify a corpse far more efficiently than could the high priests of ancient Egypt."

The ponies had been shot in the head.

*O*ur interview with 1924 Everest expedition members Colonel Edward F. Norton, medical officer R. W. G. Hingston, Dr. Theodore Howard Somervell, Captain John B. Noel, and Noel E. Odell—the last three men particular friends of the Deacon's—takes place in October, after the official memorial service for Mallory and Irvine. These former team leaders and members are attending an Alpine Club function at the Royal Geographical Society at 1 Kensington Gore, and we are told to meet them in the Map Room on that Saturday afternoon.

"I hope that they left word at the entrance that we're expected," I say as we get out of our taxi across from Kensington Gardens, evening shadows lengthening, the huge dome of the Albert Hall looming over the brick building of the Society. It's sunset, and the October-colored leaves on the countless trees in the park across the boulevard seem to be catching fire from the reflected light from the dome.

"I'm a member," says the Deacon. "There should be no problem getting up to the Map Room."

J.C. and I glance at one another.

Other than a bust of the explorer David Livingstone set into a niche on a wall outside the courtyard, there's no clue that this sprawling brick building is, for geographers and explorers, the center of the universe.

Inside, someone takes our hats and coats, and an older, silver-haired man in tails and white tie says, "Mr. Deacon. Welcome back, sir. It has been too long since we've had the pleasure of your presence here."

"Thank you, James," says the Deacon. "Colonel Norton and some others are awaiting us in the Map Room if I'm not mistaken."

"Yes, sir. Their meeting ended just a few minutes ago, and the five gentlemen are waiting for you in the Club Room annex to the Map Room. Shall I escort you, sir?"

"We'll find our way, thank you, James." The wide hallways with their highly varnished floors and glass-cased displays make me want to whisper as if I'm in a church, but the Deacon's tone remains the same as it had been outside.

The Map Room is beautiful—mezzanines with leather-bound books, long tables with maps set on wooden display wedges, a globe large enough that an acrobat could have balanced on it while rolling it down Kensington Boulevard—but it is not as huge a space as my imagination has been drawing. To one side of the main room is one of the 1875 building's many-windowed porch annexes, a lighted fireplace set into one wall. Hingston, Noel, Norton, Somervell, and Odell stand as we approach, the Deacon introduces J.C. and me, and the three of us take the last deep leather chairs in the arc of eight chairs facing the fireplace. Through the windows behind us, the sunset light has mellowed into a general golden glow.

During the Deacon's introductions and our handshakes, I realize that while I've met none of these men in person before, I thought I knew what they looked like through published photos of their various expeditions. But almost all of them had been sporting beards—or at least rampant whiskers—in those photographs, and now most are clean-shaven except for a couple of well-trimmed mustaches, so I probably would have walked right past them on the street without recognizing them.

Colonel Edward Felix "Teddy" Norton is exceedingly tall—at least an inch or two taller than my 6 foot 2, I realize—and everything about him, from his quiet, competent demeanor to his cool stare, reflects a military man who has long been comfortable in positions of command. Dr. Richard Hingston, 37 years old, is a slim man—not a climber (he'd served as both physician and expedition naturalist on last spring's '24 expedition)—but I knew that he'd pushed himself as high as Camp IV on the North Col to take care of snow-blinded Norton and other ailing patients stuck there. He'd served as a doctor in France, Mesopotamia, and East Africa during the Great War, and had been awarded the Military Cross for his courage under fire. Hingston may not be a climber, but I look at him with great respect.

Theodore Howard Somervell—called Howard by his friends and introduced as such to us by the Deacon—is also a surgeon as well as a former missionary, but looks as rugged as a stevedore. The Deacon has told us that Somervell never really returned to England after the 1922 Everest expedition and has chosen to live and work at a medical mission in Neyyoor in southern India ever since. Somervell is in London now only for the Mallory-Irvine memorial tribute and this round of Alpine Club and RGS meetings and banquets.

Somervell's a handsome man, even without the thick dark beard he'd sported in photographs from Tibet, and his curly hair, deeply tanned face, expressive dark brows, and sudden white flash of a grin make him appear almost rakish. But that's not his nature. The Deacon almost never spoke about his own experiences during the War, but he had mentioned one night while we were bivouacking high on an alpine peak last year that Somervell—a particular friend of his—had been turned into a deeply religious pacifist while serving in a surgical tent as one of only four doctors trying to deal with the thousands of wounded soldiers, many mortally wounded and knowing it, on the first morning of the Battle of the Somme. The Deacon said that Somervell had spoken with many of the hundreds of men lying outside the tent on their bloody stretchers or rain ponchos, each man undoubtedly knowing that waiting even moments longer for medical treatment might well cost him his life, but *not one injured man* had asked to be treated before the others. Not one.

As I shake Somervell's hand—calloused for a surgeon—and look into his clear eyes, I consider the probability that such an experience might turn any sensitive soul into a pacifist overnight. The Deacon also has told us that while Somervell was a devout Christian, he certainly wasn't a dogmatic one. "The only problem with Christianity," Somervell had told the Deacon as they shared a two-man tent high on a snowy pass during the '22 expedition, "is that it's never really been tried."

Captain John Noel is a thin man with a lined face and deep-set eyes that seem filled with worry. There may be reason for that: Noel had paid

£8,000, the full cost of the 1924 expedition, in exchange for all film and photo rights—had brought specially devised still and cine cameras as high as the North Col to get long shots of the summiteers, presumably Mallory and Irvine, reaching the top of Everest—and had even brought a full darkroom tent to Everest Base Camp with him the previous spring. He'd paid for a series of runners to carry his developed photographs from Everest to Darjeeling for mailing to the major London papers. Now he is putting out his motion picture *The Epic of Everest*—but because clouds had obscured any last views of Mallory and Irvine, at least from the North Col, it was being whispered that Captain Noel had no satisfactory ending to his film. He somehow had managed to bring to London with him a troupe of dancing lamas from a Tibetan monastery—not the Rongbuk Monastery near Mount Everest—to liven up his showings, but that, along with "objectionable scenes showing Tibetans eating head lice" in his proposed film, seems already to be causing diplomatic problems. Unless Noel's motion picture turns out to be a huge hit here in England and in America, the poor man is looking at losing the majority of his £8,000 investment.

As I stare at Odell, I realize that he has good reason to look worried and distracted this autumn evening in 1924.

Captain John Noel had been the last man to receive a note from George Mallory, but it is the last man we greet this night, the geologist and climber and the Deacon's particular friend Noel E. Odell, who always will be known as the last man to see Mallory and Irvine alive.

Odell had been alone at Camp V the night before Mallory and Irvine made their attempt from the precarious tent higher at Camp VI, and as he ascended alone to Camp VI that day—what should have been the auspicious summit day—it was Odell who'd clambered up a 100-foot crag at about 26,000 feet at 12:50 p.m. and, as he recorded in his journal that night, "saw M & I on ridge, nearing base of final pyramide."

But had he?

Already, only days after the memorial service for Mallory and Irvine and the jam-packed Alpine Club meeting which had set all of England abuzz, climbers—even other members of the same expedition—were casting doubts on what Odell said he'd seen. Could Mallory and Irvine *possibly* have been surmounting the so-called Third Step and silhouetting themselves against the final snowy Summit Pyramid, as Odell claimed, as early as 12:50 p.m.? It was possible, but seemed doubtful. Their climbing rate, even with oxygen, would have been very impressive indeed. No, argue some, it must have been the *Second Step* which Odell had seen them climbing. No, no, argue other experts who weren't within 5,000 miles of the mountain at the time, it could only have been the *First Step* that Mallory and Irvine were passing that early in the day. Odell must be wrong, even though he'd pointed out via photographs and terrain maps that the rise of ridges and the bulk of the mountain blocked his view of the First Step from his particular vantage point on that crag. But the clouds had parted for only a minute, granting him just a glimpse of the two climbing human figures—if human figures they were ("mere rocks in a snowfield," argued many alpinists)—before closing in to obscure his view.

We were all seated and another servant in white tie and tails had taken our orders for whiskeys when Colonel Norton broke the silence.

"It's good to see you, Richard. I'm sorry we have only twenty minutes or so before the formal Alpine Club dinner begins. Since you're a fellow in the RGS and former expedition member, we could always find room for you..."

The Deacon waves that away. "I'm hardly dressed for it, Teddy, and it wouldn't be appropriate at any rate. No, my friends and I only want to ask a few questions of you gentlemen, then we'll be on our way."

Our drinks arrive: whiskey, neat and amber-colored and aged eighteen years in sherry casks. It is warm going down. My hands aren't shaking, but I realize that they want to. I also realize that I probably will never be in such an august company of world-class climbers again, which must be the cause of this tension. I'm not afraid of trying to climb Mount Everest, but I'm almost frightened to be in the presence of these men who've become world-famous by attempting and failing to do so.

"About Mallory and Irvine, I presume?" says Norton to the Deacon, his tone—I think—rather cooler. How many times has this group been asked questions about the disappeared "heroes" in the past four months?

"Not at all," says the Deacon. "I had a visit with Lady Bromley this summer and promised that I would help her find out as much as I can about the disappearance of her son."

"Young Percival Bromley?" says the filmmaker Noel. "How on earth can we help her? Bromley wasn't *with* us, you know, Richard."

"I was under the impression that he traveled from Darjeeling to Rongbuk with you." The Deacon sips his whiskey, his aquiline profile lighted by the fire from where I sit.

"Not *with* us, Richard," says Howard Somervell. "Behind us. By himself. Just himself on a Tibetan pony and his gear on a single mule. Always a day or two behind us. He caught up with us and visited our camp...what, John?" He is asking the filmmaker, Noel. "Three times?"

"Only twice, I believe," says Noel. "The first time at Kampa Dzong, where we spent three nights. The last time at Shekar Dzong, before we turned south toward the Rongbuk Monastery and Glacier. We spent two nights at Shekar Dzong. Young Bromley never seemed to spend more than one night camped anywhere. He had a simple Whymper tent. One of the smaller, lighter kinds."

"Should he not have passed you, then, on the trek in?" asks Jean-Claude. He is obviously enjoying his whiskey. "I mean, if you spent multiple nights in certain spots and Bromley would camp only one night..."

"Oh, I say," says Dr. Hingston with a laugh. "I see your point. But no...Bromley seemed to be making little side trips. South along the Yaru Chu River, for instance, after we spent two nights at Tinki Dzong. Possibly to get a glimpse of Mount Everest from the low mountains there. At any rate, he was behind us again when we arrived at Shekar Dzong."

"Strangest thing," says Colonel Norton. "Whenever young Lord Percival did drop in for a visit—both times—he brought his own food and drink. Would accept no hospitality from us, though God knows we had enough food to spare and left a ton of tinned goods behind at the end."

"So he was well provisioned?" asks the Deacon.

"For a weekend camping trip in Lincolnshire," comments John Noel. "Not for a solo expedition into Tibet."

"How could he have traveled alone without official permission from the Tibetan government?" I hear myself asking. I feel the blush rising to my cheeks, as warm as the whiskey in my belly. I'd not planned to speak tonight.

"Rather good question, Mr. Perry," says Colonel Norton. "We wondered ourselves. Tibet is in a state of relative barbarism, but the local *dzongpens*—the tribal and village headmen—as well as the government, do post guards and soldiers here and there, especially on the high passes which one cannot bypass. Guards checked our papers there, so I have to assume that Lord Percival had some formal permission papers—perhaps received through the governor of Bengal. The Bromley plantation there near Darjeeling—Bromley-Montfort now—has long been a friend of the Tibetans and whoever is in charge of Bengal and Sikkim."

"I rode over to Lord Percival's camp once or twice," Noel Odell says. "Early in the expedition, just after we'd crossed into Tibet after cresting Jelep La. Young Percival seemed very content to be alone—not overly welcoming, but certainly friendly enough once I sat by his fire. I was worried about his health, you see—so many of us had either dysentery or the beginnings of real mountain lassitude by that point—but Bromley appeared perfectly fine. Every time we saw him, he seemed healthy and in high spirits."

"And did he follow you from Shekar Dzong to your Base Camp at the foot of the Rongbuk Glacier?" asks the Deacon.

"Oh, heavens no," says Colonel Norton. "Bromley continued on west the dozen or fifteen miles to Tingri after we turned south toward Everest. We never saw him again. I had the impression that he was set to explore farther west and north beyond Tingri. Much of that area is essentially unexplored, you know, Richard. Tingri itself is a rather frightfully crude former Tibetan military garrison on a high hill. You were there with us when everyone went out of their way to Tingri Dzong in 'twenty-two, as I recall."

"Yes," says the Deacon, but adds nothing else.

"I also had the impression from young Bromley," says Dr. Hingston, "right from the time we met him at the family's tea plantation, that he was going into Tibet to meet up with someone. It was as if he had just enough food and gear to get to a rendezvous somewhere beyond Shekar Dzong."

"What about climbing gear?" asks the Deacon. "Bruno Sigl has told the German press that Lord Percival and another man died in an avalanche high on Everest. Did any of you see climbing gear with Lord Percival?"

"Some rope," says Norton. "One always can use some good rope in Tibet. But not nearly enough rope for an attempt on Everest...nor enough food, nor tents, nor Primus stoves, nor any of the other things he would have required to get even as far as Camp Three, much less up onto the North Col...much, much less the huge mass of material he would have needed to get up to Camp Five or out onto the Face."

"This Bruno Sigl...," begins the Deacon.

"Is a liar," interrupts Colonel Norton. "I'm sorry, Richard. I did not mean to be rude. It's just that everything Sigl has told the press is sheer rot."

"So you never saw Sigl or any other Germans, including this possible Austrian Meyer, who's supposed to have died with Lord Percival?" asks the Deacon.

"Never heard the slightest whisper that any Germans were within a thousand miles while we were on the mountain or glacier," says Colonel Norton. There are pink spots high on his sharp cheekbones. I have to think that the Scotch he is finishing is not his first of the evening. Either that, or the idea of Germans having been anywhere in the area during their attempts on Everest this year is somehow infuriating and intolerable to Norton.

"I confess to being confused," says the Deacon. "The last of your party left Base Camp...when? On sixteen June, some eight days after Mallory and Irvine's disappearance, no?"

"Yes," says Odell. "We took time to let the most fatigued climbers rest, and to build the memorial cairn for George and Sandy—and for the porters lost in 'twenty-two—but the last of us were out of the Rongbuk Valley by the afternoon of the sixteenth. We were all in bad shape, except for me, strangely enough: heart conditions, the aftereffects of Colonel Norton's snow blindness, frostbite, fatigue, constant altitude sickness, headaches for everyone. Everyone coughing constantly."

"My cough almost killed me on the mountain," says Howard Somervell.

"At any rate, we left in different groups—invalids, most of us—and the majority went with Colonel Norton to explore the never-before-visited Rongshar Valley under Gaurishankar—we had permission to do so—and to recuperate for ten days at lower altitudes before the hard march back."

"I had to get my film back, so I came straight back to Darjeeling with the porters and mules," says Captain Noel.

"John de Vere Hazard, our primary cartographer, wanted to finish up the survey your 'twenty-one expedition had begun, Richard," says Colonel Norton. "We gave him permission to accompany Hari Sing Thapa of the Indian Survey to the West Rongbuk region for a few days. We waved good-bye to them as they and their few porters went west on sixteen June, the day most of us went north and east."

"And I had my own detour," says Odell. "I wanted to do a little more geological work."

The other four famous men laughed. Odell's geological ardor, even at altitudes above 27,000 feet on Everest, had evidently become a bit of a joke amongst these otherwise somber survivors.

"I told Odell he could have his little hundred-mile diversion during our trip back if he took our transport officer, E. O. Shebbeare, with him," says Norton. "There are bandits in that Tibetan hill country. At least Shebbeare spoke some Tibetan."

Odell looks at the colonel. "And Shebbeare admitted to me a week later that you warned him, Edward, that after our little trip was over, he would never want to set eyes on me again. I believe that was the precise quotation he gave me of your words—'My dear Shebbeare, you may never want to set eyes on Odell again.'"

Colonel Norton looks down at his glass, and the two pink circles high on his cheekbones seem to glow a darker red.

"But Shebbeare and I enjoyed every day of the geology survey together," continues Odell. "We became even faster friends than before. And thanks to the ten days of recuperation the main party had taken at Rongshar Valley in the shadow of Gaurishankar, we caught up to the main party just as it arrived in Darjeeling, and just before Hazard got back with Hari Sing Thapa and the porters they'd taken to the West Rongbuk on the mapping expedition."

The Deacon takes his watch out of his waistcoat pocket, glances at it, and says, "We have only a few minutes before you all have to go to the dinner, my friends. And I confess that I've completely lost track of Lord Percival, much less the Germans—Meyer and Sigl. The report of Lord Percival's death on the mountain—of him and this Meyer person—was in *The Times* the same week as the full report about Mallory and Irvine. I believe you telegraphed that report from Darjeeling. If you never saw Bromley after twenty-four April, when your expedition went south toward Everest and Bromley continued on toward Tingri, then how...."

"We apologize, Richard," says Colonel Norton. "It is a rather tangled narrative, but it was a tangled narrative that brought us news of Bromley's death. Let me explain. Just as John Hazard and Hari Sing Thapa were approaching the West Rongbuk region to do their survey, religious pilgrims met them and told them, translated through Hari Sing Thapa, that two English sahibs in Tingri—one named Bromley, the other a 'non-English-speaking English sahib' named Meyer—had rented six yaks to take with them as they headed south and then east along the river to Chobuk, then south to the Rongbuk Glacier and Chomolungma."

"The Tibetans definitely said that Bromley and this Meyer were traveling together toward Mount Everest?" The Deacon has finished his whiskey, and now he carefully sets the empty glass on a wicker table next to his chair.

"They did," says Colonel Norton. "Two more pilgrims—all headed toward the Rongbuk Monastery—told Hazard and Hari Sing Thapa the same news as our two men were headed back to the northeast, toward Pang La Pass and Shekar Dzong on their way home. But they added that there were seven other 'non-English-speaking English sahibs' who'd arrived in Tingri the day after Bromley and Meyer left, but who'd immediately left the village again, to the southeast, as if following Bromley."

"How odd," says the Deacon.

"But more than that," continues Norton, "Hazard and Hari actually *saw* Bromley and Meyer. *And* the seven men following them."

"Where's John Hazard now?" asks Jean-Claude.

John Noel makes a vague gesture with his left hand. "Oh, back to doing government map work somewhere in India, I believe."

"And Hari Sing Thapa?" asks the Deacon.

"Also doing map work in India," says Colonel Norton. "But not with John."

"Could you tell us what Hazard saw?" says the Deacon.

Dr. Hingston is the first to speak. I can feel a tension in my neck and back grow worse as our few minutes with these men are ticking away before we get any solid information.

"Hazard and Hari were headed northeast and had just begun to climb the old trade route trail toward the Pang La when Hari—who has the sharper vision of the two—said he saw two sets of riders headed south. Many miles away, but the day was perfectly clear—Hazard said that they could see Mount Everest smoking worse than ever, the spindrift spread thirty miles or more above the summits to the east of our mountain. Hazard and Hari actually diverted to a nearby hillside so that John could use military field glasses to confirm what they were seeing. Furthest south were two men—John said that he could definitely identify Bromley's pony and the mule he'd brought from Darjeeling, but now Bromley and his new partner also had six yaks in train—and many miles behind them, perhaps five to seven hours' ride, were seven men on larger ponies. Either real horses or—as Hari identified them—those big, shaggy Mongolian ponies."

"Did it seem like a pursuit?" asks the Deacon.

"It seemed merely damned strange to Hazard," says Norton. "He told us when they caught up to us in Darjeeling that he thought later that he and Hari Sing Thapa should have headed back south to Rongbuk to see what the devil was going on—if Bromley and these other men following might be poaching on our mountain, as it were. But Hazard was already several days behind us due to the mapping. He wanted to catch up before we got to Calcutta, and in the end he and Hari turned north over the Pang La."

"What was the date of this sighting?" asks the Deacon.

"Nineteen June," replies Norton. "Just three days after we'd divided the party while leaving the Rongbuk Glacier valley."

"This is all fascinating," says the Deacon. "But it hardly supports announcing that Lord Percival died in an avalanche on Mount Everest. I presume you received more information through some other reliable source?"

"We did," Odell confirms. "As Shebbeare and I were finishing up our rather enjoyable geology excursion and heading north to the main route east, we ran into three of the Sherpas who'd accompanied us to Mount

Everest and who'd been very important in the high-altitude carries. Perhaps you remember the one Tiger from 'twenty-two, the one who spoke the best English... Pemba Chiring, but everyone called him 'Kami' for some reason."

"I remember Kami well," says the Deacon. "He carried heavy loads to Camp Five... without supplementary oxygen."

"Exactly," says Odell. "And he was just as reliable during this year's sad expedition. But Shebbeare and I were surprised to see Kami and his two non-English-speaking cousins, Dasno and Nema, as we were turning northeast again. They were literally whipping their little Tibetan ponies in their haste... and you know that the Sherpas rarely do that. They'd returned to the Rongbuk Glacier and were now fleeing as if for their lives."

"What date was this?" asks the Deacon.

"Twenty-two June," says Odell.

Colonel Norton clears his throat. "Kami and his cousins had started back with us but requested permission to detach from the main body. I granted it, thinking they would be heading home on their own. Evidently they had it in mind to return to our Base Camp... perhaps even to the higher camps."

"For looting purposes?" asks Jean-Claude. "Or perhaps I should say... scavenging?"

Norton frowns. "It would appear that way. Although there's precious little of value that we left behind, unless one were to count the caches of barley and tinned food we left at various camps."

"Kami later insisted to me that they'd left a religious talisman behind by accident," says Odell. "He thought he'd left it at Base Camp or perhaps tucked in one of the *sanga* rock walls at Camp Two. He said they couldn't return to their family and village without it. I believed him."

"What did they say they'd seen?" asks the Deacon.

I surreptitiously glance at my own watch. We have only three minutes or less before these esteemed climbers are expected at yet another Royal Geographical Society formal banquet here in the RGS's Lowther Lodge. A glance over my shoulder shows me that the electric lamps along Exhibition Road where it runs into Kensington Road are burning. The October night has fallen.

"Kami said that he and his cousins reached our old Base Camp on twenty June," says Odell. "They searched, but the talisman wasn't there. What they did find there shocked them...seven hobbled Mongolian ponies down below the memorial cairn, down where there's a bit of that tough grass a few hundred yards below the melt pond."

"No one tending the ponies?" asks the Deacon.

"Not a soul," says Odell. "And a bit further up the valley, before one gets too deep into the *penitente* ice pinnacles, they came across what Kami immediately identified as Lord Percival Bromley's Whymper tent—the same one he'd slept in every night we'd seen him during the trip in—and two dead Tibetan ponies. The ponies had been shot in the head."

"Shot!" cries out Jean-Claude.

Odell nods. "Kami told us that he and his younger cousins were alarmed. Nema would go no further, nor stay near the murdered ponies, so Desno took Nema back down the valley to Base Camp, while Kami kept climbing up the glacier toward Camp Two. He *had* to find the talisman, he said. He was also curious and somewhat alarmed for Bromley, who had been kind to him during his few visits to our camps during the trek in."

"Did he see Bromley again?" I ask.

"No," says Odell. "Kami found his talisman—set into the stones in the *sanga* they'd set up at Camp Two, right where he thought he might find it."

"What exactly is a *sanga* again?" asks Jean-Claude.

The Deacon responds. "The rock walls we and the porters build at Camp One and above. They enclose the tents we use and keep things from flying away when the winds rise. The porters often sleep within *sangas* that have only a ground cloth and a pole-supported tarp for a roof." The Deacon turns back to Odell. "What did Kami see?"

Odell rubs his cheek. "Kami admitted to us that he should have turned back to his cousins as soon as he found his talisman, but instead, out of curiosity, he continued climbing toward Camp Three."

"That must have been dangerous with the monsoon snows covering the crevasses," says Jean-Claude.

"That's the odd thing," comments Colonel Norton. "We'd expected the monsoon to hit full force by the first week in June...indeed, there were some serious flurries during the last days before Mallory and Irvine's final effort. But the monsoon hadn't arrived at Rongbuk when we finally left on sixteen June, nor had it arrived when Kami says he was back there on the twentieth of June. Some snow, very strong winds, but no actual monsoon. It didn't really strike until we were all back in Darjeeling. Very odd."

"Kami said that when he was at Camp Two, long before he got the last four miles up the glacier and through the last field of high *penitentes,* he heard what sounded like thunder from higher on the mountain, above the North Col," says Odell.

"Thunder?" asks the Deacon.

"Kami found it very odd," says Odell, "since it was a totally clear day—bright blue sky, snow plume off Everest's summit clearly visible—but he said that it sounded like thunder."

"Avalanche?" suggests J.C.

"Or pistol or rifle shots with echoes?" says the Deacon.

Norton looks shocked at that suggestion, but Odell nods. "Kami spent the night bivouacked on the glacier and in the morning light saw new tents at our site for Camp Three and, he said, more tents up on the ledge on the North Col where we'd set Camp Four. He also said that he'd seen three figures high up on the mountain, above where the Northeastern Ridge runs into the North Ridge. Far to the west, he said, between Steps One and Two...where a boulder was, he said. A boulder that looked like a mushroom. Three tiny black figures stood near that rock and then, suddenly, only one figure. Hours later he watched men coming down the sheer ice face from the North Col, using the rope ladder Sandy Irvine had cobbled together. He thought there were four or five descending."

"It wouldn't have been possible for even a sharp-visioned Sherpa to see figures so high on the ridgeline without field glasses," muses the Deacon.

"Oh, yes," says Colonel Norton with a smile. "Kami admitted that he'd 'borrowed' a good pair of Zeiss binoculars from one of the Germans' empty tents at Camp Three."

"And you left Irvine's rope ladder behind?" the Deacon asks Norton. "Still in place on the ice cliff to the North Col?"

"We considered taking it down because it was dangerous, frayed and overly used," says the colonel. "But in the end it was too much trouble to take it down, and some thought it might even last till our next expedition, so we left it where it was. Partially as a memorial to Sandy, truth be told."

The Deacon nods. "I know you all must go in a moment, but what did Kami tell you that made you report the death of Lord Percival as told by a certain Bruno Sigl from Germany?"

Odell clears his throat. "Kami was frightened at the thunder, but stayed near Camp Three that second day just to see who the down-climbing figures turned out to be—hoping it was Bromley—but just as he was about to give up and leave the Camp Three area, he was shouted at in heavily accented English to stop. The man who shouted at him was holding a black pistol. A Luger, Kami thought. He stopped."

"A pistol on Mount Everest," whispers Jean-Claude. I could hear the revulsion at the idea in his voice. I felt it myself.

"At least it answers the question of who shot Bromley's and Meyer's little ponies," I suggest.

The Deacon shakes his head. "They might have gone lame. Bromley or Meyer may have put them down themselves, planning to walk back to Tingri or Shekar Dzong with the yaks."

"At any rate, poor Kami thought he was going to be shot for trespassing and for the theft of the Zeiss glasses," continues Odell, "and he told us that he'd only hoped that his cousins would be brave enough to find his body and to bury it there in a crevasse with the proper ceremonies. But instead the German man with the Luger demanded in English—Kami had spent enough time in Calcutta that he could hear the German accent—to know who Kami was. Kami told him that he was a Sherpa with the Norton-Mallory Expedition and that he'd returned with others to retrieve a few forgotten items and that he was expected back.

" 'How many others?' the German demanded.

" 'Nine,' lied Kami, 'including two sahibs waiting at the Rongbuk Monastery.' "

"Clever man," the Deacon says.

"At any rate," says Odell, "the German put his pistol away, identified himself as a European explorer, Bruno Sigl, and said that he was there simply reconnoitering the area with two friends—a number Kami did not believe because he'd seen the seven riding Mongolian ponies and four or five figures still on Irvine's rope ladder—and that he, Sigl, had seen Bromley and an Austrian with Bromley, Kurt Meyer, carried to their deaths by an avalanche just twenty hours earlier.

"Kami had the presence of mind to ask where Sahib Bromley had died, and Sigl said that it had been on the mountain, above Camp Four on the North Col. Kami said that he was very saddened by the news—indeed, he wept in front of Sigl, partially, Kami admitted, because he knew the German had lied to him about where Bromley had died, and Kami still thought the chances were great that he himself would be shot dead by the German; but then Sigl merely waved him away and told him to stay away from Rongbuk.

"Kami complied," concludes Odell, "literally glissading down dangerous stretches of the glacier until he picked up Nema and Dasno. The three cousins whipped their little ponies away from there and rode all through the night before coming across Shebbeare and me headed north toward the trade routes."

"So we telegraphed tentative word of Bromley's fatal accident to *The Times* from Darjeeling in our first full report," says Colonel Norton. "Less than two days after we all took the train to Calcutta, Sigl himself showed up in Darjeeling and telegraphed his version of Bromley's death to the *Völkischer Beobachter* in Germany."

"That is one of the right-wing fascist newspapers, is it not?" asks Jean-Claude.

"Yes," says Somervell. "A National Socialist Party paper. But Sigl was a respected German mountain climber, and the story was picked up almost immediately by the *Deutsche Allgemeine Zeitung,* then the *Berliner Tageblatt,* and then the *Frankfurter Zeitung.* Sigl's story was repeated almost verbatim by *The Times* less than a day after our own sketchy first report—and folded within our report in a way I did not much care for, to be honest."

Norton and the others nod at this.

"But you do have Hazard's, Hari Sing Thapa's, the Tibetan pilgrims', and Kami's reports to back up Sigl's claim that Bromley had gone to Everest and started climbing," responds the Deacon. "I can give little hope or comfort to Lady Bromley about the reports of his disappearance on the mountain somehow being a mistake."

"Perhaps not," says Howard Somervell, "but it's all deucedly strange. It leaves a bad taste in one's mouth, no? And not just because young Percy was a nobleman." Somervell slaps the leather arms of his deep chair. "Well, gentlemen, I believe it is time..."

We rise.

"One last thing," asks the Deacon, after again thanking his former associates and climbing partners for their time. "We all know something about Bruno Sigl—he's been a German alpine climber for years, but never an explorer to my knowledge. But what about Kurt Meyer? Why would Bromley have chosen to try to climb Everest, even a little way up, with this Austrian or German?"

Colonel Norton shrugs. "The Alpine Club has been in touch with the German and Austrian alpine and climbing clubs, but they say they have no record whatsoever of a Kurt Meyer as a registered climber. It's strange."

"It's all very strange, if you ask me," says Dr. Hingston as we all walk through the Map Room on the way to the banquet hall. "Damnably strange."

And then there are all-around handshakes and farewells to us that are much warmer than the first greetings.

Outside, a north wind is blowing in from Kensington Gardens across the broad avenue. It's scented with plants and flowers still blooming, but there's also a stronger, sadder scent of leaves fallen and moldering. The not unpleasant smell of death in autumn. The clouds are low, and I can smell rain coming.

"We'd best find a cab," says the Deacon.

None of us says a word during the entire ride back to the hotel.

This is one hell of a stupid place to leave a pipe.

*A*fter the October memorial services and Alpine Club reports and our interview with Norton, Somervell, Noel, Odell, and Hingston, but before our November trip to Munich to meet Sigl, Jean-Claude and I want to start packing for Everest. The Deacon overrules us. He says that there are two things we have to do before we start planning the matériel and logistics for such an expedition.

First, says the Deacon, we have to learn about George Mallory—something that will show us something important about the challenge of climbing Everest that's ahead of us—and for that we have to drive to Wales. (I know nothing about Wales except that I seem to remember that they use no vowels in their spellings there. Or was it *all* vowels? I'll soon find out.)

We have a few weeks until the Deacon and I leave for Germany. He's arranged a meeting with Bruno Sigl in Munich in November. In the meantime, the Deacon has reminded me that Jean-Claude lost not only all three of his older brothers in the Great War but also two uncles and a half dozen other close male relatives.

With that background, I find it surprising that Jean-Claude accepts German clients in his Chamonix Guide work and, the Deacon says, is as careful, protective, and polite to them as to any of his French, Italian, British, American, or other clients. But down deep, J.C. does, the Deacon says, deeply hate *les boches*.

But the Munich trip lies ahead in November.

"First," says the Deacon after we've filled most of the backseat and all of the boot of a borrowed automobile with full rucksacks and climb-ing gear, including a *lot* of expensive new rope of the Deacon's own design—the Deacon's Miracle Rope, J.C. and I call it, since its blend of rope materials gives it a much greater tensile strength than the easily snapped climbing rope we are used to in the Alps—all of which I as-sume will go with us to Mount Everest, "we go to Pen-y-Pass."

"Penny Pass?" I say, even though he hadn't pronounced it that way. "That sounds like some place in a Tom Mix western."

Rather than answering, the Deacon ignores me as he starts the engine and drives us out of town and west toward Wales.

It turns out that Pen-y-Pass is an area of tall crags and vertical rocky slabs in the region near Mount Snowdon in north Wales. We pass a hotel situated at the summit of the pass that—according to the Dea-con—used to host many climbing parties in the early days of British rock climbing, many of them brought there by the preeminent rock climber of the time, Mallory's older friend Geoffrey Winthrop Young, whom Mallory met way back in 1909.

I wouldn't mind a big lunch and a pint at the hotel, but we keep driv-ing. We've packed sandwiches and water in our rucksacks, but I secretly hoped for something better.

There have been plenty of climbable, fun-scrambling crags right along the dirt road we've been driving on for an hour now, but the Dea-con keeps driving past them until, in an absurdly remote area, he finally parks the coupe and says, "Get your rucksacks and all that gear out of the boot, chaps. And tie it on well. It's going to be a long hike in." It is. More than two hours of covering rough country to get to his chosen crag. (I can't remember now whether it was named Lliwedd or Llechog, but it is a *big* crag, at least 400 vertical feet to the summit, with a daunt-ing overhang running the width of it about 50 feet below the summit.) All we're given to understand is that the Deacon climbed here before the War with Mallory and his wife, Claude Elliott, David Pye, the better climber Harold Porter—who did a lot of first ascents and new routes on these crags in 1911—and the best climber of the time and perhaps Mal-lory's closest climbing friend, Siegfried Herford.

Jean-Claude and I are ready to sit, study the face of the crag—which is daunting—and eat our pathetic lunches, but the Deacon insists·we wait and walk just a while longer.

Surprisingly, he leads us around the massive crag to a backside where getting to the summit would be child's play, just scrambling up tumbled boulders and easy ledges to the top. This is precisely what we do, which irritates me. I hate taking the easy way to a summit, even though that's often the best way to do reconnaissance on a vertical rock face. Many great rock climbers do it, even rappelling down to check things out before starting their climb—although the Deacon tells us that after George Mallory did just that on this crag, after his rappelling recon, he let his climbing partner at the time, Harold Porter, take the lead.

The Deacon doesn't allow us to eat even after we've hauled our loads to the top of the crag. The narrow summit, it turns out, is all but useless for climbing reconnaissance because of that view-obscuring overhang just 40 or 50 feet below the summit.

"Belay me," says the Deacon and hands me one of the longer coils of rope we've dutifully hauled to the summit. It makes sense that I belay him—I'm by far the heaviest, tallest, and probably the strongest of the three of us, and there's really nothing good to tie on to for a belay from up here—but it's still irritating. It will waste energy I'll need for any scrambling on the face of this crag that the Deacon might be planning for us.

Luckily there's a ridge of rock along the summit line where I can wedge both feet solidly, adding some non-skid insurance to my one-man belay. I feel Jean-Claude behind me pick up the rope, although if both the Deacon and I get pulled off, the odds are almost zero that the smaller, lighter Jean-Claude could arrest our fall. He would simply join us in the 300-foot tumble.

The Deacon is nonchalantly smoking his pipe as he rappels backward and out of my sight over the edge of the summit. He rappels quickly, bouncing down eight and ten feet at a hop, and the load on the rope is significant. I brace myself in the classic belay pose, the rope over my shoulder as well, and am glad for the crack in the crag-wall summit in which I can dig my booted heels.

Still holding the moving end of the rope, Jean-Claude steps up to the edge of the drop, leans over, looks, and says, "He's out of sight under the overhang now."

Then, shockingly, the rope goes slack. He's still moving—I have to feed some more rope out—but he's moving horizontally, along some ledge, requiring no full belay. Then the rope stops moving and I hold my position and Jean-Claude leans further over the drop and says, "I can see smoke coming up over the overhang. The Deacon's sitting on some damned ledge and smoking his pipe."

"While I'm starving," I say.

"I want the wine I brought," says Jean-Claude. "This is no fun at all. What does any of this rock climbing have to do with our climbing Everest—no matter what Mallory and the Deacon may have achieved on these stupid rocks before the War? Mount Everest is not a rock-climbing challenge—it is snow and ice and glacier and crevasse and ice walls and high ridges and steep snowfields. This trip to Wales is a waste of our time."

As if he's heard us, there's a warning tug on the rope, and then I'm on full belay again, leaning back to take the Deacon's full weight—which is not great, thank heavens, since he has a Sherlock Holmesian thinnesss to him—as he climbs back up over the overhang and the 50 or so feet of rock, leaning back almost horizontally as he ascends.

Then he's up over the summit ledge, standing with us, untying the knots of his belay rope, no longer puffing on that damned pipe, which must be in his shirt pocket now, and saying, "Let's eat before we go back down to do what we came for."

"I want the two of you to climb it," says the Deacon as J.C. and I stare up at the forbidding face of the crag.

"To the summit?" asks Jean-Claude, looking down at the heap of ropes, carabiners, pitons, and other gear we've hauled in to this distant site. It will take pitons driven in—German style—for some sense of safety, stirrups, and some sort of suspended cord ladder to hang under that formidable overpass, then Prusik-climbing it loop by loop, and trying to find a handhold or place to spread-eagle yourself on the broad edge to climb over it.

The Deacon shakes his head. "Just to where I forgot my pipe," he says and points to a grassy ledge about three-fourths of the way up the face, just under the overhang. "I want it back."

As tempted as J.C. and I are to say "Then go get it yourself," we both stay quiet. This has to have *something* to do with Mallory and our attempt on Everest.

"And no iron," adds the Deacon. "Just the two of you, ropes, and your ice axes if you wish."

Ice axes? Jean-Claude and I exchange worried glances again and look up at the slope.

The grassy ledge where the Deacon left his damned pipe is about 250 feet above us, sheltered nicely by the overhang but wide enough that one could dangle one's legs, smoke a pipe, and stare out at the view from 25 stories high. Which is exactly what the Deacon had done.

It took him a couple of minutes to rappel down from the summit to that ledge, including the mildly tricky rappel move over and then under the overhang. But climbing it from here...???

The crag is the kind of just-beyond-the-possible challenge that causes even temperate climbers to use harsh descriptive language.

"I know," says the Deacon as if reading our minds. "It's a daunting bugger."

Everything under the grassy ridge, for a width of 50 to 75 feet and more, is a huge, smooth, steep stone bulge—like the underbelly of some giant stone sow or an ex-prizefighter gone completely to seed. I'm good on rock—I started with countless rock climbs in Massachusetts and elsewhere and have taken those skills to rock-climbing challenges in Colorado and Alaska. I fancy that I can climb almost any climbable rock face.

But the part of this accursed face under the grassy ridge just isn't climbable. Not by 1924 standards, equipment, and ability. (Perhaps the Germans could do it with all their pig iron—carabiners, pitons, and the like, which we've hauled this long way in—but the Deacon has ruled out using such Teutonic hardware on this climb.) I see no ridges, no cracks, no fingerholds or creases in the rock where booted feet can find a hold, and the smooth sow's belly curls far out and then back in toward the bottom where we stand. The only thing that will hold a climber onto a vertical rock face (above the underbelly curve) like that in the first place is speed and friction—sometimes spread-eagled friction with every part of your body, including your palms and cheek and torso, trying to force

itself into the rock, to become part of the rock, so you don't keep sliding 200 feet to your death. But this curled-in sow's belly won't allow
a friction scramble on a third of its lower face—one would be hanging
out almost horizontally without any holds, sans pitons. A fall would be
inevitable. Even with pitons allowed, I see no cracks or crevasses or soft
areas of the nasty, solid-faced granite where any could be driven in.

So good-bye to the *direttissima* route—direct to the grassy ledge
where the Deacon's pipe sits. That's out.

Which leaves the crack that runs up the majority of the face about 50
feet to the right of the grassy ledge up there above 250 feet.

Jean-Claude and I move to the base and look up. We have to lean back
to see how it runs all the way to an ever-narrowing mini-crack as it peters out not far beneath the great overhang.

The first 30 feet or so of this climb will be easy enough—erosion has
exposed boulders and rubble and ridges for this first short section—but
beyond that it's all this narrow crack and prayers for finger- and footholds
that we can't see from here.

"I hate cunt-crack climbing," Jean-Claude mutters.

I'm shocked. To date I haven't heard either of my new climbing
friends use real obscenity or such a vulgar comment as this. I put it down
to Jean-Claude not fully understanding what an unacceptable word this
is in English.

But I look up again and understand Jean-Claude's intense dislike of
such a climb. For more than 200 feet our ascent will depend upon jamming our wedged hands, raw forearms, bloodied fingers, and the tips of
our boots or shoes into an ever-narrowing and zigzagging crack. I doubt
if there will be half a dozen decent belay points anywhere up this miserable little crack—and I still can't see any decent handholds or footholds
on either side of the fissure.

"You will lead, Jake," says Jean-Claude without making it a question.
Superb on snow and ice, brilliant on high mountain ridges and faces,
the gifted young mountain guide simply doesn't enjoy this sort of rock
climbing.

He says, "Shall we even bother roping up?"

I look again at the face and crack—the 50-foot separation from the
grassy "pipe ledge" to the highest points we must traverse from the

crack, if it's even possible to do so—and ponder the question. In truth, we'd probably be safer—especially I would—if we each climbed solo. With so few belay points, there's little to no chance that if one of us falls, the other can hold him.

But some chance is better than no chance.

"Yes," I say. "Ten meters of rope between us should do it."

Jean-Claude groans. Such a short tether slightly increases the chance of holding a fallen fellow climber—since if the lead climber, me, falls, it'll be 60 feet of falling inertia that the man on belay (Jean-Claude) will have to hold against, as well as far less weight-energy against the lead climber (should I have a solid hold) if the second man, Jean-Claude, falls. But the short rope will mean a slow ascent, with many stops for each man going on belay for the other. A sloppy, slow, dangerous climb, the antithesis of quality speed work on rock.

"But we should haul up a hell of a lot of rope," I add. "For the rappel down from the pipe ledge. I don't want to down-climb the damned crack."

Jean-Claude stares angrily at the almost invisible "pipe ledge" nearly 250 feet above us, glares at the Deacon, and says, "That's a *lot* of rope for a full rappel."

"We'll do it in two stages, J.C.," I say with far more enthusiasm and confidence than I feel. "There has to be at least one decent belay point in that crack about halfway down or more, and we'll swing the lead man on rappel to it and he'll set up the second rappel from there. Easy as pie."

Jean-Claude only grunts.

I turn to the Deacon and find that my voice is as angry in tone as was J.C.'s gaze at our "leader." I say, "I presume that you're going to explain to us why this miserable and dangerous save-the-pipe climb has something to do with Mallory or our attempt on Everest."

"I shall explain *after* you deliver my pipe to me, old man," says the Deacon in that smug British tone that makes Americans want to punch Brits.

Jean-Claude and I sit down, our backs against the crag, and start coiling the extra rope—we're going to have to carry a lot of it looped over our backs and bellies—and emptying out our rucksacks to carry even more rope. I'm using the rucksack mostly as a way to hold my ice axe, which I can imagine a use for even though Jean-Claude thinks I'm crazy to haul it up this iceless, snowless mass of rock.

And he stares in shock—now truly convinced of my insanity—as I take off my mountain boots and put on an old pair of sneakers that I'd hauled in with me in my rucksack, holes worn in them from my years of tennis at prep school and college and on summer clay courts. I understand my French friend's incredulity. Crack climbing demands the heaviest and most rigid climbing boots you can find; wedge a toe of that mountain boot in on the slightest spur or foothold, and the stiff sole of the boot gives you a stable platform on which to stand as you go for your next hold. My tennis shoes all but guarantee that my feet are going to be as bruised and bloody as my bare hands after this climb.

But all I can think about is that 50-foot traverse to the pipe ledge across that smooth and seemingly hold-free sow's-belly curve of rock 250 feet up. On that sort of rock, I've always used the softest shoes I can find—my American equivalent to the grippy-soled soft shoes that the new generation of German rock climbers call *Kletterschuhe.* So today it's my old tennis shoes with the holes in them.

Jean-Claude and I rope up and begin the climb. We're soon using the crack, and it's even nastier than I'd thought. My hands—already toughened and well calloused for such rock work—are bleeding profusely before the end of the first pitch. My tennis shoes soon have more holes in them, and I feel as if my bruised and torn feet do as well.

But we've found our rhythm, and very soon we're climbing as quickly as the frequent stops for belays in the crack allow. Jean-Claude watches for the improbable places where I jam my hands or set my toes for a hold, follows my lead well, and our climbing soon flows smoothly upward. Only our occasional curses—in American English and more expressive French—echo down to where the Deacon lounges against a tree, only occasionally watching us.

When we're three pitches and about 100 feet up the crag, something that had been in the back of my mind comes to the forefront of my thoughts: most rock climbers prefer crags and rock challenges close to a road. Falls from vertical rock faces can be terrible for the victim, and if the man survives the fall but is immobilized with broken bones and an injured back, it's important to get him to medical help quickly—if he can be moved at all—or to get medical help to him quickly if he can't be moved without killing him or snapping his back or neck. The two-hour rough hike in to this crag, no way to get a car or even a horse-drawn buckboard in here across the boulders, showed me that Mallory, the Deacon, Harold Porter, Siegfried Herford, and the others had been displaying impressive confidence and courage climbing here before the War. Or perhaps a certain arrogant stupidity.

I should talk about other people's arrogant stupidity, I think as I clench my aching and bloody left hand, turn it into a wedge blade again, and jam it into the crack as far as I can reach above my head. Then, feet secure on nothing, I begin pulling myself up yet again.

When I find spurs in the crack where I can get at least one of my torn tennis shoes set, and find a real hold for at least one hand, something better than a mere friction wedge, I call "On belay!" and wait while Jean-Claude closes the ten meters or so until his head is just below my free, dangling sneaker.

At about 200 feet up the crag, we pause to catch our breath—hanging too long in such temporary holds will just tire us out more, but we have to stop for a few seconds—and Jean-Claude says, *"Mon ami,* this climb is *merde."*

"Oui," I say, using up half of my collection of conversational French. It's possible that the little finger on my left hand is now broken—it *feels* broken—and this does not bode well for a Mount Everest attempt, even though such an attempt would have to be at least eight months away.

"Jean-Claude," I call down, "we're going to have to go all the way to the top of this damned crack to have any chance of a traverse. All the way to the overhang."

"I know, Jake. You'll have to half-free-climb swing, half-down-slide your way to the pipe ledge. But it has to be almost twenty meters across that bad patch of smooth, almost vertical rock. We'll tie on an extra rope between us—if we can find a belay point for me up there—but if you want my opinion, I do not believe it can be done. When you slide off the dome, you'll pluck me out of my belay point in the crack like a cork out of a wine bottle."

"Thanks for the image and the encouragement." Then, in a louder tone, "Climbing!" I wedge my possibly broken left hand as deep as I can in a three-inch crack far above my head and let that support all my weight as I scramble for another fingerhold, or a crack spur for my tennis shoe.

Pressing our bodies against the rock here just under the six-foot-wide overhang feels oppressive, as if that ceiling might force us out of our tenuous holds in the last skinny remnants, now almost horizontal, of this damned crack. The view from twenty-five stories up is fine, but neither of us can take the time or attention away from our tenuous and painful holds to appreciate it. Since we're only 40 feet or so higher than the grassy ledge—which seems about half a mile away across the smooth curve of near-vertical rock—the friction-sliding I have in mind is going to be trickier than I'd hoped.

Gingerly, only one hand free, I remove my until-now-useless ice axe from its rucksack loop and set the long, curved pick side of it as deep into the horizontal crack as I can. Luckily there's a downward V to the crack. Then I release my handhold and put my full weight on it. There's a downward-sloping camber in the slot that nicely matches the curve of the ice axe's pick.

It holds, but I wouldn't bet the farm—well, I guess I already am, in truth—on its holding too long.

"Here's your belay point," I say to Jean-Claude, who's moved to my right along the dying crack, actually ahead of me, and eye to eye with me for the first time in the climb.

"Hanging. From your ice axe," says Jean-Claude in a flat tone.

"Yes. And with your left boot in this part of the vertical crack that just tore up the front of my tennis shoe."

"My legs aren't long enough to reach the crack while hanging from your axe," J.C. says without unneeded emphasis. This climb has taken a lot out of us already. I know in my heart that Jean-Claude would prefer to try to free-climb this impossible overhang to reach the summit than try to help get me lower to that accursed pipe ledge.

"Make one of your legs longer," I say and hand him the end of the second 50-foot coil of rope I've hauled up the crag. J.C. is better at tying knots than I am.

We get ready, and tied in to the new rope, I have 80 feet of tether between Jean-Claude and me. It's necessary for the amount of naked rock I have to traverse, 60 feet to the ledge and some slack for up-and-down work, but it would mean that J.C. would have to arrest me after an 80-foot fall. I look at his belay stance. He's made his left leg longer but only by hanging almost horizontally, one boot on a ridge higher in the crack than I'd been, his body hanging from his left hand gripping the ice axe and his right forearm holding much of his weight along a three-inch-wide ridge he's found below the crack.

I think of the image that Jean-Claude's provided: if I fall, he'll be plucked out of his tenuous hold like a cork out of a wine bottle—or in this case more violently, more like a champagne cork.

But if I'm going to belay him over once I get to the pipe ridge, we need the connection. I think that if I were J.C., in my free right hand I'd have my knife unfolded and ready to cut the belay rope before it goes taut when I fall. Perhaps he does; I can't see that hand well because of the rock and position of his body.

"Okay," I say. "Here goes nothing."

The Deacon and Jean-Claude usually enjoy my more American Americanisms, but this time it's wasted: the Deacon looks like he's dozing 250 feet below us, his back to a warm rock and his tweed hat pulled down over his eyes, and Jean-Claude is in no mood for my chirpy vernacular.

I step out of the crack and onto the near-vertical smooth rock face.

I slide only a foot or two before friction stops me, spread-eagled on the rock, shirt and face and belly and balls and thighs and very tensed lower legs begging for friction, most of which is being provided by the toes of my tennis sneakers, which are bent almost at right angles to the rest of my shoe and foot. This is a bit uncomfortable, but not as uncomfortable as falling 250 feet.

I can't stay there. I begin slipping and sliding to my left, toward the damned pipe ridge, which is about 25 feet lower than I am and perhaps 60 feet away.

My fingers seek holds, even the slightest wrinkle in the rock, but this is an obscenely wrinkle-free rock face. I keep moving to the left, held against the near-vertical cliff just by friction and speed. If you're fast enough, sometimes gravity doesn't immediately notice you. My tennis shoes are doing 80 percent of the job of holding me onto the sow's belly of curved rock.

It's tricky playing out the rope to Jean-Claude as I crab-shuffle to the left. Most of it is in my rucksack, which keeps trying to pull me back and off the face with just the weight of the extra rope and a few other small things in it, but some I've had to loop over my right shoulder to keep playing out to J.C. The coil of rope itself pushes me away from the arresting friction of the cliff, and every time I play out more to Jean-Claude, I slide down a little bit until I'm free to slap my palms and fingers and forearms against the rock again.

I've made it a little more than halfway to the pipe ledge when I slip. My body just comes away from a glazed section of the great rock face.

I try to self-arrest madly, my fingers clawing toward any grip, any ridge, any irregularity in the rock, but I keep sliding, slowly at first, and then picking up speed. I'm already below the level of the pipe ledge still far to my left and sliding toward a part of the face that curves in enough below to be called a drop-off. I go off that, I go all the way down to where the Deacon is napping. Dragging J.C. with me if he's not smart enough to cut the rope with the knife. I think I should scream at him to do just that—he's only about 40 feet away and shifting in his impossible position to put more weight on his right arm along the thin ridge—but I'm too busy to scream. If he cuts it, he cuts. If he doesn't, he dies with me. It'll be decided in seconds.

The slide is cartwheeling to my left and within seconds I'm head down, still spread-eagled, upside down, my face and upper body being scraped bloody across suddenly rougher rock.

Rougher rock.

My bloody fingers become claws, trying to find a ridge big enough to grab and stop this quickening fall and swing me around. My claws lose a fingernail or two but don't stop or slow me—the upside-down position doesn't help matters.

I'm already about 20 meters below the face I'd been traversing and I'm picking up speed—the rope hasn't gone taut yet, the remnant is flying off my shoulder still slack for Jean-Claude, and when it gets to the extra 40 feet or so of tied-on rope in my rucksack, I'll be over the edge only a few meters ahead of me and in freefall.

Suddenly the toe of my right sneaker finds a deep part of one of these rough wrinkles in the stone just above the drop-off and I slam to a stop. "Ummphh!"

The rucksack tries to keep going over my head but doesn't pull me off.

For long seconds—hours, maybe—I hang there upside down, still spread-eagled, blood from my hands and torn cheek riveting down the rock just below me, and then I begin the slow process of figuring out how to get right side up from that one tennis shoe toehold above me and then what to do next.

The first part offers one real option, and I don't like it much. Somehow keeping the one toehold, I have to bend the rest of my body into as tight a U as I can, arms and bloody fingers fully extended vertically, and before that ridiculous posture pulls my sneaker out of the fault line and J.C. and me off the face, I have to get a hand jammed in there. It will be a curved-body flailing lunge as my foot comes out and I start sliding again.

Not good alpine form, by anyone's standards. I'm suddenly happy that the Deacon, still 200 feet below, isn't watching what very well might be my last seconds.

The upside-down position is just going to sap my energy, blur my thinking with blood rushing to my head, and make me weaker every second I think about this. The toe of the right sneaker may not continue its jammed hold for many more seconds.

I twist myself as hard right across the rock as I can, using the roughness for fingerholds as I bend myself into the tight U. The toe of my sneaker comes out before I want it to and my legs slide free again, nothing to stop me now before the drop-off, but I've gained inertia in the U-turn and I scrabble and lunge upward toward the ridge my foot has found.

Thanks be to God it's not just one narrow ridge but an actual fissure, deep enough to accommodate both hands jammed into it, and as I hang head-up vertical again, my hands deep in the fissure, even my sneakers finding some toeholds on the rough rock below where my head had been a few seconds earlier, I see that this fissure—about six inches from top to bottom and eighteen inches or more deep—keeps running to the left all the way to a spot about 25 feet beneath the pipe ledge. The horizontal crack even accommodatingly climbs a bit toward the end, getting me closer to the pipe ledge.

I hear Jean-Claude shouting down — the curve of the face is hiding me from him: "Jake! Jake?"

"I'm fine!" I shout back as loudly as I can. An echo returns from surrounding crags.

Am I fine? I can shinny my way left using my hands in this crack, but there's a better alpine way.

I carefully study the rock and find the ridges above the crack that could be sufficient for fingerholds. Keeping one hand in the crack for emergency arrest, I lunge at one of the wrinkles with my right hand. It's more than arm's length, so I have to push up toward it with knees and sneakers scrambling like a character in one of those new short Disney features from America where a live-action "Alice in Wonderland" interacts with clumsily drawn cartoon characters. In this instance *I am* the clumsy cartoon character, all rubbery legs and wildly pedaling feet.

I find the handhold wrinkle, it's adequate, I lunge up to my left — this one is less secure but it holds me as I pull and scramble my weight up above the fissure, using speed and friction again to temporarily defy gravity.

It works. My feet are now in the fissure below, and moving to my left is just a matter of shuffling slowly. Even when there's no fully secure cleft or ridge for either of my hands, upper-body contact with the curved stone works. I'm on a shuffle-fast highway now, and within a few minutes I'm at the high point of the crack, still about 15 bare-rock feet beneath the beginning of that goddamned pipe ridge.

I look up at it. I don't want to take my feet out of this life-saving fissure. I don't want to go back to spread-eagle friction and a prayer. To my right, the long rope to Jean-Claude curves up and out of sight. There's just enough bulge to the rock to hide my climbing partner from sight.

Slowly confidence flows back into me. I learned to climb on rock scrambles — in Massachusetts and other climbing spots in New England, and then twice in the Rocky Mountains, and once on a summer expedition to Alaska. After two years with my climbing friends from Harvard, I was *the* rock man of our group.

And this is a lousy 15 feet of smooth rock ascent. Come on, Jake, sheer vertical inertia, teeth, knees, sneaker toes, and then teeth again—if need be—can find enough three-second-type holds to get you up 15 feet.

I lunge up, arms wide, fingers clawing, pull my feet from the safety of the wonderful fissure, and crawl and clamber and climb.

I'm so tired when I reach the pipe ledge ridge that I have to pause, dangling a moment, before lifting myself up and over, onto grass.

God *damn* the Deacon. He risked both Jean-Claude's and my life for—what?

His damned pipe is lying in the grass about ten feet to my right as I stand looking out at the truly impressive view that the Deacon enjoyed just by rappelling down here at my expense. There's also a thin boulder curving up and back that will make a wonderful rappel anchor. I loop some of the rope around that, step back to my left, and wave at Jean-Claude, who has moved back to the vertical crack, my ice axe jammed in beneath his feet now. His new belay position, one arm deep in the crack, teetering atop the curved steel of the ice axe, *might* have stopped me if I'd gone over the edge.

Maybe.

Probably not.

I catch my breath for another moment and shout, "Ready! On belay!" The echoes return.

Jean-Claude waves his positive response. I've tightened the 60 or so feet of rope connecting us.

J.C. has a very complicated moment getting *off* the skinny shelf of my ice axe, using the vertical crack to climb below it, retrieving the axe, and sliding it into the loop on his own rucksack.

Then he waves again from that strangely great distance, shouts "Climbing!" and moves out onto the face.

He falls after this third traverse pitch. He just begins sliding as I had, but at least the rope between us keeps Jean-Claude head up as he hurtles down toward the overhang and freefall.

He's not going to get there. There's less than 40 feet of rope between us now, and I plant one foot on a boulder for extra leverage and easily hold him on the belay I'd worked around the short spire rock behind me. That will fray the rope as we pull Jean-Claude higher, but there's nothing to be done about that. We'll inspect it and use shorter rope on the rappels if we must.

Jean-Claude gives up on trying to self-arrest—saving his fingers and nails and knees from much damage—and just swings beneath me in a wide arc, easily held by my belay, until he swings back directly beneath me.

Then I do brace myself, even with the spire rock for backup, as J.C. pulls himself upright while holding the rope until his boot soles are on the rock face. He begins climbing that way—the tense and fraying rope his only hold—and I belay him up as quickly as I can, not wanting that rope to fray against the rock longer than it has to. It's good Manila rope, the most expensive the Deacon could find, but it's only a half-inch-thick lifeline.

Then he's up, pulling himself over the final ledge, and collapsing onto the grass.

I coil the rope, inspecting it carefully.

"Fuck the Deacon," J.C. says in French, gasping out the words.

I nod. That phrase is the second half of my tiny French vocabulary. And I agree with the sentiment.

Jean-Claude disentangles himself from the last coil of rope and walks over and picks up the Deacon's pipe. "This is one hell of a stupid place to leave a pipe," he says in English. He puts the damned thing in his large buttoned shirt pocket, where it won't fall out.

"Shall we set up and start the rappel?" I ask.

"Jake, give me about three minutes to enjoy the view," he says. I see that his ascent has sapped all of his energy.

"Good idea," I say, and for five or ten minutes we just sit with our legs dangling over the drop, our butts on soft grass, and our backs against the sun-warmed curved spire stone that we plan to use as a rappel anchor.

The view from almost 250 feet up this rock slab—like looking out a big window on the 25th floor of some skyscraper in New York—*is* beautiful. I see other crags that are taller, thinner, and more of a climber's challenge, and idly wonder if George Mallory, Harold Porter, Siegfried Herford, and Richard Davis Deacon had climbed *them* as well in those years between the time Mallory and the Deacon graduated from Cambridge in 1909 and went to war in 1914.

As for me, I've just done the only Welsh crag I'm going to climb this summer—perhaps this lifetime. Great fun, but just once, thank you.

It feels good to be alive.

After enjoying the view for a while and letting Jean-Claude get his wind back, we secure the ropes for the rappel. The section I'd used to pull J.C. using the rock as belay anchor looked okay, but we set it apart in my rucksack, to be used only if absolutely necessary.

The rappels down are fun. At the end of our first 80-foot descent, we swing our bodies right across the smooth rock—actually in a standing, boot-sole-running pendulum move—until Jean-Claude finally grips the edge of the vertical crack we'd climbed and stops his motion. A second later he is in the crack, with the really decent footholds and craggy bits we remember from the climb up—the one dependable platform in the whole vertical crack—and a few seconds later I swing up and join him.

J.C. has tied a good knot for our two-rope rappel—a stuck and irretrievable rope can be a nightmare on such a long rappel, and we need that extra twice-80-feet-each 160 feet of rope for the final single-rope descent from the crack here.

"Left rope to be pulled!" Jean-Claude and I shout out in unison. Pull the wrong rope, and J.C.'s beautiful knot will jam in the rappel sling we'd rigged, and we're in trouble.

I check the ends of the ropes and remove a couple of small twists and the safety knots we'd tied at the end of the strands. Then—taking the left rope we'd both just shouted about as a reminder—I give it a steady pull. As it starts to travel freely and fall, I shout "Rope!"—an old habit and a necessary one. Eighty feet of falling rope can knock a climber off even the best narrow platform.

We pull the first strand and coil it as I shout "Rope!" once more and bring down the second length.

There's no jam. There's no debris falling with it. We retrieve the second rope, coil it, and J.C. begins knotting the two together in that flawless Chamonix Guide knot he does when he unites ropes.

Five minutes later we're on the ground, retrieving the long rope and getting out of its way as the mass of it hits the ground, tossing up dust and pinecones.

Instead of inspecting and coiling it immediately, as would be proper, we both walk over to the boulder where the Deacon still appears to be sleeping.

I don't believe it. I think he has been watching us during the hard parts of the climb and traverse.

But I use my jagged, torn sneaker to kick him on the knee to get his attention.

The Deacon shoves his cap up and opens his eyes.

I hear my voice coming out as an actual growl. "Are you going to tell us what the fu— . . . what the hell . . . this has to do with Everest?"

"Yes," says the Deacon. "If you've brought my pipe back."

Not smiling, Jean-Claude retrieves the pipe from his pocket. I'm sort of sorry to see that it hasn't been snapped in two during the rappels.

The Deacon puts it in the chest pocket of his jacket, stands, and looks up at the face. All three of us are staring up at it.

"I climbed this with George Mallory in nineteen nineteen," he says. "Five years, for me at least, of no climbing—four during the War and one when I was trying to get a job after the War."

Jean-Claude and I wait, not happy. We don't want old tales of heroism, whether about climbing or war. Our hearts and minds are aimed at Mount Everest now, a climb of snow, glaciers, crevasses, then ice walls, glazed rock slabs, windblown ridges, and a huge North Face that we won't want to get very far out on.

"Mallory had done the rappel recon down from the top and had stopped to smoke his pipe on the grassy ridge," says the Deacon. "It was only Mallory, me, and Ruth—his wife—on this climb, and Ruth didn't want to do the full ascent. To the left of the grassy ridge, Mallory found the only indentation in the overhang that we might be able to climb without pitons, rope ladders, and all the modern overhang equipment.

"I went. But the move from the crack to the grassy ledge and then up again to and over the overhang took everything I had and more. We were roped together, but the belay points were as impossible as you just discovered them to be. Mallory and I had to do the same traverse across the same rock."

"What does this have to do with Everest other than telling us that George Mallory is . . . was . . . a good rock climber?" There's a bit of a growl still in my voice.

"When we came down the backside and around here to get our gear and hike out," says the Deacon, looking back at the crag, "Mallory told his wife and me that he'd forgotten his pipe up on that grassy ledge, and before I had time to tell him that he had other pipes, that I'd buy him a new damned pipe, George is scrambling up the crack again, all the way to where you belayed, Jean-Claude, and then did that smooth rock traverse alone . . . by himself."

I tried to imagine it. All I could see was a big black spider scuttling across the rock. Alone? No hope of belay or help? Even in 1919, such solo climbs, without protection of some sort, were considered bad form, showing off, and anathema to the protocols of the Royal Geographical Society's Alpine Club, to which Mallory belonged.

"Then he took the sixty-foot coil of rope he'd climbed and traversed with, and rappelled down," the Deacon continues. "With his pipe. And with Ruth furious at him for essentially doing the entire climb, except the overhang bit again, solo."

J.C. and I wait in silence. There's something here that might yet make sense of the day.

"On their last day, Mallory and Irvine left Camp Six at twenty-six thousand eight hundred feet about nine in the morning. They were slow to get started," says the Deacon. "You've both seen the photos and maps of Everest, but you have to be *on* that ridge, in the high winds and bone-shattering cold, to understand it."

Jean-Claude and I keep listening.

"Once you get on the North East Ridge," the Deacon says, "and if the winds allow you to stay on it, it's like climbing steep, ice-covered, downward-tilted slabs to the summit. Except for the Three Steps."

J.C. and I exchange glances. We've seen the Three Steps on the ridge maps of Everest, but on the map or in the photos taken from a great distance, they were just that—steps. Not a real barrier.

"The First Step you can work around along the North Face, just below it, then scramble back up to the ridge again if you're good," says the Deacon. "The Third Step no one alive knows about. But the Second Step—I've reached it. The Second Step . . ."

The Deacon's expression is strange, almost pain-filled, as if he is telling some terrible tale from the Great War.

"The Second Step you can't work around. The Second Step comes at you out of the whirling clouds and blowing snow like the gray bow of a dreadnought. The Second Step Mallory and Irvine—and the three of us—would have to free-climb. And this at twenty-eight thousand three hundred feet or so, where to take one step makes you stop to gasp and wheeze for two minutes.

"The Second Step, my friends, this bow-front gray hull of a battleship in our way on the North East Ridge route to the summit, is about a hundred feet high—much less than your scramble for the pipe today—but it is composed of steep, brittle, treacherous rock the whole way. The only possible route I could see before the wind and my climbing partner, Norton, growing ill, forced us down—the only possible climbing route I could see on the Second Step is a fifteen- or sixteen-foot perpendicular slab on the upper part of the free climb, which in turn is split vertically with three wide cracks running up towards the top of Step Two.

"This climb you just did, if you'd also done the overhang to the summit, is rated 'Very Severe.' The technical free climb of the Second Step—above twenty-eight thousand feet, please recall, where even when one is hauling heavy oxygen equipment, your body and mind are dying every second you stay at that altitude or increase it—the rating of the Second Step is beyond the Alpine Club's 'Very Severe' rating system. It may be impossible to climb such a rock face at such an altitude. And then there is the Third Step waiting for us higher on the ridge, the last real obstacle, I believe, except for a pyramid snow slope that one has to climb just below the last summit ridge—that Third Step may be even more impossible."

Jean-Claude just stares at the Deacon for a long silent moment.

Then J.C. says, "So you had to see if we—or actually if *Jake*—could do such a comparable free climb. And then haul me up like a bag of laundry. And he did...so...I don't understand. Does this mean you believe we can do the same sort of climbing above twenty-eight thousand feet?"

The Deacon smiles in earnest now. "I believe we can try without it amounting to suicide," he says. "I believe I can do the crux of the Second Step, and now I think that Jake can as well, and that you will be an able third partner, Jean-Claude. This doesn't give us the summit of Everest—we simply don't know what's beyond the Second Step, save for perhaps Mallory's and Irvine's frozen corpses, which might also be at the base of the Second Step—but it means we have a fighting chance."

I coil the last of the rope, secure it over my shoulder and rucksack, and think about this. In my angry heart I forgive the Deacon somewhat for putting us through this go-get-my-pipe charade. Mallory had free-climbed that solo, after climbing it following the Deacon—the sporting thing to do, Mallory had said, according to the Deacon, since he, Mallory, had the advantage of the rappel recon.

We head out toward the distant car, almost two hours of rough hiking after our climbing day, and I feel like my insides are flying. My heart—or soul, or whatever's in there at the core of who each of us is—has taken happy flight and is soaring above us.

The three of us are going to climb Mount Everest.

Whatever the outcome is of finding the remains of Lord Percival Bromley—and I assign that a very low probability—the three of us are going to make our attempt, alpine style, at the summit of the tallest mountain in the world. And the Deacon now thinks that we can climb that dreadnought bow of the vertical face of the Second Step. Or at least that *I* can.

From this moment on, a new fierce fire burns in me, and it continues to burn in the weeks and months ahead.

We are going to climb that goddamned mountain. There is now no other choice or alternative.

The three of us are going to stand on the summit of the world.

Der Mann, den wir nicht antasten lassen.

I haven't been to Germany in the year I've spent in Europe, doing almost all of my climbing in France and Switzerland, although we met more than a few German climbers in Switzerland: some Germans were friendly; many more were not. When I first met Jean-Claude and the Deacon, the three of us staring at the North Face of the Eiger and agreeing that the face was simply beyond the climbing techniques and technology of our day, there was a team of five very intense, very self-serious, very unfriendly Germans nearby who were talking as if they were actually going to try to climb *die Eigerwand*—the wall of the North Face. They didn't, of course. They barely got beyond the Bergschrund and scrambled around a bit on the first 100 feet or so of slope before abandoning their bold quest.

For our trip to Germany, the Deacon and I first travel back to France, where he has to conclude some financial business, cross Switzerland to Zurich and then north to the border, where we change trains, since at the time railroad stock ran on different-gauge rails in Germany than in all the surrounding countries. This was a defensive military measure on the part of Germany's neighbors, of course, even though the former land of the Kaiser had been defanged by the Versailles Treaty. The Deacon tells me in soft tones, even though we have a private compartment to ourselves (thanks to Lady Bromley's expense account), that the current Weimar Republic government is a rather inefficient and mostly left-wing debating club.

Then on to Munich in the morning.

It is a rainy day, low gray clouds moving quickly westward, in the opposite direction of the train, and my first impressions of November 1924 Germany are a bit confused.

The villages are tidy—overhanging eaves, some modern buildings mixed in with homes and public buildings that look like they were there in the Middle Ages. Cobblestones wet from the rain reflect what little daylight there is. Some of the men visible walking the village streets are dressed like peasant farmers or overall-clad factory workers, but I also catch glimpses of men in modern double-breasted gray business suits carrying leather briefcases. But everyone I see out the train windows—peasants, workers, and businessmen alike—looks... weighed down. As if the gravity here in Germany is greater than in England, France, and Switzerland. Even the young men in business suits hurrying under their rain-slicked umbrellas look slightly bent, slightly stooped, heads bowed, gazes lowered, as if each were carrying some invisible burden.

Then we move through an industrial area that is all long, dirty brick and cinderblock buildings amidst mountains of slag. A few towers and industrial chimneys throw up great fingers of flame that seem to cast an orange spotlight on the scudding rain clouds. I see no human beings in this landscape as I watch mile after mile of these ugly industrial monoliths and their mountains of cinders, slag, sand, and sheer refuse slide past my train car windows in the rain.

"In January of last year," the Deacon says, "the German government fell behind on reparation payments that were part of the treaty. The mark dropped from seventy-five to the dollar in nineteen twenty-one to seven *thousand* to the dollar by the beginning of nineteen twenty-three. The German government asked the Allies to grant a moratorium in reparation payments, at least until the mark began to regain some value. The response of the Allies was given by the French. Former Premier, now Prime Minister Poincaré sent in French troops to occupy the Ruhr and other industrial sites throughout the heart of Germany. When those troops arrived last year, January of 'twenty-three, the mark dropped to eighteen thousand to the dollar and had reached one hundred sixty thousand to the dollar and then a clear one million marks to the dollar by August first last year."

I try to understand this. Economics always bored me, and while I'd read that French troops had gone into Germany to occupy the industrial area, I certainly hadn't paid any attention to what effect such an occupation would have on Germany's economy, such as it was after the Great War.

"By November of last year," says the Deacon, leaning close to speak in little more than a whisper, "it would have taken a German *four billion marks* to buy a dollar. With the Ruhr French troops overseeing all industrial production, river traffic, and steel exports, Germany was effectively cut in two. So the German industrial workers, essentially working while under armed guard and supervision of the occupying French troops in each of those factories we're passing, declared a general strike last year—and in most of these factories, as in the Ruhr, real production of steel or anything else has come to a stop because of the German workers' passive resistance, active sabotage, and even guerrilla warfare. The French keep arresting and deporting and even lining up and shooting the presumed leaders of this slowdown, but it makes no difference."

"My God," I say.

The Deacon nods toward the men and women in the street. "Last year those people knew that even if they had millions of marks in their bank account, it wouldn't be enough to buy them a pound of flour or a few raggedy carrots. Forget being able to pay for several ounces of sugar or a pound of meat."

He took a deep breath and pointed through the rain-streaked window toward the suburbs of Munich we were entering. "There's a lot of frustration and anger out there, Jake. Be careful when we go to meet Sigl. Americans, even though they helped win the War, are an oddity. But many, not all, hate the British and French on sight, and Jean-Claude might not have been physically safe here in Munich."

"I'll be careful," I say, without even being sure of what "careful" will demand or amount to in this strange and sad and *angry* country.

The Deacon has not even booked us into a hotel. We have tickets for sleeping berths on a train leaving for Zurich at ten p.m. I'm curious about this, since it would have been easy to put the cost even of luxury hotel rooms in Munich on Lady Bromley's advance money expense account. I know that unlike Jean-Claude, the Deacon doesn't hate Germany or Germans—I'm also aware that he's traveled here frequently since the War—so it isn't anxiety or fear that is rushing us out of town tonight even before we can get a good night's sleep. I sense that there is something about this simple interview with climber Bruno Sigl that bothers the Deacon on some level I don't understand.

In a curt telegram, Sigl has agreed to meet us—briefly, he says, for he is a very busy man (his phrase)—in Munich at a beer hall called the Bürgerbräukeller way out on the southeastern fringes of the city. The appointment is for seven p.m., and the Deacon and I have time to stow our luggage, such as it is, at the train station, freshen up there a bit in the first-class lounge lavatory, and wander the strangely shopless streets of downtown Munich for an hour or two under our dark umbrellas before taking a cab to the edge of town.

Munich looks old but not picturesque or attractive to me. It is still raining hard against the slate-shingled rooftops, and the streets are as dark and chilly as on any November evening in Boston. All my conscious life I've thought my first real encounter with Germany would be strolling down the Unter den Linden in rich summer evening light, with hundreds of well-dressed and friendly Germans strolling along nodding *"Guten Abend"* to me.

The rain pours down as the cab's window wipers slap uselessly against the rivulets on glass. We cross a river on a broad, empty bridge, and a few minutes later the surly cab driver announces in broken English that we are *"hier"*—at *die Bürgerbräukeller* in *den Haidhausen* neighborhood on *Rosenheimer Strasse*—and demands what has to be three times the legal fare. The Deacon pays it without protest, counting out the huge stack of high-numbered marks as if it were play money.

The stone entrance arch to the beer hall is huge and has the words

> *Bürger-*
> *Bräu-*
> *Keller*

tacked one atop the other in the middle of a circular, heavy-handed wreath, a sort of lumpy stone oval with an arch key design at the bottom.

All of it is dripping water running from a steep slate roof and from several overflowing gutters. Through that arch toward the actual doorway, and it's like we are entering a train station rather than a bar or restaurant. But at least it's not raining in the foyer.

When we are actually inside the Bürgerbräukeller, both the Deacon and I stop in a kind of shock.

Besides the fact of two or three thousand people — mostly men, guzzling beer out of huge stone mugs at tables so rough-hewn that they look as if they'd been carved in the forest that very afternoon — the place is gigantic, echoing, more a huge auditorium than any sort of restaurant or pub that I've ever seen. The noise of conversation and accordion music — unless that's people screaming while being tortured — hits me like a physical shove. The next shove is the *smell:* three thousand partly or totally unbathed Germans, mostly working men, judging from their rough clothes, and mixed with that wall of sweat smell washing over us like a rogue wave, an accompanying stink of beer so strong that I feel like I've fallen into the actual beer vat.

"Herr Deacon? Come here. *Here!*" It's a shouted order, not a request, from a man standing at a crowded table about halfway across the crowded room.

The standing man, who I assume to be Bruno Sigl, watches us approach through the bedlam with an unblinking, cold, blue-eyed stare. Sigl has a European reputation as a good climber — especially good, according to the alpine journals, at route finding on previously unclimbed faces in the Alps — but except for the massive forearms visible because his dark tan shirtsleeves are rolled up, he doesn't look like a climber to me. Too self-consciously overmuscled, too top-heavy, too stocky, too blocky. Sigl's blond hair is cut so short that it's almost flat as a bristle brush on top and is actually shaved on the sides. Many of the larger men sitting along the table with him sport similar haircuts. For Sigl, it's not a good look because of the jug ears that jut out from his granite block of a face.

"Herr Deacon," Sigl says as we approach the table. The German's deep voice cuts through the beer hall babble like a knife through soft flesh. "*Willkommen in München, meine Kletterkollegen.* I have read of many of your brilliant first ascents in the *Alpine Journal* and elsewhere."

Bruno Sigl's English has the expected German accent but sounds easy and fluent to my untutored ear.

I was aware that the Deacon spoke fluent German as well as French, Italian, and some other languages, but I'm still surprised at how quickly and strongly he replies to Sigl: *"Vielen Dank, Herr Sigl. Ich habe ebenfalls von Ihren Erfolgen und Leistungen gelesen."*

During the night trip home on the train later that night, the Deacon will translate from memory everything that Sigl and the other Germans said, as well as what the Deacon replied in German. Here my guess is right that the Deacon is returning Sigl's compliment by saying that he's read of Sigl's mountaineering exploits and successes as well.

"Herr Jacob Perry," says Sigl, shaking my hand in a granite-crunching grip through which I can feel his rock-calloused hand. "Of the Boston Perrys. Welcome to *München.*"

Of the Boston Perrys? What did this German climber know about my family? And Sigl somehow had made the "Jacob" with its German Y-sound pronunciation sound very Jewish.

Sigl is wearing lederhosen—leather shorts and bib—over his military-looking brown shirt with the sleeves rolled high, and the whole getup should look ridiculous amidst all the rumpled business suits in this gigantic beer hall, but his massive, sun-browned bare thighs, arms, and oversized Rodin-sculptured hands make him look powerful instead—almost godlike.

He waves us to the bench opposite him—several of the men there move down to make room, never pausing in their drinking as they do so—and the Deacon and I sit, ready for the interview. Sigl waves over a waiter and orders beer. I'm disappointed. I expected Fräuleins with low-cut peasant blouses to be serving the beer, but it's all men in lederhosen carrying trays of the giant stone mugs. I'm also hungry, and it's been a long time since the Deacon and I had a light lunch on the train, but the tabletops here and all around us are empty except for beer steins and hairy male German forearms. Evidently the eating time here has either passed or is yet to come or simply doesn't happen except for beer.

Our beers arrive almost immediately, and I must admit that I've never before drunk good, strong German beer from an icy-chilled stone stein.

After lifting the thing three times, I begin to understand why all the men on this side of our table have huge biceps.

"Gentlemen," says Sigl, "allow me to introduce some friends of mine here at the table. Alas, none of them is confident enough in your language to speak English this evening."

"Although they understand it?" asks the Deacon.

Sigl smiles thinly. "Not really. To my immediate left is Herr Ulrich Graf."

Herr Graf is a tall, thin man with a thick and absurd black mustache. We nod toward one another. My guess is that there'll be no more handshaking.

"Ulrich was *his* personal bodyguard and shielded *him* with his own body last November, receiving several serious bullet wounds. But you see that Herr Graf has recovered nicely."

I hear the odd, almost reverential emphasis on "his" and "him" but don't have a clue as to who they are talking about. It appears that Sigl's not going to enlighten me, and rather than break into the ongoing introductions, I turn to the Deacon for a hint. But the Deacon is looking at the men across the table being introduced and won't acknowledge my questioning gaze.

"To Herr Graf's left is Herr Rudolf Hess," Sigl is saying. "Herr Hess commanded an SA battalion in last November's action."

Hess is a strange-looking man with oversized ears, a dark five o'clock shadow—the kind of man who probably has to shave twice or three times a day if he has a decent job or interacts with the public—and sad-looking eyes under heavy, cartoonish eyebrows that are either kept raised in evident surprise during the time I observe him or lowered to a glowering position. To be honest, Hess reminds me of a madman I saw once in the Boston Public Garden when I was a boy—a madman who'd escaped from a nearby asylum and who was peacefully captured by three white-coated attendants not thirty feet from me. That crazy man had been shuffling along straight toward me around the lake as though he were on a mission which only he could carry out, and Hess gives me the creeps in the same way as I'd felt looking at that man coming toward me past the Swan Boats pavilion.

I still have no clue as to what "last November's action" was, but it sounds military. It may explain why so many men at the table are wearing quasi-military brown shirts with epaulets.

I search my memory for news from Germany in November 1923, but I'd spent that month climbing on and around Mont Blanc and couldn't recall hearing any radio news or reading any pertinent reports in newspapers—most of which were in French or German—the few times we stayed in Swiss hotels. The past year has been a climbing vacation almost completely out of time for me—up until we read of Mallory's and Irvine's disappearance on Everest—and whatever "action" happened here in Munich the previous November hadn't caught my attention. I presume it was some more of the political idiocy that Germany has been cranking out from both sides of the political spectrum ever since the weak Weimar Republic came into power after the toppling of the Kaiser.

Whatever it was, it's irrelevant to the reason we came all this way to Munich to interview Bruno Sigl.

What *isn't* irrelevant are the names of the six mountain climbers whom Sigl is now introducing—the six hairy-armed men sitting on the bench along our side of the long table.

"First, allow me to introduce our co-lead climber, along with myself, among my climbing colleagues," Sigl is saying, palm out toward the tanned, thin-faced, solemn-looking bearded man to my immediate right. "Herr Karl Bachner."

"Meeting you is a true honor, Herr Bachner," says the Deacon. Then he repeats it in German. Bachner nods slightly.

"Herr Bachner," continues Bruno Sigl, "has been the mentor of many of Munich's and Bavaria's top climbers—which, of course, means the top climbers in the world—at the *Akademischer Alpenverein München,* the climbing club of the University of Munich..."

How many times during my years at Harvard had I wished that my college had a *formal* climbing club such as Munich's? While there were a few professors who climbed and helped us organize our Alaskan and Rockies expeditions, the founding of the Harvard Mountain Club was still a few years in my future.

"Herr Bachner is also a leader in the now merged *Deutscher und österreichischer Alpenverein,*" says Sigl.

This is German that even I can understand. I knew from the alpine journals that Karl Bachner had been the prime mover in uniting the German and Austrian alpine clubs.

Sigl gestures toward the next two young men beyond Bachner. "You have read, I presume, of the recent ice-climbing exploits of Artur Wolzenbrecht..."

The man closer to me nods in our direction.

"...and his climbing partner, Eugen Löwenherz."

I know that the young men were famous for designing the much shorter ice axes—ice *hammers,* really—and thus, with the help of pitons and ice screws, what climbing Brits like Deacon derisively tend to call "the dangle and whack school," rapidly climb straight up ice walls that would defeat our old-fashioned attempts to carve steps in the ice.

"Artur and Eugen climbed the direct route up the North Face of the Dent d'Hérens last week in sixteen hours," says Sigl.

I whistle in astonishment. Sixteen hours for a direct North Face ascent of one of the most difficult faces in all of Europe? If it is true—and the Germans never seem to lie about their ascent claims—then these two men drinking beer to my right have opened a new era in the history of mountaineering.

The Deacon says in a rapid-fire German something he later translates for me as "Gentlemen, does either of you have one of your new ice axes with you?"

It's Artur Wolzenbrecht who reaches under the table and brings out not one but two short ice axes, their shafts less than a third the length of my own wooden axe's, their blades far more pointed and curved. Wolzenbrecht sets the two revolutionary climbing instruments on the table in front of him, but he does not hand them to the Deacon or me for closer inspection.

It doesn't matter. Just looking at the shortened ice hammers (for want of a better term), I can imagine the two men hacking their way straight up the icy North Face of the Dent d'Hérens, driving in long pitons or their newly designed German ice screws all the way for their safety. And I'm sure that they used the 10-point crampons as well—invented in 1908 by the Englishman Oscar Eckenstein but rarely used by British climbers. Now *frequently* used by this new generation of Bavarian ice climbers. Cramponing and short-ice-hammering their way up a giant ice face. It's beyond ingenious—it's brilliant. I'm just not sure if it's *fair,* if that makes any sense.

Sigl introduces the last three climbers—Günter Erik Rigele, who, two years ago, in 1922, successfully adapted the German piton for use on ice; a very young Karl Schneider, about whom I'd read amazing things; and Josef Wien, an older climber—his head shaved bare for some reason—whose stated goal in the alpine journals was to lead joint Soviet-German expeditions to Peak Lenin and to other impossible climbs in the Russian Pamirs and the Caucasus.

The Deacon expresses, in smooth German, his and my sense of being honored to meet these great Bavarian climbers. The six men being complimented—seven including Bruno Sigl—don't even blink in response.

The Deacon takes another long drink of beer from the heavy stein and says to Bruno Sigl, "Can we begin our discussion now?"

"It will not be a 'discussion,' as you call it," snaps Sigl, his Bavarian courtesy suddenly and totally absent. "It will be an interrogation—as if I'm in a British courtroom."

I gape at this, but the Deacon only smiles and says, "Not at all. If we were in an English courtroom, I would be wearing a funny white wig and you would be in the dock."

Sigl frowns. "I am only a witness, Herr Deacon. It is the defendant—the usually guilty party—who sits in the dock in British courts, no? The witness sits...where? On the chair near the judge, *ja?*"

"*Ja,*" agrees the Deacon, still smiling. "I stand corrected. Would you prefer that we speak in German so that all your friends can understand? I'll translate for Jake later."

"*Nein,*" says Bruno Sigl. "We will speak English. Your Berlin accent grates on my Bavarian ears."

"Sorry," says the Deacon. "But we agree that you were the *only* witness to see Lord Percival Bromley and his fellow climber Kurt Meyer swept to their death by an avalanche, is this not true?"

"By what authority, Herr Deacon, do you interrogate...or even *interview* me?"

"No authority whatsoever," the Deacon says calmly. "Jake Perry and I came to Munich to speak to you as a personal favor to Lady Bromley, who, understandably, simply seeks more details about her son's sudden death on the mountain."

"A *favor* to Lady Bromley," Sigl says, the sarcasm audible in his voice even through the heavy German accent. "I presume there is money changing hands as part of this...*favor.*"

The Deacon merely continues smiling and waits.

Finally Sigl slams down his empty stone stein, waves the attentive waiter over for a new one, and grumbles, "Everything I saw of the accident I reported both to German newspapers and in the German alpine journal and in a letter to your Royal Geographic Alpine Club journal."

"It was a very short report," the Deacon says.

"It was a very quick avalanche," snaps Sigl. "You were on both of Mallory's earlier Everest expeditions. I trust you saw snow avalanches? Or at least in the Alps?"

The Deacon nods twice.

"You know, then, that one second the person or persons are *there,* the next second they are *not.*"

"Yes," agrees the Deacon. "But it is difficult to understand what Lord Percival and the man named Meyer were doing on the mountain at all. Why were they there? Why were *you* and your six German friends there? Your report in the journals said that you and several other German...explorers...had come south to Tibet through China. That your permit was Chinese, not Tibetan, but for some reason the Tibetan *dzongpens* accepted it as they would an official pass. You told the *Frankfurter Zeitung* that you'd diverted your route when you heard in Tingri that a German and an Englishman had rented yaks and purchased climbing equipment in the Tibetan town of Tingri Dzong, and that you and your friends had gone south to investigate...out of sheer curiosity. Nothing more."

"Everything I told the newspapers is correct," Sigl says in a dismissive tone. "You and your American comrade came all the way to Munich to hear me confirm what I have already explained?"

"Much of it makes little or no sense," says the Deacon. "Lady Bromley—young Percival's mother—will be very appreciative if you can help us discover the missing facts. That's all she wants."

"And you have come all this way to help the old lady learn a few more...how do you say it in England?...tit-bits about her son's death," says Sigl with an expression very close to a sneer. I marvel that the Deacon keeps from losing his temper.

"Was this Kurt Meyer from your . . . ah . . . exploration group?" asks the Deacon.

"*Nein!* We had never heard of him before the Tibetans in Tingri Dzong told us his name . . . and that he had ridden southeast toward Rongbuk with Lord Percival Bromley of England."

"So Meyer was not a climber?"

Sigl drinks a long gulp of beer, belches, and shrugs. "None of us had ever heard of Kurt Meyer. We heard his name only from the Tibetans in Tingri who had spoken to him. Between those of us at this table, we know almost all of Germany's and Austria's real climbers. *Ja, meine Freunde?*" He is addressing the question to his fellow Germans. They nod, and several of them say "*Ja*" even though Sigl just told us they didn't understand English.

The Deacon sighs. "Rather than my directing questions to you that make you feel like you're in a courtroom, Herr Sigl, why don't you just tell us the full story of why you were there at the approaches to Everest, and what you saw of Lord Percival Bromley and Kurt Meyer? Perhaps you even know why the two men's ponies had been shot."

"We saw the ponies lying there dead when we arrived," says Sigl. "The Camp One area, as you know, Herr Deacon, is very rough moraine. Perhaps the ponies had both broken their legs. Or perhaps Herr Bromley or Herr Meyer had gone mad and shot the ponies. Who knows?" The German climber shrugs again.

"As for our reason for 'following' Bromley and Meyer to Rongbuk Glacier," continues Sigl, "I shall reveal to you what I have told no one—not even our local newspapers. My six friends and I were merely interested in meeting George Mallory, Colonel Norton, and the other climbers we had heard were attempting Everest that spring. Obviously, since we were in China during most of our trip, we heard no news of Mallory's and Irvine's deaths, or even that the expedition had reached the mountain. But when the Tibetans in Tingri told us that Bromley was headed for the mountain they call Chomolungma, we decided—as you British and Americans say—'Why not?' And so we went southeast rather than back north."

(*Und zo ve vent soudeast razzer zan back nord.* Sigl's accent is beginning to grate on me for some reason.)

"But certainly," said the Deacon, his tone polite but insistent, "when you saw that Norton's and Mallory's Base Camp had been abandoned, except for scraps of tents and dumps of uneaten canned food, you must have known that the expedition had already departed. Why then continue up the glacier all the way to the North Col and above?"

"Because we saw two figures descending the North Ridge, and it was obvious they were in trouble," snaps Sigl.

"You could see that from Base Camp, twelve miles away from Mount Everest?" asks the Deacon, more in a tone of wonder than one of challenge.

"*Nein, nein!* We had gone up to Camp Two after finding the dead ponies, thinking that Bromley and this Meyer person whom we'd never heard of might be in some difficulty. We saw them on the ridgelines from Mallory's Camp Two. We used fine German field glasses—Zeiss—the best in the world."

The Deacon nods his acknowledgment of this fact. "So you set up your own tents at the site of Mallory's old Camp Three just below the thousand-foot ascent to the North Col, then climbed onto the Col itself. Did you use the rope ladder that Colonel Norton's group had left behind for the last hundred-some vertical feet?"

Sigl waves away that suggestion with a flicking motion of his fingers. "We used no old ladder or fixed ropes. We used our own ice-climbing axes and other German techniques to ascend the ice wall."

"Kami Chiring reported seeing several of your men coming down from the Col using Sandy Irvine's rope ladder," says the Deacon.

"Who is this Kami Chiring?" demands Sigl.

"The Sherpa you met and aimed a revolver at near Camp Three that day. The one you told the story of Bromley's death to."

Bruno Sigl shrugs and sneers. "Sherpa. There you have it. Sherpas lie constantly. As do Tibetans. My six friends and I went nowhere near that worn-out rope ladder. We had no need to, you see."

"So you were on a purely exploratory trip through China, but you brought your mountain- and ice-climbing gear with you," says the Deacon, getting out his pipe and beginning to fill it. The huge room cannot get much smokier than it is already.

"There are mountains and steep passes in China, Herr Deacon." Sigl's tone has gone from surly to contemptuous.

"I did not mean to interrupt your narrative, Herr Sigl."

Again Sigl shrugs. "There is very little...narrative, as you call it...left, Herr Deacon. My friends and I climbed to the North Col because we could see that the two figures descending the North Ridge were in trouble. One appeared to be snow-blind and was being led, almost held up, by the other."

"So you set up camp on the North Col?" says the Deacon, lighting and breathing his pipe alive.

"We did *not!*" cried Sigl. "We had no camp on the North Col."

"Kami Chiring saw at least two tents on the same ledge on the Col that Norton and Mallory had used for their Camp Four," says the Deacon. Again, his voice is more curious than challenging. A man simply trying to ascertain a few facts to help a grieving mother get over the confusing disappearance of her son.

"The tents were Bromley's," says Sigl. "One was already in tatters from the high winds. The same winds that forced the retreating Bromley and Meyer off the ridgeline onto the unstable snow of the face just above Camp Five. I shouted at them in both English and German not to go onto the face—that the snow there was not stable—but either they did not hear me through the wind or they ignored me."

The Deacon's heavy eyebrows rise slightly. "You were close enough to speak to them?"

"To *shout* to them," Sigl says in tones one would use with a slow child. "We were still thirty meters or more apart. Then the snow under them simply shifted and fell thousands of feet down the face in one roaring mass. They disappeared completely in the avalanche and I heard no more from them."

"You didn't attempt to go lower to see if they might have survived?" There is no accusation in his voice, but Bruno Sigl still bridles and glowers as if he's been insulted.

"It was impossible to go lower on that face. There was no face left. All the snow on it had disappeared with the avalanche, and it was obvious that young Bromley and Kurt Meyer were dead—buried under tons of snow thousands of feet below—gone. *Hinüber.*"

The Deacon nods as if he fully understands. I remember that he had seen—and warned George Mallory against trying to ascend—the long snow slope leading to the North Col, a slope that had killed seven of Mallory's porters in the avalanche on Everest in 1922.

"You wrote in your newspaper reports and in fact have just repeated that the wind on the ridge leading up to Camp Six was so terrible that both Lord Percival and Herr Meyer had to retreat to the rock bands and ice fields of the North Face for their descent to Camp Five," says the Deacon.

"*Ja,* that is accurate."

"Presumably, Herr Sigl, you were also forced off the ridge and onto the face during your ascent in searching for the two men. That means you met them, saw them, and shouted to them, and they to you, while on the face rather than the ridge. Which would explain the avalanche that would not have happened on the ridge itself."

"Yes," says Sigl. His tone around the English word has a finality to it, as if the interview is now over.

"And yet," says the Deacon, steepling his long fingers, "you tell me that both you and the doomed men were able to shout and be heard at a distance of over thirty meters—a hundred feet apart—even with such a wind roaring over the ridge."

"What are you suggesting, *Englander?*"

"I am suggesting nothing," says the Deacon. "But I'm remembering that when I was on that ridge at that altitude in nineteen twenty-two and then forced off the ridge with two other climbers and onto the rocks of the North Face by the wind, we couldn't hear each other's shouts at five paces, much less at thirty meters."

"So you are calling me a liar?" Sigl's tone is very low and very tight. He's taken his hands and forearms off the table, and his right arm moves as if he is taking something—a small pistol, a knife—from his broad belt.

The Deacon sets his pipe down carefully and lays both of his long-fingered, rock-scarred hands palm down on the table. "Herr Sigl, I am not calling you a liar. I am trying to understand Bromley's—and his Austrian climbing partner's—last minutes alive so that I can report in detail to Lady Bromley, who is beside herself with grieving. So much so that she has fantasies that her son is still alive on the mountain. I presume that once you left the ridgeline to continue climbing along the face, the force and roar of the wind died enough that you were able to shout thirty meters to Bromley."

"*Ja*," says Sigl, his face still closed with anger. "That was precisely the situation."

"What," asks the Deacon, "did you shout to them, especially to Bromley, and what did they say in return before the avalanche? And which of the two appeared to be snow-blind?"

Sigl hesitates, as if any more participation in this interview will be too much of a surrender for him. But then he speaks. His friend with the strange eyebrows and haunted eyes, Herr Hess, appears to be following all the exchanges in English with absorbed comprehension, but I can't be sure. Perhaps the thin man is merely straining to understand a word or two, or is waiting impatiently for Sigl to translate. At any rate, he seems quite interested in the exchange.

I'm convinced, though I'm not sure why, that the man to my immediate right—the famous climber Karl Bachner—*does* understand the English being batted back and forth.

"I called to Bromley, who seemed to be leading the snow-blinded and staggering Meyer, 'Why are you two so high?'" says Sigl. "And then I shouted up at them, 'Do you need help?'"

"Were your six German explorer friends with you on the ridge then when you were shouting toward Bromley?" asks the Deacon.

Sigl shakes his cropped and shaven head. "*Nein, nein.* My friends were more affected by the altitude than was I. They were either resting at Camp Three—as your English expedition had called it—or just come up onto the North Col. I had climbed the North Ridge to Camp Five and above alone. As I explained in my various newspaper and alpine journal reports, I was alone when I encountered Bromley and his snow-blind partner. Certainly you have read my statements before this?"

"Of course." The Deacon resumes smoking his pipe.

Sigl sighs, seemingly at the perverse slowness of his English interlocutor.

"If you don't mind my asking, what was your destination, Herr Sigl? Where were you originally headed with those Mongolian horses and mules and gear?"

"To see if I could meet George Mallory and Colonel Norton and perhaps reconnoiter Mount Everest from a distance, Herr Deacon. Just as I explained earlier."

"And perhaps to climb it?" asks the Deacon.

"*Climb* it?" repeats Bruno Sigl and laughs harshly. "My friends and I had only basic climbing equipment—nowhere near enough to lay siege to such a mountain. Also, the monsoon was already weeks overdue and might descend upon us at any minute. It was your Bromley who was foolish enough to think that he could climb Everest using the few left-over tins of food, fraying rope ladders, and snow-covered fixed ropes that Mallory's expedition had left behind. Bromley was a fool. To his last steps onto the unstable snow, he was a total fool. He killed not only himself but a fellow countryman of mine."

Several of the German climbers to the right of me nod in agreement, as does the Rudolf Hess fellow. The big man with the shaved head next to Sigl, the fellow introduced as *someone's* bodyguard, Ulrich Graf, continues to stare straight ahead through all this banter as if he is drugged. Or simply totally uninterested.

"My dear Herr Deacon," continues Sigl, "by all accounts Mount Everest is not the mountain for a solo ascent." He looks at me hard. "Or even for two...or three...ambitious alpine-style climbers from different countries. Mount Everest will never be climbed alpine style. Or by solo ascent. No, I only wanted to see the mountain from a distance. Besides, it is a *British* hill, is it not?"

"Not at all," says the Deacon. "It belongs to whoever climbs it first, whatever the Royal Geographical Society's Alpine Club might think about the matter."

Sigl grunts.

"When you shouted at Bromley and Meyer on the face, that last day," continues the Deacon. "Could you describe again what you said to them?"

"As I said, it was very brief," says Sigl. He looks impatient.

The Deacon waits.

"I asked them—shouted to them—'Why are you so high?'" Sigl says again. "And then I asked if they needed help...they obviously did. Meyer was obviously snow-blind and so exhausted that he could not stand without Bromley's help. The British lord himself looked confused, lost...dazed."

Sigl pauses to drink more beer.

"I warned them not to step out onto the snow slope, they did, the avalanche began, and that was the end of all conversation with them...forever," says Sigl. It's obvious he is not going to repeat the story again.

"You said that you called to them in German as well as in English," says the Deacon. "Did Meyer respond in German?"

"Nein," says Sigl. "The man the Tibetans in Tingri had called Kurt Meyer seemed too exhausted and in pain from his snow blindness to speak. He never said a word. Right up until the avalanche took him away, he never uttered a word."

"Did you say—shout—anything else to them?"

Sigl shakes his head. "The snow shifted under them, the avalanche carried them off the face of Everest, and I made my way back to the more solid ridge—almost crawling in the howling winds—and retreated down to Camp Four and then the North Col and then away from the mountain."

"You couldn't see any hint of their bodies below?" asks the Deacon.

Sigl *is* angry now. His lips are thin and his voice is a bark. "The drop from that point on the North Face to the Rongbuk Glacier below is more than five of your *verdammte* English *miles!* And I was not looking for their corpses eight kilometers below, Herr Deacon, I was using my ice axe to get off my own loose slab of snow—which might join the rest of the avalanche any second—and back to the ice-covered slabs of the North Ridge so that I could descend to the North Col as quickly as possible."

The Deacon nods his understanding. "What do you think those two were up to, then?" The Deacon's voice sounds sincerely curious.

Bruno Sigl looks down the table toward Bachner and the other German climbers and I wonder again *How many of them are following this conversation in English?*

"It's obvious what the truth was," says Sigl, a tone of audible contempt in his voice now. "I stated it a few minutes ago. Were you not listening, Herr Deacon? Do you not see it as obvious yourself, Herr Deacon?"

"Tell me again, please."

"Your Bromley—veteran of a few guided climbs in the Alps— decided that he could use the remnants of ropes and camps left behind by Norton and Mallory's group to climb Mount Everest on his own, with only the idiot Kurt Meyer as his porter and fellow climber. It was pure *Arroganz... Stolz...* what is the Greek word... *hubris.* Pure *hubris.*"

The Deacon nods slowly and taps his lower lip with the pipe stem as if a serious mystery has been cleared up. He says, "How high do you think they got before turning around?"

Sigl snorts a laugh. "Who on earth *cares?*"

The Deacon waits patiently.

Eventually Bruno Sigl says, "If you're thinking that the two fools might have summited, put it out of your mind. They'd been gone from our sight far too few hours to have gone much further than Camp Five... perhaps Camp Six if they'd used some of the oxygen apparatus left at Camp Five, if there *was* oxygen apparatus left there. Which I doubt. Not as high as Camp Six, I am certain of that."

"Why are you certain?" asks the Deacon in a reasonable, interested voice. He is still tapping his lower lip with the pipe stem.

"The wind," says Sigl with total finality. "The cold and wind. It was unbearable on the ridgeline where I met them just above Camp Five. Up near Camp Six, above eight thousand meters and then out onto the exposed higher North East Ridge or bare face up there, it would have meant death to try to proceed. There is no chance they had got that far, Herr Deacon. No chance at all."

"You've answered my questions with great patience, Herr Sigl," says the Deacon. "I thank you in all sincerity. This information might help Lady Bromley put her mind at rest."

Sigl only grunts at that. Then he looks at me. "What are you staring at, young man?"

"Your red flags on that wall in that roped-off corner," I admit, pointing behind Sigl. "And the symbol in the white circle on the red flags."

Sigl stares at me and his blue eyes are as cold as ice. "Do you know what that symbol is, Herr Jacob Perry from America?"

"Yes," I say. I'd studied a lot of Sanskrit and the Indus Valley cultures at Harvard. "It's the symbol from India, Tibet, and some other Hindu, Buddhist, and Jain cultures meaning 'good luck,' or sometimes 'harmony.' The Sanskrit word for it, I believe, is *svastika.* I'm told that one finds it everywhere on old temples in India."

Sigl is glaring at me now, as if I might be making fun of him or of something sacred to him. The Deacon lights his pipe and looks at me but says nothing.

"In today's *Deutschland*," Sigl says at last, barely moving his thin lips, "it is the *swastika*." He spells it for me using English-sounding letters. "It is the glorious symbol of the NSDAP—*Nationalsozialistische Deutsche Arbeiterpartei*—the National Socialist German Workers' Party. It and the man in those photographs will be the salvation of Germany."

I have good vision, but I can't make out the "man in those photographs." There are two rather small framed photos on the wall under the red flags in that roped-off corner, plus another furled red flag directly in the corner, rising about six feet high on a staff. I assume it's a flag similar to the two hanging on the wall.

"Come," orders Bruno Sigl.

Everyone—the Germans, including Hess and the baldheaded man next to Sigl on the opposite side of the table and Bachner and all the climbers on our side, followed by the Deacon still puffing at his pipe—get up as I follow Sigl to the corner.

The rope that sets off this little corner memorial area—it looks like an ad hoc shrine—is simply quarter-inch climbing rope painted gold and anchored on two of those little posts that maître d's keep their short velvet ropes hooked to at the entrance to fancy restaurants.

One man appears in both photos, so I have to assume that he—as well as this socialist party with the swastika flag—is the "salvation of Germany." In the photo below the red flag on the wall to the right, it is just the one man. At a distance one might think it's a photo of Charlie Chaplin because of the silly little mustache under his nose, but it's not Chaplin. This man has dark hair parted severely in the middle, dark eyes, and an intense—one might say furious—gaze at the camera or photographer.

The photograph on the left shows the same man standing in a doorway—the doorway of this beer hall, I realize—with two other men. The other two are in military uniforms, the Charlie Chaplin–mustached fellow in baggy civilian clothes. He's the shortest and certainly least imposing of the three men in the photograph.

"Adolf Hitler," says Bruno Sigl and looks closely at me for my response.

I have none. I think I've heard the name in reference to some of the constant unrest here in the Germany of November 1924, but it has made no real impression on me. Evidently he's a Communist leader within his National Socialism workers' party.

Behind me, the great climber Karl Bachner says, *"Der Mann, den wir nicht antasten lassen."*

I look to Sigl for some translation, but the German climber says nothing.

"The man we will not see impugned," the Deacon translates, the pipe in his hand now.

I see now that the red flag with the white circle and swastika on the staff has been torn—as if bullets had passed through it—and bloodied, if the dried brown spots are indeed blood. I lift my hand toward it to ask a question.

The baldheaded, round-faced muscleman who sat silent next to Sigl through the entire discussion at the table now moves quickly to slap my hand down and away so that I don't actually touch the torn fabric.

Shocked, I lower my hand and stare at the glowering wrestler-type.

"This is the *Blutfahne*—the Blood Flag—sacred to followers of Adolf Hitler and of *Nationalsozialismus*," says Bruno Sigl. "It must not be touched by non-Aryans. Never by an *Ausländer*."

The Deacon does not translate the word for me, but I can guess the meaning from context.

"Is that blood?" I ask stupidly. Everything I've done, said, or felt this evening feels stupid to me. And I'm starving to death.

Sigl nods. "From the massacre of nine November of last year, when the Munich police brutally opened fire on us. The flag belonged to the Fifth SA *Sturm*—much of the blood on it is from our comrade, the martyr Andreas Bauriedl, who fell atop the fallen flag when he was murdered by the police."

"The unsuccessful Beer Hall Putsch," the Deacon explains to me. "It started from this beer hall, as I remember."

Sigl glares at him through my friend's pipe smoke. "We prefer the term *Hitlerputsch* or *Hitler-Ludendorff-Putsch*," snaps the German climber. "And it was not—as you say—'unsuccessful.'"

"Really?" says the Deacon. "The police put down the uprising, scattered the marching Nazis, and arrested its leaders, including your Herr Hitler. I believe he's currently serving a five-year sentence for treason in the old fortress prison of Landsberg, on a cliff above the river Lech."

Sigl smiles strangely. "Adolf Hitler has become a hero of the German people. He will be out of prison before the end of this year. Even while there, he is treated like royalty by his so-called 'guards.' They know that he will someday lead this nation."

The Deacon taps out his pipe, sets it in his tweed jacket pocket, and nods appreciatively. "Thank you, Herr Sigl, for tonight's information and for setting me straight, as they say in Jake's America, about my misperceptions and faulty information regarding the *Hitlerputsch* and the current status of Herr Hitler."

"I will walk you to the door of the Bürgerbräukeller," says Sigl.

Our train to the border on the way to Zurich leaves the station promptly at ten p.m. Promptness, I'm learning, is a German trait.

I'm glad that we have a private compartment in which we can stretch out on the padded benches and doze, if we choose, before we change rails and trains at the Swiss border later in the night. On the cab ride from the Bürgerbräukeller to the Munich train station, I realize that I've sweated through my undershirt, through my starched shirt, and into my thick wool suit jacket. My hands are trembling as I watch the lights of Munich recede into the relative darkness of the countryside. I don't think I've ever been happier to see the lights of any city disappear behind me.

Finally, when I can speak without a tremor in my voice that would match the earlier shaking of my hands, I say, "This Adolf Hitler—I have read the name but remembered nothing about him—is he a local Communist leader calling for the overthrow of the Weimar Republic?"

"Rather the other way around, old boy," replies the Deacon from where he is stretched out on the compartment's other long, padded bench. "Hitler was—is, since his trial gave him a national audience for his rants—famous and much loved for his very far-*right-wing* views, virulent anti-Semitism and all."

"Ah," I say. "But he *is* in prison for five years for the treason of his attempted coup last year?"

The Deacon has sat up to light his pipe again and opens the train window a bit to reduce the smoke in the compartment, although I don't mind it. "I believe that Herr Sigl was right on both counts about that...that is, that Hitler will be out before the new year, with less than one year served, and that the authorities are treating him like a royal guest in that prison above the river."

"Why?"

The Deacon shrugs slightly. "Nineteen twenty-four German politics is far beyond my poor powers to understand, but the extreme right wing—the Nazis, to be precise—certainly seems to be speaking for a lot of frustrated people since this superinflation struck."

I realize that I'm not really interested in the little man with the Charlie Chaplin mustache.

"By the by," adds the Deacon, "that bald, round-faced, scowling gentleman who sat across from you at the table and who slapped your hand when you seemed about to touch their sacred Blood Flag?"

"Yes?"

"Ulrich Graf was Herr Hitler's personal bodyguard—which may be why he took several bullets aimed Hitler's way during last November's absurd botch of a *putsch*. But Graf is a hardy fellow, as you saw tonight, and will probably live to be the savior of Germany's Nazi hero once again, I am sure. Before becoming a Nazi and bodyguard to their leader, Graf was a butcher, a semi-professional wrestler, and a for-hire street brawler. Sometimes he would volunteer to beat up—or even kill—Jews or Communists without charging his bosses."

I think about this for a long moment. Finally I speak in just above a whisper, despite the compartment walls around us.

"Do you believe Sigl in his account of how Lord Percival and the Austrian Meyer died?" I ask. Personally, as much as I disliked Sigl and some of his friends, I can't see an alternative to believing him.

"Not a word of it," says the Deacon.

This causes me to sit up straight from where I've been half-reclining.

"No?"

"No."

"Then what do *you* think happened to Bromley and Meyer? And why would Sigl lie?"

The Deacon shrugs slightly again. "It is possible that Sigl and his friends were ready to make an illegal bid for the summit after they heard in Tingri that the rest of Mallory's team had left. Sigl certainly had no Tibetan climbing or travel permit himself. Perhaps Sigl and his six friends caught up with Bromley somewhere below the North Col and pressed him and this Meyer person to go with him on the climb in the tricky near-monsoon weather. When Bromley and Meyer fell to their deaths—or perhaps died some other way on the mountain—Sigl had to retreat and make up the Lost Boys story of the other two men climbing alone and being carried away by an avalanche."

"You don't believe in his avalanche story?"

"I've been on that part of the ridge and face, Jake," says the Deacon. "That section of the face rarely accumulates enough snow for the kind of massive slab-slide avalanche Sigl described. And if it did, my feeling is that Bromley had garnered enough avalanche-avoidance experience in the Alps to know better than to venture out onto such a slope."

"If the avalanche didn't kill Bromley and the Austrian, do you think they fell while climbing above Camp Six with Sigl?"

"There are other possibilities," says the Deacon. "Especially since the little I remember about Percy Bromley would not include the possibility of his being bullied into an Everest summit attempt by a German political fanatic intent upon bagging Mount Everest for *das Vaterland*."

The Deacon studies his pipe. "I wish I'd known Lord Percival better. As I told you and Jean-Claude, I was brought to the estate—rather as nobility would send out for any other commodity to be delivered—to be an occasional playmate for Percy's older brother, Charles, who was about my age, nine or ten at the time. Young Percival always wanted to tag along. He was—what is your American term, Jake?—a right pain in the arse."

"You never saw Percival after that?"

"Oh, I'd bump into him from time to time at English garden parties or on the Continent," the Deacon says vaguely.

"Was Percival really...inverted?" It's hard for me to say the word aloud. "Did he really frequent European brothels where young *men* were the prostitutes?"

"So it's rumored," says the Deacon. "Is that important to you in some way, Jake?"

I think about that but can't make up my mind. I've led a sheltered life, I realize. I've never had any inverted friends. Or at least none that I knew about.

"How else might Bromley and Kurt Meyer have died?" I ask, embarrassed and eager to change the subject.

"Bruno Sigl may have killed them both," says the Deacon. There is a blue haze between us, but it hovers and then moves for the open window. The sound of steel wheels on metal rails is very loud.

I'm profoundly shocked at this. Is the Deacon saying this for effect? Just to shock me? If so, he's succeeded beautifully.

My mother is Catholic—a former O'Riley and another stain on the escutcheon of the old-line Boston Brahmin Perry family—and I was raised to understand the difference between venial and mortal sins. Killing another climber on such a mountain as Everest would be, to me, somewhere *beyond* a major mortal sin. For a climber, it adds a sense of blasphemy to the mortal sin of murder. "*Kill* fellow climbers? Why?" I manage at last.

The Deacon taps his pipe out in an ashtray set into the end of an armrest. "I rather imagine we shall just have to go climb Mount Everest and do what we're supposed to be doing—that is, find the remains of Lord Percival Bromley—to find out."

The Deacon pulls a tweed hat down over his eyes and goes to sleep in seconds. I sit upright in the clacking train compartment for a long time, thinking, trying to sort out things which simply defy sorting.

Eventually I shut the window. The air outside is getting colder.

The ledge was about the width of that bread tray...

⬥⬥⬥

*I*t is on another train, this one a narrow-gauge railway climbing 7,000 feet from miasmic Calcutta to the high hills of Darjeeling at the end of March 1925, that I finally take time to think back about the busy winter and spring months before our departure.

In early January of 1925, all three of us had traveled back to Zurich to visit George Ingle Finch, who, with the possible exception of Richard Davis Deacon, was the finest British alpinist still living.

And while Finch had been a fellow Everest expedition climber with Mallory and Deacon in 1922, he shared the Deacon's bad fortune of falling out of favor with the Powers That Be—twice, in Finch's case, not just running afoul of George Leigh Mallory's sensibilities, but alienating the entire Mount Everest Committee, the Alpine Club, and two-thirds of the Royal Geographical Society.

Finch had studied medicine briefly at the École de Médecine in Paris and then switched to the physical sciences while studying at the Eidgenössische Technische Hochschule in Zurich from 1906 to 1922, then served as a captain in the Royal Field Artillery in France, Egypt, and Macedonia during the Great War, and after the War had returned to mostly Swiss alpine climbing, in the process bagging more first ascents in the Alps than the rest of the chosen Everest expedition members combined. He was much more aware of German and other new European climbing techniques than any of the Everest Committee or other British climbers—but he'd been left off the 1921 roster, officially because of poor results on his physical. The real reason was that although he, Finch, was a British citizen and decorated Great War artillery officer, he'd spent so many years climbing and living in the German-Swiss-speaking part of Switzerland before and after the War that he was more comfortable speaking German than English. As Brigadier General Charles Bruce had described the selection committee's choices, "If at all possible, they, we, wished to keep the Everest expeditions all an Old Boys' Club, you see. 'BAT' we called it amongst ourselves—'British All Through.'"

According to the Deacon, General Bruce, the same Everest Committee man and 1922 expedition leader who'd argued for a BAT climbing team, had once written to other potential committee and team members (including the Deacon) that George Finch was "a convincing raconteur of quite impossible qualifications. Cleans his teeth on February 1st and has a bath the same day if the water is very hot, otherwise puts it off until next year."

But Finch's primary sin in the various BAT-eyes of the committee, according to the Deacon, was, besides a frequently unkempt appearance and an odd German accent, the "impossible qualifications" part—that is, George Finch kept coming up with climbing innovations for conquering Mount Everest. Neither the Royal Geographical Society nor the Alpine Club (nor, for that matter, the Mount Everest Committee) liked "innovations." The old ways were the good ways: hobnailed boots, nineteenth-century-style ice axes, and thin layers of wool between the climber and the almost-out-of-the-earth's-atmosphere sub-zero-degrees-Fahrenheit temperatures at 28,000 feet and above.

One such absurd Finch innovation, said the Deacon, was an overcoat the successful alpinist had designed and had made—just for Mount Everest conditions—consisting of a goose-down-layered (rather than regular wool or cotton or silk) overcoat. Finch had experimented with many materials, finally settling on a thin but very strong balloon fabric, to create a long overcoat with many sewn compartments of goose down to trap air pockets of a person's warmth much as the down had done for the goose in the Arctic.

The result, explained the Deacon, was that at altitudes of 20,000 feet and above on the 1922 expedition, Finch was the only man not freezing in the high-altitude winds and cold.

But the death knell for George Finch's inclusion in the 1924 expedition, despite his excellent climbing record in the previous Everest attempt (he and young Geoffrey Bruce briefly set a high-altitude climbing record on their bold but unsuccessful May 27, 1922, summit bid), was that it had been Finch who proposed and adapted the Royal Flying Service oxygen equipment that members of the team had used—to very good effect—in 1922 and '24. (Mallory and Irvine were wearing Finch's oxygen apparatus, although much redesigned by the tinker-genius Sandy Irvine, when the two heroes disappeared in their summit attempt on that final 1924 expedition.)

Arthur Hinks, the Everest Committee man most in charge of spending (and hoarding) the expeditions' funds, had written of Finch's oxygen apparatus—long after it had been proven in altitude-chamber experiments, on the Eiger, and upon Mount Everest itself—with this much-repeated official comment: "I should be especially sorry if the oxygen outfit prevents them going as high as possible without it. If some of the party do not go to 25,000 ft to 26,000 ft without oxygen they will be rotters."

Rotters?

"Easy enough for a man who never leaves London's sea level to say," commented the Deacon as we traveled by rail to Zurich in January of 1925.

"I'd like to transport Mr. Hinks to twenty-six thousand feet on Everest and watch him gasp, retch, and flop around like a fish out of water," continued the Deacon, "and *then* ask him if he considers himself a 'rotter.' I certainly consider him such, even when he stays at sea level."

This was why we were tentatively planning to take twenty-five sets of the Irvine-improved Finch oxygen rigs and one hundred tanks of oxygen on our own expedition. (This was more than the ninety tanks that Mallory and his team had taken along for their 1924 expedition to serve dozens of the climbers and high-altitude porters. And there would be only the three of us.) "What about 'Cousin Reggie'?" Jean-Claude had asked, reminding the Deacon of Lady Bromley's condition that we take Bromley's tea plantation cousin with us.

"'Cousin Reggie' can bloody well stay at Base Camp and breathe the thick yak-scented air at sixteen thousand five hundred feet," said the Deacon.

And now, in the cold first month of the year in which we'd try or die on Mount Everest, the Deacon wanted us to meet and speak with George Finch in his adopted hometown of Zurich. (The Deacon had invited him to London, offering to pay his expenses, which made sense since there were three of us and only one Finch, but the irascible climber had cabled back, "There's not enough money in all of England to induce me to return to London now.")

We met George Ingle Finch at the Restaurant Kronenhalle, an upscale place even by Zurich's high standards for fancy restaurants, and one well known throughout Europe. The Deacon had informed us that, despite its once proud history, Kronenhalle had become pretty run-down in recent years and during Germany's era of hyperinflation, the old restaurant floating by on its nineteenth-century reputation for excellence. But then a certain Hilda and Gottlieb Zumsteg had recently purchased and renovated the place, bringing the whole large establishment, including a new chef, a menu that was a combination of the best Bavarian, classic, and Swiss cuisine, and superlative service, up to the true standards of Swiss and Zurich excellence. So while Germans were starving a few miles across the border, the Swiss bankers, merchants, and other upper-class citizens could dine in luxury.

Restaurant Kronenhalle was situated at Rämistrasse 4, less than a mile southwest of the University of Zurich (where two of Jean-Claude's three older brothers attended classes before returning to France to die in the Great War) and precisely where the Limmat River flows into Lake Zurich. The late January wind blowing off that lake, blocked only intermittently on the broad Rämistrasse by softly rumbling streetcars, froze me to the bone despite my heaviest wool formal overcoat.

It's at this moment that I found myself wondering, *If I'm freezing with chattering teeth just crossing the Rämistrasse in Zurich in a slight breeze from a Swiss lake for a few moments exposed to the wind, how in God's name am I going to survive and conquer the space-blown sub-arctic winds of Mount Everest above 26,000 feet?*

I thought I'd dined well in Boston, New York, London, and Paris—all on my aunt's bequest money or through the largesse of Lady Bromley with the Deacon picking up the actual tab—but the Kronenhalle certainly had to be the largest and most formal-feeling restaurant

I'd ever set foot in. The day we met Finch was the only day of the week when they served lunch, and still the waiters, maître d', and other personnel were dressed in tuxedos. Even the tall potted plants configured here and there, in this corner and next to that pillar and over near that window, looked too formal to be mere vegetable matter; they seemed to wish they were also wearing tuxedos.

I was wearing the dark suit that the Deacon had purchased for me in London, but crossing the vast open spaces of Zurich's Restaurant Kronenhalle, its luncheon tables filled mostly with formally dressed men but also a few elegant women, made me realize how insecure I still felt in European high society. Even though I was wearing my best (and only) pair of highly polished black dress shoes, I suddenly thought how clodhopperish and scuffed they must look to everyone in the huge restaurant.

Sitting alone at the white-linen- and silver-service-covered table to which we were led was a short, thin, sharp-faced man. He was ignoring the glasses of wine and water already poured and seemed to be lost in a book he was reading. Finch was the only man in the room wearing a regular daytime-wear tweed suit and waistcoat—neither looking all that clean at the moment (there were cigarette ashes on his waistcoat)—and his posture was the comfortable, oblivious, cross-legged sprawl that I associate with the very, very rich or simply the very, very self-confident. The Deacon cleared his throat, and the gaunt-faced man looked up, folded the book, and set it on the table. The title was a long one in large-word German that I couldn't translate.

Finch removed his reading glasses and looked up at us as if he had no idea who we were or why we were standing by his table. I couldn't be sure if the smudge under his nose was the rough sketch of a brownish mustache on his tanned face or simply more of the brownish stubble that already stippled his jaw and cheeks.

The Deacon reintroduced himself, although the two men had spent the entire 1922 Mount Everest expedition in each other's company, and then introduced each of us. Finch didn't bother to get to his feet but raised what looked like a limp hand dangling—almost as if he expected it to be kissed rather than shaken. Still, his handshake was surprisingly firm—almost shockingly firm, given the long, thin fingers. Then I noticed the damage to those hands and fingers and nails; if nothing else this man was an alpinist who'd spent years jamming his bare hands into cracks and holds in granite, limestone, and sharp ice.

"Jake, Jean-Claude," continued the Deacon, "I'd like to present Mr. George Ingle Finch. You both know that two and a half years ago, Mr. Finch and I were on the expedition that climbed to just above twenty-seven thousand three hundred feet on the East Ridge and North Face of Everest...without oxygen. It was an altitude record at the time. But even though we climbed without the tanks that day, George helped design the oxygen apparatus that Mallory and Irvine were using when they disappeared last June, and he's been kind enough to offer to take us to his workshop here in Zurich after lunch to show us how it works...and to give us some advice on various aspects of our...recovery expedition."

The Deacon seemed embarrassed to have used so many words and—most rare for the Deacon—not sure of what to say next. Finch rescued the moment by lazily waving us to the three empty chairs.

"Sit down, please," said Finch. "I took the liberty of ordering a wine but we can certainly get a different bottle for the table...especially if you're paying, Richard." Finch's brief flash of smile showed small, slightly nicotine-stained but strong teeth. Despite the Alpine Club's discriminatory insults about Finch, it was obvious that he brushed those teeth more than once a year. "This joint has good food and I can rarely afford to dine here, even for lunch," he continued in his slightly German-accented British English, "which is why I suggested we meet here when you said you would be picking up the tab." He casually waved over the headwaiter and—surprising, considering how Finch was dressed—the tuxedoed gentleman responded with alacrity and obvious respect. Perhaps people in Zurich were well aware of Finch's alpine successes. Or perhaps the waiters simply assumed that anyone who could afford to dine at Restaurant Kronenhalle was wealthy enough to deserve such respectful treatment.

I admit that I was bridling a bit as we all ordered our lunches (I simply said that I'd have whatever the Deacon had just ordered) and while Jean-Claude and Finch conversed animatedly about which kind of wine to order for the table. I was irritated because I wondered if Finch used that "this joint has good food" vernacular because I was so obviously an American and a not-very-successful-looking one at that. (I soon learned that this was not the case; George Ingle Finch spoke many languages and mixed their vernacular into his sentences, even Americanisms, with casual enjoyment. By the end of that day in Zurich, I would see that Finch, though a man of great personal dignity, probably took the fewest pains to impress others with his knowledge, prowess, and personal achievements than any climber I'd ever met.)

The food *was* good. The wine, whatever it was (and to the limited extent I could judge wine when I was 22), was excellent. And the waiters whom I'd expected to be ostentatious, even Deutsch-Schweizer imperious toward our little group of foreigners, treated us with great courtesy and were all but invisible during their silent delivery and whisking away of courses and dishes. (This idea of capable-waiter invisibility equaling quality service was an opinion I'd picked up from my father: one of the few unsolicited opinions I ever heard him venture other than on the day he and Mother dropped me at Harvard and he took me aside and said sternly, "All right, Jake. You're a man responsible for yourself from this point on. Try to keep your whiskey bottle out of the bedroom, your pecker in your pants as much as possible, and your head in your books until you get a degree. Any degree.")

I set down my wineglass and realized that Finch, Jean-Claude, and the Deacon were discussing our plans, such as they were at that point, for our upcoming "recovery expedition" to bring back Bromley's personal possessions to his mother, or, since we all knew that the odds of that were close to nil, at least return with some clear report about how young Percival had died. The Deacon had assured us that Finch understood that news of our private expedition was not to be shared with anyone else. "And," the Deacon had added, "there's currently so little love lost between Finch and the Alpine Club, the Committee, and the entire Royal Geographical Society that he certainly won't be eager to tell them anything...much less our secret."

"So you knew Percival...Lord Percival Bromley?" Jean-Claude was asking.

"The first time I met him was when he hired me as a guide some years ago," said Finch in that rather pleasant educated-British tone with its slight German accent. "Bromley wanted to traverse the Douves Blanches..." He paused and looked at me for the first time. "The Douves

Blanches is a spur, Mr. Perry—a sharp, spiky one all the way—off the main chain of the Grandes Dents on the east side of the Arolla Valley."

"Yes, I've been there," I said, my voice a shade impatient. I was no longer a novice at alpine climbing, after all. I'd done the Douves Blanches traverse the previous autumn with Jean-Claude and the Deacon.

Finch didn't seem to have picked up on my tone. Or perhaps he had and didn't care one way or the other. He nodded once and continued, "Young Percy was capable even then of doing the traverse, but he'd come to attempt what he called a 'delectable' series of rather impressive chimneys that split the two-thousand-foot rock wall above the upper Ferpècle Glacier, and he wanted someone on the rope with him."

All three of us waited, but Finch seemed to have lost interest in Bromley and the conversation and returned his attention to his steak and wine.

"How did you find him?" asked the Deacon.

Finch looked up as if the Deacon had spoken in Swahili. (Which is a bad comparison, I realize, because it turned out that George Ingle Finch *could* speak some Swahili and understood more of it than he spoke.)

"I mean," said the Deacon, "how did he handle himself?"

Finch shrugged noncommittally, and that might have been the frustrating end of the discussion, but perhaps he realized that we'd come a long way, and there was a real chance that we would soon be climbing very high on the shoulder of Mount Everest to find Percy Bromley's corpse, and that we were, after all (or Lady Bromley was), paying for Finch's meal in one of the most expensive restaurants in Switzerland. Perhaps in all of Europe.

"Bromley was all right," said Finch. "Climbed very well, for an amateur. Never complained, even when we had to spend a long, cold night on a very narrow ledge, without food or proper equipment, on that steep south ridge just a short but difficult pitch below the summit. Not a good overcoat or bag between the two of us, nor a bump in the rock face to tie ourselves on to. The ledge was about the width of that bread tray..." Finch nodded toward the narrow silver tray. "We had no candles to hold lighted under our chins in case we dozed, so we took turns through the long night sitting watch, as it were, making sure the other didn't fall asleep and pitch forward three thousand feet to the glacier."

Perhaps to make sure that we got the point, Finch added, "I trusted the boy with my life."

"So Lord Percival was a better climber than some others are saying now?" The Deacon was finishing his *Tafelspitz*—an excellent meal consisting of tips of choice beef simmered along with root vegetables and various spices in a rich broth and served with roasted slices of potato and a mix of minced apples and sour cream combined with horseradish. I always marveled at how the Brits could lift a fork with something like morsels of meat and sauce on the back of the utensil, and make it look not only easy but proper. Eating in England and Europe, I thought, must be like going to China and getting used to chopsticks.

"Depends on which 'others' you have in mind," responded Finch after another significant pause. He was looking carefully at our team leader. "Anyone in particular?"

"Bruno Sigl?"

Finch laughed—a harsh bark of a sound. "That bully-boy Nazi fanatic friend of Herr Hitler?" he said. "Sigl's an accomplished climber—I've never climbed with him but I've run into him on almost a dozen alpine ascents over the years. He's a smooth, careful, competent man on rock or ice—but he's also a lying *Scheisskerl,* one who tends to get his younger climbing partners killed."

"What is this...*Scheisskerl?*" asked Jean-Claude.

"Brainless, untrustworthy fellow," said the Deacon quickly, glancing over his shoulder at the hovering waiters. To Finch he said, "So if Herr Sigl told you that Percival Bromley ventured out onto a risky Everest North Face, walking onto an obviously avalanche-prone slab of snow with an Austrian fellow in tow, you wouldn't believe him?"

"I wouldn't believe Bruno Sigl if the bastard told me that the sun would be coming up tomorrow," said Finch, pouring himself the last of our wine.

"Richard, weren't you one of the first to see the monster's tracks on Lhakpa La when you led Mallory up to that pass in 'twenty-one?" asked George Ingle Finch between large bites of his crème-covered *Apfelstrudel.* Jean-Claude and the Deacon were having only thick, rich coffee for dessert. I'd tried a chocolate pudding.

"Monster?" said Jean-Claude, perking up. I'd watched as the heavy Bavarian meal, so unusual for the athletic French mountain guide, made him sleepy. "Monster?" he said again as if unsure of the English word.

"*Ja,*" replied Finch, "the tracks of some huge biped our friend Richard here and the late, overly lamented George Mallory found above twenty-two thousand feet on Lhakpa La, the high pass from where Richard had suggested to Mallory—correctly suggested, as it turned out—that they might be able to see a possible approach route to Everest. But on the way up—this is in late September nineteen twenty-one, I believe—they found the tracks of the monster instead of a view. True?" He turned toward the Deacon.

"Twenty September," said the Deacon, setting down his coffee cup with great precision. "Deep into the monsoon season. The snow was pure powder and hip-deep."

"But you made it to the summit of this little mountain—more a peak of its own than a pass, *ja?*—despite the snow," said Finch. It was not a question.

The Deacon scratched his cheek. I could tell that he wanted to light up his pipe but was refraining from doing so while Finch was still enjoying his dessert. "Mallory and I cleared the icefall all right, but the deep snow slowed us down and made the porters with our tents turn back eight hundred feet below the summit. We all—Mallory, me, Wheeler, and Bullock, with Wollaston, Morshead, and Howard-Bury in reserve—made it to the top and set up camp on the twenty-second."

"What about the tracks of a monster?" insisted Jean-Claude.

"Yeah, what about the *monster?*" I asked. It was one of the first times I'd spoken, except to ask for something to be passed to me, during the entire meal.

"Above the icefall, on both the twentieth and twenty-second, where none of our climbers or porters had gone before, there were deep marks both in the loose snow and in the firmer, frozen-over parts of the ascent, where we could climb without fully breaking through the crust," said the Deacon, his voice very soft. "They *appeared* to be from a two-legged creature."

"Why say 'appeared'?" demanded Finch. A slight smile was forming under his fuzz of a mustache. "Mallory, Wollaston, Howard-Bury, and all the others who made it up to the saddle summit of Lhakpa La swore that they were the giant clawed footprints of some mammal-like, two-legged living thing."

The Deacon sipped the last of his coffee. The waiter bustled over, and we all accepted more coffee so we could keep the table longer.

"How large *were* the prints in the snow?" I asked.

"A paw print of a human-like foot fourteen to sixteen inches long?" said Finch, turning it into a question as he turned toward the Deacon.

Our friend only nodded. Finally, setting the coffee cup down again, he said, "By the time Wollaston and the others got up to the saddle of Lhakpa La, our porters—Mallory's and mine, since we were leading that second attempt—had stomped all over the original tracks we saw. There was no way for any of the British climbers to be sure of what was what or the precise length of any track in the snow."

"But George Mallory took photographs," said Finch.

"Yes," said the Deacon.

"And those photos were almost identical to tracks reported and photographed on a high pass in Sikkim way back in eighteen eighty-nine," said Finch.

"So they tell me," said the Deacon.

Finch chuckled and turned toward Jean-Claude and me. I am sure I looked as goggle-eyed as Jean-Claude did.

"The porters knew exactly what the tracks were and who or what had made them," said Finch in his soft German accent. "They were made by *Metohkangmi . . . a yeti.*"

"By whom?" I said, my cup of coffee still frozen in space as if I could neither drink from it nor set it back on its saucer. "By what?" said Jean-Claude almost in unison.

"*Yeti,*" repeated Finch. "Not one of the many demons who the locals believe live in or on the mountain, but a real, living, breathing, blood-eating man-thing . . . a creature-monster, eight feet tall or larger. Huge feet. A gorilla-like or manlike monster that can survive at altitudes of twenty-two thousand feet and above near Everest."

Jean-Claude and I looked at each other.

Finch ate strudel and smiled again. "I saw tracks myself the next year, in nineteen twenty-two, when Geoffrey Bruce and I climbed all the way to the North East Ridge for the first time. They were in an icy snowfield at about twenty-five thousand feet—a snowfield that none of our people had yet climbed to—clearly tracks of a biped like us, but with almost twice the stride of even the tallest man, and in the shallower parts of the snowfield where the tracks were embedded mostly in soft ice, we could see the actual outline of the foot—almost sixteen inches long, with what looked to be claws on the toes." He looked at the Deacon. "You were there at the Rongbuk Monastery when we talked about the *yetis* in nineteen twenty-two, yes?"

The Deacon nodded.

Finch looked at Jean-Claude and me again. "Rongbuk Monastery is a very sacred place since it's near the village of Chobuk, right across from the entrance to the valley that leads eventually to Chomolungma..."

"Chomolungma?" interrupted Jean-Claude.

Finch had turned back toward the Deacon and for some reason continued to look at him as he answered J.C. "The locals' name for Mount Everest. It means something like 'Goddess Mother of the World.'"

"Ah, *oui*," said Jean-Claude. "I had forgotten. Colonel Norton had mentioned that name when we spoke to the climbers at the Royal Geographical Society."

"So the monks at the Rongbuk Monastery knew about this...*yeti* creature?" I asked. I didn't want to let the subject of the "monster" drop.

Finch nodded and said to the Deacon, "You were there with me right at the end of April in nineteen twenty-two and you heard what the Rongbuk lama and his priests said about *yetis* on Everest. Was it four of the creatures that the lama said lived there?"

"Five," said the Deacon. "Bruce kept pressing them on the tracks and the creatures, and the head lama—Dzatrul Rinpoche—told us calmly that he and the monks had seen five *yeti*. He said that they lived in the upper reaches of the valley, up to the North Col and even above that. The Rinpoche said that the *yeti* were more feared than the mere mountain demons, which might or might not exist. He said that the *yeti* were manlike, but taller, larger, with huge chests and powerful long arms. He said that the *yeti* were covered with long hair and had yellowish eyes. The lama told Bruce and us—you were there, Finch, I know you remember—that sometimes the *yeti* raided the village of Chobuk, but never the

Rongbuk Monastery itself, drinking the blood of yaks, killing men with one swipe of their clawed paw-hands, and—I believe Geoffrey Bruce found this most interesting—carrying off the Chobuk women."

"What would the monsters want with human women?" asked Jean-Claude in a small, almost childlike voice.

The other three of us had to chuckle, and J.C. blushed a bright crimson.

"The lama went on to say that when the village sent men up the glacier valley with weapons," said Finch, his voice low so that none of the hovering waiters would hear, "they never found the *yeti* or the women, alive at least—always just the women's gnawed skeletons and skulls. The women's bones, said the lama, had always been sucked free of all their marrow. The eye sockets in the skulls looked, he said, as if they had been licked clean."

I finally had to set my coffee cup down into its saucer. They both rattled. The sound made me imagine Mount Everest winds blowing through gnawed ribcages and the hollowed-out eye sockets of a skull.

The last of his coffee drunk, glancing to make sure that our silent trio had finished, George Ingle Finch gracefully waved over the waiter, his rock-ravaged fingers writing in air to signal for the bill. When the bill came, he gestured, with equal grace, for it to be presented to the Deacon.

We came out the front door of Restaurant Kronenhalle and turned left onto Rämistrasse and into the full force of the freezing wind blowing in off the lake. A teeth-chattering block and a half later we reached the Quaibrücke bridge but turned left onto an empty avenue named Utoquai and trudged southeast along a frozen lakeside walkway. A low concrete railing to our right was guarded by fangs of icicles. A constant rumbling below reminded us that the ice—the lake was frozen solid near the shore, icy but liquid water starting a hundred yards or so out—was grinding up against the cement breakwater below that railing. The wind was roaring hard enough to raise whitecaps far out along the white-iced and white-watered expanse, and the same wind would have thrown me down had not the ever efficient Swiss cleared all the ice and snow along the Utoquai Boulevard sidewalk and sprinkled it liberally with salt. Finch had informed us that his storage warehouse was less than half a mile away, but as Jean-Claude and I plodded along behind the Deacon and Finch, trying to overhear their conversation through the freezing wind, half a mile seemed too far to walk.

Jean-Claude and I walked faster to close the distance to the two men in front of us.

"I know what you're trying to do," George Finch was saying, "and it's just not possible, Richard."

"What am I trying to do, George?"

"Climb Mount Everest alpine style," said the shorter man. "Instead of the Mallory-Bruce-Norton military-siege style of attack—one slow camp at a time, attack, retreat, attack again—you and your young friends want to take it in one swift alpine assault. But it won't work, Richard. You'll all die up there."

"We've been paid by Lady Bromley to carry out only a search and recovery operation—at least to find and bury her son's body," said the Deacon. "With luck, we'll find some trace of him far lower than Bruno Sigl was talking about, way up high between Camps Four and Five—that made no sense. But I've mentioned nothing about the three of us trying to *climb* the mountain."

George Finch nodded. "But you *will* try, Richard. I know you. So I tremble for the fates of you and your two fine friends."

The Deacon did not reply to this. We passed the Opera House and turned left on a street called Falkenstrasse. At least the wind was at our backs now.

"You must remember in 'twenty-two," continued Finch, "the day we reached Pang La Pass—at seventeen thousand two hundred feet—and caught our first glimpse of Everest."

"I remember," grunted the Deacon.

"The wind was so strong at Pang La that we had to lie down, gasping for air and clinging to rocks to keep from being blown away," continued Finch. "But suddenly there was that view of a hundred miles of the Himalayan range. Mount Everest was still forty bloody miles to the south, but that monstrous hill dominated *everything*. You remember the cloud trailing from it, Richard? You remember the snow plume stretching out for miles to the west? That bloody mountain creates its own *weather*."

"I was there with you, George," the Deacon said. We turned right onto a narrower street of closed-front warehouses and bleak old apartment buildings—*Seefeldstrasse,* read the ice-encrusted street sign.

"Then you know that an alpine-style assault is impossible," said the alpinist, removing a fat, heavy key ring from his overcoat pocket and finding the right key for a warehouse door. "Climbers sick, porters sick, terrible winds, sudden heavy snows, the monsoon season arriving early, injuries, avalanches, rockfalls, tents torn, oxygen apparatuses not working properly, dysentery, altitude sickness, frostbite, stoves malfunctioning...any single setback, and there *will* be many, Richard, you know that as well as I do...any setback will destroy the entire alpine-style effort. And cost some or all of you your lives. Here we are."

Finch entered the black maw and fumbled for a light switch.

The first floor—first floor by my American way of thinking—of this warehouse wasn't the huge storage space I'd expected. Or, rather, it was, but it had been partitioned. Nine-foot walls without ceilings had created dozens of such storage areas, each entrance with a metal-grill door and heavy padlock. We followed Finch halfway down the echoing space, he produced yet another long key from his key ring, and then he held the iron-grill door open as we entered his storage space, which was perhaps 25 feet by 20 feet.

Inside, a long workbench along the far wall was stacked with oxygen tanks.

To our left was a wall with more than a dozen different-sized ice axes hanging. Shelves held a myriad of hobnailed and felt-lined boots, and a long rack showed varieties of wool climbing jackets, arctic anoraks, and a whole line of distinctive long padded jackets or overcoats. I counted ten there on the rack, and I was surprised that Finch needed so many.

Finch had closed the door when I walked over, lifted the eiderdown-filled fabric of the closest long coat on the rack, and said, "Is this your famous balloon jacket?"

Finch glowered at me. It was obvious that he'd endured too much teasing about that particular article of clothing. "It's the goose-down-filled outer jacket I devised for Everest," he snapped. "Yes, it's balloon fabric—the only material I could find that wouldn't tear or rip and which could be easily sewn for the compartments of eiderdown. It kept me *warm* at almost twenty-four thousand feet below the North East Ridge."

The Deacon chuckled. "I can vouch for that. The three of us—George, Geoffrey Bruce, and I, and Bruce was a neophyte climber then—used 'English air,' George's oxygen apparatus, to press through the Yellow Band to a point just below the North East Ridge. We would have made the ridge had Bruce's oxygen outfit not quit working. There was a broken glass tube in Bruce's set. Luckily, George carried a spare glass piece, but he had to stop and tinker with his own oxygen rig to allow it to feed oxygen to both Geoffrey and himself while he repaired Bruce's rig. All that at twenty-seven thousand three hundred feet...at the time, the highest point humans had ever reached on foot."

"And then we had to turn back," growled Finch. "Surrendering our summit attempt because of Bruce's temporary trauma at not getting oxygen. And he'd been one of the adamant ones about reaching the summit without 'artificial air.' Had he been an experienced climber..." The growl trailed off, but the sadness and anger etched on George Ingle Finch's face remained.

The Deacon nodded acknowledgment of Finch's frustration. I realized then, fully for the first time, what an insult and disappointment it had been for these two men, each having climbed higher than Mallory or anyone else on the 1922 expedition, not to have been given another chance in 1924. What fury they must have felt when they were informed that they had not been chosen for the 1924 Everest attempt. While holding Finch's balloon coat in one hand, I suddenly imagined the bile that must have brought a constant taste of rejection to these two proud men.

The Deacon said, "My point was only that when we returned to Camp Four that evening, Geoffrey Bruce and I were frozen to the bone, but George had stayed warm climbing in his eiderdown jacket. This is why I asked each of you to bring two empty Gladstone bags. I've paid George to make up nine of these coats for us."

"Nine?" said Jean-Claude. He looked at the coat rack with its line of bulging down jackets. "Why so many? Are they that fragile that they wear out so soon?"

"No," said the Deacon. "I figure that we'll each have two high-climbing porters with us to get to the high camp for our summit attempt. I've ordered the extra oxygen sets and eiderdown coats for them as well.

Nine in all. They compress nicely. We'll pack them in our Gladstones today and take them back ourselves so that nothing gets lost in shipping."

Finch grunted. "Mallory listed a copy of my eiderdown coat as possible outerwear for the climbers in last year's expedition," he said. "But no one ordered one. They chose to climb—and die—in silk, wool, cotton, wool, wool, and more wool."

"Wool is warm in layers," Jean-Claude said tentatively. "It has kept me alive through high bivouacs many nights."

Instead of arguing, Finch only nodded and touched two of his worn wool outer jackets and then one of the Shackleton windproof gabardine anoraks hanging there. "Wool is wonderful, until it gets wet. Wet from our sweat as well as from snow or rain. And then you're carrying another forty pounds of sodden wool with you when you climb, in addition to the forty or fifty pounds in your rucksack and thirty-some pounds of your oxygen apparatus. And then, when you pause in the high winds, your sweat freezes on the lower layers..." He shook his head.

"Doesn't your eiderdown jacket absorb sweat and lose its loft when wet?" I asked.

Finch shook his head again. "I wear the usual wool underlayers, but the sweat buildup is less because of the breathing capabilities of the eiderdown. The eiderdown *would* lose its insulating qualities when soaked—it's the pockets of air it creates that kept the goose, and now me in the jacket of the goose's down, warm—but the balloon fabric I chose resists water short of a full immersion in a lake." He managed a small smile. "There aren't many lakes above twenty thousand feet on Everest...unless one slips."

"I wasn't aware that there were lakes or standing water on the upper reaches of the Rongbuk Glacier," said Jean-Claude, still looking hard at Finch. "Just melt pools down at the entrance to the glacial valley."

George Finch sighed at my French friend's apparent literalism and shrugged ever so slightly. "If you fall two vertical miles from the North East Ridge or Everest summit ridge, your impact velocity might be enough to melt some ice and create a serious puddle."

Finch knew better than we did—but all alpinists know from experience—that a falling climber almost never falls the full distance off any mountain. The body hits many rocks, boulders, ice slags, ridges, and other protuberances on the way down...enough that whatever remains make it to the glacier below are in many small, naked pieces and barely recognizable as having once been human.

"Or not," he added and gestured to the cluttered worktable. "Richard, the coats are indeed ready for you to take today. I also thought we might look over the oxygen apparatus that we used in 'twenty-two, then the rigs that Sandy Irvine changed for his and Mallory's final attempt, and now the final version you and I decided on. I need your approval before I ship them to Liverpool for loading on whichever ship you sail on next month."

February departure was just a month away. Jean-Claude and I had known since November, of course, that the Deacon had been ordering oxygen tanks and breathing equipment for our small-scale expedition. And we knew that he'd decided not to use Siebe Gorman in England for the equipment, even though—or actually, because—Siebe Gorman had done all the oxygen rigs for the '21, '22, and '24 official expeditions. The Deacon had explained that the risk was too great that Siebe Gorman might leak out word of another expedition outfitting itself with oxygen for the Himalayas—and of that word getting back to the directors of the Royal Geographical Society, the Alpine Club, and the Mount Everest Committee. He said that he knew of no oxygen-supply company in England that could be entrusted with our secret. Instead he'd gone to a "source in Switzerland."

Now J.C. and I knew that the source was named George Ingle Finch.

But when I said this aloud, Finch only chuckled and shook his head. "No, Mr. Perry, our friend Richard Davis Deacon has been sending Lady Bromley's money to me, but I have been sending it on to *Zürcher Werke für wissenschaftliche Präzisionsinstrumente und Geräte*—a scientific instrument manufacturing firm I know here in Zurich."

I must have looked doubtful. Finch said, "I am a scientist by trade, Mr. Perry. A chemist. I do business with such firms for scientific instruments all the time. They are Swiss—which means that discretion is bred into their genes."

The long worktable was piled high with oxygen cylinders, frames for the tanks, valves, tubes, regulators, and a variety of face masks, while the wall above the worktable was pegged with tools both common and exotic.

Finch dragged the one oxygen rig across the table toward us. To the Deacon he said, "Look familiar, Richard?"

The Deacon only nodded.

"We each hauled one of these to twenty-seven thousand three hundred feet, didn't we, Richard?" said Finch. "And we would have gone higher if the glass tube in Bruce's mask hadn't shattered from the cold."

"Not so much higher," the Deacon said. "We wouldn't have made the summit that day, George. Just not possible."

Finch showed his strange, clenched smile. "You and I might have made the summit with these tanks if we'd left Bruce to get back to Camp Five on his own and we'd pressed on to the ridge and higher...and if we'd been willing to die up there. I think we would have reached the summit around sunset."

The Deacon shook his head again. I realized that he wasn't denying that they might have done it—the two of them making the summit of Everest by sunset or just after sunset on that day in late May of 1922—only that he, the Deacon, hadn't been willing to die doing so.

I decided to ask the obvious question (but possibly insulting to Finch, who had championed the use of oxygen on Everest). "Does this oxygen stuff really help? Most of the English climbers I know are against using it on Everest."

Surprisingly, it was the Deacon who answered. "Most English climbers have never climbed as high as even the lower North Col of Everest. If they had, they would know the benefits of bringing oxygen along...it can be as necessary as bringing food along, or a stove to melt snow for hot water."

Perhaps Jean-Claude and I looked skeptical—I know that I did—because Finch then began talking specifics. He paused almost at once. "Are you gentlemen more comfortable in metric measurement or English feet?"

"Either will work," Jean-Claude said.

I admitted that metric wouldn't work as well for me. Despite the constant use of meters and kilometers in my French, Italian, and Swiss climbing, I still had trouble translating the figures into feet or miles.

"I shall use both, then," said Finch. "Just one illustration, perhaps. In the nineteen twenty-two expedition, there were two serious summit attempts from Advanced Base Camp, which that year was at five thousand one hundred and eighty meters—that's seventeen thousand feet, Mr. Perry. George Mallory and Howard Somervell, in their attempt, climbed to eight thousand three hundred and twenty meters, approximately twenty-seven thousand feet, in fourteen and a half hours. This is without oxygen, remember. So Mallory and Somervell's ascent rate was one hundred twenty meters—approximately three hundred and ninety-three feet—per hour. Is this clear so far?"

J.C. and I both nodded, but I was lying with my nod. I'd lost the mathematical thread somewhere around the first altitude high point.

"Then Richard here, Geoffrey Bruce, and I, also starting our summit attempt from Advanced Base Camp, climbed to eight thousand three hundred and twenty meters...the twenty-seven-thousand-three-hundred-foot level that I've mentioned before and will refer to again since it was the human high point on Everest until Mallory and Irvine's disappearance last year. It took us twelve and a quarter hours with oxygen to reach that altitude. That gave the three of us, with the crude oxygen apparatus, an ascent rate of one hundred fifty-five meters...some five hundred seventeen feet...per hour. This is clearly a superior climbing rate to that of Mallory or Somervell, and Richard and I have agreed that the rate and final altitude would have been even higher had we not moved out on a slow traverse of the North Face because of the terribly high winds on the ridge."

Jean-Claude held up one finger as if he were a student begging to ask a question of his instructor. "But you had to turn back because of a valve failure in Bruce's equipment. So in the end, the oxygen tanks ruined your chance of reaching the summit."

Finch smiled. "I'll discuss the valve problem in detail when we get to it. But please remember, Monsieur Clairoux, that there was another advantage to carrying the oxygen tanks so high." He looked at the Deacon. "It saved all three of our lives."

"How so?" I asked.

"On twenty-four May, Richard, Bruce, and I had sent our porters down and set up our tent on an exposed area at twenty-five thousand six hundred feet of altitude—seventy-eight hundred meters. We ended up being trapped there for more than thirty-six hours by high winds that literally lifted our tent off the ground. The tent had become a sail on the edge of a three-thousand-foot drop. Sleep was impossible as we spent day and night trying to hold the groundsheet down, now and then one of us venturing out into the hurricane gale to add another rope tie-down to a boulder. When the storm did begin to die down, we should have retreated to a lower altitude immediately, but none of us wanted to, even though we were short of food and our bodies were becoming numb from the cold. That night we were so weakened that all three of us were showing early signs of frostbite that would have been fatal by morning. None of us could have made the descent to a lower camp after another sleepless night of that insidious cold. Then I remembered the oxygen tanks we'd brought up."

We looked at the Deacon. His nod was almost imperceptible. "The oxygen saved our lives that night," he said. "All through the night, when we felt the coldest, we passed the oxygen cylinder around, and even a few breaths of the richer air got us warmer...the effects were immediate. It allowed us to sleep and kept us warm and alive through the worst night I've ever spent on any mountain."

"The next morning was when we made our summit bid," said Finch. "The three of us left the tent at six thirty a.m. and started climbing strongly. The oxygen sets had not only saved us from freezing to death in the night but restored our resolve to try to reach the summit—or at least the North East Ridge—the next day. And remember that this was after a record-setting forty-eight hours at an unprecedented altitude, and with almost no food or adequate water. The wind had blown so hard that for most of the time we could not even scoop a pan of snow from outside or light the stove. But the oxygen allowed us to climb toward the ridge that day anyway. At the ascent rate I mentioned earlier, we had climbed to twenty-five thousand five hundred feet, using bottled oxygen for many hours at a climbing rate of six hundred and sixty-six feet per hour, as compared to Mallory and Somervell's three hundred sixty-three feet per hour. Almost twice their rate of ascent, gentlemen."

"All right," I said to both the Deacon and Finch. "That makes sense even to me. We climb with oxygen packs. How do they work, Mr. Finch?"

Finch started to explain the equipment to Jean-Claude and me, speaking mostly to me, but then he paused. "Mr. Perry, you are the tinkerer-mechanic for this expedition, are you not?"

"Not me!" I said, almost alarmed. "I can barely change sparkplugs. Jean-Claude's our technical person."

Finch blinked. "That was stupid of me. Perhaps, Mr. Perry, I assumed you were the technical boffin because you so closely resemble Sandy Irvine, who did all the technical work for Mallory's expedition last year, even rebuilding this oxygen apparatus. You are the same age, I believe. Twenty-two? Same height. Same weight. Same confident look. Same athletic college rower's build. Same blond hair. Same smile." He turned to J.C. *"Pardonnez-moi, monsieur. J'aurais bien vu que vous êtes l'ingénieur du groupe."*

"Merci," said Jean-Claude with a nod. "But I fear that I am a mere tinkerer, Mr. Finch. Not a brilliant young engineer as Monsieur Irvine showed himself to be. My father was a blacksmith much of his life and then opened a small steel fabrication company before the War. During the War, the company grew quickly and *mon père* began working on much more complicated metal fabrication for the army. I used to watch...and help sometimes...but I am no engineer."

"I imagine you will be for this group," Finch said and propped up the heavy oxygen rig.

He paused before beginning what I assumed would be a lecture on the equipment.

"I know that Richard understands this," Finch said. "But do both of you know the difference in the actual amount of oxygen and air between sea level and, say, twenty-eight thousand feet?"

Again I felt like a schoolboy caught unawares by a surprise quiz. Desperately, I tried to remember the amount of O_2 at sea level—no number came to mind—and even more desperately tried to find an equation that would give me the smaller number at 28,000 feet. Divide by 28, perhaps? But divide what? "There's almost exactly the same amount of air and oxygen at twenty-eight thousand feet as there is at sea level," Jean-Claude said confidently.

What? My French friend obviously had lost his mind.

"Very good," said Finch. He managed to avoid the pedant's annoying whining sing-song and spoke normally. "But if the oxygen is roughly the same at both altitudes, then why," he paused dramatically, "do you run easily along the beach for a mile at sea level but have to stop to pant and gasp like a fish after two steps at twenty-eight thousand feet?"

"Air pressure," said Jean-Claude.

Finch nodded. "Scientifically, we know almost nothing about high-altitude physiology, and most of what we do know has come from a few studies by the British Air Ministry in the last few years—aeroplanes have been able to climb above ten thousand feet for only a very short time, obviously—and from tests in the nineteen twenty-one through 'twenty-four Everest expeditions. But we know that it's the lack of pressure at altitudes above twenty thousand feet that kills us—literally kills our brain cells, literally kills our organs and metabolism, literally kills our ability to think rationally—and, as Monsieur Clairoux says, it is because that lack of pressure makes it harder to breathe, to pull the oxygen into our lungs, and harder for oxygen to be pushed into the lungs' little capillaries and vessels to restore the red blood cells."

He held the heavy oxygen pack higher. "The oxygen in these bottles—what the Sherpas quaintly called 'English air' during our 'twenty-two expedition—is pressurized to an altitude of fifteen thousand feet. No breathing problems there for a fit alpinist."

I remembered that the summit of the Matterhorn we'd climbed the previous June was around 14,690 feet. Indeed, I hadn't felt any problems breathing there. The air had felt a bit thinner and much colder in my lungs, but also rich enough to fuel any physical exertion the climb required.

Finch moved the heavy-looking pack of oxygen tanks in front of him. "This was pretty much the design that the Air Ministry gave us along the lines of the designs that a Professor Dreyer gave them. Notice that the frame is a strong steel Bergen pack frame, and it holds four steel bottles of oxygen, each bottle of air at that fifteen-thousand-foot pressure I mentioned. Then there was this mass of tubes, some regulator valves—all that gabble went over the shoulder and down to the climber's chest, where he could fiddle with it at the risk of losing all O-two feed—and, to top it off, no fewer than three different types of face masks, counting my own modification."

Finch shrugged into the straps of the four-tank rig. Tubes and valves and...things...hung in front of him like an uncut umbilical cord. "Each full bottle of oxygen weighs five and three-quarters pounds," he said. "Would you prefer the data in English pounds, Monsieur Clairoux, or should I speak in kilograms?"

"Pounds would be completely understandable," Jean-Claude assured him. "And please call me by my Christian name."

"*Oui, très bien,*" said Finch. "Well, I've come to think in metric, so just for the record, each tank weighs a little more than two point six kilograms. The whole rig then weighs just a bit more than fourteen and a half kilograms... thirty-two pounds to you, Mr. Perry."

"Jake," I said.

"*Oui, très bien,*" he said again. "Here, Jake... Richard knows the weight of this version of the oxygen apparatus all too well. Why don't you try it on and then give it to Jean-Claude."

I took the Bergen frame and oxygen tanks from Finch, slipped into the thick straps, and shrugged it on. I didn't know what to do with the regulator stuff, tubes, and mask, so I let all that dangle in front of me.

"Not too heavy," I said. "I've carried almost twice this weight up serious mountains."

"Yes," said Finch, smiling, "but remember, you still have to carry a rucksack or some sort of canvas carrying bag as well as the oxygen bottles and Bergen frame. Food, your clothing, extra climbing gear, tents for the high camps... how much does your regular three-man tent weigh, Jake?"

"Sixty pounds."

Finch's smile was starting to look smug to me. "Pretty soon, with these 'twenty-two-style tanks, you're off balance backwards, and just imagine climbing a rock face with all of those valves, regulators, and tubes hanging in front of your chest! With this rig, you're exhausted in ten paces above nineteen thousand feet."

Jean-Claude was running his hands over the oxygen canisters, flow tubes, and regulator doohickeys, as if he'd fathom more of the rig's purpose just through feel. I stepped back to give him more room.

"Try it on, both of you," said the Deacon. "Please."

J.C. propped the apparatus up on the bench and easily slid into the straps. He hoisted it higher and secured a cross-strap over his chest. "Not too bad," he said. "I often climb with more weight in a rucksack. But I think you may be right about the balance issue..." Then Jean-Claude surprised me by setting a foot on the bench's stool and using just his arms to lift himself and the apparatus up to a kneeling position on the sturdy workbench. He set his hands on the wall to help himself get to his feet.

Looming above us, J.C. said, "Yes, climbing sheer rock or ice would be trickier with this." Then he jumped four feet to the floor as if he weren't carrying thirty-two pounds of steel and pressurized oxygen on his back.

When it was my turn, I loosened the straps for my greater size and girth, tugged them tight again, took a few steps around the workshop and grunted noncommittally. With J.C.'s help, I shrugged out of the pack and lowered it gently to the bench. I wasn't sure whether such weight would hinder my climbing or not, but although I'd never say it out loud, I relied on my greater strength and fewer years to allow me to perform physical feats that might be beyond the 37-year-old Deacon and the much smaller and lighter Jean-Claude.

"Then there are the sad tales of the multiple face masks," said George Ingle Finch. He'd pulled three across the bench toward him. "This first thing was called the Economizer. It was designed to deal with the fact that at Mount Everest altitude, with the lower pressure, most of the oxygen you breathe in while struggling uphill is just breathed out again—without your body or red blood cells getting any benefit from it. So the Economizer here had two valves..."

Finch turned the mask around and tapped the complicated interior. "They were there to allow carbon dioxide to pass through the mask but to store the unused oxygen for reuse. But the damned valves froze up more often than not, making the whole mask useless."

He held up a second, even heavier-looking face mask. "We tried to solve that problem with this backup mask—the Standard—made of pliable copper with chamois leather over it. The idea was that it could be bent easily to fit each climber's face. And there were no valves, you see..." He tapped the empty interior. "You controlled breathing and re-breathing by biting on the end of the supply tube. Simplicity itself."

"Mallory hated that mask," said the Deacon.

Finch smiled. "Indeed he did. As much as he hated the emergency backup plan I taught everyone, which was simply ripping off the mask and sucking on the oxygen hose directly, as Royal Air Force pilots often do during their brief flights above ten thousand feet. And he hated both the mask and the bare tube for the same reason—the climber drools like a baby. Then the drool freezes. Or runs down your throat and collar and then freezes."

"So what's the third mask?" I ask, pointing.

"This was my answer to the Standard's drooling problem," said Finch. "T-shaped glass tubes, like small mouth bits, instead of rubber hoses. They minimized drool and worked far better for re-breathing the oxygen your body has just exhaled without using. There was one problem, though, as Geoffrey Bruce discovered during his, Richard's, and my high-altitude-record ascent toward the North East Ridge in nineteen twenty-two..."

"They break," said Jean-Claude.

"Indeed." Finch sighed. "The glass becomes brittle in the extreme cold and can break...or clog...either way shutting off all oxygen to the climber. Before the 'twenty-one and 'twenty-two expeditions, a lot of atmospheric scientists thought that with a climber using bottled air pressurized to fifteen thousand feet, if that O-two flow suddenly stopped at altitude—say, at twenty-seven thousand three hundred feet, where Bruce, Richard, and I were when Bruce's valve broke—the climber would die immediately."

"But no one died from such a failure," said Jean-Claude, obviously aware of the oxygen rigs' history in the Himalayas.

"Not at all. At least two of our climbers and three porters climbed all the way to our Camp Five at twenty-five thousand feet on the East Ridge with oxygen rigs that weren't working at all. But Bruce's valve failure that day, as Richard and I discussed earlier, did cause all three of us to turn back before we reached the North East Ridge."

"So this version of the pack with the glass valves in the mask is what we'll be using on Everest?" I asked, looking first at the Deacon and then at Finch.

"No," said both men at once.

Finch dragged a third Bergen pack frame from the pile of rigs propped against the back of the bench. This one looked different somehow.

"This is Sandy Irvine's so-called Mark Five version," said Finch, tapping the steel canisters. "You can see the difference."

It looked different to me but I was damned if I could see exactly how...wait, there were three oxygen tanks in the frame rather than four, I realized. I smiled at how perceptive I was.

"Almost everything is different," said Jean-Claude, again running his hands across frame and tanks and dials and tubes. "To start with, I can see that Irvine inverted the tanks so that their valves are at the bottom rather than on top..."

Well, I'll be damned, I thought. So he had.

"Irvine got rid of almost all the pipe work," continued Jean-Claude, "and radically simplified this flow meter, setting it right at the lower center of the pack so the rig's balance would be better."

Without asking permission, J.C. tugged the Sandy Irvine version of the oxygen rig onto his back. "The hose goes over the shoulder now, rather than under the arm and through all those valves and tubes that used to be hanging in the front. Those are gone. The air feed should be better and the climbing should be easier. And it feels lighter."

"Yes," said Finch, nodding. "The late Mr. Irvine's Mark Five version is almost five full pounds lighter than its predecessors, while working much better and being infinitely less awkward."

Well, I'll be damned, I thought again.

"Mr. Irvine did most of this redesign while he was still at Oxford," continued Finch. "He sent all the modification plans to the company manufacturing them—our proud Siebe Gorman—and in almost a year, they made none of the changes he had requested."

"None?" I repeated.

"None," said Finch. "They ignored his and the Everest Committee's orders to make such modifications and shipped precisely the same clumsy, leaking, bulky kits that Richard, Mallory, Bruce, and I had used in nineteen twenty-two. My good friend Noel Odell, who was the last person to see Mallory and Irvine climbing high, told me that when the expedition's ninety cylinders arrived in Calcutta, fifteen were empty and twenty-four had already leaked so badly that they were useless on the climb. Mr. Irvine told Odell that he, Sandy, had broken one kit just by carefully removing it from its packing case. It was the same thing I found when we reached Base Camp at Mount Everest in 'twenty-two—not one of the ten apparatuses shipped was usable. The soldered joints all leaked, washers had become so dry during the high-desert trip in to the mountain that joints could no longer be made gas-tight, and the majority of the gauges didn't work. Some of it was fixable—and I fixed what I could—but essentially, the judgment on the Siebe Gorman apparatus is that they were all...junk."

Jean-Claude removed the Irvine Mark V version and set it on the workbench with a resounding thump. "Then how did Sandy Irvine get this improved version?"

Finch showed his small smile. "He fiddled with it all during the three-hundred-and-fifty-mile march in, then at Base Camp, then at the higher camps, and didn't quit fiddling and improving it—with the few tools and parts he had—until the morning he and Mallory left Camp Six and disappeared."

"So I assume we shall be receiving the Irvine Mark Five versions?" Jean-Claude said.

"One further modified to my specifications, yes. And you will be getting them not from Siebe Gorman but, as I said, from *Zürcher Werke für wissenschaftliche Präzisionsinstrumente und Geräte.*" The smile widened almost imperceptibly. "And I guarantee, gentlemen, that they will be engineered properly and up to and exceeding the late Sandy Irvine's standards."

The Deacon stepped forward and touched the Mark V tanks. "George, you said that you had a couple of final modifications of your own that you asked for."

Finch nodded again. "I asked the Zurich engineers to make the Bergen pack frame, the flow meters, and several other elements of the apparatus out of aluminum"—he pronounced it British style, "alu*min*ium"—"a strong metal derived from bauxite ore. I wish I could have made the oxygen canisters out of this aluminum as well, but facilities did not exist for attaching the proper valves or pressuring aluminum tanks, so the oxygen is still carried in steel canisters. But with three tanks maximum, not four, and the new aluminum components, the overall weight will be significantly lower."

Finch pulled out yet another oxygen rig. This looked much like Sandy Irvine's Mark V design but was somehow...different...at the same time.

"How *much* lower is the weight?" asked the Deacon, running his hand over the aluminum frame.

Finch shrugged, but his pride was obvious. "Down from Siebe Gorman's thirty-two pounds to just over twenty pounds."

"And you also did something with the face mask valves," said the Deacon.

Finch lifted the mask of his Mark VI pack. The mask seemed simpler in design than all the others and more pliable in Finch's scarred hand. "Instead of glass, I redesigned the breathing/re-breathing mouthpiece valves to be made out of a very high grade of rubber," he said. "We've tested that rubber at altitudes up to and above thirty thousand feet—and in ultra-dry air—and the rubber does not become brittle or leak. I took the liberty of replacing all of the leaking Siebe Gorman gaskets and valves with this higher-quality rubber as well." Finch looked down, and his voice sounded almost embarrassed or ashamed. "I had no time to test all the new components on a mountain, Richard. I wanted to...I had planned to...I had thought the ridges along the North Face of the Eiger might make for a good test...it is not right that you will find if everything works only once you're high on Everest...but the fabrication of the new design took so long...."

The Deacon patted Finch on the back. "Thank you, my friend. I'm sure your tests here in Zurich have ensured that the tanks we ordered will work and not leak as the earlier ones did. Thank you for all your work and advice, George."

Finch showed his small smile, nodded, and put his hands in his pockets.

The Deacon looked at his watch. "We'd better be off if we're going to meet our train."

"I'll walk with you to the *Eisenbahn* station," said George Ingle Finch.

The train was on time, which, of course, is redundant. It was a *Swiss* train.

The Deacon and I were going back through France to Cherbourg and then to England to continue our preparations. Jean-Claude was returning to Chamonix briefly—mostly to say good-bye to the girl he was planning to marry, was my hunch—and would be joining us in London just before it was time to go to Liverpool and depart for India. On the train from Zurich, we each would be carrying our two leather Gladstone bags filled with the nine compressed eiderdown coats.

As we were preparing to board, Finch—who had been silent during the cold walk to the station—suddenly said, "There is one other thing I should tell you about the reason you are going to Everest...about Lord Percival Bromley, that is."

We hesitated. The Deacon had one foot up on the lower step of the train car. There was no one behind us. We stood there holding our light valises and listened as steam from the train wrapped us in shifting folds of warm vapor.

"I did see Bromley one other time after I climbed with him years ago," continued Finch. "He visited me here in Zurich—came to my home—in the spring of nineteen twenty-three. April. He said that he needed to ask me about one aspect of our 'twenty-two expedition..."

Finch seemed to be hunting for words. We waited in silence. Down the platform, the final passengers were boarding the train.

Letting out a breath in a small cloud that mixed with the steam, Finch went on, "It's rather absurd, actually. Young Bromley wanted me to tell him everything I knew, everything we'd seen or heard, about...well...the *Metohkangmi*."

"The *yeti* critter?" I said, surprised.

Finch managed a final smile. "Yes, Mr. Perry. Jake, I mean. The *yeti* critter. I told him about the tracks I'd seen high on the Rongbuk Glacier near the North Col, showed him photographs Mallory had taken the year before of the tracks he'd found on nearby Lhakpa La, and related what the lama at Rongbuk Monastery had said about the five *yetis* they were sure inhabited the upper reaches of the valley. That was all I had to show or tell young Bromley—hardly worth a trip to Zurich from Paris, where he was staying at the time—but he did not seem disappointed. Merely thanked me for my time and the information, finished his tea, and returned to Paris that same afternoon." The conductor was waving his hands at us, pointing emphatically at his watch.

The Deacon said quickly, "Did Bromley tell you why he was interested in this *yeti* story?"

Finch merely shook his head. Then he stepped forward, bowed slightly, clicked his heels together in a formal manner that was almost Prussian, shook each of us by the hand, and said, "Good-bye, gentlemen. I somehow feel that I will never see any of you again, but I wish you all good fortune in your travels, in your adventure on Everest, and in your...search."

Seek out Messrs. Burberry, Haymarket
("ask for Mr. Pink").

*T*he Deacon had informed us the previous November that for the 1921 through 1924 expeditions, the Alpine Club and Everest Committee had allocated £50 per man for his full "kit." He also told us that most of these upper-class gentlemen had spent additional money of their own for their outfitting, so he had taken it upon himself to allocate £100 of Lady Bromley's budget for each of us in our outfitting and would add to that if necessary.

Even with the Deacon's personal checklist from his '21 and '22 expeditions, as well as the updated 1924 gear list given to him to by his friend the filmmaker-climber Captain John B. L. Noel, finding and purchasing our clothing and specialized climbing gear for Mount Everest was almost the precise equivalent of preparing for a trip to the South Pole. But then, of course, the entire British effort to climb Everest to this date—up to and including the final disappearance of Irvine and Mallory the previous year—had used South Polar expeditions as their template: i.e., using porters to set a series of food and matériel caches in stages along the way to the Pole—or, in our case, at different altitudes on the mountain—and then shifting backward and forward through these camps until a smaller, select group, given a window of good weather, could make their dash for the summit, as Robert Falcon Scott had toward the South Pole thirteen years earlier, just him and his handpicked group of four good men planning to sledge their 1,600-mile round trip to the Pole and back. Since Scott and all four of his men had died during that ill-advised and bad-luck-plagued attempt, it was an analogy I tried not to dwell on.

Still, the clothing and materials we were buying now were very similar—with a few wonderful modern improvements—to what Scott and his men had worn to their cold deaths in the Antarctic.

The first item on the sacred List was windproof clothing, and for that, the List said, we should "Seek out Messrs. Burberry, Haymarket ('ask for Mr. Pink')." Jean-Claude and I were a little intimidated by what was reputed to be one of the ritziest of all London haberdashers—"outfitters to Ernest Shackleton" and all that. So J.C. and I went together on a day when the Deacon was busy with other expedition preparation business.

"Mr. Pink," it turned out, was indisposed and not at the Messrs. Burberry establishment on Haymarket that particular day, but a formally dressed and impeccably polite "Mr. White" spent nearly three hours helping us choose clothing and sizes before we left with a receipt for our purchases and a promise that they would be delivered to our hotel that very afternoon. It turned out that the parcels beat us back to the hotel, and we'd only stopped for a single post-Burberry pint on the way.

The majority of what we purchased at Messrs. Burberry was in the Shackleton line of windproof knickerbockers, smocks, and gloves. We purchased fingerless woolen mitts that went inside larger mitts made of Shackleton gabardine. We added thick woolen mufflers to our Burberry-buying list.

We also needed protection for our heads and faces at Everest altitudes—or even at the 17,000-foot and higher altitudes of the many passes on the 350-mile hike through Tibet *to* the mountain—and, rather amazingly I thought, Messrs. Burberry sold leather flying, or perhaps motorcycle, helmets with rabbit or fox fur linings and earflaps that tied under one's chin. Also available—and we each bought one—were face masks made of a thin, soft, breathable, leather-lined chamois. This awe-inspiring combination of leather flaps and straps and fur and brass toggles was topped off with massive goggles made of Crooke's glass which could be sewn into the leather face mask and helmet if we so chose. The thick glass darkened our view and would shield our eyes from the terrible sunlight at high altitudes. Every climber knew the story of Edward Norton, who'd left his goggles off during his and Somervell's daring 1922 traverse across the North Face and their failed attempt to climb up the snow-filled great gully that runs down the face of the mountain from the summit. The climbing was so technical that Norton removed his goggles for hours to make sure he could see where he was setting his hands and feet. He'd assumed that since he was climbing on bare rock more than on reflective snow or ice, the sunlight wouldn't hurt his eyes.

They didn't succeed in climbing the treacherous couloir, but that night upon descending to Camp IV, Norton was hit with blinding pain in both eyes. He'd given himself ophthalmia—snow blindness with an accompanying infection—and the pain and blindness afflicted him for sixty straight hours after that. They had to help the blinded man down to Advanced Base Camp and put him in a tent covered with sleeping bags to hold out the painful light. Norton's suffering in that tent was said to have been terrible.

The Shackleton jackets—they were waxed-cotton anoraks, really—had helped keep the wool clothing from earlier expeditions from getting soaked through, but they did very little to hold in warmth, despite their theoretical resistance to wind. The Deacon had this wild idea that a climber—at least the three of *us* climbers—might be able to survive in the open after dark on Everest with the combination of Finch's goose down jackets and our waterproof Shackleton jackets. Perhaps—not probably, but just perhaps—we would have clothing warm enough to keep us alive all night in an open bivouac above 25,000 feet.

The few layers that Irvine and Mallory had been wearing when they disappeared, said the Deacon, wouldn't keep them alive for an hour of sitting still after sunset on the North East Ridge. "I can't guarantee that Mr. Finch's eiderdown coats will make the difference between life and death up there," the Deacon had said when we'd been deciding on outerwear (actually, when *he* had been deciding), "but I know Finch was warmer than all the rest of us in 'twenty-two, plus the eiderdown is lighter than more layers of wool, and the Shackleton overjackets should keep the down loft dry, so it's worth the wager."

I never liked the word "wager" used when it applied to our lives on the highest mountain on earth.

The day after our visit to Messrs. Burberry, Jean-Claude and I joined the Deacon on a boot-purchasing trip to Fagg Bros. on Jermyn Street. There all three of us were fitted for a recently designed—for polar exploration, of course—leather-soled felt boot that was intentionally made oversized to accommodate at least three pairs of thick wool socks. Few of the 1924 climbers had chosen to wear the felt boots once they were above the lower glacier, which meant that no one knew for sure how the boots performed for rock and ice climbing at real altitude.

"Why can't I use my own climbing boots?" asked Jean-Claude. "They have served me well for years. They only need re-soling from time to time."

"All of us in the first two expeditions, even Finch, and all of the high-climbers on last year's expedition, wore our own hobnailed boots," said the Deacon. "And we all suffered from cold feet, several had frostbite, and some lost toes. Sandy Irvine told John Noel last year that the reason is that these specialized alpine climbing boots not only have the hob-nails—in whatever pattern you choose, and Mallory and everyone chose different ones—but also have little metal plates driven between the in-ner and outer soles to give extra grip. And some of the 'nails' on the hobnails are serrated."

"So?" I said, impatient at last with our team leader. "*Did* these expen-sive hobnailed boots give better grip? If so, the metal plates are a good idea, right? They can't weigh that much."

The Deacon shook his head in that way that always meant *No, you don't understand.*

"Irvine did suggest we use fewer hobnails, for lightness's sake," he said. "In the army, we were told that every pound of weight on our feet was equal to ten on our back. Our leather boots during the War were substantial, but designed to be light—for maximum marching. But it's not the weight that Sandy Irvine was warning Noel about, it was the transmission of cold."

"Transmission of cold?" repeated Jean-Claude as if not sure of the English phrase.

"Leather soles and thick socks insulate against the terrible cold of the rock and ice high on the mountain to some extent," said the Deacon. "But Irvine had a theory that the hobnailed boots everyone was wearing were conducting heat from the body through the feet via those metal plates and the hobnails themselves. Heat always flows to cold, of course, and that, according to Irvine's theory, is why there were so many cases of near-frostbitten toes and some of the real thing. On our expedition, Henry Morshead had to have a toe and several fingertips amputated when we got back to India. He applied to the nineteen twenty-four expedition, but was turned down because of those injuries. So I agree with Sandy Irvine that the hobnailed boots lose body heat to the rock or ice."

"Then why are we here?" I said. "I might as well wear my trusty old climbing boots if these more expensive hobnailed things are just going to get my feet colder sooner." That sentence sounded childishly petulant even to my own ears.

The Deacon unfolded several papers from his jacket pocket. On each sheet were carefully diagramed pencil or ink drawings, with columns of handwritten text to either side. The spelling was terrible, but the instructions were clear—Sandy Irvine had made his own revision of the standard alpine climbing boot design, showing where layers of felt should be added between the welt and the nailed sole. Irvine's summary (the Deacon confirmed that these were his actual notes, given to Captain Noel during the last days before Irvine disappeared with Mallory) concluded in precise handwriting but in terrible spelling, *Boots shulde be spareingly naild for liteness—everry ouns counts!*

"This spelling," I said to the Deacon, holding up the folded note as if it were evidence. Everyone knew after the months of newspaper accounts and funeral oratory that Andrew "Sandy" Comyn Irvine had gone to Merton College, Oxford. "The result of high-altitude oxygen deprivation?"

The Deacon shook his head. "Noel said that Irvine was one of the cleverest young men he'd ever met...a near-genius at engineering and in-the-field tinkering...but there was some problem that never allowed the boy to learn to spell correctly. It didn't seem to hold him back in any way. He rowed crew for the OUBC—Oxford University Boat Club—and was a member of the rather infamous Myrmidon dining club at Merton."

"Infamous?" said Jean-Claude. He'd been carefully examining Irvine's diagrams for the special boots and looked up in surprise. "Irvine was part of something...infamous?"

"A dining club of rich boys, most of them excellent athletes, who specialized in breaking university rules and windows," said the Deacon. He took back the folded sheets of paper and handed them to the attentive Fagg Brother who had been discussing boots with us. "Now our decision is whether to go with Irvine's design for the newer, possibly warmer alpine climbing boots, or stick to the new felt ones, or get the super-rigid types of boots that Jean-Claude has asked us to use with his newly designed crampons, or just bring our own."

"Can we not do all four things?" asked Jean-Claude. "Soon I will show you why the very rigid boots I requested may be necessary on Everest. So the four types of boots—high felt for cold, extra-rigid for my new crampon design, Irvine's felt and hobnail boots, and our own old boots, perhaps resoled, for backup. If Lady Bromley's money allows?"

"It allows," said the Deacon. He pointed to the diagrams and said to Mr. Fagg, "Two pairs of these specialized boots with the extra felt layer and metal-plates-not-touching-metal-nails for each of us. Two pairs of the extra-rigid boots—Jean-Claude has a page with the specifications. And two pairs each of the Laplander Antarctic felt boots. We have time to be measured now."

But it was not Finch's balloon coat or the Irvine-designed new boots that were the largest change made in outfitting our tiny new expedition in 1925.

As soon as J.C. had rejoined us after his last trip to France, he asked urgently for two days of our time before the end of January. The Deacon replied that it was impossible; he simply didn't have two days to waste between January and late February, when we were destined to sail for India.

"It's important, *Ree-shard,*" said Jean-Claude. At this point J.C. used the Deacon's first name only on rare occasions, and I was always amused when he used the French pronunciation. *"Très important."*

"Important enough that the success or failure of the entire expedition may depend upon it?" The Deacon's tone was not friendly.

"Oui. Yes." J.C. looked at both of us. "I think that, yes, these two days may be so important that the success or failure of our entire expedition may depend upon it."

The Deacon sighed and pulled out a tiny notebook-diary with calendar that he kept in his jacket pocket. "The last weekend in the month," he said at last. "The twenty-fourth and twenty-fifth of January. I have several important things...I'll move them. That's a full-moon weekend...will that make any difference?"

"It might," said Jean-Claude. He flashed his sudden, wide, boy-like grin. "The full moon may well make some difference. Yes. *Merci, mon ami.*"

We left at sunrise—or what passed for sunrise on that freezing, gray, foggy, snow-spitting late January day—on Saturday the twenty-fourth. None of us owned an automobile, so the Deacon had arranged to borrow one from a friend of his named Dick Summers. It was a Vauxhall, and in my memory the vehicle was about thirty feet long—it had three rows of seats with plenty of legroom and tires that came up almost to my chest. (The mild irony, explained the Deacon, was that Dick Summers had used this same Vauxhall less than two years before to make the first-ever automotive crossing of the rough gravel road—little more than a trail, said the Deacon—in both directions over the difficult Wrynose and Hardknot passes in the Lake District. When I commented that I didn't see much irony in this, the Deacon lit his pipe and said, "True. I forgot to add that while Summers did the driving on that adventure, Sandy Irvine rode in the third-row seat with two attractive young ladies.")

We learned within moments of leaving Summers's storage garage that the huge Vauxhall was better suited to summer expeditions over high passes than it was to winter driving. It was a convertible—what the Brits called "a ragtop" or "topless"—and although it had taken the three of us only thirty minutes of swearing and smashed fingers to get the impossibly complex roof apparatus properly raised and locked, and then another half hour to get the soft side and rear windows buttoned and snapped in properly, as soon as we were on a London street heading northwest out of the city, we realized that the damned machine had more gaps in its superstructure than a cheap colander. Within ten minutes of getting the huge auto onto the streets, snow was blowing in our faces and piling up along the wooden floorboards, on our feet, and in our laps.

"How long a drive did you say this is?" the Deacon asked Jean-Claude, who was at the wheel. J.C. hadn't yet revealed our destination, which irritated the Deacon all the more. (Not that he seemed to need many reasons those days for being irritated; the amount of logistical work he was doing for our limited little "recovery expedition" was leaving him no time for sleep or food, much less relaxation or exercise, and was visibly wearing him down.)

"Less than a six-hour drive, I am told, on a nice summer day," replied J.C. happily, both wool-gloved hands firmly on the giant steering wheel, and spluttering a bit of snow off his lips. "Perhaps a little longer today."

"Ten hours?" The Deacon's voice was a growl as he tried to light his pipe. It was difficult for him since he was wearing our new fingerless gloves under our new wool and then Shackleton-cloth mittens. At least we had dressed for the South Pole for the *drive* to this outing.

"May be lucky if we get there in twelve hours," chirped Jean-Claude. "Please sit back, as you say, and relax."

No chance of that for two good reasons: first, the Vauxhall had a theoretical heater in the dash, and all three of us were huddled forward toward it, me from the second-row seat, even though the thing blew out only *cold* air; and second, Jean-Claude was not used to driving *any* automobile, but especially not in England, so the trip on snow and ice was terrifying even *between* his lapses as to which side of the road to drive on.

The snow fell harder. We continued on northwest—the only other vehicles foolhardy enough to be on the roads this day were lorries—through Hemel Hempsted, then Coventry, then the smoky-black city of Birmingham, then on toward Shrewsbury.

"We're going to northern Wales," said the Deacon with a sigh, long before we got to Shrewsbury. Somehow he managed to make "Wales" rhyme with "Hells."

The wide third seat, and half of my second seat, were taken up with huge and heavy duffel bags which J.C. had needed our help to lift into the car. They were *heavy*. And the steel clank and heavy metal bangs coming from the bags as we slewed left and right in dizzying attempts to find a straight line down the road again over the snow and ice made me guess that there was a lot of *serious* equipment in those bags.

"Is this the oxygen apparatus you brought with us?" I asked from where I gripped the front seat ahead of me like the restraining bar on a roller coaster.

"*Non,*" said Jean-Claude absently, chewing his lower lip while he tried to thread the needle with a twelve-foot-wide Vauxhall between an on-coming lorry and an impenetrable hedge and deep ditch to the left of our steeply crowned and snow-covered road.

The Deacon removed his pipe for a second. I'd just decided that I should lean closer and hold my hands out to *it*—his pipe—as a source of warmth rather than toward the car's so-called "heater."

"Can't be the oxygen sets," said the Deacon glumly. "You remember that Finch will be sending those straight from Zurich to the ship for loading."

It grew dark. Our dinner had consisted of freezing—literally freezing; there were ice crystals in them—sandwiches we'd packed in a now mostly snow-filled hamper and a thermos flask of hot soup that had lost all of its heat somewhere around when we did, ten hours earlier in the northwest suburbs of London.

The snow continued to fall. The Vauxhall's flickering headlights put out almost as much light as two sputtering candles. No matter; there was no one else idiotic enough to be out on these roads this night any-way. Perhaps the full moon that Jean-Claude wanted had risen while we drove on. We'd never know. The world was a whirling white mass through which Jean-Claude drove firmly ever onward, blinking unmelt-ing snowflakes out of his eyes as he squinted into the white-darkness ahead.

"We're going to Mount Snowdon," said the Deacon. His pipe would no longer stay lit in the gale blowing through the flapping sides and roof and window panels.

"Non," said Jean-Claude grimly. The last time I'd seen his smile had been somewhere just after Birmingham.

We didn't get to his destination that night. The first of two tire punc-tures that we were to enjoy during the trip made sure of that. Luckily, Dick Summers had had the foresight to have two workable spares lashed to the Vauxhall's left-rear running board. (I could get in and out of my rear seat only on the right side.) Less luckily, the jack and other tools needed to change the spare in the roaring blizzard—we had broken down in mid-road, so if a lorry or other vehicle came barreling out of the snowy darkness, it was all over for all of us (we didn't even have a flash-light—or "torch," as the Deacon called it—to carry down the road to warn other cars, nor even a candle, much less a road flare)—we finally realized must be buried in the tiny boot of the huge Vauxhall. And the boot was locked. And the ignition key would not open it.

We wove a tapestry of obscenities so thick that night I'm certain that it's still floating somewhere near the England-Wales border.

Finally one of us thought of merely banging the hinged boot cover, *hard,* thinking that perhaps it was merely frozen closed rather than locked, and the tiny flap of metal swung up as easily as you please, revealing a jack, tire iron, and so forth that looked to have been made for an automobile a fifth the size of the hulking Vauxhall.

No matter. We had the tire changed in under ninety minutes.

We spent the night in an overpriced and not very clean local hostelry in a place called Cerrigydrudion. We arrived too late for the warm food they'd served earlier, and the owner wouldn't open the kitchen to allow us to forage. The public room did have a fireplace, and although the owner, on his way to bed, stepped forward as if to tell us not to put any more coal on the fire, one glance at the glares from all three of us froze him in his tracks.

We stayed by the tiny fire until midnight, trying to thaw out. Then we dragged ourselves to tiny, strange-smelling rooms that were almost as cold as the Vauxhall had been. We'd brought our best down sleeping bags—after J.C. had told us that we'd be camping out this Saturday night—but the cold and evil smell of the tiny cells was too much, and somewhere around three a.m. I pulled on more outer layers of clothing and trudged back out to see if I could get the fire relit.

There was no need. J.C. and the Deacon had got there before me, had the tiny coal fire burning brightly, and were both snoring as they lay in contorted positions sprawled in and across two wing chairs. There was a third ancient wing chair in the room. I dragged it over—the screech waking neither of my climbing partners—got it as close to the little fire as I could, pulled the down bag over me like a comforter, and slept soundly until the inn's host rousted us out of our happy nests at six in the morning.

That Sunday, January 25, 1925, was one of the most beautiful days in my life, albeit at the tender age of 22, when so much of my life still lay ahead. But to be honest, none of my "most beautiful days" in the almost seven decades since have been shared with anyone quite the way I shared that day—and then more such days and moments during the following months—with my friends and brothers of the rope, Jean-Claude Clairoux and Richard Davis Deacon.

There was deep snow everywhere, but the day was blue-skied and sunny. Perhaps the sunniest day I remember during my time in England, with the possible exception of that perfect summer one when we visited Lady Bromley. It was still very cold—at least ten degrees below freezing—so the snow wasn't melting, but the huge Vauxhall, with its powerful engine and gigantic, strangely knobbed tires, was in its element. Even on the provincial Welsh roads where no other vehicles had traveled that morning, we barreled along at a comfortable and safe thirty miles per hour.

After only a few miles, we all realized that we couldn't stand being entombed in the top-up Vauxhall again, so we stopped the car in the middle of the empty, blindingly white road—our two tracks behind us disappearing over the last pass like black railroad tracks in a domed white world—and we deconstructed the ragtop's rag top, storing pop-off windows, canvas sides, and the rest on the floor next to J.C.'s huge bags riding next to me.

We'd each pulled on our five layers of wool, then the personal-use eiderdown balloon-fabric parkas we'd brought back in our Gladstone bags from Mr. Finch's Zurich, and finally the Shackleton-Burberry anoraks. J.C. and I also donned our leather flying or motorcycle helmets and face masks, complete with Crooke's glass antiglare goggles.

I wish to this day that someone had been there to take a photo of us as we passed by all that Mount Snowdon–area emptiness. We must have looked like Mr. Wells's Martian invaders.

But it turned out that our destination—Jean-Claude's secret destination—was not the frequently-climbed-in-winter Mount Snowdon or George Mallory's Pen-y-Pass slabs where we'd rock-climbed the previous autumn; our destination, reached mid-morning that January Sunday, was the lake Llyn Idwal and its surrounding moraines, *roches moutonnées* (Jean-Claude's description but familiar to me from our many alpine climbs during the previous year), brilliant striations in the cliff sides, wild moraines and scree slopes, erratics (boulders brought there by long-gone glaciers and left sitting on the rocky flatlands like huge hurling stones forgotten by a race of giants), and exposed deep-rock strata on vertical faces and slabs and slopes everywhere around us. The Llyn—the lake, frozen then—was surrounded by hard-rock verticality. J.C. pointed out the high peaks of Y Glyder Fawr and Y Garn as we got out of the car and stretched our legs in the snow. Jean-Claude and I were wearing waxed-cotton gaiters to keep our high socks dry. The Deacon, also in knickerbockers, wore old-fashioned puttees—though of the finest cashmere—and looked like the rather fussy-looking British climbers in the photos of the '21, '22, and '24 Everest expeditions. Also, with his khaki knickerbockers and khaki wool shirt visible through the opening of his unbuttoned balloon coat, the Deacon looked like the military man—Captain—he'd been during the Great War.

There was something almost disturbing in seeing the Deacon in brown and khaki and high puttees like that. If it brought back harsh memories of the War to him, he certainly didn't show it as he got out of the big car, stretched, craned his head back to look at the surrounding peaks and icefalls, and then got his pipe out of his tatty old wool-jacket pocket and proceeded to light it up. I remember that the smell of his tobacco in the cold air was like a powerful drug.

I was worried that it would be another two-hour hike to our climbing spot—as with Mallory's damned pipe-ledge rock—but Jean-Claude had parked the gigantic Vauxhall only a hundred yards or so from his true destination.

He'd been after vertical summer waterfalls that had turned to icefalls; he'd been after 200-foot walls of ice over rock that ended in daunting ice-over-rock-slab overhangs. He'd found them. Frozen waterfalls and spectacular icefalls filled the entire valley at this far end of the mostly frozen Llyn Idwal and under the cliffs of Cwm Idwal. We lugged the heavy bags to the base of one of the largest, steepest, and most overhanging-at-the-top vertical icefalls, where he dumped his load in the snow and waved for us to do the same. And then he began to explain something that would change alpine and Himalayan climbing forever.

"First you must change into the new boots Messrs. Fagg created for us," said Jean-Claude. He pulled two pairs of the stiff boots from one of the heavy canvas bags. J.C. was already wearing his.

The Deacon and I grumbled but found separate boulders to sit on while we took off our comfortable and broken-in new alpine boots and tugged on the ridiculous stiff ones. We'd tried walking in these new things in London, and they were hideously uncomfortable. (The Lap-lander high-and-fuzzy felt-and-leather boots were best—like walking in knee-high, extra-warm Indian moccasins. Unfortunately, the rocks and boulders we'd be walking on in Tibet, usually while carrying heavy packs, on the 350-mile hike in to Everest would bruise the soles of our feet too much if we wore the fuzzy boots all the time. But they'd be per-fect as in-camp boots.)

The Deacon and I took a few clumsy steps in the full-shank "stiff boots," frowned at each other, and scowled at Jean-Claude. Those stupid boots had almost no flex at all. They'd never break in to become com-fortable hiking or climbing shoes.

J.C. did not seem daunted by our glares. Also, he was too busy remov-ing a host of metal and metal-and-wood items from his three heavy bags of tricks. "What are these?" J.C. asked us, holding up two old crampons I'd seen him use many times.

"Crampons?" I said, hating the schoolboy rise in my voice at the end. "Crampons," I repeated more firmly.

"And what are they used for?" he continued in his schoolmarmish, only slightly French accent.

"Crossing glaciers," I said even more firmly. "Sometimes going up snow slopes—if they're not too steep."

"How many points does each have?"

"Points?" I said stupidly.

"Spikes on the bottom," said the Deacon. He was fumbling with his damned pipe again. I wanted to hit him with one of the four-foot-long icicles dangling from the lower part of the icefall ahead of us.

"Ten points," I said. I'd had to envision my crampons at home and mentally count the spikes. Stupid. I'd used them since I was a teenager. "Ten."

"Why don't we use them more while climbing?" asked Jean-Claude. "Why won't we use them high on Mount Everest?" His soft, innocent voice sounded treacherous to me. There was some trap here. I looked at the Deacon, but he was suddenly very busy getting his pipe relit.

"Because the damned things are no good on rock," I said at last. I was losing patience with this dunce-schoolboy role.

"Is everything underfoot high on Everest rock?"

I actually sighed. "No, Jean-Claude, not everything underfoot high on Everest is rock, but enough is. We can use crampons for the occasional snowfield, if it's not too steep. But hobnailed boots are better. More grip. More traction. The North Face of Everest, and most of the North East and East ridges, according to the Alpine Club's reports and what the nineteen twenty-four expedition high-climbers say, consists mostly of downward-tilting rock slabs—like slate shingles on a steep roof. A *very* steep roof."

"So crampons would be inadvisable there?"

I had a geometry teacher in prep school who used to lead class instruction and discussions in that tone. I hated him as well.

"Very inadvisable," I said. "It'd be like walking on steel stilts." That hadn't been easy to say clearly.

Jean-Claude nodded slowly as if finally coming to a basic understanding of Himalayan and high-alpine climbing. "And what about Norton's Couloir?"

"Norton's Couloir" was what climbers were now calling the great slab-and-snow-filled gully that runs straight up the central North Face of Everest to the Summit Pyramid. A year earlier, Edward Norton and Howard Somervell—Norton in the unroped lead—had blazed a route off the East Ridge onto the North Face above the so-called Yellow Band of rock above 28,000 feet. Norton, with Somervell not feeling well and trailing far behind, had reached the great snowy gully and tried to fight his way almost vertically up the couloir. But the snow was almost waist deep. And where it wasn't, the downward-tilting slabs were covered with ice. Norton finally began to realize how precarious his position was—one glance under his sliding feet showed a direct drop to the Rongbuk Glacier some 8,000 feet below—and he was forced to end his summit attempt, descending *very* slowly to Somervell and asking in a shaky voice if they could rope up. (This sudden loss of nerve after daring attempts, in climbs with terrible exposure, wasn't uncommon, even in the Alps. It was as if the brain, suddenly clicking on a survival instinct, finally overrode the adrenaline and ambition of even the most courageous climber. Those who didn't heed this "loss of nerve" in truly dangerous situations—such as George Mallory—often didn't return from climbs.)

Norton's couloir effort had been an astounding attempt. A new altitude record of 28,126 feet—surpassed, if it all, only by Mallory and Irvine on their fatal final attempt along the windy North East Ridge.

But most would-be Everest climbers had written off Norton's Couloir as impossible. Too steep. Too much loose snow. Too much vertical climb. Too serious a penalty for a single slip after too many hours at too high and cold a place under the most extreme exertion possible.

"Why not use crampons to climb Norton's Couloir?" asked Jean-Claude. "Or even along the steep snow ramps above twenty-seven thousand feet on the East Ridge or North East Ridge, where only Mallory and Irvine have gone?"

The end of that sentence chilled me. But then, I'd taken off the Finch balloon coat and a cold breeze was coming down Cwm Idwal and across Llyn Idwal.

"Crampons don't work on a snowfield as steep as Norton's Couloir," I said irritably. "Or even on the high-ridge snowfields below where they established high camp at around twenty-seven thousand feet."

"Why not?" asked Jean-Claude with that maddening Gallic smugness.

"Because human feet and ankles don't bend that way, God damn it!" I said loudly. "And because crampons can't keep a grip on steep snow slopes when the climber's weight isn't above them, bearing down on them. You *know* that, J.C.!"

"Yes, I know that, Jake," he said, dropping his old crampons onto the snow.

"I think our friend has something to show us," said the Deacon. His pipe was puffing along well now, and he spoke through gritted teeth.

Jean-Claude smiled, bent to his big bag, and pulled out a single, shiningly new metal crampon. It took me a few seconds to see the difference.

"It has front spikes...points," I said at last. "Like horns."

"Twelve-point crampons," said Jean-Claude, his tone brisk and businesslike now. "The German ice climbers were talking about them. I had my father design and manufacture them."

We all knew that Jean-Claude's father had gone from being a blacksmith to running one of the biggest metal-pouring and forming companies in all of France, certainly in Chamonix. M. Clairoux Sr.'s business had grown by leaps and bounds thanks to French government (and some British and one American) contracts during the Great War. Now they produced everything from specialized steel pipelines to dental instruments.

"That looks dangerous," I said.

"It is," said Jean-Claude. "To the mountain that does not want to be climbed."

"I think I understand," said the Deacon, stepping forward to take the scary-looking 12-point crampon in his hand. "You kick these points in, put your weight on the solid, almost unbending shank of your new stiff boots, and use it as a platform. Even—theoretically—on near-vertical ice."

"*Oui,*" said Jean-Claude. "But not just on 'near-vertical,' my friend. On sheer vertical. And worse than vertical. I have tested them in France. We shall test them here today."

I confess that my heart started pounding rapidly. I've never enjoyed ice climbing. I hate surfaces where my boots can't get a grip, however tenuous. J.C.'s "we shall test them here today" made my cold skin go clammy.

"There is more," said Jean-Claude. "Show me your ice axes, my friends."

We'd brought ours with us, of course. I pulled mine out of the snow and set it in front of me: long wood shaft and metal adze and pick on top. The Deacon retrieved his ice axe from the snow and leaned on it.

"How long is your ice axe, Jake?" asked J.C.

"Thirty-eight inches. I like that shorter length for cutting steps on a steep slope."

"And yours, Richard?" *Ree-shard.*

"Forty-eight inches. It's old-fashioned, I know. But so am I."

Jean-Claude merely nodded. Then he reached into the bulging bag in the snow and brought out a series of "ice axes" that weren't ice axes at all. The longest couldn't have been much more than 20 inches or so in length. They were hammers, for God's sake. Only with different adzes and picks atop each wooden or...dear Christ...*steel* shaft.

J.C.'s daddy had been busy at his steel-fitting plant.

"Your designs?" asked the Deacon, hefting one of these absurd hammer-things.

J.C. shrugged. "Based on what the Germans have been doing this year—you two told me so yourselves after you returned from Munich last November. So I climbed icy routes with them in Chamonix in December—with some young Germans, that is—saw their new techniques, used some of their new equipment. Then I made my own variations at *l'usine de mon père* to improve what they had."

"Those aren't ice axes!" I was almost spluttering.

"No?"

"*No,*" I said. "You couldn't hike with any of those, couldn't lean on them, couldn't even cut ice steps on a steep slope."

Jean-Claude held up one finger. "*Au contraire,*" he said softly, lifting one of the five short axe-hammer-things he'd left lying on the canvas bag. The one he was holding up looked most like a regular ice axe—wood shaft and all—but like a real ice axe that had been left out in the rain and shrunk by two-thirds. But instead of there being an adze on one side, as our ice axes had, the short end was as blunt as a hammer. It *was* a hammer.

"This ice hammer, my father and I call it 'straight drooped,'" said J.C., "is superb for cutting steps on a steep ice or snow slope. And one does not have to lean out of balance as one would with either of our old longer ice axes."

I just shook my head.

"The shortest one is there," said the Deacon, pointing to a large hammer-sized thing made entirely of steel with a pointed and sort of threaded base and a long, flat pick on one side and very short adze on the other.

J.C. smiled and lifted it, then handed it to the Deacon, who took it in his free hand. "Light. Aluminum?"

"No, steel. But hollow in the shaft. This is what Father and I called the 'technically curved' short ice axe. For use on steep ice slopes, perfect for carving steps. This slightly longer one with the wooden handle, the one which looks more like a shortened version of a regular ice axe but with this long, curved, serrated pick, we called the 'reverse curved' axe. It is used"—he turned to the impossibly vertical ice wall behind him—"for *that.*"

The Deacon had handed the two short ice axes to me and was rubbing his stubbled cheeks and chin. He hadn't bothered to shave that morning, though we'd finally procured some hot water at that execrable inn.

"I'm beginning to see," he said.

I was making axe-weapon downward swings with both sharp-picked... things. I imagined the long, curved picks penetrating a French skull.

"How did you find this place... Cwm Idwal?" asked the Deacon. He was craning backward to look up at the vertical ice cliff, now glistening wickedly in the late-morning sun. Its terrifying slab of rock and ice hung directly above us like a giant weight that could drop 200 feet onto us at any time. The overhang was just too broad and thick to free-climb—the width of rock twice Jean-Claude's entire height, at least, and the slabs of ice extending another five or six feet. There would be no sane way to get to the vertical rock and ice above the overhang for the last icy pitch of eight feet or so.

"I asked British ice climbers for the best place in England and Wales," responded Jean-Claude.

"There *are* British ice climbers?" asked the Deacon. I didn't know if he was faking his tone of wonder and surprise. I'd always assumed that the Deacon personally knew *all* British climbers. And most of the French and German ones as well.

"A very few," said J.C. with a small smile.

"What next?" asked the Deacon, pointing to the still mostly full bag, sounding eager to see the next weird thing to pop out.

Jean-Claude Clairoux turned around, stepped back, shielded his eyes, and joined the Deacon in looking up at the sheer ice wall and terrifying overhang. "Next," he said, his voice almost lost in the rising breeze, "...next, all three of us climb that wall today. All of it. Including the overhang. To the top."

All right, I'll be honest. I would have pissed my silken underwear and new woolen knickerbockers at that moment if I hadn't been sure it would have frozen into a long and very uncomfortable icicle.

"You...can...*not*...be...fucking...serious," I said to my diminutive French ex-friend. It was only the second time in my life that I'd ever used that word and certainly the first time in the presence of my two new climbing partners.

J.C. smiled.

From the largest bag, J.C. had pulled out three sturdy but light leather..."harnesses" is the word that comes to mind—although there were metal carabiners on the front of the belt, where straps met in the center of the chest, and more loops and carabiners around the wide belt—and while the Deacon and I were tugging our harnesses on, dubiously, Jean-Claude simply lifted his left leg as high as it would go, kicked his new forward crampons of the 12-point set into the wall of ice, hammered in the pick end of both of his short ice axes—connected to his wrists, I noticed now, by short leather straps and loops—and pulled himself up until he was supporting himself just on that rigid left foot. His harness jingled because he was carrying a variety of self-designed steel implements on it—an extra ice tool of some sort set in its holster, a mass of shiny carabiners, a large bag of ice screws, other bags of jangly things set around his belt. A huge coil of rope was slung over his shoulder and across his chest, and now he slowly let it out beneath him as he started to climb.

He pulled the short ice axe in his right hand down, jiggled it, pulled it out of the ice, and hammered the pick head in deep another four feet up. Still holding his weight on that left foot—easily, I thought—J.C. kicked his right foot into position several feet higher, wiggled the forward crampons of his left foot out of the ice, and pulled himself upward with the strength of both arms. He banged the left ice axe deep in the wall higher than the right axe, lifted his left foot, and kicked it into the ice.

Standing as casually and easily six feet up the ice wall as he might have on a city sidewalk, J.C. looked over his shoulder at the Deacon—who'd finally got the harness rigged right—and said, "If this were the ice wall below the North Col and we had to prepare it for other climbers and porters, how long do you think it would take to hack out the necessary steps?"

The Deacon squinted upward. "It's too steep for steps. And the overhang...it's impossible. Porters wouldn't do it, even with fixed ropes."

"All right, then," said J.C., not even breathing hard as he stood on that vertical face, "we'll bring something like the hundred-foot ladder that Sandy Irvine strung together for the porters last year. For the porters to use when they follow us."

"That was after Mallory had free-climbed the chimney—a fissure in the ice wall," said the Deacon. "They also rigged a pulley to pull up loads."

"But assuming one could climb this wall just by cutting steps," persisted Jean-Claude. "How long for the first ascent?"

The Deacon looked upward again. The sunlight on the vertical ice was blinding. He tugged his goggles on. "Three hours," said the Deacon. "Maybe four. Maybe five."

"Seven," I said. "At least seven hours."

J.C. smiled and began kicking and hammering his way up the ice wall again. Every 30 feet or so he would stop, create a tiny hole in the ice above or in front of him by tapping with the pointed end of his pick, remove a 12- to 18-centimeter ice screw from the bag on his belt, and screw it in by hand, the screw always angled uphill—that is, downward into the ice—with an angle of what I judged to be 45 to 60 degrees against the direction of his weight and pull. Sometimes, when the ice was so hard that the screw would not go in fully, J.C. used the sharp point of his ice axe pick or some sort of ice tool from his belt inserted into the eye of the screw to gain greater leverage for screwing it in.

Each time he finished fastening a deep ice screw, he would snap on a carabiner and test it with his weight, his boot crampons never leaving the ice.

Even with the pauses to put in the ice screw protection every ten yards or so, Jean-Claude was scrambling up the ice wall like a spider. Sometimes he would bang both ice hammers into the ice—connected only by a bifurcated tether running from the carabiner set into the chest piece on his harness to the wrist loops—and use both hands to secure a tough ice screw.

As he climbed higher and higher, it became harder and harder for me to watch these moves. Theoretically, his rope—which he'd run through a complicated series of knots on the chest and belly side of his harness—would break his fall if he came off the wall, but if he did come off at the high point of his next pitch, before he'd put in the next ice screw, it would be a 60-foot vertical fall before the rope would catch on the eye of the inset ice screw. Very few climbers, even given good footing and a possible belay point, could belay a man who'd fallen 60 vertical feet. Too much mass. Too much velocity after that long a fall.

Besides, climbing ropes in 1925 almost always snapped when put under that much pressure.

This was when I noticed that Jean-Claude's huge coil of rope looked so large not only because he had more than 200 feet of it across his chest when he started, but also because the rope that now spiderwebbed down the ice wall was *thicker* than the kind we always used.

Jean-Claude continued scrambling vertically up the impossible ice wall, shifting a few feet or yards left and right when he had to avoid rotten ice or outcroppings, so that the fixed rope behind him did begin to look a little spiderwebby.

The Deacon had taken his gold watch out of his waistcoat pocket and was looking at it. I knew the watch was also a chronometer. He was timing our friend.

When the now diminutive figure reached the 15-foot rock-and-ice overhang 180 or so feet up the vertical wall, he clipped his chest or waist harness carabiner (it was hard to tell which from this distance) to a thick strap attached to the last ice screw he'd just put in at the junction of wall and overhang, and shouted down (sounding only a little breathless), "How much time?"

"Twenty-one minutes," the Deacon shouted back, putting his watch away.

I could see Jean-Claude shake his head. He was wearing a floppy red stocking cap, not quite a beret. "I could do it in half that time with more practice. And...," he looked straight down through the V of his widened legs, "...fewer ice screws, I think."

"You've shown us, Jean-Claude," shouted the Deacon. "You've proven your new hardware! It's brilliant. Now come on down!"

The figure leaning back in his harness straps almost 200 feet above us shook his head. He shouted something that neither the Deacon nor I could make out.

"I said—'to the top,'" he shouted again, looking straight down at us between his legs again.

I was actually wringing my hands with anxiety, which made little sense since I was the sheer-face rock climber of the three of us. I was supposed to love this kind of vertical test—lots of exposure and fissured rock and even some modest overhangs for an extra challenge. But this... *this* was suicide.

I realized then that I really *hated* ice. And the idea of going up Mount Everest with these stupid harnesses and all this clanking metal—"bloody ironmongers" was what the British climbers derisively called the Germans and the few French who were using metal carabiners, pitons, and such on tough rock faces and slopes—seemed suddenly obscene. Obscene and absurd.

I also realized at that moment how nervous I was. I'd never felt this tense climbing on high alpine ledges, ridges, faces, summits, or slopes with these two men.

I looked up expecting J.C. to begin his descent. He had enough rope left that he could rappel a good part of the way. *If* he trusted those damned ice screws.

Instead of rappelling or scuttling down the way he'd gone up, Jean-Claude Clairoux then did something that to this day, more than sixty-five years later, I do not believe.

First, a strap still connecting his chest harness to the ice screw he'd just put in at the topmost section of the vertical part of the wall, J.C. leaned back until it was just the tension of that five-foot leash holding him almost horizontally on the ice. He then drove both hammers into the overhang ice as far out as he could reach. Then J.C. raised his feet—I had to look away it was so appalling, then looked back to watch him fall—and planted his crampons and toe crampons firmly in the corner where vertical wall and horizontal overhang came together.

Somehow he hung there horizontally with one arm supporting the weight of his entire body while he drove in a deep screw—he had to bang on it to get it in the last few centimeters, and I heard steel going into solid rock under the ice—then he clipped a carabiner and a sort of double tether leash to that and let himself down until he was hanging horizontally only from the ropes, perhaps seven feet beneath the overhang.

Then, using his steel crampon tips against the vertical wall on each inward oscillation, he began to pendulum-swing back and forth, completely dependent upon that one ice screw and the rope, no point of his body in contact with the wall or overhang except when he kicked harder each time to pendulum out further.

"Mother of God," whispered the Deacon. Or perhaps I did. I really no longer remember.

But I do remember Jean-Claude's outer pendulum motion under that 20-foot-wide overhang stopping when he banged both ice axes into the ice ceiling above him. Only one held, but he pulled himself higher so that there was slack in the rope tether, from which he was dangling horizontally. He kicked until both sets of points at the front of his rigid-shank boots were attached to the ceiling again. Then he pounded in the other ice axe.

All good climbers have to be strong. Look at our forearms and you will see bulk and muscles rare in any other athlete and missing from almost all "normal" people. But to hang there like that, suspending the full weight of his fully horizontal body—more than horizontal, since his head was lower than his boots cramponed into the ice—to hold on using only the strength of his hands on two short ice axes, the strength of those two forearms and upper arms. Impossible.

But he did.

Then he released one of the ice axes. His left hand fumbled on his harness belt for an ice screw from the dangling bag of hardware.

It slipped out of fingers that must have been close to nerveless by then, and fell 200 feet. The Deacon and I stepped aside as the long screw bounced off a low boulder between us, sending up sparks against the snow all around.

J.C. calmly reached for another screw, righting the carrying bag so no more hardware tumbled out. Shifting hands on the embedded ice axes so his weight was now supported by his left hand, Jean-Claude calmly screwed in that final ice anchor. He had to use the small steel ice tool from his belt to get it through the last of the ice, then pound it into the underlying rock. Why he didn't come off the overhang when he did that work, I'll never understand.

His next move—after letting out another seven or eight feet of harnessed leash—was to dangle, head and feet lower than his supported torso, and swing wildly back and forth. The far point of his outer swing took him out further than the edge of the overhang. Back and forth he went, and I waited for the sight and sound of both of the screws set into the ice ceiling popping out, sending him hurtling 30 or 60 feet down and back into the ice wall, almost certainly rendering him unconscious. One of us would have to ice-climb the fixed rope to retrieve our unconscious or dead friend. I didn't want it to be me.

Instead of peeling off, Jean-Claude's arc went beyond and above the edge of the overhang, and on the second swing at that distance, he banged in the curved picks of both ice hammers.

Freeing one at a time, he pulled himself higher, again just with the strength of arms and forearms that must be shaking with tension and toxins by now.

Seven feet up the 12-foot outside vertical wall of the ice overhang, he kicked the toes of his new-style ice-climbing crampons into the ice and calmly screwed in the last piece of steel protection he needed. The only sign of J.C.'s great fatigue — or perhaps the backwash of adrenaline that always gets a climber's hands and fingers shaking after the fact in a truly terrifying situation — was that after he'd clipped in a carabiner and used Y tethers to tie into both his chest and belt harness, he leaned back from the short ice wall at about 40 degrees to rest a couple of minutes. His short ice axes dangled from his wrist straps. Even from more than 200 feet below, I could see him clenching and unclenching the fingers of both hands.

Then he grasped both ice axes, straightened up, and began hacking and climbing again.

The Deacon and I watched him lean over the top of the overhang, sink his right ice hammer point into something, and then he pulled himself up and out of sight over the edge.

A minute later he was standing near that edge, taking the remnants of the coil of rope from over his shoulder, and shouting down at us.

"I have about a hundred feet left," came the echoing, triumphant shout. "I've tied both off — we'll want two ropes for belay — so bring up around another hundred feet of rope, the thicker stuff, the Deacon's Miracle Rope, that I brought, in the second bag, and you can tie it on halfway up. Who's next?"

The Deacon and I looked at each other.

Again, I was the "big face" rock climber of the trio. I was the one who would be expected to free-climb rock on Everest, say, if we ever reached that battleship prow of the so-called Second Step near the summit along the North East Ridge above 28,000 feet.

But for the moment, I was terrified.

"I'm next," said the Deacon and, shrugging on a 100-foot coil of J.C.'s "good rope," walked up to the ice wall with both ice hammers raised.

None of us wanted to stay in that pathetic inn again in Cerrigydrudion or anyplace close to Wales, so the Deacon drove us all the way back to London through the dusk and long, dark night. The Vauxhall's headlights were still little more than useless, but once on the real highways again after dark, he tucked the Vauxhall in behind various lorries and we followed them closely, using their tiny little red taillights as our guide. We'd taken time to wrestle and button and snap the roof, windows, and side flaps back into place. Somehow the heater seemed to be working at last (or perhaps it was just our overheated bodies), and Jean-Claude was sprawled across the cushions and gear bags in the backseat, snoring all the way home. When the Deacon and I talked, it was in low, almost reverent voices. I kept thinking about the incredible day and the incredible revelations Jean-Claude had given us.

My own climb, when my time came, wasn't nearly as bad as I'd feared. The ice hammers and 12-point crampons with the deep-digging front points gave one a feeling almost of invincibility. Also, the Deacon had brought up an extra 100 feet of what J.C. called "the Deacon's Miracle Rope" and tied on to his second line, so—counting the first fixed rope—I was essentially under double belay the whole way up.

This came in handy when twice I was a little too eager to remove my crampons before securing my next hold with three solid points and came unglued from the wall, but while it might have been a thrill to drop the 50 feet or so to arrest (or non-arrest) by the last ice screw below me, the second belay rope, tied to a massive tree somewhere out of sight above the overhang and physically belayed by the Deacon, caught me in five feet or so.

The overhang itself, which had so unnerved me while watching from below, was sort of fun. I was worried about my extra weight on the two ice screws that had held for the two lighter climbers before me, but the Deacon had taken time—while hanging horizontally under the ice-rock overhang—to secure a third and even longer screw in place, banging the hell out of it to get it the last five or six centimeters into the rock itself.

So I actually enjoyed swinging out wide, nothing beneath me at the outer arc of my swing but 200 feet of empty air to the rock below, and I successfully smashed both ice hammer picks into the outer, vertical section of the overhang on my first try. Those years of serious rock climbing, it turned out, were not wasted on ice: I pulled myself the last ten feet to the top using only the strength of my arms fiercely gripping the ice hammers. Once I was on top—the view of Llyn Idwal and Cwm Idwal and the peaks and lakes beyond was fantastic—Jean-Claude reprimanded me for not using my crampons on that last bit, but all I could do was grin at him.

We'd rappelled down one after the other, leaving the second belay rope in place, and then practiced for the rest of the day on the lower slopes. Only the Deacon's new rope—a thicker-diameter blend of hemp, regular climbing rope, and some secret ingredient he wouldn't reveal to us (but which gave the rope greater elasticity and a much higher breaking point)—gave us the confidence to rappel that way. In 1924–25, few alpine climbers trusted their ropes—what the Deacon now called "our old clothesline ropes"—for such long rappels.

Trying to stay awake during the long drive back to London—just to keep the Deacon company as he drove, so *he'd* stay awake—my tired mind kept going over and over the French terms that J.C. had tried to drill into us about this new type of glacier and ice climbing.

Pied marche—just marching across flat ice or a shallow slope up to 15 degrees, as if across a glacier—we'd all done that together on regular 10-point crampons many times before.

Pied en canard—"duck walk"—a careful 12-point cramponing on slopes up to 30 degrees. It looked and felt as silly as it sounded, but we could use our old, longer ice axes for that.

Pied à plat—literally "flat-footed," with the bottom 10 points on each crampon holding your body upright on slopes up to 65 degrees or so, with your ice axe dug in uphill. A good way to rest.

Then there were the regular ice axe moves themselves: *piolet ramasse* (cross-body) on slopes from 35 to 50 degrees (an elegant way to cut steps in a steep slope) and *piolet ancre,* the anchored way one could cut steps or do hand work (such as sinking ice screws with one's free hand) on steep slopes, 45 to 60 degrees and steeper.

The ice hammers had their own vocabularies—angle of pick entrance, whether to hold the tools high or low while climbing, etc.—and the ones I remember from that first day were *piolet panne* (low dagger) for steep slopes 45 to 55 degrees; *piolet poignard* (high dagger), which we used on steeper slopes of 50 to 60 degrees; and the most common one we used that day, *piolet traction* (traction), on 60 degrees to vertical to overhanging.

Since these last techniques were all used with the "front-pointing" crampons, techniques which I was sure Jean-Claude had said he'd learned from the Germans and Austrians while ice climbing with them the previous December, I was a little confused as to why there weren't any terms in German. The answer was simple: the Germans and Austrians had kept using the old French 10-point crampon and long ice axe terms and simply added more in French. Ahh, Europe.

What we began learning on shallower—but still deadly slick—ice slopes around Llyn Idwal that Sunday afternoon is what I think of (to this day, after using them thousands of times since) as the "dance steps": *pied à plat–piolet ramasse,* for instance—flat-footing upslope while simultaneously using the short ice axe in a graceful cross-body position to find the next anchor. J.C. did this so beautifully on a steep but less-than-vertical slope that it was a delight to watch—left leg bent inward until he was slightly knock-kneed, short ice axe held in both hands and pressing down higher up the slope, then the right leg crossing over the left as if in a tricky dance step, and then, when the tip of the ice axe and 10 of the 12-point crampon steel teeth on the right boot were all pressing down into the ice again, swinging the left leg higher upslope until 10 crampons on the bottom of *that* foot got a solid bite.

And then starting the dance all over again.

Jean-Claude showed us various ways to rest on such an exhaustingly steep slope, but my favorite was the simple *pied assis*—leaning back on the slope until your butt almost (but not quite) touched the ice, left leg bent and left foot under you with all crampons pressing down, right leg further outward with ankle turned so the right boot and its crampons were at almost a 90-degree angle from the direction one's right knee was pointing. You didn't need your ice axe or ice hammers to hold this position, and the result was that, as long as the muscles in your legs and thighs didn't start cramping, you could hold this position for an extended time, ice axe in both hands, giving yourself plenty of time to look out over the slope and up and out at the landscape below.

But the bulk of the afternoon into the lovely Welsh sunset was spent learning how to use the shortest ice axe and the ice hammers in basic low-dagger and high-dagger positions, front-pointing (using only the forward two crampons of the twelve) in anchor positions, front-pointing in traction positions, front-pointing in high-dagger position (the way we'd climbed the vertical ice wall), the three-o'clock position using both ice hammers ahead of you on a steep slope with the right leg curved and slammed down behind you, front-pointing on a terribly steep slope so that your weight was over the ice hammers with picks down in a low-dagger position (climbing with both at once, essentially under you), and so forth.

Traverse and descent techniques on the ice—especially the rapid descent (I'd always loved glissading down a steep snowfield, using only my regular ice axe as a rudder and then for self-arrest near the bottom, and J.C. showed us how we could flat-foot down on crampons, using the cross-body position with the short axe or trailing the axe behind us in anchor position, almost as quickly and on much more dramatic inclines)—took most of the rest of the afternoon.

Later that afternoon, on a steep snowy slope below a rock face, Jean-Claude showed us his last technological tour de force.

It was a small and relatively light metal wedge-shaped device that had steel springs—released by hand pressure, tightening automatically when you exerted no pressure—that could slide along a fixed rope. J.C. had laboriously climbed the slope in his new 12-point crampons, attached the Deacon's Miracle Rope to a long ice axe driven deep into the ice under the boulders some 150 meters above us, reinforced that belay with several ice screws, and then removed his crampons and expertly glissaded down the steep slope to us. The rope lay like a long black fault line on the blindingly white snow.

Then J.C. showed that he had one of these hand clamps for the rope for each of us.

"It is simple, *non?*" he said. "Release the hand pressure completely, and it locks tight to the rope. One could dangle if one chose. Squeeze ever so slightly with one hand, and the mechanism glides along the rope as if the rope were a guide. Squeeze hard, and the mechanism—and you—no longer has...how do you pronounce it? *Friction? Friction* on the rope."

"What do you suggest we use this gadget for?" I asked, but I saw that the Deacon had grasped the idea.

"It would be best if it were attached to some light climbing harness," said the Deacon. "So that one could have both hands free while staying attached to the fixed rope."

"*Exactement!*" cried Jean-Claude. "I am working on precisely such light leather and canvas harnesses. For today, though, we try the one hand, no?"

And with that J.C. clamped his little device onto the fixed rope and began sliding it up as he climbed steadily, even without crampons. The Deacon went next, getting the hang of when to apply pressure, when to release it, within a few paces. It took me longer, but soon I realized the added security of climbing with this silly little spring-driven device gripping the fixed rope harder than one's heavily mittened hand ever could. It would give even more assurance if it were attached, say, by a line and carabiner, to the climbing harness that he and the Deacon had been talking about.

At the top of our 150-meter 50-degree slope, we huddled together as a cold wind rose. The sun was setting behind peaks to the west. The moon was rising in the east.

"Now we use it for a controlled descent," said Jean-Claude. "You will see, I believe, that one could use this device even on vertical fixed ropes. It is, how do you say it? Proof for fools?"

"Foolproof," said the Deacon. "Show us the fast descent."

So J.C. unclamped his device from the double line of fixed rope—double so we could retrieve the rope after our rappel down the slope—retrieved the ice axe so that only the deep screws held the doubled line on belay, re-clamped onto the line below me, and began a rapid, no-crampon glissade that he controlled only by the spring pressure of the device in his hand.

"Incredible!" I gasped as the Deacon and I reached the bottom after one of the fastest glissades I'd ever experienced.

"We shall practice more later before we leave and during the trek in to Everest," said Jean-Claude.

We were in twilight shadow now and it suddenly became very cold. J.C. was already pulling the rope free of its needle-eye ice screws and retrieving the long line.

"Do you have a name for this device?" asked the Deacon.

J.C. grinned as he expertly wrapped the long coil of Miracle Rope from his fist to his elbow, coil and coil again. "Jumar," he said.

"What does that mean in French?" I asked. "What does it stand for?"

"Nothing," says J.C. "It was the name of my dog when I was a boy. He could climb a tree after a squirrel if he chose. I have never seen a better dog-climber."

"Jumar," I repeated. Odd word. I wasn't sure that I'd ever get used to it.

"I've been worrying about that last ice wall between the Rongbuk Glacier to the North Col on Everest for some months," the Deacon said quietly as we approached London and the murky winter sunrise.

I nodded awake. "Why?" I whispered. "In 'twenty-two, you and Finch and the others found snow slopes up to the Col and cut steps for the porters. Last June there weren't any snow slopes, but there was that fissure—the ice chimney—that Mallory free-climbed and dropped fixed ropes and then Sandy Irvine's jury-rigged rope ladder down."

The Deacon bobbed his head slightly. "But Rongbuk is a *glacier*, Jake. It rises, subsides, fissures, faults, moves, crumbles, creates its own crevasses. All we know for sure is that it won't be as it was last year for Mallory—a chance to show off his climbing techniques—or for Finch and us the year before that. This spring that ice wall may have climbable fissures or new snow slopes—or it may be two hundred feet of vertical ice."

"Well, if it is sheer vertical ice," I said, tiredly but with a new sense of bravado, "J.C. and his front-point crampons and silly little ice axes and the whatchamacallems—jumars—have given us a way to climb it."

The Deacon drove in silence for a moment. I could see the dome of Saint Paul's coming over the horizon with the sun.

"Then, Jake," he said, "I shall have to assume that we are ready to go climb Mount Everest."

I just wish this Lord Bromley-Whatsis, his serene bug-
gering Highness, had bloody well buggered himself down
to Calcutta from the hills and helped us bandobast *these*
buggering great heavy crates to the bloody freight depot a
full buggering day earlier, is what I damn well wish.

---

*C*alcutta is a terrifying city, with Kipling's "sheeted dead" underfoot on an evening walk—not dead bodies, it turns out, but
people wrapped in their sheets and sleeping on what passes for side-
walks—and everything smelling of incense, spices, human piss, cattle,
the not unpleasant sweat-and-breath scent of multitudes, and fragrant
smoke from burning cow dung. All the dark-skinned men's stares are curious, dismissive, or outright angry, while the women's stares—even the
Mohammedan women's eyes peering out from beneath and above the
black cloth covering them from head to foot—are alluring, inviting,
and, for me, filled with sexual promise.

It is only the twenty-second of March, 1925, far from the terrible
summer pre-monsoon heat and the downpours of the later-summer monsoon rains, but the air of Calcutta already feels like a wad of wet blankets
wrapped around me head to toe.

At least these have been my impressions so far during our two and a
half days here.

Everything is strange to me. Even though I'd crossed the Atlantic
in a liner from Boston to Europe last year, the five weeks of travel on
the HMS *Caledonia* from Liverpool to Calcutta seemed a thousand times
more exotic. The first days were rough going—the tugs barely got us
out of Liverpool harbor against the wind and waves—and I was surprised to find out that I was the only one of the three of us who did not
succumb to seasickness at some point on the voyage. The pitching and
rolling seemed like a fine game, a simple challenge in getting from Point

A to Point B and then onward and upward to the wooden deck, where I ran my twelve miles daily and nightly in a pitching, rolling oval, and I never had a hint of the nausea that all but ruined the early part of the voyage for Jean-Paul and the Deacon.

Except for the slow boredom of transiting the Suez Canal and the storm in the western Mediterranean that kept me belowdecks for a day, the voyage to Calcutta was a pleasant experience. At Colombo—a small white town seemingly being besieged by ferocious, impenetrable jungle on all sides—I bought some lace and mailed it to my mother and aunt in Boston. Everything was new and exciting. And I knew—but did not then fully appreciate—that everything was prelude.

The 1921, '22, and '24 Everest expeditions all came through Calcutta on the way to their official starting point—Darjeeling—but funded and backed as they were by the Mount Everest Committee of the Alpine Club and that club's parent, the Royal Geographical Society, there were always agents in Calcutta ready to sort out the crates of supplies and matériel, so that when the climbers arrived, everything they needed was either already loaded onto the train for Darjeeling or ready to be loaded.

We, of course, being a secret and illicit expedition, have no agents waiting in Calcutta. The Deacon is in charge of spending Lady Bromley's money—at least until "Cousin Reggie" takes over here in India—and the Deacon soon tells Jean-Claude and me the Hindi word *bandobast,* meaning "arrangements." Evidently *bandobast* in Calcutta (where most of the people speak Bengali, not Hindi, but the word is still used here, it being, I assume, almost a universal concept in all of multilingual and multiethnic India) means the same as *baksheesh* in the Middle East—i.e., bribes necessary to get even the simplest thing done.

But since the Deacon was on the two earliest Alpine Club expeditions with Mallory and others and was interested in all aspects of them, including this administrative greasing of the wheels to get things done in Calcutta (and, Jean-Claude and I can only hope, later in both Darjeeling and Tibet), our twelve heavy crates—amongst other things we had to bring from Europe, we're bringing *a lot* of the Deacon's new high-quality rope on this expedition for reasons I'll explain later—have been moved

from the docks to the train station freight depot by early this third afternoon of our stay in Calcutta.

There is a night train from Sealdah Station just beyond Calcutta
called the Darjeeling Mail that we'll be taking in a few hours, but that
train—a real train, as it were—only goes as far as Siliguri, a little trading station out in the middle of nowhere which we're supposed to reach
about 6:30 the next morning. There we'll have to switch to the Darjeeling Himalayan Railway, by all accounts a narrow-gauge toy of a train
that has to chug its way 7,000 feet up the mountain foothills of the
southernmost Himalayas to Darjeeling, where the Bengali English government of the Raj spends its summers. The entire train voyage will be
about 400 miles, and the Deacon informs us that it will probably be too
hot and dusty to get any sleep during the Darjeeling Mail part of it.

No matter. I don't plan to spend much of the time on the train sleeping at any rate.

We receive a telegram from "Cousin Reggie" on our first morning
here:

MEET AT HOTEL MT EVEREST DARJEELING TUES. 24 MARCH.
I WILL ASSUME COMMAND OF THE EXPEDITION AT THAT
POINT.
    L./ R. K. BROMLEY-MONTFORT

"'Assume command of the expedition,' my arse," says the Deacon, crum-
pling the telegram flimsy in his long-fingered hand and throwing it on
the ground.

"What does the 'L.-slash' in this thing stand for?" asks Jean-Claude,
who is retrieving and flattening out the crumpled telegram.

"'Lord,' I presume," says the Deacon, biting down so hard on the stem
of his unlighted pipe that I expect it to snap. "Lord Reginald K.-some-
thing Bromley-Montfort."

"Why does he keep the Bromley in his name?" I ask. The ways of British near-royalty are still a mystery to me.

"How the hell should I know?" snaps the Deacon. He is rarely this
short-tempered. Both Jean-Claude and I take a step backward, shocked
by his tone. "I just wish this Lord Bromley-Whatsis, his serene bugger-

ing Highness, had bloody well buggered himself down to Calcutta from the hills and helped us *bandobast* these buggering great heavy crates to the bloody freight depot a full buggering day earlier, is what I damn well wish. This is *his* lousy country, *his* culture where bloody damn venal bribery is necessary everywhere to get the least bloody thing done, and where no one can keep a simple bloody appointment on time. So where *is* this 'commander of the expedition' when we actually *need* his fat arse?"

Jean-Claude and I look at each other and I think we are thinking the same thing. When George Mallory came this way a year earlier, he had no administrative responsibilities until they reached Tibet and the team leader, Geoffrey Bruce, fell ill during the five-week trek in to Everest Base Camp. Because of Bruce's heart problems and trouble adapting to altitude even on the Tibetan passes long before Everest came into sight, the expedition's doctor ordered the 58-year-old Bruce back to Darjeeling, and Colonel Norton, who had been the climbing leader, assumed overall command of the expedition with Mallory becoming climbing leader.

But even with the responsibility of planning the climbing logistics, Mallory had been free of the heavier administrative responsibilities of overseeing the entire expedition, renting mules and porters, handling all the Tibetan governmental and other requirements, and — most tiring — dealing with the personalities and sudden illnesses and weaknesses of the entire British climbing team and its mélange of more than a hundred porters.

Jean-Claude and I stare at each other after the Deacon's sudden outburst — as I say, in the more than year and a half I've known Richard Davis Deacon, I've never heard anything like this from him (his usual response to logistical or climbing setbacks is a shrug and an ironic smile, followed by the lighting of his pipe) — and I know we're both thinking that while Jean-Claude and I had been free to enjoy the ocean voyage here (or, for J.C., "enjoy" it between brief bouts of debilitating seasickness in the choppy parts), the Deacon had been dealing with thousands of unsettled money, administrative, logistical, and climbing details.

During the trip on the HMS *Caledonia,* although the Deacon did some daily exercising to stay in shape, he never had the time to go jogging miles around the pitching deck as I did each day. Usually he could be found at his tiny first-class stateroom desk, poring over topographic maps of Everest and its vicinity, photographs, and the private and public accounts of the three previous British expeditions—including a score of notebooks that the Deacon himself had filled during the '21 and '22 expeditions before he'd fallen out of grace with Mallory.

We are only on the first step of the trip—preparing for the train ride from Calcutta to Sealdah to the little town of Siliguri and then uphill to Darjeeling, where the real trek to Everest always begins—but the Deacon is exhausted.

And it's even more than that, I also realize. The Deacon has been infuriated by this Lord Bromley-Montfort's arrogant telegram. This "Cousin Reggie" was supposed to finance our expedition from Darjeeling on to Everest, not "take command of it." I don't blame the Deacon for his reaction—I'm seriously worried about what will happen when the two men actually meet sometime in the next forty-eight hours—and I have the sickening sense that our entire Mount Everest expedition may be in imminent danger of collapsing. It certainly wouldn't be the first major mountaineering expedition that failed early because of conflict between two would-be leaders. (Nor, as I will notice over the next sixty-nine years, would it be the last.)

But then we're leaving Sealdah Station in the loud, infernally hot, and eternally dusty first-class section of the equally loud, infernally hot, and eternally dusty first leg to Siliguri, and I find myself staring out at some of the most boring landscape I've ever traversed: endless rice paddies, interrupted only by plantations of various kinds of palm trees. It is also a chaotic train, with second- and third-class and non-paying passengers hanging from every door and window and many more on the rooftop of every car except the first-class ones. As darkness falls, the number of villages we're passing on this great, flat plain becomes obvious by the thousands of campfires and lantern lights we glimpse. A million people appear to be preparing their dinners at the same time, most over simple open fires in or near their open-doored homes, and—from the not totally unpleasant scent that fills the air even with our windows closed, the air moving only because of small electric fans set high on the walls turning slowly—it becomes obvious, and is confirmed by the Deacon, that most of the cooking fires we pass in the encroaching dusk are fueled by dried cow dung.

The Deacon does not apologize for his earlier outburst of temper at the Calcutta staging area, but as our Siliguri-bound night train moves deeper into the countryside and real darkness punctuated by hundreds or even thousands more fires in villages and isolated homes, his manner suggests both apology and embarrassment. After we dine on a basket of hotel-roasted chicken and a decent white wine in our small compartment where all three of us will be sleeping on fold-down cots, the smell of the Deacon's pipe tobacco mixes with the cow dung scent of India's humid air.

This is strangely calming. We say little to each other, all of us more interested in the tableaus glimpsed briefly as the now hurtling little train passes villages and homes lighted by open fires and the occasional lantern. We are climbing a little, but we know that narrow-gauge Darjeeling Himalayan Railway train tomorrow morning will have to pull itself and us from near sea level to Darjeeling—the town and the Bromley-Montfort tea plantation are set in the Mahabharat Mountain Range, also known as the Lesser Himalayas—at an average altitude of around 7,000 feet.

The heat eventually forces us to open the windows to allow more dust, smoke, and flying cinders in, but that thick, humid air becomes a tiny bit cooler as we roll through more coconut and banana plantations and the cooking-dinner scent of cow dung campfires is slowly balanced, if not replaced, by the thickly sensuous tropical funk of irrigated palm trees.

We are three or four hours out of Calcutta when the Darjeeling Mail express roars and clatters its way across the famous Sara Bridge which spans the Padma. After that, all is darkness, broken only by the dim constellations of the hundreds upon hundreds of distant villages across the plain.

All three of us are in our thinly cushioned fold-down beds by eleven p.m., and from the sounds my climbing partners are making, they are soon sleeping deeply. I'm plagued by thoughts and doubts for a while—the meeting with Lord Bromley-Montfort at the Mount Everest Hotel tomorrow night or Tuesday morning may be as disastrous as I fear—but then I also fall asleep to the swaying of the train and the soothing sound of its iron wheels on the Darjeeling Mail rails.

* * *

Early the next morning in Siliguri—after tea, coffee, and a good Western breakfast in an area of the station reserved just for British and other white passengers—we transfer to the narrow-gauge railroad that always departs for Darjeeling precisely thirty-five minutes after the mail train arrives in Siliguri. Seven miles up this line—the train really is so tiny that it seems a slightly overgrown toy train of the kind boys dream of owning—we reach the Sukhna station and begin the absurdly steep (and absurdly slow) switchback climbing to Darjeeling. The humid scents of the crowded Bengali plain are soon replaced by refreshing breezes and the thick, green, rain-scented forest that punctuates rolling plantation rows of tea plants. We are scheduled to arrive by noon, but two rockfalls onto the tracks put us hours behind schedule.

The engineer and fireman of the little Coney Island toy train roust out dozens from the third- and even second-class cabins to move the rocks fallen from the rain-drenched cliffs, but Jean-Claude and I enthusiastically join in the work, prying with crowbars to lever small boulders off the tracks.

The Deacon stands to one side, arms crossed, and glowers. "If you hurt your back or legs or hands now," he says tightly, "you've ruined your chance at climbing Everest for *nothing*. Let the other passengers do it, for God's sake."

J.C. and I smile our agreement but ignore him, helping clear the track while the engineer and fireman and useless conductors (who collected all our tickets before the Darjeeling Himalayan Railway toy train started, since one cannot walk from one of the tiny cars to the next, but who have done no work since) lazily watch with crossed arms and frowning faces. From time to time they shout instructions and criticism in Bengali and Hindi and some other dialect. Eventually we're finished, the rails are clear, and J.C. and I stagger back to our coach.

Twelve miles further on, we stop for another rockfall, this one with even larger rocks and boulders heaped all over the tracks. "Heavy rain," says the engineer, shrugging and looking above us at the vertical cliffs from which run a thousand miniature waterfalls. Jean-Claude and I again join the second- and third-class passengers in levering off a few tons of rocks. Pointedly, the Deacon stays in his bunk and takes a nap.

So we arrive hours late in Darjeeling, not at noon as the schedule promised, but toward dusk. And in a heavy rain which has prevented us from catching views of the summits of Kanchenjunga or any of the other high Himalayan peaks usually visible—according to the Deacon—during the approach to Darjeeling. Two of us are sore and bruised from moving tons of rock, our muscles aching despite being honed for climbing, our climbing-necessary fingers torn and bloody; the third member of our party is also bloody—bloody disgusted with us.

We walk back to the fifth and last car on our Coney Island Express—the so-called "freight car," in reality just a flatbed with our many crates and boxes hastily lashed down and covered with tarps—and wonder how we are going to get the tons of stuff to the Hotel Mount Everest. (Expedition members, especially their leaders, are often invited to stay up the hill at Government House, but our expedition is so totally unofficial that we want to be invisible. So the hotel it is.)

Suddenly, miraculously, a tall man with an umbrella appears out of the pounding rain. He's followed by more than a dozen porters pouring out of three Ford trucks with wooden beds behind their cabs. The station platform has no roof. The rain is cold up here at 7,000 feet, and steam rises from the Fords' hoods still ticking with heat.

The tall man is wearing a finely made cream-colored cotton robe with long wool vests hanging down like brown scarves. On his head is perched an elaborate and carefully fitted cap unlike anything I've seen so far in India. He doesn't look either Indian or Tibetan—not quite Asiatic enough for the latter nor brown and short and dark-haired enough for the former—and while he might be one of the mythical Sherpas I've heard so much about, I know that Sherpas also tend to be short, and this man's brown-eyed gaze is exactly level with mine—and I'm 6 foot 2. Without saying a word or making a gesture, he somehow projects a powerful sense of dignity and self-respect. He obviously has what some call "a commanding presence."

The Deacon walks forward through the rain, water cascading from his fedora, and the other man extends the umbrella so that the Deacon can stand close under the broad black circle.

"Are you sent by Lord Bromley-Montfort?" asks the Deacon.

The man stares at the Deacon. Long, silent seconds pass in the pouring rain.

The Deacon points at his own chest and says, "Me... Richard Davis Deacon." He points at the tall man's chest. "You?"

"Pasang." The voice is so soft that I can barely hear it under the pounding of rain on the umbrella fabric.

"Pasang what?" asks the Deacon.

"Pasang... Sirdar."

I step closer through the rain and extend my hand. "Pleasure to meet you, Pasang Sirdar."

The tall man makes no move except to shift the umbrella a bit so that it offers me some protection.

"No, no, Jake," says the Deacon, almost shouting over the downpour. "*Sirdar* means something like 'head man.' He'd be in charge of the porters. Evidently it's just Pasang for now." He turns back to the tall man. "Pasang... can... you... get these?" The Deacon gestures dramatically to the heaps of tarp-covered crates that J.C. and I had only begun to untie. "To... the... Hotel Mount Everest?" The Deacon gestures vaguely uphill toward the dark, multi-terraced hill city of Darjeeling, all but invisible in the rain, and says again, more loudly, "Hotel... Mount... Everest?"

"That shouldn't be a problem, Mr. Deacon," Pasang says in a perfect Oxbridge accent. The soft, deep voice sounds as upper-class British as the Deacon's. Perhaps more so. "We shan't take more than five minutes."

Pasang hands the umbrella to me and steps out into the rain to shout in both Hindi and Bengali to the dozen or so porters waiting silently in the downpour. The men rush to untie the crates and quickly load them onto the backs of the Ford carryalls. Somehow—I'll never know how, except that J.C. is half-perched on my left knee while I am pressed sideways against the passenger-side door—the three of us squeeze into the cab of the first truck along with Pasang, who is driving. The downpour increases, and since the only working windshield wiper is banging away to clear the tiniest possible arc in front of Pasang, I can't see a damned thing out the front, side, or back as the truck bounces, bucks, and grinds gears around unseen turns and up a seemingly endless series of steep and invisible switchbacks. Whatever Darjeeling looks like, I'm not going to see it this night.

Not one of the four of us says a single word during the ride up.

* * *

I'd expected the Hotel Mount Everest to be an old stone building set amidst other old stone buildings—gray, gray, gray. Instead we stop at a well-lighted and splendid-looking three-story Victorian structure perched high on a hillside. The hotel might fit an American's mental image of Olde London Towne for all of its gables, rafters, towers, more gables, the elaborate porte-cochère with its brick drive and Elizabethan-style pillars, a shingled turret rising to the right of the main entrance, a garden out front with a white-graveled walkway, small leafy trees (not the great multi-trunked banyans of the lower elevations we'd climbed through on the tiny train) along the front of the hotel and elegant tall pines behind.

As we reach the hotel entrance, it stops raining so suddenly it's as if someone has switched off a spigot. A full moon emerges from behind quickly scurrying clouds and illuminates the snowy summits of tall peaks to the north and east and west behind the hotel.

"We're not *that* close to the Himalayas here, are we?" I ask as the three of us step further back from the hotel and its overhangs to look at what surely must be more clouds, not mountain peaks. Not so near to Darjeeling.

"That is moonlight on snow and ice," Jean-Claude says. "Peaks and ridges."

Despite the late hour, four handsomely attired bellboys have hustled out from the lobby and are now carrying in our personal baggage—some suitcases, but mostly rucksacks and duffels. The Deacon insists we go around back with Pasang and the other porters in the Ford trucks to make sure our gear is stored somewhere safe. That turns out to be in the large building that had obviously once served as the Hotel Mount Everest's extensive stables. Pasang oversees the porters' careful delivery and re-tarping of our crates into what had been three large stalls with high swinging doors.

"I think one of us should stay out here and keep an eye on our...," begins the Deacon.

But with our crates counted and inspected, all tarps tied down, Pasang closes the stall doors, locks a heavy padlocked chain on the front of each, and silently hands the keys to the Deacon. "Everything should be quite secure for the night, Mr. Deacon. And I've posted a trusted servant from the plantation to sleep here and keep watch, just in case. One never knows."

We trudge back to the front of the hotel amidst a wild myriad of almost overpowering scents: wet leaves and grass, rich soil, the richness of the flower gardens on both sides of the drive, wet mosses along a stream trickling down under an arched bridge, moist bark that makes up the driveway where the bricks and paving stop, and—perhaps most powerfully—the mountain-breeze-borne scent of hundreds of thousands of ripened and dampened tea plants growing along tens of thousands of green terraces on the steep hillsides now illuminated in moonlight above, around, and below the hill town of Darjeeling. Lights are coming on all over, many of them electric.

The hotel night manager is Indian, formally dressed in a cutaway and a high nineteenth-century collar, and he seems very excited to have us arrive in his establishment. The wide lobby is strangely empty except for the hovering bellboys, Pasang, and the three of us.

"Yes, yes, yes," says the manager in his thick Indian accent, opening and swiveling the huge register and proffering a fine pen. The mahogany counter glows almost gold with its patina of age and use. "The Bromley Expedition, yes, yes," continues the smiling manager. "We offer a very warm welcome indeed to the esteemed Bromley-Montford Expedition."

The Deacon's glower is almost, not quite, enough to extinguish the manager's huge smile. "We are *not* the...Bromley Expedition," our head climber says softly. "Our group doesn't have a name. But if it did...it would be the Deacon-Clairoux-Perry Expedition."

"Yes, of course, yes, yes," says the manager, looking nervously at Pasang, who doesn't so much as blink. "Half of our topmost floor, the Mallory Wing we call it now, our finest suites, sir, yes, yes, has been set aside for the Bromley Expedition."

The Deacon sighs. We're all tired. He signs the register, hands the pen to J.C., who signs and hands it to me. The liveried bellboys—not the same dark men who'd acted as porters with our crates—leap forward to lift our suitcases, rucksacks, and duffel bags. The three of us and a bellboy crowd into a single cage elevator—ancient, wrought-iron, electrically powered by God-knows-what, an intricate but workable mass of chains and gears. An operator begins to slide the cage doors shut.

"Just a moment," the Deacon says, walking back to the registration desk. The manager snaps to attention like a Prussian officer being inspected by the former Kaiser.

"Is Lord Bromley-Montfort here already?" demands the Deacon. His voice is thick with an oncoming cold or mere fatigue. "I need to meet with him tonight if he's still awake."

The manager's broad grin freezes in place, becomes a rather terrible rictus, and while his head both bows and shakes at the same time—yes, no, yes, no—his eyes flick to where Pasang has been standing silent in the same place amidst all the commotion with baggage and bellboys.

"The meeting is set for tomorrow morning," says Pasang.

"Yes, yes, yes," breathes the relieved manager. "The breakfast room is set aside for...yes...in the morning."

The Deacon shakes his head, runs his hands through his thinning hair, and walks back to where the rest of us wait in the lift. We may be preparing to climb the tallest mountain in the world, but this night we're too tired to climb three flights of stairs to our waiting luxury suites.

Ultramarine is a strange and rare color: beyond sea blue,
even beyond the deeper blue artists call marine blue.
When my mother included ultramarine in her paintings,
which was rarely, she would use her thumb to crush
small balls of pure lapis lazuli into powder, wet the
powder with drops of water from a glass or with her
own saliva, and then, using strong, sure jabs of her
palette knife, mix tiny amounts of that overpoweringly
strong tone—ultramarine—*into the seascape or*
skyscape on which she was working. In the slightest
excess, it's disturbing, unbalancing. In just the right
amount, it's the most beautiful color in existence.

⸺⸺⸺∞⸺⸺⸺

The suites in the Hotel Mount Everest are actual suites, which include sitting rooms with overstuffed Victorian furniture. Our corner suite has tall windows looking both southeast to the buildings of Darjeeling staggering down the hillside beneath the hotel, and when we part the drapes, glimpsed through ever-shifting clouds, high mountains with snowy, moonlit peaks rising like ramparts to the north and northeast. "Which one is Everest?" I ask the Deacon in reverent tones.

"That stubby low-looking little peak to the left center...the one you can't really make out," he says. "The closer giants like Kabr and Kanchenjunga block a good view of Everest from here."

There is a bedroom for each of the three of us in this roomy suite, and...most wonderful of all...feather beds.

Jean-Claude and I would be happy to sleep late this next morning—when will be the next time we'll be sleeping in feather beds?—but the Deacon, fully dressed down to the thumping lug soles of his alpine boots, ruins that plan by banging on both our doors, opening them, waking J.C., then stomping into my bedroom, throwing wide the heavy drapes to let in the high-altitude sunlight, and rousting me out just as the sun is rising.

"Can you believe it?" he snaps as I sit groggily on the edge of my wonderfully comfortable and warm bed.

"Believe what?"

"He wouldn't let me in."

"Who wouldn't let you in where? And what time is it?" My tone is surly. *I* am surly.

"It's almost seven," says the Deacon and goes into J.C.'s room to make sure he's also getting up and dressed. By the time he returns, I've splashed soapy water from a basin on my face and under my arms—I'd taken a long bath the previous night before going to bed, actually falling asleep in the hot water—and now get into a fresh shirt and trousers. I have no idea how one should dress for this surprisingly posh Hotel Mount Everest, but the Deacon is in twill trousers, mountain boots, a white shirt, and linen vest, so evidently one doesn't have to dress formally to go to breakfast here. Still, I pull on a tweed jacket and knot a cloth tie. Even if the hotel is so informal as to tolerate the Deacon's mountain-climbing attire, one has to doubt that Lord Bromley-Montfort will be.

"Who wouldn't let you in where?" I repeat when we meet again in the hallway. When the Deacon is truly angry, his lips—already thin—become an even thinner line. This morning they have all but disappeared.

"Lord Bromley-Montfort. He has closed off the whole wing just down the hall from our suites, and he has that *sirdar* Pasang and two other oversized Sherpas standing in front of the doors, arms folded across their chests—*guarding* the doors, Jake, as if it were a bloody harem in there."

The Deacon shakes his head in disgust. "Evidently Lord Bromley-Montfort is sleeping late this morning and does not wish to be disturbed. Even by the climbers who have come thousands of miles to risk their lives to find the body of his beloved cousin."

"*Was* he beloved?" asks Jean-Claude as he joins us by falling into line on the surprisingly narrow stairway.

"Who?" snaps the Deacon, obviously still distracted by being turned away from Lord Reggie's suite.

"Young Lord Percival," says J.C. "Cousin Percy. Lady Bromley's wastrel of a son. The fellow whose frozen corpse we've come to find. *Was* young Percy beloved by Darjeeling's Lord Bromley-Montfort...by his cousin Reggie?"

"How the devil should I know?" barks the Deacon. He leads us downstairs to the large breakfast room.

"I suggest we get a good breakfast," I say so there'll be no more Deaconesque snarling. India has certainly brought out the dark, impatient side of our friend, one we've never seen before. It's been my conviction during the months that I've known Richard Davis Deacon that he would choose his own beheading before allowing himself to commit an emotional scene in public.

I will very soon find out just how wrong I've been about that.

The long breakfast room is empty except for a table that has been set for seven. The same manager who'd greeted us in the middle of the night leads us to that table and sets five menus down. J.C. and I sit on one side of the table, the Deacon opposite us, and we leave the chair to my right at the head of the table and the one to the left of the Deacon empty. I've expected a British buffet, serve-yourself upper-class sort of breakfast, but evidently that's not how the Hotel Mount Everest is going to feed us. The five menus set down suggest that Lord Bromley-Montfort and someone else—perhaps *Lady* Bromley-Montfort—may be joining us. This is not exactly a Sherlockian-level deduction, but then, I'm still groggy with sleep and without my morning coffee.

After twenty minutes of waiting for them—mostly in silence save for the sounds of our stomachs rumbling—we decide to order. The breakfasts are very English. Jean-Claude orders only muffin-biscuits and black coffee—a large pot of black coffee. The clerk/waiter pouts. "No tea, Monsieur?"

"No tea," grunts J.C. "Coffee, coffee, coffee."

The clerk/waiter nods dolefully and shuffles closer, looming over me, pen poised again. "Mr. Perry?"

I should find it unusual that he remembers my name from our checking in during the night, but then again, other than Lord and Lady Bromley-Montfort and their retinue, we seem to be the only three people in the hotel. I'm hesitating because I've had trouble in England finding breakfasts I can really enjoy, and this menu is most definitely English.

The Deacon leans my way. "Try the Full Monty, Jake."

I don't see it on the menu. "The Full Monty?" I say to the Deacon. "What is that?"

The Deacon smiles. "Trust me."

I order a Full Monty with coffee, the Deacon orders the same with tea, Jean-Claude again mumbles "Coffee," and the three of us are alone in the long room again.

"Not much business these days in the ol' Mount Everest Hotel," I say as we wait.

"Don't be naive, Jake," says the Deacon. "It's obvious that Lord Bromley-Montfort has rented the entire hotel so that our meeting here today can be private."

"Oh," I say, feeling stupid. But not so stupid that I don't ask, "Why would he do that?"

The Deacon sighs and shakes his head. "There goes our attempt to keep a low profile and to pass through Darjeeling without really being noticed."

"Well," I persist, "if Lord Bromley-Montfort cleared the place out so that we could meet this morning...where *is* he? Why keep us waiting?"

The Deacon shrugs. J.C. says, "Evidently English lords in India prefer to sleep late."

Our breakfasts arrive. The coffee tastes like slightly warmed ditchwater. My breakfast plate is heaped so high with fried foods that bits keep slopping off as if trying to escape; the heap includes half a dozen burned-black pieces of bacon, at least five fried eggs, two gigantic pieces of fried bread slathered in butter, some sort of semi-ambulatory black pudding, fried tomatoes crouching next to grilled tomatoes, a row of sausages bursting through their burnt-fried skins, fried onions dolloped here and there at random, and a heap of leftover vegetables and potatoes from the previous evening's dinners now all shallow-fried and jumble-piled together: bubble and squeak, I know the jumbled part of this mess is called. I hate bubble and squeak.

I've had large English breakfasts before, but this is...ridiculous.

"All right," I say to the Deacon. "*Why* is this called 'the Full Monty'? What does 'Full Monty' mean?"

"It means, approximately—'everything' or 'the whole thing.'" He is already busy forking the fried stuff into his mouth in that insufferable way the Brits do—fork upside down and held in his left hand, blob of food teetering impossibly on the fork's backside, keeping the knife in his right hand to carve through the gelatinous mass.

"What does 'Full Monty' *mean?*" I persist. "Where'd the phrase *come* from? Who's *Monty?*"

The Deacon sighs and sets down his fork. Jean-Claude, obviously more interested in the view of the mountains than in his food, is looking out through the window at the bright Darjeeling morning.

"There are different etymological theories on 'the Full Monty,' Jake," intones the Deacon. "The one I think most likely to be true comes from the tailoring business of a certain Sir Montague Burton, begun, I believe, shortly after the turn of the century. Burton offered that most oxymoronic of things—well-tailored suits for the common bourgeois man."

"I thought all you English fellows had tailored suits... what did you call it when you bought mine in London?" I said. "Bespoke."

"That certainly applies to the upper classes," said the Deacon. "But Sir Montague Burton sold such tailored suits to men who might wear a suit just a few times in their adult lives—one's own wedding, one's children's weddings, friends' funerals, one's own funeral, that sort of thing. And Burton's stores specialized in lifelong tailoring of the same suit, so as the bourgeois gent expanded, so did his suit. Nor was the cut ever of such a sort that it would, as you Bostonians would say, 'go out of style.' Burton started with one shop, in Derbyshire, I believe, and within a few years had a chain of stores all over England."

"So asking for the Full Monty means... what? I want the whole suit? The whole thing?"

"Exactly, my dear chap. Coat, trousers, waistcoat..."

"Vest," I correct.

The Deacon squints again. Actually, this time, I *have* squirted him with juice as I knifed into one of the sausages.

I start to say something sarcastic but stop with my mouth open as the most beautiful woman I've ever seen—or *would ever* see—walks into the room.

* * *

I can't adequately describe her. I realized that decades ago when I first attempted to write these memoirs without the death sentence of cancer hanging over me. I had to abandon the attempt then when I came to describing...her. Perhaps I can tell you a little bit about what she was by describing what she was *not*.

This is 1925: stylish women have a certain look. To be stylish in 1925 means the woman has to be flat-chested as a boy (I'd heard that there are breast bands and other such underwear sold to produce that effect for those ladies not lucky enough to come by flat-chestedness naturally), but this woman entering the room with Pasang by her side definitely has breasts, although she isn't flaunting them. Actually, her shirt—and it really is more of a shirt than a lady's blouse—is of a fine linen but otherwise cut much like a working man's field shirt. It does not hide her curves.

A fashionable woman in 1925 will have her hair cut short, parts of it curled—the floozies in Boston and New York and London go in especially for spit curls—or, better yet, especially for the smart set, bobbed short. This woman with Pasang has long hair, dropping in rich natural curls below her shoulders.

The fashionable hair color for ladies in 1925 is blond bordering on platinum; this woman has hair so dark as to be both blue and black at the same time. The highlights on the ebony curls flicker and dance with the movement of sunlight on her long hair. The sophisticated sort of society women I'd met through Harvard and the whores I'd met in Boston speakeasies had mostly plucked their real eyebrows and then penciled in the skinny, high-arched fake brows that Jean Harlow would soon make so popular worldwide. This woman striding toward our table has rich black eyebrows that arch only slightly but which seem infinitely expressive.

And her eyes...

When she is at the base of the stairway twenty-five feet away, I think that her eyes are blue. At twenty feet, I realize that I'm wrong—the color of her eyes is ultramarine.

Ultramarine is a strange and rare color: beyond sea blue, even beyond the deeper blue artists call marine blue. When my mother included ultramarine in her paintings, which was rarely, she would use her thumb to crush small balls of pure lapis lazuli into powder, wet the powder with drops of water from a glass or with her own saliva, and then, using strong, sure jabs of her palette knife, mix tiny amounts of that overpoweringly strong tone—*ultramarine*—into the seascape or skyscape on which she was working. In the slightest excess, it's disturbing, unbalancing. In just the right amount, it's the most beautiful color in existence.

This woman's eyes have just the right shade of ultramarine to complete and complement the rest of her beauty. Her eyes are perfect. *She* is perfect.

She strides across the room with Pasang to her right and only half a step behind her, and both stop behind the empty chair at the head of our table, the Deacon on her right and J.C. and me gawking from her left. The Deacon, J.C., and I stand to greet her, although I admit that my standing is more of a springing upward. Jean-Claude is smiling. The Deacon is not. Pasang is carrying a pile of books and what appear to be rolled maps, but my eyes have no time to linger on Pasang or my friends.

Besides the beautiful linen shirt-blouse, this woman is wearing a broad belt and a riding skirt—breeches, really, but looking like a skirt—of what appears to be the softest, richest suede in the world. Suede well and evenly bleached to even subtler hue and greater softness by high Darjeeling sunlight. It's almost as if she's here in tea plantation work clothes (if work clothes were ever perfectly tailored). Her equestrian boots are such as those a lady would wear while riding in tall grass or snake country and look to be made of a leather so soft that I think it can only have been formed from the hides of newborn calves.

She stands at the head of the table, and Pasang nods to each of us in turn. "Mr. Richard Davis Deacon, Monsieur Jean-Claude Clairoux, Mr. Jacob Perry, it is my pleasure to introduce to you Lady Katherine Christina Regina Bromley-Montfort."

Lady Bromley-Montfort nods to each of us as we are introduced, but she does not offer to shake hands. She is wearing thin leather gloves that match her boots.

"Mr. Perry and Monsieur Clairoux, a pleasure to meet you at long last," she says and turns to the Deacon. "And you, Dickie, my cousins Charlie and Percy used to write to me about you all the time when we were all young. You were quite the wild child."

"We were expecting *Lord* Bromley-Montfort," the Deacon says coolly. "Is he nearby? We have expedition business to discuss."

"Lord Montfort is at our plantation only a thirty-minute ride up into the hills," says Lady Bromley-Montfort. "But I'm afraid he will not be available to you."

"Why is that?" demands the Deacon.

"He is in a crypt at the tea plantation," says the woman, her amazing eyes remaining clear and fixed on the Deacon's face. She seems almost amused. "Lord Montfort and I were married in London in 1919, before we came back to India, to the plantation where I had been raised and which I had been running. I became Lady Bromley-Montfort, and eight months later Lord Montfort passed away from dengue fever. The climate in India never really agreed with him."

"But I've been sending letters to *Lord* Bromley-Montfort...," sputters the Deacon. He removes his pipe from his jacket pocket and clenches it between his teeth but makes no move to fill it or light it. "Lady Bromley mentioned a Cousin Reggie, so I naturally assumed..."

She smiles, and my legs go weaker. "Katherine Christina *Regina* Bromley-Montfort," she says softly. "'Reggie' to my friends. Monsieur Clairoux, Mr. Perry, I sincerely hope that you will call me Reggie."

"Jean-Claude, Reggie," says my friend and bows low to her, taking her hand and kissing it even with the glove on.

"Jake," I manage.

Reggie takes the seat at the head of the table while the tall, dignified form of Pasang stands behind her like a bodyguard. He hands her a map and she unscrolls it on our table, unceremoniously moving aside used plates and cups to make room. Jean-Claude and I look at each other and then also sit. The Deacon clamps down so hard on the stem of his pipe that it makes an audible clack, but eventually he sits.

Reggie is already speaking. "Your proposed route is the standard one, and I agree with most of it. The day after tomorrow we can take some of our plantation trucks to Sixth Mile Stone, do the final loading of packs and pack animals there, and proceed on foot with the Sherpas past the Tista Bridge and beyond to Kampong, where some of our other Sherpas will be waiting for us with more mules..."

"Us?" says the Deacon. *"We?"*

She looks up at him with a smile. "Of course, Dickie. Since my aunt agreed to fund your search for Cousin Percy's body, it's always been understood that I would accompany you. It's an absolute condition for any further funding of the expedition."

The Deacon must realize that he is going to bite through the stem of his favorite pipe, for he removes it with a violent motion that almost catches Reggie in the head. Rather than apologize, he says, "You on the expedition to Everest? A woman? Even to the Base Camp? Even into Tibet? Absurd. Ridiculous. Out of the question."

"It was an absolute condition of the funding for this—my—expedition to recover Cousin Percival's remains," Reggie says, her smile still in place.

"We'll go on without you," says the Deacon. His face is very red.

"You'll do so without a shilling more from the Bromley estate," says Reggie.

"Very well, then, we'll forge ahead on the funds we have," barks the Deacon.

What funds? is my thought. Even the tickets from Liverpool to Calcutta have been paid for by Lady Bromley...evidently out of the money earned by Reggie's tea plantation.

"I'll give you two reasons for my going on this expedition besides the absolute necessity of my funding," Reggie says calmly. "Will you be so kind as to listen, or will you continue to interrupt me with those barnyard noises?"

The Deacon folds his arms and says nothing. Everything about his expression and posture says that nothing will convince him.

"First...or, rather, second, after the funding," says Reggie, "is the appalling fact that you've provided no doctor for your expedition. All three of the previous British expeditions had at least two physicians, one of them a surgeon, and usually they had more than two medical men along with them."

"I learned some important first aid during the War," says the Deacon through gritted teeth.

"I'm sure you did," says Reggie with a smile. "And if any of us were to receive a shrapnel wound or be shot by a machine gun during this expedition, I have no doubt that you could prolong our lives for entire minutes. But there are no Aid Stations behind the battle lines in Tibet, Mr. Deacon."

"You're going to tell us that you're a competent nurse?" says the Deacon.

"Yes, I am," says Reggie. "With more than thirteen thousand local people working on our two plantations, I've had to learn some nursing skills. But that's not the point I was going to make. I intend for us to have an excellent doctor and surgeon on our team."

"We can't afford to add people...," begins the Deacon.

Reggie stops him with a gracefully raised palm. "Dr. Pasang," she says to her *sirdar.* "Would you like to tell these gentlemen your medical credentials?"

Dr. Pasang? I thought. I confess—and it *is* a confession, a shameful one—that vague images of Indian fakirs and holy men, not to mention Haitian voodoo witch doctors, dance through my brain in the few seconds before Pasang speaks in that smooth and cultured English accent.

"I attended one year at Oxford and one at Cambridge," says the tall Sherpa. "But I then trained a year at Edinburgh Medical Centre, three years at the Middlesex Hospital Medical School, eighteen months studying surgery with the famous thoracic surgeon Herr Doctor Claus Wolheim in Heidelberg...that's Heidelberg, *Germany,* gentlemen...then, after returning to India, I served another year of residency in the Karras Convent Hospital in Lahore."

"Cambridge and Oxford would never allow...," begins the Deacon and then bites down on what he was about to say.

"A wog in their midst?" asks Dr. Pasang without rancor. He shows the first broad, bright smile we've seen from him to date. There is no malice in it. "For some strange reason," he continues, "both worthy institutions were under the odd illusion that I was the eldest son of the Maharaja of Aidapur, as were the medical schools in Edinburgh and Middlesex I mentioned. This was a short while before your days at Cambridge, Mr. Deacon, and the maintenance of friendly relations with the royalty of India was very important to England then."

We are silent for a long moment, and then Jean-Claude asks in a very small voice, "Dr. Pasang, if you don't find it impertinent of me to ask, why—after such excellent medical training and after becoming a licensed physician—did you return to work as a...*sirdar*...here at Reggie's...at Lady Bromley-Montfort's tea plantations?"

Again the white smile. "*Sirdar* will be my title only on this expedition to the Tibetan sacred mountain Chomolungma," he says. "As Lady Bromley-Montfort has explained, there are more than thirteen thousand men and women in her direct employ. Those employees have extended families. My skills as a physician here in the hills between Darjeeling and the southern Himalayas do not go unpracticed. We have two plantation infirmaries, one for each large tea plantation, which are...if I may be so bold...somewhat superior in both equipment and medicines to the small British hospital in Darjeeling."

"How can the people do without you while you're on expedition, Dr. Pasang?" I hear myself asking.

"Lady Bromley-Montfort has, most graciously, sent younger men than I for medical training in England and New Delhi. And several of our Sherpa women have completed comprehensive nurse's training in both Calcutta and Bombay and, to honor their benefactress as I did, returned to the plantation to offer their services."

"You're really a surgeon?" asks the Deacon.

Pasang shows a different, sharper sort of smile. "Allow me time to fetch a scalpel and lancet from my bag and I will show you, Mr. Deacon."

The Deacon turns back to Reggie. "You said there were three reasons we'd have to accept your company. We could take Dr. Pasang along—with our gratitude—but having a woman on an Everest expedition..."

"I imagine you'll find it very difficult traveling through Tibet without official Tibetan permission," Reggie says.

"I...we...," begins the Deacon. He hits the table with his fist. "Lady Bromley promised that she would obtain such permission and that we should receive the documents here in Darjeeling."

"And so you shall," says Reggie. She lifts her hand over her right shoulder and Pasang puts another rolled-up document into it. She smooths the thick parchment out over the map of our planned five-week trek from Darjeeling to Rongbuk and then Mount Everest. "Would you all care to read it?" she asks, turning the document.

All three of us half-stand to lean over the table to read. It is a handwritten document, in beautiful script, and affixed with half a dozen stamped and waxed seals.

TO THE JONGPENS AND HEADMEN OF PHARIJONG, TING-KE, KAMBA, AND KHARTA:

You are to bear in mind that a party of Sahibs are coming to see the Cho-mo-lung-ma mountain, even though the Dalai Lama has set a temporary ban on such travels by foreigners due to bad manners after the 1924 so-called "Mt. Everest Expedition." This exception is given by the Sacred Dalai Lama only because this party's leader, Lady Bromley-Montfort, has long been a friend of the Tibetans and of the many jongpens and we wish her to be able to travel with her associates to and onto Cho-mo-lung-ma in an attempt to retrieve the body of her deceased cousin, British Lord Percival Bromley, whom many of you have met. He died on the sacred mountain in 1924 and our friends the Bromleys would like to see him properly buried. We trust that Lady Bromley-Montfort's group will, in the tradition she has long established at her Darjeeling planta-tion, continue to evince great friendship and generosity towards the Tibetans. Therefore, on the request of the Great Minister Bell, and by the express wish of His Holiness the Thirteenth Dalai Lama, a letter of passage has been is-sued requiring you and all officials and subjects of the Tibetan government to supply transport, e.g., riding ponies, pack animals, and coolies as required by Lady Bromley-Montfort and her Sahib helpers, the rates for which should be fixed to mutual satisfaction. Any other assistance Lady Bromley-Montfort may require, either by day or by night, on the march or during the halts, in or near their encampments or in our villages, should be faithfully given, and their requirements about transport or anything else should be promptly at-tended to. All the people of the country, wherever Lady Bromley-Montfort and her Sahib helpers may happen to come, should render all necessary assistance in the best possible way, not merely to re-establish friendly relations between the British and Tibetan Governments, but to continue the long amity between Lady Bromley-Montfort's tea plantation — long famed for its hospitality to our travelers — and all the people of Tibet.

Dispatched during the Water Dog Year
Seal of the Prime Minister

The Deacon has nothing to say. His expression is as blank as I've ever seen it, even blanker than on the day nine months earlier atop the Matterhorn when we learned of Mallory's and Irvine's deaths.

Reggie—I take the liberty of thinking of her with that name almost immediately—rolls up both the prime minister's document and the large map, hands them to Pasang, and says, "I've told the valets to have your clothes packed. We should leave now for the plantation so that we can have the rest of the day to discuss your proposed route, the climbing details, food for the trip, plans for our dealings with the Tibetan *jongpens,* and all the rest. Then tomorrow morning you shall choose your personal Sherpas and your ponies. I have enough good men waiting that we should be able to choose the sixty or so porters we need by teatime tomorrow, and they'll have the gear loaded on pack animals before nightfall."

She stands and strides out of the room, Pasang—Dr. Pasang, I remind myself—keeping a step behind her and not falling farther behind only because of his liquid, giant strides. After a moment, J.C. and I stand, stare at each other a second, manage not to grin outright in front of the silent Deacon, and go up to supervise the final packing of our luggage.

Eventually the Deacon follows us up the stairs.

The monks have turned into quite the performing troupe,
some dancing while others play drums and blow on
thigh-bone trumpets. It's been very popular with
English cinema-going audiences.

———❧———

The maps are spread out all over the long reading table in the library at Reggie's main plantation house. I've seen few libraries this extensive, either in the homes of rich Boston friends or in England. Even Lady Bromley's library did not extend to so many multiple levels, mezzanines, iron circular staircases rising toward broad skylights, or movable ladders. The reading table is probably fourteen feet long and flanked by globes of the earth—one showing ancient geography, one showing quite current—that must be six feet across. We stand around one end of the table as more colored maps are set under and beside the map of our proposed route Reggie showed us in the hotel.

We traveled up to the plantation that morning in style. At least Reggie and two of us traveled in style. Three trucks, the lead one driven by Dr. Pasang, hauled our food and gear up into the hills, but J.C. and I rode with Reggie in the plush compartment of a 1920 Rolls-Royce Silver Ghost. The chauffeur's front seat was open to the elements—and it had started to rain—but Jean-Claude was comfortable on the thick cushions of the rear seat next to Reggie under the black top, not crowding her, while I sat opposite J.C. on a little jump seat that was no more than a leather-wrapped panel that folded down from the firewall separating us from the driver's front seat. Every time we hit a deep pothole or serious bump—and the dirt road was all potholes and bumps—I'd fly up in the air off my little springboard, my bare head contacting the hard canvas of the roof, and come crashing down again. My long legs were all but intertwined with J.C.'s shorter ones, and I kept apologizing after every bounce.

The Deacon had chosen to sit up front, to the left of the chauffeur—a silent, short Indian man named Edward, so short that I wondered how he could see over the Silver Ghost's endless hood. It was called the "Silver Ghost" but it was more a pale cream color than silver, except for the gleaming radiator, headlight mounts, five chrome stripes running down from the radiator to the equally gleaming bumper, windshield frame, and a few other shiny odds and ends, including the gleaming chrome spokes of the enclosed spare tires riding forward of the front doors on the low parts of the fenders.

The sliding panel that allowed Reggie to talk to the chauffeur opened only on the right side, the driver's side. Between the roar of the engine and the roar of the sudden downpour on the thick roof, any of us would have had to shout for the Deacon to hear us. The glass on the panel behind the Deacon was frosted and etched with the same Bromley crest of a gryphon holding a jousting pike that I'd seen on the flag flying at Lady Bromley's estate in Lincolnshire.

"How large is your plantation, Lady...Reggie?" asked Jean-Claude over the drumbeat of the sudden squall.

"This primary plantation, closer to Darjeeling, is around twenty-six thousand acres," said Reggie. "We have a larger and higher plantation to the northwest, but the small train from Darjeeling doesn't run to its fields the way it does here at the main plantation, so it costs more to get the tea leaves to market."

More than fifty thousand acres, I'd thought. *That's a hell of a lot of tea.* Then I remembered how Brits both in England and here in India drank the stuff morning, noon, and night, not to mention the hundreds of millions of Indian people who'd taken up the habit.

The steep hills were terraced here and there and green with rows of plants grown about as far apart as in a good vineyard, but much shorter. I caught glimpses of men and women in wet cotton saris and shirts working along the endless green rows that followed the curves of the hills like curving parallel lines on a topographic map. The shades of green were almost overwhelming.

After about twenty minutes, we turned off the steep dirt-rut road onto a long, rising lane of white gravel. I'm not sure what I expected at the end of that long driveway—perhaps another stone estate like Lady Bromley's in Lincolnshire—but while Reggie's home was appropriately large and surrounded by stables and other well-constructed outbuildings, it was more in keeping with the colors and style of a large Victorian-era farmhouse. The trucks followed us to the broad driveway but turned off toward the stables and garage before the Silver Ghost reached a wide gravel circle in front of the house, its center and fringes green with wet tropical plantings of all sorts. We stopped, and Edward rushed to open the door on Reggie's side.

To this day, that remains my only ride in anyone's Rolls-Royce.

The tropical darkness has fallen, we've eaten an excellent meal of veal along a dining room table even longer than the fourteen-foot reading table where we'd left the maps, and by the time all four of us—five if one counts the tall, silent form of Dr. Pasang—retire to that same library with brandy for everyone and cigars for J.C. and me, the Deacon is puffing away on his pipe and obviously still silently attempting to come up with some argument or reasons why Reggie cannot accompany us when we leave in 36 hours or so. Rather than gather around the map table again, we're sitting at the hearth of a giant fireplace where the servants have lit a fire. It's chilly above 8,000 feet here at the plantation.

"It's simply out of the question, taking a woman *on* to Everest," the Deacon is saying.

Reggie looks up from rocking the brandy in her snifter. "There is no question *involved,* Mr. Deacon. I am going. You need my money and you need my Sherpas and my ponies and my saddles and Pasang's medical skills and my permission from the Tibetan prime minister—and you would need me to gain access to Tibet this year even if there weren't the crisis of the lice and the dancing lamas."

The Deacon shows a sour expression. *At least she's no longer calling him "Dickie,"* I think.

"Crisis of the lice and dancing lamas?" inquires Jean-Claude between sips and puffs.

I've almost forgotten that J.C. hadn't spent the autumn and winter in

London as the Deacon and I had. I look to the Deacon to explain, but he shrugs and gestures for me to speak.

"You remember," I say to Jean-Claude, "that the Deacon's friend we met at the Royal Geographical Society, the photographer and filmmaker John Noel, paid the Everest Committee eight thousand pounds for all cinema and still photo rights to last year's expedition."

"I remember because I thought it was an extraordinary amount of money," says J.C.

I nod. "Well, Noel was sure he could make a profit if the expedition were successful last year, but he couldn't really make a dramatic film showing Mallory's and Irvine's disappearance since there was only one photograph taken of them before they left Camp Four, and clouds got in the way of Noel's long twenty-inch telephoto cinema lens, so Noel made one of the cinema releases more of a travelogue—*The Roof of the World,* he called it. The Deacon and I saw it in January before you returned from France."

"So?"

"So there were things in the film—including a scene where an old man is finding fleas in a beggar child's hair and then crushing them between his teeth—that the Tibetan government evidently objected to. Others objected to a bit where Mallory's widow is quoted in titles as saying that she regretted the whole enterprise. But mostly the Tibetans have been objecting to the dancing lamas."

"Dancing lamas?" repeats Jean-Claude. "Noel filmed them at Rongbuk Monastery?"

"Worse than that," says Reggie. "John Noel paid a group of lamas to leave the Gyantse Monastery and to perform—live in cinemas in London and other British cities—what Noel in the film calls a 'devil dance.' The monks have turned into quite the performing troupe, some dancing while others play drums and blow on thigh-bone trumpets. It's been very popular with English cinema-going audiences. Quite different from the usual fare. At the same time, the lamas were introduced as 'holy men' to the Archbishop of Canterbury. The uproar between Tibet and His Majesty's Government has been ample enough for the Everest Committee to be turned down, by Tibet, for its proposed 1926 Everest expedition. It may be a decade or more before the British Alpine Club and Everest Committee receive another climbing permission."

"Ahh," says J.C. "I can see why the Tibetans feel humiliated. But how did the Tibetans learn what was happening in English cinema houses?"

Reggie smiles as the Deacon irritably repacks his pipe. "It isn't really the Tibetans who are causing this moratorium on British expeditions to Everest," she says. "It is Major Frederick Marshman Bailey."

"Who the devil is Major Frederick Marshman Bailey?" I ask. This is the first I've heard of either the man's name or the fact that it was he, not the Tibetans, who were throwing a spanner into the Everest Committee's efforts to get a future climbing permission.

"He's Political Officer for Sikkim," says the Deacon from around his pipe stem. He sounds very angry. "Remember our maps? The eastern-most province of the Raj in India, the one we have to trek through to get to Tibet? It's a quasi-independent kingdom called Sikkim. Bailey got the Dalai Lama at Lhasa to back him on all this 'the Tibetans are outraged' nonsense, but in truth, it's Bailey who's stopping all British climbing permits except ours. He's stopping German and Swiss permit attempts as well."

"Why would he want to do that, *Ree-shard?*" asks Jean-Claude. "I mean, I see why a British Political Officer would try to head off the Germans and Swiss, to keep Everest an English hill, but why on earth is he stopping permission for English expeditions?"

The Deacon seems too angry to speak. He nods to Lady Bromley-Montfort.

"Bailey is a former climber, having achieved some lower summits here in the Himalayas," Reggie says. "He's far past his prime—and he never got close to Mount Everest even in his prime—but many of us believe that he's stirring up and exaggerating the Tibetan anger over the dancing lamas as a pretext to save the mountain for himself."

I have to blink rapidly at this news. "Will he try this spring or summer?"

"He'll never try," says the Deacon through gritted teeth. "He just wants to spoil it for the others."

"Then how did Lady . . . Reggie's . . . request get approved by the Tibetan prime minister and the Dalai Lama at Lhasa?" asks Jean-Claude.

Reggie smiles again. "I went straight to the Dalai Lama and the prime minister for personal permission," she says. "And ignored Bailey completely. He hates me for it. We shall have to transit Sikkim as quickly and quietly as we can, before Bailey finds some way to block us. He is a malevolent man. Our only advantage is that I've done several things by way of misdirection to make him believe that our expedition will be attempting transit to Chomolungma in August, post-monsoon, rather than now during the pre-monsoon months, and that we would be using the direct northern route—over Tangu Plain and up over the Serpo La—rather than the traditional route farther east."

"Why would Bailey be so foolish as to believe that someone would attempt Everest in August again?" asks the Deacon. His 1921 recon expedition had done just that, only to find how deep the snow could be in August. But then again, it had been June 5 when Mallory, Somervell, and the others—minus the Deacon, who thought the snow conditions too dangerous—had lost seven Sherpas and Bhotias in an avalanche during Mallory's stubborn attempt to return to Camp III on the North Col after heavy early monsoon snows.

"Because Pasang and six others and I did just that in August a year ago," says Reggie.

All three of us turn to gaze at her in silence. Dr. Pasang's presence is only half-registered in the flickering firelight as he stands behind the wingchair in which Reggie leans forward over her brandy. Finally, the Deacon says, "Did what?"

"Went to Everest," Reggie replies, with an edge to her voice. "In an attempt to find Cousin Percy's body. I would have gone earlier in the summer, but the monsoon was at its worst right after Colonel Norton, Geoffrey Bruce, and the others in Mallory's former party beat their retreat back this way. Pasang and I had to wait until the worst of the rains—and the snows on Chomolungma—stopped before we trekked in with six Sherpas."

"How far did you get?" says the Deacon, sounding dubious. "As far as Shekar Dzong? Further? Rongbuk Monastery?"

Reggie looks up from her brandy, and her ultramarine eyes seem much darker in her anger at the tone of the question. But her voice remains firm and under control. "Pasang and two of the other Sherpas and I spent eight days above twenty-three thousand feet at Mallory's Camp Four. But the snow kept falling. Pasang and I did press on to Mallory's Camp Five one day, but there were no supplies left there, and the storm grew worse. We were lucky to get back down to the North Col and were trapped there for four more of the eight days, with no food for the last three."

"Mallory's Camp Five was at twenty-five thousand two hundred feet," Jean-Claude says in a very small voice.

Reggie only nods. "I lost more than thirty pounds during those eight days on the North Col at Camp Four. One of the Sherpas, Nawang Bura—you shall meet him tomorrow morning—almost died from altitude sickness and dehydration. We finally had a break in the weather on eighteen August, and we retreated all the way back to Mallory's Camp One—the four Sherpas who'd remained at Camp Three below the Col all but carried Nawang down the glacier—where we regrouped before trekking out. The snows never stopped. The downpour continued as we clumped back through the steaming Sikkim jungles in mid-September. I thought I would never get dry."

The Deacon, Jean-Claude, and I exchange glances in the firelight. I am sure my thoughts are being echoed. *This woman and that tall Sherpa climbed to above 25,000 feet on Everest at the height of the monsoon season? Spent eight consecutive days above 23,000 feet?* Almost no one in the three previous Everest expedition spent so much time so high.

"Where did you learn to climb?" the Deacon asks. The brandy seems to be affecting him, which is something I've never seen before. Perhaps it's the altitude here.

Reggie gestures with her empty glass, Pasang nods toward the darkness, and a servant moves into the light to refill all of our brandy snifters.

"I've climbed in the Alps since I was a girl," she says simply. "I've climbed with Cousin Percy, with guides, and solo. My trips back to Europe from India were more often to the Alps than to England. And I've climbed here."

"Do you remember the names of your alpine guides?" asks Jean-Claude. There is no sound of challenge in his voice, only curiosity.

Reggie gives the names of five older Chamonix Guides so famous that even I know them well. Lady Bromley had named three of those guides as having climbed with her son Percival in years past. Once again, as he'd done when Lady Bromley had given three of these five names, Jean-Claude whistles softly.

"What summits did you do solo?" asks the Deacon. His tone has changed.

Reggie shrugs slightly. "Pevous, the Ailefroides, the Meiji, the north face of the Grandes Jorasses, the north east face of Piz Badille, the north face of the Drus, then Mont Blanc and the Matterhorn. And some peaks around here—only one eight-thousand-meter summit."

"Alone," says the Deacon. His expression is strange.

Reggie shrugs again. "Believe it or don't, it makes no difference to me, Mr. Deacon. What you need to understand is that when my aunt, Lady Bromley, wrote me last autumn asking me to seek permission for access to Chomolungma, for your expedition to—and I quote—'find Percival,' I had already been to Lhasa to receive permission from the Dalai Lama and the prime minister...for another attempt this spring. *My own* second attempt—with Pasang and more Sherpas this time."

"But the permission refers to 'other Sahibs,'" says the Deacon.

"I expected to find some on my own, Mr. Deacon. Indeed, I had contacted them and invited them to join me on the recovery expedition this spring. I would have paid them, of course. But when Aunt Elizabeth sent me your names, I did some research and found you...adequate. Plus, you had been a friend of my cousin Charles and you'd met Percy. I thought it best to give you a chance."

I suddenly realize that the tables have been turned, that we are now supplicants to *her* for this trip, not the other way around. I can see in the Deacon's somewhat glassy gaze that he has accepted that fact as well.

"How is your cousin Charles?" he asks, as much to change the subject, it seems, as to receive an answer.

"I received a cable from Aunt Elizabeth only a week ago," says Reggie. "Charles finally died from the progressive lung failure while you were in transit to Calcutta."

All three of us express our condolences. The Deacon seems especially disturbed by the news. There follows a long silence broken only by the crackling of the log fire.

J.C. and I finish our cigars and I follow his example of tossing the cigar butt into the fire. We set empty glasses on tables.

"We have to make some changes to the route and your plans for provisions," says Reggie, "but we can do that in the afternoon, after you've chosen your Sherpas and ponies. The Sherpas will be here at first light—they're camping less than a mile from here tonight—and I want to be outside to greet them. I'll have Pasang knock you up in case anyone sleeps late. Good night, gentlemen."

We rise as Reggie stands and leaves the circle of firelight. A few minutes later, still silent, we follow one of the male servants to our rooms on the second floor. I notice that the Deacon seems to be having trouble lifting his feet as we climb the wide, winding stairway.

But how do you keep a chicken carcass fresh over weeks if
the snows hit you at Camp Three below the North Col,
Mr. Deacon? Do you plan to carry ice with you? An
electric refrigeration unit?

We awake early at Reggie's estate. The plantation house has a neatly manicured backyard as trim and broad and long as a cricket field. Above and below the house, morning fogs seem to be rising like respiration from the green rows of tea plantings, and suddenly I can see silhouettes of men moving between and then out of those rows, onto the yard, as if the fog had congealed itself into human forms. I count thirty figures as the sun brightens and the fog begins to dissipate. Beyond the plantation hills rise the distant white peaks of the Himalayas so brilliant with the dawn's sunlight that I have to squint toward them, and yet still their white glare makes my eyes water.

"Too many men," says the Deacon. "I'd planned on only a dozen or so Sherpa coolies."

"Just 'Sherpas,' not 'coolies,'" says Reggie. "'Sherpa' means 'people from the east.' They came over the nineteen-thousand-foot Nangpa La generations ago. They've fought a thousand years for their land and independence. And never have they been anyone's 'coolies.'"

"Still too many," says the Deacon as the ragged forms of men solidify more fully and move across the grassy expanse toward us.

Reggie shakes her head. "I'll explain later why we need at least thirty. For now I'll introduce all of them and pull aside the dozen or so that I think will make excellent high-climbers. 'Tigers,' your General Bruce and Colonel Norton liked to call them. Most of the chosen speak English. I'll let the three of you interview them and choose whomever you want as your two co-climbers."

"You know all their names?" I ask.

Reggie nods. "Of course. I also know their parents and wives and families."

"And these Sherpas all live near Darjeeling?" asks Jean-Claude. "Near your plantation?"

"No," says Reggie. "These men are the best of the best. Some live in the Solu Khumbu region of Nepal, near the southern approaches to Mount Everest. Others come from the Nepali district of Helambu or the Arun Valley or Rowaling. Still others from Kathmandu. Only about a fourth of these climbers live within four days' walk of Darjeeling."

"Previous expeditions have always chosen a few Darjeeling Sherpas and then added more porters from the Tibetan villages along the way," says the Deacon.

"Yes," says Reggie and smacks her leather riding crop against her gloved palm. She had come in from her morning ride as the three of us were gathering in the huge kitchen for coffee just before sunrise. "That's why the first three English expeditions had some good Sherpa climbers but many porters not at all fit for climbing. Tibetans are wonderful people, proud and courageous, but when pressed into duty as porters, as you probably remember from your two expeditions here, Mr. Deacon, they tend to act rather like unionized Englishmen and go on strike for better wages, more food, fewer carrying hours...and always at the worst time. Sherpas don't do that. If they sign on to help, they help until they die."

The Deacon grunts, but I notice that he doesn't argue the point.

Pasang has put the thirty Sherpas in a rough line, and one by one they come forward, bow to Lady Bromley-Montfort, and are then introduced to us by Reggie herself. As the strange names wash over me, I wonder how she can tell the little brown men apart, but then I realize my own American astigmatism: this Sherpa is heavier than the others, this one has a full dark beard, that one a few wispy whiskers, this one is clean-shaven but with brows grown together into a single black line above his eyes. This man has missing front teeth, the man after him a dazzlingly brilliant white smile. Some are burly, some thin. Some are dressed in fine cotton, others in little more than rags. A few wear Western-style hiking boots; far more are in sandals; some are barefooted.

Introductions completed, Pasang waves more than half the men into a more distant part of the yard, where they squat amicably and speak softly amongst themselves.

"I've never interviewed a Sherpa for a job position before," whispers Jean-Claude.

"I have," says the Deacon.

But in the end it is Pasang and Reggie who help us make up our minds. As the three of us make little more than small talk, Pasang might say, "Nyima can carry more than twice his weight all day without tiring," or Reggie might comment, "Ang Chiri lives in a village situated above fifteen thousand feet and seems to have no trouble with greater altitudes," and that sort of information, along with a man's ability to speak or understand English, is what helps us decide, especially on who our personal Sherpas will be.

After twenty minutes, we realize that Pasang will be Reggie's sole Sherpa—as well as *Sirdar* or boss-man of all the Sherpas, even while serving as the expedition's physician. J.C. has chosen Norbu Chedi and Lhakpa Yishay as his Sherpas. The two men, while from different villages and evidently not related, look enough alike as to be brothers; both have let their bangs grow down over their eyes, and Reggie explains that these long bangs take the place of darkened goggles to protect against snow blindness where the men live high up amongst the glaciers.

The Deacon has chosen Nyima Tsering—a short, stout Sherpa with a loud giggle he uses as prelude to his pidgin English answer to each question, and who can carry more than twice his own weight. The Deacon's second choice is a taller, thinner, more English-proficient man named Tenzing Bothia who never went anywhere without his own assistant, young Tejbir Norgay.

I choose a smiling, roly-poly, but obviously healthy and happy fellow named Babu Rita to be one of my two Tigers and Ang Chiri of the high-altitude village as my other co-climber. Babu's wide grin is so infectious that it's everything I can do not to grin back at him all the time. He has all his teeth. Ang is a relatively short man but with a barrel chest so broad that my father would have described it as "doing a Kentucky thoroughbred justice." I can imagine Ang Chiri climbing all the way to the summit of Everest without ever needing oxygen from anyone's tank.

We spend a few more minutes chatting, and then Reggie announces

that the jovial little fellow named Semchumbi—no last name evidently—will be the head cook for the expedition. A tall, serious, relatively light-skinned Sherpa named Nawang Bura will be in charge of the
pack animals.

"And speaking of pack animals," says Reggie, "we need to start appor-
tioning the gear into bundles for the mules." She claps her hands, Pasang
makes gestures, and all thirty of the men rush toward the lower stables,
where our trucks are parked with the gear.

"And, gentlemen, you need to get about choosing your riding ponies
and saddles," says Reggie, leading us briskly toward the larger upper
stable.

"You've got to be kidding." I'm sitting on the white pony and my feet
are flat on the ground.

"They're Tibetan ponies," says Reggie. "Much more surefooted than
regular horses or ponies on the icy mountain trails we'll be taking, and
able to graze where a regular horse or mule would find no forage."

"Yes, but...," I say. I stand up and let the pony walk out from under
me. Jean-Claude is laughing so hard he's holding his sides. His legs are
short enough that he can hitch them up his pony's flanks and look as if
he's actually riding. The Deacon has chosen a pony but hasn't bothered
getting on the thing.

When I saw Reggie's big roan gelding trotting into the stable at dawn
after her ride, I assumed we'd be riding *real* horses into Tibet. After all,
Bruce's equipment list for the 1924 expedition had recommended each
Englishman bring along his own saddle.

I look at the miniature white pony walking out from under my bowed
legs. Hell, even an English saddle would weigh the poor thing down; an
American western saddle would crush it.

As if reading my mind, the Deacon says, "You can ride with just a
blanket pad on the poor beast, but you'll get tired holding your legs up,
Jake. Sliding off the pony on some of the narrow mountain trails we'll
be on would be a bad idea...it might be three or four hundred vertical
feet to the river below. There are wooden Tibetan saddles that Mallory
wanted us to use in 'twenty-one, but I would not recommend them."

"Why not?" I ask.

"They're shaped like a wooden 'V,'" says Reggie. "They'll crush your testicles after two or three miles."

I've never heard a woman say *testicles* before, and I realize that I'm blushing wildly. Jean-Claude doesn't help by laughing.

"I'm going down to help Dr. Pasang supervise the loading," says the Deacon.

Reggie is telling the liveryman which small pony saddles should go with which small pony. I get the largest saddle.

"Luncheon is at eleven sharp," she calls after the Deacon. "We have to settle the provisions problem then."

The Deacon stops, turns, opens his mouth to say something, but then pulls his unlit pipe from his tweed jacket's pocket and bites down on the stem. Making a military turn on his right heel, he walks quick time out of the stable and down toward the garages and smaller stable, from which direction we can hear the shouting of Sherpas and the braying of mules.

The Deacon and Reggie argue loudly during lunch, continue the argument over sherry in the afternoon when the gear and provisions finally have been apportioned to packs for quick loading on the mules in the morning, and resume the arguments again during dinner in the grand dining room.

They argue over provisions, about the route, over alternate plans for the search for Percival Bromley's corpse, about methods of climbing once we get to Everest, and—most central to all of the arguments—about who is in charge of the expedition.

In the middle of the arguing at lunchtime, the Deacon brings up a mystery that we haven't been able to solve despite all of the Deacon's contacts with the 1924 expedition: i.e., how on earth had Percival Bromley been allowed to tag along *behind* the expedition? Both General Charles Bruce, before he became ill and had to leave the expedition, and Colonel Norton, who took over general command of the expedition, were sticklers for staying with the plan they'd laid out. Even the addition of one more person to be responsible for would have fouled up their plans, and certainly young Percy wasn't such a renowned climber that Mallory and the others wouldn't have objected strongly to his nearby presence, even if he weren't a member of the expedition. Even the Deacon's good friends Noel Odell and the moviemaker who'd caused such controversy with his dancing lamas, Captain John Noel, had told the Deacon that they had no idea why Percy had been allowed to tag along. All they knew was that both General Bruce and Colonel Norton insisted that it was all right, against all logic—and each climber that the Deacon queried had said that Percy was such a nice and unassuming chap that as long as he simply followed the expedition, perhaps a half day's march behind, he was tolerated.

But there had been no plans for young Lord Percival Bromley to go with them even as far as Everest Base Camp at the foot of the Rongbuk Glacier. Everyone had understood that.

In the middle of arguing over provisions, the Deacon returns to this issue of how and why Percival Bromley was allowed to tag along to Mount Everest.

Reggie is weary of the talk, and her tone is of the sort that ends most conversations. "Listen one last time, Mr. Deacon. Cousin Percival was visiting here when the 'twenty-four expedition leaders were invited to the plantation to have dinner with Lord and Lady Lytton, as well as Percy and me. Lord Lytton, as you may remember, was Governor-General of Bengal, and he and General Bruce and Colonel Norton met alone with Percy for the better part of an hour in the study. When they emerged, both Bruce and Norton announced that Percy would be allowed to follow the expedition—not travel *with* them, you understand, and never be on the official rolls, but strictly travel *behind* them—the condition being that Percy provide his own pony, tent, and foodstuffs. The last was no problem because Percy had been assembling his kit here at the plantation for two weeks before the expedition arrived in Calcutta."

The Deacon shakes his head. "That makes no sense. Let someone just follow the expedition into Tibet? Someone with no official clearance to *be* in Tibet? Even if Lord Percival were following a day behind the real expedition, as an Englishman, his arrest or detention might have put the entire expedition at risk with the *dzongpens* and Tibetan authorities. It makes no sense at all."

"What are these *dzongpens* I've been hearing so much about?" asks Jean-Claude. "Just local headmen? Village chiefs? Tibetan warlords?"

"None of the above, really," says Reggie. "Most Tibetan communities are run by *dzongpens*—usually two men—one an important lama and the other an important layperson from the village. But sometimes there's a single *dzongpen* chieftain." She turns back to the Deacon. "It's getting late in the afternoon, Mr. Deacon. Have all your questions been answered to your satisfaction?"

"All save for why your cousin was trying to climb Everest after the Norton Expedition had left the area," presses the Deacon.

Reggie laughs with no humor in her voice. "Percy never attempted to climb Mount Everest. Of that I am certain."

"Sigl told both the *Berliner Zeitung* and *The Times* that he had been attempting precisely that," says the Deacon. "Sigl says that when he and the other Germans arrived at Camp Two—just exploring out of an original intent to meet Mallory and then from sheer curiosity—he, Sigl, and the other Germans could see your cousin and Kurt Meyer staggering down the North Ridge. Obviously in some difficulty."

Reggie shakes her head with absolute certainty. Her blue-black curls slide across her shoulders. "Bruno Sigl lied," she says sharply. "Percy may have had a reason to go up onto the mountain, but I know for a certainty that he did not go into Tibet in order to attempt a climb of Mount Everest. Bruno Sigl is a common German thug who lies."

"How do you know Sigl is a common German thug?" asks the Deacon. "Do you know him?"

"Of course not," snaps Reggie. "But I had inquiries made in Germany and elsewhere. Sigl is a dangerous climber, dangerous to himself and anyone with him, and in his regular life in Munich he's a fascist thug."

"Do you think that Sigl was somehow complicit in your cousin's and this Meyer's death?" asks the Deacon.

Reggie fixes her ultramarine gaze on the Deacon but does not answer.

In the calmer part of the afternoon, we show Reggie J.C.'s modified 12-point crampons and the shorter ice axes for vertical travel. Then Jean-Claude demonstrates the jumar climbing mechanism and the caver's rope ladders we've brought.

"Brilliant," says Reggie. "It all should make getting onto the North Col infinitely easier—and safer for the porters with the fixed ropes and ladders. But I don't have boots rigid enough for the pointed crampons, I fear."

"You'd need them only if you were leading the climb," says the Deacon. "And I guarantee you will not be doing that."

"I brought an extra pair of rigid boots," says Jean-Claude. "And I think they may fit you. I'll run and get them and we'll see."

They did fit her. She made some practice swings with the short ice hammers. The Deacon did not roll his eyes, but I could see this took some effort.

"Now I have an innovation for all of you," says Reggie. She goes into a storeroom and returns a few minutes later with four pairs of what look to be leather-strap football headgear, or perhaps leather bands that a coal miner might wear. But there are two insulated batteries in the back and an electric miner's lamp on the front.

"I had these made up after I returned from Everest last September," she says. "Lord Montfort had extensive mining operations in Wales. These are the newest thing—electric headlamps instead of carbide flames that might trigger an explosion. The batteries are a bit heavy, but they power the lamps for hours...and I have a lot of extra batteries."

"What on earth for?" asks the Deacon, holding the leather straps and lamp and heavy batteries at arm's length.

Reggie sighs. "According to Norton, Noel, and others I spoke to as their defeated party retreated through Darjeeling last year, Mallory and Irvine had planned to depart their high tent at six or six thirty a.m., but the slowness of everything—getting boots on properly, trying to melt snow on the stove for water for a hot drink and hot gruel before departing but overturning the cooker, getting their oxygen apparatus on and working, everything done so terribly *slowly* at that altitude—kept them in their camp until eight a.m. or later. That's far too late to leave camp for a summit bid. Even if they reached the summit, there was no way they could have gotten back down to their Camp Five before nightfall. Probably not even back down to the Yellow Band."

"How early do you suggest a summit team should leave camp with these...these...*things* on their heads?" asks the Deacon.

"No later than two a.m., Mr. Deacon. I would suggest closer to midnight the night before the actual summit attempt."

The Deacon laughs at the thought of climbing at that altitude at night. "We'd freeze," he says dismissively.

"No, no," says Jean-Claude. "Remember, *Ree-shard,* that thanks to you, we have Monsieur Finch's lovely warm goose down duvet jackets, enough for all of us and for our Tiger Sherpas. And I believe that Lady Brom...that Reggie has a good point here. There are fewer avalanches at night. The snow and ice are firmer. The new crampons would work better with the colder snow and more solid ice. And if these headlamps truly show the way..."

"They do for hundreds of modern Welsh miners," interrupts Reggie. "At least the engineers and supervisors. And Welsh miners don't have the advantage of starlight or moonlight in their dark holes."

"Magnifique!" says Jean-Claude.

"Very interesting," I say.

"Leave high camp at midnight for the summit," says the Deacon. "Absolutely absurd."

There are 40 mules allocated for the trek in to Everest, and each mule is capable of carrying a double pack weighing some 160 pounds. One Sherpa porter can handle two mules even while carrying his own heavy loads of our excess baggage.

Reggie has argued for more prepared food for the expedition. The Deacon is adamantly against it. As we're eating a delicious dinner of pheasant under glass set off with a very fine white wine, the two erupt at each other again.

"I don't believe you understand my theory behind this expedition, Lady Bromley-Montfort," the Deacon says coolly.

"I understand it all too well, *Mr.* Deacon. You're attempting an alpine assault on the tallest mountain in the world, dealing with it as if it were the Matterhorn. You plan to buy as much food as you can in the Tibetan villages along the way and hunt for more: wild goats, rabbits, *goas*—Tibetan gazelle—white deer, Himalayan blue sheep, whatever you can find and shoot."

"That *is* the idea," says the Deacon. "And since you claim to have climbed both in the Alps and here in the Himalayas, you know that such an alpine assault has never been tried against Everest."

"For good reason, Mr. Deacon. Not only the size of the mountain, but the weather. Even in this pre-monsoon season, the weather on the mountain can change in a matter of minutes. The mountain creates its own weather, Mr. Deacon. And you simply don't have enough portable food to last weeks on the mountain if weeks are called for. You can't just keep running back from the Rongbuk Glacier over Pang La to Shekar Dzong to go shopping when you run low, you know. And the tiny village of Chōdzong on the Everest side of Pang La doesn't have enough extra food this time of year anyway."

I've learned by now that *La* in Tibetan means "pass." Pang La is the 17,000-foot pass south of Shekar Dzong: the last such high pass before one approaches the Rongbuk Monastery, the Rongbuk Glacier, and Mount Everest. Most expeditions take four days or more trekking from Shekar Dzong to Everest Base Camp at the opening of the Rongbuk Glacier valley...then many more days finding a way up the glacier and onto the North Col.

"We can buy extra food from villagers on the way in," insists the Deacon.

Reggie laughs. "The average Tibetan villager will sell you his last chicken even if it means his own family will go hungry," she says, showing her very white teeth. "But how do you keep a chicken carcass fresh over weeks if the snows hit you at Camp Three below the North Col, Mr. Deacon? Do you plan to carry ice with you? An electric refrigeration unit? And once you're past Rongbuk, don't plan to survive on what the party may shoot. Except for a few rare *burrhel*—mountain sheep—and even more rare *yeti,* there's nothing up there. You'd spend your days hunting rather than climbing...and still likely starve."

The Deacon ignores the *yeti* comment. "I've been there, please remember, Lady Bromley-Montfort. I've spent many more weeks exploring the north side of the Everest approaches than you could have."

"You only spent so much time there in 'twenty-one because you and Mallory could not find the obvious way in via the East Rongbuk Glacier, Mr. Deacon."

The Deacon's face darkens.

"Listen," says Reggie, turning to J.C. and me as well as toward the Deacon, "I am not suggesting that we provision ourselves the way Bruce, Norton, and Mallory did...Good Lord, I watched them leave Darjeeling. Seventy Sherpa porters—a hundred and forty porters by the time they added Tibetans across the border—and more than three hundred pack animals, carrying not just oxygen and tents and necessary supplies, but scores of cans of *foie gras* and smoked sausages and beef tongue."

"Appetite wanes with altitude," says the Deacon. "You need foods that stimulate the appetite."

"Oh yes, I know." Reggie smiles. "I lost more than thirty pounds on the North Col last August, you may remember my telling you. Above twenty-three thousand feet, the very idea of food becomes repugnant. And one does not have the energy to prepare it. That is why I've added the supplemental canned goods, simple staples, bags of noodles and rice that will warm up in the boiled water, in case we're pinned down by weather."

The Deacon looks at J.C. and me as if we should jump in to support him in this argument. We smile at him and wait.

"Instead of three hundred pack animals," continues Reggie, "we'll travel with only forty and buy replacements along the way if need be. Instead of seventy Sherpa porters, we'll use only thirty. Instead of hiring another hundred and fifty porters in Shekar Dzong, I've arranged for us to trade the mules there for yaks and to continue with just our thirty Sherpas as porters. But we *must* have enough food. The search for Cousin Percy may take weeks. We simply can't return without finding him because we've run out of *food*."

The Deacon sighs. He can't tell her the real reason that he, Jean-Claude, and I have signed up for this expedition. A wait for good weather and then an alpine dash for the summit and then . . . home.

Reggie looks at each of us in turn. "I know your real reason for coming on this expedition, gentlemen," she says as if reading our guilty minds. "I know that you hope to climb Everest, that you're using my aunt's money and the excuse of searching for Percival's remains only as a way to get yourselves onto the mountain and, with luck, to the summit."

None of us replies. And none of us can meet her cool gaze.

"It doesn't matter," continues Reggie. "It's more important to me to find Percival's body than it is to you—perhaps for reasons you don't yet understand—but I also want to climb Mount Everest."

We all do look up at that. A woman on the summit of Everest? Ridiculous. Yet none of us speaks.

"It's nine p.m.," says Reggie as clocks throughout the great plantation house chime at the same second. "We should all get to bed. We'll be leaving at dawn."

J.C. and I rise with Reggie, but Deacon remains seated. "Not until we settle this issue of who is in command of the expedition, Lady Bromley-Montfort. An expedition cannot have two leaders. It simply won't work."

Reggie smiles at him. "It worked well enough last year when General Bruce grew ill with malaria, Mr. Deacon. Colonel Teddy Norton—who probably knew he would not end up on the summit team—took overall command of the expedition, while Mr. Mallory was in charge of the climbing plans and sorting out who would make the summit bid. Naturally that turned out to be himself and his healthy if inexperienced assistant Sandy Irvine...a nice boy. I enjoyed having him as a guest in my home. Now I suggest we use the same system. I shall be in charge of the expedition per se; you shall be climbing master on the mountain, answerable in terms of climbing decisions only to any sound suggestions I might have in the search for Cousin Percy's remains."

I can see the Deacon struggling to find the proper words to rebut this suggestion once and for all. But he is too slow.

Pasang...*Dr.* Pasang...pulls Reggie's chair out of her way.

"Good night, gentlemen," she says softly. "We leave for Mount Everest at dawn."

PART II

THE MOUNTAIN

Saturday, April 25, 1925

*E*verest is still 40 miles away but already it dominates not only the skyline of white-shrouded Himalayan high peaks but the sky itself. I suspect that the Deacon has brought a British flag to plant at the summit, but I see now that the mountain already bears its own pennant—a mist of white cloud and spindrift roiling in the west-to-east wind for 20 miles or more, from right to left, a white plume swirling above all the lesser summits to the east of Everest's snow massif.

"Mon Dieu," whispers Jean-Claude.

The five of us, counting Pasang, have trekked ahead of the porter-Sherpas and yaks and climbed a low hill to the east of the pass, and while Pasang stands a few yards behind us and below the high point of the pass, holding the reins of J.C.'s little white pony, which is spooked by the winds here on Pang La—the last pass before Rongbuk and Everest—the four of us have to lie on the boulder-strewn ground or be blown away.

We lie unceremoniously on our right sides, like Romans on their couches at a feast, the Deacon furthest from me, propping himself on his right elbow as he attempts to hold his military binoculars steady with his left hand; then there is Reggie, who is lying prone, her boot soles looking like inverted exclamation marks, using both hands to prop a naval-type telescope against a low boulder in front of her; then Jean-Claude, sitting more upright than the rest of us and squinting southward through his snow goggles; finally me, reclining on my right elbow and somewhat behind the other three.

We're all wearing wide-brimmed hats against the Tibetan sunlight, ferocious at this altitude—burning and peeling has been my bane the last weeks, as evidently it had been Sandy Irvine's—and while the three of us men have simply jammed the hats as far down on our heads as we can in order to outwit the wind, Reggie is wearing a strange fedora—broad-brimmed on the left, front, and back, buttoned up on the right, which has an adjustable strap that goes under her chin and holds the hat tight. She said she had picked it up during a visit to Australia years ago.

We call out the names of mountains to one another like children exclaiming over Christmas presents: "Moving to the west, that tall one is Cho Oyu, twenty-six thousand nine hundred and six feet..." "Gyachung Kang, twenty-five thousand nine hundred ninety feet..." "That peak throwing its shadow on Everest is Lhotse, twenty-seven thousand and...I forget..." "Twenty-seven thousand eight hundred ninety feet." "To the east there, Chomo Lonzo, twenty-five thousand six hundred and four feet..."

"And Makalu," says the Deacon. "Twenty-seven thousand seven hundred sixty-five feet."

"My God," I whisper. One could take the highest peaks of America's Rocky Mountains and they would be lost in the foothills of these white-fanged giants. The cols—the saddles—that were the low points connecting Everest and the other peaks started above 25,000 feet—3,000 feet higher than any mountain in North America.

Usually, according to Reggie and the Deacon, members of previous expeditions had been able to catch glimpses of Everest at other times during the trek west toward Shekar Dzong—especially if one was willing to detour up the Yaru Valley west of Tinki Dzong and do a little climbing—but we've spent the last five weeks trekking under thick, low clouds, often against freezing rain and blowing snow, so this sunny day atop Pang La is our first view of the mountain.

Reggie beckons me forward, and I lie prone next to her on the reddish soil and hard rocks—a strangely intimate moment—and she steadies the barrel of the telescope as I peer through it.

"My God." These seem to be the only syllables I'm capable of this day.

Even at my young age—I'd turned 23 somewhere in Sikkim on April 2—I've had enough mountaineering experience to know that a mountain that seems unclimbable from a distance can reveal routes, perhaps even easy routes, once one gets close enough to it or actually on it. But the summit of Everest looks...just too large, too tall, too white, too windy, too infinitely far away.

Jean-Claude has crawled up to use the Deacon's binoculars.

"You can't see the North Col or the high point on the East Rongbuk Glacier from here because of the intervening hills," says the Deacon. "But look along the North East Ridge. Can you see the First Step and Second Step nearing the summit?"

"All I can see is an endless plume of spindrift," says J.C. "What must those winds be like *on* that North East Ridge right now?"

Instead of answering that, the Deacon says, "You can clearly see the Great Couloir—or what they're calling Norton's Couloir now—stretching down to the left from beneath the Summit Pyramid."

"Ah, yes...," breathes J.C.

It's impossible for me to tell through Reggie's slightly jiggling telescope whether or not that couloir is deep in snow and a pure avalanche deathtrap or not.

"The strong spring winds are good," Reggie says, her voice almost lost beneath the Pang La wind hooting and whistling between boulders. "They clear away the monsoon and winter snows. They will give us a better chance of finding Percy."

Percy. In my growing eagerness to get on the mountain and to start climbing, I've almost forgotten about Lord Percy Bromley and our ostensible reason for coming so far. The thought of the young man's corpse up there somewhere on that unassailable, inhuman mountain with its impossible winds makes me shiver.

Pasang's powerful voice comes up to us. "The lead porters are approaching the summit of the pass behind us."

Reluctantly, eyes watering from both the wind and the fatigue of squinting so hard at the distant peak in the unrelenting light, all four of us stand, brush dust and pebbles from our heavy layers of goose down and wool, turn our backs to the wind from the west, and walk—half-staggering in the gusts now at our backs—toward the narrow trail leading across the saddle of this pass.

* * *

Sikkim had been all hothouse flowers, jungles of rhododendrons, air almost too thick and humid to breathe, steaming overgrown valleys, camping in clearings that weren't really clearings, salting leeches off our bodies at the end of long days hiking through wet vegetation and avoiding the *daks*—tidy little bungalows that the Raj had placed every eleven miles, a long day's march, on the long main route into Tibet toward the closest Tibetan trade capital, Gyantse. *Daks,* according to Reggie and Dr. Pasang, came complete with fresh food, beds, books to read, and a permanent servant, called a *chowkidar,* in each bungalow. But our group camped a mile short of each *dak* or two miles beyond, never taking advantage of the bungalows set there for precisely the purpose we needed them.

"British expeditions stay in the *daks*," said the Deacon as we sat around one of our early campfires in the Sikkimese jungle.

"So do hundreds of other Englishmen," said Reggie. "Trade representatives going north to Gyantse. Officials of the Raj. Naturalists. Cartographers. Diplomats."

"But we're none of those things," said the Deacon. "One look at our climbing gear and miles of rope and the servants will send the word about us forward into Tibet."

"How?" asked Jean-Claude.

The Deacon removed his pipe and smiled thinly. "We're not quite as far off all maps as we feel, gentlemen. Even here in Sikkim. The Raj has run telephone and telegraph wires all the way north to Gyantse, across even the high passes."

"It's true," said Reggie. "We won't be off the main north-south trade route until we turn west toward Kampa Dzong, well into Tibet. But in the meantime, I believe the only ones we're fooling with our rugged camping rather than spending relatively comfortable nights in the *daks* are some of the leeches we've encountered."

Our starting out had been all downhill from Darjeeling to the Tista Bridge. The Sherpas had left before dawn on March 26 with the ponies and loads, and we brought our rucksacks and extra provisions as far as 6th Mile Stone in two rugged trucks, one driven by Pasang and the other by Reggie. There we joined the trekkers while Edward the chauffeur and another man returned the trucks to the plantation, and we and the thirty

Sherpas and our ponies and mules continued steeply downhill to and across the Tista River to the Sikkim village of Kalimpong.

We camped beyond Kalimpong because Reggie did not want to give advance notice to the crotchety governor of Sikkim, Major Frederick Bailey, the official who (according to Reggie) had been sabotaging the Everest Committee's permissions to enter Tibet just so that he might someday get a chance to climb the mountain himself. There was a border guard as we entered Sikkim—a lone Gurkha—who accepted Reggie's Tibetan travel permit without protest, and we were all amused at the lone guard shouting orders to himself—"Right hand salute!" "Left turn!" "Quick march!" The Deacon informed us afterward that when a Gurkha lacked an officer or NCO to give him orders, he was quite happy ordering himself around.

Twice during our six days crossing Sikkim did brown men in police uniforms catch up to our line of Sherpas and mules and small white ponies, but in each case Reggie took the official aside, spoke to him privately, and—I can only guess—gave him money. In any event, no one tried to stop us in Sikkim, and in just under a week of breathing the over-sweet scent of rhododendrons while pulling leeches off any unprotected parts of ourselves after wading through waist-high wet grasses, we were approaching the high pass—Jelep La—that would bring us into Tibet. We were not sorry to put Sikkim behind us; it rained constantly, and soon all our clothes were sodden; not a day of pure sunlight in which we could lay our clothes and socks out to dry. I thought I was the only one who'd picked up a light case of dysentery during our Sikkim crossing, but I soon realized that it was bothering J.C. and the Deacon as well. Only Reggie and Pasang seemed immune to the embarrassing disability.

I'd been dosing myself with lead opium for several days before the Deacon noticed my illness and referred me to Dr. Pasang. The tall Sherpa nodded when, embarrassed as I was, I admitted to my intestinal problems, and then gently suggested that the lead opium would have some effect on the dysentery but that the side effects from the nightly dosings might be worse than the disease. He gave me a bottle of sweet-tasting medicine that quieted my guts within a day.

At first I would walk ahead of my white pony, carrying almost 70 pounds of gear in my pack, but Reggie convinced me to ride when I could and to let the mules carry most of my load. "You'll need your energy on Everest," she said, and I soon realized that she was right.

Weakened some by the dysentery from which I was just beginning to recover, I became used to our expedition's habit of stopping in early evening, the Whymper tents and larger cooking tarp tent already erected for us by advance Sherpas and our sleeping bags laid out, and accustomed also to awakening to the soft tones of "Good morning, Sahibs," as Babu Rita and Norbu Chedi brought J.C. and me our coffee. Next door, the Deacon would be drinking his coffee, and Reggie, always up and dressed before any of us, would be having her morning tea and muffins with Pasang by the fire.

It wasn't until we climbed 14,500-foot Jelep La that I realized how the illness in Sikkim had weakened me. In Colorado with Harvard climbing friends a few years earlier, I'd all but galloped up the 14,000-plus-foot Longs Peak and felt great at its broad summit, able to do handstands, but climbing the switchbacks and then the wet and slippery stones—a sort of endless natural staircase—toward the summit of Jelep La, I found myself taking three steps, then leaning on my long ice axe and gasping for breath. Then three more steps. Since the high point of the pass was less than half the altitude of the summit of Everest, this was not a good omen.

I could see that Jean-Claude was also breathing a little harder and moving a little slower than usual, although he'd been atop enough 14,000-foot summits. Only the Deacon from our original party seemed already acclimated to the altitude, and I noticed that he had some trouble keeping up with Reggie's fast hiking and climbing pace.

We reached Yatung in Tibet, and the differences between Tibet and Sikkim could not have been much greater. It had snowed on us at the high point of Jelep La, and the snow and driving winds from the west continued as we headed out onto the high, dry Tibetan plain. From the jungle riot of colors in Sikkim—pinks and rich cream colors and colors I didn't even have names for but which Reggie or the Deacon identified as mauve and cerise—we'd emerged into an essentially colorless world, gray clouds low above our heads, gray rocks to either side, and only the dull native red of the Tibetan soil to add a little color to the universe. Our faces were soon muddy with that windblown red soil, and when the cold wind made my eyes water—before I learned to wear my goggles even at that relatively low altitude—the tear streaks would run like bright blood down my mud-caked cheeks.

We spend our last night of the approach trek outside the small, windswept village of Chōdzong on Monday, April 27, then the next day we head down the eighteen-mile-long valley to the Rongbuk Monastery only some eleven miles from the entrance to the Rongbuk Glacier, the proposed site of our Base Camp.

"What does Rongbuk mean?" asks Jean-Claude.

The Deacon either doesn't know or is too preoccupied to answer. Reggie replies, "Monastery of the Snows."

We stop at the windswept monastery long enough to ask for an audience with and a ritual blessing from the Holy Lama, *ngag-dwang-batem-hdsin-norbu,* the high lama Dzatrul Rinpoche. "The Sherpas aren't as superstitious about this as Tibetan porters would be," Reggie explains as we wait, "but it's still a good idea to get such a blessing before we proceed to Base Camp, much less attempt to climb the mountain."

But we're to be disappointed. The Holy Lama with the title sounding like a tin can tumbling down concrete steps sends word that it is "inauspicious" for him to meet with us now. Dzatrul Rinpoche will summon us back to the monastery, his lama representative says, if and when he, the Holy Lama, feels it is auspicious to grace us with his presence and blessing.

Reggie's surprised at this. She's always had a good relationship with the monks and chief Holy Lama at the Rongbuk Monastery, she says. But when she asks a priest she knows why the Dzatrul Rinpoche is refusing to see us, the bald old man answers—in Tibetan, which Reggie translates for us—"The auspices are bad. The demons in the mountain are awake and angry, and more are coming. The *Metohkangmi* on the mountain are active and angry, and..."

"*Metohkangmi?*" asks Jean-Claude.

"*Yeti,*" the Deacon reminds us. "Those ubiquitous hairy manlike monsters."

"...your General Bruce assured us three years ago that all the British climbers belonged to one of England's mountain-worshiping sects and that they were on a holy pilgrimage to *Cho-mo-lung-ma,* but we know now that General Bruce lied. You English do not worship the mountain." Reggie is interpreting as fast as the old monk is speaking.

"Is this about the dancing lamas and Noel's damned motion picture?" asks the Deacon.

Reggie ignores the question and does not translate it for the monk. She says something in singsong Tibetan, bows low, and all five of us, including Pasang, back out of the monk's presumably holy presence. The old man returns to spinning a prayer wheel.

Outside in the wind again, she lets her breath out. "This is very bad, gentlemen. Our Sherpas—especially our chosen Tiger high-climbers—very much want and need this blessing. We'll have to set up Base Camp and then I'll return and try to convince the Holy Lama that we do deserve a blessing for the mountain."

"To the Devil with him if the old man doesn't want to grace us with his damned blessing," growls the Deacon.

"No," says Reggie, gracefully swinging herself aboard her tiny white pony. "It will be to the Devil with *us* if we don't get that blessing for our Sherpas."

It was back in late March when we were camped just past the first major Sikkim village of Kalimpong that the Deacon had his visit from the Mysterious Stranger.

I'd noticed the tall, thin man when Dr. Pasang led him into camp and Reggie started chatting with him, but between the traditional Sherpa-Nepalese clothing, the brown cap that was really more turban than cap, the brown skin and huge black beard of the stranger, I assumed that this was an unusually tall Sherpa, or perhaps a relative of Pasang's, visiting us. I did note that he was wearing solid, if very worn, English hiking boots.

It turned out not only to be a white man, an Englishman, but a very famous Englishman.

Before a whisper of the stranger's identity started buzzing around the camp, the Deacon's personal Sherpa, Nyima Tsering, had come to fetch our friend. "A sahib is here to see you, Sahib," said Nyima to the Deacon with his habitual giggle.

The Deacon and J.C. were both fiddling with the oxygen apparatus flow valve. When he looked up toward our visitor, the tall, bearded man in Nepalese peasant clothing but wearing solid English hiking boots, the Deacon leaped to his feet and jogged over to shake his hand. I assumed that the Deacon would bring the stranger over to the fire and introduce him to Jean-Claude and me, but instead the two men—rather rudely, I thought—walked away toward the nearby stream that flowed into the Tista River we'd just crossed. There we could just see through the screen of trees that the stranger squatted in a Sherpa-like manner, the Deacon sat on a small river boulder, and the two immediately became lost in conversation.

"Who is that?" I asked Reggie when she finally strolled over to see if we wanted some more coffee.

"K. T. Owings," she said.

I couldn't have been more dumbstruck if she had announced that the stranger was the Second Coming of Christ.

Kenneth Terrence Owings had been one of my literary idols from the time I was twelve years old. The so-called "climber-poet" had been one of the top five living British alpinists before the Great War, but also one of England's more celebrated free-verse poets, easily ranking with Rupert Brooke and even the other great poets who'd died in the War—Wilfred Owen, Edward Thomas, Charles Sorley—or those few who'd survived to write about it, including Siegfried Sassoon and Ivor Gurney.

K. T. Owings had survived the War, after being promoted all the way from lieutenant to major, but he'd never written a word about the fighting. In fact, as far as I knew, Owings had never written another word of *poetry* since the War. In that sense he was very much like the Deacon, who'd been rather famous for his verse before the War but hadn't published—or evidently written—a word since the fighting began. Nor had Owings returned to the Alps, where, like George Mallory and the Deacon (and often in the company of the Deacon), he'd become so famous as a climber before the War. K. T. Owings had simply disappeared. Some newspapers and literary journals reported that Owings had gone to Africa, where he'd climbed Mount Kilimanjaro by himself and simply refused to come back down. Others were certain that he'd gone to China to climb unnamed mountains and been killed by bandits there. The most recent authoritative word was that K. T. Owings—to cleanse himself of his experiences in the Great War—had built a small sailing ship, attempted to sail around the world, and drowned in a terrible storm in the South Atlantic.

I looked through the branches again. There was K. T. Owings, dressed in something like clean rags, black beard with swatches of gray in it, squatting on his haunches and chatting away a mile a minute with the Deacon. It was hard to believe.

I stood, took my metal water bottle, and began walking toward the stream.

"Mr. Deacon wanted to be left alone with him," said Reggie.

"I'm just going to get some water," I said. "I shan't bother them."

"Make sure you boil it before drinking," said Reggie.

I, all but tiptoed down to the stream, keeping a thick screen of branches between me and the two men. Leaning to my left toward the screen of branches, the better to eavesdrop as I filled my large metal water bottle, I realized that the Deacon was speaking too softly to be heard but Owings's voice was a deep rasp.

"...and I've reconnoitered high enough to see that there's a serious step in the ridge, a rock face about forty feet high, just below the summit ridge...I can see it from the valley with binoculars and caught another glimpse climbing above the Cwm..."

What was this? Owings seemed to be warning the Deacon about the First or Second Step...probably the Second Step, since the summit ridge lay just beyond...on the North East Ridge of Everest. But we all knew about the First and Second Steps, although no one—with the possible exception of Mallory and Irvine on the day they disappeared—had yet gone high enough on the ridges to tackle them (especially the larger, steeper-looking Second Step). The two Steps had been visible in photographs taken since the 1921 expedition. Why would Owings be cautioning the Deacon about such an obvious thing now? And for some reason he'd used the term "Cwm" rather than Col for the North Col. Perhaps the poet-climber had his own names for various features that had been named since the 1921 recon expedition. Had Owings tried to climb Mount Everest on his own and been turned back by these formidable rock-step obstacles high on the North East Ridge? The Steps were a main reason—along with the terrible winds along the ridgeline—why Norton and others had moved onto the North Face to try ascending the near-vertical Great Couloir.

"...with fixed rope perhaps..." was all I could hear of the Deacon's hushed reply.

"Yes, yes, that might work," Owings concluded. "But I can't promise a camp or cache right below that..."

The Deacon said something in low tones. He might have warned Owings to keep his voice down, since the famous poet-climber's words were barely audible when the conversation resumed.

"...the worst part of all is almost certainly the Ice Fall...," Owings was saying urgently.

Ice Fall? I thought. Was he talking about the near-vertical snow and ice face below the North Col at the head of the East Rongbuk Glacier? That was difficult, certainly—seven Sherpa porters had died in the avalanche there in '22—but how could it be the "worst part" of an Everest expedition? Two expeditions had already climbed high above it, even transporting heavy loads up the ice face daily. Scores of trips. Last year Sandy Irvine had jury-rigged that rope and wood ladder to make the climb easier and safer for the porters. Even Pasang and Reggie, if she was to be believed—and I believed her—had free-climbed it, laboriously cutting steps into the ice face, and had been able to get to the North Col campsite and briefly above before bad weather pinned them down. We'd brought caving ladders and J.C.'s new 12-point crampons and his jumar doohickey to make the porters' climb to the North Col easier and safer.

"I have the sequence," Owings said, his voice a rasp. "White, green, then red. Make sure...keep them high, very high, and..."

This made no sense to me at all. Suddenly my boot slipped on a stone as I squatted by the stream, my bottle already full, and I heard the Deacon say, "Shhh, someone's nearby."

Red-faced, faking nonchalance, I capped my bottle, stood, and strolled as innocently as I could back up to the campsite, not sure if the Deacon and his famous friend could see me through the leafy branches or not.

The two moved a bit downstream, further out of sight and into a clearing where no one could crouch nearby unseen, and their intense exchange continued for another thirty minutes. Then the Deacon came back to camp alone.

"Isn't Mr. Owings going to join us for dinner?" asked Reggie.

"No, he's headed back this evening. Hopes to reach Darjeeling by tomorrow night," replied the Deacon and looked sharply at me where I sat with my incriminating water bottle still in my hands. I looked down before I started blushing.

"Ree-shard," said Jean-Claude, "you never told us that you knew K. T. Owings."

"It never came up," said the Deacon, taking his ease on one of the packing crates and resting his elbows on his wool-covered knees.

"I would very much have liked to meet Monsieur Owings," continued J.C., his tone a shade accusing, I thought.

The Deacon shrugged. "Ken is a rather solitary fellow. He wanted to talk to me about something he did, and then he needed to get back."

"Where does he live?" I managed to ask.

"In Nepal." It was Reggie who answered. "Near Thyangboche, I believe. In the Khumbu Valley."

"I didn't think that white men—Englishmen—were allowed in Nepal," I said.

"They aren't," said the Deacon.

"Mr. Owings went there after the War," Reggie said. "I believe he has a Nepalese wife and several children. He's been accepted there. He rarely crosses into India or Sikkim."

The Deacon said nothing.

What's the white-green-red sequence stuff all about? I wanted to ask the Deacon. *Why is the ice face, or Ice Fall, as Owings called it, supposed to be the most dangerous part of the climb? Why was he talking about camping sites and caches? Has he found or left something on the north side of the mountain that the three previous English expeditions hadn't stumbled upon?*

"Did you happen to know Major Owings during the War?" asked Reggie.

"Yes, I knew him then," said the Deacon. "And before." He stood up and slapped his knees. "It's getting late. Are we going to get Semchumbi busy cooking something tonight or just turn in hungry?"

*   *   *

Leaving the Rongbuk Monastery with many of the Sherpas grumbling about the lack of a blessing—grumbling at least until Dr. Pasang shouts them into a surly silence—the thirty-five of us trudge two miles down the valley and across the river toward the mouth of the Rongbuk Glacier until we reach the site of the three earlier expeditions' Base Camp about an hour or so before sunset. The futile waiting at the monastery for the head lama Dzatrul Rinpoche to see us has wasted too much of our day.

I confess that I'm feeling somewhat depressed by the time we reach the Base Camp site. All three expeditions have camped at exactly this spot—within the glacier valley but shielded from the worst winds by a 40-foot-high moraine-rock ridge to the south, view open to the north whence we've just come, flat spots for the tents (some even free of larger rocks), and a small melt lake where the ponies, mules, and yaks we've traded for can drink. A glacial stream runs nearby, and although the water has to be boiled before drinking because of the nearby animal and human waste, and we prefer to melt clean snow to drink, the stream gives us water for bathing.

But there's also filth and debris from the three previous British expeditions: tatters of torn tent canvas and broken poles; a litter of discarded oxygen tanks and frames; low rock walls that the wind has managed to tumble in places, heaps of not-yet-rusting discarded tin cans by the hundreds, some still full of rotting uneaten delicacies from last year's expedition; and to the left of the main camping area, an obvious spot for the latrines along a line of flat stones. We're greeted by hundreds of freeze-dried human turds lining a trench neither dug deep enough nor filled in when Norton and the others retreated from this spot.

Even more depressing, just downhill from the trashy site of Mallory's base camp rises the tall pyramid of stones that the previous expedition raised as a memorial to those who've died on the mountain. The top inset boulder had been painted to read IN MEMORY OF THREE EVEREST EXPEDITIONS and below that is a boulder inscribed 1921 KELLAS in memory of the physician who died during the 1921 reconnaissance expedition that the Deacon had been part of. Below that, Mallory's and Irvine's names are inset there, as are the names of the seven Sherpas who died in the 1922 avalanche. The rock-pyramid memorial seems to turn the entire Base Camp area into a cemetery.

But grimmest of all somehow is the un-Matterhorn-like massif of Mount Everest itself, still some twelve miles up the windblown Rong-buk Glacier valley. We can see its western flanks and ridges glowing in the evening light during a break in the snow and near-constant cloud cover, but even at this distance, the mountain seems misshapen and far too large. Rather than a distinct mountain like Mont Blanc or the Matterhorn, Everest seems more like one infinitely huge fang along an impossible barrier of gigantic teeth. The wind spume from its summit and ridges now extends beyond the horizon to the east, streaming high above nearby Mount Kellas and the taller—and also too large, too tall, too steep, too massive, too distant—Himalayan peaks which stretch like a wall built by gods to block our path.

I can sense the Deacon's distaste at setting up a camp here, but the Sherpas will carry no further this long day. The Deacon had always wanted to set up our first Base Camp more than three miles farther up the valley, where Camp I or Advanced Base Camp had been in the earlier efforts. But this Base Camp is already at 16,500 feet—more than 12,500 feet below Everest's impossible summit but still high enough to leave most of us gasping with our 60-pound loads. Camp I, according to what both the Deacon and Reggie have said, is at 17,800 feet, and—while it is said to catch the most sun of any of the Everest camps—it is often much more exposed to the winds whipping down off the North Face of Everest and scouring the glacier. There's more ice than moraine rock up there, and Dr. Pasang has pointed out that it will be harder to recover from altitude sickness with even just another 1,300 feet of altitude beneath us. Reggie's made a good argument during the five weeks of camp evenings that we should establish the first line of tents here—someplace to retreat to when altitude sickness strikes—and the Deacon no longer seems interested in arguing the point. He plans to cache almost all of the high-climbing equipment at Camp II, six miles above Base Camp.

Now he dumps the heavy load he's been carrying, pulls an almost empty rucksack from it, and says to Reggie, "Go ahead and supervise the establishment of Base Camp here, if you will, Lady Bromley-Montfort. I'm going to reconnoiter up the valley as far as Camp One."

"That's ridiculous," says Reggie. "It will be dark before you get there."

The Deacon reaches into the almost empty rucksack and pulls out one of Reggie's leather battery-lamp headpieces. He flicks its headlamp on and then off. "We'll see if this Welsh miner contraption works. If not, I have an old-fashioned hand torch in my rucksack."

"You should not go alone, *Ree-shard,*" says Jean-Claude. "And especially not onto the glacier. The crevasses will be impossible to see in the twilight."

"I won't have to climb onto the glacier proper just to reach Camp One," says the Deacon. "I have some biscuits in my jacket pocket, but would greatly appreciate it if you would keep some coffee and soup warm for me."

He turns and disappears up the valley of gathering shadows.

Reggie calls Pasang over, and within minutes they are organizing the tired Sherpa porters, unloading the yaks and mules, and deciding which tents to erect where in this strangely sad place. Pasang directs the lifting of a large Whymper tent rainfly inside one of the crumbling *sangas,* or rock walls, hangs curtains on the side, and declares this the medical tent. Several Sherpas line up for consultation and treatment almost at once.

Our valley is in darkness, but Everest blazes far beyond and above us in a cold, powerful, self-contained isolation. That strikes me as terrifying.

It was our last night in Sikkim—April 2—right before we crossed over the Jelep La into Tibet, when I celebrated my 23rd birthday. I hadn't told anyone about the date, but someone must have noticed it on my passport, because we definitely had a celebration.

I don't even remember the name of the tiny village some 12 or 13 miles between Guatong, where we stayed that night, and the border—perhaps it had no name, it certainly had no *dak* bungalow—but it did have what I called a Ferris wheel and what the Deacon called "a miniature version of the Great Wheel at Blackpool" and what Reggie called "a little version of the Vienna Wheel." The thing was crude, built out of raw lumber, and consisted of four "passenger cars" that were little more than wooden boxes one crawled into. At its high point, this "Great Wheel" couldn't carry a person's feet more than ten feet above the ground, and the mechanism to make it work, once I'd been coaxed into sitting in one of the boxes, consisted of Jean-Claude pulling the next car down on one side and the Deacon pushing up on the other. The contraption must have been built for the village children, but we'd seen no children on our way into the village and would see none before we left in the morning.

Then they stopped me at the nominal high point—all eight of the village huts were spread out in panorama, their rooftops just a little higher than my knees—and Reggie, the Deacon, Jean-Claude, Pasang, and several of the English-speaking porters began singing "For He's a Jolly Good Fellow" followed by a ragged chorus of "Happy Birthday." I confess to blushing wildly as I sat there with my wool-stockinged legs dangling.

Reggie had packed in all the makings for a seriously civilized cake, even icing and candles, and she and Jean-Claude and the cook, Semchumbi, baked it in one of the Primus and stone stoves before we all ate dinner that night. The Deacon produced two bottles of good brandy, and the four of us drank each other's health deep into the night.

Finally, when everyone had staggered off to their sleeping bags in their own tents, I stumbled outside mine and looked up at the night sky. It was one of the few times during our days in Sikkim when it wasn't raining.

Twenty-three years old. It seemed so much older, but no wiser, than 22 for some reason. Had Sandy Irvine been 22 or 23 when he died on Everest the year before? I couldn't quite remember. Twenty-two, I thought. Younger than I was that night in Sikkim. The brandy fumes made me dizzy, and I rested against one of the splintery support props for the Not-So-Great Wheel as I continued looking beyond black treetops at a half-moon rising above the jungle. It was a Tuesday, and I was one day from dropping off most nations' maps, into the high-desert wilderness of Tibet.

I thought of Reggie. Had she brought a nightgown? Or did she sleep in some combination of her clothes and underwear or in pajamas as most of us did? Or in the nude as the Deacon did, even in places where centipedes and snakes had been common?

I shook my head again to rid myself of that image of Lady Bromley-Montfort. At the very least, Reggie was a decade older than I—probably more.

So what? asked my brandy-liberated brain.

I looked at the half-moon rising—bright enough to paint the upper rain forest leaves silver and diminishing stars to invisibility in its slow climb toward the zenith—and imagined various acts of heroics I might perform during the coming trek or climb, something that would endear me to Reggie in some manner greater than, or at least different from, the mere friendship we seemed to enjoy now.

She baked me a birthday cake. She'd known the date of my birthday and carted in all that flour and sugar and canned milk—and found eggs somewhere in this village or the last—and worked with Semchumbi and J.C. over an open kitchen fire to bake it. I had no idea how that was done, but the cake had been delicious, down to its chocolate icing. And there had been a small conflagration of twenty-three small wax candles burning on it.

She baked me a birthday cake. In my calf love, I edited out J.C.'s and Semchumbi's contribution to the cake and the Deacon's hearty singing and back-clapping and the rare gift of the brandy. *She baked me a birthday cake.*

Before I started blubbering, I managed to crawl back into my tent, remove my boots, and struggle into the sleeping bag, trying to keep that single thought—*She baked me a birthday cake*—as my last before dreaming, but my actual last thought before falling asleep was—*Now I'm 23. Will I survive to be 24?*

My first morning at Everest Base Camp, I wake with a splitting headache and nausea. This is profoundly disappointing since I've only recently felt 100 percent after the bout of dysentery that Dr. Pasang cured more than a month earlier in Sikkim. I always thought, since I was the youngest, that I'd be the healthiest during this expedition, but it's turning out that I'm the invalid of the group.

For a moment I can't remember what day it is, so before crawling out of my warm sleeping bag into the terrible cold—our thermometer will show us later in the day that the high temperature will be minus nineteen degrees Fahrenheit—I check my pocket calendar. It is Wednesday, April 29, 1925. We'd fallen behind Norton and Mallory's trekking time way back in Sikkim but made up for that with shortcuts Reggie showed us in the long trek west across Tibet to the mountain-fortress village of Shekar Dzong before turning south to the Rongbuk. We also spent only one night in villages where the previous expeditions had spent two. It was precisely one year ago that Mallory, Irvine, Norton, Odell, Geoffrey Bruce, Somervell, Bentley Beetham, and a few other high-climbers with hopes of reaching the summit had awakened to their first day in Base Camp at this very spot.

I realize that Jean-Claude is already out of his bag and stirring, and he wishes me a good morning as he lights our small Primus stove. He's already dressed and has been out far enough from the campsite to bring back clean snow for melting for our first coffees. No Sherpas are showing up at our tent door with hot morning drinks as they had during the trek in, but presumably Semchumbi is using the largest, multiple-grill Primus to prepare our breakfasts in the large, round experimental tent which Reggie brought along and which we've been using for our common mess tent when a mere large tarp isn't enough to shelter us from the increasingly harsh elements.

We are carrying three basic types of tents on this expedition: the heavier A-shaped Whymper tents used for so many years and on previous expeditions, which we plan to pitch only at the lower camps; the lighter but sturdy Meade-pattern A-type tents for the upper camps; and this igloo-shaped experimental tent of Reggie's. It is a prototype of a specially framed hemispherical tent made by the firm of Camp and Sports, with its outer shell double-skinned in a Jacquard material. "Reggie's Big Tent," as we call it, has eight curved wooden struts, each of which can be folded in the middle for easy hauling. The groundsheet is sewn in, and up here in the cold, I've watched Reggie and Pasang supervise the setting out of a separate and thicker groundsheet that Reggie says was made especially for her by the Hurricane Smock Company. There are two mica windows in this exceptional domed tent—of course our other tents all have only tied-up openings and no windows—and the Big Tent has rather complicated but almost windproof lace-up doors. The Big Tent also has a ventilating or stovepipe cowl that can be turned in any direction to accommodate the winds. It's made for four or five people to sleep in—comfortably—and we can easily squeeze in eight or nine during mealtimes.

The first day Reggie and Pasang erected this igloo-tent on our trek, the Deacon sourly announced that the contraption looked like a Christmas plum pudding minus its sprig of holly.

But, as it turns out, the Big Tent will be warmer and more windproof than any of our Whymper or Meade-pattern tents. I will make a note of this during our first days at Base Camp: future expeditions should bring smaller versions of the hemispherical tent, perhaps four hinged and curved struts rather than eight, for the most dangerous camps—IV, V, and VI, even VII if such a higher camp is ever pitched—up on the mountain where tent platforms have to be hacked out of snow and ice or laboriously created by moving stones. Not only would such a round footprint be smaller on the mountain, but the howling winds today will flow over and around the Big Tent, while our A-tents are already flapping with a noise like multiple rifle shots.

"What's the weather like?" I sleepily ask J.C. as I accept my first cup of hot coffee from him.

"Look," says my friend.

Taking care not to spill my coffee, I crouch next to the tightly ribbon-tied tent opening and peer out.

It is an absolute whiteout of a blizzard. I can't see the other tents pitched nearby, not even the central Big Tent.

"Oh, damn," I whisper. I'd thought it cold in our tent, but the high winds blowing in chill me through two layers of long underwear and the third layer I'd slept in. "Did the Deacon make it back from his reconnoiter toward Camp One last night?"

How ironic and sad would it be if our experienced climbing leader had been caught by the storm and died on his first night out from Base Camp.

J.C. nods and sips his coffee. "He came back about midnight, shortly before the heavy snow and higher winds started up. His face mask was covered with ice, and, according to Tenzing Bothia, *Ree-shard* was *very* hungry."

"So am I," I say as I finish the coffee. The nausea and headache are still there, but I'm convinced that I'll feel better if I eat something. "I'll finish dressing, and what do you say we see if we can make it over to the Big Tent for breakfast?"

* * *

It was April 18 during our trek in to Everest when the bandits struck.

We were more than halfway through our five-week trek. We had spent two nights camping near the larger Tibetan town of Tinki Dzong and had just decided not to divert down the Yaru Chu Valley on the chance of getting a glimpse of Everest—the weather was terrible, constant clouds, sleet, snow, and wind. We were on the main trade route trail approaching the 16,900-foot pass of Tinki La, when suddenly horsemen clattered downhill and surrounded our group, herding the Sherpas and trailing mules up to the front with us.

There were about sixty men on horseback, all wearing elaborate leather, wild furs, and long-flapped hats. Their faces and eyes and skin color were more Asian-looking than the villagers we'd seen during our two and a half weeks in Tibet. Most of these bandits wore mustaches or wispy beards, and the leader was a big man, barrel-chested, ham-fisted, with cheeks as hairy as his hat. They all carried rifles, ranging from what looked to be muskets from the last century to ancient Indian Army breechloaders to modern Enfields from the Great War. I knew that Reggie and Pasang had each brought a rifle in a scabbard—for hunting—and I'd accidentally glimpsed the Deacon packing what must have been his Webley service revolver in his rucksack in Liverpool, but none of these three made any move to go for their weapons as the bandits galloped, trampled, and swooped around us, herding us together like sheep.

Many of our Sherpas—especially the non-Tigers—looked frightened. Pasang looked disdainful. The mules made an uproar at this interruption of their daily routine and then quieted. My little white Tibetan pony tried to bolt, but I planted my feet, grabbed its saddle, and half-lifted it off the ground until it calmed down.

The bandits' larger Mongolian ponies were shaggy, but their manes and tails were elaborately braided, and they were closer in size to a real European horse than to our ridiculous ponies.

When the red dust settled, we were surrounded in two groups: the majority of the bandits encircling the Sherpa porters and ponies, and the leader with about a dozen armed men surrounding Reggie, the Deacon, J.C., Pasang, and me. The many rifles weren't exactly pointed *at* us, but they weren't pointed *away* from us either. All I could think of as I looked at these men was that we'd somehow traveled centuries into the past and come across Genghis Khan and part of his Horde.

Reggie stepped forward and began talking to the leader in rapid Tibetan—or some dialect of Tibetan. It didn't sound quite like the Tibetan she'd used when talking to the *djongpen* headmen and villagers in Yatung, Phari, Kampa Dzong, and the many smaller villages we'd passed, bargained with for food, or camped near.

The bandit leader showed strong white teeth and said something that made his fellow bandits laugh. Reggie laughed with them, so I had to assume the comment wasn't at her expense. (At J.C.'s, the Deacon's, and mine, perhaps.) I didn't care as long as the bandits didn't shoot us—but even as I cravenly thought those words, I realized that when these bandits carried away our mules with all our gear and oxygen tanks and tents and food and Reggie's and Lady Bromley's money, our expedition would be over for good.

The bandit leader barked something, still grinning like a madman, and Reggie translated: "Khan says that it's a bad year to go to *Cho-mo-lung-ma*. All the demons are awake and angry, he says."

"Khan?" I repeated stupidly. Perhaps we *had* gone through some sort of hole in time. For whatever reason, it didn't seem that odd to have Genghis Khan's Mongol hordes descending upon us.

"Jimmy Khan," said Reggie. She said something to the oddly named leader, turned, went back to the mule that Pasang always kept tethered right behind her white pony, and returned with two small packing boxes. After bowing slightly and saying something with a smile, she offered the first box to Khan.

He took a curved blade not much shorter than a full scimitar from his leather belt and pried the box open. Inside, cradled in straw, was another, smaller box, this one made of polished mahogany. Khan tossed aside the packing crate, and several of his men—all smelling to high heaven of horses, human sweat, smoke, dung, and horse sweat—crowded their mounts closer so that they could see.

Khan sheathed his knife and pulled two chrome-plated, ivory-handled American western-type revolvers from the mahogany box. Boxes of cartridges were inlaid in red velvet. The other bandits gave up a collective "*Ahhhhhrrrhhh*"—half admiration, half anger or jealousy, it sounded like—and Khan snarled something at them. They fell silent. The other group of bandits surrounding our clumped-together Sherpas were watching carefully.

Reggie said something in this Tibetan dialect and offered Khan the second, larger box. Again he ripped open the carton and this time he held up a box and shouted at his men.

In the crate were stacked box after box of the distinctive Rowntree's English chocolate samplers. Khan started tossing the boxes to his men. Suddenly the majority of the bandits shouted and fired off their rifles, and our Sherpas had to hold on to the ponies and mules for dear life. I lifted my panicked pony's front hooves off the ground again.

Khan opened the first box, lifted an oval chocolate delicately out of its paper wrapper—his filthy fingers almost the color of the chocolate—and daintily tasted it.

"Chocolate over almond," he said in English. "Very very good."

"I hope you will all enjoy them," said Reggie, also speaking English now.

"Be careful of the demons and *yeti*," said Jimmy Khan. He fired his rifle, spurred his shaggy horse, and the Mongol Horde disappeared in a red dust cloud back toward the northeast whence they'd come.

"Old friend?" asked the Deacon as we managed to re-form our long line and begin the trek toward the Tinki La again.

"Sometimes business associate," said Reggie. Her face was red with the dust that had been kicked up by the horses. I realized that we were all dust-covered and that the layer of dust on us was quickly turning to red mud in the freezing drizzle.

"*Jimmy* Khan?" I heard myself asking. "How on earth did he end up with that first name?"

"He was named after his father," Reggie said and tugged at her stubborn pony's reins to lead it up the first steep part of the trail toward the 16,900-foot-high pass called Tinki La.

For the first three days we're pinned down at Base Camp. The Deacon is going nuts. I'm going nuts in my own way—worried to death that the altitude keeps giving me headaches, causing me to vomit at least once a day, stealing my appetite, and keeping me awake at night. Even rolling over—on the rocks under the tent floor, each one of which my body has memorized by the second night—sends me gasping up out of my light doze, laboring to breathe. It's ridiculous. Base Camp is at a mere 16,500 feet of altitude. The real climbing doesn't begin until we're above the North Col, almost half again as high as this low base. Sixteen thousand five hundred feet isn't that much higher than the alpine summits I've frolicked on in the past year, I keep telling myself. Why the trouble here and not there?

You usually spent less than an hour on those summits, idiot, my rational self explains. *You're trying to* live *here.*

I don't really want to hear from my damned rational self these miserable three days. I also do my best to hide my condition from the others, but J.C. shares the Whymper tent with me and has heard me vomiting, has heard me gasping in the night, and has seen me on top of my sleeping bag panting on all fours like a sick dog. The others must notice my lassitude when we share meals and planning sessions in Reggie's Big Tent, but no one says anything. As far as I can tell, neither Reggie nor the Deacon is bothered by the altitude, and Jean-Claude was over his light symptoms on the second day here at Base Camp.

Despite the terrible cold, wind, and weather, we don't spend all of our first days at Base Camp cowering in our tents. The first full day there, despite the blizzard and temperatures twenty below zero Fahrenheit, saw us staggering around in the whiteout, unpacking and sorting all the gear. The mules were sent back to Chōdzong with a few Sherpas since there was no grass here for them, and the yaks were tethered in a sheltered spot a half mile closer to the river north of us, where the poor hairy beasts could paw through the drifting snow on the riverbanks for what little forage they could find.

A large Whymper tent has been set aside as J.C.'s workshop, where he checks the oxygen tanks, their frames, the Primus stoves, and our other equipment. He has a better set of tools than poor Sandy Irvine had a year ago, for all of Irvine's excellent fixes and repairs and jury-rigging of ladders and O_2 sets, but the current tool kit is still relatively primitive. Jean-Claude can solder but not weld; take cameras, watches, stoves, lanterns, crampons, and other things apart and reassemble them with the right tools, but has a minimum of spare parts for replacement; he can bang metal back into shape but not forge new pieces if something is damaged seriously enough to warrant it.

Luckily, after two days of testing, J.C. informs us that only fourteen of our hundred oxygen tanks have lost pressure, and nine of them only partially, as opposed, the Deacon tells us, to more than thirty out of a total of ninety of the oxygen canisters in Norton, Mallory, and Irvine's expedition the year before. Their thirty tanks had leaked so much by the time they got to Shekar Dzong and took inventory, the tanks were essentially worthless. Sandy Irvine's redesign to the Mark V oxygen system during his trek in last year, combined with further improvements, especially in gaskets and valves and flow meters, via the talents of George Finch, Jean-Claude, and J.C.'s blacksmith-turned-industrialist-steel-manufacturer father, have evidently done the trick. If we fail on this expedition—fail even in our limited goal of finding Lord Percival Bromley's remains on the lower half of the mountain—it shouldn't be for lack of what the Sherpas call "English air."

As I say, we aren't idle. On the second day, after our yak and mule loads have laboriously been repacked into porter loads, other crates set out to stay here in Base Camp or set aside to be cached at Camps I, II, or III, we four sahibs and Pasang meet alone in Reggie's Big Tent to finalize our strategy.

"Our date for summiting remains May seventeenth," says the Deacon as the four of us crouch over the topographic and hand-drawn maps laid out on the circular floor of Reggie's tent. A hanging lantern hisses above us. Pasang stands in the shadows, guarding the laced-up entrance from any random intruders.

"What's your date for finding Cousin Percy?" Reggie asks.

The Deacon taps his cold pipe against his teeth—the air is already too thick in here and redolent of wet wool for him to add smoke—and says, "I've built in search days from each camp along the way, Lady Bromley-Montfort."

"But your goal is still to summit Everest," she says.

"Yes." The Deacon clears his throat. "But we can spend time *after* the summit parties succeed—until the monsoon really hits—to continue the search for Lord Percival's remains, if necessary."

Reggie smiles and shakes her head. "I know the condition of the men who've achieved the high-altitude records here and *not* summited. Bruce with heart problems and traumatic shock and frostbite after his oxygen set quit working. Morshead, Norton, and Somervell too weak to descend safely in 'twenty-two and falling toward the overhang, saved only by tangled ropes and Mallory's impossible belay of all three. High-climbing porters dead from brain embolisms and broken legs, others sent home due to terrible frostbite. Norton's sixty hours of screaming in pain from snow blindness last year..."

The Deacon waves away her objections. "No one says the mountain's not going to take a toll on us. We may all perish. But odds are good that even if we summit by seventeen May, some or all of us should be in good enough shape to direct the Tiger Sherpas in the search for Percy. We have advantages that none of the previous expeditions had."

"Pray tell," says Reggie. I can see Jean-Claude's curious interest, and I admit that my own is fairly keen as well.

"First of all, the oxygen sets," says the Deacon.

"Two of the three previous British expeditions used similar oxygen apparatus," says Reggie. Her voice is calm.

The Deacon nods. "They did, but with apparatus not nearly as good. And not as many tanks. George Finch is sure that the problem was that most of the previous climbers, including me, used too little, too late. The altitude sickness begins eating away at our energy and reserves even here at Base Camp. You and I are acclimated, Lady Bromley-Montfort, but you can see the effect that just seventeen thousand feet has on some of the Sherpas and...others."

His glance my way is just a flick of the eyes.

"Above the North Col," he continues, "especially above eight thousand meters, our bodies and brains begin dying. Not just becoming fatigued and tired, but literally dying. Previous expeditions tended to dole out the oxygen tanks, even to porters, only when they were well above the North Col. And then almost always only when climbing. I plan for us to go on oxygen from Camp Three and beyond—including the Tiger Sherpas when needed—even when stuck in the tents. Even when sleeping."

"Pasang and I spent two weeks on the North Col and climbed above it without oxygen," says Reggie.

"And were you miserable the entire time?" asks the Deacon.

She looks down. "Yes."

"Did you sleep well . . . or at all some nights?"

"No."

"Did you have any appetite even when you still had food reserves?"

"No."

"Did you rouse yourselves enough every day—after a while at that altitude—to get snow and to fire up the Primus when you needed to melt it for soup or drinking water?"

"No."

"Were both of you dehydrated, sick with headache, and vomiting after a few days?"

"Yes." Reggie sighs. "That comes with being on Mount Everest, does it not?"

The Deacon shakes his head. "It comes from our bodies beginning to die on Mount Everest near and above eight thousand meters. Oxygen from the tanks—just breathing a few liters at night while we sleep—can't stop that slow dying, but it can slow it down a bit. Give us a few more days at altitude in which we can think clearly and function properly."

"So we're definitely going to use English air all the way up after the North Col, *Ree-shard?*" asks Jean-Claude.

"Yes. And on the North Col when we have to. I don't like being stupid, my friends—and this mountain makes *everyone* stupid. And often causes hallucinations as well. At least above Camp Three at the base of the Ice Fall. In 'twenty-two, I climbed for two days with a fourth man on our rope . . . a man who didn't exist. The use of oxygen, even at a low flow rate, day and night, will reduce that fatal stupidity a bit. Enough, I hope, to give us the edge for reaching the summit *and* for finding Bromley's remains."

I can tell that Reggie is not totally convinced, but what choice does she have? She's always known that the Deacon's—and Jean-Claude's and my—primary goal is to reach the summit (although in the past two days of illness, I've been very discouraged about the odds of reaching that goal). She just has to believe that we'll do our best in searching for Percy on the way up and back down—if there *is* a "back down."

*　*　*

On the morning of the fourth day, as the snowstorm finally shows signs of relenting, we reconvene in the Big Tent and go over the Deacon's strategy. "There's a reason that all the English expeditions have been led by military men," the Deacon is saying as we huddle over the map of the mountain. His gaze rests more on Reggie's face than on J.C.'s or mine, and I understand he's making a final effort at persuasion. "This way of attacking the mountain—carrying to Camp One, then Camp Two, and so forth up to Camp Six or Seven before attempting the summit—is classic military siege strategy."

"Such as the sieges in the Great War?" asks Reggie.

"No," says the Deacon with a tone of absolute finality. "The Great War was four years of trench warfare insanity. Tens of thousands of lives lost in a day for a few yards of ground gained...yards that would be lost the next day at an equal price. No, I'm talking about classical sieges from the Middle Ages on. The kind of siege of Cornwallis at Yorktown that *your* general, Jake...Washington...was taught by his French friend"—a nod at J.C.—"Lafayette. Surround the enemy where he can't retreat—a peninsula worked fine as long as the French ships didn't allow the Royal Navy to save Cornwallis and his men. Then bombard. Under bombardment, advance your trenches yard by yard, mile by mile, until you're right up against the enemy's defenses. Then a final quick assault and...victory."

"But none of your English generals here on Everest," says Jean-Claude, "have moved their trenches close enough to the summit for that successful final assault."

The Deacon nods agreement, but I can tell he's distracted. Perhaps by Reggie's unwavering gaze. "The 'twenty-two and 'twenty-four expeditions both planned to establish a Camp Seven at around twenty-seven thousand three hundred feet, but neither achieved that goal. Mallory and Irvine and all the rest of us before them started our summit assault from Camp Six at about twenty-six thousand eight hundred feet."

"That's only five hundred feet difference," says Reggie, moving her gaze down to the map of the Rongbuk Glacier and the mountain.

"Five hundred vertical feet can mean half a day's worth of climbing at those altitudes." The Deacon plays with his unlit pipe. "There's no *only* to it."

"Didn't Norton and Mallory fail to establish a Camp Seven because the porters gave out?" I ask. I've heard and read all the reports. "Were just unable to carry tents higher?"

"In part," says the Deacon. "But the sahib climbers also gave out, in terms of carrying loads, above Camp Six. And that includes Finch and me in 'twenty-two. Besides, Camp Seven was always the plan for a final assault without oxygen; when Mallory decided that he and Irvine would make an attempt with the O-two apparatus, the extra five hundred vertical feet didn't seem to make that much difference."

"But you think it did," says Reggie.

"Yes." If she'd been attempting irony, the Deacon's tone suggests he hadn't noticed it. He presses his pipe stem down on a point on the map above our inked-in Camp VI and below the juncture of the North Ridge with the long North East Ridge. "The problem isn't just altitude up there—although that's debilitating enough. The slabs are steeper as one approaches the North East Ridge, and there's much less packable snow—very few places to carve out a platform for even one tent, and the climber doesn't have enough energy to be moving stones to create a platform. But mostly it's the wind up there. Camp Six is bad enough, but closer to the North East Ridge, that wind rolls over and down most of the time. It can carry away a climber, much less his tent."

"You originally wanted a rapid alpine assault from Camp Five at twenty-five thousand three hundred feet or lower, *Ree-shard*," says J.C. "The three of us climbers carrying just a rucksack, bread, water, chocolate, and perhaps a flag to plant on the summit."

The Deacon smiles wryly.

"And maybe a bivouac sack," I say. "For when we get caught by the sun setting while we're descending the Second or First Step on the way down."

"Aye, there's the rub," says the Deacon, audibly scratching his stubbled cheek. "No one's ever survived a night bivouac at those altitudes. It's hard enough to survive in a tent with a working Primus at Camps Four, Five, and Six. That's why I've decided that we have to make the assault from Camp Seven, or, failing that, from a high Camp Six, as Mallory and Irvine did. But start earlier. Perhaps even at night as Reg . . . as Lady Bromley-Montfort has suggested. Those little headlamps work pretty well. But I haven't worked out how we avoid freezing to death while attempting to climb before dawn—or after sunset, for that matter."

"As far as surviving," begins Reggie. "Excuse me a moment..." She leaves the tent and snow blows in. Pasang remains behind, retying the door cords.

The Deacon looks at us but we shrug. Perhaps he's said something to upset her.

A few minutes later she's back from her own tent, brushing snow out of her long black hair, her arms full of what we first think are extra Finch goose down duvet balloon jackets.

"You three have laughed at me bringing my treadle sewing machine on the trek," she says. And before we can speak, she insists, "No, I've heard you complaining. Half a mule's total load, you said. And I heard you sniggering in the evenings along the trek when I was in my Big Tent sewing and you heard the treadle going."

None of us can deny that.

"Here's what I was working on," she says and hands out the bulky but light items.

Three pairs of sewn and hemmed goose down trousers. *So that's why she took our measurements back at the plantation,* I think.

"I believe that Mr. Finch solved half of the problem," she says. "There's still too much body heat lost through the silk and cotton and wool of the climber's underwear and trousers. I've made enough of these for all of us, Pasang, and eight of the Tiger Sherpas. I can't promise that it will allow any of us to survive a night bivouac above twenty-eight thousand feet, but it gives us a fighting chance to keep moving before dawn and after sunset."

"They'll rip and tear," says the Deacon. J.C. and I are busy shedding our boots and squirming into our new goose down trousers.

"They're made of the same balloon cloth that Finch used on the parkas," says Reggie. "Besides, I have a waxed-cotton outer shell for all the trousers. Not heavy. Tougher than the anoraks you wear over the Finch duvets. Notice that all of your trousers, inner and outer, have buttons for braces and a button fly. That last was extra work, I tell you."

I blush at this.

"I'm also using the last of the balloon fabric to make buttoned-on goose-down-filled hoods for our Finch duvet jackets," says Reggie. "And I must say that using that sewing machine treadle at this altitude is hard work."

The Deacon clamps down on his cold pipe and scowls. "Where on earth did you get balloon fabric?"

"I sacrificed the plantation's hot-air balloon," says Lady Katherine Christina Regina Bromley-Montfort.

Jean-Claude and I spend twenty minutes or so parading around Base Camp through the blowing snow and minus-fifteen-degree temperatures while wearing our three layers of mittens, Finch coat, Reggie trousers, Shackleton windproof anoraks, Reggie's just-finished button-on goose down hoods, and our tough duck trouser shells. With our three layers of glove-mittens and our leather and wool aviator caps pulled down under our new hoods, balaclavas and goggles on, it's a strange feeling to be so warm in such terrible conditions.

Reggie comes out in her full gear. She no longer looks like a woman, I think. In truth, she no longer looks quite human.

"I feel like the Michelin Man," says Jean-Claude, laughing through the mouth flap in the wool-lined balaclava covering his face. Reggie and I also laugh. I'd seen the Michelin Man on posters and billboards, a pudgy shape made all out of tires advertising the brand, that had been on show in Paris since 1898.

"Add the oxygen gear," says Reggie, "and we'll feel like men from Mars."

"We shall *be* men from Mars," says J.C., laughing again.

It strikes me then that we might well feel very removed from the human act of climbing—of interacting with rock, snow, and the world—in the days and weeks to come.

The Deacon emerges from his tent. He has his long ice axe and is wearing his Finch duvet, full mittens, and headgear, but from the waist down he is still all stout English woolen knickers, puttees, and leather boots.

"Since we're all outside anyway and the day's promising to clear," he says, "what do you say to the four of us hauling some Whymper tents up to Camp One and then taking a look at the glacier above there? We won't need crampons or the short axes."

"No Tigers?" says Reggie.

The Deacon shakes his head. "Let's make this first recon a sahib-only outing."

We go back to fetch our larger rucksacks, some ropes, and long ice axes. The Deacon supervises loading each of us with about forty or fifty pounds of tent parts, stakes, more ropes, loose oxygen tanks, Primus stoves, and some canned food; even Reggie gets her full load. Pasang—wearing only the cotton robes and scarves he had on in the Big Tent—stands outside with his arms crossed and a powerful scowl of disapproval on his face as the four of us sahibs lean into the wind and snow to stagger around our rocky ridge-barrier and then up the boulder-and-ice-strewn valley of the Rongbuk Glacier.

Saturday, May 2, 1925

*I*t says something about the altitude and cold—and perhaps about the poor condition I'm in—that it takes a little under two hours for us to haul our loads three miles up the glacier bed to the site of Camp I.

The snow was letting up as we climbed, and I'm surprised to find only an inch or two on the moraine rocks beneath our boots, just enough to make footing treacherous. For this first stage of our "siege" of Everest—based more on South Polar expeditions' cache-dump attempts than on our original plan for a quick alpine ascent, is my silent opinion—we don't have to climb onto the glacier proper, but we do waste time winding our way through a bewildering series of 50- to 70-foot-high ice pinnacles that are called *penitentes:* they do look rather like giant religious pilgrims in white robes. In addition to the pinnacles that have turned the rocky moraine trough into an obstacle course, there are also innumerable ice-melt pools, frozen over but frequently so thinly frozen that we'd break through and soak our boots if we tried to cross the slippery surfaces.

This seems to make no sense, given the far-below-zero temperatures we've been suffering since we arrived at the mouth of the Rongbuk Glacier valley, but it is a part of the weirdness of Mount Everest and its environs; in places where the ridge walls and even ice walls shield the valley from the coldest winds, the early May sunlight can heat up sheltered places fifty degrees and more above the temperatures at Base Camp. The worst will be on the glacier itself, but on this first day we stay off

the glacier, trudging along the rocky moraine bottom that previous expeditions have called the Trough.

My rucksack is heavier than any load I've carried for some time, and
as we trudge uphill, I stay 50 feet behind the Deacon and Reggie so they
won't hear my labored breathing and occasional retching. But through
my discomfort, I realize now why Mallory and Bullock missed this approach to the North Col for so many weeks and months during the late
summer and early autumn of 1921. They found that the main avenue
of the primary Rongbuk Glacier headed up to Lho La below the West
Ridge of Everest and was impassable in its higher reaches. The broad
Kharra Glacier comes down from the North East and North faces of the
mountain, but careers off almost due east to the Lhakpa La Pass, where
the Deacon had finally dragged Mallory and where the team had finally
seen the true way to the North Col—this East Rongbuk Glacier.

But the East Rongbuk Glacier is a tricky, sneaky thing, converging
with the main Rongbuk Glacier valley way down at Base Camp but
snaking to the east, then northeast, and then sharply northwest—parallel to the Kharra Glacier—from Camp I to the North Col. The 1921
expedition had tried following ridges to the North Face, but the most
promising ridge, one that led along the eastern side of the main Rongbuk Glacier, had led them to a dead end at what they called the North
Peak—the mountain we now call Changtse.

In the monsoon mess of late summer 1921, Mallory and Bullock simply couldn't believe that such a major glacier could give birth to such
a miserable little trickle of a stream—the one that flows past our Base
Camp now—and they kept circling back and forth along the northern
approaches, swinging ever further west and east and then west again,
looking for the kind of roaring stream or small river worthy of a glacier
that ran all the way to the North Face or North Col.

It doesn't exist. Our little trickle-stream at Base Camp, as the Deacon
had guessed in 1921 (and for which correct guess—plus the recon to
Lhakpa La, where they'd found the *yeti* footprints in the new snow as well
as the glimpse of the proper route—I believe Mallory never fully forgave
him), is all that the East Rongbuk Glacier is giving up.

We'd have been wasting more time today, since so many of the
corridors through the five-story-tall *penitentes* lead to glacier walls or

moraine-ridge dead ends, but the Deacon had brought bamboo wands with him during his recon on our first night at Base Camp, and the irregular line of these in the patches of snow keeps us on the right path. Since we're not yet on the glacier or any real slope with crevasses, we're not roped up, of course, but we settle into a single file with the Deacon leading, Reggie behind him, J.C. walking easily behind Reggie, and me bringing up a very distant rear. There are times when I lose them amongst the ice pinnacles, and only the bamboo wands and faint footsteps in the thin scrim of ice and snow show me which way to turn.

Finally we reach the site of Camp I, and the four of us dump our loads and sit panting with our backs against boulders. It is the same site that expeditions have used going back to 1921, and it shows the same tawdry signs of use as Base Camp, but it is also situated in the sunlight right where a wide rivulet of fresh water runs out of a moraine ridge of rock. The previous expeditions have built no *sangas* here—those low rock walls for extra wind protection within which you pitch a tent or tarp—but the multiple tent sites, places where rocks have been moved and the ground made as smooth as possible, are obvious.

"We'll set up the Whymper tent and one smaller one, eat lunch, and head back," says the Deacon.

"What was all this about, Mr. Deacon?" asks Reggie.

I'm still gasping for breath hard enough that I couldn't join in this dialogue if I wanted to. I don't want to. Jean-Claude seems to be breathing easily, his elbows on his knees as he uses his knife to cut up an apple he's eating, but he also shows no interest in jumping into this discussion.

"All what, Lady Bromley-Montfort?" says the Deacon, eyes wide with feigned innocence.

"Our doing this useless hauling of these heavy loads to Camp One," snaps Reggie. "Norton and Geoffrey Bruce last year had the porters do *all* the hauling to Camps One, Two, and Three, while the British climbers remained at Base Camp and saved their energy for the North Col and above."

"Didn't you and Pasang haul your own gear to this point last August?" asks the Deacon.

"Yes, but we had half a dozen Sherpas to help. And Pasang and I were carrying only light tents which we brought along with us to each camp...that and a minimum of food."

The Deacon drinks from his canteen and says nothing.

"Was this some sort of test?" presses Reggie. "A cheap test of Jake and Jean-Claude and me, as if we hadn't just trekked in more than three hundred fifty miles over passes up to nineteen thousand feet? Testing whether we *can* haul forty-plus-pound loads up the valley?"

The Deacon shrugs.

Reggie calmly takes a heavy can of peaches out of her overloaded rucksack and throws it at the Deacon's head. He ducks, but *just* in time. The can of peaches bounces off a boulder but does not explode.

Jean-Claude laughs heartily.

The Deacon just points over Reggie's and J.C.'s heads and says, "Look."

Not only has the snow stopped, but the clouds have parted to the south. The high reaches of Everest may still be nine dangerous miles away up the glacier and Col and almost two vertical miles above us, but the Himalayan air is so clean and clear that it looks as if we could reach out and touch the visible First and Second Steps, run our finger down Norton's Couloir, and press our palm down on the snowy spike of summit.

No one says anything. Then Reggie dumps the contents of her overstuffed rucksack out on the ground, stands, says, "You can set up the tents and stack your food tins here, *Mister* Deacon. I'm going back to Base Camp to get the loads apportioned for the Sherpas for tomorrow's double carry."

Then J.C. dumps his pack out, tent fabric flapping in what's left of the wind—little more than a breeze now. "I'm going back to Base Camp to finish instructing the Sherpas on crampon and jumar technique." He disappears downhill behind *penitentes* some minutes behind Reggie, although he seems to be making no obvious effort to catch up to her.

I continue to sit, my pack propped next to me.

"Go ahead and dump it and go, Jake," the Deacon says. He lights his pipe. "Reggie was absolutely right. It *was* a sort of test, and it was wrong of me to have put the three of you through it."

It's one of the few times I've heard him call her "Reggie."

"I don't have anything pressing to do at Base Camp," I say. I admit that I'm irritated not only at his testing us during our first days at this altitude, but also for smoking that goddamned pipe when I can't get a full breath of air in my lungs. "I'll help you set up the two tents," I hear myself say.

The Deacon shrugs again but slowly gets to his feet, his gaze still fixed on the ever more visible massif that is Mount Everest.

Trying not to wheeze too loudly, I dig through the heaps of stuff for the Whymper tent's larger ground cloth.

———∞∞∞———

Tuesday, May 5, 1925

e reach the site for Camp III around noon, and as we emerge from the forest of ice pinnacles in the Trough below the glacier and get our first real look at the sight and the North Col beyond and above it, I say, "Dear God, what a terrible place." It's made more terrible by a rough pyramid of rocks set closer to the great snow and ice wall leading up to the North Col—a monument to the seven dead porters from the 1922 avalanche, I realize—and made even more pathetic by the seven empty oxygen tanks stacked next to the rock pyramid.

I have no way of knowing that Camp III will someday be a haven of thicker air and respite from impossible hardships for all of us, but in the meantime will become a terrible test of my endurance.

It is just Jean-Claude and me leading and our personal Tiger Sherpas, Lhakpa Yishay and Norbu Chedi climbing roped with J.C., Ang Chiri and Babu Rita roped with me, who have made this first trip from Camp II to Camp III. We stop a bit short of the actual campsite—marked, as always, by the fallen tentpoles and torn canvas of demolished and snow-covered old tents and other expedition detritus—and look ahead at the more than 1,000-foot wall of ice and snow leading to the North Col that connects the North Ridge of Mount Everest to the south ridges of Changtse. "Col" is a Welsh word meaning "saddle," but this is certainly the highest mountain saddle I've ever set eyes on.

While the Sherpas sit on boulders and pant, worn out, J.C. and I look through his binoculars at the huge wall of snow and ice that rises beyond the Camp III site. I feel happy to be with just my French friend and the Sherpas. Reggie is back at Camp II today, supervising the Team Two Sherpas with their loads to carry up here to Camp III now that Jean-Claude has marked the way across the glacier with bamboo wands. The Deacon's all the way back at Base Camp, shuttling back and forth to Camps I and II with Tiger Team Three.

"Mallory's ice chimney is gone," Jean-Claude says and hands me the small field glasses.

A year ago, Mallory had free-climbed those last 200 feet or so up through the ice chimney to the North Col, and it was in that crack in the vertical ice face that they'd dropped Sandy Irvine's ingenious rope and wood ladder—the same one that Bruno Sigl had lied about his men using; the same one that Reggie had admitted to climbing with Pasang, despite the ladder's frayed appearance, a year ago this coming August. The ladder had allowed the scores of porters on last year's huge expedition to climb to the North Col without someone constantly cutting steps for them.

Now both ice chimney and ladder are gone, folded into the churnings of the ever-shifting ice wall and glacier. The last 200 vertical feet to the ledge on the North Col where both previous expeditions have set their tents is once again a slick, solid 90-degree ice wall. But the more than 800 feet of snow and ice below that look bad as well.

"The snowfields look deep headed up to the ice wall," I say between ragged gulps for air. We've been climbing this last hard bit between Camps II and III without oxygen—the last such oxygen-tank-free climbing we'll be doing if the Deacon sticks to his plan—and I understand why the Tiger Sherpas with us have all but collapsed where they sit, lying back against their loads, too tired to remove the bulging thirty- to forty-pound packs from their backs.

J.C. removes his Crooke's-glass goggles and squints up at the wall.

"Don't go snow-blind on me," I say.

He shakes his head but continues studying the 1,000-foot snow and ice wall while holding his hand above his eyes and squinting. "More fresh snow there than on the glacier," he says at last, pulling up his goggles. "It's probably as bad as . . ."

Jean-Claude stops before finishing his thought, but I can read his mind well enough by now to hear the unspoken parts of that sentence:

It's probably as bad as the snow slope conditions in 1922 when the avalanche killed seven Sherpas. We won't know that for sure until the Deacon finally gets up here to Camp III, but I suspect the worst.

"Let us get our friends back on their feet before we lie down beside them and we all take a cold final nap," says Jean-Claude. He turns and starts coaxing the four exhausted Sherpas to their feet, the men sagging under their loads. "It is only a few hundred more yards and downhill from here," he says to them in English, knowing that his Sherpa Norbu and my man Babu will translate for the other two.

As we stagger out onto the moraine from the forest of huge ice pin-nacles at the base of the glacier, all of us wearing crampons today—10-point for the Sherpas and full 12-point for J.C. and me—and keeping them on even though we're now ready to cross moraine rocks, I point to the open spot just ahead of us and about 200 feet short of the camp-site and say, "This must be about where Kami Chiring confronted Bruno Sigl a year ago."

Jean-Claude only nods, and I sense how very tired he is.

The three miles of climbing between Rongbuk Base Camp and Camp I amounts to hiking uphill on lateral moraine beds and across fields of shallow ice between hundreds of the *penitente* ice pillars. The three uphill miles between Camp I and Camp II are a mixture of moraine and actual glacier crossing, but the majority of the way is along the Trough among and between the ice pinnacles at the bottom of the valley. But almost all of the almost five hard miles uphill from Camp II here to Camp III at the base of the wall is on the ever more steeply rising glacier.

And the glacier is filled with hundreds of crevasses covered over with new snow.

I've followed J.C. for two days now as he's threaded our route through those invisible crevasses, leaving only our footsteps in the deep snow—much of the time Jean-Claude was breaking trail through snow up to his thighs or waist—but also marking that route with wands and fixed ropes for the steeper parts.

Both days have been sunny, and through my goggles the glacier snow-fields are merely a maze of *sastrugi* drift-ripples and corresponding blue shadows everywhere. Some of those blue shadows are shadows. Many are crevasses under their thin coverings of snow—gaps that would drop a man (or woman) hundreds of feet into the heart of the glacier. Somehow Jean-Claude always seems to know which shadow means what.

Twice between Camps II and III we've had to detour around crevasses too extensive to flank. The first time, yesterday, J.C. finally found a snow bridge that he judged would hold our weight. Jean-Claude crossed first while I belayed, my ice axe sunk deep in the ice, and then we rigged two strong, waist-high guide ropes across along with jumars that would carabiner onto the Sherpas' new climbing harnesses.

The second crevasse had no snow bridges, and trying to detour around it either way just led us into endless fields of more hidden crevasses. Finally I belayed J.C.—while the Sherpas belayed me—with an extra ice axe laid across the lip of the crevasse so the rope would not cut into the snow. Jean-Claude used his new, short ice axes and 12-point crampons to descend 60 or 70 feet into the terrible crack until he reached a point where the walls were close enough together that he could take one huge step (for a short man) and slam his right ice hammer and right crampon front blades into the opposing ice wall. Then he swung his left arm and leg across a widening abyss that dropped into absolute darkness, kicked both crampon fronts into the blue ice wall, and began climbing with his short axes smacking into ice, each one higher than the other, up the opposite wall.

Once J.C. climbed out and was standing on the other side of the crevasse, I threw a coil of strong rope across and then two of the long ice axes, which he used to anchor the ropes. Then I used two axes and several long ice screws to anchor the ropes on our side of the crevasse. J.C. was wearing one of the climbing harnesses that none of us had tried on the mountain yet, and now he clipped carabiners from the harness onto one of his jumar thingies, lifted his cramponed boots up and over the rope, and just scooted hand over hand, butt first, back toward us along the doubled rope across the bottomless drop as if he were a child on a playground.

"The Sherpas can't do that with their loads," I gasped out when he unclipped from the ropes and moved away from the treacherous edge.

Jean-Claude shook his head. He'd been doing all the climbing and work, and I was still the one gasping and panting. "We have our fine fellows dump their loads here for now and we go back to Camp Two. Reggie should have had her team of nine porters bring up the ladders to Two by now. We lash two of the ten-foot ladders together, provide guide ropes as we did on the snow bridge, and... *voilà!*"

"*Voilà*," I repeated with less enthusiasm. It had been a long, hard, dangerous climb up the glacier to this point, we were less than two-thirds of the almost five miles to Camp III, and now we had to head back down to Camp II to start hauling up ladders and more rope. The Sherpas with us were grinning. They'd had enough of hauling loads for one day and were more than happy to dump their heavy loads and walk unencumbered back down the safely wand-marked glacier.

The Deacon had warned us that this was how all the previous expeditions' planning and schedules, including Mallory's the year before, ended up in disarray, with loads being dumped up and down the entire eleven-mile Trough and glacier trek up to Camp III and the North Col. All the military planning in the world, he said, can't overcome the inherent chaos of crevasses and sheer human exhaustion.

"We need more wands anyway," J.C. said. It was true. There were so many crevasses that Jean-Claude's route up the glacier twisted this way and then that, rarely a simple straightforward route along the three and a half miles or so we'd covered. We'd underestimated the number of bamboo wands we'd need to mark the route accurately enough for porters following—especially in a snowstorm.

But by early afternoon of this Tuesday, the fifth of May, we have our loads safely delivered to Camp III. Crossing 15 feet or more of the lashed-together wooden ladders above the endless crevasse drop with only the waist-high guide ropes to steady us on our crampons had been an experience I didn't look forward to having again (though I knew I would have to, many times). We've erected J.C.'s and my small Meade tents and Reggie's hemispherical Big Tent in anticipation of the scheduled rush of men and matériel to come. For tonight, the four Sherpas can sleep in it.

The plan is for us to spend this one night here, waiting for Reggie's Tiger Team Two with nine Sherpas and their loads, scheduled to arrive before noon tomorrow, and then some of us are to continue waiting—and acclimating—at Camp III until the Deacon comes up the next day, Thursday, May 7, with Tiger Team Three. Only then, according to the plan, and perhaps with even one more day of acclimation for some of us, can anyone attempt to tackle the 1,000-foot slope and wall up to the North Col. Mostly, I think to myself, because the Deacon doesn't want anyone to climb onto the North Col until he's present and—presumably—leading the climb.

The real headache hits me before darkness fully falls on this Tuesday night.

I've had a headache since we reached Base Camp far below, but suddenly it feels as if someone is driving an ice screw into my skull every thirty seconds or so. My vision flutters, dances with black dots, and begins to constrict into a tunnel. I've never had a migraine headache in my life—only two or three serious headaches of any sort that I remember—but this is terrible.

Not bothering to layer into my goose down or outer jackets or to pull on my gloves or overmittens, I crawl on all fours out of the flapping tent, turn away from where we'd staked out the other, larger tent, and vomit behind the closest boulder. The headache makes me continue to dry retch even after my stomach is empty. Within seconds, my hands are freezing.

Dimly, distantly, I realize three things: first, the wind has come up so strongly that the small Meade tent J.C. and I have been crouching in is flapping and banging like wash hung out to dry in a hurricane (I'd thought the noise was only in my throbbing skull); second, that along with the wind have come deeply freezing temperatures and a blizzard so intense that I can barely see the Big Tent eight feet away; third and finally, that Jean-Claude has pulled on his Finch duvet jacket and, leaning out of our tent's opening, is screaming for me to come back inside.

"Vomit in here, Jake, for the love of Christ!" he is shouting. "We'll toss the basin out. If you stay out there another minute you'll be fighting frostbite for a month!"

I can barely hear him over the gale-force winds and the flapping of canvas. If my head weren't pounding with pain and my insides weren't busy turning themselves inside out, I would have found his invitation amusing. But rather than be amused now, I am almost too exhausted to crawl back into the wind-pounded tent we're sharing. I can no longer see Reggie's Big Tent with the four Sherpas huddling in it only eight or nine feet away, but I can hear its canvas fighting the wind. Between that tent and ours, it sounds like two infantry battalions exchanging fire. Then I'm back inside and J.C. is rubbing my frozen hands and helping me crawl back into my sleeping bag.

My teeth are chattering too hard for me to speak, but after a minute I get it out—"I'm d-d-d-dying and...wha...w...we're...n...not even...o...on...the fucking mountain y-y-yet."

Jean-Claude starts laughing. "I don't believe you are dying, *mon ami.* You just have a healthy dose of this altitude sickness that I, too, have been fighting."

I shake my head, try to speak, stutter, and finally get the word out. "Edema."

I wouldn't be the first man attempting Everest to die of a pulmonary or brain edema on the way up. I can imagine nothing else that would cause this level of headache pain and nausea.

J.C. sobers up at once, brings the electric torch out of his rucksack, and passes the light in front of my eyes several times.

"I think not," he says at last. "I believe it is altitude sickness, Jake. Combined with the terrible sunburn you received in the Trough and on the glacier. But we shall get some hot soup and tea into you and see how you feel."

Except we can't heat any soup. The Primus stove—the larger type we'd brought up to cook for up to six people—simply will not light.

"*Merde,*" whispers J.C. "A few minutes more, my friend." He begins expertly to disassemble the complex mechanism, blowing into tiny valves, checking small pieces, using the flashlight to look down narrow cylinder parts as my father used to peer down the gun barrel after cleaning his rifle.

"All pieces are present and accounted for and looking proper," he announces at last. He reassembles the Primus as rapidly as a U.S. Marine would reassemble his rifle after fieldstripping it.

The damned thing still won't light.

"Bad fuel?" I manage to suggest. I've curled up in my sleeping bag so my voice is muffled by folds of canvas and down. Even watching J.C. do such fine work with his bare hands in this terrible cold has made my head hurt worse. I desperately do not want to have to crawl outside to vomit again—not as long as I can lie absolutely still and just roll up and down these waves of headache pain and stomach cramps like a small dinghy on hurricane-driven waves.

"We used almost all the water in our bottles and canteens during the long trek up from Camp Two," Jean-Claude says. "We can go days without warm food, but if we can't melt snow for hot tea and drinking water, we may be in some trouble if we're stuck here for several days." He's pulling on his outer layers.

"What do you mean stuck here for several days?" I manage to say through the frost-rimmed opening in my sleeping bag. "Reggie and her Tiger Team will be arriving tomorrow before noon and the Deacon and his Sherpas before nightfall. This place is going to look like Grand Central Station by this time tomorrow—we'll have food and fuel and Primuses enough for an army."

At that second a gust that must exceed a hundred miles per hour hits the north side of the tent, slides under the ground cloth, and is about to lift us into the air and carry us away when Jean-Claude throws himself spread-eagled across the tent floor. After half a moment when it seems undecided whether we are going to become airborne or not, we bounce once, hard, in the same spot, while the tent walls start whipping back and forth and cracking like renewed volleys of rifle fire. I guess that a couple of our carefully rigged tie-downs have ruptured or stakes have pulled out. Or perhaps the wind has just blown away the half-ton boulders we'd tied guy ropes onto for extra security.

"Perhaps they will not be arriving tomorrow after all," Jean-Claude says loudly enough to be heard over the volley fire. "But we *will* need a way to melt snow for tea and drinking water before then. And we need to check on the Sherpas next door."

It looks from the outside as if Reggie's hemispherical Big Tent is handling the wind better than our A-shaped Whymper tent, but once we're inside, we immediately see that the four Sherpa inmates in the Big Tent aren't doing so well. Jean-Claude and I have brought some frozen tins of food as well as dragging the dead Primus along in the vague hope that one of the Sherpas will be able to repair it. Snow blows in behind us as we enter, and we hurry to lace the entrance back up.

The only light in the tent comes from the stubby little open-flame ghee-butter candle of the sort that Hindus use for their religious services. Ghee is clarified butter, and the stench from the tiny candle adds to my already adequate nausea. The four Sherpas look pathetic; Babu Rita, Norbu Chedi, Ang Chiri, and Lhakpa Yishay are all huddled together in a wet goose down Finch-jacket heap in the center of the tent space. Two of them have crawled half into their down sleeping bags—also damp—but the other two don't even have their bags with them. There's no gear or food from their loads in the tent—not even an extra blanket—and all four men, earlier thought to be some of our sure-to-be-named Tiger Sherpas, look at us the way the terminally lost look at possible rescuers.

"Where are your other two sleeping bags?" demands J.C.

"Lhakpa lightened the load in his pack at Camp Two," says Norbu Chedi, his teeth chattering. "He left his and my bags and the extra ground cloth behind...by accident, Sahib."

"*Merde!*" says Jean-Claude. "Sleeping bags were the lightest things in your loads. Do you have any water?"

"No, Sahib," says my personal Sherpa, Babu Rita. "We drank it all from our bottles during the climb to this camp. We were hoping that you had already melted us some."

J.C. plunks the recalcitrant Primus down in the middle of our crowded little huddle and explains the problem. Babu and Norbu translate for Ang Chiri and Lhakpa Yishay.

"Where's the food?" asks Jean-Claude. "The soup and the food tins?"

"We could not get to the pack loads," says Norbu. "Buried too deep in snow."

"Nonsense," snaps J.C. "We dumped those loads just a few yards from here only hours ago. We need to go out now and bring in the food and packs, see what there is for us to use. Was there a second Primus packed, by any chance?"

"No," Babu says in a hopeless tone. "But I carried many cans of Primus fuel up the glacier."

Jean-Claude shakes his head. I would do the same but my head hurts too much. The small cans of kerosene are useless unless we can get the Primus working. "Get your gloves, mittens, and Shackleton overjackets on," orders J.C. "It's snowing too hard—and getting too dark—to sort through the loads out there, so we're going to pull the packs and load bags into the tent."

It *is* getting dark outside, and the blizzard still restricts our vision to only a couple of yards. I'm wondering whether we should have roped up for this effort when Jean-Claude shouts over the howling wind for Babu and Ang to hang on to each other and me, and for Norbu and Lhakpa to keep a grip on each other and him. We stagger and feel our way the few yards from the Big Tent to the general vicinity of where we think the Sherpas dumped their packs. J.C.'s rucksack and load bags, as well as mine, are weighted down by rocks right at the entrance to our tent. Of course they're empty, since, with the exception of a few food tins, we hauled the two heavy tents, tent staves and poles, and the nonworking Primus stove up in our loads. So our lives now depend on what we find in the Sherpas' loads. Camp III is supposed to be sheltered—compared to Camp IV up on the North Col, much less compared to any camps exposed up on the North or North East ridges higher up—but the wind whipping down the 1,000-foot slope of ice and snow is so strong that it literally knocks me over. Babu Rita and Ang Chiri dutifully fall into the snow with me. On all fours, I flail around trying to find their rucksacks and pack loads amidst the drifts, snow-covered boulders, and the growing heaps of snow on this side of the tents.

"Here!" I can barely hear J.C.'s voice, but the two Sherpas and I crawl toward it.

We all grab some part of the load masses now under ten inches or more of new snow and begin dragging them back to the Big Tent...but where *is* the Big Tent? Luckily, Lhakpa Yishay had left burning the one tiny ghee candle they had set on the floor—foolish to leave it unattended, since fire is always a danger in these canvas tents—and we all crawl and tug and grunt and swear in the direction of that tiny light.

Inside—it was impossible to unload the packs and rucksacks and load bags outside in the wind and snow—things are a real mess.

Enough snow has come in that our down jackets and trousers (the Sherpas chose not to wear the extra down trousers we had for them) and the two spread sleeping bags are covered with snow that body heat soon will melt into moisture. The wetter goose down gets, the less insulating property it has, until, when soaked enough, it will provide all the insulating warmth of a cold, wet washrag.

Dizzy, trying hard not to be violently sick again, I curl up on the driest part of the tent floor I can find and shiver, my head hurting worse with each shiver and shake. The sudden, overpowering stench of the kerosene doesn't help matters.

Jean-Claude is going through the packs and load bags: several more tins of frozen food and sealed packs of what the Royal Navy has called "portable soup" since the early 1800s, but no water. Five more Primus-fuel-sized cans of kerosene.

We now have enough kerosene to blow up a German pillbox or burn a hole in the wall of the North Col, but the damned Primus stove won't ignite it.

J.C. clears a space in the middle and lays down an extra wool shirt of his as a work area. He has brought a flashlight from his personal rucksack and adds the beam of its light to the ever-diminishing blue flicker of the tiny ghee-candle lamp.

He sets up the Primus again. We have two big pots for boiling, and each of us has his tin cup for drinking. J.C. makes sure that the fuel tank is two-thirds filled with fresh kerosene as the instructions suggest, primes it with a bit of burning alcohol in the tiny spirit cup below the burners, pumps up the pressure, and tries again to ignite the burners.

Nothing.

J.C. allows himself a torrent of French so picturesque that I can pick up only one vulgarity in twenty. He begins disassembling the damned thing again, taking great care not to spill the kerosene or remaining alcohol.

"How can it *not* work?" I manage to say from my fetal position and through my throbbing headache.

"I...do...not...know," Jean-Claude says through gritted teeth. Wind batters the wall of the Big Tent so hard that four of us grab the wooden ribs of the dome, trying to hold the tent down with our weight and waning strength. While outside, J.C. had swung his little steel-tubed instrument, and he whispered the results to me inside: the barometer was frighteningly low and still falling; the temperature at nightfall outside was minus thirty-eight degrees Fahrenheit. We had nothing but our bodies, tents, and fears with which to measure the velocity of the wind down here in the "sheltered" area at the base of the North Col, but these winds have to be hurricane velocity. Some must be a hundred miles per hour or more.

I force myself to sit up and look at the disassembled brass pieces of the Primus now gleaming faintly in the weak light from the single flashlight and the dying ghee-candle dish.

I'm thinking, *There may be no more idiot-proof piece of machinery in the world than a Swedish-built Primus stove.*

The Deacon had bought mostly the new 1925 models, but except for being improved for high altitudes—some of the improvements suggested by a certain George Finch—they differed very little from earlier pressure stoves going back to 1892. We'd used Primuses from our stores for cooking all the way through Sikkim and across Tibet. None had ever failed to light.

As J.C. holds the burner up to the light yet again, making sure there is no blockage, I dully paw through the other pieces.

The simple little machine is a brass 1925 (O) Primus 210 model—the new kind with fixed legs. The procedure for lighting it is the same as for all the other Primuses I've used over my years of hiking and climbing. Primuses have always worked at any altitude I've been at.

First, one uses the pumping mechanism set into the main fuel tank to pressurize that fuel tank. This rise in pressure forces the kerosene in the main tank up and along the tube that rises to the burners. To preheat those burner tubes, one lights a small amount of methylated spirits—alcohol—in the built-in spirit cup encircling the burner tube.

We've done all that a dozen times this afternoon and now darkening evening with no luck.

Once those burner tubes reach a high enough temperature, a fine, almost invisible spray of hot paraffin gas is emitted through the central jet in the burner. When air mixes with that gas—even the thin air of Mount Everest—the stove's simple and sturdy little flame ring forces the gas into a circle. Technically, it's not the kerosene burning in the blue-flame ring of a Primus stove, it's the plasma paraffin gas generated from the spray of kerosene. The noise from those flame-ring burners has always been loud enough that many climbers and campers have called their Primuses "roarers." Indeed, there are few sounds more reassuring to an exhausted mountain climber than the roar of a Primus stove as it melts snow for drinking water, heats soup or stew, and generally adds to the warmth of a cold tent pitched high in the snow and rock.

Now . . . nothing.

"We can make tea and maybe even some soup on the little spirit burner stove," I say. "Heat up some sardines." The small alcohol-burning stoves are meant for the high camps—mostly to make hot tea—but are supposed to be included as a backup stove for every camp.

"There was no spirit burner in any of the packs," says Jean-Claude. We exchange guilty glances, and I realize we're sharing our sense of shame at having supervised our loads, Sherpas, and selves so poorly on this, our first real outing toward the mountain.

"So it has to be the Primus," I say.

I stupidly move the brass tank in both hands but find no holes or leaks. Since kerosene would be spilling out if the circular tank had been breached, it isn't the most clever troubleshooting I've ever done. As if hypnotized, I count eleven languages imprinted on the side of the metal tank. Only eight years after the Great War, and this Swedish company—B. A. Hjorth & Co., Stockholm, as it says on the Primus as well as on an accompanying card advertising "Practical Accessories for the Primus" (e.g., a spirit can with a nozzle, part No. 1745; a cleaning needle case, No. 1050; and, of course, a Wind Shield, No. 1601)—is selling the stove in at least these eleven countries.

This version of the Primus has only a triangular plate as a "wind shield," but J.C. has blocked the wind with his body huddled over the stove each time he's tried to light it, so the wind shield is not the problem. Technically, we're supposed to use Primuses outside the tents, but there's no hope at all of getting this thing lighted in the gale-force winds ripping at even the entrances to our tents.

"Not at fault," says Jean-Claude as he inspects each disassembled piece: the burner nipple for heat and quench, the reserve cap parking boss, the burner collector collar, the flame ring, the nitrile seals, the lead seal in the burner itself, or the leather for the pressurizing pump.

He whispers under his breath, uses the few tools he's brought with him—a screwdriver, small wrench, some wire probes—to reassemble the stove, and tries again to light it. Nothing.

"It's not building up pressure in the tank," he says at last.

"How can that be?" I force myself to say. One pumps a Primus and it builds up the pressure to force the kerosene up into the tiny pipes. It's always worked for me.

Jean-Claude shakes his head.

Norbu Chedi speaks softly, almost apologetically: "On the Dongkha La, long before Kampa Dzong, Nawang Bura dropped his load down a steep incline. No sahib saw, since Nawang was back with the rear pack mules. There was a Primus that bounced free off large rocks for many yards downhill. Nawang Bura retrieved it and the other materials and repacked them without mentioning the accident to Dr. Pasang or Sahib Deacon or to Lady Bromley."

"That was weeks ago," I say. "Surely we would have used that... *this*...Primus since then."

"Maybe not," Jean-Claude says wearily. "We got into the habit of using the same Primuses at each camping spot. This one was taken out of reserve stores to go up the mountain. It's one of the 1925 models adapted for higher altitudes."

"Can't you fix it?"

Our lives may depend upon his doing so if we're trapped here many days. Hot soup and tea will be important, but melting the snow for drinking water is imperative.

"The tank isn't leaking," says J.C. "I've taken the pressurizing pump apart and inspected it and the leather bits more than a dozen times. I can't see anything wrong or broken anywhere. It just...won't...fucking...work."

None of us says anything for a very long moment, but the silence is filled in with a wilder, louder howl of wind that makes all of us grab on to the floor cloth or tent walls to keep from flying away.

"Sandy Irvine fixed dozens of things, built the rope ladder up to the Col, and repaired and redesigned the entire oxygen apparatus at Base Camp or above," mutters J.C. "And I—a Chamonix Guide and the son of a blacksmith and inventor and steel industrialist—can't even fix a *putain* Primus stove on our second night out above Base Camp."

"Without the Primus or spirit burner, what are our other options to get a controlled flame to melt some snow, heat some soup?" I ask. "We have the two pots. We have our tin cups. We have plenty of matches. We have some more alcohol. We have *lots* of kerosene."

"If you're thinking of dumping some kerosene into a cup and lighting it to put our pots on, forget it, Jake," says Jean-Claude. "Kerosene by itself doesn't burn in the way we need to heat things. To get a good blue flame we need..." Suddenly J.C. falls silent and takes the brass tank from my hands. He's already pulled off the pressure-pump mechanism, but now he tries the permanent screw that I've always used to turn the flame up at the beginning of a cooking session and then turned the other way to shut the Primus off after its use.

"The damned vent screw," says Jean-Claude. "It turned when I tried it each time, but it's cross-threaded...it's not opening to allow the pressurized kerosene jet to rise. In fact, the damned thing's cross-threaded and bent enough that the tank won't even hold pressure. The *goddamned vent screw!*"

He sets his wrench and small pair of pliers to work on the screw, but it won't thread properly. And now it is stuck. I see him using all of his massive arm and hand strength to get the screw to turn. It does not.

"Let me try," I say. I'm larger than Jean-Claude, my hands are much larger than Jean-Claude's, and I'm probably stronger than the Chamonix Guide, but I can't get the vent screw to turn either with my bare hands or with the wrench or pliers.

"Totally cross-stripped, the tank unpressurized and not able to be pressurized with the vent screw broken," says Jean-Claude. It sounds like our death sentence, but what's left of the logical parts of my brain reminds me that we can do without water for a few days, without food for weeks if need be. But my guess is that lots of snow-melt water and some hot soup would have gone far to reduce this headache and the other altitude sickness symptoms I'm feeling.

Meanwhile, the hemispherical tent walls are trying to rip themselves away from the curved wooden interior staves holding them in place. The thin ground cloth—the Sherpas hadn't bothered with setting down the thicker one before raising the tent—is trying to rise up under us even with all six of us, and the heavy food loads and kerosene cans, spread about on it. I've never been in an earthquake, but it must feel like this. Only not as loud. We're still shouting at each other to be heard.

"Jake and I are going back to our own tent to sleep," Jean-Claude tells Babu and Norbu. "It'd be a little too crowded in here with six men trying to stretch out. Get some sleep—tell Ang Chiri and Lhakpa Yishay not to worry. This storm may break by morning and either Lady Bromley-Montfort will be here with her Sherpas and supplies, or we'll just walk back down to Camp Two."

Since we've kept our boots and Shackleton jackets on, we just crawl out the door. But J.C. says, "Wait a minute, Jake," and begins handing out the cans of kerosene to me. He also brings the reassembled but still unworkable Primus. "We'll stack the cans just outside your tent," he shouts to Babu Rita.

But he doesn't. J.C. motions to me to carry my armloads of miniature cans with him to the far side of our poor sagging tent. There he sets his behind a boulder and I do the same. He puts his mouth near my ear so that I can hear him over the wind. "Some of the worst injuries I've seen in the mountains came from tent fires. I don't trust our friends to keep from experimenting with burning cans of kerosene when they're thirsty enough."

I nod, understanding that on a calm day or night, such experiments—especially if done just outside the tent—might be worth the risk. But not in a tent that's leaping and shaking under and around you.

Our own small tent, seven feet by six, is sagging and pitiful-looking. J.C. holds up one finger, telling me to wait outside a moment, and then he crawls in just far enough to pull a coil of the Deacon's Miracle Rope from his rucksack. He cuts different lengths and we use the heavier rope to add more tie-downs to the wind-whipped tent. The long stakes don't work worth a damn here on the lateral moraine, so we're adding to the already existing spiderweb of lines to rocks frozen into the moraine, boulders, and even to one ice pinnacle.

By now I'm frozen through and relieved when we're finished and can crawl into the low tent.

We crawl deep into our still dry goose down sleeping bags, removing our boots but putting them in the bags with us so that they won't be too frozen to get into in the morning. At this temperature, if a climber leaves his boots outside his bag, the laces tend to snap off when he tries to tie them in the morning. With George Finch's goose down duvet still on under the sleeping bag down, plus Reggie's hood and Michelin Man goose down trousers, what little body heat I have left builds up again quickly enough.

"Here, Jake, put these in your bag as well." J.C.'s left his bulky hand torch on, and I can see that he's handing me a frozen tin of spaghetti, a smaller tin of meat lozenges, a solid brick of the rubber-protected "portable soup," and the can of peaches (I can see the dent) that Reggie threw at the Deacon's head the hundred years ago that was Saturday.

"You're kidding," I say. How am I supposed to sleep with these freezing cans against me?

"Not at all," says Jean-Claude. "I have twice as many in my bag. Our body heat may melt—or at least soften—some of the food. The tin of peaches has syrup in it and we'll share it with the other four in the morning to...how do you say it in English?...*slake* our thirst."

Let's open it and drink it now, just the two of us, is my unworthy thought. But nobility wins out. That and my sure knowledge that the fluid in the peach can is frozen as solid as a brick at the moment.

J.C. flicks off the hand torch to save the batteries but then says in an almost perfect imitation of the Deacon's voice, "Well, what lessons have today's events taught us, my friends?"

The Deacon asks that after almost every climb and certainly after every problem we have with a climb, but J.C.'s mimicry of the vaguely tutorial Oxbridge accent is so dead-on that I laugh hard despite the pain it causes to my aching skull.

"I suppose we should check the contents of our loads more carefully when carrying to any higher camp," I say into the loud darkness.

"*Oui.* What else?"

"Double-check that none of the porters has tossed out something essential—such as his and his mate's sleeping bag."

"*Oui.* What else?"

"Probably have an Unna cooker in each camp as well as a roarer." The Unna cookers we've brought to Everest, smaller and lighter than Primuses and using a solid fuel to burn, were generally used in higher camps when weight in the load had to be kept to a minimum. I'm fairly certain that Mallory and Irvine had an Unna cooker at their Camp VI.

"Primuses almost always work," is J.C.'s response. "Robert Falcon Scott hauled one nine hundred miles to the South Pole and most of the way back."

"And look what happened to Scott and his men," I say.

We both start laughing. As if in response, the wind off the North Col roars more loudly. I feel as if our little two-man tent is going to shake itself to death despite—or perhaps because of—the spiderweb of tie-downs we've added outside.

There's no more talk between us until I ask, "Do you think Reggie will be here with the Sherpas and extra loads by late morning?"

Jean-Claude's silence goes on so long that I almost decide he's fallen asleep. Then he says, "I doubt it, Jake. If the blizzard continues this cold and this hard, I think it would be foolhardy to try to come up those last three and a half miles of glacier. Remember, they don't know that we have a damaged Primus. They assume that we are eating and drinking all right and... what is your American phrase that I like so much in Mark Twain? Ah, yes—hunkering down. Yes, just hunkering down here and waiting, as they are. My guess is that Lady Bromley-Montfort wisely retreated from Camp Two at the first signs of the blizzard hitting them. It's a cold, windblown site at the best of times."

He is right about that. Camp II is supposed to be pleasant because earlier expedition members said that, unlike Camps I and III, it's positioned to catch any sunlight the Himalayan skies might offer. But in our time there, it has been cloudy, windswept, and bitterly cold. Its only advantage is its beautiful view of Mount Kellas, named after the physician who died during the 1921 reconnaissance expedition.

"With the fixed ropes we've set along the way," I say hopefully, "they might come up from Camp One or even from Base Camp in a few hours."

"I think not," says Jean-Claude. "The snow was more than knee-deep when we broke trail this morning. Now those tracks are gone—swept away and filled in. I suspect that many of the fixed ropes will also be buried by morning. This is a hard snowstorm, my friend. If Reggie or the Deacon should try to come up, they and the porters would be... what is your word?..."

"Fucked?" I say.

"*Non,* postholing, at least all the way from Camp One, when they must leave the moraine and come onto the glacier. It is exhausting and terribly dangerous in a storm like this when one cannot see the trail or crevasses."

"We left bamboo markers all along the way."

"Many of which, we must assume," says J.C., "will be buried or blown over by morning." He switches to the Deacon's slow, deep, educated British accent. "Another thing we have learned, my friends, is that at least every other bamboo marker or wooden rope guide must have a red flag on it."

This time my head hurts too much to laugh. Also, I'm growing a bit frightened.

"What do we do if this storm keeps up all day tomorrow, Jean-Claude?"

"Experience tells us that we should stay here—hunkered down—until the storm finally passes," he says over the gunshots of crackling canvas walls. "But I'm worried about the Sherpas who are missing sleeping bags. Already they do not look so well. I hope their friends can keep them warm enough tonight. But if this continues longer than another day, I think we should try to get down to Camp Two."

"But as you said, it's almost as windy and cold as this damned Camp Three."

"But there should be at least six tents there by now, Jake. Odds are good that they will have left food supplies and at least one Primus and an Unna cooker with Meta solid fuel in a load stashed for a higher camp."

"Ah, hell... all right," I say.

I roll over, right into a frozen can of something. I also can feel every moraine rock beneath the tent, most of them pressing into my spine and kidneys. When we'd pitched the tent, there hadn't been enough snow here in the spot furthest away from any avalanche danger to provide a comfortable, melt-your-body-form-into-it padding below the tent. Now the snow is mostly on top of the tent or drifted up to either side.

I'm just drifting between miserable, cold wakefulness and miserable cold sleep when Jean-Claude says, "Jake?"

"Yes?"

"I think we need to climb the ice wall straight up, not even go near the slope that avalanched in 'twenty-two. There's too much new snow there. It'll be harder, but I think we have to go straight up the nine-hundred-foot slope, setting fixed ropes as we go, and then climb the sheer blue-ice wall where Mallory's chimney used to be."

He must be joking, I think. *Hallucinating out loud.*

"Okay," I say.

"Oui," says J.C. "I was afraid you would want to go the old way."

Jean-Claude starts to snore. I am asleep in ten seconds.

Sometime later—we eventually figure it to be about three a.m.—I awake to icy pellets being flung into my face, even though I've crawled down deep within my bag. To that and to Jean-Claude screaming at me over an infinitely louder wind roar.

The wind has finally ripped open the entire seam along the north wall of our guaranteed windproof new Meade tent and torn the canvas there to rags. The full force of the storm is blowing in on us.

"Quickly!" shouts Jean-Claude. The hand torch is lit, showing a blinding wall of snow blasting between the two of us. J.C. is tugging on his boots and then grabbing his rucksack in one hand and his flashlight and lumpy, food-tin-filled sleeping bag in the other, shouting at me all the time.

Boots unlaced, face stinging with minus-forty-degree cold, forgetting to put on my various gloves and mittens, dragging my own lumpy-with-cans sleeping bag in one hand and the almost empty rucksack in the other, I stumble after him and out into the maelstrom.

If Reggie's Big Tent has blown down, we're all dead.

Thursday, May 7, 1925

*I*t's time to pack and go down," says Jean-Claude as it begins to get light after two miserable, endless, restricted-to-the-tent days and two even more endless, wet, cold, sleepless nights at Camp III.

I lift my hands to where strips of my face are coming off and think, *Maybe it's past time we left.*

We'd brought no mirrors in our personal kits. "Give it to me straight, Jean-Claude...leprosy?"

"Sunburn," says J.C. "But you *are* a mess, my friend. Your sunburned skin is coming off in red and white strips, but your lips and the flesh underneath the peeling skin are almost blue—cyanotic, I think—from lack of oxygen."

"Red, white, and blue," I say. "God bless America."

"Or *Vive la France,*" says Jean-Claude, but he does not laugh. I notice that he and three of the four Sherpas, all but Babu, also have a blue tinge to their lips, faces, and hands.

For breakfast, lunch, and dinner yesterday I'd tried to suck on a tin-shaped frozen wedge of potatoes and peas. It tasted of kerosene, as did everything else the Sherpas had carried in their mixed loads. I'd crawled outside to vomit again and have not tried to eat anything since then. (We had been able to thaw the tin of peaches enough that all six of us got one tiny, icy sip of the peach juice. The tantalizing hint of liquid was almost worse than having nothing at all to drink.)

I'm freezing. J.C. and I had assumed the first night that Ang Chiri and Lhakpa Yishay would be able to wriggle into a sleeping bag with

315

one of the other Sherpas—the bags were made for European-sized male bodies, not the diminutive Sherpas—but they weren't able to manage it. These bags are sewn like a cocoon, not buttoned or zippered, so there is no way to open them up to spread one above and one below like eiderdown duvets. So that first night, Ang Chiri tried to sleep wearing just the wool outer clothing they'd chosen to keep on rather than wear the "Michelin" Finch goose down suits that J.C. and I had climbed into (and had been forced to shed our first hot day in the Trough and on the glacier where I received my terrible sunburn). The result was that Ang Chiri and Lhakpa Yishay both had frostbitten toes and feet. J.C.'s English-speaking Sherpa, Norbu Chedi, had been gasping for air so hard both nights that he chose to sleep with his face outside the folds of his sleeping bag; the result is white patches of frostbitten cheeks for Norbu.

So last night Jean-Claude and I gave our Finch down jackets and trousers to Ang Chiri and Lhakpa Yishay, and I didn't sleep a wink all night. Under the new down coat and trousers, I was wearing just a regular Mallory-style wool Norfolk jacket and sweater and wool knickers and socks, and now even the eiderdown sleeping bag couldn't keep me warm. I would begin to doze off despite the physical misery, but then slam awake either from the intense chill or with a sense of someone strangling me. Or both.

It feels better to be moving now, dragging on my boots and packing the high felt Laplander "slippers" deep into my empty rucksack. But every move uses up my energy and makes me have to stop and gasp for breath. I see Jean-Claude taking the same pauses as he labors to tie his frozen bootlaces. The Sherpas are moving even more slowly and ponderously than J.C. and me.

But eventually we're all packed, booted, cramponed, and layered—Jean-Claude and I have taken back our Finch outer clothing for the descent—and then J.C. makes me moan and the four Sherpas slump silently when he says, "We have to pack the tent and staves and ground cloths as well."

"Why?" I ask plaintively. Reggie's experimental Big Tent has survived the two days and nights of hurricane winds, but the damned thing is *heavy.* I'd carried only parts of it uphill and the weight had been oppressive. Now, I thought, everything depended upon our getting down to

Camp II or lower *quickly. Leave the damned tent where it is for the next Tiger Team,* is what I think but do not say aloud.

"We may need it for shelter on the glacier," Jean-Claude explains.

I stifle the urge to moan again. The idea of bivouacking anywhere on the open glacier seems like death to me. But if for some reason we *do* have to bivouac . . .

I realize that J.C. is right and I say to Babu Rita, "All right, you heard the man. You and Ang Chiri begin taking down the staves. Norbu, you and Lhakpa get outside and pull up all of the stakes and untie all the tie-downs. Don't cut them unless you have to and then only right next to the tie-down knot—and leave all the ropes attached."

If we have to pitch this tent on the glacier, I don't think we'll have the energy to attach new ropes. And there won't be these friendly rocks and boulders around.

It's strange to be standing outside and wearing a pack load again. The winds haven't abated, and the blizzard is coming down as heavily as it has the past two days and nights, but Jean-Claude's handy combination aneroid barometer and thermometer tells us that the low pressure is climbing along with the temperature, which is up to a balmy ten degrees Fahrenheit.

"Good for the crampons on the glacier snow," J.C. says into my ear under the wind roar and buffet.

Nothing is good.

J.C. and I are both surprised that there's only about two feet of new powder on the glacier rather than the four or five feet the intensity of the three-day storm made us fear, but the crust is not frozen solid enough to keep us from crashing through up to our knees or waist every dozen steps or so. And none of us ever seem to fall through at the same time. We descend the glacier like six blind men with palsy.

We've decided to rope up, all together, using the Deacon's hideously expensive Miracle Rope that was his personal invention (at Lady Bromley's expense) for this expedition. For things like casual guiding ropes on the glacier, on the way up we'd strung the alpine-standard three-eighths-inch cotton rope—what I think of as "the Mallory-Irvine rope," since they were last seen using it on this very mountain—but for vertical fixed ropes and for roping up in dicey situations, the Deacon insisted on this new blend of cotton, manila, hemp, and other material for his rope. It made the rope thicker and heavier—five-eighths of an inch rather than the three-eighths that had been standard for so many years in alpine climbing—and thus heavier to haul and harder to knot quickly, but his Alpine Club contacts led the Deacon to a commercial rope-testing facility in Birmingham: the three-eighths-inch standard cotton rope, even when new and unfrayed in any way, would snap at 500 pounds of pressure. This sounds like a lot, but when a normal-sized male is free-falling, say, while leading on a 30-foot belay, his mass plus velocity after falling 60 feet will almost always snap the standard three-eighths-inch cotton rope. "I think we use the damned stuff more as sympathetic magic rather than as a real safety precaution," the Deacon said.

That low tensile strength was also the reason, the Deacon had pointed out to us the previous winter when he'd had us testing his new rope in Wales, why so many climbers—in the Himalayas now as well as in the Alps—lost their lives while descending steep slopes again rather than rappelling down with any real assurance of safety. The Deacon's new Mixed Fibre Rope, as he liked to call it, had tested out to more than 1,100 pounds' strain before snapping. Not yet satisfactory to the Deacon—he envisioned what would later become the 5,000-test-pound average nylon-blend rope of the future, without knowing how it could be manufactured with the materials of 1924–25—but decidedly better than the three-eighths-inch cotton "clothesline rope" (as the Deacon called it) that Mallory and Irvine had tied onto on their last day.

But even with the new, improved rope, J.C. and I have had to sort out the order in which we should all descend the mountain. Obviously Jean-Claude should go first, but then who? Of the other five of us, Ang Chiri and Lhakpa Yishay can barely stand and stagger along on their frostbitten and swollen feet—neither had been able to tie the laces to his own boots, and J.C. and I had attached their crampons—so neither can be expected to hold a belay if Jean-Claude were suddenly to disappear into a hidden crevasse. And neither I nor the Deacon's new Miracle Rope could be expected to hold the weight of three free-falling men on belay, no matter how quickly I could get my long ice axe into the glacier snow.

So we've compromised, with J.C. going first, then Babu Rita—the healthiest of the Sherpas this awful day—and then me (in the slight hope I might belay two men), and then Ang and Lhakpa staggering along, holding each other up, and finally with Norbu Chedi, frostbitten cheeks and all, as our anchorman. Theoretically I could belay Ang and Lhakpa if one or both of them fell into a crevasse behind me.

It is understood, at least by Jean-Claude and me, that if it reaches the point where Norbu Chedi has to belay all or most of us, we are dead men anyway.

So we follow J.C. up and away from our quickly disappearing wreckage of Camp III, back onto the East Rongbuk Glacier, and then down the glacier's surprisingly steep slopes. How, in this never-ending blizzard, Jean-Claude can find his way and avoid the hundreds of crevasses he'd pointed out during the climb up in sunlight two days ago I'll never know. Most of our route-marking bamboo wands either have blown away or are covered with snow, but occasionally J.C. reaches down and tugs one up, reassuring all of us that we are on the right track.

And although I believe in nothing supernatural, I will always—after this day—ascribe a weird but real sixth sense to Jean-Claude Clairoux in his ability to sense the presence of crevasses that would have been invisible even on a sunny, shadow-assisted day, much less in this blinding blizzard. Several times he holds up his arm telling us to stop where we are, and then he turns around and retraces his quickly disappearing steps in the snow, leading us back up and then around and then down past crevasses that sometimes become slightly visible to the rest of us in the passing, but more often than not remain unseen and unsensed by anyone other than Jean-Claude.

So, after the agonizingly slow hours of dressing, tying our bootlaces, getting our crampons on, and packing up the tent in different loads (J.C. hauling most of it), we suffer four more hours descending the glacier in this stop-and-start way before we get to the ladder-crossed crevasse that had been less than an hour short of Camp III on our way up on Tuesday.

Jean-Claude holds up his snow-covered arm and we stop, then approach slowly.

The combined 15-foot span of the two roped-together ladders has slipped out of place.

"Merde," says J.C.

"Yeah."

It's still snowing so hard that we have trouble seeing the far side of the slumped span of the ladder only 15 feet away, but after a few minutes the flurries clear just long enough for us to assess the problem.

There's been a subsidence on the far, southern lip of the crevasse, as if a column of ice supporting the far side has shifted downward six feet or so. One of our Miracle Rope guy lines is missing, and the other one—the one to our left as we look south—is slumping under its weight of snow and ice in a way that suggests that the eyelet stake and ice screws holding it on that side have come loose. We'd left two climbing rigs for the heavily laden porters who were to follow us up on Wednesday to put on for security—clipping the carabiner on the harness into one of the guy lines—to use as they crossed the rickety ladder, but the harnesses are now lost, either buried under the new snow or fallen into the widened crevasse.

We untie from our common rope, and Babu Rita ties back in as lead man of the four connected Sherpas. I tie on to Jean-Claude, who sinks to his hands and knees to crawl closer to the ladder and the edge of the crevasse.

I borrow Ang Chiri's and Norbu Chedi's long ice axes, and J.C. and I drive them as deep into the snow and solid ice as we can, running about 30 feet of free Miracle Rope to Jean-Claude so that the axes will be the primary anchor system should he fall. I gesture for Ang and Norbu to come around to the crevasse side of the ice axe anchors and to lean their weight on them. Borrowing Lhakpa Yishay's long ice axe, I lay it along the edge of the crevasse, anchoring its curved pick deep into the ice; if J.C. falls, I want both the anchor rope and my belay rope to be running over the smooth wood of the ice axe shaft rather than cutting into the lip of the crevasse. Babu Rita retains his ice axe to sink behind us and has run a loop of rope around it should a hole open up under Ang, Norbu, and Lhakpa. He's their belay man now.

Then I sink the steel point of my own ice axe as deep into the snow and ice as I can—there's too much powder snow to make it feel truly secure—and back away from the edge as I play out the 30 feet of rope I've left between J.C. and me.

He begins his crawl out onto the now steeply inclined ladder. I brace myself for the sudden belay shock of his fall.

Jean-Claude has only one free hand with which to grip the ladder in front of him, since he's using the short ice hammer that has been lashed onto his rucksack to bang snow and ice off the rungs and ladder rims ahead of him as he crawls. He's left on his full rucksack load; he and I hadn't even needed to speak out loud before both deciding that—if the ladder holds—we want the Sherpas also to cross with their loads still on their backs. It would just take too damned long in this freezing world of continually falling temperatures and whirling spindrift to send the loads across by hand. So it will be all or nothing.

At one point, when J.C. is about halfway across, his feet and backside higher than his head as he crawls downhill, the ladder drops another six inches or so in its snowy niche across the crevasse, and I brace again for the full, spine-jarring shock of his drop.

It does not come. The new ledge of snow and ice on the far side stays solid long enough for Jean-Claude to finish his crawl. Amazingly, he stays out on the ladder while he bangs some ice screws into the blue-ice wall of the little debris chute he's crawling toward. He takes two precut six-foot strands of the Deacon's rope and ties the ends onto the stakes and then wraps the other ends around each side of the ladder until the lines are taut.

It's not much protection, but it's a start.

Now I can barely see Jean-Claude through the heavy snowfall, but I can hear him panting heavily as he pulls his own long ice axe off his rucksack and sinks it into the snow and ice about ten meters beyond the crevasse. He ties longer strands to this new ice anchor and—incredibly—crawls back out onto the ladder to lash these new support lines onto the middle section of the ladder. I toss him two more lines that we've tied around our own ice anchors, and he moves forward to tie them onto this end of the ladder. Then, rather than stand up on our side of the crevasse, he laboriously backs his way across the steeply inclined ladder again, crampons first.

Standing in the debris chute, he uses his ice hammer and mittened hands to sweep away some of the snow debris so that it will be easier for the porters to stand upright and walk the eight vertical feet up the rough ramp to the glacier proper.

Then he throws his own belay line and the last coil of Miracle Rope across the crevasse to me and backs away to loop his ends around his ice axe anchor before he takes up his belay stance. Just watching my friend exert himself like this above 20,000 feet has made me gasp for breath.

"All right," I say with as much authority as I can muster. "Lhakpa first. Babu, you keep the other two on belay while I tie my belay rope and Sahib Clairoux's onto Lhakpa. And please instruct Lhakpa and the others to approach the ladder on their hands and knees—with pack loads remaining on, if you please—and to move slowly. Tell them that there's no danger. Even if the ladder were to give way, which it won't with its new tie-downs, Sahib Clairoux and I both will have you on belay. All right...Lhakpa first..."

For a moment the terrified Sherpa won't come forward, and I'm sure that we'll have a mutiny on our hands.

But in the end, after much gesticulating from me and shouting in Nepalese from Babu Rita, Lhakpa crawls forward an inch at a time, out onto the ladder, trying to keep his knees on the ladders' still icy rims, moving only one mittened hand at a time. It takes forever, but finally Lhakpa is across and being untied by Jean-Claude. The frostbitten Sherpa is laughing and giggling like a child over there.

Four more of us, I think wearily. But I smile and beckon the hobbling Ang Chiri to drop to all fours and come crawling forward to be tied in on both our ropes.

About a century later, when all of the Sherpas are across and tied in to their own climbing line again, I wrestle with all my might to dig up the three ice axes I've driven in and then hurl them across the crevasse. J.C. retrieves all three.

I'll have only Jean-Claude on belay for me, but the second line he tosses me will run to where his own axe is still being used as an ice anchor. I tie a loose strand of the Miracle Rope around me, to make a Prusik sling for my feet should the ladder give way under me. It's infinitely better for the climber fallen into a crevasse to Prusik-knot his way up and out under his own power—creating little climbing stirrups with the knotted loops—than to have the man or men on the other side try to use brute force to haul him up.

I make the mistake of staring down into the swirling blue-to-black depths of the crevasse as I shuffle across the ladder. The drop beneath the shaky, ice-rimmed, tilted ladder looks to be, quite literally, bottomless. The downward-forward incline seems steeper when one is *on* the ladder. I feel blood rushing to my head.

Then I'm across and eager arms are helping me to my feet. Tying on to the main rope again, I look back at the spiderwebbed, jury-rigged mess of a ladder-bridge we've all just crawled across and I laugh, just as Lhakpa Yishay had earlier, with a weary sense of sheer elation at the mere fact of being alive.

It's getting late in the afternoon and we have far to go. Jean-Claude takes the lead, I tie in to the line in third place behind Babu Rita, where I'd been before, and we resume the slow descent of the glacier in the snowstorm. I can tell that Ang Chiri and Lhakpa are stumbling along with no sensation in their frostbitten feet at all; they might as well be walking on wooden stumps.

Somehow, I will never understand how, J.C. keeps us to our route. As we get a bit lower, moving between the towering and oppressive ice pinnacles again, there's less new powder, and we see more of the bamboo wands appearing like quick, careless ink scratches on a perfectly white sheet of paper. There is no separation between snow and sky this gray afternoon, and the giant seracs appear suddenly before and beside us like white-shrouded ghost-giants.

Then we reach the last obstacle between us and Camp II and fresh water to drink and warmed soup and real food to eat—the final crevasse less than half a mile above the camp, the crevasse with the wide and thick snow bridge and our rope guy lines to clamp on to for a sense of security as we cross.

Both guy lines are in place, although slumping from the weight of ice on them. The snow bridge is completely gone, tumbled into the broad crevasse.

Jean-Claude and I huddle and compare watches. It's after 4:30 p.m. The glacier will be in full shadow from Everest's ridges, and it will be growing dark in forty-five minutes or less. The snow and temperature continue to fall. In coming up, we'd gone both right and left for more than half a mile in each direction before deciding that the snow bridge was the best way to get across. There will be no bamboo wands to guide us between snow-covered crevasses if we try that kind of traverse again. We'll have to wait for morning and—if God be pleased with us—better weather.

We look each other in the eye and Jean-Claude says loudly to Babu and Norbu, "We dump our loads here, about thirty feet away from the crevasse. And we will set up the tent *here.*" He drives his ice axe into the snow about ten meters back from the lip of the crevasse.

The porters pause, stunned at the thought of spending another night on the glacier.

"Quickly! *Vite!* Before darkness falls and the higher winds return!" J.C. claps his mittened hands so hard that the echo returns to us as loud as a gunshot.

The noise brings the Sherpas out of their shock, and we all work as well as we can to unload both ground cloths, set up the tent, and drive in as many jury-rigged stakes and ice screws as we can. I realize that if the winds come as they did the last two nights, odds are poor that our tent—and we—will survive. I can imagine Reggie's Big Tent with all six of us huddled in it tonight, fingers trying to self-arrest through the ground cloth, as the hurricane winds just slide us, tent and all, across the ice like a hockey puck, until we go hurtling into this no-bottom crevasse.

Within an hour we're inside the tent and huddled together for warmth. We make no attempt to eat anything. Our thirst is terrible beyond any words I have to describe it. All six of us are coughing that high-altitude cough that sounds so terrible—"like a barking jackal," J.C. has called it. The second time he uses the phrase, I ask my friend directly if he's ever actually *heard* a jackal bark. "All last night, Jake," is his reply.

Jean-Claude and I have given Ang and Lhakpa our eiderdown sleeping bags this night while we sleep in our Finch duvet coats and Reggie goose down trousers, thin blankets pulled over us. I use my boots in a weatherproof sack as a pillow.

Both J.C. and I are exhausted, but we're too cold and anxious even to pretend to sleep. We try to huddle closer, but the other's shaking and chattering teeth just seem to make it worse for each of us. Perhaps our bodies have just quit putting out any heat.

That would mean that you're both dead, Jake. I don't like the tone of my own voice in my head. It sounds like it's given up.

"In the m-m-morning," whispers Jean-Claude as full darkness falls and the winds grow stronger, "I'll cross on one of the fixed ropes, ankles and hands, and g-g-get down to Camp Two and bring everyone back with me early with ladders and food and hot b-b-beverages."

"Sounds...okay," I manage between teeth chattering. Then, "Or I could try it tonight, Jean-Claude. Take the hand torch with me and..."

"No," whispers my friend. "I d-d-don't believe the rope will h-h-hold your wuh-weight. I'm lighter. Too t-t-tired to b-belay tonight. In the m-morning."

We curl closer, close our eyes, and pretend to sleep. The wind has grown in ferocity so the machine-gun battle sounds of the canvas slapping have returned with a vengeance. I imagine that I can feel the entire tent sliding south toward the crevasse, but I'm too exhausted and dehydrated to do anything about it and just remain curled where I am, the other bodies pressing close.

Jean-Claude's slow breathing has the bad habit of just stopping for what seems like minutes on end—no sound, no inhaling or exhaling—until I shake him back into a semblance of breathing again. This goes on deep into the black night. It gives me a good reason for staying awake in the cold darkness. Every time I shake him back into life, he whispers, "*Merci,* Jake," and then passes into his irregular, semiconscious breathing again. It's like a deathbed watch with a dying man.

Suddenly I sit straight up in the darkness. Something terrible must have happened. I can hear J.C.'s and the other men's gasping breaths, including my own, in the near-absolute darkness, but there's something essential missing.

The wind has stopped. The noise is gone for the first time in more than forty-eight hours.

Jean-Claude is sitting up next to me, and we shake each other's shoulders in some sort of mute celebration or simple hysteria. I fumble around until I find the boxy flashlight, turn its light onto my watch. Three-twenty a.m.

"I should try the rope now," rasps J.C. "I won't have the strength to cross come sunrise."

Before I can answer, there come a scrabbling and tearing at our tent door—which we've learned to leave partially unlashed since totally closing off the tent adds to our inability to breathe—and I begin hallucinating bright lights shining in on us. Norbu Chedi's cheeks are frostbitten pure white and black in the sudden glare of brilliance. Something large and powerful is clawing to get in.

The Deacon's and Lady Bromley-Montfort's heads poke into the tent. I can see the flashlights in their mittened hands and more lights behind them—lanterns, several of them. The two are also wearing Reggie's Welsh miner headgear, and those lights also illuminate the tawdry, ice-dusted interior of our tent and our staring faces.

"How?" I manage to say.

The Deacon grins. "We were ready to set out as soon as the blizzard died down. I have to admit that these miner's lamps work passably well..."

"Better than passably," interrupts Reggie.

"But how did you cross...," begins Jean-Claude.

"The glacier's been busy," says the Deacon. "About six hundred meters—a quarter of a mile—to the west, both sides collapsed a debris field to the shallow bottom there. About a hundred and fifty feet down and then back up, but ramps, really. No terribly serious climbing involved. We left some fixed ropes. Make room, gentlemen, we're coming in."

Besides the Deacon and Reggie crowding in to fill our tent to overflowing, Pasang comes in on his knees. He removes a medical bag from his rucksack.

The Sherpas outside crouch by the doorway, their own headlamps burning, at least three lanterns casting a wide light on their grins as they pass in thermoses of warm Bovril, tea, and soup. A larger thermos holds only water, and each of us takes a turn drinking deeply.

Dr. Pasang is already inspecting Norbu's face, Lhakpa's and Ang's frostbitten feet. "These two will require carrying on Tejbir's and Nyima Tsering's backs," says Pasang. He begins rubbing smelly whale oil on the two men's bare, blackened feet and on Norbu's face.

"We're going now?" I manage to say. I'm not sure I can stand, but already the water has revived something that had been close to being extinguished in me.

"Now's as good a time as any," says the Deacon. "There's a Sherpa to help each of you. We also have headlamps for all of you. Even with the—what's your American word, Jake?—even with the *detour* down to the new route across the crevasse, we'll be back to Camp Two in forty-five minutes or less. We've marked the way with wands."

"Come, Jake, I'll help you to your feet," says Reggie and puts my arm over her shoulder. She lifts my two-hundred-plus pounds as if I were a child and all but carries me out into the night.

The stars are very bright. There is no hint of snow or cloud, other than the spindrift I can see hurling itself from the summits and ridges of Everest, a mere three miles and 10,000 feet above us.

Jean-Claude also looks up at Everest and blazing star fields as he's helped out of the tent. *"Nous y reviendrons,"* he says to the mountain.

I may be wrong, but I think I've picked up enough French to translate that as "We shall return."

Saturday, May 9, 1925

*I*t's unspeakably hot.

There's not a breath of air in the two-man Meade tent that Jean-Claude and I slept in last night after being released from the Base Camp "infirmary," and although the canvas doors to the tent are tied back and wide open, lying in here is like being buried in the Sahara in a shroud smelling of overheated canvas.

J.C. and I have stripped to our underwear but are still sweating profusely, and now we see the Deacon striding toward us across the uneven moraine-rock field.

Yesterday morning, Friday before dawn, when the Deacon, Reggie, Pasang, and the others had come to our rescue, they'd brought us down to Camp II, where both J.C. and I continued to drink cup after cup of cold water.

I'd assumed that they'd leave J.C. and me at Camp II while they helped carry Ang Chiri and Lhakpa Yishay down to Base Camp to have Pasang deal with their frostbite in the medical tent "infirmary" he'd set up there, but the Deacon insisted that all of us—including Norbu Chedi, with his frostbitten cheeks now liberally smeared with whale oil and axle grease—go all the way back down to Base Camp. After drinking so much water and then some hot soup, Jean-Claude and I were perfectly able to hike down the Trough with Pasang and half a dozen other Sherpas, but Ang Chiri needed to be carried on a jury-rigged stretcher, and Lhakpa Yishay hobbled down with a Sherpa friend sup-

328

porting him on either side. It was testimony to the severity of our earlier dehydration that, even after gulping down so many cups of water, neither of us had to stop to pee during the descent.

The air at Base Camp—at only 16,500 feet—seemed rich and thick enough to swim in after two days and nights at Camp III's altitude of 21,500 feet. Besides that, Dr. Pasang had "prescribed" that all six of us take some "English air" from one of the oxygen rigs being carried up to Camp III by porters. After dismissing Jean-Claude and me from the infirmary on Friday afternoon, he'd sent one bottle rigged to two mask sets—the regulator timed to dispense only one liter of oxygen per hour—and told us in no uncertain terms to use it during the night whenever we woke gasping for air or feeling cold.

With the English air to help us, J.C. and I had slept for thirteen hours.

The Deacon crouches next to where Jean-Claude and I sprawl half outside the tent, lying on our sleeping bags in the hot sunlight. The Deacon is down to his shirtsleeves, although he continues to wear his thick wool knickers and high puttees.

"Well, how are my last two hospital patients?" he asks.

J.C. and I both insist that we're feeling excellent—great sleep, wonderful appetite at breakfast this morning, no signs of frostbite or the "mountain lassitude" remaining—and we're telling the truth. We say that we're ready to head back up the Trough and glacier to Camp III right now, immediately.

"Glad you're feeling better," says the Deacon, "but no hurry to come up to Camp III. Rest another day. One thing that Lady Bromley-Montfort and I heartily agree upon is the idea of climbing high, sleeping low. Especially after the winds and cold you chaps put up with for three nights."

"You've climbed the ice wall to the North Col without us," says Jean-Claude, and his voice sounds both disappointed and accusatory.

"Not at all," says the Deacon. "We spent yesterday and this morning continuing to make the trail up to Camp Three safer and supervising the Sherpas as they haul more loads up there. Reg...Lady Bromley-Montfort is at Camp Two now, and we'll be working on shuttling things all the rest of the day. Tomorrow, she and I thought we'd acclimate some more at Camp III, and if you fellows come up by late tomorrow afternoon, we'll give that ice wall to the North Col a try on Monday morning." He pats Jean-Claude's arm. "You're our official snow-and-ice man, old sport. I promised you that we wouldn't take on the North Col until you were ready. Besides, the wind's too high on the Col today. Perhaps it will die down tomorrow and the next day."

"Wind?" I say. There's not a breath of it down here at Base Camp.

The Deacon shifts to one side and extends his left arm as if introducing someone. "See how she smokes," he says.

J.C. and I had been marveling at the blue sky and blindingly white snow on the North Face of Everest, but now we notice just how high the winds must be at altitude. The spindrift from the summits and North Ridge disappear beyond our field of vision to the left.

"Incredible," I say. "Is the Trough this bloody hot?"

"Twenty degrees hotter," says the Deacon with a grin. "My thermometer registered over one hundred degrees Fahrenheit among the *penitentes* between Camp Two and Camp One. Even hotter up on the glacier. We've been giving the porters plenty of rest time and water, and still they stumble into Camp III too exhausted to stand or to eat."

"How heavy are the loads, *Ree-shard?*"

"None more than twenty-five pounds between Camps Two and Three. Most around twenty."

"Many trips up and down needed, then," says Jean-Claude.

The Deacon merely nods absently.

"How are our four guys this morning?" I ask, realizing that I should have asked after our Sherpas first thing.

"Babu Rita and Norbu Chedi are carrying again already," says the Deacon. "Lhakpa's feet are black, but Dr. Pasang says perhaps he won't lose his toes. Ang Chiri, on the other hand—well, Pasang says it's *sayonara* to at least all of Ang's toes and probably two or three fingers."

I'm shocked to hear this. Ang's feet had been swollen and hard-frozen white when we'd helped him squeeze those malformed feet into his boots at Camp III on Thursday morning, and I know that Dr. Pasang spent a lot of time with both Sherpas when we were all in the infirmary tent yesterday, but I had no idea that it would come to amputations.

"Some of the other Sherpas are already preparing Ang's new 'sahib boots' with wedges at the end to make up for his soon-to-be-missing toes," says the Deacon. "Ang's morale is wonderful. Pasang will probably remove the toes and fingers—Ang's three fingers look especially bad, as brown and shrunken and wizened as an Egyptian mummy's—by Wednesday. Ang insists that he'll be carrying again by next weekend."

A sober silence follows this announcement. Finally Jean-Claude says, "Are you sure you don't want us to come up to Camp Three today, *Reeshard?* Jake and I feel well enough to climb, and we can haul some loads from here."

The Deacon shakes his head. "I don't want you hauling loads even tomorrow when you come up. It's going to take an extraordinary amount of energy to get up that hill to the North Col...the snow is waist-deep on much of the slope, and you saw the blue-ice wall where Mallory's beloved chimney used to be. Reggie and I are both leaving the trailbreaking on Monday morning to you two lads. We'll be poking along behind, rigging the fixed ropes and cavers' ladders."

"Don't forget my bicycle," J.C. says.

The Deacon nods. "You can bring your bicycle up with your personal kit tomorrow," he says. "Nothing heavier."

Jean-Claude's "bicycle"—its bicycle seat, pedals, and handlebars only rarely glimpsed when the mule or yak loads were being repacked—has been a source of some teasing and some real curiosity during the entire five weeks of our approach to Everest. I know that it's not actually a bicycle—there's been no glimpse of bicycle tires or wheels, and several people swear to have spotted strange folding metal flanges attached to the bicycle frame—but only J.C. and the Deacon seem to know what the damned thing really is.

"I only hope that this beautiful weather holds," says Jean-Claude. "Minus this terrible heat, of course."

"I'm sure that air temperature in the sun—out of the wind, at least—is well over one hundred degrees on the sunny parts of the North Col today," says the Deacon.

"Tuesday and Wednesday nights at Camp Three," I say, "it was thirty below and we were all certain that the monsoon had arrived."

"Not yet," says the Deacon. "Not yet." He slaps his wool-covered thighs and stands from his long crouch. "I'm going to look in on Ang and Lhakpa again, chat with Dr. Pasang for a moment, and take a few of these boys uphill with me. We'll be carrying loads to Camp Three until well after sunset this evening."

"*Ree-shard,*" says J.C. "Did you not forget to ask us something?"

The Deacon grins. "Well, gentlemen," he says. "What lessons have we all learned from your little carry-to-Camp-Three adventure?"

After Jean-Claude and I laugh, but before we can speak, the Deacon waves one hand and strides back toward the infirmary tent.

Monday, May 11, 1925

*I*t is a perfect day for an attempt to summit Mount Everest.

Unfortunately, we are just beginning our assault on the mountain's flanks, trying to reach the North Col and establish a foothold there before the end of the day. We leave Camp III a little after 7:00 a.m. Tied in to our first rope are just Jean-Claude, then me, then the Deacon, then the Deacon's strongest-climbing personal Tiger Sherpa, Nyima Tsering. The second rope is led by Reggie, followed by my smiling Sherpa Babu Rita and three more Tiger Sherpas after him, the string anchored by the Deacon's big man, Tenzing Bothia. Pasang is still at Base Camp watching over Ang Chiri and Lhakpa Yishay.

It turns out that the Deacon hasn't been quite as lazy over the weekend as he'd promised us. With soft snow, just the trek from Camp III to the base of the huge slope could have taken two totally exhausting hours or more of wallowing through waist-deep snow. But the Deacon, Reggie, and some of the Sherpas broke trail yesterday in the heat, so we are at the base of the actual slope and ready to climb within thirty minutes.

Our hope of all hopes over the past few days has been that the sun would melt the outer inches of snow during the day and the freezing-cold nights above Camp III would harden that surface snow to something like the consistency of ice for our new 12-point crampons. Now is the test...and J.C. and I are soberly aware that we're no longer horsing around in Wales, pretending to be real Himalayan mountaineers. Jean-Claude's newly designed crampons, ice hammers, jumars, and other devices — not to mention the Deacon's Miracle Rope, which we'll be bet-ting our lives on each time we set up a rappel rather than chop steps for a descent—will either work and save us days of repeated effort, or prove to be a costly, perhaps fatal mistake. One fact looms large: achieving the North Col soon is absolutely essential if we are to come close to meeting the Deacon's summiting date of May 17.

The first 300 feet or so of elevation consists of little more than a steep slope. Mallory and the others before him—including the Deacon—had spent entire days using their ice axes to hack footholds into the icy snow crust for the porters. Even then, the steps would soon fill with spindrift and new snowfall and would require more days of "maintenance" hacking—heavy work above 21,000 feet. And to minimize the exertion of the porters, the climbers had hacked the steps back and forth across the face of the snow slope in easy switchbacks.

Not today.

Jean-Claude is as good as his word and forges a crampon-kicked path straight up the 1,000-foot incline, keeping the line a hundred yards or so to the right of where the seven Sherpas had died in the avalanche in 1922. Even this close to the bottom, we're putting in fixed ropes—the lighter three-eighths-inch cotton "Mallory rope" for this more casual incline at the base of the steeper slope—and every 50 feet or so Jean-Claude pauses as I use a wooden mallet to pound in tall, sharpened wooden stakes with eyelets atop them. We're all carrying heavy coils of rope (with more in the rucksacks), and the thinner cotton rope goes quickly.

Even though "breaking trail" with 12-point crampons is infinitely easier than wallowing waist-deep in snow and hacking out steps, I can soon hear Jean-Claude's heavy breathing. All of us fall into the rhythm of three paces, pause, gasp, then three more steps up.

"It's time to go to the gas," cries the Deacon the next time both ropes pause in our long vertical line.

This is the Deacon's Rule—above 22,000 feet, all possible summit climbers will go to oxygen tanks. Rather than have us all climb with a full O_2 rig, J.C. has separated out one tank of English air for each rucksack carried by us four sahibs, and one tank each for Tenzing Bothia, Nyima Tsering, and the other three Tigers climbing with us. Those full sets we'll save for assaults above the North Col.

"I don't really need the English air yet," calls up Reggie.

"I'm still all right," calls down J.C. from his perch above us.

The Deacon shakes his head. "Feel free to set the valves at their lowest flow, but we go on oxygen from this point on while doing heavy climbing."

I feign reluctance, but in truth the headache I'd gotten rid of yesterday is trying to creep back in—the pain throbbing to my pulse as I gasp for breath during each short rest break—and I'm relieved when, with the mask covering my face below my goggles, I hear the soft hiss of air. The flow valve can be set to 1.5 liters of air per minute—the lowest setting—or 2.2 liters per minute. I choose the lower rate of flow.

Within a minute, I feel as if someone has given me a shot of pure adrenaline. J.C. doubles his climbing speed even as the snow slope becomes much steeper and more treacherous and a gap begins to open between the four of us on the first rope and Reggie and her four Sherpas. Babu Rita and the other three porters are carrying and climbing stolidly enough, but they soon can't match the pace of those of us on oxygen.

We run out of the Mallory-type clothesline rope precisely where we'd planned to, and the Deacon signals for us to switch over to his heavier Miracle Rope. The slope is steep enough now that we could rappel down it—if we learn to trust the new rope for such previously unheard-of long rappels—and we begin feeding it out minus the eyelet stakes.

At our next pause around 11:00 a.m., as we wait for Reggie and her Tiger Team to catch up, I realize that we're more than 600 feet up the 1,000-foot snow and ice wall. The exposure is severe—the Camp III tents look very small and distant from here—but the combination of fixed rope anchored by ice screws at intervals and the almost unbelievable grip of our 12-point crampons and short ice hammers gives us a sense of real security.

It's during this rest about 200 feet below the beginning of the sheer ice wall that the Deacon gestures for J.C. and me to trade places. Jean-Claude signs that he still has plenty of energy to spare, but the Deacon merely repeats his hand commands. For a minute both J.C. and I are untied and unbelayed as we trade places in the vertical line. In the lead now, I switch my oxygen tank regulator from the 1.5-liter minimum flow to the 2.2-liter-per-minute full flow rate. There should be enough to get me to the North Col all right, but I'll be lowering that flow before too long. I'm sure that the Deacon will want Jean-Claude to take the lead on the vertical face of blue ice looming above us.

I admit that my thrill at finally taking the lead on this expedition is mixed with some disappointment that I won't be the first to climb an ice wall at this altitude with nothing more than 12-point crampons and a short ice hammer in each hand. J.C. had enjoyed that honor.

As we stay stuck to the steep wall below the vertical section, even though I've stripped off all goose down garments and stowed them in my rucksack and have been climbing with only a wool shirt and cotton undershirt on, I'm all but drenched with sweat. The entire upper basin of the East Rongbuk Glacier and the North Col have been in direct sunlight now for some time; the Camp III area more than 60 stories beneath us is a glaring basin of bright light.

Reggie and her Tigers—I can see Babu Rita's white grin from 50 feet away—catch up, a heavy coil of Miracle Rope is passed up to me, and after we've all had another minute or two of rest, I tighten my oxygen mask and start my own crampon-and-ice-hammer ascent.

Fifteen minutes into this I realize that I've never felt stronger on a mountain. My headache is gone. My arms and legs are suffused with a new energy even while my spirit is filled with a renewed sense of confidence.

This new type of ice climbing which J.C. says he's stolen from the top German climbers is *fun.* I pause every 30 feet or so to set out and anchor the next strand of fixed rope—now dangling almost vertically past us—but I no longer need the rests to gasp for air after only four or five kicked-in steps. I feel as if I could climb like this all day and all night.

For the first time I'm beginning to believe that our little band might have a real chance at summiting Mount Everest. I know that the Deacon has been considering moving out onto the North Face from Camp V or VI, duplicating Colonel Norton's 1924 attempt on the Great Couloir—traverse off the ridge to the right above the Yellow Band until reaching the scar of snow that stretches straight up to the snowfield below the Summit Pyramid—and if the quality of the frozen snow in that couloir is anything like that of the North Col face here, such a plan would seem to make sense. Climbing on oxygen, leaving the tent before sunrise—trusting our Finch-and-Reggie down clothing to keep us alive in the unrelenting cold—we could easily make the summit and be back before sunset if the climbing were as straightforward 12-point crampon and ice hammer work as today's has been.

I pause in such thinking before my dreams outrun reality's headlights. Even now, part of me knows that nothing really will "come easily" on Mount Everest. I've learned from listening to the Deacon and through reading and listening to others—as well as through our hard experience at Camp III—that everything this mountain gives, she plucks away just as quickly and certainly. Perhaps the Great Couloir will be part of our plans, but I remind myself that no part of this ascent will turn out, in the long run, to be "easy."

Suddenly we're at the vertical ice. I pause again, breathing heavily but not gasping into my mask, allow the Deacon just below me to bang in the ice screws for the last section of fixed Miracle Rope, and—trusting my crampon points and the sunken adzes of the two ice hammers far more than I would have thought possible before today—lean far back to stare up at the gleaming wall of ice that is the North Col's last full barrier before we beat her.

It seems impossible. To my right a few yards, I can see various cracks and tumbled ice boulders—all that is left of the ice chimney that George Mallory had free-climbed a year ago. I'd seen one photograph of that climb and heard Deacon's description of it—Mallory's moves being one part spider to two parts gymnast, his fast, vertical scuttle impossible to imitate even by the expert climbers coming up behind him. That's where Sandy Irvine's rope ladder had come in so useful to the porters and later climbers. We'd brought rope and wood caver's ladders for just that purpose, but the plan was to lower them from the top of the North Col ledge, not fix them as we ascend.

I give the Deacon a thumbs-up—I can still take the lead onto the vertical ice if he wants—but he shakes his head and looks up and beyond me at J.C., who is directly above both of us now on the extremely steep slope. One gloved palm up—the Deacon is questioning whether Jean-Claude has enough energy for this final assault. I know that the Deacon himself will lead this 200-foot vertical pitch if Jean-Claude can't. It's the main reason that the Deacon hasn't yet taken the lead on this morning's climb.

J.C. gives a thumbs-up—his oxygen mask, goggles, and leather fly-ing helmet hide his expression and features—and passes his rope and other loads down to Nyima Tsering next in line.

Once again he and I trade places, but much more gingerly this time since a slip here would lead to an almost certainly fatal fall. These ice hammers are wonderful for such frozen-crust and real-ice climbing, but none of us has adequately practiced self-arrest with them.

Then we're both tied in again, and I let out a breath I haven't even noticed that I'd been holding. This reminds me to dial my O_2 flow back to the lowest 1.5-liter level.

The Sherpas behind Reggie, except for the always grinning Babu Rita, look exhausted and anxious. They all wear our experimental climb-ing harnesses, and Reggie has helped them each clip a carabiner onto the fixed rope, but I notice that each Sherpa (again except for the trusting Babu Rita) is also hanging on to that rope more tightly than is really good for our group's sense of security.

Suddenly Reggie unties from the Sherpa rope and quickly ties a 30-foot strand of Miracle Rope onto Tenzing Bothia's harness. Thus freed, she moves up and down the line, using her long ice axe to dig more substantial cups in the snow for each of the porters. She then shows them how, by shifting hands without totally relinquishing their reas-suring grip on the fixed rope, they can slowly turn around and lower their behinds into the cup-shaped depressions, all while keeping their regular 10-point crampons embedded in the frozen snow beneath them. Watching them take their assigned seats in the snow on that near-verti-cal hillside, I'm glad that we've brought underwear for the Tiger Sherpas as well as thick woolen trousers with a covering of Shackleton gabardine. Babu Rita giggles and laughs at the beauty of the views.

Now it's time for the ultimate test of Jean-Claude's new climbing ap-paratus and techniques.

My neck hurts from craning and I find that I'm leaning ever further backward, trusting, perhaps, too much to my crampon points and ice hammer adzes. But it's hard *not* to watch Jean-Claude in this, his *tour de force.*

As he'd done on much safer ice in Wales, J.C. kick-scrambles his way up the sheer wall of ice like some gecko on a *dak* bungalow wall. For the first 50 feet or so he's still tied on our rope—both the Deacon and I with our full-length sunken ice axes braced for belay—but at the end of that extra-long rope length, he drives in an ice piton, unties from our belay, and ties in his Miracle Rope for protection. He'll do this every 50 feet or so on the 200-foot climb, since if he falls it will be vertical free fall, and not even the Deacon's Miracle Rope could hold his weight without snapping after a 400-foot vertical fall.

About two-thirds of the way up the icy wall, J.C. pauses, fumbles in his rucksack, and pulls out his oxygen tank. The Deacon and I exchange guilty glances; the plan had been for Jean-Claude to do this part of the climb with a new oxygen tank, opened to its full flow of 2.2 liters per minute. We'd all forgotten to make the exchange; even Jean-Claude in his eagerness to start the most dramatic part of our day's climb had forgotten.

Now he removes his oxygen mask and free-hanging regulator with its various tubes and carefully sets them in his rucksack, even while pulling out the empty tank, pinning it against the ice wall with his body while using just his free right hand to unscrew the connections.

Shouting "Watch out below!" J.C. swings the empty tank one, two, three times and then hurls it to our right. We all watch, delighted and horrified at the same time, while the heavy oxygen tank bounces first off the ice wall itself and then off snow and ice for the full 1,000-foot drop to the glacier below. The noise it makes in its bouncing—especially its final ricochet off a snow-hidden boulder—is wonderful.

The Deacon pulls his own mask down. "Want to change leads?" he shouts upward.

On a windy day, I have no doubt that the shout would have been lost under wind roar, but today is almost perfectly still. I'm using the undershirt over my forearm to mop away sweat, even as we just stand here on the hillside below the vertical face, one arm around the fixed rope, both forward sets of crampon points and our left ice hammer holding us in place.

Jean-Claude grins, shakes his head, and looks up at the rest of the climb above him. Then he begins moving again, pausing more frequently now, moving a bit more slowly, but still climbing steadily.

Fifteen minutes more and we watch him thrust himself up, weight on his crampon points, and lean far over the lip of the North Col, sinking his right ice hammer deep into horizontal ice we can't see. Then he's gone.

A moment later, when he's obviously tied in to some anchor he's set on the surface of the Col, his head and shoulders reappear and a second rope begins snaking down.

"Send up the ladders!" shouts Jean-Claude.

We do, but not before all eight of us sitting and standing on the ice cliff below the last vertical wall send up a cheer for him.

The caving ladders are in 50-foot sections, and it takes all four of them to reach the lip of the Col. Not trusting just the attachments from one section to the next, J.C. comes down each 50-foot section and secures the next with short-cut strands of Miracle Rope, ice screws, and more pitons. It's hard work, and J.C. is pouring perspiration as the last ladder is fixed in place. Then he's at the bottom of the ice wall with us and we're pounding him on the back and shoulders, voices hoarse in the high, thin air but filled with our congratulations.

The Deacon shows the Sherpas and the rest of us his total confidence in the rope ladders by unhooking from the common rope and clambering up, his crampons biting into the wooden rungs. One by one we follow, Reggie falling back to come up last behind the final Sherpa. I fall in behind my old friend Babu Rita, who clambers monkeylike up the rope-and-wood ladders, looking down and grinning at me until I become nervous for him. I want to shout up to him to remember the three-point rule—always keep three parts of you in touch with something solid while climbing (e.g., two feet, one hand; two hands, one foot; whatever)—but I'd have to remove my oxygen mask to make the shout and I'm still enjoying the benefits of English air. Babu completes his ascent without incident, and his hand is stretched out and waiting for me as we make the last, mildly nervous-making lurch up and over the lip of the North Col from the ladder. Babu grasps my hand and forearm in both of his strong hands and helps me to my knees and then up.

I move a few paces away from the top of the ladder and look at the dizzying sight.

We've climbed to the "Shelf," where previous expeditions had set their tents—a sort of slumped area on the north side of the North Col where the upper ice ridge makes a nice protective wall. But where there had been room for dozens of tents in 1922, shrunken to a 30-foot-wide ice shelf good for only a thin row of tents in 1924, now the shelf is less than ten feet wide. Too exposed to the drop and too narrow now to serve as our Camp IV.

Still, it's a good place to rest, and almost everyone is sitting slumped along the south wall of the shelf. I find my way down to the end of the line and slump along with them until Reggie comes up with the final three Sherpas. She warns them in Nepalese and Tibetan not to shed their loads yet—that they have to climb up and off this thin but sheltered shelf—and then she sits down next to me and tells me what she's just told *them.*

Winds and avalanches have swept the ice shelf free of all the previous expeditions' tents and signs of occupation other than for one collapsed green tent—wind-torn to rags, one tentpole still sticking up at a wild angle—right at our feet. I poke at the green canvas with my crampons and say to Reggie and Jean-Claude, "Just think—Mallory may have slept in there."

"Not bloody likely," says Lady Bromley-Montfort. "That's the tent that Pasang and I brought up and shared last August when we were stuck up here for a week."

I'd shut off my oxygen flow and pulled the mask down to my chest, but now I wish I'd left it in place; it might have hidden this sudden, absurd blush. For a long moment we all just sit there staring out at the incredible view—most of the East Rongbuk Glacier winding away at our feet (we can see all the way back to Camp I from here) and the mass of Changtse seeming to hurl itself skyward to our left, the overhanging bulk of Everest's shoulder and North East Ridge cutting the skyline into steep, serrated segments to our right.

Jean-Claude looks around at our sitting line of Sherpas and says, "Where is *le Diacre?*"

"Mr. Deacon?" says Reggie. "He went off with Nyima Tsering, Tenzing Bothia, and a stack of bamboo wands to find a better place for Camp Four."

"What are we sitting here for?" I ask.

J.C. and I laboriously get to our feet, I turn my oxygen flow back on, and we walk on a narrow strip of ice separating the Sherpas' outstretched legs and crampons from the 1,000-foot drop to the glacier to where we can follow the Deacon's and his two Sherpas' footsteps up and out of the shelf area, onto the North Col proper.

When we reach the level of the actual Col, Jean-Claude and I both have to stop and gape for a few seconds. The full North Face of Mount Everest is now revealed to us as if someone had drawn back a theater curtain. To our left, beyond the last giant snow seracs, the North Ridge rises from this saddle of the North Col in a 4,500-foot-high spur to where it meets the North East Ridge—what the Deacon still calls the North East *Shoulder* of Everest—at an altitude of 27,636 feet. From that juncture of the North Ridge and North East Ridge so far above us, it's another mile's trek along the ridgeline to the right to the actual summit of Everest. The North Face of the mountain, including Norton's Great Couloir, looks absolutely vertical from this viewing spot, but I know that such looks are deceiving from the base of any mountain. That couloir might still be our best bet, especially if high winds keep us off the ridgelines.

Without fumbling for binoculars, J.C. and I can clearly see about two-thirds of the way up the North Ridge in front of us to a weakly pronounced recline, the point where the Deacon has been planning to set our Camp V. Below that area, the North Ridge is composed of an irregularly rounded rock buttress that soon blends into the humpbacked extension of snow and ice that connects to our low, snowy saddle here on the North Col.

It's weird. We can easily see the spindrift blowing off the summit like a 20-mile-long white scarf set against the brilliantly blue sky, and more spindrift being lifted off the North East and upper North ridges as if by hurricane winds, but there's hardly a breath of wind down here on the North Col. I remember the Deacon saying that when he, Mallory, and the others had first reached this spot in their 1921 reconnaissance mission, the winds everywhere atop the Col, except on the ice shelf behind us that's now dwindled so much, had been too strong for a man to stand in for more than a few seconds. To stand where Jean-Claude and I were walking now would have been certain death. This, I thought, is the difference between climbing to the North Col in that narrow window of time between winter and the onset of the monsoon, and climbing *during* the monsoon season.

The cramponed boot prints of the Deacon and his two Sherpas are quite clear in the snow, and we follow them up and further west beyond the ice shelf. Behind us, Reggie has got Babu Rita and the three other Sherpas in motion, although they are plodding slowly under their loads here at 23,000 feet. Should any of the Sherpas get ill at this altitude, the plan is to give them oxygen; otherwise, only the four of us high-climbers are to use oxygen at North Col altitudes.

For some reason, I'm not prepared for all the yawning crevasses up here on the North Col. It makes perfect sense that they should be here; the ice of the North Col keeps breaking off and dropping onto the East Rongbuk Glacier proper far below. But I guess—despite reading and rereading all the earlier expeditions' accounts and listening to the Deacon talk about how we'd have to pick our way through crevasses atop the North Col—for some reason I'd expected the Col to be more of a smooth surface.

It's not. I realize that we're climbing again as I follow the three men's boot prints along narrow ridges between deep crevasses, up and over one massive ice bridge that the Deacon's just marked minutes before with red-flagged bamboo wands, around and through a series of giant tumbled seracs leading out to a broader, more crevasse-riddled rising slope, and finally to where we can see the Deacon, Nyima Tsering, and Tenzing Bothia setting up tents in the lee of some giant drifts and seracs near the south edge of the North Col, right below where the Col meets the rising ice and snow of the North Ridge spur.

My gaze keeps rising to the North Ridge and North Face of the mountain. I can clearly see the downward-tilting black granite slabs on both the ridge and face, some partially snow-covered, others glistening as if covered with ice. Most alpine climbers—myself included—dislike climbing on such downward-tilting rock slabs; it's too much like attempting to climb slick, slippery, treacherous tiles on the steep roof slope of some Gothic church. Sometimes the slab tiles themselves will give way beneath you.

Because of the maze of crevasses, the route through them marked only with the few red-flagged bamboo wands, J.C. and I rope up with the three Sherpas and Reggie on a single line as we continue to plod uphill toward this new site for Camp IV.

When we come up to the Deacon and his two Sherpas, our guys dump their loads and collapse in the snow while those who've come before us finish their job of erecting one heavy Whymper tent and two lighter Meade tents. Still staying on the last of my oxygen, I empty my own rucksack of the one 10-pound Meade tent and three sleeping bags I've hauled up with me today.

We've brought lots of water, thermoses with warm drinks, and some light food stocks with us—mostly chocolate, raisins, and other high-energy snacks—but most of our load carrying today has centered on bringing the tents and sleeping bags needed for Camp IV and, with luck, Camp V. One of the Sherpas has brought up a Primus stove—for serious cooking—but each campsite has been under orders, after J.C.'s and my near debacle at Camp III, also to have at least two spirit stoves and, more important, multiple Unna cookers with their Meta solid fuel to burn. The Deacon isn't taking the chance of other advanced camps not being able to melt snow for drinking water, tea (however tepid at these altitudes), and soup.

Reggie, after telling her Sherpas what to set up where, is standing next to the Deacon and looking rather dubiously at the giant seracs that hide the view of the North Ridge from us here. "Are you sure that this will block the worst of the wind?" she asks.

The Deacon shrugs. There's a glint of real joy in his eyes that I've noticed on the Matterhorn and elsewhere when he's enjoying climbing to a soul-deep extent. "In 'twenty-one and 'twenty-two, we always noticed less wind in the lee of large seracs here on the west end of the North Col," he says. His oxygen mask is dangling unused on his chest. "And Teddy Norton told me that other than the ice shelf, this would have been his choice as a site for Camp Four last year."

Reggie does not look totally convinced. I remind myself that she and Pasang were kept prisoner here on the North Col for a miserable, windy week, waiting at every moment for their tent—the green canvas rags and broken poles I'd noticed back on the shelf—to blow over the edge of the Col. The North Col has to be a source of anxiety to her.

"It will be convenient for climbing to the North Ridge," she says at last. "And better for anyone descending late from Camp Five or higher than the old ice shelf camp was...too many crevasses to avoid in the dark."

The Deacon nods. Reggie gives more instructions to the Sherpas in both English and Nepalese. She wants the openings of the tents to face toward the great sunrise-reflecting bulk of Changtse to the north.

As the Sherpas finish their work, the four of us find something to sit on. J.C. and the Deacon are sitting on rolled-up sleeping bags, eating chocolate and staring westward above the seracs to the visible sections of the North Ridge. I join them.

"Any further today?" I ask.

The Deacon shakes his head. "This is a good day's work. We'll go back to Camp Two, get a good night's sleep, and try to get at least three ropes of Sherpas up here tomorrow with food and other supplies, including for the high camps. Hope the weather holds for the next three days."

"You're thinking of a summit bid for day after tomorrow?" Jean-Claude says to the Deacon. This would be four days earlier than our original May 17 goal.

He smiles but does not reply.

It is Reggie who speaks. Her voice is determined. "You forget, we have to look for Bromley."

"I did not forget, *Madame*," says J.C. "I merely assumed that such a search will be part of our climb."

Into the moment of somewhat awkward silence that follows, I say, "What about the crevasses up here on the North Col? Shouldn't we check them out for...for...Bromley?"

"Kami Chiring reported seeing three figures far up on the North East Ridge," says Reggie. "Then only one figure. I suspect we shall have to go that far before seeing any possible sign of my lost cousin. I know that there was no sign of anything between here and Mallory's Camp Five last August. Also, Pasang and I lowered lanterns into all the crevasses that were here last summer. Nothing. Obviously we do not need to search new crevasses."

"So all we have to do today," I say, "is finish our lunch, finish setting up Camp Four, and head downhill for a good night's sleep at Camp Two."

"That's all," says the Deacon, and I'm not surprised at the slight tone of irony in his voice.

The Deacon leads us down. The descent takes less than an hour and would have been even faster than that if the Sherpas could have rappelled down the way J.C. and I did for entire sections, testing the Miracle Rope. Above us at the westernmost reach of the North Col, we'd left six heavily anchored tents—two Whympers and four Meade tents—buttoned up and provisioned with sleeping bags, blankets, various types of cookers, Meta solid fuel, and kerosene cached outside.

Jean-Claude and I had volunteered to come down last so that we could test the rappel strength of the fixed ropes (although we cheated a bit by taking turns belaying while the other climber rappelled), and a rappel from that kind of exposed altitude is always a thrill. J.C. and I had expected an easier climb this day, but neither of us had imagined having so much fun.

Finally, when we come off the fixed ropes of the lower slope—the last 200 feet or so down to the level of Camp III didn't need fixed ropes, we'd decided that morning, since it's a relatively gradual snow slope—we find Babu Rita standing there waiting for us in the growing evening shadows, stamping his booted feet to stay warm. He's removed his crampons (the only remaining problem with them and our new rigid boots is that the crampon straps still tend to cut off circulation, which leads to cold feet despite the extra layers of felt we'd put in the newly designed "stiff" boots), and now J.C. and I do the same.

"Very good day, yes, Sahibs Jake and Jean-Claude?" asks Babu, grinning from ear to ear.

"A very good day it's been, Babu Rita," I say. All three of us start down in the sunken footsteps in the snow, but then, on a whim, I say, "Would you like to see how real climbers go down a slope like this, Babu?"

"Oh, yes, Sahib Jake!"

Making sure that my crampons are secured safely outside my rucksack in a spot where they won't stab me if I fall or have to go to self-arrest, I hop up out of the trough made by the party's earlier ploddings, keep my long ice axe out, and begin glissading down the long snow slope, my hobnailed boots kicking up a rooster tail behind me, guiding myself with the pick end of the long axe.

"Race you!" cries J.C. and jumps onto the snow surface firming in the shadows. "Stay here, Babu. Look out, Jake!"

Jean-Claude glissades faster than I do and is soon trying to pass me. Damn Chamonix Guides! We slalom our way lower, swerving to miss the few boulders near the base of the slope, and J.C. comes across the imaginary finish line on the flats at least 15 feet ahead of me.

Laughing, stamping our cold feet here at the edge of the moraine, we turn to watch Babu Rita posthole his way down the trough path of deep footsteps.

"I, too, also!" cries the short Sherpa, and he steps out of the footsteps onto the snow crust, sets his ice axe behind him like a tiller, and starts imitating our glissade.

"No, don't!" cries Jean-Claude, but it's too late. Babu is glissading quickly down the slope and laughing like a madman.

Then he pushes too hard on the pick or adze of his ice axe, a common beginner's mistake in glissading—the guiding point must touch the snow ever so lightly—the pick embeds itself deep into the snow, Babu is jerked around violently, and then he's on his back, arms spread wide, picking up speed as he hurtles down the slope on his back, his rucksack spilling personal items as he slides. If anything, he's laughing even harder now.

"Self-arrest!" I bellow, cupping my hands to make a megaphone. "Self-arrest, Babu!"

He's lost his ice axe, but he still has his hands—and when the mittens get pulled off, he should be able to dig his gloved fingers deep enough into the snow to slow his rate of descent. We've trained and rehearsed all the Sherpas in self-arrest techniques.

But Babu's splayed body is spinning around in circles now, first head up, then down, hands and heels merely slapping at the ice-crusted snow. All this time he's laughing even louder as he hurtles closer to us.

Fifty feet from the bottom of the slope, Babu goes over a hidden snow ramp. "Oopsies!" he cries in English as he flies eight feet into the air, still headfirst.

There's a strange sound as he strikes what looks to be a large pillow of snow and he quits laughing. His splayed form spins a final three times and slides to a stop not 30 feet from us. J.C. and I are running now, postholing our way over to the suddenly silent Sherpa. I'm praying that he's just had the wind knocked out of him.

Then we notice the long smear of red on the otherwise white snow. The "pillow" of snow Babu had hit, headfirst, is a snow-covered boulder.

Tuesday, May 12, 1925

abu was unconscious when we evacuated him from Camp III last night, Monday night. The others had come out of their tents at the sound of our shouts—reacting first to his laughter, then to our calls for help—and we'd gathered and knelt around the still splayed, supine, and unconscious Babu Rita.

Reggie took one look at the knot and spreading bruise on the Sherpa's temple, tossed the first-aid kit to the Deacon, pointed to two other Sherpas while giving orders in their Nepalese language, and then ran with them back to the tents to put together a stretcher out of spare tent canvas and poles. The Deacon crouched next to Babu, carefully lifting his heavily bleeding head. He quickly set two gauze pads against the freely bleeding areas on Babu's scalp, then lashed them into place with quick loops of a gauze bandage. He cut the bandage with his pocketknife and knotted it with swift, sure movements.

"Will he be all right?" I asked. Everything about me, down to the lifeless tone of my voice, was signaling guilt and responsibility for my porter's accident. Jean-Claude looked equally guilty.

"Head wounds are weird things," said the Deacon. He'd been lifting Babu gently by the shoulders, gingerly touching the short man's neck and back, down to his tailbone. "I don't think there's any spinal damage. We can move him. The best thing we can do is to get him down to Base Camp and to Dr. Pasang as quickly as we can."

"Is it really safe to move him?" asked J.C., who'd long ago told me that Chamonix Guides were trained not to move a fall victim if there was any chance at all of spinal or serious neck injuries.

The Deacon nodded. "His neck isn't broken, as far as I can tell by touch. His back feels all right. I think there will be less danger in moving him than in leaving him up here all night."

Reggie and Nyima Tsering returned with the jury-rigged stretcher, its canvas doubled over and lashed tight to the two six-foot poles.

"We'll need someone to carry him down," said the Deacon. "Six men, I think. Four to carry and two more along to spell the others."

"We'll carry him," Jean-Claude and I said in pathetic, guilty unison.

The Deacon nodded. "Pemba, Dorjay, Tenzing, Nyima, you four go down with the sahibs."

Reggie quickly translated to the three Sherpas who spoke no English. I saw that she had also brought back from the tents two lanterns and two sets of the headlamps. She waited until we crouched next to the unconscious Babu and—on the count of three and with infinite gentleness—transferred him from the snow to the unfurled stretcher.

The snow remained caked with Babu's blood, and his bandages were already bleeding through.

Silently, Reggie handed lanterns to Pemba and Dorjay and the headlamp rigs to J.C. and me. "Tejbir!" she called to the tallest of the watching Sherpas. I remembered that Tejbir Norgay spoke English. "You go ahead as runner as quickly as you can. Tell those in Camp Two and Camp One that we may need new volunteers to carry as we get to each camp. But don't waste time at those camps—hurry straight on down to Base Camp and see if Dr. Pasang can come up and meet the stretcher bearers along the way. Tell Dr. Pasang exactly what Babu Rita's head wounds are like and what caused them. There's a third lantern outside the big tent here—pick it up as you go."

Tejbir nodded once and jogged off the snow slope, snatched the lantern as he ran past on the rough, snow-covered moraine at the campsite, and within seconds had disappeared behind the ice pinnacles and was up and onto the glacier path.

Jean-Claude took the left front end of a pole and I grasped the right rear. Nyima Tsering grabbed the right front and Tenzing Bothia was at the rear with me. On the count of three again, we lifted the stretcher waist-high. Babu Rita seemed to weigh nothing at all.

"We'll follow you down as soon as we get things sorted out here at Camp Three for tomorrow's carries," said the Deacon. "Tell Dr. Pasang that I'm bringing everyone down to Camp One or Base Camp."

The trip back down the glacier was grueling, especially since it came at the end of our long climbing day. Before we'd climbed onto the glacier for our descent, Reggie had handed Pemba a full oxygen rig with three full tanks on the frame. The idea was that as we grew tired, we'd fall out and take some English air from two of the tanks, while Pemba or Dorjay filled in for us. Babu Rita would breathe from the third tank all the way down. It just added 22 pounds to the weight of the stretcher.

But neither Jean-Claude nor I dropped out during the four-hour descent through the camps, even while the Sherpas took turns relieving one another. Once or twice after a difficult bit—such as the detour down into the glacier and up and out its steep slopes again—Pemba held the oxygen mask up to J.C.'s face, then mine, and we drank in some rich English air and continued on. Babu Rita looked asleep behind his chamois-cloth mask.

Dr. Pasang met us at Camp I and had us set the stretcher on some crates while he did a preliminary assessment of Babu by lantern light.

"I believe your Mr. Deacon was correct about there being no immediately obvious neck or spinal injury," said Pasang. "But we do need to get him down lower. Can you carry him again—as far as Base Camp—or shall I get fresh porters?"

Jean-Claude and I had no intention whatsoever of allowing anyone to take our respective corners of the stretcher. Of course, that attitude was absurd since it was as if we were punishing ourselves, but I thought then—and believe to this day—that we, especially I, *deserved* punishment. If we hadn't acted like idiot schoolchildren—if I hadn't started that behavior with my stupid, playground-level showing off, Babu Rita would have been eating dinner at Camp III right then and laughing with his Sherpa friends.

We reached Base Camp a little before eleven p.m. The infirmary tent had its side curtains raised, and the night was surprisingly warm for an altitude over 16,000 feet. There was no wind. Half a dozen kerosene lanterns hung hissing from the tent eaves, and I could see why Dr. Pasang would want to do any serious medical work here, where the air was relatively thicker and warmer and the light was much better than at any of the other camps.

The four Sherpas who'd come down with us went off to their tents, and J.C. and I collapsed on the floor of the medical tent while Pasang began his careful inspection of Babu Rita's wound. My arms were so tired I felt that I'd never be able to lift them again.

After the thirty-minute examination, which included Dr. Pasang taking Babu's blood pressure, pulse, and other vital signs before he cleaned the wounds and put on fresh bandages, not a word was said. Finally, when Pasang had put an oxygen mask in place over Babu's face, turned it to full flow, pulled two blankets up to the Sherpa's chin, and moved away one of the lanterns and both of the mirrors he'd been using, I said, "How bad is it, Dr. Pasang?"

"His respiration is very shallow, pulse is weak, breathing labored," said Pasang. "I'm ninety-five percent sure that Babu has a hematoma—a blood clot on the brain—where his head hit the boulder."

"Can you do something for that?" asked Jean-Claude. I knew the guide had seen men die in the mountains from brain embolisms before this—some from injuries, some from high-altitude illness that triggered a blood clot in the lungs or brain. For me, it was only a phrase.

Dr. Pasang sighed. "The oxygen should help a little. In a regular hospital setting, I would do my best to identify the precise location of the clot or clots and then, if the patient did not awaken and the vital signs grew weaker, might perform a craniotomy. Here, in these conditions, the best I can do is an old-fashioned trephination."

"What's the difference?" I asked.

Pasang moved his large hand above the bandaged areas on Babu's skull. "For a surgical craniotomy, I'd shave this part of Babu's scalp and then make a surgical cut through the scalp—with no X-ray machine, I'd have to make my best guess where the blood clot is and where to cut. Then I'd drill a small hole in his skull and remove a piece of the skull...we call that a bone flap. Then I'd remove any skull fragments that are pressing against Babu's brain and drain off the solidified and pooled blood. If his brain is swollen by the injury, I might leave the bone flap off—that would technically turn the operation into a craniectomy. If there's no serious swelling, I'd use small metal plates or wires or sutures to put the bone flap back in place."

"That sounds sort of primitive," I managed to say over the feeling of gorge rising in my throat.

Pasang shook his head. "That's the modern version. In these conditions, and with the surgical tools I have with me, I'd have to do a trephination."

"What's that?"

Pasang seemed lost in thought. Finally, he said, "Trepanning's been done since Neolithic days. It's just drilling a hole in the patient's skull to expose the dura mater, thus relieving the pressure on the brain that bleeding or a blood clot or skull fragments from the injury can cause. I did bring a trephine with me." Pasang crossed to the small crate of his surgical supplies and lifted out an instrument.

"That's just a hand drill," I said.

The Sherpa doctor nodded. "As I say, they've used such trepanning instruments for centuries. It sometimes works."

"How would you seal up a drill hole like that?" asked Jean-Claude. I could hear the revulsion in his voice as well.

Pasang shrugged. "Such a hole, by definition, will be larger than the bone flap entry, but I could use wire sutures to replace the disk of skull material, or even screw in something so prosaic as a coin the right size. The skull has no nerve endings, of course."

"Are you going to do it?" I asked. "The trepanning, I mean."

"Only if it's absolutely necessary," said Pasang. "Such a surgical procedure at this altitude—and under these unhygienic conditions—would be very, very dangerous. And because at least three points on his skull and scalp made contact with the boulder, I wouldn't be sure where the blood clot may lie. I'd hate to have to drill three holes in Babu Rita's skull and still not find the right place."

"*Pardonnez-moi,*" said Jean-Claude and left the tent. I hadn't known that my French friend was so squeamish.

"We'll give Babu ten to twelve hours," said Dr. Pasang. "If he comes out of this coma, then we'll just take care of him until he can travel on a litter and then get him back to Darjeeling as quickly as possible."

I thought of the five-week trek in. There were shorter routes over higher passes, directly into northern Sikkim, but the passes were very high and open only during brief parts of the summer season. Neither the long way through the filthy Tibetan hill towns nor the dramatic short-cuts over blizzard-threatened high passes seemed appropriate for a man suffering from brain injury or a recent trephination.

Jean-Claude returned with our two Base Camp sleeping bags. "May we sleep on the floor of the infirmary tonight, Dr. Pasang?" he said.

Pasang smiled. "We can do better than that. There are two empty camp beds in the rear curtained section here in the infirmary tent, near where Ang Chiri and Lhakpa Yishay are sleeping. I'll help you carry the beds out into this main area. You can stay near Babu Rita tonight."

I sleep late—until after sunrise—and awaken with that terrible sense that something is wrong. I peek out of my sleeping bag and see that Babu Rita is sitting up, eyes open, and smiling broadly. Pasang stands nearby, his arms folded across his chest. I jostle J.C. awake in the cot next to mine.

"Oh, Sahib Jake and Sahib Jean-Claude," cries Babu Rita. "Such fun before I never have had!"

I manage to return the Sherpa's grin. J.C. just stares.

"I am so lucky that I am dying so close to the beloved Dzatrul Rinpoche," continues Babu Rita, still grinning broadly. "I ask that you let His Holiness the abbot of Rongbuk decide what kind of funeral I should have."

"No one's going to be dying...," I begin but stop when I see that Babu Rita has collapsed back on the high padded table where Pasang has watched over him through the night. The Sherpa porter's eyes are still open, the grin still on his face. But I can see that he's not breathing.

Dr. Pasang tries resuscitation for several endless minutes, but Babu Rita's battered body and tremendous spirit do not respond. He is gone.

"I'm sorry," Dr. Pasang says at last. He closes Babu's staring eyes.

I can't help but look at Jean-Claude. I can see in his gaze that he agrees: we've killed this good man with our boyish nonsense and lack of common sense.

Thursday, May 14, 1925

he last two days have been perfect summiting days. Mount Everest has stopped "smoking" for the first extended period since we've come in sight of it. Even winds along the North East Ridge have appeared to die down to a point where no spindrift is rising. The temperature on the North Col this day is in the seventies. High winds the previous week have blown much of the snow off the ridge rocks, and even the Great Couloir appears to have contracted in size.

But none of us are on the mountain today. All of us—all the Sherpas, Dr. Pasang, Lady Bromley-Montfort, the Deacon, J.C., and I—are trudging the eleven miles up the valley to the Rongbuk Monastery from Base Camp for a blessing ceremony from Dzatrul Rinpoche.

The Deacon's anger at this self-inflicted loss of the two best climbing days of the month—perhaps of the year—shows itself through thin, pale lips and his expression of rigid control. Jean-Claude and I both are waiting for the Deacon to turn that fierce anger on us.

The Sherpas look and sound happy, as if it's a holiday from school for them. None had seemed especially saddened by Babu Rita's sudden death. I ask Pasang about this and the *sirdar*-medic says, "They feel that if it was Babu Rita's destiny to die on the mountain, then his death on the mountain was inevitable and there is no special reason to mourn it. Today is a new day."

I shake my head at this. "Then why are they so eager to get this blessing from the monastery's holy man, Dzatrul Rinpoche? If everything's predestined for them anyway, what difference will the abbot's blessing make?"

Pasang smiles his small smile. "Do not ask me, Mr. Perry, to make sense of the internal contradictions that are so common in all religions."

Yesterday we'd wrapped Babu's body in the cleanest and whitest tent fabric we could find, the Base Camp Sherpas had put the body on a litter and strapped that litter to the back of a yak, and six of the Sherpas, led by Dr. Pasang, had ridden ponies up the valley to the monastery, escorting Babu's corpse.

Unsure of what to do or if we'd be invited to the funeral ceremony that Dzatrul Rinpoche, at Babu Rita's last request, might choose for him, Jean-Claude and I took loads of food and oxygen—and J.C.'s mysterious "bicycle" bundle—and carried them the eleven miles up the Trough and East Rongbuk Glacier to Camp III. Learning that Reggie and the Deacon were still on or above Camp IV on the North Col—we'd gotten word to the Deacon about Babu's death, of course, but he'd sent back a note saying that since we weren't going to be responsible for Babu's burial service, he'd stay at the high camps—J.C. and I reduced our loads a bit (Jean-Claude carrying little more than his clumsy "mystery bicycle" in his oversized-load bag) and followed the fixed ropes and caving ladders up to the North Col. Feeling guilty about many things, we decided—without discussing it—not to use oxygen during this ice-wall climb, but to save it for others in the days to come. Two Sherpas followed us up.

J.C. kept the two Sherpas with him at the lip of the ice shelf and said, "Go ahead to Camp Four...I'm going to set up my bicycle here with Dorjay's and Namgya's help. I'll join you when we're finished here."

When I'd crossed the white-burning expanse of the North Col to Camp IV, I learned from Reggie that the Deacon and four Sherpas, including Tenzing Bothia and Tejbir Norgay, had just returned to the North Col after climbing the first section of the North Ridge and pitching two tents at the chosen Camp V site, just where the North Ridge leveled out ever so slightly at an altitude of a little more than 25,000 feet.

His face burned almost black by the high-altitude ultraviolet rays of the sun, the Deacon grinned at us and said, "If this calm holds, we can make the summit bid from Camp Five tomorrow."

Reggie—who'd just come up an hour earlier with more loads carried by four Sherpas from Camp III—looked doubtful. The North Col behind her and to every side of us was a blaze of heat and white light. I made sure to keep my goggles of darkened Crooke's glass on.

The Deacon was ravenously devouring lunch—heated potato soup, tongue, rich chocolates, cocoa—when he suggested we retreat to Camp III this afternoon, come back up to IV the next day, and push on to spend Thursday night at Camp V. From that high camp, if the weather remained anywhere near as calm as it was this Wednesday, we could leave in the middle of the night for the summit attempt on Friday, May 15.

"So my Welsh miner's headlamps may be of some use after all?" asked Reggie with a certain ironic edge in her voice.

Too excited to argue, the Deacon only grinned again and said, "The two Meade tents we set up today at Camp Five can hold four people, maximum. I suggest that we leave on two ropes in the early hours of Friday, Tenzing Bothia and me on the first rope, you—Jake and Jean-Claude—on the second rope. All of us using oxygen. At the lower flow rate, we should have from fifteen to sixteen and a half hours of bottled air. Time enough to summit and get back to Camp Five before sunset."

"Where do I fit into this plan?" demanded Reggie.

The Deacon only stared at her.

"You promised that we would all look for Percival's remains on the way up," continued Reggie. "Well, I have to be along to make sure that we actually *look*."

The Deacon frowned and continued to eat chocolate. "Your going to the summit was never part of the plan, Lady Bromley-Montfort."

"It's part of *my* plan, Mr. Deacon."

I was fighting for breath after the climb with no oxygen tanks and wasn't part of this argument. My thoughts weren't on the summit of Everest; they were still fixed on Babu Rita's dead face and staring eyes.

At that moment we noticed Pemba Sherpa, traveling alone, trudging up and out of the shelf area along the marked traffic way across the North Col to our westernmost camp. No one spoke until Pemba reached us.

The news was staggering. Dzatrul Rinpoche had sent word that we were all to come to the Rongbuk Monastery the very next day, Thursday, to receive his blessing. Babu Rita's sky burial, said Pemba, would be at sunrise on Friday, but only Babu's immediate family would be invited to stay for that.

"God *damn* it!" snarled the Deacon. "The best damned weather of the entire year... we're *this* close to being able to climb the mountain... in weather better than George Mallory *ever* had....and that damned old Buddhist abbot sends word for all of us to appear before him. To hell with it. I'm not going."

"We're all going," said Reggie.

"It's not Babu's *funeral*," insisted the Deacon. "Just another damned blessing that we'll have to pay for—pay each Sherpa two rupees so that he can have money to pay the bloody head lama for each damned blessing—and I've done it twice before and I feel damned well blessed enough and I'd rather be summiting Mount Everest in this weather than sitting in that stinking monastery all day tomorrow."

"We all have to go down," said Reggie. She sounded almost... relieved.

"I won't do it." The Deacon tossed his cooking pot aside, the pan clanging on ice next to the little Unna cooker.

"You're going to do your summit climb without any Sherpa support?" said Reggie.

"If that's what I have to do, that's what I'll do," said the Deacon. He looked at J.C. and me. "It'll be the three of us on a rope, my friends, and we haul just oxygen sets and extra clothes and food in our pockets to Camp Five tomorrow."

Reggie shook her head. "Not only would it be an insult to Dzatrul Rinpoche, Mr. Deacon, but your attempting the summit on the day of the holy man's blessing would cost you the loyalty of all your Sherpas. They've been very patient for this blessing as it is. Snub the lama and attempt to climb the mountain without Dzatrul Rinpoche's blessing, and many of the Sherpas will leave the expedition here and now."

"God damn it!" said the Deacon. "Jake, Jean-Claude, you'll come with me, won't you?"

I knew what Jean-Claude was going to say even before he spoke. "No, *Ree-shard.* We are going down with Reggie and the men for the blessing and to honor Babu Rita."

* * *

It is a perfect day as we all leave Base Camp early on Thursday morning for the 11-mile hike down the valley for the lama's blessing. Even the frostbitten Ang Chiri and Lhakpa Yishay—since Lhakpa's frostbite was worse than first thought, the amputations of certain toes and fingers for both Sherpas were put off for another day—are riding mules led by their friends. Dr. Pasang is riding a small pony next to Reggie's larger one. The Deacon walks alone, easily keeping pace with the plodding ponies, his face as fiercely closed as a castle's main door with an enemy army outside.

I kick my pony's ribs, catch up to Reggie and Pasang, and ask about the monastery and its abbot.

"Dzatrul Rinpoche is the incarnation of Padma Sambhava," she says. At my blank gaze she adds, "You've seen images of Padma Sambhava along the way across Tibet, Jake. He's the god with nine heads."

"Okay."

"Rongbuk Monastery is the highest monastery in all of Tibet...in all the world, for that matter," continues Reggie. "The faithful make pilgrimages there all the time, many of them prostrating themselves every few yards...for hundreds of miles. And the hills all around us here are filled with caves holding holy men who've renounced the world. Some of the lamas at the monastery say that after many years, many of these holy men—they're all but naked through the terrible winters here—can survive on three grains of barley per day."

I turn to Dr. Pasang beside us and say, "Do you believe all this?"

Pasang smiles slightly. "Don't ask me, Mr. Perry. I'm a Roman Catholic. I have been since I was a child."

He is polite enough to pretend not to notice my gawking amazement.

Reggie looks at me. "How old do you think the Rongbuk Monastery is, Jake? Take a guess."

I remember how ancient the temple and its crumbling *chortens* and other shrines had looked when we'd paused there on the way to Base Camp. "A thousand years old?" I venture.

"The current head abbot, Dzatrul Rinpoche, started building the place just twenty-four years ago," says Reggie. "He was thirty-five years old, and his name then was Ngawang Tenzin Norbu. He managed to get the patronage of traders in Tingri and of the Sherpas living and teaching across the Nangpa La and other passes in Solu Khumbu in Nepal. Some here called him Sangye Buddha, the Buddha of Rongbuk. The name he's settled on is Dzatrul Rinpoche, a living embodiment of the legendary Guru Rinpoche—the Great Teacher—and a spiritual master of *chöd.*"

I have to ask. "What's *chöd?*"

"It's a Buddhist spiritual practice," replies Reggie. "In literal terms it means the 'cutting through' of attachment to this illusion that is the world. *Chöd* was first practiced here in the Rongbuk Valley by Machig Labdrön, an eleventh-century *yogini*...a sort of tantric wizard. Machig Labdrön was known as a leading Buddhist scholar by the time she was seven years old, and she dedicated the rest of her life to freeing her mind of all intellect."

"Sometimes I feel that I've been doing the same thing," I say. The guilt in my gut about Babu's death, not to mention Ang's and Lhakpa's imminent amputations, all due to J.C.'s and my poor shepherding skills, grows stronger by the hour.

Reggie glances sharply at me. "Machig Labdrön came to Rongbuk nine hundred years ago to shatter all orthodoxy with her *chöd* techniques," she says. "She taught that only in such fearful, inhuman places as Rongbuk and its frozen hills—or in the haunted wildness of charnel grounds, cemeteries, sky burial sites—the foulest and most ragged and exposed of environments, could the catalyst for true spiritual transformation be found."

I bounce along on my tiny pony and think about this. The low rooftops of Rongbuk Monastery are just now visible above and ahead of us.

Pasang says, "Machig Labdrön once wrote, *Unless all reality is made worse, one cannot attain liberation.... So wander in grisly places and mountain retreats...do not get distracted by doctrines and books...just get real experiences...in the horrid and desolate.*"

"In other words," I say, "face your demons."

"Exactly," says Reggie. "Make a gift of your body to the demons of the mountains and wilderness. It's the best way to destroy the last vestiges of one's vanity and pride."

"I can vouch for that," I say.

"As *chöd* spiritual master of Rongbuk," says Pasang, "Dzatrul Rinpoche has dispatched more than a thousand seekers of wisdom into the mountains here to confront demons. Most never return and are assumed to have achieved enlightenment in their caves and high places."

"I guess we can add four more names to that list," I mumble. I'm thinking of Mallory, Irvine, Bromley, and now Babu Rita. More loudly, I ask, "Does Dzatrul Rinpoche give any advice on how to deal with *yetis?*"

Reggie grins. "As a matter of fact, one young would-be ascetic did once ask the Rinpoche what he should do if a *yeti* appeared at his cave. The master responded, *Why, invite him in to tea, of course!*"

With that image fresh, we fall silent for the rest of our approach to Rongbuk Monastery.

We're kept waiting in a downstairs antechamber for about ninety minutes, but the lama's high priests bring us a lunch of yogurt and rice and the very thick, almost nauseating butter tea they drink. The wooden bowls are clean, but the chopsticks have been nibbled down to sharp points by countless teeth other than our own. They also serve us radishes dipped in hot black pepper; these make my eyes water and my nose run.

Eventually we're shown up the stairway, our Sherpas following us with heads bowed, to a sort of half-enclosed veranda on the rooftop, where Dzatrul Rinpoche awaits us on a metal throne that looks for all the world like a red iron bedstead. We sahibs and Pasang are ushered in to sit on elaborately upholstered benches on either side of the alcove, but most of our Sherpas go onto all fours on the cold stone, their gazes and faces downcast. I begin to understand that it's not the proper thing to look into the eyes of a man-god.

But I stare anyway.

My first impression of Dzatrul Rinpoche, the incarnation of the man-god Padma Sambhava, is that his head is weirdly large, and is shaped rather like a huge, squat pumpkin. The Deacon has told me that what he remembered of the Holy Lama was his wide, engaging, delightful smile. The god-man's smile is still very broad in that far-too-wide face, but it looks as if he's lost some major teeth since the Deacon saw him last.

The Rinpoche's voice is very low and rough, as if grown hoarse from endless hours of chanting, and I suddenly realize that he's not chanting some prayer now but asking a question of either the Deacon or Reggie or both. In any case, Reggie translates the query: "Dzatrul Rinpoche would like to know why we are again trying to climb *Cho-mo-lung-ma* after the deaths of so many earlier sahib explorers and Sherpas."

"You could tell him...'because it's there,'" the Deacon suggests to Reggie. Our English friend's face is still grim and tight.

"I could," said Reggie, "but I don't think I shall. Any other answer you want to give him before I create my own?"

"Go ahead," growls the Deacon.

Reggie turns back to the Holy Lama, bows, and speaks in rapid, melodic Tibetan. The Rinpoche smiles even more broadly and bows his head slightly.

"You just told him that we're here to find and honor the body of your cousin, Percival," accuses the Deacon.

Reggie flashes him a look. "I'm aware, Mr. Deacon, that you know *some* Tibetan. If you don't want me answering, go ahead and talk to His Holiness without my translations."

The Deacon merely shakes his head and looks even more dour than before.

The Rinpoche speaks again. Reggie nods to him and translates for the Deacon, J.C., and me. "His Holiness reminds us that the high places of *Cho-mo-lung-ma* are very cold and filled with forces dangerous to those who do not follow the Path. There is nothing of value to be done up there, he tells us, except for the practice of *dharma*."

"Humbly ask for his blessing and protection," says the Deacon. "And assure His Holiness that we will kill no animals during our stay on Rongbuk Glacier."

Reggie does so. The Rinpoche nods as if satisfied and then asks a question. Without conferring with the Deacon, Reggie answers it. The head lama nods again.

"I didn't catch that," whispers the Deacon.

"His Holiness says that he and the other monks are doing a very powerful ritual of sanctification here at the monastery over the next two weeks and warns us that such a ritual always stirs up the demons and angry deities of the mountain."

"Please thank him for the warning," says the Deacon.

Reggie conveys this to the Rinpoche, who speaks at length. Reggie listens, bows her head low, and answers the Holy Lama with a short burst of almost musical Tibetan.

"What?" says the Deacon.

"His Holiness has praised me," says Reggie. "He says that each time he meets me, he is more certain that I am the reincarnation of the eleventh-century tantric sorceress Machig Labdrön, and he says that if I were to perfect my *chöd,* I could be the master-mistress of *Cho-mo-lung-ma* and all of its adjacent mountains and valleys."

"What was your response?" asks the Deacon. "I only understood the Tibetan word for 'unworthy.' "

"Yes, I said that I was unworthy of such a comparison," Reggie says. "But I admitted that the discipline of *chöd* was very attractive to me right now, since, as I've said before, at the present the world is too much with me."

"May I ask a question?" whispers Jean-Claude.

"Just one, I think," says Reggie. "We need to get on with the blessing ceremony if we're to get back to Base Camp by suppertime."

"I just wondered," whispers J.C., "if this *Cho-mo-lung-ma* really means 'Goddess Mother of the World' the way Colonel Norton and the others said it did."

Reggie smiles and passes the question along to the Rinpoche with the huge head. The old man—he's in his sixties but seems older—smiles again and answers in his melodic prayer-rumble.

"Not really, according to Rinpoche," says Reggie. "And His Holiness thanks you for asking. He says that the sahibs tend to take the translation they like for the names of sacred places here and ignore the places' true names. The name *Cho-mo-lung-ma,* he says, can be twisted to mean 'Goddess Mother of the World,' but for those like us, he says, who live *near* it, he says, the more common name for the mountain in Tibetan is *Kang Chomolung,* which means something more akin to 'The Snow of Bird Land.'

"But he says that this translation of the Tibetan name for our Mount Everest is also too simplistic," continues Reggie. "A better translation for *Cho-mo-lung-ma,* says His Holiness, is 'the tall peak you can see from nine directions at once, with a summit you cannot see as you draw near, the mountain so high that all birds flying over the peak instantly become blind.'"

Jean-Claude and I look at one another. I think we both believe that His Holiness is having us on.

Dzatrul Rinpoche rumbles his bass tones again. Reggie translates: "His Holiness has decided that our dead man, Babu Rita, will receive a sky burial tomorrow at dawn. The Holy Lama asks if there are any members of Babu Rita's immediate family here who might wish to stay for the ceremony."

Reggie translates the question into Nepalese, but the Sherpas continue to look down. Evidently none of them count Babu as family.

Without conferring, or even looking at one another, Jean-Claude and I both stand and step forward, our heads lowered in respect. "Please," I say, "my friend and I would like to be considered Babu Rita's family and would be honored to stay for his funeral rites in the morning."

I can hear the Deacon hiss through his teeth. I can almost hear his thoughts. *Another lost morning and day for the climbing effort.* I don't care and I'm sure that J.C. doesn't either. Babu's needless death has shaken me to the core.

Reggie translates, and His Holiness grants permission. Then Reggie instructs Norbu Chedi, who speaks some Tibetan as well as some English, to stay with us tonight in order to help interpret.

Dzatrul Rinpoche nods, rumbles again, and Reggie says, "It is time for the blessing."

The actual individual blessings for all of us, sahibs and Sherpas combined, take less than forty-five minutes. Dzatrul Rinpoche rumbles melodically—I never can tell if he is speaking in sentences or chanting (or both)—and then one of the head lamas gestures the soon-to-be-blessed to step forward to receive his or her blessing. Both Reggie and the Deacon are called forward at the same time, and the Holy Lama gestures for gifts to be given to them: an image of the Thirteenth Dalai Lama and a piece of silk for each, the silk too short to be used as a scarf. Both Reggie and the Deacon bow deeply, but I notice that they don't go to their knees the way the Sherpas have. Reggie claps her hands, and four of the Sherpas bring in her gift for the Rinpoche: four bags of ready-mix cement. Dzatrul Rinpoche again smiles broadly, and I realize that the cement will go far toward mending the *chorten* and other relatively new structures on the monastery grounds that are falling apart because they'd been built with little more than mud, rock, spit, and good intentions. The four bags had been an entire mule load during the trek in—yet another source of conflict between the Deacon and Reggie—but to judge from the happy response from His Holiness and his high priests, it is a much-valued gift.

When I'm gestured forward, I bow deeply as the Rinpoche touches my head with what looks like a white metal pepper pot, but which J.C. has told me is yet another form of prayer wheel. Soon we sahibs are all properly blessed and it is time for the Sherpas to receive their blessings. This takes a while longer since each man prostrates himself on the cold stone floor and worms his way closer to the Rinpoche, without raising his head or meeting the holy man's gaze, to receive his blessing.

The only one who seems to have the attitude that he'll be damned if he'll be blessed this day is Pasang, who watches everything with a smiling, faintly amused yet respectful countenance, but who is not gestured forward by the monks and who obviously has turned down this offer of a blessing before. Dzatrul Rinpoche doesn't seem to mind a bit.

Finally the ritual blessings are over, the Sherpas file out—never turning their backs on the Rinpoche or the high priests—and Dzatrul Rinpoche says as Reggie interprets, "Those of the dead man's family may stay behind for tomorrow morning's sky burial." Then His Holiness also leaves.

J.C. and I step outside the main monastery building to say goodbye to Reggie, Pasang, and the Deacon. The Sherpas have already begun their long trek back to Base Camp.

"You may be sorry that you chose to stay for the sky burial," is all that the Deacon has to say.

I ask why we'd be sorry, but he ignores me and prods his little pony into a semblance of a canter, moving quickly to catch up to the Sherpas.

"Tell us about this Padma Sambhava that the current Rinpoche is supposed to be a reincarnation of," Jean-Claude says to our tall doctor. "Was he a man or a god?"

"He was both," says Pasang.

"In the eighth century, Padma Sambhava brought Buddhism to all of Tibet," adds Reggie. "He overpowered *Cho-mo-lung-ma* with Buddha-truth and then defeated the evil power of all the mountain demons and gods and goddesses, turning them all into *dharma* protectors. The darkest and most powerful of all the demon-goddesses, the queen of the *dakini* sky dancers, was turned into the pure white peak *Cho-mo-lung-ma*, her skirts reaching here to the Rongbuk Valley itself. The first temple built in this region was constructed on her left breast. Beneath her vulva was buried a white conch shell from which all *dharma* doctrine and Buddha-wisdom flow to this day."

I find myself blushing wildly again. First "testicles" and now "vulva." This woman is likely to say *anything* out loud.

Jean-Claude says softly, "If Guru Rinpoche—the Great Teacher, the Great Master, Padma Sambhava himself—defeated all the gods and demons around here and turned them into acolytes for the Buddha, why does Dzatrul Rinpoche say that they're angry and that he'll intercede for us?"

Reggie smiles as she hops onto her white pony. "The mountain gods, goddesses, and demons have been largely tamed for those who follow the Way, Jake," she says. "Those who've mastered *dharma*. But nonbelievers and those of small faith are still in danger. Are you two sure you want to watch the sky burial?"

J.C. and I nod.

Reggie speaks to the Sherpa Norbu Chedi, and then she kicks her pony into motion and hurries to catch up to the line of Sherpas and the Deacon. They are already disappearing into the gray evening. Dr. Pasang nods to us and strides to join the others. "A storm is coming" are his parting words.

And it *is* gray. Clouds and snow have moved in again, and the temperature's dropped at least thirty degrees.

"Monsoon?" I say.

J.C. shakes his head. "This front is coming in from the north. The monsoon will come from the south and west, piling up against the Himalayas until it pours over the peaks like a tsunami over a low breakwater."

Two priests come outside and say something to Norbu Chedi.

"These two will show us where we'll sleep," says our Sherpa. "And there will be a light repast of rice and more yogurt."

The old priests—they have perhaps five teeth among them—lead us to a small, windowless (but terribly drafty) room where, according to Norbu, we are to spend the night before being wakened for Babu Rita's sunrise funeral. There is a single candle for us to light, three bowls of rice, a communal bowl of yogurt, and some water. Three blankets have been spread out on the stone floor.

Before leaving, the two monks pause at a dark niche and hold their candles high so that we can see the wall mural there.

"Holy Christ," I whisper.

A series of devils, complete with cloven hooves, are throwing climbers into a deep abyss. Instead of Dante's fiery Hell, we are looking at a zone of damnation that is all snow, rock, and ice. The mural shows a whirling vortex, a sort of snow tornado, that is carrying the hapless climbers down, down, down. The mountain is obviously Everest, and to either side of it are growling, slathering guard dogs of immense proportions. But the most disturbing part of the mural is a single human figure lying at the base of the mountain the way a human offering would lie prostrate on an altar. The single body is white with dark hair—obviously a sahib. He has been speared, and one shaft still passes through him. Horned demons surround him, and J.C. and I step closer to see that the white man has been eviscerated. He is still alive, but his guts are spilling out onto the snow.

"Nice," I say.

The two monks smile, nod, and depart with their candles.

We sit on the cold stone, wrap the blankets around ourselves, and try to eat our rice and yogurt. All through the temple, the rising wind howls with a woman's terrified scream. It is very cold and growing colder.

"I wonder how old that mural is," says Jean-Claude.

"It was painted only last autumn, Sahibs," says Norbu Chedi. "I heard the other monks speak of it."

"After Mallory and Irvine disappeared," I say. "Why?"

Norbu Chedi pokes at his rice. "Word spread both at the monastery here and at Tingri and other villages that the sahibs had left much food behind at their higher camps—rice, oil, *tsampa*, much food."

"What is *tsampa?*" I ask.

"It is barley flour, roasted," says Norbu Chedi. "At any rate, when some of the villagers and some of the herders from the valley went up the East Rongbuk Glacier to claim this abandoned food, but about where you and Sahib Deacon have put our Camp Three, seven *yetis* leaped out of their hiding place in the caves in the ice and chased the young herders and villagers all the way off the glacier, all the way out of the valley. So Dzatrul Rinpoche had this mural painted as a warning to the greedy and foolish who would follow the foreign sahibs into such dangerous territory."

"Wonderful," I say.

We curl up in our respective blankets, but it is too cold to sleep. The monastery echoes to wind whistles, the distant slap of sandals on stone, the occasional dismal chanting, and the unceasing whir of prayer wheels spinning.

Without saying anything to one another, we decide to leave the candle burning between us and the mural.

Friday, May 15, 1925

The high priest comes for us—I can't say "wakes us" because neither J.C. nor I has slept a minute all night—sometime around 4:30 a.m. Norbu Chedi has chosen to sleep outside in the cold and wind, and I can't say I blame him. The candle the priest is holding, like so many others in the Rongbuk Monastery, consists of ghee butter in a tiny bowl. It smells terrible.

I've realized through the endless night that I hate the smell of everything in this supposedly sacred place. It's not because of filth—Rongbuk Monastery is one of the cleanest places I've seen in all of Tibet—but rather because of some mixture of the underlying scent of unwashed bodies (Tibetans tend to bathe once a year, in the autumn), the reeking ghee lamps, a heavy musky odor of incense, and the very stones of the building, which seem to have a coppery smell, like freshly spilled blood. I chastise myself for this last thought, for the Tibetan Buddhists here are nothing if not nonviolent. In the *beyuls* nearby—the sacred valleys made loci of *dharma* energy by the white magic of Guru Rinpoche so many centuries ago—the animals have been left unmolested for so many generations, the Deacon has told us, that undomesticated mountain sheep will come into your tent, wild swans will come to eat out of your hand, and the white wolf of the Himalayas is said not to kill his prey there.

A monk appears in the dimness, and we follow him and his flickering ghee lamp through the labyrinth of rooms. Norbu Chedi is still knuckling his eyes as a second priest joins us.

I'd assumed that the funeral rites would be in the monastery proper, but the priests lead us out a back door and down a path worn into the very stone. Our silent procession passes through a maze of high boulders, and we begin climbing. Wherever this ceremony is going to be held, it's at least half a mile from the monastery.

Finally we stop in an open area where four Tibetans—very poor by the look of their rags—wait near a strange flat stone. Behind the large altar stone (for so I think of it), higher boulders rise on edge and seem to have some sort of large gargoyles carved into them.

The first priest speaks, and Norbu Chedi translates: "The priest says that these four men are the grandfather, the two sons, and the grandson from the family of the Ngawang Tenzin, and they are the Breakers of the Dead for Babu Rita. The priest says that you may sit there during the ceremony." Norbu Chedi gestures to a long, flat boulder and turns to leave.

"Wait!" says Jean-Claude. "Aren't you going to stay for the ceremony?"

Norbu speaks over his shoulder. "I cannot. I am not of Babu Rita's family. And I do not choose to see a sky burial." He continues on into the dark maze of boulders, disappearing with the two acolytes who'd led us here.

It's getting vaguely light in the east now, but it's going to be a cloudy, cold day. I've brought an extra sweater which I'd tugged on during the night, but neither it nor my flannel shirt nor the thin Norfolk jacket keeps me warm. I wish to hell I'd brought my Finch duvet in my rucksack rather than just a few bars of chocolate and the sweater. I see that J.C. is also shivering.

We nod a greeting to the Ngawang Tenzins—an old man, presumably the grandfather, with white bristles sprouting everywhere on his wrinkled face, two overweight, middle-aged men with only two eyebrows between them, and a rail-thin boy who might be a teenager but who looks very young. None of the Ngawang Tenzins shows any response to our nods. We seem to be waiting for someone.

Eventually four other priests, obviously higher in the monkish hierarchy than the acolytes who led us here, appear from the boulder maze. The monastery itself is out of sight somewhere downhill behind us. For some reason, I'd expected Dzatrul Rinpoche himself to officiate at the sky burial. But evidently the mere Sherpa of white sahibs doesn't rate funeral officiating by the Holy Lama and reincarnation of Padma Sambhava.

Behind these priests come four lower-caste acolytes carrying the body of Babu Rita, still on the improvised stretcher on which we'd brought him to the monastery. The priests have the four ends of the litter on their shoulders, and the white tent canvas that had served as a shroud for Babu has been replaced by a white gauze, perhaps silk.

They set the stretcher on the broad, low stone around which the Ngawang Tenzin family—whose title Norbu Chedi had interpreted as "Breakers of the Dead"—stand waiting.

Meanwhile, the predawn light has come up enough that I now see that what I thought were gargoyles carved into the tall boulders behind the altar stone are nothing of the kind. They're living bearded vultures. Huge ones. They do not move. Their rapacious gazes remain fixed on the small form under the white gauze sheet.

J.C. and I stand there in a brief but freezing drizzle while the four priests and the four acolytes sing their harmony-free chants while two of the high priests circle the great stone holding Babu Rita's shroud-wrapped body, occasionally sprinkling some white powder onto it.

Finally the priests quit chanting and step back into the shadows of the boulder maze where the stretcher-bearer acolytes wait in silence. But no one leaves. The three generations of the Ngawang Tenzin family—the Breakers of the Dead—have stayed respectfully removed from the stone circle, barely visible in the shadows, through the entire ceremony.

"Is that *it?*" I whisper to Jean-Claude. "Is the sky burial *over?*"

"I don't think so," my friend whispers in turn. I sense something ominous in his voice.

The Ngawang Tenzins open several tanned leather bags and black cloths that are filled with sharp-edged tools: long, curved filleting knives, meat cleavers, handsaws, a small axe, a large hatchet, and other blades as well as massive stone-headed hammers.

Immediately they set to work.

They pull off the white shroud to show poor Babu Rita naked beneath the sheet. His brown form, lying on his back, palms down, eyes already somewhat sunken into their sockets, looks very small indeed. J.C. and I instinctively look away, trying to afford our Sherpa friend a shred of dignity. We needn't have bothered.

The grizzled grandfather Ngawang Tenzin works quickly with a long filleting blade in one hand and a large hatchet in the other. In less time than it takes to write about it, he's cut off both of Babu's hands, then both feet, and then decapitates him with two strong blows of the hatchet.

The middle-aged Ngawang Tenzin hacks and saws off what is left of Babu Rita's arms and legs. The sound of the saw cutting through bone and joints echoes off the high boulders. The teenaged Ngawang Tenzin now gets busy, using a smaller hatchet to cut off the dead Sherpa's fingers, then using one of the stone hammers to smash those fingers into even smaller pieces. And then the pieces are pounded into pulp.

The three older men are now working on Babu's torso. Our Sherpa comrade's heart, lungs, liver, intestines, and other internal organs are unceremoniously scooped out and tossed into a stone bowl. The grandfather Breaker of the Dead uses a metal bar to crack the ribs into pieces. Flesh is flensed from bone. The Ngawang Tenzin men and boy turn what's left of Babu Rita onto his front and pry and chop and leverage away what had been his vertebrae. These they also smash and mash. The sounds these efforts make are...unique.

When all the morsels are small enough and pulverized enough, the boy has the honor of tossing the pieces, one at a time, to the waiting vultures. The ugly carrion eaters will flap down to a piece that's dropped between their high boulders, but there's none of the usual vulture fighting and flapping associated with their dining on the dead I've heard described in Africa or somewhere. It's as if these bearded vultures, old veterans of sky burials, know that there will be enough to go around.

When Babu Rita has been reduced to bite-sized pieces—including his head and skull pounded flat, the eyes gouged out and thrown to the waiting vultures, his brain mashed to a gray gruel by the teenaged Breaker of the Dead—they wash off the worst gore from the butcher's stone with several pails of water thrown across it.

And then the four Breakers of the Dead leave. The eight monks and acolytes from the monastery have already left—sometime while J.C. and I were watching the butchers' work in silent horror.

Jean-Claude nods and we also leave, making a wide arc around the monastery proper, silently joining Norbu Chedi down the hill a bit, where he waits with our three ponies. No one says a word as we begin kicking the little ponies in the ribs to hurry them back north toward Base Camp and into the maw of a coming storm.

In the past, the trip between Rongbuk Monastery and Base Camp on our little ponies has taken us less than two hours. But today in the whirling, blinding snow, even with the strong, cold wind at our backs, it takes us more than three.

Neither J.C. nor I speaks during the first half of the trip home.

Finally Norbu Chedi says, "I have seen several sky burials, Sahibs. I did not wish to see another."

Jean-Claude and I have nothing to say to that.

In the last hour, as we approach the half-frozen river not far below the moraine and Base Camp, J.C. says to me, "I suppose it makes sense, culturally, practically, since the ground in most of Tibet is frozen solid ten months of the year."

"Yeah," I say. But I don't really mean it.

After a long silence, Jean-Claude turns to me. When he's sure that we're out of earshot of Norbu Chedi, who's gone ahead, he whispers, "If I buy it on this mountain, Jake, make sure I'm buried in a crevasse or just left where I lie. All right?"

"I promise," I say. "And you do the same for me, okay?"

J.C. nods and we say nothing else during the last fifteen minutes of our snowy pony ride to Base Camp.

Friday, May 15, 1925

*B*ase Camp is almost deserted when we arrive there before
noon.

Dr. Pasang is still there, of course, with both his frostbite patients
resting in their tents. Pasang carried out the amputations when everyone
returned from the monastery yesterday: all ten toes for Ang Chiri, four
toes and three fingers on the right hand for Lhakpa Yishay. Normally,
Pasang told J.C. and me, he would have waited much longer before operating, but the rot from Ang Chiri's toes was spreading to his entire foot,
and gangrene also threatened Lhakpa's right hand and left foot.

Jean-Claude and I look in on both men; Ang Chiri is more cheerful
than ever and, he says, is looking forward to trying the new wooden
wedges in the toes of his hiking boots to see how well he can walk with
no real toes. Of course, J.C. and I think but do not say aloud, a Sherpa
spends most of his life at home in sandals, not wearing English-made
hiking boots. But evidently Ang isn't worried about that fine distinc-
tion.

Lhakpa, who's lost less than Ang, is far gloomier. Both men have
their feet bandaged with yellow-red iodine stains leaking through. He
is cradling his now two-fingered right hand and all but weeping and
repeating the mantra—according to Pasang's interpreting—that he'll
never find work again.

Outside the tents, J.C. and I comment on Ang Chiri's high morale
and Pasang says softly, "Never discount the power of a little post-surgical
opium to cheer one up."

There are only about five other Sherpas in Base Camp, and Pasang tells us that yesterday Reggie and the Deacon assigned most of the men carrying tasks—hauling loads to the "upper camps," Camp III at the base of the last ice slope and Camp IV on the North Col. Also according to Pasang, a messenger brought word today that high winds and heavy snow up there were keeping everyone except the Deacon, Reggie, and two Tiger Sherpas lower than the North Col, and Pasang guesses that even those four may have retreated to Camp III by now. At least Camps II and III now have plenty of tents, sleeping bags, and food for the mobs moving in and through.

Pasang tells us that he is eager to get to the higher camps himself, once his two patients are better. That freedom for him, of course, depends upon no more injuries so severe that he has to take the injured man or men all the way back down here to Base Camp. My own guess is that Pasang doesn't like being separated from his employer—Lady Bromley-Montfort—for such long periods.

Jean-Claude and I decide that we're going to do a carry to the highest camp we can reach today, despite the relatively late hour for departing from Base Camp. I think we both need some high, clean climbing and carrying to get rid of the terrible taste of that dawn's "sky burial." I know I do.

While many of the oxygen rigs have already been transported higher by Sherpas, J.C. and I test the tank integrity of two such backpack-frame rigs—almost no leakage in any of the six tanks—and we shrug into the harnesses to haul the O_2 sets up as high as we can get by nightfall.

With the Irvine-Finch-modified oxygen rigs on our backs—we won't be breathing any of the English air today, so the masks and valves are tucked into the metal frame there—we're hauling close to the Deacon's guideline carry-load total of 25 pounds, but we also have to haul some personal stuff up with us if we're going to be staying at any of the high camps—perhaps stay there until the summit bid itself. So we grab two off-the-shoulder, hang-in-front "carry bags"—actually gas mask containers (minus the masks) from the Great War which the Deacon had purchased both cheap and by the dozens. They're perfect for cramming in our personal effects of some extra clothing, shaving kit—which I haven't used for a week, since I hate shaving in cold water—camera gear, toilet paper, and all the rest. It's probable that there are extra sleeping bags waiting at the high camps, but J.C. and I aren't going to take any chances: we roll the bags tight, put on their protective waterproof covers, and tie them onto the outer metal bars of the oxygen rig frames.

We have our assortment of odd-sized ice axes (keeping only the long axes out and unlashed) as well as two of J.C.'s jumars, we've strapped on our 12-point crampons (despite the fact that most of the way to Camp II is on moraine rock), and it's cold enough and snowy enough today that we're wearing our Finch duvet jackets and Reggie eiderdown pants under our outer Shackleton anoraks and snow pants.

We shake hands with Pasang when we leave, and then we're walking up the stony valley between walls of dirty moraine ice and the occasional ice pinnacle. The weather remains lousy, and visibility is down to about 15 feet. The wind is even stronger here than out in the Rongbuk Valley, and while the falling snow doesn't seem to be accumulating much, hard pellets of the stuff sting our faces like buckshot.

Tied together by 40 feet of the Deacon's Miracle Rope, more rope slung over our shoulders, with me in the lead, Jean-Claude and I head up the twelve-mile valley and glacier to the North Col.

J.C. and I exchange only a few necessary words during our long trek up the Trough, then the glacier above Camp II. We're each lost in our own thoughts.

I'm thinking about death in the mountains. Beyond my real sense of guilt at Babu's useless death during our clowning around, I'm remembering other mountain deaths and my reaction. I'm not totally new to sudden death on a mountain.

I've mentioned before that the Harvard Mountaineering Club didn't formally come into existence until last year, 1924, but when I attended Harvard from 1919 to 1923, there were a few of us — the Harvard Four, as we were known in climbing circles — who spent every vacation and spare moment climbing in the nearby Quincy Quarries in the spring and autumn and in the New Hampshire mountains during the winter.

Instructor Henry S. Hall, who would found the formal club in '24, was our informal leader, and our ad hoc climbing group met in his home. The other two members of our little group were Terris Carter (same year as me) and Ad Bates, a year behind us and a tough little mongrel of a climber, all knees and elbows and flying heels, but strangely skillful.

Professor Hall, with his older and more experienced mountaineering pals, specialized in climbing in the Canadian Rockies and, on rare occasions, in Alaska. During a school break in the early autumn of my junior year, the four of us were climbing on Mount Temple in Alberta, doing the East Ridge—which today would be classified IV 5.7 or so—when Ad slipped, snapped the 60-foot rope connecting him to Terris and me, and fell to his death. We hadn't been set for belay, and Ad's fall was so sudden and so vertical that if the rope hadn't snapped, Terris and I would almost certainly have gone over the north face to fall with him.

We mourned Ad's death, of course, in the way that only the young can mourn the death of someone their own age. I'd tried to talk to Ad's parents when they came to Harvard to pick up his things, but all I could do was sob. I started missing classes when school resumed, just sitting in my room and brooding. I was sure I'd never climb again.

That's when Professor Hall came to see me. He told me either to get back to my classes or drop out of school. He said I was just wasting my parents' money the way it was. As to climbing, Hall told me that he'd be taking student climbers to Mount Washington as soon as the first snow fell and that I should make up my mind whether to continue climbing—he thought that I had some skill at it—or run away from it now. "But dying's part of this sport," Professor Hall told me. "That's a hard fact—unfair—but it's a fact. When a friend or partner on the rope dies, if you're going to continue to be a climber, Jake, you have to learn how to say 'Fuck it' and move on."

I'd never heard a teacher or professor use that word before and it hit me hard. So did the lesson he was imparting to me.

But over my last few years of climbing, I've learned—at least partially—how to say "Fuck it" and move on. During my months in the Alps with the Deacon and J.C., we'd been involved in no fewer than five attempted rescue missions, three of which ended in tragedy for someone. It's true that I didn't know any of the dead climbers well, but I did get to know the terrible damage an alpine fall will do to the human body: fractured, splayed limbs, clothes torn off by jagged rocks on the way down, blood everywhere, crushed skulls or heads missing altogether. Death by falling from a great height is never a dignified thing.

Babu Rita hadn't fallen from any height; he'd just followed two idiots in glissading down a slope that one could find with a toboggan run in any snowy American city's municipal park. Only toboggan runs don't usually have boulders concealed under the snow.

"Fuck it," I hear myself whisper. "Move on."

The wind howls between the ice pinnacles of the Trough, and once up on the glacier, we have to dig out fixed ropes for security between crevasses, but the flagged bamboo poles show us the way.

We get to Camp III before daylight starts to fade, but Reggie and the Deacon aren't there. There are now six tents at Camp III—two of them oversized Whympers—but we find eight Sherpas curled up and sleeping in the smaller Meade tents. Pemba moans that none of them feel well: all have been struck by "mountain lassitude"—our word for altitude sickness in 1925. Those not in sleeping bags are wrapped in heavy layers of blankets. Pemba says that Lady Memsahib and Deacon Sahib are up at Camp IV on the North Col with Tejbir Norgay and Tenzing Bothia. The winds up there, says Pemba, are very terrible.

Jean-Claude and I step back out of the odiferous Meade tent and confer. It's late in the day, and it will be dark by the time we reach Camp IV. But we've brought our Welsh miner headlamps, I have an extra hand torch in my gas mask bag, and we both feel strong and impatient.

The hardest part of the climb, oddly enough, is the postholing from Camp III to the base of the slope and then trudging up the two hundred yards or so to the steep part where the first fixed ropes begin. The heavy snow and dimming day hide the boulder that killed Babu, but I can't help imagining a layer of frozen blood under the new-fallen snow, like strawberry jam spread thin beneath white bread. When we reach the steeper fixed-rope part of the route, we have to use our ice axes to dig through the new snow until we can find the fixed rope and tug it up and out. Then we dig through our canvas bags and don our headlamp rigs and take out the ascender device that Jean-Claude named "jumar" after a dog he had as a kid. Or so he's said.

As J.C. double-checks to make sure I've clipped the jumar onto the Deacon Miracle Rope properly, I say, "Did you really invent this doodad?"

My friend grins. "I did, but in collaboration with my father, who was helping a young French gentleman named Henri Brenot, who wanted some sort of mechanism for climbing free-hanging ropes in caves. Since it was just for one person, my father didn't think to patent it, nor did Brenot, who called his larger cave rope-ascender devices *singes*—monkeys—so I decided to modify it, make it smaller and safer with stronger, lighter metal, added the curved handle and its handle guard, which we can fit our mittens into, and designed a sturdier cam to lock on to the rope without fear of slipping or shredding the line, and...*voilà!*"

"But 'Jumar' was really your dog's name?"

Jean-Claude only grins more broadly and begins mechanically ascending—I've already begun thinking of it as "jumaring"—up the fixed rope.

A year ago, it would have taken Mallory or Irvine or Norton or any of the others four or five hours to get up this ice wall to the North Col, especially in a swirling snowstorm such as J.C. and I have just climbed through. Mallory would have spent much of his time on the ice face bent almost double, dutifully and exhaustingly using an ice axe to chip new steps out of the snow and ice. J.C. and I kicked in the front spurs of our new 12-point crampons and jumared up in less than forty-five minutes—and that included a time-out halfway up to hang from the rope and eat bars of chocolate. We did use our long ice axes, but only to stab into snow with our left hands for balance on the way up or to bat away the ice and snow covering the next few yards of fixed rope above us.

The traverse from the ice shelf across the North Col to Camp IV at the northwest corner under the tall seracs should have been worrisome in so serious a storm, but the Deacon and others have done such an excellent job of setting out permanent bamboo wands and red pennants that even in high winds and the near whiteout, it's as easy as walking along a well-marked eight-foot-wide highway between invisible 100-foot drops into crevasses.

Camp IV now consists of one medium-sized Whymper tent, brought up in separate loads, as well as the RBT—Reggie's Big Tent—and two smaller Meade tents in which the Deacon planned to store loads for higher carries. When some of this stuff goes up to Camps V and VI, the

Meade tents as well as the Whymper tent here will host Sherpas on their way up or down in the theoretical supply line.

The Deacon and Tejbir Norgay look up in surprise as we come through the Whymper tent door, shaking snow off our outer layer into the small vestibule before joining them. I imagine we're a sight in our high-cinched eiderdown hoods, full-face leather flying helmets, glowing headlamps, iced-over goggles, and snow-rimmed Shackleton anorak shoulders. The two men obviously aren't expecting company as they huddle over an Unna cooker, the Meta fuel boiling up a big pot of something—at the pathetically low temperature it takes to boil things at 23,500 feet. Water boils at somewhere around 170 degrees Fahrenheit at this altitude, as opposed to 212 degrees at sea level. Although 170 degrees may sound hot, by the time the cold air hits it, our "boiled" liquids are down to around body temperature.

When we reveal our faces, the Deacon says, "Just in time for dinner, gentlemen. Beef stew. And we've made plenty."

J.C. and I are surprisingly ravenous. Evidently the nausea we shared after the morning's sky burial has worked itself out during our hours of trekking and climbing.

I've expected a rebuke from the Deacon regarding Babu Rita's death, but it never comes—not even a pointed question as to whether we enjoyed the sky burial or had an interesting time with the Breakers of the Dead. I know that the Deacon himself has attended such terrible rites, but he makes no mention of it, ironic or otherwise. My guess is that he sympathizes with our reaction to the horrors we've seen. I know that Richard Davis Deacon also liked Babu very much.

"What is the climbing plan, *Ree-shard?*" asks J.C. when we've finished the last of the stew and reheated biscuits and are sipping our tepid coffee.

"In the morning, unless the weather gets actively worse, we'll try the North Ridge to Camp Five," he says. "I managed to get the two Meades up there a few days ago...we can only hope they haven't blown away or been carried all the way down to the glacier by an avalanche." He points to where J.C. and I have dumped our oxygen rigs in the corner of the tent. "Did you use any of that on the way up?"

We shake our heads.

"Good," says the Deacon. "But we have extra sets cached here at

Camp Four, and I recommend that you have one tank between you during the night...use the double-breathing hookup. If you get cold or really start feeling bad, a little oxygen at the one-point-five-liter flow rate will help out. We'll all need some sleep if we're going to climb in the morning. Speaking of which, did you bring extra batteries for those miner lamps?"

I nod.

"Good," he says again. "When I say 'in the morning,' I mean around three-thirty or four a.m."

I'm tempted to say *So you're following Reggie's advice after all,* but I decide against it and ask only, "Where are Reggie and Tenzing Bothia?"

"In the RBT," says the Deacon. Suddenly he grins. "Lady Bromley-Montfort challenged me at Camp Three this morning when she overheard me talking about the RBT with a couple of the Sherpas there. She demanded to know what this 'RBT' she's been hearing from various men stood for. When I told her 'Reggie's Big Tent' and apologized for the familiarity with her name, she just said 'Oh' and blushed like mad. I have to wonder what she *thought* we were talking about."

I have to think about this for a minute before a possibility strikes me..."Reggie's Big...," and then it's my turn to blush. I pour more coffee to hide my embarrassment.

The wind claws at the walls of the Whymper, but there's no sense of imminent collapse as there'd been a week ago at Camp III. And even if this tent were to tear free, we have the two unused Meades and Reggie's Big...Tent...as lifeboats in the storm.

Unless, of course, we don't have time to get *out* of the tent when its tie-downs and stakes pull free in the gale. In that case we'll just all try to claw through canvas as the Whymper slides over the edge into a bottomless crevasse or a thousand vertical feet down onto the glacier proper.

We're settling into our sleeping bags and still sipping the last of our coffee when I take out the book I'd packed up with me. It's the popular wartime anthology of English verse *The Spirit of Man,* and I begin reading a Tennyson poem aloud to everyone when the Deacon suddenly says, "Excuse me, Jake. May I see that book?"

"Of course." I stop reading and hand it to him.

The Deacon stands, still in boots, tugs on his down jacket, furls up his sleeping bag, grabs his personal rucksack, and goes out the tent door into the maelstrom.

Confused, smiling to myself thinking it's some joke—perhaps having to do with toilet paper, although we've all brought some with us—I stick my head and shoulders out of the Whymper tent just long enough to see the Deacon hurling *The Spirit of Man* into one of the deeper crevasses. Then he disappears through the swirling snow toward one of the gear-crowded Meade tents.

I close the tent flap and turn toward J.C. and Tejbir. Both men look as startled and confused as I feel.

I'm shaking my head, trying to think of something to say, wondering if the altitude has driven our older English friend temporarily mad, when the flaps are suddenly unlaced and Reggie steps through. She's not wearing her down outer layers but is carrying them and her eiderdown sleeping bag and inflatable sleeping cushion.

"May I come in?" she asks after she's already inside and re-lashing the door shut behind her.

"Please...yes...please do...of course," J.C. and I are babbling. Tejbir continues staring and I remember that his grasp of English tends to slip when he's upset or confused.

We make room as Reggie lays out her sleeping pad and bag, takes off her unlaced boots, and slithers down into her bag while still sitting up. She speaks to Tejbir in rapid-fire Nepalese and the Sherpa nods, gets into his boots, folds his sleeping bag, grabs his rucksack, and goes out into the storm.

"I just suggested to Tejbir that since I'd be sleeping in this tent tonight—if it's all right with you fellows—Tenzing Bothia might be lonely in my dome tent. Tejbir took the hint. This will give us more room to spread out."

Sleeping in here tonight, I think giddily. Then I realize the absurdity of my Victorian-era shock. Besides the mummy-style sleeping bags themselves, all three of us are still dressed in multiple layers of cotton, wool, and goose down. I'm reminded of a tale I'd heard in England about Sir Robert Falcon Scott at the South Pole. Evidently Scott was rather stuffy about rank and social class—he's said to have hung a blanket between the enlisted men's and the officers' parts of the single room in the large shack they built near the coast—but during the early part of his push to the Pole, while there were others there who would return to the shack and survive the experience, someone deferentially asked Scott why he took more time than the others when he stepped out into the terrible cold at night to attend to the call of nature. "Basically," Scott is reported to have said, "it's the problem of getting two inches of business out of seven inches of clothing."

In other words, Lady Bromley-Montfort was safe with us tonight. Of course, she would have been even if we'd all been sleeping naked.

"I was out going to the loo when I saw Mr. Deacon throw a book over the side of the cliff and then take himself off to make room in the Meade tent we half-filled with provisions for the upper camps," she says.

This gives me pause. *Going to the loo?* For urinating in storms like this, we male climbers don't leave the tent—we're not as particular about such things as Scott was—but merely use what we politely call "a piss bottle." We covertly—or not so covertly—dump it outside when conditions improve, but I've never thought about the problems a woman climber might have with even the simpler form of..."going to the loo." I find myself wondering if she teeters on the edge of crevasses, and I also worry about her getting frostbite.

I won't admit to blushing again, but I do look away until I regain my composure.

"What was the book?" asks Reggie. I realize that J.C. is waiting for me to answer.

"Oh, the Robert Bridges anthology of English verse, *The Spirit of Man*," I say quickly. "I'd heard that George Leigh Mallory had read aloud from it to his tent mates here at Camp Four and thought it might be...appropriate...if...," I trail off.

Reggie nods. "I understand why Mr. Deacon tossed the book off the Col."

I look at J.C., but he looks as confused as I feel. Has the Deacon gone a bit mad because of the altitude? Are we supposed to believe that he's still angry at Mallory—or jealous of him? Nothing seems to make sense.

Then Reggie asks something that takes me from the realm of the surreal directly to the impossible.

"Have either of you seen your friend Richard Davis Deacon naked?" she asks in a calm voice.

Jean-Claude and I look at each other again, but neither of us can muster more of an answer than a headshake toward her.

"I didn't think so," she says. "I have."

My God, she and the Deacon have been lovers since we met her in Darjeeling, I think. *All the irritable banter has been a smokescreen.*

J.C. somehow manages to ask the important question. Perhaps it's easier for a Frenchman. "May I ask when have you seen him naked, my lady?"

Reggie smiles. "The first night you were all at my Darjeeling plantation. But it's not what you're thinking. I had Pasang deliberately drug Mr. Deacon's brandy with a draught of morphine so that he'd sleep deeply. Pasang and I then examined his body using only candles for light. Luckily, in warmer climes, your Mr. Deacon sleeps in the nude. It was nothing personal, you understand. Purely a medical necessity."

Now, there's absolutely nothing to say to this, so I don't. It's not only crazy but outrageous. *Nothing personal?* What could be more personal than someone drugging you to inspect you while you're naked? I find myself wondering if she and Pasang inspected all of us that night—I remember sleeping deeply. But why would she?

Neither J.C. nor I ask that question aloud, but Reggie answers it.

"Did either of you know Mr. Deacon before the War?"

We shake our heads.

"Did either of you know him during the years immediately after the War?"

Again we signify we did not. Sometimes I forget that Jean-Claude met and began climbing with the Deacon just two months before I did.

Reggie sighs. "Captain R. D. Deacon was cited in no fewer than fourteen official despatches during the War," she says softly. "Do you get the full import of that information?"

"That *Ree-shard* is very brave?" J.C. says tentatively.

Reggie smiles. "Amidst all that carnage and bravery," she says, "to be singled out for praise in four or five despatches is extraordinary. To be mentioned in seven or eight is usually associated only with those so courageous that they invariably died in battle. Captain Deacon—he refused multiple attempts to promote him to major or colonel, you know—was in the thick of the battle at Mons, when they inserted the British Expeditionary Forces into the hole in the front at the First Battle of the Marne, at Ypres—which many British soldiers pronounced 'Yippers'—at Loos in the Battle of Artois in nineteen fifteen, at the Somme in February nineteen sixteen when the British lost fifty-eight thousand men before breakfast the first day, in the crater at the Battle of Messines, and finally in some of the worst fighting at both Passchendaele in nineteen seventeen and the Second Battle of the Marne in nineteen eighteen."

"How do you know all this?" I ask.

"My late cousin Charles was one source," says Reggie. "Cousin Percival was an even better source."

"I thought that Percival—young Bromley—hadn't fought in the War," says Jean-Claude.

"Percival did not *fight* in the War," says Reggie. "At least not as a soldier in uniform in the way Captain Deacon and my cousin Charles did. But Percival's contacts in the government and the War Department were...let us say...extensive."

"But your cousin Percy was dead by the time you knew that *Ree-shard* was coming on this mission," persists J.C.

"Oui," says Reggie. "But dropping Percival's name opened certain doors...or I should say file drawers...for me in the last few months."

"I don't understand," I say, the protest more than audible in my tone. "How on earth does the Deacon's admirable war record justify you and Pasang drugging him and looking at him naked as he slept?"

"I had already made arrangements for this spring's expedition to find Percival's remains," Reggie says. "I had three alpine guides—Swiss—lined up to come back here to the mountain with me. When I heard that you and Jean-Claude were coming with Mr. Deacon—who saw his chance to use my aunt Elizabeth's wealth to fund you all—and that you'd actually landed at Calcutta, I had to know if Mr. Deacon was physically fit."

"Of course he is," I say, not even trying to hide the indignation I feel. "You've seen him trek and climb. He's almost certainly the strongest of us all."

Reggie shrugs slightly, but not enough to show apology or regret. "I knew from Cousin Charles—and the classified War Department records Charles's and Percival's contacts had got for me—that Captain Deacon was wounded no fewer than twelve times. At no time did he allow himself to be invalided home to England the way, say, George Mallory did. Mallory was a second lieutenant in the Fortieth Siege Battery at the Somme—he served all of his time at the Front in an artillery unit behind the front lines, as such—and while he saw men killed near him, Second Lieutenant Mallory was never posted directly at the Front for any length of time the way Richard Deacon was in the infantry. Mallory was invalided out and back to England for surgery—it was an old ankle injury which occurred before the War, the result, I believe, of a fall while rock scrambling in a quarry. He was invalided out of France on eight April nineteen seventeen, the day before the Battle of Arras, in which forty thousand British soldiers died. And the battle in which Captain Deacon was wounded for the fifth time. George Mallory—who had friends on high, no pun intended—spent most of the rest of the War in England, both recuperating and working in training units. He was still on convalescent leave when he felt well enough to go climbing at Pen-y-Pas in Wales with friends. Mallory was ordered back to his artillery battalion in time for the terrible Battle of Passchendaele, but he missed arriving there on time due to another injury in England—this time damage to his foot and thumb when he had an accident with his motorcycle in Winchester. You might say, if such things were possible to say, that Second Lieutenant George Mallory had an easy war.

"Captain Deacon, on the other hand, kept returning to the Front in spite of his injuries. He never allowed himself to be invalided back to England. As far as I know, he never returned to England during the entire War—very, very unusual for an officer. It was only a day's travel from the Front to London or home, and officers took advantage of almost every leave to make that trip. As for the despatches and wounds, I was also aware that, at least twice, Captain Deacon had been directly exposed to mustard gas."

"His lungs are fine," I say. "His eyes are fine."

"Ahh," says Jean-Claude as if he finally comprehends something.

Reggie shakes her head. "You don't understand, Jake. Mustard gas not only attacks the eyes and lungs and mucous membranes in a person but—as it did with poor Cousin Charles—when it's spattered directly upon one's body, the yellow powder of the gas eats directly into flesh and muscle in a wound that will never heal. Sufferers from mustard gas contact have bleeding, suppurating wounds that have to be re-dressed every day of their lives. My dear cousin Charles suffered from precisely such suppurating wounds. Do either of you remember the name John de Vere Hazard?"

"Hazard was on last year's expedition," says Jean-Claude. "He's the fellow who left four Sherpas behind here on the North Col in a storm—a storm like this one—and made Mallory, Somervell, and the others risk their lives going up from Camp Three to get them down."

Reggie nods. "Mr. Hazard received the Military Cross during the War. A very serious decoration for exemplary service and for receiving wounds in the line of duty. Mr. Deacon won it *four times* during the War. Mr. Hazard came on the Everest expedition last year with his wounds—especially bad were the ones caused by contact with solid mustard gas, but he also had shrapnel in his back and wounds from machine gun fire in his thigh and hips. Hazard's wounds opened while he was climbing here. Beneath his wool and cotton, the poor man was bleeding constantly. When he was most needed, he was most incapacitated."

"How can you know all this?" I say again.

"My cousins Charles and Percy had many contacts," says Reggie. "I've also had a long history of exchanging letters with Colonel Teddy Norton, whom you met last autumn at the Royal Geographical Society digs."

"So," says J.C., "you felt that you had to...*vet*, I believe is the legal language in English...vet Richard Deacon by having Dr. Pasang look at his wounds while the Deacon slept under the influence of morphine at your plantation?"

"Yes," says Reggie. There's no defiance in her tone, but still no sound of shame, either.

"What did you find?" asks Jean-Claude.

I turn to shoot a harsh glance at J.C.

"Scar tissue in more than a dozen places, as you might imagine," replies Reggie. "Some muscle in his left calf missing due to a machine gun wound there. At least three sets of scars on his torso where shrapnel or bullets passed all the way through Captain Deacon, obviously not striking any vital blood vessels or organs. Naked, your Captain Richard

Davis Deacon's scars, front and back, look like a spider has been weaving white webs in his flesh."

"That took one hell of a lot of cheek to spy on him like that," I say, my voice as harsh as I can make it while still speaking to a lady.

Reggie nods. "It did. It was an almost unforgivable violation of Mr. Deacon's privacy. But I had to know. The three Swiss alpine guides I'd contacted to help me in the retrieval of Percival's body had already set sail from Europe, and I had to cable them in Colombo if I was going to cancel their participation and climb here with the three of you instead."

"Did *Ree-shard* pass your muster?" J.C. doesn't sound angry, only a little bemused. I doubt if he'd use the same tone if it had been *him* whom Reggie had been peering at naked. Or, on second thought, perhaps he would.

"He did," says Reggie. "But Pasang informs me that due to the placement and severity of some of the old wounds, your Mr. Deacon must be in constant pain."

"So what?" I say. "A lot of world-class alpinists climb through pain."

"Probably not this much pain," replies Reggie. "And I regret that I lied to all of you about my dear cousin Charles succumbing to his wounds while you were in transit to India. In truth, he took his own life. According to my aunt Elizabeth—Lady Bromley—after more than seven years of bravely tolerating his wounds, he simply could no longer bear the pain. He used his service revolver."

This silences us for several long minutes.

"Just out of curiosity," Jean-Claude says at last, "would you tell us again the names of the three Swiss guides you'd hired?"

Reggie names them again and Jean-Claude whistles, eyes wide with awe or respect. "I am surprised, Lady Bromley-Montfort, that you turned them back and have come with us."

Reggie smiles. "I paid the three Swiss guides a fee for their time, sent them a generous cheque when they turned back from Colombo, but you three were *already* being paid by my aunt. And my aunt receives her income from the plantation in Darjeeling which I've run since I was fourteen years old. Going ahead with you three—and Pasang and the Tiger Sherpas—seemed like the most economical thing to do. But I had to know about Mr. Deacon's wounds...whether his body was up to this climb or not. He's thirty-seven years old, you know."

"George Mallory was thirty-seven when he disappeared last year," I say idiotically. No one responds.

Jean-Claude shrugs his upper body out of the cocoon of his sleeping bag. He has to free his hands. He cannot talk earnestly without the use of his hands.

"But, Madame, you asked us if we had known *Ree-shard* Deacon in the years right after the War. Is that period somehow relevant to your concerns about our friend's leadership?"

"Do you have any knowledge of Mr. Deacon's actions right after the War?" asks Reggie.

"Only that he came to the Swiss and French Alps and spent most of his time climbing," says J.C.

Reggie nods. "Mr. Deacon's mother died some years before the War. His father died of a heart attack in nineteen seventeen. Mr. Deacon had an older brother, Gerald, but he was killed as an RAF pilot in early nineteen eighteen. That left Richard Davis Deacon not only in total possession of his two huge estates—Brambles, the larger home, makes my aunt Elizabeth's Bromley House look like a shack in comparison—but also an earl, a peer of the realm, and a member of the House of Lords."

"Earl Deacon?" I say.

Reggie laughs. "I love Americans. No, Mr. Deacon is, despite his objections, the ninth Earl of Watersbury." She pronounces it in that slurry British way . . . *Watrsbreee.*

"Despite his objections?" says J.C., his palms upward now.

"Mr. Deacon cannot legally renounce his hereditary title," says Reggie. "But he refuses to answer to it, has given away most of his estates, and will not take his seat in the House of Lords."

"I didn't know that someone would not want to be an earl," I say. "Nor that he *has* to be, even if he doesn't *want* to be."

"Neither do many people in the United Kingdom," says Reggie. "In the meantime, in nineteen eighteen, from France, I believe, Mr. Deacon donated his two estates and twenty-nine thousand acres and the estates' revenues to the Crown. He suggested they turn his nine-hundred-year-old primary home, Brambles, into a convalescent home. He never returned to it after the war. He has a small income—I believe derived from royalties coming in now and then from novels or poetry he wrote under various *noms de plume* before the War—and he's stayed in the Alps almost constantly since nineteen eighteen."

"Are you saying that Richard Davis Deacon is nuts?" I ask her.

Reggie looks straight at me, and those ultramarine eyes are narrowed. "Nothing of the sort," she says sharply. "I am trying to explain why your friend took your book of poetry and threw it over the ice cliff."

"I don't get it," I say.

"Mr. Deacon knows that in September nineteen fourteen, when war with Germany was barely under way, the newly created—and top-secret—War Propaganda Bureau had a secret meeting with some of England's top writers and poets at Wellington House, Buckingham Gate. Thomas Hardy was there, as was Mr. H. G. Wells..."

"War of the Worlds!" I cry.

Reggie nods and goes on. "Rudyard Kipling, John Masefield—the Catholic writer—G. K. Chesterton, Arthur Conan Doyle...G. M. Trevelyan, J. M. Barrie..."

"Peter Pan!" cries J.C.

"Evidently Mr. Deacon was a well enough respected poet that he was also invited," she says softly. "Along with his poet friend Robert Bridges. All they were asked to do during the War—even the relatively younger men such as Mr. Deacon—was to be exempted from the military call-up and to use their literary talents for the war effort. Primarily in keeping the British public's morale up and never...*never*...allowing them to know how terrible the actual fighting might turn out to be."

"But the Deacon enlisted instead," says Jean-Claude, his fingers now folded together as if in prayer.

"Yes," says Reggie. "But his poet friend Robert Bridges stayed behind and didn't write another word of his own poetry throughout the War. Instead, Bridges edited an anthology of inspiring English verse—the very *Spirit of Man* that George Mallory read from twice here at Camp Four and which you tried to read from this evening, Jake."

I'm confused. "But it's all good English verse," I say. "Classic stuff. There's even one of the Deacon's early poems in it."

"And no mention whatsoever of war," says Reggie.

"That's correct," I say. "A lot of topics but no English verse about war. And..."

Suddenly I stop. I think I'm beginning to understand.

"The newspapers were part of the propaganda effort," says Reggie. "Of course they had to be, hadn't they? Casualty lists had to be published there, but the real war was never described in its terrible detail...not once. All newspapers were willing subjects of the Propaganda Bureau. My cousin Charles wrote me in nineteen seventeen that Lloyd George had told C. P. Scott of the *Manchester Guardian* that, and I think I quote correctly, 'if the people really knew'—he meant what the slaughter in France and Belgium was really like—'if the people really *knew,* the War would be stopped tomorrow.'"

My voice, when I try to speak, is slow and cautious, as if my words were threading their way through a crevasse field. "So *The Spirit of Man*...was part...of the Propaganda Bureau's...effort to keep the War going no matter what the cost in lives."

Reggie says nothing and doesn't even nod, but I can see that she's proud of me for catching up to things. I'm not used to being the slow pupil in the class, but I pride myself on being smart enough to know if and when I am.

Jean-Claude looks troubled. "Reggie—Lady Bromley-Montfort," he says just loudly enough to be heard over the noise of the wind rattling the tent walls, "you must have another reason for telling us this incredibly personal information about *Ree-shard.*"

"I do," says Reggie. "I know how eager all three of you are to use my aunt's money to get a chance to climb Mount Everest. But you see, I'm not totally convinced that dear Mr. Richard Davis Deacon wants to *return* from the mountain."

Saturday, May 16, 1925

*T*he Deacon's plan, before he stole my book and stalked off, was for us to wake in the middle of the night, make some hot tea and get dressed by our hissing lanterns, and be out of the tent and climbing toward Camp V somewhere around four in the morning, so as J.C., Reggie, and I crawl deeper into our mummy bags to get some sleep, I set my pocket watch to vibrate me awake at 3:30. The watch is a beautiful and expensive thing, a gift from my father upon my graduation from Harvard, and whatever else happens on Mount Everest, I most dearly want no harm to come to it. It has a clever little feature whereby one can set a time and the watch will soundlessly announce that set time with the insistent flutter of a small metal arm set into the back of the device.

I keep the watch in a waistcoat pocket, and at 3:30 a.m. there comes the frenzied flutter over my heart. Despite my fatigue, I awake at once.

Oddly, I've managed to sleep quite a bit during the few hours allowed us. Once Jean-Claude had shaken me awake and whispered, "You're not breathing, Jake," and I'd taken a snort of English air from the bottle we'd rigged between us, but other than that, it has been my best sleep so far at altitude. At Camp III, just the exertion of rolling over had led to my gasping awake, panting from the effort, and I'd kept rolling over onto irritating patches of my own frozen breath, but here, 1,500 feet higher, I've slept like a baby.

Well, we aren't leaving for Camp V this morning. The sides of the tent are still rippling and snapping, and I can clearly hear the rattle of countless snow pellets on canvas. *Another day to sleep and catch up on rest,* I think gratefully while burrowing back into my bag, even while the more conscious part of my brain knows that staying another day at this altitude isn't a good idea.

The term "Death Zone" wasn't used much in 1925, but the basic understanding of it was just becoming known after three British expeditions to Everest.

Here at Camp IV our bodies are already suffering the consequences of altitude. I mentioned earlier in this narrative that there's as much oxygen at altitude as at sea level — 20.93 percent, to be pedantic — but with the decreasing atmospheric pressure, our lungs and bodies can't gain access to that precious resource. Way down at Camp I, at only 17,800 feet of altitude, the atmospheric pressure — and thus the oxygen our bodies can normally drag into our lungs — is half that at sea level. If we make it to the summit of this mountain at just over 29,000 feet, the pressure will be one-third that at sea level, barely enough oxygen to allow one to stay conscious and not enough to prevent headaches, nausea, severe "mountain lassitude," and — perhaps the worst thing from a climber's point of view — severe mental grogginess, hallucinations, and impaired judgment.

So above 8,000 meters — a little more than 24,000 feet, not much more than 500 feet higher than where we are sleeping this night on the North Col — the once-and-future term "the Death Zone" becomes an absolute imperative not to linger. At and above 8,000 meters, your body is dying — literally dying, more so every minute you stay at such an altitude. The technical term is *necrosis.* Not only will brain cells be dying by the millions, Dr. Pasang has explained, but the rest of the brain fails to function properly in the fog of oxygen deprivation, even while our circulation becomes thick and sluggish and major organs begin to swell (as our hearts already have for all of us, even the Sherpas), literally swelling toward bursting, or generally just shut down and cease to work at all.

Our average heartbeats have long since quickened to 140 beats per minute or more, making every upward step or simple physical activity dangerous as well as difficult. In a vain attempt to get more oxygen to our muscles and brains, our blood has already dramatically thickened in our veins, increasing the likelihood of fatal strokes or thrombosis every hour we stay at this altitude or climb higher. Ironically, because the blood in our veins has turned a much darker red due to oxygen shortage, our faces, lips, and extremities tend to glow blue.

Only the occasional whiff of English air helps us ward off some of these more severe problems.

And we're still 5,500 feet below the mountain's summit.

Thinking *We have to get down lower soon,* I nonetheless burrow deeper into my eiderdown bag and drift back to sleep. I admit to taking a long inhalation from the oxygen tank first. It warms my frozen feet and toes.

Then someone or something is crashing through the tent doors and I snap awake, trying to sit up. It takes three attempts to do so.

Reggie is gone. *Out to the loo?* I think but then notice that her sleeping bag is missing.

It's the Deacon coming in through the door flaps amidst a flurry of snow and a moving wall of cold air. If it weren't for the red bands he'd earlier wrapped around the arms of his goose down duvet, I wouldn't recognize him: he's absolutely coated with snow and ice, his flying helmet, balaclava, and goggles are rimmed with icicles, and his huge outer mittens make cracking-ice noises when he tries to remove them. He has an ice-covered oxygen rig on his back, but the mask isn't over his face, and I'm sure the regulator has been switched to *Closed.*

"Chilly morning," he says, panting.

I pull my watch out. It is a little after seven a.m.

"Where have you been, *Ree-shard?*" J.C.'s beard, I notice, is coming in much more nicely than mine. I seem to be all stubble and itch.

"Just seeing if the North Ridge will go," answers the Deacon. "It won't."

"The snow?" I say.

"The wind," says the Deacon. "It must be well over one hundred and twenty miles per hour. I was trying to walk up the slabs while leaning forward so far that my nose was almost touching granite."

"Climbing alone?" says Jean-Claude, a hint of rebuke in his voice. "Not what you would advise us to do, *Ree-shard.*"

"I know." The Deacon has fumbled our Unna cooker into place just inside the Whymper's outer vestibule, and is trying to use his frozen hands to get a match lit indoors and transferred to the cooker. The wind blows it out each time. "To hell with it," he says and brings the cooker inside—another total breach of fire safety protocol. I light the Meta for him, and he sets a cauldron of snow in the most sheltered part of the small vestibule.

"I don't think we'll get to Camp Five," he says, unzipping outer layers as if the below-freezing temperature in the tent were some tropical climate.

"I poked my head in to wake them all," continues the Deacon. "Reggie's been up for a while, working on a stove that won't bring water to boil. Evidently this morning's giving them some insomnia, headaches, breathing problems, cold toes, sore throats, and sour thoughts."

The Deacon shows white teeth through the icicles still dangling from his new beard. "I think this beautiful bitch of a mountain has already declared war on us, my friends. God or the gods or destiny or chance grant that we be worthy of the challenge." Suddenly he pulls off his inner mitten and silk glove and thrusts his bare, bluish right hand toward me. "Jake, I apologize sincerely and completely and without reservation for my idiocy in taking and tossing your book last night. There's no excuse for such behavior. I shall buy you a new copy—perhaps get Bridges to autograph it for you—as soon as we get back from this adventure."

Since Robert Bridges has been the Poet Laureate of England since 1913, I consider that one hell of a decent offer.

I don't know what to say, so I just shake his offered hand. It's like grasping a slab of frozen beef.

Reggie comes in and laces the tent flaps behind her. She's wearing every bit of goose down outerwear we had available. The only thing that would prevent her from climbing the mountain dressed as she is now is the high Laplander furred boots that several of us prefer to wear in camp while our mountain boots dry. The Laplander boots have relatively soft soles that won't work on near-vertical snow, rock, and ice.

"Tenzing Bothia's sick," she says without greeting or prelude. "He's been vomiting the last six or seven hours. We need to get him down...at least to Camp Three but preferably lower."

The Deacon sighs. We have a tough decision pending. If we stay here at Camp IV on the Col, we get weaker by the hour, but we're in a good position to make a break for Camp V high on the North Ridge if the weather moderates. Then again, that may not happen for a week or more. But if we all go down, there'll be hell to pay in terms of logistics. Camp III at the bottom of the ice wall is already overflowing with Sherpas, every tent filled. Some of them are probably already suffering from mountain lassitude and also may have to be evacuated down the mountain to Base Camp. Our loads—meant for Camps V and VI and our search for Percival up there—are spread out between Camps I and IV, with the carefully planned schedule of alternating Sherpa carries now shot to hell.

I know that every Everest expedition so far—all three of them—has run into this same problem, no matter how careful the planning or how large the number of porters, but that's little solace to us now as we huddle in this flapping Whymper tent at 23,500 feet.

"I'll take Tenzing down," says Jean-Claude. "And I'll take Tejbir Norgay with me."

"Tejbir's feeling all right," says Reggie. "Just tired."

"But he can help me with Tenzing on the ropes," says J.C. "And the two of us can help him down to Camp Two or One if we have to go that far."

The Deacon thinks a moment and nods. "If we all go down now, we'll be bumping six Sherpas out of the tents at Camp Three."

"We'll only have three of your jumars left for descending or ascending fixed ropes if we have to follow you or fix ropes higher," I say. My mind feels like it's been wrapped in fuzzy wool.

"I still know how to rig a friction knot," says Reggie.

I want to slap my forehead. How quickly we get addicted to new devices. A friction knot on the fixed ropes is probably safer during descent than the mechanical doohickey that J.C. has built. Not as convenient, but surefire.

"Well, the three of us—Jake, Lady Bromley-Montfort, and I—still have to decide how long we should stay up here," says the Deacon through iced whiskers. "We're using the oxygen tanks for sleep and to help us when we feel seedy at night, but it's a losing game just to stay here using up the English air. It'll just mean more O-two rigs will have to be portered up for our real work at Camps Five and Six...not to mention any chance at a summit bid or for a sustained search for

Lord Percival and Meyer... and we have only so many in reserve. Any thoughts about what we three do next?"

I'm actively surprised that the Deacon is putting this to a vote, or seeming to. Both his military background and personality usually lead him to take charge in any situation. And in Darjeeling we'd all agreed—even Reggie—that he'd be in charge when it came to the climbing part of the expedition.

Into the brief silence Jean-Claude says, "I think I can get Tenzing as low as he needs to be today and still climb back up here to Camp Four before nightfall. I can also relay orders to Pasang and everyone else as to who carries what up in relays as soon as the weather clears a little."

"You can do all that descending and re-climbing," says Reggie, "in this blizzard? In this wind? In this cold?"

Jean-Claude shrugs. "I believe so. I've done similar trips in similar weather in the Alps... and without the fixed ropes that we have in place now on both the ice wall and glacier. I'll get new batteries for my Welsh miner's lamp for the last part up here in the dark."

"All right," says the Deacon. "I suggest we follow Jean-Claude's plan, get Tenzing as low as he needs to be today, move Tejbir down so we have some extra space for the next group of Sherpas carrying from here to Camp Five. But only for the next twenty-four to thirty-six hours—the four of us shouldn't stay here longer than that. What do you all think?"

Again I'm surprised he's putting it to a vote. I tell myself that it shows how much the Deacon respects our opinion.

"I agree," says Reggie. "It's Saturday morning. If this wind and snow haven't disappeared or died down sufficiently by Monday morning, I vote we all go down—at least as low as Camp Two. The Sherpas can just damned well make room for us or go down to Base Camp."

"Tomorrow, Sunday, is the seventeenth of May," Jean-Claude says in a small voice.

The Deacon only stares at him.

"The day you designated as our summit day, *Ree-shard.*"

The Deacon's only response is to run his bare hand through his wet beard. Much of the ice has remained there, but some has melted.

J.C. begins pulling on his outer layers. "I'll go get Tenzing and Tejbir and start down now. Reggie, it's your choice, but I suggest that you move into the Whymper here until we get more people back up the mountain to the Col. Every little bit of body heat helps the cause. When I get back, it will be four of us here. The Sherpas I bring can have the other tent."

"I agree," she says. "I'll go get my things and let Tenzing and Tejbir know they're going with you, Jean-Claude. I'll be back in a minute and...oh...I'm bringing a book to read...Dickens's *Bleak House.* I presume that it will be safe from search or seizure?"

The Deacon only smiles ruefully and scratches at his wet beard.

I awaken the next morning at 3:30 a.m. to the tripping of the little brass watch hammer vibrating over my heart. Immediately I become aware that there's something missing...something wrong.

The wind has died away. Not a sound except the rasp of the others breathing. The tent walls are lined with the frost from our breath, but those walls aren't moving. The air is very, very cold. I listen harder but can hear neither wind nor the previously constant background noise of blowing snow hitting canvas.

I pull on my boots and down jacket as quietly as I can, slither out of my bag, and try to slip out the door without waking anyone. Jean-Claude had returned after dark, at almost ten p.m. He reported that he'd delivered Tenzing to four Sherpas at Camp II to be brought down to Base Camp with no difficulty, and then he drank nearly two full thermoses of water we'd set aside for him and fell asleep almost before he was in his bag.

Outside, I stretch and take a few careful steps away from the snow-heaped tents. Too many steps and I'll be in crevasse territory or near the edge of the Col. When I'm sure I'm on safe ground, I pause and look down and up and around.

What an incredible sight.

The moon is waning somewhere between half and quarter full, but there's enough light from that bright sliver and from the full sky of stars to make the snow slopes and summit of Changtse behind me and Everest above me glow white and bright as if generating their own cold lunar radiance. To the north, below the Col, heavy moonlit cloud masses churn in the milky light, surging as thick as overflowing cream to within 200 or 300 feet of the top of the North Col. Camp III and every-thing below is socked in — as I would later hear my biplane-pilot friends use the term — but the sky up here is bright with stars and the moon. Farther to the north, rising out of the clouds like the finned spine of some great glowing saurian thing, I can see a procession of snow-topped 8,000-meter peaks marching deep into Tibet, perhaps into China.

"An impressive view, isn't it?"

I just about jump off the Col at the sound of the soft voice behind me. The Deacon's been standing there all this time.

"How long have you been up?" I whisper.

"A while."

"Is that the monsoon piling up down there?"

The Deacon-shadow shakes its head. "Remember, the monsoon comes from the west and south. That's just the storm from the north that's been bothering us. There's a lot of weather from the north until about ten days to a week before the monsoon arrives from the west. That week or so is the best climbing weather of the year for Everest."

He pours something from a thermos and hands me the cup. I drink it greedily: tepid Ovaltine.

"Do you think we're in that window of good weather?" I whisper.

"Hard to tell, Jake. But I think we should push on to Camp Five to-day."

I sip my drink and nod. "Shall I wake the others?"

"No, let them sleep," whispers the Deacon. "Jean-Claude's worn out. I notice that Reggie's not sleeping well... had to use the oxygen repeat-edly. I'll make breakfast for you climbers starting in an hour. You can sleep until five or so."

"'You climbers'?" I repeat. "Aren't you climbing to Camp Five to-day?"

"I don't think so." He's speaking to me, but his eyes are constantly scanning the moonlit North Ridge, the North East Ridge, and the sum-mit of Everest. "With luck, the two Meade tents that we positioned there will still be up there waiting for you. You and Reggie and Jean-Claude can settle in and prepare for the search for Bromley. I think to do a search in the right way, we'll also have to have a Camp Six as close to twenty-seven thousand feet as we can. I'll go down when you three start climbing and come back up later today with Pasang and the strongest Tigers. We'll use Jean-Claude's bicycle apparatus to get heavy loads up to the North Col and then repack food, oxygen rigs, and at least one tent for the highest camp and get it to you tomorrow morning. Monday."

"Today's summit day," I whisper. "The seventeenth."

I can see the Deacon's teeth gleam in the moonlight. "If it weren't for this search, it could be. All four of us push straight on and make the bid for the summit, returning to Camp Five by dark."

"But you're not going to do that? I thought you—the three of us—were going to make a dash for the summit and search afterward. What made you change your mind?"

The thin shadow shakes its hooded head. "I could lie to Lady Bromley-Montfort and tell her that we'd look for her cousin's remains on the way down from the summit, but I've been up above twenty-six thousand feet, Jake. She was right in Darjeeling. One shot at the highest ridges on Everest and this damned mountain just takes everything out of you. One day you're filled with adrenaline and ready to go for the summit come hell or high water. The next day, Sherpas are helping you stagger down to Base Camp—your energy gone, your heart enlarged, your eyes half-blinded, and your toes and fingers frozen. I almost set the summit dash for today, but I promised the lady that we'd search for Percival, and we'll spend a couple of days doing just that before we decide if we're still strong enough for a summit attempt."

I look up at the snow-to-black whaleback of the North Ridge rising steeply above us. I haven't brought an oxygen rig out, and I find myself gasping for breath just to keep standing there. Part of me is relieved at this reprieve—I don't want to disappear up on those heights the way Mallory and Irvine did last year—but a larger part of me is bitterly disappointed. This may be the end of our summit dreams. *Why has the Deacon changed his mind at this late date? Our goal has always been to climb the damn mountain.*

"That will mean a lot of time spent above eight thousand meters," I finally say aloud.

"Probably too much." He seems to be acknowledging that he's decided to throw away our best chance at climbing Mount Everest, but he's not telling me why he's decided this. Especially so late in the game. I can *see* the North East Ridge gleaming like a highway of diamonds far above us. All the way to the summit. And no hint of the usual killer winds.

"Do you think there's much chance of actually finding Lord Percival?" I manage at last.

"No," says the Deacon. "Not one chance in a hundred would be my guess. But we promised we'd try. We took Lady Bromley's money."

I have nothing to say to that. I hand back my empty cup, and he screws it onto the top of the thermos.

"Go get some more sleep, Jake. Take a few whiffs of good old English air, stay warm, and sleep if you can. I'll wake you when I get breakfast heating on the Unna cooker."

Before crawling back into the tent, I take a final look around at the magical landscape: Everest and its lesser attendant peaks glowing in the starlight, clouds clustered below the level of the North Col, only the slightest visible streamer of spindrift coming off the summit of the ultimate peak we're climbing toward in a few hours. For the first time since we've set out from England, part of me feels, with real assurance rather than abstract bravado—*We could have climbed this damned mountain today. We still can climb it in the next couple of days if we don't waste a lot of time hunting for a dead man. It's possible.*

Sunday, May 17, 1925

As it turns out, it's just Reggie and me plodding up this granite-slabbed rib toward Camp V today.

Jean-Claude had admitted that he wasn't feeling so well—"a bit seedy," he'd said, borrowing the Deacon's English phrase—and we all decided that he should go down with the Deacon to help organize the load carrying to the North Col and then come up to Camps V and VI the next day.

"It will give me a chance to use my bicycle," says J.C.

I don't believe I've taken the time to describe the contraption that Jean-Claude hauled all the way across Tibet in pieces and dutifully assembled our first day up on the North Col. The device did have bicycle parts—a bicycle seat, pedals, gears, bicycle chains—but it also had an upholstered backrest (since the person on the contraption would be pedaling it while lying almost on his back, knees higher than his head) and metal support struts that went out six feet in four directions, each anchored deeply into the ice shelf with ice screws, hammered pitons, and a spiderweb of ropes. That bicycle-doodad wasn't going to fall off that narrow shelf unless the North Col glacier itself calved off a huge piece.

A meter or so above the pedals, a nine-foot metal arm—J.C. had brought the components in three-foot sections—had been bolted together to become a sturdy horizontal flange, also reinforced by multiple tie-downs, which held a third bicycle gear and pulley assembly.

We'd only had time to test it with two loads before the storm came in on Friday, but the bicycle worked well, in its own crude way. In the

1924 expedition, Sherpas had dropped ropes to haul loads up the chimney Mallory had climbed in the final 200-foot ice wall, but the loads had to be fairly light. Pedaling with one's legs and feet, with leverage gained through reduction gears, was infinitely easier than using one's back and arms, and the loads tied onto the continuously circulating 400-foot strand of Deacon's Miracle Rope could weigh up to fifty or sixty pounds. The bicycle was serious exercise above 23,000 feet, there was no denying that, but we'd each tried it out, and with two men—one to pedal and the other to untie and dump the loads as they came up to the level of the ice shelf—moving entire tons of matériel up to the North Col was now a real possibility, without endless lines of load-hauling Sherpas gasping and wheezing and constantly resting on the rope ladder or fixed ropes.

"If I'd just been able to haul in a small petrol-powered generator," said Jean-Claude.

But J.C. is ill and recovering lower today, so it is just Reggie and me working our way up the slabs toward sunrise and Camp V this fine Sunday morning. The last thing Jean-Claude whispered to me before we left camp, Reggie yards away and preoccupied with getting the flow valve working right on her hissing oxygen set, was—"Besides, *mon ami,* the Deacon, Tenzing, and Tejbir put only two small two-man tents up at Camp Five. With my luck, I'd end up sleeping alone."

Reggie and I haven't roped up and I'm not sure why. I suppose it is because the first few hundred yards up the snowfields from the North Col were just a kick-step exercise, and above that we've been on these damned black granite slabs that require little more than giant steps up very high curbs to ascend. The few arêtes and serious rock outcroppings we've come up against on the ridgeline are easily avoided by traversing out onto the equally downward-tilting granite slabs of the North Face until we've climbed up and around the rock outcroppings and moved back left to the broad ridgeline.

This is not to say that a fall from this North Ridge—or what the Deacon sometimes calls the North East Shoulder (as opposed to the North East Ridge far above that leads to the summit)—would not be a serious problem.

The winds are intermittent this predawn morning, unlike the constant gales that the Deacon and his two Sherpas encountered on Friday. Those three had been forced to lean forward into the hurricane-force wind so far that their heads were lower than their knees and their noses almost touching the rock slabs in front of them. Reggie and I can walk hunched forward just slightly—like French and British infantry I've heard about at the Battle of the Somme leaning forward as if into a wind while walking into enemy machine gun fire—but the occasional gust rocks us back on our heels and makes us pinwheel our arms for balance. Of course, a backwards topple here will be one hell of a topple. At one place on the ridge, the winds suddenly seem to batter us from both directions at once, and Reggie has to fall forward, her mittened hands seeking a grip on the icy slab in front of her, rather than let the wind tumble her backward for a long, long, long fall.

We should be roped up. I *know* it—every bit of mountaineering sense and experience I have tells us that we should—but for some reason I can't seem to suggest it to her or insist upon it. Maybe it seems like too personal a suggestion.

For the first time, I appreciate the problem that the Deacon and his two Sherpas—and both the high-climbing British expeditions before this—had dealt with in finding a place for tents. To our right, the west, the edges of the steep ridge and the North Face itself are exposed to the full force of the near-constant winds perpetually blowing from the northwest. A tent wouldn't survive an hour there. But there is no flat place to pitch a tent, even a small tent, on the west side of the North Ridge at any rate.

To our left, the east, the ridgeline blocks some of the wind, but there is nothing on that side of the ridge other than very steep and very exposed slopes, snow couloirs that end abruptly in 5,000-foot drops to the main Rongbuk Glacier, the couloirs dappled with a giant jumble-maze of tilted rock in which a climber could quickly get lost, especially in bad conditions.

The Deacon and Mallory in '22 and Mallory in '24 had been worried about descending climbers taking a wrong turn into one of these dead-end, sheer-drop couloirs, and for that reason, Reggie and I are carrying more red-flagged bamboo wands this morning, embedding them deep along the main route wherever someone descending in a snowstorm might be tempted to take a wrong turn toward eternity.

We continue climbing toward the sunlight, our Crooke's glass goggles still up on our leather-covered foreheads. The summit of Everest has been glowing gold since not long after we moved from snow to rock on the North Ridge, and now the tips of Changtse, Makalu, Chomolonzo, and other nearby high peaks blaze with light even while snowy summits far to our north also begin to welcome the morning. I'm eager for the band of morning light to reach our lower altitude along the ridge because it's just so damned cold; even with all the new down clothing and felt-layered boots, only near-constant motion fights off the body's insistence on losing core heat at this altitude, and near-constant movement is all but impossible.

The Deacon has demonstrated for all of us his and Mallory's high-altitude trick of taking a deep breath—inhaling deeper and for a longer time than seems natural—then taking a step, exhaling while you pause, then inhaling deeply for the next step. But since both Reggie and I are using oxygen at the lower flow rate of 1.5 liters per minute, we can't do this as dramatically as the Deacon has demonstrated for us. The regulators won't allow it. Still, early on, Reggie and I loosen our masks long enough to try to make a full twenty paces before stopping completely to wheeze and gasp, but the best we've been able to do—on snow or these rock slabs—is thirteen short paces. And our pausing-to-breathe stops are growing longer and more frequent with every 100 feet of altitude we gain.

I keep looking down and around, rather than watching my feet as I should. I can't help it. I've always loved the views from anywhere high, and nothing in my experience—nothing in my short life—has come close to this view from the North Shoulder of Everest as we approach 25,000 feet. The East Rongbuk Glacier valley, which holds our Camps I through III behind us, is still filled with heavy gray clouds that broil and roil and tumble over each other in the lower storm's unsuccessful attempt to haul its heavy moisture-filled mass as high as the North Col. The air is so clear up here above those clouds that peaks 50 miles away look like they're almost within reaching distance below and behind us. When I lean far over, I can see Camp IV on the North Col through the

V of my down-covered and duck-canvased legs, the green tents already mere dark specks on the white snow saddle.

At the Deacon's and J.C.'s urging, Reggie and I are doing this entire climb—including all the steep hiking up these interminable rock slabs—while wearing our 12-point crampons. At first I felt nervous climbing on rock with crampons rather than having solid boot soles beneath me—and the danger of catching the front points and tripping *is* always there if you quit thinking about how to lift your feet at each step—but after two or three hours of ascending, I'm clearly seeing the advantage of staying in crampons. There's as much real contact with the rock as there would be with hobnailed boots, but the transitions to patches of snow and ice are much easier; you can kick your toe points in and keep climbing at the same rate as on bare rocks. Also, few of these rocks are actually bare; despite the high winds, the snows have left a thin glaze of ice on most of them. The crampons cut through and into that ice in a secure way that no hobnails ever could.

We're using our long ice axes, of course, and every thirteen steps both of us pause and bend almost double, leaning on the axes as we hungrily let the oxygen sets hiss air into our laboring lungs. We're carrying three O_2 tanks each—planning to use only one each on our way to Camp V—but rather than climbing with the metal oxygen rigs, we're using the special rucksacks that Jean-Claude has adapted. It took a few more minutes to get ready with the rucksacks—oxygen lines and regulator valves have to be slipped through strategically placed holes that then lace up tightly—but we're carrying extra food, clothes, and several other items that would have been unwieldy crammed into gas mask holders dangling on our chest or from our shoulders. I certainly feel the weight of the three tanks and their associated valves, hoses, and gear, but the total, thanks to both Mr. Irvine's and Monsieur Clairoux's alterations, is still under 30 pounds even with our load of extra items. And that includes another 10-pound Meade two-man tent we're each carrying segments of.

The sun reaches us. I realize that the Michelin Man figure next to me is gesturing for me to put on my goggles; hers are already in place. I hate to do it because the special glass distorts colors and makes me feel—along with the damned oxygen mask—locked away in a different world, like a man in a heavy, metal-helmeted diving suit. But she's right. We're on a long stretch of rising slabs and low rock pinnacles now, not a snowfield around, but that won't save us from snow blindness at this altitude. The ultraviolet rays alone will blind you if you climb too long, even on dark rock. Under our top layer of Shackleton anoraks, Reggie and I are carrying undersized military binoculars. These aren't usually necessary for climbing on Everest, but they may help in the search for her cousin Percival. She hasn't brought her glasses out yet, and I've seen nothing on the North Face to my right to make me reach for mine. Once when we pause to break a piece of chocolate and try to melt it in our mouths, I ask her if she's been looking.

"Both sides of the ridge," she gasps around the chocolate. "But... remember... Pasang and I looked... carefully... up to... Camp Five... last August. No sign... then... either."

I'd almost forgotten that this climb to Camp V, so novel for me, was old territory for Lady Bromley-Montfort.

When we'd asked the Deacon how long it would take us to reach Camp V from the North Col, he'd given us the almost laughably precise number of five hours and ten minutes. But as with all things Deaconish, he's actually gone through the records of the men in '22 and '24, including himself, climbing between Camp IV and Camp V while using oxygen, and come up with that exact figure.

After five hours and twelve minutes of climbing, we see the two small tents of the Deacon-established new Camp V just a few dozen yards above us.

My first thought is *You must be kidding.*

This is the worst campsite I've ever seen. In truth, there's no campsite *here.* There's a slight broadening of the slope, and in an area partially protected from rockfall and the wind by a high rock ridge, the Deacon and Tenzing Bothia and Tejbir Norgay have moved a few rocks to create two absurdly tilted platforms *smaller than the tents that are set on them.*

And the two small Meade tents aren't even at the same level. One is off to the right of our line of ascent, tilting on the edge of nothing, and the other is in an even more precarious position 30 or so feet higher and to the left. This second tent literally hangs out over nothing—5,000 feet of open air to the main Rongbuk Glacier. For a moment I think this is some sort of sick joke prepared by the Deacon and his two Sherpas. *We can't spend a night here,* I think. *This is fucking impossible.*

But then I see why the Deacon's chosen the places he did; the rock ridge is good protection for the lower tent, while the more exposed-looking higher one has a web of heavy rope lines wrapped around three large boulders set next to it. There is new snow piled up on the windward side of each green tent, but neither one has collapsed or blown away.

Still, I can't believe that we're going to trust our lives to, much less actually close our eyes for a moment of sleep on, the slab slope of either of these insanely positioned sites.

But scan the ridge and mountain face as I may through my thick goggles, I can find no other possible tent sites.

Reggie turns around and sits on one of the large down-tilting slabs next to the lower tent. She turns off her oxygen flow and pulls down her mask. I do the same. The effect of drowning—of not getting enough oxygen to draw a full breath—is immediate and panic inducing. But it passes.

In slow motion, like one of the undersea divers I'd been imagining earlier, Reggie unlaces the tent's door—the opening is toward the rock wall and *away* from the steep drop—and bends over to peer in.

"Sleeping...bags...and...everything's here just where...the Deacon... and the porters...left it," she says between audible pants. "Unna cooker and...Meta bricks, too. But...lots of...spindrift. Inside the...sleeping bags...we may be wet."

Shit. Well, we've brought our own bags. The sun is so bright now that, out of the wind, it's almost warm. I unzip my outer down jacket.

"Whisk...broom," I manage and pat an outside pocket on the left side of my rucksack.

Reggie nods, retrieves the tiny broom, and somehow finds the energy to lean into the tent and brush most of the snow out. She turns the sleeping bags inside out and drags them out into the sunlight, weighting them down with rocks as protection against the occasional gusts of wind.

Then she pulls an altitude barometer from some inside pocket and consults it. "Twenty-five thousand two hundred fifty feet plus or minus two hundred feet or so given the weather," she says and has to pant for air. I realize that she's pointing downhill toward something to our left.

It takes me a minute to see it. Two patches of torn and tumbled green canvas on a snowy steep patch of rock. "Camp Five...in 'twenty-two...," she says.

It gives me a certain stupid sense of satisfaction to know that we've come 200 or 300 feet higher than the iron men of the 1922 expedition before setting up our own camp.

"Where are the...tents...from...'twenty-four?" I ask.

Reggie shrugs. She's said that she climbed to the site of the '24 Camp V with Pasang last summer, so I suspect she knows where that site was but is too tired to tell me at the moment.

Whichever tent or tents we choose to spend the night in—and the thought of being in either precarious perch in a high wind makes my scrotum contract—I have a good sense from the Deacon's and Norton's and the others' reports as to what the rest of this day will be like.

First, Reggie and I will get out our little list of necessaries—there's already an Unna cooker here, so we'll save ours for the higher camp to-morrow—and crawl into or onto our sleeping bags, luxuriating in the false sense of warmth under the sun-warmed tent canvas. Too exhausted to do anything constructive, we'll just lie in our respective bags and stu-pors for forty-five minutes to an hour, perhaps taking the rare shot of English air to offset the headaches already roiling in our skulls like the shifting cloud mass in the East Rongbuk Glacier valley so far below.

Then one of us—I hope to God it's Reggie—will find the energy to crawl, with frequent rests and more frequent groans, out of her bag, out of her daytime tent, and across the terribly steep slope to the near-est patch of clean snow—about ten paces from this tent, only about four paces from the hanging-over-nothing tent above us to the left—and will use the last of her energy to fill two big aluminum pots with snow.

Then we'll take turns groaning and moaning as we work together to light the damned Meta burner and to open some tins and bags of food—not a small accomplishment at this altitude—taking two hours to prepare a dinner we don't want: pemmican, perhaps, or some bully beef (which the Deacon must be fond of, since he packed so much of it), and then "boil" some lukewarm tea with lots of sugar and condensed milk.

I gag just thinking about it. Perhaps I'll just sleep all day and night instead. We still have water in our thermoses. That will do me until to-morrow. Or forever. Whichever comes first.

So I'm amazed—beyond amazed—when Reggie says, "What do you say . . . to going . . . up to . . . Camp Six?"

"Today?" I manage in little more than a squeak.

She nods, pulls a delicate lady's watch from somewhere under her unzipped Finch duvet, and says, "It's not quite noon. The Deacon says . . . they climbed from Camp Five . . . to Camp Six . . . in just un-der . . . four and a half hours. We can be there long before . . . . dark."

For a moment I'm certain that this is sheer bravado, that Reggie can't be serious, but then I look at her sunburned face and beautiful eyes above the tugged-down oxygen mask and beneath the raised goggles and real-ize that she's totally serious.

"They made that climb . . . starting . . . in the morning," I say. "When they were rested."

Reggie shakes her head, and I see curls of her blue-black hair trying to escape the wool cap she wears under the goose down hood. "You don't really rest . . . up this high. Just . . . hurt. Lie . . . awake. We might as well do it . . . seventeen hundred feet . . . higher . . . tonight. Start hunting for . . . Percy . . . in the morning. Come *down*hill."

"The Deacon and J.C. will expect us to be here . . . at . . . Camp Five," I manage.

Reggie shrugs. "I'll write them a note." She takes a small leather note-book and small pencil from an inner pocket.

Jesus Christ, I'm thinking. *She really means it!*

I play my trump card. She will have no answer to this. It will save our lives . . . or at least *my* life. "There's no . . . Camp Six . . . *up there,*" I say, trying to fake a sound of regret in my voice. "We wouldn't know where . . . to put one. We couldn't . . . get one . . . set up before nightfall. We'll die . . . of exposure."

"Oh, nonsense," says Reggie. She's writing busily. Then she pushes the partially dried sleeping bags back into the tilted tent and shows me the note before setting it atop the closest bag, weighting it with a rock. The brief note, our death warrant I am sure, reads *At Camp V at noon. Both well. Decided to go up to establish VI around 27,000. Will begin search on Face in morning. —Reggie.*

She ties the tent flaps closed, and we gasp and moan getting to our feet. I have a second of vertigo that almost sends me headfirst the 2,000-plus feet down to the North Col, my arms flapping like vestigial wings on some flightless bird. Nothing between here and the drop-off beneath us would stop me if I did tumble backward. I continue to teeter groggily, flailing my arms in a vain attempt to find my balance, and then feel Reggie's firm hand on my upper arm, holding me in place.

When I find my balance and some semblance of normal breathing, she slaps me on the shoulder as if nothing had happened.

"We can dump the first oxygen...tank...when it empties," she says before pulling her mask back up. "Maybe we should use less...of the air...for the second part...of the climb. Have more...for...tomorrow."

"Sure," I pant over the top of my own mask. "Whatever...you say...ma'am."

We turn around, facing up the impossibly steep heap of murderously slippery black granite slabs and snow, and prepare to take our first thirteen steps. Almost 6,000 feet above us, the West Face of Everest's snowy Summit Pyramid begins to glow in the very cold and increasingly low early afternoon light. Spindrift is again being hurled out for miles to the southeast. I start to imagine what the wind will be like up at 27,000 feet, our destination just a few hundred feet below the Yellow Band that is the last physical landmark and dividing line beneath the North East Ridge and that straight—if almost certainly impossible—ridgeline route to that summit. But then I have to shut down my imagination or just sit on a boulder and start weeping like a child.

We take our first of thirteen steps.

Monday, May 18, 1925

"Jake," Reggie says softly, "if you're awake, you might want to see this."

I'm awake all right. Our "Camp VI" is a sad joke—the small 10-pound two-pole Meade tent precariously perched on a tilting slab so steep that we had to set our feet against the boulder that anchored the downhill end of the tent and sleep on an incline so steep that it felt as if we were half-standing. At least I'd thought to tie down an extra blanket on the flat face of the slab while we were lashing and weighting the tent to the side of the mountain, so the pure cold of this alien world at 27,000 feet hadn't completely flowed up and into us from the cold rock all night.

I'd slept a few minutes during the darkness. I'd also been vaguely aware that, cocooned in our bags as we were, Reggie and I were still huddling together—rather like two passengers crowding together for warmth on the packed upper deck of an oddly tilted British double-decker bus on a London winter day. At least the winds were mild during the night. The suspense of waiting to be blown off this ridiculous excuse for a perch wouldn't have allowed me even my few moments of half-sleep.

"Okay," I say and sit up for the terrible ordeal of pulling on outer layers and boots that have stayed with me in the bag all night. My only concession to hygiene is to put on the last pair of clean cotton undersocks that are in my rucksack. It helps psychologically, if in no other way.

I crawl out of the uphill end of the tent. It's like coming up and out of a hoar-frosted tunnel. Or perhaps it's more like being born and finding out that you're on the moon.

The band of sunlight has just moved down across our happy little home at 27,000 feet and I realize that the hissing noise I've been hearing for a while now isn't snow, it is the last of the Unna cookers and Meta fuel blocks working to melt pathetically small pots of snow, one after the other. It must have been working for a while now, because Reggie — decked out in all her layers and sitting on her folded-up sleeping bag, boots braced against a ridge in a slab to keep her from sliding off the mountain — has already filled three of our thermoses with...something tepid.

I try to remember the boiling point of water at 27,000 feet — 164 and some decimal degrees Fahrenheit? 162? — anyway, something so cool that before long, if we keep climbing, it seems the water will be boiling in the pot without any burner under it.

Actually, I vaguely remember George Finch saying that if we humans ever managed to get into outer space — totally above the atmosphere — our blood would boil in our veins and brains even while the temperature on the shaded side of our bodies might be more than 200 degrees below zero Fahrenheit. "Of course," Finch had added to make us feel better (it was while we were eating dessert at the four-star Zurich restaurant), "you wouldn't have to worry about your blood boiling in outer space, since your lungs and bodies would already have exploded like those poor deep-sea creatures we dredge up from the depths from time to time."

That had put me off my pudding.

I haul my sleeping bag up the slab slope to sit next to Reggie. As I'm tucking it under my butt, my boots slip — I haven't put on crampons yet because my fingers aren't up to all the strap-tying — and Reggie has to steady me with a firm hand again before my heels can find another wedge of rock to hold the rest of me in place. We'd had to move slightly onto the North Face to find even this pathetic campsite. There'd been no sign of Mallory and Irvine's Camp VI from last year; we may have missed seeing it in the long shadows, rock mazes, and swirling snow at dusk. And while the Face here next to the North Ridge and just below the Yellow Band doesn't seem all that steep — perhaps the 35- to 40-degree slate roof of the church that George Mallory had so famously climbed as a boy would be a good comparison—one real slip might well keep one falling the 6,000 feet or so to the East Rongbuk Glacier.

"How do you feel, Jake?" I realize that she's not using oxygen, and I'm glad I haven't yet dragged my overnight oxygen tank out of the tent.

"Great," I say dully. If my skull had been stuffed with wool down at Camp V altitude, up here at Camp VI it was mostly empty except for pain . . . and thinking or speaking is enough to cause that pain to leap and cavort.

"You coughed all night," says Reggie.

I'd noticed that. The constant cough—caused, I presume, by the un-believable dryness that reaches into the smallest vesicles in your lungs and dries up the mucus in your throat at this altitude—sometimes makes you feel that you're literally going to cough your guts up.

"Just the cold air," I say. In truth, I feel that there's something solid stuck in my throat. It's a nauseating thought and I try not to dwell on it.

Reggie opens her arms. "I thought you might like to see the sunrise."

"Oh . . . yeah . . . thanks," I mumble.

My God, it's beautiful. Part of my malfunctioning brain and warmth-desiring soul is dimly aware of this beauty. After a moment, both the reality of what I'm seeing and a bit of the rising sun's warmth begin to sink into the semi-ambulatory chunk of frozen, coughing, shivering flesh that I've become.

At this moment, Lady Katherine Christina Regina Bromley-Montfort and I are, without any doubt, the highest people on the planet to be touched by the rising sun. I look to my left and crane my aching neck to gaze up at the summit of Everest—so close! so infinitely far away!—just 2,000 impossible feet above, less than a mile of ridgeline to the west of us now, and the radiance of the sun shining a benediction on the reddish rock of the summit. The gleaming snowfields of the Summit Pyramid below the final vertical section to that summit look like something di-vine, something not of this world.

This altitude is not *of this world,* I think dully. *We humans are not meant or evolved to be up here,* I think, with some small sense of panic stirring in me. At the same time, a totally contradictory thought rises to the sur-face: I'm *meant to be here. I've waited all my life for this.*

What had John Keats said about Negative Capability—holding two opposite ideas in one's mind at the same time without straining to reconcile them? Beats me. Maybe it hadn't been Keats at all...maybe it had been Yeats or Thomas Jefferson or Edison. Wait...what was I just thinking about?

"Here, drink some of this," says Reggie and hands me one of the thermoses. "It's not hot, but it has caffeine in it."

The tepid coffee almost makes me gag, but I decide that vomiting this stuff all over Reggie wouldn't be the proper way to thank her for getting up before dawn at the top of the world to heat my morning coffee.

I realize that from time to time Reggie has been using the binoculars slung around her neck to scan the slopes below us.

"Anything?" I say.

"There's just enough snow on the North Face...to make...every rock and boulder in it look like a human body at first glimpse." She lowers the binoculars. "No. Nothing to see yet. Except those two human beings climbing directly towards us."

"What?" I say and borrow her binoculars. It takes me a minute to find what she's talking about, even with her pointing to help, since the objects are just gray specks moving slowly against gray-black rock along the ridge. It's only when they move in front of the occasional small snowfield that I actually realize that the specks are alive and climbing.

"The Deacon leading," I say.

"And Jean-Claude?"

"No, the second man on the rope is too tall for J.C. It must be a very tall Sherpa whom the Deacon is...wait! It's Pasang!"

She takes the glasses back. I watch her face light up with pleasure. Somehow, that view is a perfect complement to the world of warming blue sky, clouds far below us in the valleys, huge glaciers visible winding back upon themselves where there are no low clouds, and scores of summits 20,000 feet and more in altitude igniting with the sun's rays one after another like a series of tall, white candles being lit by an invisible altar boy. Below each newly lighted candle lies the white altar cloth of countless glaciers, ridges, and pristine snowfields.

It takes another half hour for the two figures to reach us—during much of the last part of that climb they are hidden from us as they work their way through the maze of gullies that starts about 1,000 feet below the Yellow Band and continues to the ridgeline above us—but then, suddenly, they're with us. Waiting for our friends to reach our altitude has given Reggie and me time to eat a hearty breakfast—some English biscuits, bits of chocolate, a few spoonfuls of semi-thawed macaroni, and then a bit more chocolate and coffee. Reggie and I haven't been conversing—the silence is what a writer type such as I'd once imagined myself to be (at least until I met that Hemingway fellow in Paris) might describe as "companionable." So I content myself with trying to get my groggy brain in gear by naming the summits already glowing with light: the cliffs and North Peak of Everest itself, of course; the snowy top of what must be Kanchenjunga far to the east; Cho Oyu to the west; Lhotse just beginning to catch the light to the south; the more distant Gyankar range slowly changing from intangible shadow to granite solidity in the sun's rays; and far, far away, peering at us over the now visible curve of the earth, some incredibly high peak in Central Tibet. I have no idea what it might be.

Then the Deacon and Pasang are here, still roped together on 60 feet of Deacon Miracle Rope. Reggie and I exchange pleasurably guilty glances about this—we never did rope together during the previous day's climb, not even after we moved out onto the North Face or had to claw our way up through the gullies, using our hands in some steep places. I can't quite understand why that little secret between us pleases me so much.

"It's not even seven a.m.," says Reggie. "When on earth...did you leave? And from where?"

Pasang's oxygen mask has been dangling free of his face for the entire time I'd been able to see him through the binoculars. I doubt that he's run out of O_2, since I can see the tops of two tanks poking out of his rucksack. Those should easily have got him up from the North Col, even at the high-flow rate. And it's certainly not like Dr. Pasang to show off. Perhaps he can just climb higher than us Europeans without *needing* the bottled oxygen. Whatever the fact of it may be, the Deacon has been wearing his mask until they arrive at our slab and find solid footing, but now shuts off the flow valve, lowers his mask, and stands gasping for a long moment before replying to Reggie's question.

"Left...a little after...two a.m.," he manages. "Camp...Five. Got there...yesterday...afternoon."

I look at the Welsh miner's lamp rigs still strapped over their wool caps just under their goose down hoods and have to smile. Between George Finch's goose down garments, J.C.'s crampons and various other inventions, the Deacon's new ropes and careful logistics, and my dashing, daring enthusiasm, we've all brought something special to this fourth and by far smallest expedition to Mount Everest. But it's been Lady Bromley-Montfort's damned miner's lamps and idea of beginning the climb in the middle of the night, whether there's a full moon out or not, that's probably made the biggest difference in how high we'll get.

"You made good time," says Reggie. She unfurls her sleeping bag so that it's at the Deacon's feet. "Have a seat, gentlemen. But make sure your boot soles and heels have a good grip on something first."

Pasang grins and continues standing, turning to look out at the view, then turning again to look at the Yellow Band, North East Ridge, and Summit Pyramid of Everest itself all looming so deceptively close above us. The Deacon takes great care in removing his rucksack—in 1922, he'd once told us, Howard Somervell had been somewhere around 26,000 feet when he'd carelessly set his pack down only to watch it fall 9,000 feet to the main Rongbuk Glacier—and propping it between two small boulders behind him as he slowly seats himself. Neither man has put on goggles yet; the Deacon's face is burned so dark by high-altitude sunlight that he and Pasang might have passed for brothers.

"We...made good time," the Deacon says at last, "because some...incredibly thoughtful...persons strung...hundreds of feet of...fixed rope on the few steep...parts." He nods his thanks in our direction. "The red-flagged bamboo wands...through the...gullies were also...a...welcome touch."

"It seemed the least we could do since we were coming this way anyway," says Reggie with another warming smile.

"It's good you...came up here a...day early," says the Deacon. "Gives us a full extra day for searching the North Face."

"We're not going to search the *entire* North Face, are we?" asks Reggie. I know she's not serious.

The Deacon smiles thinly and gestures downward. I notice that his lips are cracked and bleeding.

"We'll follow the plan...of imagining a huge trapezoid...running down from the North East Ridge from...where the North Ridge meets it near the First Step." He shifts awkwardly to look up toward the First Step, only the top of which is visible from this vantage point, and says, "My God, it all seems possible from here, does it not, Jake? But that *verdammte* Second Step..."

Reggie hands him her binoculars and the Deacon studies the Second Step the way I had earlier. "A bit of a rock-climbing problem, that," he says. "But of course, that's why we brought you along, Jake. You're our leader on rock."

"'A bit of a rock-climbing problem'!" I exclaim. "I've been looking at that damned Second Step through the glasses for...the better part of an hour...when I haven't been enjoying the sunrise...and it's just as Norton or whoever it was at the RGS described it. The hundred-foot-tall vertical prow of a goddamned dreadnought coming out of the mists at you." I take a few gulps of breath. "I apologize for the language, Reggie."

"As you goddamned well should," she says.

"Anyway," continues the Deacon, shucking off his overmittens and opening gloved hands toward the steep expanse of rock below us, "we'll search the trapezoid we...decided on earlier, but starting down from here, Camp Six, will be easier than climbing...from Camp Five."

"Will you two have the energy to search today?" asks Reggie.

Pasang grins again. The Deacon makes a slightly sour face.

"We still have two full oxygen tanks left," says the Deacon. "How about you two?"

"Two each," I confirm.

As if reminded, the Deacon pulls his recently depleted tank out of his rucksack and disconnects it from the valves and rubber tubing. He starts to set it carefully between jagged rocks but Reggie stops him.

"Jake and I discovered something...fun...when we discarded our first tank yesterday evening," she says.

The Deacon's eyebrows rise slightly toward his miner's lamp.

Reggie takes the tank from him, holds it high over her head with both gloved hands, and hurls it out and away from the North Face.

It hits about 60 feet down the slope, bounces another 50 or 60 feet before touching rock again, and keeps hurtling lower—a silver blur in the rich morning light—with echoing clangs that seem to go on forever. Then it disappears.

The Deacon shakes his head but grins. "If that lands on one of our Sherpa friends a mile below on the North Col, *I'm* not taking responsibility," he says. "That reminds me. There's that sheer drop-off on the Face not too far below the level of Camp Five straight below us—all the way over to the Grand Couloir. That sets... the lower boundary of our search area."

"I'll say what I said before," Reggie says softly. "That's still hundreds and hundreds of acres. *Vertical* acres."

"Not quite vertical," says the Deacon. "Thank heavens." He reaches under his now unzipped down outer layer and pulls a folded sheet of paper from some pocket. As the Deacon unfurls it, I see a more formal version of a diagram he had drawn and which we'd discussed during the trek across Tibet and again at Base Camp.

Four horizontal lines in different-colored inks go zigzagging left to right and then back again across a sketch of the North Face of Everest stretching roughly between the North Shoulder, now to our east, and the Grand Couloir hundreds of yards to our west.

"Lady Bromley-Montfort," the Deacon says formally, "you've been our prime climber so far, so if you'd be so kind as to continue on up about four hundred feet to the bottom of the Yellow Band above this basin and search from east to west along the ridge there below the Yellow Band gullies. I don't believe...you'll have to clamber up into any of the...gullies themselves. Just use your binoculars. The shelf up there sort of peters out just short of Norton's Great Couloir, so please don't go further than that. You can use the First Step on the ridge above as a guideline...just turn back before you get very far west beyond it."

Reggie nods but says, "You're not giving me the bottom of the Yellow Band because it's the widest and safest and easiest ledge to traverse up here, are you?"

"On the contrary," says the Deacon, his expression serious, "I'm giving it to you because that search route offers the longest fall. And also"—now his expression is mischievous rather than serious—"because it involves climbing and all the rest of us get to *descend.* Dr. Pasang?"

"Yes?" Pasang says. It's the first word I've heard from him today. He sounds no more breathless than if we were chatting at sea level.

"Would you be so kind as to descend a couple of hundred yards to that ill-defined rock rib..." The Deacon pauses and points it out. The "rib" is so ill-defined that it takes us all minutes to see it properly, but my guess is that it's the same traversable "horizontal ridge" that Norton and Somervell had returned from the Grand Couloir on when Norton set the world's highest climbing record of 28,600 feet last year—*known* record, that is, since no one knows how high Mallory and Irvine had climbed before dying.

"Please take that as far as it stays solid to the west, then drop down a few hundred feet and follow the best line back east toward the North Ridge," continues the Deacon. He looks up at the tall Sherpa. "You did this morning's climb brilliantly without oxygen, Pasang, but you might want to go onto English air for parts of the search. Just to help you stay alert."

"All right," says Pasang. He's shielding his eyes and looking down at the steep rooftop slabs far below that will be his broad search area.

"I'll take this large area of the basin between Dr. Pasang's so-called ill-defined rib to the level of Camp Five," says the Deacon.

"That's a large area, Richard," says Reggie. "And very steep. Very exposed."

He shrugs. "And I'll be very careful. Don't forget to keep your goggles on, my friends. Even if you're just on dark rock, remember..."

"Colonel Norton," I say.

"Yes," says the Deacon. "We'll use one tank of oxygen apiece and try to keep the second tank in reserve for tonight, but we should be back at Camp Five together by two p.m. I don't think any of us had adequate rest last night, and I...don't want...any more altitude health problems if we can help it." He looks at me. "Your cough is getting worse, Jake."

I shake my head irritably. "It'll go away when I go back on bottled air." I know it won't—my throat still feels like I've got a chicken bone caught in it—but I don't want to argue or whine.

The Deacon nods, obviously not convinced, and opens his pack. "I have something for each of you," he says and pulls out what look to be three short, wide-barreled black metal pistols.

"Dueling pistols?" says Reggie, knowing better. I'm the only one who laughs, and that soon turns into my hacking cough.

"I did not know that Very signal pistol came in such a small size," says Pasang. The Deacon is setting out colored Very shells, each not much bigger than a shotgun shell—both shells and pistols much smaller than any nautical or military Very gear I've ever seen. I'd seen the Deacon write the word on a list in London. I hadn't known why at the time, and he spelled it "Verey" for some reason (evidently it was an English thing), but I'd always seen such pistols spelled "Very," after the name of the fellow who first designed the flare guns.

"My Webley and Scott Mark Three flare pistol in the War was a blunderbuss of a thing," the Deacon is saying. "Big brass flared barrel. Fired a one-inch-caliber flare—the kind of one-inch-bore Very pistol you've probably seen, Jake. But some German boffin designed these smaller twelve-gauge Verys for night patrol work. We captured a few." He pulls his larger British-made Very pistol out of his pack to show us the comparison. It and its flare cartridges are easily twice the size of the smaller German ones laid out on the rock before us. Even in smaller size, the flare pistols have that ugly, black metal, totally functional German look to them.

"So," I say, feeling sarcastic this fine morning at 27,000 feet on the North Face of Mount Everest, "the army just let you walk off with three of the smaller German ones and your larger British Very pistol? How generous!"

"I admit I did walk off with the big one," says the Deacon. "No one thought to ask for it back and I didn't remind them. A lot of that was going on during the demobilization. The smaller ones for you—and I gave Jean-Claude his yesterday—I purchased via mail order from the Erma-Erfurt Company before they went out of business."

"How do we use them?" asks Reggie, all business now. She's picked up one of the pistols and—showing her familiarity with firearms—has broken open the breach to make sure it isn't loaded. She fingers the smaller, color-coded 12-gauge shells lying atop the flat rock next to the Deacon's hand.

"You see, the flares come in three colors—red, green, and what we called 'white star' during the War," continues the Deacon. I have to admit that he doesn't sound like he's lecturing: just explaining something to friends. "I suggest that we use green to signal that we've found something and that the others should come to you. Red to signal that you're in distress in some way and need help. White to signal that everyone should return to Camp Five."

"So if I fall off the mountain," I say, still feeling a little lightheaded and silly, forgetting completely for the moment the grim purpose of our search, "I should fire a red flare on the way down?"

The other three look at me as if I've grown a second head.

"Couldn't hurt, Jake," the Deacon says at last. "You're lowest—closest to the drop-off."

Then we're all busy for a moment, pulling on our rucksacks and setting the Very pistols and their cartridges in the outside pockets, reachable without having to remove the packs, but safely away from our oxygen tanks.

"About searching in the area so low on the Face," says Reggie when we're all loaded up and standing. "Do you really think that Percival could have fallen that far from the North East Ridge or from the Face just off the North Ridge?"

The Deacon doesn't shrug, but there's the sound of a shrug in his soft tones. "Once a body begins falling on a slope this steep, Reggie...it tends to continue falling for a long way. If the fall started with a snow avalanche the way Sigl says it did, then Percy's and Meyer's bodies would have picked up vertical velocity right from the beginning of the fall."

"So their corpses probably wouldn't be here on the Face still at all," says Reggie.

The Deacon doesn't answer, but we can all hear the silent *Probably not.* That sudden drop-off some 2,000 feet below us, the more-than-8,000-vertical-foot fall, is terrible even to think of.

"But I don't think Bruno Sigl told us the truth about an avalanche being the cause of your cousin's and that Meyer fellow's death," the Deacon adds. It's the first time I've heard him that decisive on the subject.

"But if Percy and Meyer fell off the other side, the south side, of the North East Ridge above us...," begins Reggie.

"We won't find them," the Deacon says with a flat finality. "More than twelve thousand feet almost straight down to the Kangshung Glacier. Even if we climb this mountain along the...North East Ridge...the way Mallory said he was going to...there'll be very little reason to look off the south side. We couldn't make out bodies—or parts of bodies—from that altitude. Especially after a year of snowfall down there. And I'm not going anywhere near the inevitable snow cornice up there."

"What about me?" I ask.

"What about you?" says the Deacon.

"The actual parameters of my search area."

"Oh," says the Deacon and points to the line of blue ink farthest down on the search-grid map. "I gave you the most dangerous bit, Jake. This lowest area just above the drop-off. I wouldn't think that you'd have to go too far below the level of Camp Five—not right down to the drop-off lip itself—since any human body that had fallen that far from the North East Ridge would be in small pieces. Or at least terribly mangled. Food for the goraks... the high-altitude ravens that fly even this high. Oh, I apologize, Lady Bromley-Montfort."

"For what?" Reggie asks coolly.

"For being so stupidly insensitive," says the Deacon. He looks down.

"I've seen corpses in the mountains before, Mr. Deacon," says Reggie. "And I'm well aware not only of what a long fall does to the human body but that even at these altitudes, some scavenger will have gotten at Meyer's and my cousin's bodies if they're still somewhere on the mountain."

"Still," says the Deacon, almost certainly still being insensitive in his clumsy effort to ameliorate the harshness of his earlier comment, "the North Face at this altitude is a high desert. Even after only one year, there should be some mummification."

I feel that I have to change the subject toward something more pleasant. Craning to look up at the tall Sherpa, I say, "Dr. Pasang, I'm surprised you were able to come climbing away from your patients. How is Tenzing Bothia?"

"He died," says Pasang. "A pulmonary embolism—a blood clot caused by altitude that had moved and blocked the main artery to his lung. There was nothing I could have done to save him even if I'd been in the tent with him on the North Col that night. He died as he was being evacuated to Base Camp from Camp One."

"Jesus," I whisper to myself.

Reggie looks visibly shaken. "Amen," she says.

Monday, May 18, 1925

ince the Deacon is descending about half the catchment basin with me here on the North Face below the Yellow Band in order to reach *his* search area, he suggests we rope up for the part we'll be descending together. I quickly agree.

I'm reminded again that many more climbers die descending mountains than trying to ascend them. As I'd also been reminded on the Matterhorn, when descending, one is facing outward rather than leaning into the mountain, so on steep but not vertical slopes a climber tends not to use his hands on descents when he might on the climb up, and you're already going in gravity's direction, no matter how slowly and carefully you try to move downward. This steep slab and snow slope stretching out below the "ill-defined rock rib" that the Deacon has asked Pasang to check isn't as steep as the part of the Matterhorn where four of Edward Whymper's comrades slipped and fell to their deaths on his triumphal first climb, but this damned down-sloping granite is still slick and dangerous—and much more difficult out here on the North Face than descending the better-defined and rather less dramatic pitch of the North Ridge.

We've traversed back to the east, toward the North Ridge, and I realize that the Deacon really wants to keep doing the east-west, back-east, west-again search patterns that he'd drawn for us.

We reach the steep pitch near our ridgeline furthest east. Our solo tent constituting Camp VI is invisible in the boulders above us, but we can clearly see the tents of Camp V (three now, the Deacon and Pasang

424

having pitched Reggie's Big Tent on a boulder about 80 feet above the other two the night before) hundreds of feet lower on the North Ridge. This is where the Deacon will start his search zone. We unrope, and I loop my part of the line and set it into my rucksack, being careful not to tangle it with the oxygen hoses. We've been on English air since starting our descent, and now the Deacon lowers his mask and lifts his goggles.

"Take care down there, Jake. No slips today." A strong breeze has come up during our descent and the wind almost steals his words, but I'm watching his lips through my thick goggles. I simply nod and move off downhill. My search area begins at almost the same level as the three tents at Camp V, but further to the west on the North Ridge.

When I get to what I think is my designated altitude, I turn back toward the Grand Couloir and begin a careful traverse, my long ice axe usually in my left, uphill hand and always finding a grip for it before taking my next step. It's hard searching for a dead body when one is always watching one's feet and preparing for the next step.

I've put my crampons back on—even though the straps cut off circulation enough that my feet do get colder faster—and in the last two days of climbing I've noticed that it feels almost natural to have rocks and scree under the crampons rather than pushing up against the hobnailed soles of my boots. There are enough patches of snow and ice still on the North Face that the crampons come in handy every few yards.

Occasionally I stop, bend, lean on my ice axe, and crane my neck to look uphill to see if my friends are all right. Because of the distance and rocky-snowy background clutter, it takes a minute or two to see any of the three figures moving back and forth across their search areas; Reggie, the furthest away, stands out most clearly against the Yellow Band, that 700-foot-high band of what the geologist Odell had called, in his report to the Alpine Club, "a Middle Cambrian diopside-epidote-bearing marble, which weathers a distinctive yellowish brown." Translated into English, that means that layer upon layer of little sea creatures, fossilized and locked in marble, were stacked here sometime in the Middle Cambrian period when the Himalayan Range was at the bottom of some ancient ocean. Even I—a C student in geology at my university—can understand that this was one hell of a long time ago. Now I see Reggie moving along that ridgeline just beneath the Yellow Band far above, stopping diligently from time to time to use her binoculars to peer up into the maze of gullies above her. Those gullies create mazes not far below the actual North East Ridge—our (and Mallory and Irvine's) theoretical highway to the summit—and are a logical place to find Bromley's and Kurt Meyer's bodies if they fell off the ridge to this, the north side. I'll feel bad if she's the one to find her cousin's corpse.

Or maybe Reggie, just like me, is simply using the binocular stops as an excuse to breathe. Even with the oxygen apparatus, these traverses are exhausting. I'm suddenly very glad that the Deacon has insisted that the search—including the walk back to Camp VI, or Camp V if we need the extra room—is to go on no longer than the contents of one oxygen tank, about four and a half hours. I feel like I could sleep for a week, but know that I won't be able to do so in the cold, rocky angles of Camp V or VI, especially VI. Nor, for that matter, will I get any real rest anywhere up here above 8,000 meters. Fatigue on Mount Everest, I'm beginning to realize, is a cumulative thing. It just keeps building until it kills you or until you get the hell off the mountain.

I begin walking again, then suddenly realize that I'm getting too close to the Grand Couloir. I'm far west of where the First Step rises so far above me on the North East Ridge and almost have reached a point below the terrible Second Step. That's the end of my search zone. Any further in this direction and I'll be wading in the deep snows and steep exposures of Norton's Couloir. I turn and angle downward as I zigzag back toward the east and the North Ridge, where the tilted tents wait.

The drop-off 100 or so feet below me now is a constant sense of menace at the back of my mind. One slip and I'll be over the edge in a few flapping, screaming, helpless seconds. I'm sorry now that I made that stupid joke about shooting off a red flare as I fell; the fall to the glacier below would be the worst and last conscious moments of my life. I can think of few deaths more terrible.

What does one think about when falling thousands of feet through the air?

I try to banish that question by assuming that I will strike a rock and be safely unconscious before catapulting off the lip of this cliff to my death so much further below. That cheers me up a bit. But I don't really believe it. Part of my altitude-stupid brain tries to calculate the actual arithmetic of how many minutes and seconds I'll be conscious during the free fall.

"To hell with that," I say aloud and spend my mental energy watching my boots and the snow-patched mountainside ahead of me.

I'm just thirty or so minutes into the search when I find myself wishing that the Deacon had provided us with individual wireless sets rather than these ugly flare pistols. Of course, the 60 pounds or so of each wireless might be a tad tiresome to carry at these altitudes, and the fragile vacuum tubes would require lots of padding and tender loving care to avoid breakage, but the real problem would be the 300 miles or so of electrical cord that we'd each have to trail behind us as we...

I stop and shake my head to clear the fuzziness away. Something seems to be fluttering downhill from me, like branches shaking on a bush or shards of silk blowing in the wind. Or some spectral thing waving at me. Beckoning to me.

I can also see something green in the same small patch of snow below and ahead of me where I'd seen some sort of motion.

That's odd. My mind works dully, shifting its gears through high-altitude molasses. *I didn't think green plants grew this high.*

Wait. They *don't* grow this high.

I stop and raise my binoculars. My hands are so unsteady that I have to crouch, almost losing my balance in doing so, and then steady the glasses on my planted ice axe.

The "green plant" is a single green leather boot on the right foot of a corpse lying facedown on the steep slope, his arms stretched above him as if he were still trying to arrest his slide. The left foot is bare except for remnants of stockings. The "small patch of snow" isn't snow at all. It appears to be marble-white flesh visible through rents in the corpse's shirt and trousers. The motion is rags or fragments *(or flesh?)* blowing in the rising wind.

My second muddled thought is *Is this Lord Percy Bromley or the Meyer fellow, or could it be the Deacon or Pasang or even Reggie? Did one of my friends fall without my seeing or hearing them?* Such an unnoticed event is all too possible, locked away as I am beneath my layers of leather and goose down, oxygen mask and goggles, with the regulator burbling air at me audibly with every breath. A marching band might have fallen behind me without my hearing or seeing them.

No, neither the Deacon nor Pasang—nor Reggie for that matter—is wearing green leather boots today. And now I can tell, even from hundreds of feet away, that this dead body has been there awhile. I notice that the waves of scree—those small, loose rocks that make up so much of the North Face here—have slid down to cover parts of the head of the corpse.

Moving more carefully than ever, I'm quite aware of the Very flare gun in my rucksack pocket, but I'm not yet willing to use it until I get a closer look. Working to watch my feet rather than the distant apparition, I begin the steep descent toward the corpse and the terrible drop-off beyond it.

Monday, May 18, 1925

*E*ventually I fire the green flare—it doesn't seem to go very high, and it burns for only a few seconds before arcing down onto the steep slope above me and fizzling out with a final hiss. Then I collapse next to the corpse. My legs will no longer support me, although I don't know whether that's due to my excitement or near-total exhaustion.

It has to be either Bromley or Kurt Meyer. Or so I was certain when I was looking down at the dead man a few seconds earlier. But then I noticed the ragged and raveling puttees on the lower legs and realized that he had to be British. Germans and Austrians don't climb in puttees.

I've found Percival Bromley.

That's when I fired the flare gun—having to remove two layers of mittens and still almost dropping the green-cased 12-gauge flare cartridge because of fingers as stiff with shock as with the cold. After setting the pistol away, I realized that my knees were weak and that perhaps I'd better sit down.

Because of the two oxygen tanks and some fragile things in the rucksack, I don't sit on it the way I normally would on a mountainside, and within minutes the deep-space cold of the granite here on the North Face of Everest is working its way through my layers of silk and cotton and wool and goose down up to my rear end and then through my thighs and upper legs. I'm quickly and deeply chilled. Now that I've recognized the English puttees on the corpse, I also note the tattered wool knickerbockers and Norfolk jacket and am even more sure that this must be Percival Bromley. As I'd seen through the binoculars, he's lying facedown with

429

his arms raised and long, thin, bare, and sun-browned fingers sunken deep into the frozen gravel above his head and face, which are both half-buried in the loose scree.

Right now, I have no interest whatsoever in seeing the dead man's face. As I mentioned, I've seen dead bodies in the mountains, but I'm not eager to see this one's face until I must. I actively hate the thought that, responding to my flare, Reggie will be down here in a few minutes and will have to see her much-loved cousin looking like this.

Part of that feeling is embarrassment. The corpse is still mostly clothed and intact save for the visible bone of a broken right lower leg—a classic boot-top break, I think—and a few rips in the fabric across his surprisingly broad and muscled back, but goraks have been at his buttocks, and these are completely exposed. The birds—*gorak* just means "raven" in Tibetan, but I imagine that they actually must be some variant species of alpine choughs—have eaten their way through poor Lord Percival's rectum and begun hollowing out his insides. I consider laying my jacket over the obscene damage to the body, as one would cover the face of someone who died suddenly on the street in London or New York, but I'm already shivering with the cold. I need that wool layer. I also know that I'd better take my crampons off, stand up, stamp my frozen feet back into circulation, and walk around until I warm up a bit.

In a minute.

The corpse's hands look deeply tanned, an unusually dark brown. For a moment I wonder if this is the result of decomposition, but then I realize it's just the same high-altitude dark tan that J.C., the Deacon, and even Reggie and I have had after <u>five</u> weeks and more of hiking across Tibet and shuttling loads up the Trough and the glacier here on Everest. This high-altitude UV turns even white British, French, and American skin a deep brown quickly enough. I also notice that there's no sign of frostbite on any of the exposed skin—even on the bare backbone and shoulders revealed where his shirt and Norfolk jacket have split in the middle. And those are *powerful* shoulders. I hadn't realized that Cousin Percival was such an athlete.

Dead bodies don't develop frostbite, Jake. Only the living suffer that indignity.

I know this. My brain is still working, just in absurd slow motion—thoughts and insights arriving rather like the muted sounds of some distant explosions reaching one long after the initial flashes.

Bromley's left leg is crossed over his right just above where the terrible break in his lower right leg shows white bone and the ripped remnants of semi-mummified ligaments.

He was alive when he came to rest here, I realize. *At least long enough to cross his good leg across the broken one in an attempt to relieve the pain.*

The thought makes me ill enough that I tug down my oxygen mask in preparation to vomit. But the urge passes quickly. I realize that I'm being an absolute child—what the hell would I have done if I'd been old enough to serve in an American regiment in the Great War? Those fellows were knee-deep in decomposing bodies and dying men for the better part of a year.

So what? comes the answer from that more conscious part of my mind. *It's only poor Percival Bromley I'm dealing with here. You were never a soldier, Jake.*

I can see through the rip in the Norfolk jacket that young Bromley had been wearing seven or eight layers of clothing: an outer anorak that has turned to tatters in a year's cold wind, the wool Norfolk jacket, at least two sweaters, some layers of cotton and silk. What I'd first taken through the binoculars for a bare and browned skull is actually a leather motorcycle helmet similar to the thin flying helmet that I'm wearing. The dead man's leather helmet is torn and ripped in places, and I think it somewhat odd that the visible tufts of Bromley's hair are almost white-blond at the ends but dark brown further down. Do men ever dye their hair the way women do?

I don't see any goggle straps on the side of his buried face.

He obviously had fought—and succeeded—in stopping his tumble and slide before he went over the drop-off just twenty or so yards below us, and his arms are in the classic mode of finger-clawing self-arrest a sliding climber uses as a last resort if he's lost his ice axe. I look up the slope but can't see Bromley's axe. Nor can I see the boot missing from his left foot.

The fluttering that first caught my eye comes from a web of three-eighths-inch rope, what the three of us, with some contempt, have come to call clothesline rope even though we'd used it enough in the Alps. It's been pulled far too tight around Bromley's waist, is looped and tangled around his left shoulder, and its broken end—I can see the frayed and splayed threads right where the rope broke—is flapping and whipping in the still-rising wind. This, then, is the "wave" I'd seen.

Bruno Sigl said that Bromley had been roped to Kurt Meyer when the avalanche carried the two of them away. I guess we have to credit the German for telling the truth after all.

But the avalanche or the sheer violence of the fall has snapped the rope. God alone knows where Kurt Meyer might have ended up. Again I scan the slope above me, but can see neither a dead German nor any of my three friends coming down to join me.

Should I fire off the other two flares? Maybe they missed the first green one. It burned for only a few seconds.

I decide to wait. My hands still haven't warmed up.

Suddenly there's motion, but it's not someone coming down from above—it's a short man in a Shackleton jacket traversing directly across the steep face toward me from the east.

It must be Kurt Meyer, I think. *He somehow survived the fall and has been waiting all this time for someone to find him and Bromley.*

Or maybe Meyer also died here, and now his mummified corpse is coming to talk to me. Or maybe it's just Percy Bromley's ghost.

It's my gasping and coughing, not the delusions, that make me realize I've been off English air for too long. I set my mask back in place and turn the flow up to 2.2 liters per minute. This clears my head almost immediately.

Just before the goggled and thickly garbed figure arrives, I recognize him: Jean-Claude. With the help of the oxygen, it takes me only thirty seconds or so to remember that the Deacon had said that J.C. would be coming up to Camp V with a group of Sherpas for a high carry today. He must have seen the green flare and come to investigate.

I stand, teetering just a bit, and lean uphill onto my ice axe, and Jean-Claude carefully steps around the corpse and hugs me before pulling down his mask and turning so that we are both looking down at the dead man.

"*Mon Dieu,*" he says over the rising wind.

I tug my own mask lower so that I can speak.

"It's definitely Bromley," I explain. "You see the puttees, J.C. Definitely British. You see the broken right leg. There are probably other injuries we can't see from this angle. But I don't think he could have fallen from as far as the North East Ridge and... you know... be in one piece like this. And definitely not from the North Ridge—this is due west, too far. He would have been almost to the Second Step, up along the ridgeline. No avalanches there."

I've talked too much and breathed too little, so when my hacking starts, I put the mask back in place and bend over until the coughing fit passes.

"His right leg is broken in other places as well, Jake," says J.C. "And you see that his right elbow looks broken too... or at least severely dislocated. I believe that the right side of this poor fellow's body took the worst of the fall..." Jean-Claude pauses, shields his eyes—he raises his goggles for a better view, which I haven't yet thought of doing—and studies the slope above us. "But you are right," he says. "It is more than a thousand feet to the North East Ridge. He did not fall that far. Perhaps from those rocks below the Yellow Band. You are correct in much of your forensic analysis, but I fear you are wrong about one thing, my friend."

"What's that?" I say, and then splutter since I've forgotten to lower my mask, and the simple re-breathing gizmo in the mask doesn't adapt itself well to transmitting human speech. I lower the damned thing and try again. *"What?"*

J.C. begins to say something but then stops and points uphill.

Three roped figures—Pasang in the lead, Reggie in the center, and the Deacon in anchor position—are using their long ice axes to pick their way slowly down the slope. They're only twenty yards or so away. I should have known that the cautious Deacon would have taken the time to get them roped together before responding to my flare rather than have everyone come rushing down solo.

"What am I wrong about?" I ask, picking up the conversation thread with J.C. He only shakes his head and steps back from the corpse as our three friends arrive, make a slow loop around the body, and create a semicircle downhill with the corpse as its focus, the easier for them to view it. I'm instantly sorry that I hadn't taken off at least my Shackleton anorak to cover the gorak-invaded buttocks and hollowed-out lower insides of Lord Percival. Now poor Reggie is leaning closer, having to see this horrible view of someone she'd grown up with almost as if he were her brother.

My mask is still lowered. "I'm sorry, Reggie," I say, realizing that there are tears welling under my thick greenish goggles. Maybe it's the cold wind bothering my eyes.

She pulls down her own oxygen mask and looks at me questioningly. Her goggles are raised. Her face is very pale in the late morning light.

"I'm sorry you have to see your cousin like this," I say again. My only wish right now is that I hadn't been the one to find him.

She cocks her head, looks at the other three men, then back at me. They're all staring at me now.

"This isn't Percival," says Reggie, having to raise her voice to be heard over the coldly quickening wind.

I take another step back out of sheer reflex. My crampons slip on something, and I have to lean on my axe or tumble. I remind my body that we're still just yards above a sheer drop-off to total oblivion. I'm very confused. It's a British climber, of that I'm certain. If not her cousin...

"I know those broad shoulders and those green climbing boots," says Reggie. "Percival is much slimmer, his upper body much less developed. And he's never owned green leather boots. Jake, I'm all but certain that you've found George Leigh Mallory."

Tuesday, May 19, 1925

*I*t's after midnight, but all five of us—the Deacon, Pasang, Reggie, Jean-Claude, and I—are sitting up in our sleeping bags in Reggie's Big Tent, which has been pitched on the slab slopes at Camp V, each of us hanging on to one of the interior struts in an effort to keep the ever-rising wind from ripping the canvas apart or hurling us off the mountain. We are very, very tired.

I feel bad that we hadn't taken time to bury George Mallory that afternoon—the previous afternoon, I realize, as I look at my watch. It's the nineteenth of May now, two whole days after the Deacon's planned summit day. The wind has grown stronger every hour, a lenticular cloud that had been hovering over Everest's summit all morning descended on us in a whirl of snow after darkness fell, and if we'd stayed on the North Face with Mallory, we would have had to spend at least an extra hour or two hacking at the frozen rocks to free enough stones to cover his body. Even piling the thinnest layer of cairn stones would have taken more energy and time than we had with the storm coming in. After we'd searched the body carefully and made note of the position and clues as to his fall and jotted down notes of landmarks, such as they were, so we could find Mallory's final resting place again when we had to, the Deacon announced that it was time to make the long west-to-east traverse to Camp V. When I objected, saying that Mallory surely deserved to be buried properly despite the approaching darkness and rising wind, it was Reggie who said, "He's lain out here under the snow and sun and moon and stars for almost a year, Jake. Another night won't matter.

We'll stay lower—here at Camp Five rather than Six—and come back to bury Mallory tomorrow."

As it happened, of course, we never did.

I still feel bad about it.

But it turned out to be wise that we turned back when we did and traversed to Camp V rather than attempted to climb to the tiny Camp VI. By two p.m., the wind was raging hard enough to have ripped one of the small Meade tents at Camp V partially off its moorings. It was now a slumped, snow-covered green mass of canvas and snapped tentpoles on the steep mountainside. We could have labored to re-erect it, possibly using our ice axes as poles, but we didn't bother. The other Meade tent had been ripped open by small falling rocks that tore through the canvas walls and roofs like canister shot. If anyone had been in that tent when those rocks hit, they would almost certainly have been killed. And there was a long night of higher winds and more hurtling rocks ahead of us.

So that leaves the five of us crowded into Reggie's Big Tent, which had been pitched atop a tilted boulder but in the rockfall-proof lee of two larger boulders when the Deacon and Pasang carried loads to Camp V yesterday. (Sunday, I amend, when I again remember that it's past midnight.) The Deacon and Pasang had not only weighted all the edges of the tent down with serious-sized stones and driven German steel pitons into solid rock for tent stakes, but also lashed the whole tent down with about twenty yards of the new high-tensile rope zigzagging back and forth over the apex of the dome and tied down to large boulders both lower than the tent and uphill.

Reggie's tent is big enough for the five of us to gather in for a meal, everyone sitting up, but stretching out to sleep is going to be a difficult proposition.

Despite not having time to excavate frozen-in-place stones to bury Mallory, we'd spent a very cold hour huddled over his corpse on the North Face. Even though we'd found tags in his clothing reading "G. Mallory," the Deacon wanted to be certain of the dead man's identity. So at one point three of us used our knives to chip away at the gravel on the left side of his body where the corpse was frozen in place until we could leverage him up a little to get a glimpse of his front and face.

That process felt precisely like lifting a log that has been frozen in place in the soil through a long, hard winter.

In the end, it was the Deacon who'd scooted closer on his back and then lain supine under the stiff, suspended body long enough to look into the dead man's face.

"It's Mallory," said the Deacon.

"What else do you see?" asked Pasang.

"His eyes are closed. There's stubble on his cheeks and chin, but no real beard." The Deacon's voice sounded weary.

"I meant in terms of visible injuries," said Pasang.

"There's a terrible puncture wound on his right temple, over his eye," said the Deacon. "Perhaps he struck a rock on the way down or the pick of his ice axe recoiled back against him as he tried to self-arrest."

"Does the wound go all the way through the bone of the skull there?" asked Pasang.

"Yes."

"Can we let him down now?" I asked, gasping for breath. We all had our oxygen masks lowered for this task. The exertion of simply lifting a partially hollowed-out frozen corpse was almost too much for me.

"Yes," the Deacon said again, sliding out and away from the dead man. And then, almost whispering, he said, "Good-bye, George."

We'd gone through Mallory's pockets and poked through a canvas bag he'd had hanging against his chest. As I mentioned, the corpse wasn't wearing the metal rig for oxygen tanks and had no rucksack—only that one small carrying bag pressed against his chest and under his arm, and a few things stuck in his pockets.

In the pocket of his Norfolk jacket there was an altimeter much like the ones we carried—specially calibrated for altitudes up to 30,000 feet—but the crystal had been broken in the fall and the altimeter's hands were missing.

"Too bad," said Reggie. "We'll never know if he and Irvine made the summit."

"There were several cameras with them, I believe," said the Deacon. "Teddy Norton told me that Mallory himself was carrying a Vest Pocket Kodak."

When we pulled the small pouch around where we could get into it, I felt, again wearing only my undergloves, something hard and metallic inside. "I believe we've found that camera," I announced.

It wasn't. The hard lump consisted of a large package of Swan Vesta matches and a metal tin of meat lozenges. We set them back in place. Other metal objects found in Mallory's pockets included an almost casual variety of personal gear, as if Mallory had just stepped out for a winter walk in Hyde Park: a stub of a pencil, a pair of scissors, a safety pin, a little metal holster for the scissors, and a detachable leather strap that had connected his oxygen mask to his leather motorcycle helmet. I knew what the last item was because I had an almost identical strap under my chin at that moment.

We returned the lozenges, matches, and other things to his pouch and pockets, but kept turning up more items: a very used—as in snotty—plain handkerchief with a tube of petroleum jelly in it (the jelly was for his chapped lips, we knew, since we each also carried one of those—same brand), and a much nicer and rather elaborately mono-grammed—G.L.M.—handkerchief in a blue, burgundy, and green foulard pattern. This handkerchief was wrapped around some papers. The Deacon looked through the papers, but they all appeared to be per-sonal letters which he did not read beyond the salutations and whatever was written on the envelopes (one was addressed to *George Leigh Mallory, Esq., c/o British Trade Agent, Yalung, Tibet*). They were personal and basic expedition business letters, not interesting save for one strange series of numbers scrawled in pencil along the margins of a letter that had been sent to him from some lady not his wife.

"Those are oxygen pressure readings," said Jean-Claude. "Perhaps notes on how far they could get on their tanks of air that last day."

"Only five pressures given here," said Reggie. "I thought they left Camp Four with more than five oxygen tanks."

"They did," said the Deacon.

"Nothing there to help us understand anything, then," said Reggie.

"Perhaps not," said the Deacon. He nodded and refolded each letter, set each back in its own envelope, wrapped all of them neatly in the monogrammed handkerchief, and set the handkerchief back in the dead man's pocket.

Even though we had taken nothing, I still felt like a grave robber. I'd never gone through the pockets of a corpse before. The Deacon seemed rather used to doing so, and I realized he almost certainly had—perhaps hundreds of times—on the Western Front

In other pockets we found only Mallory's folding pocketknife and his goggles.

"That could be important," said Reggie. "His goggles being in his pocket."

I didn't understand at once—I was too busy coughing at the moment—but Jean-Claude said, "Yes. It was either twilight or after dark when they fell...Mallory started his climb the day after he saw Norton so snow-blinded. It's all but certain that he would only take his goggles off after sunset."

"But were they climbing upward or downward when one or both fell?" asked Pasang.

"Down-climbing, I would think," said the Deacon.

"Did they have an electric torch with them?" asked Reggie.

"No," said the Deacon. "Odell found it in their tent at Camp Six and brought it down. The fact that they'd not brought their only electric torch tells almost conclusively that they left Camp Six after sunrise. Also that George Mallory was quite the forgetful sort of chap."

"Let's not speak ill of the dead," I said between coughs.

"Not ill," said the Deacon. "Just factual. George was always losing or forgetting something or leaving something behind on the first two expeditions I spent with him—his socks, his shaving kit, his hat, his roll of toilet paper. It was just his way."

"Still...," I began, and found I had nothing else to say.

The Deacon shielded his eyes—we'd been doing the search without wearing our goggles since the clouds were so heavy above us now—and looked as far up the slope as he could in the swirling snow. "Those gullies below and this side of the First Step, below the Yellow Band, would have been very hard to down-climb in the dark, without an electric torch or any flares or lanterns or candles."

We all peered up at the ridges and gullies of rocks far above this lower part of the face. "Based on how intact his body is—and the obvious fact that he was still conscious and trying to self-arrest when he came to a stop—it's obvious that Mallory didn't fall from as high up as the North East Ridge," said the Deacon, confirming my earlier hunch. "Almost certainly not from as high up as the Yellow Band. More likely he fell from one of the gullies or minor rock bands further down, closer to us here."

"So Sandy Irvine may be right up there waiting for us," said Reggie.

The Deacon shrugged. "Or it was Irvine who fell first, pulling Mallory off his footing. We'll never know unless we find Irvine's corpse as well."

You mean we're going to continue searching after this? was my exhausted thought.

That's when the Deacon brusquely ordered us all back to Camp V before the howling wind rose higher and the already snow-diminished visibility grew worse.

"So nothing we found on George Mallory can tell us whether he and Sandy Irvine reached the summit or not," Reggie is saying. "Both Mallory's watch and altimeter are broken and missing their hands."

"Perhaps it is what's missing that gives us our best clue," says the Deacon.

I rise a little from the depths of my filthy goose down sleeping bag. "The Kodak camera?"

"No," says the Deacon. "A photograph of Mallory's wife, Ruth. Norton and everyone else I spoke to said that Mallory had taken the photograph with him from Camp Four—certainly no one ever found it there or at either of the two higher camps—and he had promised Ruth that he would leave it on the summit for her."

"Or just at his high point before turning back—God alone knows where," says J.C.

The Deacon nods at that and chews on the stem of his cold pipe.

"The absence of a photo isn't proof that he reached the summit," says Reggie.

"No," agrees the Deacon. "Only that he left it somewhere. Perhaps, as Jean-Claude suggested, at their highest point before turnaround... wherever that was."

"The missing camera interests me," says Dr. Pasang. His deep voice is as gentle and unhurried as ever.

"Why?" I ask.

"Because when does one relinquish a camera to someone else?" asks the tall Sherpa.

"When you ask him to take your picture," says Reggie. "As Mallory might have—giving the Kodak to Irvine on the summit, after taking the younger man's photograph."

"Only conjecture," says the Deacon. "What isn't speculation or conjecture is the fact that if we're to have any hope at all of searching more tomorrow, we all have to get some sleep."

"Easy for you to say," I get out between coughs. "I just can't seem to sleep at these goddamned altitudes."

"Watch your language, Jake," says the Deacon. "There's a lady present."

Reggie rolls her eyes.

"I have sleeping pills with me," says Pasang. "They should guarantee at least three or four hours' sleep."

There is a silence, and I imagine that everyone else is thinking what I am—*So we'd all be snoring away when the winds blow our tent over the edge of the mountain.*

I start to give my opinion, but Reggie holds up her palm, silencing me. "Ssshh, everyone," she whispers. "I hear someone. Someone screaming."

My forearms break out in goose bumps.

"In this wind?" says the Deacon. "Impossible. Camp Four is much too far below us and . . ."

"I hear it as well," says Pasang. "Someone is out in the dark screaming."

PART III

THE ABOMINABLE

1.

Note to Mr. Dan Simmons: Up to this part, I've written out my story mostly in present tense because I was working from daily journal entries and climbing notes I'd made at the time in the summer and autumn of 1924 and spring of 1925. Writing in present tense helped bring things alive and immediate for me again. I know that wasn't very professional of me, in any writing sense, but this last section of my tale has been told to only one person, and never written down at all. Not even in my notes at the time. I write this part as I remember it now, in past tense never recorded at the time, but please understand that every word that I set down here is as true and precise as I can remember and tell it, and that you will be only the second person since 1925 to hear this part of the tale.

— Jake Perry

Within five minutes of Pasang's confirming hearing the screaming, three of us—the Deacon, Pasang, and I—were outside in the swirling snow. It had been decided that someone should remain behind to hold the tent staves; Reggie had volunteered, J.C. and I had tossed a coin, and he lost.

"Do you still hear it?" shouted the Deacon to Pasang.

"No, but I *see* something," said the Sherpa. He pointed downhill toward a point about 300 feet below us near what remained of the two tents that had been our original site for Camp V.

It took me a second because of the snow blowing in the cone of light from my Welsh miner's headlamp, but then I saw it: a hellish red glow behind large boulders 100 feet or so downhill from us.

With three of us tied onto a single rope—we hadn't taken time to put on our crampons—I led the descent down the steep boulder slope. Not much snow was sticking to the rocks because of the wind, but there was a thick enough ice sheen to make every rock more slippery than usual. It felt strange to be walking only in hobnailed boots again. Already, I lacked the sense of secure footing that the crampon blades had been giving me in recent days.

In fifteen minutes we reached our original Camp V site, the one tent destroyed by rockfall, the other collapsed, just in time to see a red flare sputter out. It obviously hadn't been one of the short-lived Very flares but rather one of the handheld, longer-lasting railroad flares we'd brought along in both red and white varieties.

Ten feet from the flare a man in one of the expedition's goose down duvet jackets lay unmoving on his back. He'd collapsed very near the tumbled opening of the intact but fallen Meade tent.

We leaned over him, our headlights playing across the man's upturned face and staring eyes.

"It's Lobsang Sherpa," said the Deacon. "He's dead."

When we'd met at Camp VI on Monday morning, the Deacon had mentioned carrying up to Camp V the day before with only a few porters and Lobsang acting as *sirdar.* Now, barely eighteen hours later, Lobsang Sherpa, a small but determined high-climbing Tiger Sherpa who'd earned his acting-sirdar position through unbelievably hard work and long carries, did indeed look dead, his mouth gaping open, his pupils looking to be fixed and dilated.

"No one else dies up here this day," said Pasang and set down his rucksack. He was the only one of us to bring a pack along. I saw in the dancing headlamps and swirling snow that his leather doctor's bag was inside his already heavy rucksack. "Mr. Perry," he added, "if you'd be so kind as to open Lobsang Sherpa's jacket and shirt layers so that his chest is bare."

I went to one knee on the steep slope, shucked off my clumsy outer mittens, and did what Pasang had ordered—not expecting any sort of resuscitation technique to do any good on a man who looked so dead, his body and exposed face already coated with a thin veneer of windblown ice crystals.

But Pasang pulled out the largest syringe I've seen since a medical-farce sketch done by Harvard's Hasty Pudding group. The needle must have been six inches long; the whole thing looked more like something a veterinarian would use on cattle than anything that could conceivably be applied to a human being.

"Hold his arms down," instructed Pasang and ran his fingers across Lobsang's bare brown chest. The Sherpa's unblinking eyes still stared up into eternity.

Why hold his arms? I remember thinking. *Is the corpse going somewhere?*

Pasang was busy counting ribs and finding the poor Sherpa's bony breastbone under the skin, and then he used both his now bare hands to lift the ridiculous syringe three feet into the air and then plunge it down through Lobsang Sherpa's skin and breastbone directly into the man's heart. The point of the needle made a sound as it pierced Lobsang's breastbone, a sickening *clack* audible even over the last hisses of the red flare and the howling of the wind. Pasang pushed down the plunger of the huge syringe.

Lobsang Sherpa's body arched upward—he would have thrown himself off the mountain if the Deacon and I hadn't been holding him down—and the little man began gasping in great gulps of air.

"Jesus Christ," the Deacon whispered to himself. I agreed. It was the damnedest medical thing I'd ever seen—and continued to be so for another six decades and more.

"Adrenaline straight to his heart," gasped Dr. Pasang. "If anything can bring him back, that will."

Pasang put his foot next to Lobsang Sherpa and pulled the needle from the man's chest the way I'd heard that soldiers were taught to remove a stuck bayonet from an enemy's carcass. Lobsang gasped, blinked wildly, and tried to sit up. After a few moments, Pasang and I worked to help Lobsang to his thick-booted feet. To me it felt like I was helping Lazarus stand.

Amazingly, Lobsang was able to support some of his own weight. If he hadn't, we would have been forced to abandon him; at that altitude, even three men couldn't carry dead weight 100 feet up a steep slope. With the Deacon and me half-supporting the blinking, gasping man and Dr. Pasang following close behind with his rucksack, the four of us staggered uphill to Reggie's Big Tent. If there'd been little hope of five of us sleeping in the domed tent earlier, there was no chance now with a sixth person joining us. I had mixed feelings about that sixth person being alive.

We'd used the Unna cooker to heat water and soup hours earlier, and now Reggie gave the gasping Lobsang some cocoa. He gulped it down. When it looked as if he might be able to answer questions, Reggie asked the first one—in English and then in rapid-fire Nepalese. "Why have you come up here in the dark, Lobsang Sherpa?"

The man's eyes widened again, and I had a flash of sickening memory of those dead eyes staring at nothing only a few minutes earlier.

He babbled in Nepalese, looked around, and repeated it in urgent English. "You must come down, Memsahib, Sahibs, Dr. Pasang. You must come down *now*. *Yeti* have killed everyone at Base Camp!"

2.

———— ∞∞ ————

omehow we all managed to sleep a few hours before the gradual, gray brightening that passed for sunrise in the center of a cloud. Lobsang Sherpa had been put on continuous oxygen, low flow, and he slept the best. The rest of us had taken some snorts of English air when the cold—or in my case the coughing—grew bad enough. Lady Bromley-Montfort was allowed to pick a lavatory boulder first, and then the rest of us went out one by one or in groups of two. The good thing about being severely dehydrated above 25,000 feet was that one's kidneys didn't require much attention.

We didn't try to fire up the Unna cooker, even though we had six more Meta fire bars. We'd make do with the two small thermoses left from what we'd filled the day before.

There was almost no talk as we got into our layers. The Deacon asked Lobsang a few questions about these *"yeti"* who supposedly attacked, but the Sherpa wasn't making much sense, and the four of us "sahibs" didn't believe in *yeti* anyway. The Deacon, who'd seen the "monster's" tracks in both 1921 and '22, was the biggest skeptic. He'd reminded us more than a few times how hot sunlight melts the tracks of a regular, run-of-the-mill quadruped into what looks to be a biped's large footprints. I guess I could say that I was a skeptical agnostic on the whole *yeti* business in 1925, but I know I didn't believe that some big two-legged beastie was eating our Sherpa porters.

All of us checked the tubes and valves of our oxygen sets as we stored them in the RBT—we fully planned to use those particular extra O_2

sets on our summit bid when we returned to Camp V—and then we filled our rucksacks with the few things we were taking down. All four of us had our Very pistols, and everyone but me had three flares left. I was the only one hauling two O_2 tanks in his rucksack—at the Deacon's request.

"We don't all have to go down," I said when we were finally standing outside the tents in what was the perfect equivalent of a freezing London fog. "I can stay up here until the rest of you get things sorted out."

"What would you do up here alone, Jake?" asked Jean-Claude.

"Bury Mallory."

J.C. didn't seem surprised by the answer. I knew he'd also felt bad about leaving the body there, exposed, on the slope where he'd died. But we both also knew that we'd done the right thing in following the Deacon's orders to retreat to Camp V when we did. If we'd been caught out in yesterday evening's wind and storm, there'd be more than one body to bury on the North Face of Everest this day.

"No, Jake," said the Deacon. "Besides the fact that you probably wouldn't even find George's body in this cloud—especially given the fact that he'd be covered by fresh snow today—we need you to lead the descent to Camp Four."

"Jean-Claude can lead," I said. My last, lame protest.

"Jean-Claude will take over when we get to the snowfields and crevasses of the North Col," said the Deacon with a climbing leader's finality. "*You* lead us down the rock. You're our rock man. That's why we paid to *bring* you here to this mountain, my American friend."

Instead of arguing, I turned my oxygen-tank regulator to the lower setting of 1.5 liters of flow, tugged my mask into place, and strapped it to my flying helmet—thinking of the similar bit of strap in George Mallory's pocket as I did so—and shrugged into my heavy pack. I wasn't carrying much besides the two oxygen tanks, my small Very pistol, the two remaining 12-gauge flare cartridges, and a chocolate bar.

Only the lead climber during the long descent was to be carrying and using the two oxygen bottles. We'd cached the other five full bottles left over from yesterday and their simple rigs there at Camp V, and between the Deacon on Sunday and J.C. on Monday, the Sherpas had portered up no fewer than six full backpacks of three tanks each, using none in their ascent. These were cached a little lower, at the level of the collapsed and rock-riddled tents, where we'd found Lobsang just last night. If we returned to these upper camps, those twenty-three tanks of English air should be more than enough to support both a search for Percy and a serious summit attempt for at least four of us. Perhaps even enough for summit attempts by two groups of three. That would be nice, I remember thinking, if we get six people on the summit.

Despite Lobsang's obvious signs of terror, *yeti* weren't even in my mind any longer.

"Two ropes going down today," announced the Deacon without asking for our opinions or advice. "Jake will lead the first rope with Dr. Pasang following and Jean-Claude at anchor. Lady Bromley-Montfort will lead our second rope with Lobsang Sherpa coming next and me last. The fixed ropes may be partially buried, but Lobsang said that he'd found and pulled most of them free of the snow during his ascent last night, so that will help us in terms of time. Unless someone gets ill, no one will be using oxygen on the way down except Jake, who will pass it over to Jean-Claude when he takes the lead through the snowfields above Camp Four."

J.C. started to protest that he wouldn't need the oxygen, that he'd climbed most of the way to Camp V without it the day before, but the Deacon silenced all further talk simply by shaking his head once.

Before we all pulled balaclavas or heavy scarves over our faces, more or less effectively shutting off talk, Reggie said, "Lobsang is a bit *non compos mentis*. I wonder what we'll find at Base Camp."

"I suspect something real frightened the Sherpas, and they may have deserted the expedition," said Dr. Pasang.

Lobsang Sherpa finally realized what we were talking about, although I was fairly sure that he hadn't understood the Latin about his not being totally mentally capable. "No, no, no," Lobsang Sherpa said in English. "Not frighten...not run off...all *killed! Yetis* killed them. All *dead!*"

"Were you there?" Pasang asked in English. "Did you *see* these *yeti* killing Sherpas?"

"No, no," admitted Lobsang. "I also be dead if there. But cook Semchumbi and head of pack animals Nawang Bura see bodies. Everybody at Base Camp dead. Very terrible. Blood and heads and arms and legs everywhere. *Yeti* kill them!"

The Deacon patted him on the back and helped him make the correct knot for tying on to the same rope with Reggie and himself. "We'll know soon," he said. "Lady Bromley-Montfort, let's remember that Lobsang Sherpa is the only one here with no crampons. We must be especially careful going down."

I pulled away my mask for just a moment. "I only hope I can find the right bamboo markers and fixed lines in this cloud-fog," I said. No one responded, so I tugged the mask back into place.

J.C. said, "We don't need to wear the damned goggles in this dim light and fog today, do we?"

"No," said the Deacon. "We'll pull the goggles back into place only if it begins brightening. It's most important we watch our footing during the descent."

J.C. and I made sure that Dr. Pasang was tied on properly—we were leaving only about 30 feet of rope between climbers, a short length, to be sure, and dangerous in the sense that a fall by anyone wouldn't give the next person on the rope much time to set himself (or herself) for belay—but I agreed with the Deacon's unspoken suggestion that the lines between each of us should be short enough that we could keep the climber behind or in front of us in sight most of the time, no matter what the wind and weather might be like.

"All right, Jake," called the Deacon from the far rear. "Start us down, please."

Using my ice axe to pick my way carefully across the down-tilting snow and ice slabs, I started weaving my way down around boulders, past the battered lower section of Camp V, and then east a dozen yards or so back toward the spine of the North Ridge and the treacherous staircase there.

3.

*N*o Everest expedition before ours had ever laid as much fixed rope as we had—and ours was the Deacon's dependable Miracle Rope blend to boot—so no expedition members had ever had such relative ease of descending from Camp V.

Or at least we *should* have had such relative ease. In truth, the clouds were so thick and the wind gusts—up to fifty miles per hour was my guess at the time—were so frighteningly powerful and sporadic that descending the ridge and ice slope and glacier of Mount Everest on that Tuesday, May 19, was a pure nightmare for me.

Some of the marker wands remained in place, but others had been blown away by the night's gales or blown sideways and covered with snow. At a hundred places during the descent on the North Ridge spur down to the North Col, I had to make the call. *Do I go straight ahead here, or right here down that familiar-looking gully, or left down that steeper part?* I kept remembering those dead-end gullies that led off to the east during our climb to Camp V in daylight, each wrong turn ending in a precipitous 6,000-foot drop-off to the main Rongbuk Glacier.

So I rarely chose a route to the right when I could find no flagged bamboo wands marking it. But twice a wrong left turn made me lead everyone out onto the North Face of Everest, and there were hidden precipices and vertical ice traps there as well. Both times I gingerly traversed backward until we were on the spine of the North Ridge again, and then I led the way down until we came across the next fixed rope and we could be sure where we were.

When we were wading through snow up to our waists on a somewhat lesser slope, I decided that we must be in the North Ridge's snowfields not too far above the North Col, and I called for a pause and for J.C. to come forward and take my place and my oxygen tank to lead us through the crevasses.

"Remember, I want the rucksack back," I said when I handed it over to him and before I slogged back to the rear of our three-person rope to tie in there. My flare pistol, cartridges, binoculars, empty water bottle, an extra sweater, and one half-eaten chocolate bar were still in the rucksack.

Jean-Claude's descent was faster than mine had been; he found an iced-over crust area of the snowfield and almost glissaded us down despite our crampons. I realized then that after Babu's death, I'd had enough of glissading for one expedition.

But a little more than two hours after setting out from Camp V, J.C. led us through the last few invisible crevasse fields to the small cluster of tents huddled in the shadow of the high seracs at the northeast corner of the North Col.

The entire camp was empty.

"Everyone scared," said Lobsang Sherpa. "Last night I volunteer to go up. Tell you. Everyone else want to go down."

"Why?" asked the Deacon. "If the *yeti* were supposed to be down below, wouldn't everyone have felt safer staying at Camp Four?"

Lobsang shook his head almost violently. "*Yeti* climb," he said. "They live up on Col in caves. They very angry at us."

The Deacon didn't bother to parse logic with the terrified Sherpa—I would at least have asked him why angry *yetis* would have started their depredations at Base Camp if they were angry at their homes on the North Col being invaded—but instead of discussing mythical monsters, we looked in the various tents for food and water. There were no water bottles or thermoses of drinks left behind—and the damned Sherpas who'd promised to stay waiting for us here at Camp IV two days earlier had taken the extra sleeping bags, Primuses, and Unna cookers with them as well—but Reggie found three overlooked Meta sticks, and we lit them and held blackened pots of fresh snow over the open fires at least to get meltwater. Then Pasang found two semi-frozen cans of spaghetti under a tangle of abandoned clothing in one of the Whymper tents, and the Deacon ferreted out a tin of ham and lima beans. We poured the mess into the last pot to cook over the waning fire.

All of us were tired and starved and dehydrated. And my coughing now that I was off oxygen was almost nonstop, the sensation that I'd swallowed a small chicken bone even more pronounced. But although Lobsang Sherpa was obviously terrified at the thought of staying at Camp IV a moment longer, and the rest of us were exhausted and had no appetite, it was imperative that we eat and drink something before heading down the ice cliff. We welcomed the tea and forced the food down.

With six of J.C.'s jumars available and so much fixed rope in place, the serious climbers among us could have rappelled down the ice face and most of the steep 800-foot slope beneath that face, but we set our pace to Lobsang's skills and scuttled down the long caver's ladder, still using the jumars and friction knots on the fixed ropes but as grips and brakes rather than aids to full-rappel rapid descents. It was still a relatively rapid and efficient descent, despite the increasing fogginess of clouds rising from the East Rongbuk Glacier valley.

"Is *this* the monsoon, *Ree-shard?*" asked Jean-Claude as our two strings of roped climbers bounced backward down the fixed ropes through ever-thickening cloud-fog.

"No, I don't believe so," said the Deacon. "The clouds are building in the south, but the wind's still blowing from the north-northwest."

J.C. nodded and saved his breath for rappelling down; he had Lobsang Sherpa more or less tied to his front, and the weary Sherpa would let out a cry at each backward bounce.

We found fourteen Sherpas—who, with Lobsang Sherpa, made up half the total complement we'd set out with—huddling at Camp III. There weren't enough tents there to shelter fifteen Sherpas, so sitting men were virtually piled atop sitting men in the Whympers and Meades in ways that would have been truly comic had not their faces reflected so much terror. Others sat outside around a roaring campfire.

"Where the hell did you get fuel for a big fire?" the Deacon asked the first Sherpa he encountered who could speak some English—Semchumbi, the cook, who was supposed to stay at Base Camp or Camp I.

Semchumbi didn't answer, but Reggie pointed to a pile of kindling to one side of the bonfire. The Sherpas had used an axe to smash up every packing crate we'd hauled to Camp III in preparation for high carries.

"Oh, that's bloody great," said the Deacon. "Just bloody great." He took Semchumbi firmly by the shoulder. "Is this fire supposed to keep away *yetis?*"

Semchumbi nodded violently and, his English evidently forgotten, kept repeating, "*Nitikanji . . . Nitikanji . . .*"

"What does that mean?" the Deacon demanded of Dr. Pasang.

"Snow men," said Pasang. "Same as *yeti,* which comes from *ya te,* which means 'man of high places'—also, as you know, called *Metohkangmi.*"

"Snowmen," said the Deacon in disgust. "Did anyone actually see these . . . *snowmen?*"

All fifteen of the Sherpas babbled at once, but Reggie and Pasang pointed out the only man who'd seen the actual monsters—Nawang Bura, who'd been in charge of all the pack animals during the trek in and who'd stayed at Base Camp the last three weeks to watch over the ponies and yaks we'd kept with us.

I knew that Nawang Bura spoke some English, but as with Semchumbi, he seemed to have lost it in his terror.

Reggie listened to the short, heavy man's explosion of syllables and then interpreted for us: "Nawang Bura Sherpa says that he is the only man who escaped Base Camp alive. The *Nitikanji* came in last night just after dusk. Tall creatures with terrible faces, fangs, long claws, long arms, and heavy gray fur everywhere on them. Nawang Bura was just returning from Camp One when he saw them slaughtering everyone at Base Camp, so he turned and ran and escaped and survived, and came all the way up here to Camp Three with the few other Sherpas who'd been at Camp One and Camp Two. No one wanted to stay in the valley with the *Metohkangmi* when the creatures were so angry and hungry."

"Hungry?" I said. "Is Nawang Bura saying that the *yeti* were killing and *eating* Sherpas down at Base Camp?"

Reggie passed the question along to the chief muleteer, Nawang Bura responded with a speech that went on for more than thirty seconds, and Reggie translated. "Yes," she said.

"How many at Base Camp?" asked the Deacon.

Nawang Bura and a dozen other men answered at once.

"Seven," said Reggie. "Seven *yeti.*"

"No, I didn't mean *yeti,* damn it all. I meant how many Sherpas were at Base Camp? Are still there?"

. Reggie spoke in Nepalese, a dozen or more men spoke at once in answer.

"Twelve Sherpas," she said. "Semchumbi said that some ran north during the slaughter, away from the mountain, toward Rongbuk Monastery, but he saw more *yeti* kill them before they reached the plain beyond the river."

"So," said the Deacon, "seven *yeti* supposedly killing a dozen strong Sherpas."

"Excuse me," said Dr. Pasang. "Two of the Sherpas there—Lhakpa Yishay and Ang Chiri—were not so strong. They were kept at Base Camp until they recovered from the amputation of toes and fingers."

"Seven *yeti* supposedly killing ten strong Sherpas and two recovering ones, then," said the Deacon. "Did anyone think to bring up any of the three rifles that were at Base Camp?"

I had to think a second before remembering how many rifles the expedition had. Reggie had brought one for hunting, as had Pasang and the Deacon. All three rifles, after our arrival, had been kept in padlocked crates in a special sealed tent. It took permission of a sahib even for the cook to use one for hunting.

"Well, we do have this weapon," said the Deacon and removed a huge pistol—not a Very pistol, but a *real* pistol—from his rucksack.

He snapped open the so-called Break-Top Revolver, showed all of us that it was empty of cartridges, and let each of us hoist it.

It was a heavy revolver, a Webley Mark VI. There was a stout leather lanyard—oiled almost black by grease and sweat and smoke—tied onto the metal loop at the bottom of the handgrip.

"It takes .455-caliber cartridges," the Deacon said, showing us a box of the large, heavy cartridges, and then took the revolver back and proceeded to load all six chambers.

"Thank God we have a weapon with us," said Reggie.

"Is it the pistol you used in the War?" I asked.

"I bought it before going to war and used it all four years. Now I only wish we'd brought the rifles up to Camp Three or Four. That was stupid of me to leave them all at Base Camp."

I hadn't paid much attention to the three rifles, even when Reggie or Pasang went out hunting with one. I assumed they were regular hunting rifles, although I remembered now that one of them—perhaps the Deacon's—had boasted a telescopic sight mounted on it.

The Sherpas were babbling at Reggie again, but I could tell by the way Semchumbi hung his head that no Sherpas had thought to break into the "sahibs' tent" and crates to get the rifles during the "yeti attack."

"That's all right," said the Deacon. "No matter. We'll get some extra tents from Camp Two to shelter the fourteen Sherpas up here, and then the five of us will go down to Base Camp and fetch the rifles. Which of you Sherpas wants to come with us to Camp Two?"

Dr. Pasang repeated the Deacon's question in Nepalese. None of the Sherpas volunteered.

"Fine," said the Deacon. "So I'll choose you, you, you, you, you, and you..." He pointed out six of the Sherpas, including both Nawang Bura and Semchumbi. "You'll come down to Camp Two with us, help us break down some tents, and haul them back up here to Camp Three."

When Pasang interpreted the command and the men started shaking their heads, the Deacon snapped to the Sherpa doctor, "Tell them it's not a request, damn it. It's an order. If they don't get at least three more tents up here tonight, some of these men will be dead by morning. Tell those six that we sahibs and Pasang will stay with them at Camp Two until they pack up at least four more tents to haul up here. We'll wait until they get safely back on the glacier before the five of us head down to check out Base Camp. And they can have my pistol to bring back up to Camp Three."

The six men sighed and hung their heads, but a couple of them brightened at the idea of getting the large Webley Mark VI pistol. Semchumbi said something which Reggie translated as "The cook says that if it is their destiny to die by the hands of yeti on Cho-mo-lung-ma, so be it."

The Deacon only grunted. "Tell those six to get their rucksacks. And also tell them to get a bloody move on."

Reggie leaned close to the Deacon and half-whispered, "Is it really wise to give up the only firearm we have?"

"I'm not giving it up," said the Deacon. "I'm only lending it to Semchumbi until we return from Base Camp. There are fourteen Sherpas here who need protection. All five of us at least will have Very pistols."

In ten more minutes we were ready. The Deacon made a small ceremony of handing his Webley revolver to Semchumbi and then set his heavy flare gun—loaded with a flare cartridge—in the large pocket of his Shackleton anorak. After a moment's hesitation, Reggie, Pasang, Jean-Claude, and I took out our smaller Very pistols, loaded them with 12-gauge cartridges—I chose the white flare, which left me only one spare cartridge, the red one—and put the pathetic little flare pistols in our outer pockets.

"Do we want to rope up for the glacier?" asked Jean-Claude.

The Deacon thought a minute and then said, "I think not. I'll lead with you alongside me to point out crevasses that may have been covered by last night's snow. Jake, you help herd the six Sherpas in a tight pack, single file behind Jean-Claude and me. Where we step, they step. Reggie and Dr. Pasang, you please bring up the rear."

To Semchumbi he said, "Tie the lanyard of my pistol to your wrist—that's right—and don't hold it by its handgrip unless you intend to shoot someone. There's no safety for it, of course."

Semchumbi handled the heavy gun as if it were a cobra, but it seemed to put some confidence back into the other five Sherpas and even in those who were to remain behind.

Everyone nodded. We left Camp III and started up onto and then down the long, dangerous glacier toward Camp II.

4.

⟨⟨⟨⟩⟩⟩

*I*t was almost dusk when we reached Base Camp.

Everything had taken too long—shepherding the six frightened Sherpas down the glacier to Camp II at 19,800 feet, checking out that the camp hadn't been harmed and didn't seem to be inhabited by *yetis* or mountain demons, helping the Sherpas break camp and then reload the tents, poles, and stakes—one big Whymper tent bound for Camp III and three smaller Meades—and finally convincing the anxious Sherpas that they'd be safe on the five-mile carry between Camps II and III. In the end, only Semchumbi's possession of the heavy Webley pistol persuaded them to head back up the glacier; their friends and relations at Camp III would be waiting for their protection with that gun.

At Camp II the Deacon asked Nawang Bura to go down to Base Camp with us since he was the only surviving Sherpa who claimed to have seen the *yeti* attack. Before leaving for Camp I and Base Camp, the six of us used the big Primus in the mess tent at Camp II to cook up a hearty lunch of cocoa—hotter than anything the five of us had drunk in days—as well as pea soup, biscuits, ham, cheese, and some fresh chocolate bars for dessert.

After the mid-afternoon meal, I was sure that all of us wanted to crawl into one. of the few remaining tents at Camp II and sleep around the clock. But we couldn't.

It was two and a half miles from Camp II down to Camp I at only 17,800 feet—relatively easy going when we'd formerly hiked up and down the bamboo-wand-marked path in the center of the Trough, but this Tuesday we stayed away from the usual trail and took twice as long descending on a rough lateral moraine that ran above the Trough and abutted the glacier itself. The high moraine route across larger stones was much harder than the usual walk down the Trough, but we were anxious not to blunder into whatever might be waiting for us at Camp I or *coming up* from that camp. We wanted to see *them* before they saw *us*.

Nothing and no one unusual waited for us at Camp I. The tents were empty, extra oxygen rigs and food stores cached right where they'd been when we'd passed this way days ago heading up to the North Col. We studied the few snowfields around Camp I, attempting to find strange boot prints—or, I admitted only to myself, the gigantic footstep imprints of a *yeti*—but other than the total absence of the few Sherpas who'd been permanently stationed there, there was nothing unusual to see at our first camp above Base Camp. I admit that after days and nights at real altitude, the air at 17,800 feet felt thick enough to swim in.

It was a final three miles from Camp I down to Base Camp at a mere 16,500 feet, and once again we stayed off the beaten trail—which prolonged both the descent and my anxiety. By the time we reached a moraine ridge that looked out and across the next lower ridge to Base Camp itself, we were all, save for Nawang Bura, carrying Very pistols in our gloved or bare hands. The Deacon's much larger Very pistol looked gigantic compared to the smaller German flare pistols carried by J.C., Reggie, Pasang, and me. Nawang had brought a large carving knife with him from Camp II.

Personally, I wished the Deacon had kept the damned revolver.

We found a place where we could all lie on our bellies along the rocky ridge that looked *over* the final moraine ridge between us and Base Camp, and we studied the camp through our binoculars.

"*Douce Mère de Dieu,*" whispered Jean-Claude.

I couldn't speak. I just let my jaw sag and worked hard at keeping the field glasses from shaking in my hands.

There were bodies spread all around Base Camp. Every tent was torn and collapsed, including the large Whymper mess and infirmary tents, and even the canvas tarps had been ripped off the *sanga*-walled low stone enclosures.

The bodies were sprawled seemingly at random, and none of them looked intact. Here there was a decapitated torso, there a body with its head and limbs intact but with all of its internal organs ripped out; far out on the plain beyond the point where the glacial stream turned into a shallow river, vultures circled and swooped over two more dead bodies. We could tell through the glasses that those two farthest-flung corpses were dressed in Sherpa clothing, but we could make no identification—especially since the low clouds kept moving along the ground like a thick fog, obscuring the bodies from our view and then suddenly revealing them again in all their gore and horror. The amount of blood at Base Camp was...*absurd* was the only word that came to mind at the time.

So we couldn't make out anyone's identity in the camp area through the binoculars, only gaze at the ungainly attitudes of death, each torn body, lopped-off limb, and decapitated head in its own pool of blood.

I didn't fully believe what I was seeing. I lowered the glasses, wiped my eyes, and looked again. The field of carnage remained the same.

Pasang stood to walk down to the camp, but the Deacon silently pulled him back low behind the moraine ridgeline. "We'll wait awhile," whispered the Deacon.

"There may be wounded men there who need tending," said Pasang.

The Deacon whispered, "They're all dead." We all sat propped against a rock while the mists opened and then closed around us. We took turns watching with binoculars until real evening gloom began setting in.

"There might be wounded men we can't see from here," whispered Pasang. I'd never seen the Sherpa so worked up. "I need to go down there."

The Deacon shook his head. "Semchumbi's body count was right. Everyone's there, and they're obviously all dead. Wait." It wasn't a request. I'd never heard former British Army captain Richard Davis Deacon's military command voice before.

Time passed. The clouds kept hiding bodies, revealing them, then hiding them again. It grew colder. Nothing living moved except the occasional gorak raven alighting on one of the ravaged corpses. The light was very dim when the Deacon finally said, "All right."

The Deacon suggested—quietly commanded—that we spread out as we approached the killing ground. I noticed that he put his own flare pistol in his pocket but gestured for the other four of us to keep ours in hand. Only later did I realize that any enemy hiding in the rocks might easily mistake our 12-gauge Very pistols for actual pistols; the Deacon's flare-barreled, military-issue blunderbuss gave away the illusion.

It was a bizarre and disturbing inspection. My instinct was to check every bloodied but intact body for any signs of life—after all, hadn't Pasang brought Lobsang Sherpa back to life at Camp V with his absurdly large adrenaline needle? But the Deacon hurried our inspections, hushed our groans and exclamations when we recognized old friends amongst the dead, and gestured for J.C. and me to join him in converging on the large Whymper tent that had held the crates of weapons.

The large tent was torn apart, rags of canvas hanging like shreds of flesh we'd seen on some of the corpses scattered about. All of the crates had been torn open as if by a wildly swung axe (or claws, I wondered?), but the crates holding the hunting rifles and all the extra boxes of cartridges—for the Webley as well as for the rifles—had simply disappeared.

The Deacon crouched so that the rock *sangas* the Sherpas had erected around this former tent would give us a little cover from any armed assassins in the surrounding rocks and hills. At the moment, the constantly shifting cloud-fog was our best (and only) friend.

"Well, the *yetis* are armed now, if they weren't before," the Deacon said softly to Jean-Claude and me. Reggie, Pasang, and a visibly terrified Nawang Bura were still out in the fog moving from body to body, kneeling briefly, and then going on to the next corpse.

"Don't cluster in tight groups," ordered the man who again struck me as Captain Richard Davis Deacon of the Yorkshire Regiment's 33rd/76th Foot Battalion. "It's better that we raise our voices from a distance if we have to than group into tight target clusters."

"Certainly no human being could do *this*," said Reggie. She was standing over the corpse of a Sherpa who'd had his heart and all interior organs scooped out of his body. His face was covered with blood but still recognizable. The absolute identifiers were the shoes, specially made by our resident Sherpa cobbler for a man whose toes had just been amputated.

"Ang Chiri," I said softly, not coming closer than ten or twelve feet from Reggie and the terrible corpse.

"I need to do a quick postmortem on one or two of these remains to find the actual cause of death," said Pasang. "Mr. Perry, Monsieur Clairoux, Lady Bromley-Montfort, could you help me carry Ang Chiri's and Norbu Chedi's bodies to what's left of the infirmary tent? Some of the operating board is still intact, and I saw a workable lantern in the debris."

To find the actual cause of death? I mumbled to myself. These men had been torn and clawed and bitten to bloody shreds and shattered bones. What could an autopsy show?

The Deacon had a different question. "You're going to light a lantern and do postmortem examinations while these killers may still be around and waiting?" he asked from where he was crouched over the headless corpse of Lhakpa Yishay. I knew it was Lhakpa because his severed head had been propped between the exposed and shattered ribs in his hollowed-out chest. I thought of the Breakers of the Dead.

"Yes, I need the light from the lanterns," said Pasang. "And, Mr. Deacon, would you please carry over Lhakpa Yishay's head...yes, just the head. Once I get the bodies within the *sanga* rock walls of the infirmary, we can disperse again according to your wishes."

The Deacon asked me to give Pasang some cover with my stubby Very pistol while Pasang was absorbed in his work under the cone of yellow light coming down from the lantern hanging on a tall tentpole he'd propped against the splintered operating table. I tried to keep my gaze averted—staring out into the shifting cloud-fog as it moved between us and the ice seracs and moraine ridges, every movement of fog looking to me like something huge and gray suddenly lurching out of the darkness—but sometimes I had to look back to where Pasang was digging in Ang Chiri's emptied-out chest cavity. I realized that Pasang was using a scalpel and tongs from his doctor's bag—most of the rest of the medical tools in the former infirmary tent here at Base Camp had been dumped and scattered but not carried away—to probe around poor Ang's all-too-visible spinal cord.

I quickly looked away, back toward the gathering darkness all around us. In the oversized gray, waterproof Shackleton anoraks worn over their bulging goose down jackets, Reggie, the Deacon, Jean-Claude, and even Nawang Bura looked too much like *yetis* standing or ambling in the roiling cloud-fog. It was beginning to snow again.

I heard a "plink" of metal on metal behind me and turned in time to

see Pasang using tongs to drop something small and dark into a white
metal basin on the autopsy-stained operating board.

"Mr. Perry, could you please help me remove Mr. Ang Chiri's
body—we'll set it over there on the ground just within the *sanga*—and
perhaps help me lift Mr. Chedi onto the table?"

I did so, donning my thick overmittens so the blood wouldn't get on
my hands. That was a mistake; I never did get the blood off those mittens.

I admit that I stared when Pasang lifted Lhakpa Yishay's disembodied
head, held it close to his own face, and rotated it under the light as if he
were inspecting a rare crystal. The entire left side of Lhakpa's face had
been gouged out—scooped out, actually—as if by a massive bear's paw
and claws. I could see something gray and glistening from the depths of
that terrible cavity.

I turned away again and fought down nausea just as the doctor set the
head down on the table, leaning it on the right side of Lhakpa's shattered face. Then Pasang lifted a thin but wicked-looking saw. I resisted
the impulse to put my hands over my ears as I heard the rasp of that saw
on Lhakpa's skull. In a minute, there was another "plink" of metal dropping into metal, and when I glanced back over my shoulder, Pasang had
moved Lhakpa's head aside and was digging around in Norbu Chedi's
disemboweled corpse.

Jesus H. Christ, I thought. *Is this really necessary? Can't we just bury
what's left of the poor bastards?*

Pasang had put on long rubber gloves from the doctor's bag he'd carried down in his rucksack, but his arms were bloody up to the elbows.

Suddenly there came a rushing, rustling noise from my right, and I
raised the German Very pistol, only barely avoiding pulling the trigger
as I realized that the silence was being broken by Reggie, Jean-Claude,
and Nawang Bura, all huddled low and moving fast behind the Deacon.
Once in the rough square of the low stone *sanga,* the Deacon silently
pointed at each person and then toward his or her appointed post along
the low wall. The sahibs still had their Very pistols in their hands.
Nawang Bura now had his knife tucked in his broad belt and was carrying a meat cleaver he'd found somewhere amidst the detritus of Base
Camp.

"Find anything?" I whispered.

"Twelve dead, just as Nawang Bura told us," hissed the Deacon from his place opposite the gap in the *sanga* that had served as the entrance to the infirmary tent.

"What about the two out on the plain?" I whispered.

"Both dead. Heads smashed in. Hearts ripped out," the Deacon whispered back.

"Who went out to check on them?" I asked.

"Me."

I tried to imagine having enough courage, even with the enveloping nightfall and fog, to walk alone and exposed those hundreds of yards out to where the two bodies lay on the plain. I didn't think that I could have done it. Then I realized that the Deacon had almost certainly done that very thing, exposing himself to enemy fire that way and worse, a hundred times or more during the four years of the War.

"Do we know who they were other than Ang Chiri and Lhakpa Yishay?" I managed to ask.

The Deacon whispered to the others crouching around the *sanga* before answering me. "Keep a sharp watch out. Try looking out, of the corners of your eyes—one picks up small motions better that way." Then to Dr. Pasang, "Will you be finished and dousing that bloody lantern soon by any chance?"

Pasang nodded, dropped a final piece of metal into the metal pan, and turned off the lantern. The relief of no longer being a lighted target . . . visible meal? . . . made me sigh audibly.

Reggie moved closer to me along the north stone wall and whispered, "Jake, we identified everyone. It wasn't easy. Besides Ang Chiri and Lhakpa Yishay, the dead were Nyima Tsering, Namgya Sherpa, Uchung Sherpa, Chunbi Sherpa, Da Annullu, Tshering Lhamo—he was the young Buddhist priest trainee you may remember . . ."

I recalled our thin, always smiling Tiger Sherpa who'd spent so much time talking to the priests at the Rongbuk Monastery.

" . . . and also Kilu Temba, Ang Tshering, and Ang Nyima. Those last two were the ones who'd run across the stream to the north."

"Were the two Angs brothers?" I whispered.

It was just light enough for me to see Reggie shake her hooded head.

"'Ang' is just a diminutive term, Jake. It can mean 'small and beloved.' Ang Tshering meant 'beloved Long Life.' Ang Nyima meant 'beloved Sunday-born.'"

I could only shake my head in sorrow and embarrassment. I hadn't even understood these men's names. To me they'd all been porters—a means to our ends, "our" being the Deacon's, J.C.'s, and mine—and I'd never even bothered to learn more than a few words of their language, and those mostly commands.

I vowed that if I got out of this mess alive, I'd be a better person.

I noticed that the Deacon had taken off his Shackleton jacket and draped it over himself and Pasang as if it were a rain poncho. Then one of the little miner's lights clicked on and I saw through the folds in their blackout mini-tent that they were looking at small, dull-colored metal objects—three of them—that were in Dr. Pasang's metal basin.

"Bullets," Pasang said just loudly enough for the rest of us to hear. "Slugs. Taken from each of the dead men. With Ang Chiri, the bullet had passed through his heart—his heart was missing, you may remember—but had lodged in his spine. The bullet is deformed from impact, but I think you can make it out, Mr. Deacon. It's similar to this one, which was in Lhakpa Yishay's brain, had not passed through hard bone, and was not deformed."

"Nine-millimeter Parabellum," whispered the Deacon, holding the larger bullet. "I saw a lot of these pulled out of British lads during the War."

"I did also," said Dr. Pasang. I remembered then that Pasang had been studying and interning and working in British hospitals during the War.

"This type was usually fired from a German Luger pistol," said the Deacon. "Seven-round magazine. Sometimes, towards the end of the War, this kind of nine-millimeter round was fired from the Luger Parabellum M-Seventeen variant—a sort of machine gun carbine, thirty rounds, longer barrel."

"We didn't hear any shots," hissed Jean-Claude. He was crouched, flare pistol in hand, and diligently looking into the foggy darkness in his sector. He didn't even turn his head toward us when he spoke.

"With the wind blowing the way it's been," said the Deacon, "and snow falling...Acoustics get very strange on the mountain."

"We heard Lobsang Sherpa shouting at Camp Five last night," whispered Reggie. "Heard him over high wind gusts."

"Which were blowing straight up the mountain toward us from where he lay in Camp Five," the Deacon whispered back. "With all the seracs and *penitentes* between Base Camp and Camps Two and Three, with the wind gusting from the west as well as the northwest last night, I wouldn't be surprised if no one, even those Sherpas still at Camp Two, heard a single shot."

"So we're looking for *yetis* carrying German Lugers?" I said, hoping to lighten the mood. Or at least to lift my own morale.

No one responded.

Under their Shackleton anorak shelter, Pasang was holding up the final bullet of the three he'd retrieved. "This one is odd. Still intact, but hard for me to identify. Not nine millimeter."

"Eight millimeter," whispered the Deacon. "Popular with the Austrians and Hungarians in pistols designed before the War by Karel Krnka and Georg Roth. The most common pistol—first used by the Austro-Hungarian cavalry, later produced by the Germans for infantry officers—was the Roth Steyr M. nineteen oh-seven semiautomatic pistol. I had one aimed at my face in a trench one day, but the hammer fell on an empty chamber."

I had to ask—"How many rounds did the thing hold?"

"Ten," said the Deacon. He shut off the small lamp, tugged his Shackleton jacket back on over his head, and gestured for all of us to duckwalk closer to him.

"I wish to God we were dealing with *yeti,* but we're not," he whispered. "We have to assume that we're dealing with several very human killers—perhaps the seven men Nawang Bura saw from a distance—at least some of whom are armed with semiautomatic pistols and perhaps even fully automatic weapons."

"Machine guns?" I said stupidly.

"Submachine guns," corrected the Deacon. "We don't know. But we do know that we have to get back up to Camp Three as quickly as we can—in case these man-monsters try to get at our Sherpas."

"But the wounds on our Tigers," hissed Reggie. "The lopped-off limbs, the damage to the tents, the decapitations, hearts torn out..."

"Most probably done with edged weapons or specialized tools—a very sharp garden claw could do some of what we saw here," whispered Pasang. "They mauled and desecrated the corpses in order to cast fear into the hearts of our Sherpas."

"It cast fear into *my* heart," whispered Jean-Claude, but he was smiling ever so slightly. *How the hell can he smile?* I wondered.

"We're not going to rope up," said the Deacon, taking time to look each of us in the eye, "but we're going to move in single file and as quietly as we can—stay in touching distance of the person ahead of you, just put a finger on his shoulder if you must—and those of you with Very pistols, carry them loaded, keep the extra cartridges in an outer pocket where you can get at them quickly."

"But our Sherpas have your Webley," said Reggie. "We're the ones with no real weapons. Shouldn't the Sherpas come down and rescue *us?*"

The Deacon smiled. "I'll ask for my pistol back when we get to Camp Three. Right now, I'm uncomfortable with the idea of one armed cook against six or seven or more armed murderers. We know what those predators are capable of." The Deacon nodded in the direction of the killing fields. I could smell the coppery stink of blood and the slight but growing stench of decomposing flesh and brains.

"Who are they?" whispered J.C.

The Deacon didn't answer. He gestured for us to get ready to leave the rock-walled protection of the infirmary *sanga.*

"We're going straight up the Trough, then?" whispered Reggie as we got into single file, the Deacon leading, Reggie next, then me, then Pasang, then Nawang Bura, and finally Jean-Claude.

"Yes," whispered the Deacon. "But not on the path. From ice pillar to ice pillar, *penitente* to *penitente,* from one moraine ridge to the next. Move when I move; stop when I stop. If I have to fire a flare at someone, check your targets before *you* fire. Remember, these Very pistols weren't built to be used as weapons. More than ten feet of distance from your target and you have sod-all chance of hitting someone. Make each shot count."

None of us had anything to add to that. One by one, following the Deacon, our left arms extended to touch the one in front of us, the Very pistols in our right hands, we moved into the swirling, snow-driven darkness and up the Rongbuk Glacier valley back toward Mount Everest.

5.

⟨∞⟩

As we walked slowly up the dark Trough, moving quickly from the theoretical cover of one ice pinnacle or moraine ridge to another (but no longer crouching or duckwalking except when the Deacon held up his arm as a signal to stop), I began to wonder when this expedition had crossed the boundary from the merely fantastic into the region of the absurdly unbelievable.

The line of the six of us slow-jogging from one 50-foot-tall *penitente* ice pinnacle to the next reminded me of when I was a kid and forced my two sisters to play Cowboys and Indians with me on a small hill set in the thick groves of trees behind our family home in Boston's old suburb of Wellesley. We'd hide, peek out, run to the next tree, and then hide again. When I could see their skirts or pinafores flash in the dappled forest light, I'd fire my carved wooden pistol at them. But my sisters, never wanting to get their frocks dirty, always refused to fall dead on the forest floor or roll down the hill when I'd clearly shot them. I, on the other hand, fell dead so violently and rolled down the hill so gracefully that eventually we'd boiled the Cowboys and Indians down to a more pure kid-activity which I thought of as "shoot Jacob and watch him die and roll."

Thinking of my sisters made me remember that none of us had sent any letters to friends or family since we'd sailed from England. This Everest expedition was supposed to be a secret—our secret—so there could be no letters or postcards stamped from Colombo or Port Said or Calcutta or Darjeeling. Quite a change from the British '21, '22, and '24

470

expeditions, when runners carried mail back and forth between Everest and Darjeeling, keeping the climbers in intermittent but solid contact with the world beyond. If someone like Henry Morshead or Howard Somervell wrote home saying that they wanted some chocolate cake, chocolate cake they would receive a few weeks later.

I knew that Jean-Claude had written a letter to his sweetheart—or was she already his fiancée?—Anne Marie, every day of this trip. Their plan, I knew, was to marry in December after J.C. received a promotion to Chamonix Guide First Class, and thus a boost of his meager pay.

I don't know if the Deacon wrote letters during this trip; I'd never seen him write anything except official expedition letters and notes in his leather-bound travel log. In the first weeks of the expedition I'd written a few letters to my parents, one to an old Harvard girlfriend, and even one to my favorite sister, Eleanor, but I got tired of packing the letters around with me, so I'd poured my writing talents into my detailed climbing journal.

The upshot of my thinking those moments scurrying up the Trough was *If we die on this goddamned glacier or mountain, no one will ever know.*

After an hour of this scuttling from one ice pinnacle to the next, never walking exactly on the bamboo-wanded and red-flagged center path, but never wandering that far to either side of it, we reached Camp I at 17,800 feet, 1,300 feet above the death fields that had been Base Camp.

Camp I had looked fine on our way down; now, just hours later, it had been torn apart. The same slashed canvas, tumbled poles, broken-open crates, and general sense of total destruction we'd seen at Base Camp. But there were no bodies at Camp I. We checked the snow for tracks, but other than those of some hobnailed boots—many of our Tiger Sherpas had been wearing hobnailed boots—there was nothing to see.

Then Jean-Claude had hissed at us, and there in a 15-foot patch of snow were three gigantic *yeti* tracks. Each was similar to a human footprint other than its absurd length—more than 18 inches long, I guessed—and the fact that the big toe curved inward, almost like a gorilla's foot or other large primate's.

"Big fellow based on his stride," whispered the Deacon. "Easily seven feet tall. Perhaps eight."

"Surely you don't . . . ," began Reggie.

"I don't," the Deacon whispered to her. "Not for an instant. You can see beneath each footprint where someone in boots stepped in the place where each fake footprint was to go, then pressed down this huge *yeti*-foot imprint when he took his next step."

"It seems an elaborate and rather silly ruse if the men doing this intend to kill us all anyway," Reggie said.

The Deacon shrugged. "I suspect that the carnage at Base Camp and this sad children's play with the footprints was aimed at scaring off all of our Sherpas. Or perhaps they plan to kill all of us, including all our Sherpas, but sell this *yeti* idea to the locals. In the end, though, it's not the Sherpas these wanton murderers want to kill; it's the four of us. Five of us, counting Dr. Pasang."

I thought that this was *very* reassuring.

Camp II was burning. They'd torched everything they could find, but they hadn't found the cache of oxygen rigs which we'd hidden behind snow-covered boulders in the maze of seracs, *penitentes,* and moraine on the glacier side of the camp on the way down.

"One could see this fire from Camp Three," said Reggie. "They've given up all pretense of being *yeti.*"

"They're *yetis* with matches and cigarette lighters," said Jean-Claude.

"Will the fourteen men we left at Camp Three climb onto the North Col to escape, do you think?" asked Dr. Pasang.

"I don't think so," said the Deacon. "It would be too much like retreating into a cul-de-sac for them."

"They may scatter," said Reggie. "Climb to the moraine ridges before descending. Try to make it down to Base Camp and back out onto the plains in small groups or one by one."

"That would be the smart thing to do," agreed Jean-Claude.

"Do you believe they will do that, Mr. Deacon?" asked Pasang.

"No."

I was looking at the sets of oxygen tanks on their frames. Their dials showed most of them were topped off with pressure. "What do we do with these things?" I asked.

"Bring them with us," said the Deacon.

"Why on earth would we do that?" I said. "Aren't we just going to fetch the surviving Sherpas from Camp Three and make a run for Rong-buk Monastery or Chobuk or Shekar Dzong?" Of the three places I'd mentioned, only the last—Shekar Dzong—seemed large enough and far enough away to feel like a place of temporary safety, even though it was a little less than 60 miles north of Base Camp by trail, less than 40 miles north as the gorak flies.

At the moment I wouldn't have minded being a gorak. But even as I thought that, I thought of the hollowed-out rectum and insides of George Mallory and felt a little sick; there were seeds or something visible in the glorious climber's opened abdominal cavity, and I thought—not for the first sickening time—that I might have been looking at the last thing Mallory had eaten on his last day alive.

I shook my head. This sort of thinking didn't help our current situa-tion. We were crouched in a rough circle around the cached oxygen rigs.

"...Sherpas probably won't flee up the fixed ropes and ladder to Camp Four because they know these...killers...would have them trapped up there," J.C. was saying. "But the same applies to us. The climbing part of this expedition is over—isn't it, Ree-shard? Why on earth would we haul these heavy oxygen sets back up the glacier?"

The Deacon sighed.

"We have to climb again if we get the chance," Reggie said softly.

"Why?" I asked. "You can't expect us to continue the search for your cousin after all this, can you? I mean...think about it, please, Lady Bromley-Montfort...fourteen of our Sherpas are dead, a dozen of them at the hands of sadistic butchers. How on earth could we even consider going back up the mountain? And for what...to summit it?"

"No, not to summit," Reggie insisted. "But it's more imperative than ever that we find Bromley's body."

"She's right," said the Deacon. Reggie blinked at him in obvious sur-prise at his quick agreement.

I didn't understand at all, but I could see that Jean-Claude was nod-ding. His glance moved from Reggie to the Deacon and back. "This expedition never was just about recovering Percival's body for the family, was it, Reggie?"

She bit her lower lip until I could see blood, black in the starlight. "No," she said at last. "It never was." She shifted her gaze to the Deacon.

"You know why it's so important to find Percy's body? Or to make sure no one else can?"

"I believe so," whispered the Deacon.

"My God," said Reggie. "Do we have a mutual friend? Someone who writes a lot of cheques?"

The Deacon smiled. "But who prefers it to be backed up by gold? Yes, my lady."

"My God," Reggie said again, running her fingers over her brow as if she were hot. "I never guessed that you also might..."

"I don't understand a word either of you has just said," said J.C. "But perhaps I should let you know that Nawang Bura has slipped away in the darkness."

The Deacon nodded. "About two minutes ago. He headed north, back towards Base Camp and, perhaps, escape."

"He's not a coward," said Pasang.

"No, none of the Sherpas have been cowards," agreed the Deacon. "They're some of the bravest men I've ever known, and that's saying a lot after the War. But Nawang and the others are up against something extraordinary that their faith and upbringing tell them is a real threat."

"What do you know about their faith, *Ree-shard?*" Jean-Claude sounded irritated.

It was Reggie who answered. "Didn't you two know that Captain Deacon has been a Buddhist for years?"

I stifled a laugh. "That's nonsense. The Deacon didn't even want to go for Dzatrul Rinpoche's blessing ceremony."

"There are Buddhists who don't believe in demons and who don't venerate or worship statues of the Buddha," the Deacon said.

My smile went away. "You can't be serious."

"Haven't you seen your friend sitting in the lotus position, in silence, every morning during the trek in?" asked Pasang.

"*Oui,*" said J.C., sounding as shocked and disbelieving as I was. "But I thought he was...thinking."

"Me too," I said. "Planning the day."

"People thinking about the coming day don't hum '*Om mani padme hum*' under their breath while they're sitting in the lotus position," Reggie said.

"Well, dress me up and call me Sally," said Jean-Claude.

I confess that I barked a quite audible laugh then. Where the hell had J.C. learned *that* phrase?

"May I ask why we're wasting time here discussing my possible philosophical peculiarities," said the Deacon, "when we have to make a decision now whether to gather the Sherpas at Camp Three and make a run for it—or to get as many Sherpas started north as we can get going—and then the five of us head up to the Col before our Luger-carrying *yeti* chums get there? Or should we also make a run for it down the valley?"

"One question first, *Ree-shard.*"

"What's that, Jean-Claude?"

"When exactly did you become a Buddhist?"

"One July nineteen sixteen," whispered the Deacon. "But luckily for all of us right now, I'm a poor excuse for a Buddhist. If I get a chance to kill these people who've murdered our Sherpa friends, I will kill them without the slightest compunction or hesitation. If I do so, you may call me a lapsed Buddhist."

For the second time in less than twenty-four hours I felt goose bumps pop up on both arms and the hair there and on the back of my neck stand straight up. *Kill all of the strangers? How could we possibly do that when they had all the guns and we had these little toy flare pistols?*

"I'll follow you anywhere," said Jean-Claude.

"Me too," I whispered. Did I really mean that? I did.

"I shall stay with Lady Bromley-Montfort wherever *she* goes," said Pasang. "And obey commands from whomever *she* follows."

The Deacon rubbed his forehead, as if he really didn't want to assume command again in any situation where people were going to kill and be killed. But he said, "Once we go back up onto that glacier headed for Camp Three, there may be no turning back. You'll just have to trust in our judgment…in this case, Reggie's and mine. She's still the overall expedition leader. I'll be the climbing and combat leader."

"Can you tell us why finding Bromley's corpse is so much more important than we thought?" whispered J.C. to Reggie.

The lady bit her bloody lip again and looked to the Deacon.

"If we get to Camp Four on the North Col all right, we'll tell you the reason," he said. "Otherwise, if we're going to make a run for Shekar Dzong and points east anyway, it's better if we don't discuss it."

"All right," said Jean-Claude, as if the Deacon had explained something.

I was totally confused but I didn't argue.

Far ahead and higher than us and to the east, a red glow suddenly grew. We watched it for several cold minutes.

"It's out on the glacier," whispered Reggie. "Closer to us than to Camp Three. A red flare?"

"It's lasted too long," said the Deacon, "even to be a railway flare."

"A horrid light," whispered Reggie.

"As if someone's opened the portals of Hell for us," said Jean-Claude.

"You know it will be a trap," Pasang said softly. "A lure."

"Yes," said the Deacon, "but we need to take some prisoners to see just what the hell is going on and who we're up against. We'll be careful, but we have to walk into their trap. Let us think of ourselves as a night patrol in no-man's-land."

"Did most of the men on night patrols in no-man's-land survive their patrols?" I asked.

"No," said the Deacon. He gestured for us to remove fifteen of the eighteen oxygen tanks and their attached valves and rubber hoses and face masks from the aluminum frames and to stick the rigs into our almost empty rucksacks. We did so with as little wasted energy and noise as possible.

Then the Deacon gestured and—the four of us still in single file behind him with J.C. bringing up the rear—moved in a half-crouching, almost running gait, crampons crunching against rock and ice, up through the maze of snow-shrouded ice pinnacles and out onto the exposed ice of the East Rongbuk Glacier.

6.

───⊛───

The red glow was coming from a forest of *penitentes* and abutting vertical ice sheets on the south side of the Grand Crevasse we'd first tried bridging with a ladder and then found a descend-and-climb route a quarter of a mile east after that ladder had sagged. The ice uplifts just east of our main route were more like high, thin, razor-sharp upright sheaths of almost transparent ice rather than the stand-alone pinnacles further down in the Trough, and it was from within this labyrinth that the unearthly red glow was emanating.

Deacon silently gestured Jean-Claude to the lead, and we followed our Chamonix Guide through a spiderweb of unseen snow-covered crevasses. We knew they were there simply because we'd seen them in the daylight every time we'd gone up or down the glacier between Camps II and III. I had no idea how J.C. managed to avoid the crevasses at night; the clouds were still low, the fog from them still curled around us in gray tentacles, and there was absolutely no moonlight or starlight. The Deacon had navigated to this point partially by feel, partially by sheer memory, and partially by strapping his Welsh miner's lamp around his right ankle and switching it on for only seconds at a time, illuminating just a few feet of ice or snow or rock ahead of him. Uncannily, almost every time he'd switched on the small light, there'd been a red-flagged wand within ten feet of him.

He didn't use his ankle light as we approached the red-glowing ice ridges, then led us around behind them to the south. The bright red glow was diffused by the shifting ice mist and had turned the very air crimson.

The Deacon gestured to us all to get down and we did, responding as quickly as well-trained war dogs. He pointed to Jean-Claude, pointed again to a low ice pinnacle to the left of the opening in the ice ridge, touched his own chest, and pointed to the ice ridge to the right. J.C. nodded. The two men moved in the same instant, running forward seemingly on the toes of their crampons, flying ice chips glinting for a second like chips of frozen blood in the cold night air.

The two leaned against their respective ice columns as if readying themselves to crash through a door into a dangerous room. Then, at the Deacon's almost imperceptible nod, both men surged around the ice walls with their Very pistols extended.

No flares were fired. For a few heart-pounding seconds they were out of sight, but then J.C. stepped back into the opening and gestured us forward. Pasang went first, then me, and then Reggie bringing up the rear. We moved carefully in the red-tinted darkness, trying to follow the Deacon's and J.C.'s footprints in the snow, and when we reached the opening in the ice ridge, we could see that the red glow was coming from a modern electric torch—essentially a black box with a bright, directed bulb in it—and that there was a red lens set over the usually transparent lens. The snowy floor of the room-like space within the cluster of ice pillars was crossed and crisscrossed by boot prints.

"A trap . . . ," began Pasang.

A tall form came whirling around a *penitente* pinnacle toward Reggie. I had time to get an impression of a tall figure covered with long gray fur and a sharp-edged gray-white face like a human skull turned inside out. Only later did I register the black steel object in his right hand.

I was frozen but Reggie was not. She dropped to one knee as the hairy form lunged in her direction, its shaggy right arm rising, and she fired her Very pistol—a red flare—directly into the figure's chest from a distance of only seven or eight feet.

The flare struck the tall man's chest, ricocheted upward into the soft flesh under his chin, the furry overjacket he was wearing caught fire, the skull-face was violently jarred up and to the side, and then a second, human mouth under the mask opened wide, emitting sputtering red flare flames rather than a scream. The tall figure whirled around once, twice, three times—its chest fur burning, the flare illuminating the contorted double face like a giant red candle set in a broken jack-o'-lantern, and then the figure just . . . disappeared.

It didn't go behind an ice ridge or pinnacle; one second it was simply whirling and on fire and hissing sparks and the next second...it was gone.

Then I saw the red glow coming up from within the glacier. I ran to Reggie's side. "Are you all right?"

"Yes, thank you, Jake," she said, her visible breath glowing red in the flare light that seemed to be coming up through the ice under our feet. She was calmly loading a new flare cartridge into the breech of her Very pistol. Turning away, I started to run forward, toward that glow at our feet, but Jean-Claude stopped me with a strong hand on my chest.

"Crevasse," he hissed. Then he handed me the end of the rope he'd lashed around himself and wormed forward across the ice on his belly. He stared down into the roughly circular hole in the snow, and I could see the fading red flicker of the dying flare reflected on Jean-Claude's face.

"It's firm to the lip," he whispered over his shoulder and gestured us forward. The Deacon and I advanced on our bellies and elbows and stared down into the crevasse. The Deacon had brought along the heavy black box of his electric torch—which cast a much brighter beam of light than did the miner's headlamps—and he held it at arm's length down the abyss, presumably to shield it from being seen by others who might be on the glacier, and turned it on.

I almost pulled my head back and away, so shocking was the view of a white skull face that seemed to be staring up at us from 40 or 45 feet down. Then I realized that the mask the assailant had been wearing had been forced to the top of his head during the fall. Because his head was sagging forward, we couldn't see his face from our vantage point. The long fur-covered jacket was still burning on his chest and around his neck, and the smell of burning flesh that rose with the smoke was sickening. I was glad that Reggie hadn't scooted forward with the three of us.

The man had fallen backside first into the crevasse, which was almost seven feet across at the top and then narrowing to less than a foot and a half at the point where the assailant's body had become stuck. It was obvious that his spine had been completely snapped; the hobnailed soles of his boots were staring at us on one side of the narrow gap, the top of his head with the crude *yeti* mask gave the illusion of his skull staring up from the other side, and by the flickering light of his burning fur jacket and in the flat glare of the Deacon's electric torch, we could see that his glove-covered hands lay limp on his lap. And there on his lap was a black 9-millimeter Luger.

The compression of the fall had turned his body into an impossibly sharp V that had jammed solidly in the narrowest part of the crevasse; we could see that beneath his grotesquely misshapen body, the crevasse opened wider again into a black and seemingly bottomless abyss.

The Deacon doused his lamp and we wriggled back and away from the crevasse opening. Pasang and Reggie joined us in a crouched circle.

"We need that pistol," whispered the Deacon.

"I'll go down," J.C. whispered. "I am the lightest. And I have my ice hammers. *Ree-shard* and Jake, you can belay me."

"No, Jean-Claude," said the Deacon after the briefest of pauses. "We'll belay Jake down. I don't want the sound of the ice hammer being used, and Jake has the longest, strongest legs of anyone here—he can deal with the crevasse as a chimney problem on the way up."

I could see Jean-Claude blink in surprise.

"We need to try to get that pistol," continued the Deacon, "but doing so will delay us in warning the Sherpas at Camp Three. It may *already* be too late. But we have to try. Jean-Claude, you're our best glacier climber. Take Pasang to interpret, and the two of you go on ahead up to Camp Three as quickly as you can. Try not to use even the headlamps unless it's absolutely necessary. If you get there before these fake *yeti* bastards do, have the Sherpas there set up a defensive perimeter... you'll have only my Webley and your and Pasang's twelve-gauge flare pistols. The rest of us will reinforce you as soon as we can get there with—I hope—that Luger on our side."

Jean-Claude nodded but Reggie said, "No, please, let me go ahead with Jean-Claude, Richard. Pasang's much stronger than I am and he can help you belay Jake. And I think the Sherpas might obey commands from me a bit more quickly."

The Deacon took about one second to consider this suggestion and then nodded. "You're right. Go ahead... be careful."

Reggie and Jean-Claude looked at each other once and slipped away to the northwest toward the wand-marked trail without giving the rest of us so much as a farewell glance. One second they were still visible in the bloody light from the assailant's red-filtered electric torch and the dying flames from the crevasse; the next they were lost in the darkness and curling cloud mist.

The Deacon removed a long coil of rope from his crowded, heavy rucksack—we were still carrying the extra oxygen tanks from Camp II—and handed the end of the line to me. Then he quickly crawled back to the round opening of the crevasse and embedded Pasang's long ice axe adze down at the edge of the ragged hole and a few inches parallel to the lip of it. A foot further back, the Deacon drove his longest ice hammer as deep into the icy snow as he could, then used his penknife to cut off a strand of rope, knotted it quickly, and lashed the head of the shorter ice axe as an anchor to the longer one.

By the time he crawled back to where Pasang and I crouched, I'd double-wrapped the Miracle Rope around my waist and upper thighs as a passable sling harness, then tied on a second time with a carefully knotted friction hitch.

The Deacon stood about eight feet from the edge of the crevasse, drove his own ice axe deep into the ice there, looped the long rope around it twice, set it over Pasang's shoulder in proper belay form, and then looped it over his own shoulder.

"Tug twice when you want us to stop lowering," the Deacon said to me. "Tug once for a little more slack. Three tugs means bring you up."

"Do you want anything other than the Luger?" I asked.

The Deacon shook his head. "I'd like the *whole* corpse so we could go through his pockets and figure out who and what we're up against. But he's wedged in there tightly, Jake, and I think we'd spend too many minutes working at hauling his corpse up after we retrieve you. But if he has any easily accessible pockets, go through them—hunt for a box of nine-millimeter cartridges and any papers or identification he might have on him. But don't put yourself in more danger than you have to. With his spine totally snapped like that, he's just a soft mass wedged there and could fall away into the abyss at any second."

I nodded my understanding, set my headlamp gear on my head, clicked on the light, walked to the very edge of the circular crevasse hole, waited until the Deacon and Pasang were on full, tight belay, leaned far back, and rappelled down into the smoldering crevasse, crampons biting into the west ice wall, the beam of my headlamp showing blue ice fragments of the crevasse wall looking as sharp as protruding daggers.

* * *

Once down to the level of the corpse—I now estimated it as being closer to 50 feet from the surface—I tugged twice on the rope above the friction hitch, spun myself around, set my back against the ice wall I'd been rappelling down, and set one long leg on each side of the body, my crampon points dug deep into the opposite wall. The corpse and I were very close to one another. I could no longer see flames coming from the lambskin or fur vest or whatever layer was covering his regular jacket, but something was still smoldering there. I realized that it was the flesh on the man's chest and neck.

I bent as low as I could toward the man's face, doing everything in exaggerated slow motion so as not to knock the Luger into the darkness below, and carefully reached the gloved fingers of my left hand for the pistol.

Got it!

I brought it up and carefully tucked it into my shirt under my sweater inside my Finch duvet jacket and under my Shackleton jacket. I might fall to the bottom of this crevasse—my headlamp beam had shown no bottom to it, only ragged ice walls and hundreds of feet of black below—but I'd be damned if the pistol was going to fall out and be lost.

I studied the mask pushed up on the man's head. It seemed to be carved out of some sort of light, white wood, then painted with exaggerated wrinkles. The carved teeth around the mouth opening were real teeth—possibly taken from wolves or huge dogs. I could see where they'd been glued into sockets in the mask.

I patted at his trouser pockets—his trousers were baggy and also covered with shaggy sheep's fleece dyed gray to look like fur—but felt nothing so solid that it could be a cartridge box. I could feel papers in his trouser pockets under the fur outer layer, but I didn't think I could get to them without dislodging the corpse from its V-shaped wedge. *Damn.*

Then I turned the headlamp full into the dead man's real face and gasped. At first glance it looked as if goraks had eaten his eyes and that someone had poured melted wax down his face, but then I realized that his eyes had exploded and partially melted from the heat of the flare. It was vitreous humor from his eyes that had run down his stubbled cheeks like melted wax.

The man's mouth was open wide—as if in a final parody of surprise at his own terrible death—and smoke from Reggie's flare that had bounced up and through the underside of his jaw was wafting out and over me like some carrion eater's terrible breath. I had to turn my head aside to the right for a minute and rest my cheek against the ice wall to breathe cleaner air there or be sick. I gulped in the clean air and fought down my rising gorge.

My movement and slight shifting of position, or perhaps some settling in the glacier itself, jogged the body slightly so that in mere seconds the man's boots folded up over his shoulders and he slipped and slid and squeezed down through a gap less than a foot wide, his body with its snapped spine and collapsed ribs folding like some obscene accordion.

Then he was gone, and for a terrible few seconds the toe points of my crampons slipped out of the opposing wall—the body must have grazed me when it fell away, but it felt more like the dead man had gripped my ankles and tried to pull me down with him. My heart was pounding wildly and I couldn't breathe in enough of the cold crevasse air to fill my lungs. Then I was suddenly hanging free on the rope, having completely lost my crampon grip on the opposite wall. I fell a foot or two before the Deacon and Pasang held me on belay. The Deacon's Miracle Rope did not snap, but I could feel it stretch more than one of our old ropes would have.

I wasted no time resting there in midair, but whirled around, planted the crampon points of my right boot on the west ice wall, dug the points of my left boot into the east ice wall, extended both arms for leverage—and began working the crevasse as a chimney climb after tugging three times on the rope. I could feel the two strong men above me keeping the rope taut, but I dug points in while spread-eagled and worked to lift myself. Any of the killers could show up at any second on the glacier above, and I damned well didn't want to be uselessly stuck in this crevasse if and when they did.

Then I was up and out of the bone-deep chill of the glacier's guts and rolling out into the open. For a second as I kept rolling, I felt under me the wood of Pasang's embedded ice axe that had kept the rope from cutting into the ice lip of the glacier. Getting to my knees, I retrieved the two anchor axes and stood, carefully backing away from the crevasse hole, still turned away from my two waiting friends. Both were panting; belaying a man who weighs a little over two hundred pounds is hard work at any altitude, but absurdly hard work there above 20,000 feet.

I let them gasp; I just bent over, put my hands on my knees, and tried to cough my guts up and out onto the glacier.

"That cough has been getting worse, Mr. Perry," said Pasang. He moved away in the flickering red gloom and dug into his rucksack and doctor's bag.

"We certainly aren't going to sneak up on any more *yetis* if you keep hacking like that," the Deacon said. "Did you get the pistol?"

I reached into my shirt to where the cold metal seemed to be burning me through several silk and cotton layers, removed the gun, and handed it to the Deacon.

He hefted the semiautomatic as if he knew how to handle the thing—I had little doubt that he did—and then he clicked a button near the trigger guard (which I later learned was the safety...the dead man in the crevasse had clicked it off), grabbed the little cylinder that tucks into the tops of Luger semiautomatic pistols, ratcheted it up and back until it locked in place, checked the now open breech, and then touched something that made the magazine that was in the stock drop into his palm.

"God *damn* it!"

The Deacon thumbed two 9-millimeter rounds out of the magazine, but that was it...two rounds.

"You couldn't feel any extra cartridges in his pockets?" asked the Deacon.

"No. Nor under that *yeti* jacket. But I couldn't reach his back pockets."

The Deacon shook his head. "Unless they've used up all their ammunition shooting everyone at Base Camp, there must be more cartridges around here somewhere—perhaps in this *yeti's* rucksack hidden somewhere here in the ice pinnacles or the ridges. What kind of total fool sets up an ambush for five or six people and keeps only two rounds in his magazine and none in the spout?"

I couldn't answer that question, so I didn't try. I wasn't even sure where or what the "spout" of such a pistol *was.*

"He probably had more rounds in his rucksack. All three of us will look around this immediate area—you can use your headlamps, I'm going to use the big electric torch—but we can't take more than five or ten minutes at the most. We don't want to fall too far behind Jean-Claude and Reggie."

I bent almost double as I started coughing and hacking again, straightening up eventually to feel Pasang's big hand on my shoulder, steadying me.

"Here, drink this, Mr. Perry. *All* of it."

He handed me a small bottle. I swallowed all of the fluid, which burned like liquid fire going down, sputtered but kept it down, and handed the bottle back to Dr. Pasang. Within thirty seconds I no longer had the compulsion to cough, and for the first time in almost forty-eight hours my throat didn't feel as if it had a turkey wishbone stuck in it.

"What is that stuff?" I whispered to Pasang as we followed the Deacon out of the rough circle of red light from our *yeti*'s ambush torch.

"Mostly codeine," Pasang whispered back. "I have more for you when the coughing returns."

We turned on our lights and searched for close to fifteen minutes, but while we found boot prints behind ridges and ice pillars, there was no sign of a rucksack with ammunition in it. Finally the Deacon called us back together and we left. I could feel the Deacon's frustration burning like a blue flame in the dark. What good was a German semiautomatic pistol with only two rounds in it?

Better than no pistol with no rounds, I told myself. I think I was trying to convince myself that my efforts down in that god-awful crevasse had been worthwhile.

Once we were back west of the crevasse and the red light and on the trail up the glacier, the Deacon turned, put a hand on my shoulder, and said, "Jake—I didn't want to tell J.C.—but mostly I wanted you going down there because I thought you might recognize our chum minus his *yeti* face. Did you?"

"I think so. Maybe. Yes...I think." Dead men's faces, I'd learned, looked different from their alive faces.

"Well, who is it, for heaven's sake?"

"Karl Bachner," I said. "Bruno Sigl's German climbing pal—the older, famous one, the one who was the president or founder of all those German climbing clubs—the older man who was at the table with us the night we met Sigl in Munich last autumn."

The Deacon was close enough for me to make out his features in the dim light; he did not look surprised.

7.

⸺ ❈ ⸺

e saw the glow from the flames and heard the gunshots when we were still more than a mile of glacier travel away from Camp III.

"Damn!" said the Deacon. I knew he was afraid that Reggie and J.C. had arrived there just in time to be caught in a massacre.

The pistol shots echoed down the long glacier valley, and they sounded strangely benign—like those last few kernels of corn popping randomly in a pan—but then the volume of shots increased. Mixed in with discrete pistol shots, there suddenly came a sound like someone ripping a long strip of thick fabric.

"What on earth…," I whispered.

The Deacon held up one finger, silencing me as we listened. None of us had gone on oxygen, and we were all panting and wheezing after trying to move so quickly here at 21,000 feet. The ripping sound came again.

"It could be a Bergmann-Schmeisser submachine gun," the Deacon said at last. "God help the Sherpas and Jean-Claude and Reggie if it is."

"How fast can it fire?" I asked even while not really wanting to know.

"Four hundred fifty rounds per minute," said the Deacon. "And the rate is limited only by the time it takes for the gunner to slap on a new thirty-two-round snail drum magazine. That bulky round magazine makes the Schmeisser MP-18/I awkward to carry, aim, and fire with any accuracy, but you don't really need accuracy with that rate of fire. You just keep spraying. The Germans loved their damned Schmeissers for close-in trench fighting."

"Jesus," I gasped.

"Let us move more quickly," said Pasang and broke into a trot, his crampons flashing in the lowered beams of our headlamps.

"I assume...no more...pretend *yetis*," gasped the Deacon as he ran along beside the long-legged Sherpa. We were still each carrying more than thirty pounds of oxygen rigs and other stuff in our rucksacks.

"No," agreed Dr. Pasang. "It is just men murdering men now."

I trotted faster to keep up with the two, but the sense of something caught in my throat had returned and from time to time I had to stop, lean over with my hands on my padded knees, and cough until I retched. Then I would run faster in an attempt to catch up. Neither man waited for me in the dark.

The flames lit up the entire valley, including the face of Changtse and the ice wall to the North Col. We were less than two hundred meters from Camp III when two dark shapes suddenly stepped out in front of us as if to block our way.

My hand came up and I almost fired my mini-Very pistol at the closer silhouette before the Deacon cried "No!" and batted down my arm.

It was Reggie with J.C. close behind her.

"This way," hissed Jean-Claude, and we followed him off the deep-printed trail as he led us north along a line of snow-covered ice pinnacles and iced-over seracs. After a few seconds of crunching along, I realized that J.C. had chosen this place to get off the main trail because the ice crust here was so thick that we left no boot prints.

"We need to get to Camp Three immediately," whispered the Deacon with a pained urgency audible in his voice. The firing had stopped several minutes earlier. The Deacon was carrying Bachner's two-shot 9-millimeter Luger in his gloved hand rather than the full-sized Very pistol.

J.C. and Reggie led us about two hundred meters north along the line of *penitentes* and seracs, then east through that icy maze until we reached a spot where we could look down on Camp III. Those of us who had binoculars in our rucksacks got them out.

"Oh...God...*damn*...it," whispered the Deacon.

* * *

The tents at Camp III were all ablaze. Bodies of Sherpas were sprawled everywhere—we counted at least nine made visible by the flames—and those stacked crates and heaps of supplies that had not been burned had been hacked to bits with axes. There were no fake *yetis* visible, but whenever the fog shifted high enough, I could see bloody boot prints leading into the forest of ice pinnacles to the south of the camp.

The five of us slumped below the ice ridge and sat staring at one another.

"We arrived too late to help," whispered Jean-Claude. "And it is all my own *être damné par Dieu* fault!"

"What happened?" asked the Deacon.

Jean-Claude emitted a stifled noise that could have been either a sob or a gasp. "I fell into a damned crevasse. *Moi!* The great Chamonix ice and glacier expert!"

"Were you using lights?" I asked.

"No," said the despondent J.C.

"Were you roped up?" I asked.

"No." He took a long, ragged breath. "I was leading, trying to keep Reggie and me on or near the path through an icy patch. Suddenly the snow opened up and I fell about twenty-five feet into the glacier until my ice axe wedged above me where the crevasse finally narrowed. I hung onto the shaft of the axe. Then I started cramponing my way back up and Lady Bromley-Montfort dropped me a rope. She pulled and I Prusiked. But it took me almost fifteen minutes to extricate myself, and I almost dropped my heavy pack into the abyss. I fell into a crevasse like some novice."

"You can't blame yourself, Jean-Claude," whispered the Deacon. "It's just too damned dark tonight and we're all exhausted. No one got more than an hour or two of bad sleep on Monday night at Camp Five and we've been on the go since then. We climbed to twenty-seven thousand feet and above on Sunday and Monday, spent the nights high too many times, haven't had enough water to keep a hamster alive, descended almost ten thousand feet in one day, and tonight climbed almost five thousand feet again. It's a miracle that any of us can function at all."

"The Sherpas here at...," began Jean-Claude and stopped. He was sobbing.

"They never had a chance," said the Deacon. "And it's all my fault. I'm climbing master on this expedition, responsible for everyone's safety. Now all of the Sherpas may be dead, and it's my fault. I was in command."

"We see only nine bodies," whispered Reggie. "There were fourteen Sherpas at Camp Three if all the porters got back safely from Camp Two after we sent them up the glacier. And Nawang Bura came with us and then disappeared. We can hope *he* made it safely out of the valley."

"With his meat cleaver against Bergmann-Schmeisser machine pistols and Luger semiautomatic pistols," the Deacon said bitterly. He rubbed the stubble on his cheek.

"How were the two who almost got away from Base Camp killed?" asked Pasang.

"Long-range rifle shots," whispered the Deacon. "From *our* stolen rifles is my guess."

"I know the hunting rifles that Lady Bromley-Montfort and I brought," Pasang said. "We both used nineteen twenty Mannlicher-Schönauer bolt-action rifles for hunting. What did you bring, Captain Deacon? It was a modified Lee-Enfield, was it not?"

"Yes," said the Deacon. "Fitted out with an offset Periscopic Prism Company 'scope. The telescopic sight is offset about three inches to the left because of the bolt action. You sight with your right eye, but can switch to your left eye while firing and working the action. I used it at the Front. It looks clumsy—it *was* clumsy—but it worked well enough."

"You were allowed to keep that after the War?" I asked.

"It was illegal, but I did," said the Deacon. "I'd paid for the telescopic sight myself."

"But *Ree-shard...*" Jean-Claude paused for several seconds. "You were an officer, no? Your only weapon was the Webley revolver that you lent to Semchumbi tonight, yes?"

"Yes and no," said the Deacon in heavy tones, as if he were a Catholic confessing a very dark secret indeed. "Even though I was an officer, I volunteered to be trained as a sniper. I grew very good at it during our weeks in the trenches between attacks."

I didn't know how to feel about this revelation. Everything I'd heard after the War suggested that *both sides* hated snipers on the battlefield. Even their own.

"A Buddhist sniper," said Reggie, breaking the silence at last. "Which means that we have to regain one of those rifles for you to use."

"We tried," said Jean-Claude. "Reggie suggested, and I agreed, that we should set an ambush here at these icy seracs for the *yetis*—these German-climber *yetis*—when they came back along this part of the glacier trail. Her idea was good. Fire flares at those carrying our rifles or the Schmeisser machine pistol, try to grab one of those weapons in the darkness and confusion, and then retreat into the ice maze here."

"They would have killed you both," said the Deacon.

Jean-Claude shrugged. "We need real weapons, *mon ami*. Did you succeed in getting the dead *yeti*'s pistol?"

The Deacon showed the black Luger. "Two rounds, none in the breech. I think Bachner was never a soldier."

"It was Bachner?" asked Jean-Claude. "The man who was with Sigl in Munich when you went there?"

"Who's Bachner?" asked Reggie.

I whispered an explanation to her, and then the Deacon interrupted. "Did you see the Germans during this slaughter at Camp Three? How many attackers were there? Is there any chance some of our fourteen Sherpas *did* get away?"

"We saw at least eight Germans in their hairy jackets," said Reggie. "They'd given up wearing the *yeti* masks once they were through slaughtering our people. After setting the tents and stores ablaze, they just tossed the masks and *yeti*-vests into the fires."

"I believe that a few of our people dragged themselves into the serac forest wounded," whispered Jean-Claude. "The boot prints show that the Germans followed them into the ice-pinnacle maze, following their blood trails. Finishing them off."

"I was hoping that some of those blood trails belonged to the Germans," I said. "Semchumbi had the Deacon's Webley revolver. I forget—how many rounds did that hold?"

"Only six," said the Deacon. "And it's a double-action revolver. But it has an automatic extractor when you break it, so someone skilled in its use, with extra cartridges at hand, can get off twenty to thirty rounds per minute."

"Was Semchumbi skilled in its use?" asked J.C.

"No," rasped the Deacon.

"Did he have extra cartridges at hand?" asked Pasang.

"No."

"Well, I still hope he shot a few of the bastards," I said.

"Amen," whispered Jean-Claude.

From time to time we popped up and looked over the ridge with our binoculars, but—save for the fires dying down—the terrible view remained the same. The Germans had not returned. None of the bodies in the snow had stirred.

"We have to go down there," said Reggie. Her voice was steadier than mine could have been.

"Why go down there?" I asked. "Why risk it?"

"We need food, kerosene, a Primus or Unna cooker, Meta bars to burn, sleeping bags, extra clothing, anything useful the Germans didn't destroy," she said.

"Let's just retreat down the glacier now," I said. "It's too risky to go near those flames. The Germans might be waiting for that. Waiting for *us*."

"They probably are," the Deacon agreed, "but Reggie's right. We need to forage what we can from Camp Three—God knows there wasn't anything left at Base Camp, Camp One, or Camp Two—and we need food, fuel, and a cooker to survive."

"Why do you think there will be stuff left here?" My voice sounded desperate and a little panicked even to my own ears.

"Remember, Jake," said the Deacon, "we had that tarp-covered cache here at Camp Three—about fifty yards west of the camp, where the boulders get jagged near the base of Changtse. Today's snow may have hidden it more. And the cache was just far enough away that the Germans may have missed it—unlike at Base Camp and the other camps where they had the advantage of some daylight, they hit Camp Three after dark tonight."

"Shouldn't we decide *what* we're doing next—which direction we're going, what our plans are—before we try to salvage anything here?" asked Jean-Claude.

"There's nothing to discuss," I insisted. "The expedition's over. It's just a question now of whether to climb west over the Changtse Ridge to Lho La Pass into Nepal, or east over the North East Ridge—no, that won't work—anyway, get out of the valley somehow and over Windy Pass, Lhakpa La, and then over Karpo La Pass down into Tibet. I think that way has to be the second choice."

"We'll discuss *where* and *what* after we forage," said the Deacon, using his command voice. "There are factors that you, Jake, and you, Jean-Claude, haven't yet heard about. First we have to get a cooker and some fuel and anything else we can scavenge. We'll also look for survivors when we're down there."

"Sherpa or German?" I asked.

"Both," said the Deacon. "But I'd give my left testicle to get one of the Germans as a prisoner."

"I'd give your left testicle for that as well," Reggie said at once.

Despite our precarious position near the glacier trail down to Camp II, we all laughed out loud. When we stifled the laughter, the Deacon said, "Who wants to come with me down to the camp?"

"I'll go," J.C. said at once.

"I shall stay here with Lady Bromley-Montfort," said Dr. Pasang.

"I'll go down to the camp with you two," I was amazed to hear myself say.

8.

———⌘———

efore the Deacon, J.C., and I found anything to salvage, we found two more Sherpas' bodies. The Germans had made no effort at *yeti*-mauling the bodies with blades or sharpened rakes or whatever the hell they'd used at Base Camp; all the Sherpas we could see in the light of the dying flames here at Camp III had been shot. Most, several times. A few had been riddled by automatic weapons fire from machine pistols at close range.

Semchumbi was one of those who'd run east and been shot in the back behind the now-burned-to-the-ground Whymper tents. There was no sign of the Deacon's revolver on him or near him. We had no idea if he'd gotten any shots off before he died. But the pistol was definitely missing.

Rather than go down into the *penitentes* where the Germans had headed after their last murder spree, the three of us took the harder route north almost to the ice wall and then circled around to the base of Changtse, where Camp III was still burning. The Deacon had guessed right; the last, snow-covered loads cache about 100 feet east of the camp had not been noticed by the Germans. Two of us crawled under the tarp and then turned our headlamps on to inventory the stores while Jean-Claude stood guard outside.

We were in luck; there were six as yet unused rucksacks and a heap of canvas carryalls in the cache. There were no more oxygen rigs, but there was a Primus stove, two Unna cookers, and twelve bars of Meta fuel. We loaded one Primus with the rest of the stuff into an empty rucksack, even though we'd already discovered the hard way that Primuses often didn't work well at altitude. But it was worth hauling the additional weight to have that extra chance of being able to melt snow for drinks.

At this point I still saw no reason to climb to the North Col and every reason in the world to head north and east to Windy Pass—the Lhakpa La, that point where the Deacon had finally led Mallory to see the East Rongbuk Glacier as the obvious approach four years ago during the '21 expedition. If we avoided these killer Germans until we reached the Lhakpa La, we could then head east along the Kharta Glacier (which the 1921 expedition had carefully mapped) and then up and over the almost 20,000-foot-high Karpo La and down into northern Tibet, turning eastward again immediately to avoid the treacherous Kangshung Glacier that ran up to the base of the near-vertical (from its southern side) North East Ridge. The Karpo La was by all accounts a treacherously dangerous pass, with its no-warning blizzards, terrible winds, and deep summer snowfalls—which was why British expeditions hadn't tried to save time by coming north into Tibet and the Everest region that way—but it seemed to me like a good (and fast) avenue of retreat for us now.

And I desperately wanted a way out. If I could come up with a good one, I was sure that I could convince Reggie and the Deacon, whatever "facts" they knew that they hadn't shared with us yet. The central fact was those men with guns who had murdered most or all of our Sherpas and who were now looking for us.

Another possibility—a less drastic way home, but one requiring a slightly longer trek in Tibet—was for us to wait till morning and climb high on the shoulder of the East Rongbuk Glacier until we could cut east to Windy Pass, get over Lhakpa La, and then traverse along the base of the great wall that was the Himalayas for some miles, and then get over the frequently traveled Serpo La down into the verdant Teesta Valley and then lower to Gangtok and straight on to Darjeeling. It would be a bitch of a trek—I wasn't sure that any white men had ever done it—but it *had* to be safer than facing crazy German killers with automatic weapons.

There was one other wild chance we could take. Lho La Pass to the west was closer—just behind Mount Changtse, which bordered our East

Rongbuk Glacier—but it would mean a long traverse climb around Changtse, a descent of unknown difficulty, then a steep ascent again to Lho La, only to have the five of us almost certainly rotting for years in a Nepalese jail for entering the country without permission...and Nepal *never* gave permission for entry by foreigners, Mr. K. T. Owings was the only exception I could think of. But the Deacon was friends with the man; maybe Owings could help us out...

So I'd argue hard for either risking the weather on high Karpo La or trekking farther east to the relative safety of Serpo La—both east of the killing ground that had been Base Camp—as far as I was concerned. I dug into the cache with a will and filled every empty rucksack we'd found there.

The tent fires had died to mere embers by the time we started our northern circle route back to the west of the camp where Pasang and Reggie waited. Less than halfway there, the Deacon said, "Dump the loads here."

This made no sense at all. We were near the part of the ice wall to the Col where we'd laid fixed ropes and—far, far above—the caver's ladder. But there was no way on earth that I was jumaring up those ropes or climbing that ladder again, not even if the Germans showed up in hot pursuit. It was the ultimate dead end. To climb to the North Col meant certain death. There was no escape from there, since the south side was a sheer drop of several thousand feet to a deep valley behind Changtse. And to go higher on either Everest or Changtse—which had never been climbed, even though it was "just" 24,878 feet high (lower than our Camp V)—only meant prolonging the inevitable. I started to voice a protest, but the Deacon said aloud, "Trust me, Jake. Dump the stuff here. *Trust* me. Please."

All thirty of our Sherpas trusted you, Captain *Deacon, and they're all dead now,* I almost said aloud. I was that tired. But I didn't speak. And because of my silence, our friendship, if that's what it was—and I've had more than sixty-five years to decide it was—remained intact.

And the Deacon—Captain Richard Davis Deacon, the man who had given thousands of commands to his men during four years of the worst war the world had ever known—had just said "please" to me.

I left all my logical arguments for retreat over the passes unspoken and dumped the load into the snow, and we continued postholing around and up onto the glacier to rejoin Pasang and Reggie.

At Camp Fort, as we'd dubbed it, we sat on our rucksacks in a rough circle, to keep our butts from freezing, and tried to talk things through. Even though the Deacon had ordered us each to take some English air at the 2.2-liter flow rate for three minutes—he kept time with his watch—our voices sounded slurred or drunken or just plain stupid. We were all beyond the point of absolute exhaustion. Merely trying to form words in my brain reminded me of newsreel film I'd seen in a British cinema of RAF fliers forced to do mathematics problems in a barometric chamber with the pressure lowered—as if they were in planes gaining altitude—until somewhere around or below this altitude we'd all been at for seventy-two hours and more. Each pilot not only quit doing arithmetic but went face forward onto his desk.

But they had the advantage of scientists and doctors watching them, ready to bring the pressure back up in their sealed chamber the moment they passed out.

The outside of our particular "sealed chamber" was either outer space or a firing squad of crazy Krauts.

My chin had dropped onto my chest and I was snoring softly when the Deacon gently jostled me awake. J.C. was saying something.

"Jake was right, my friends. Unless there's something that he and I don't know, the only sensible course of action is to start climbing out of this accursed valley at first light and head for the nearest pass into Tibet or Nepal. Since I value my freedom as well as my life, I suggest Karpo La or Serpo La into Tibet. Nepal does not treat intruders very nicely."

"There *are* things that you and Jake don't know, *mon ami,*" said Reggie. "The Deacon may not know the precise details, but I think he's guessed some...or perhaps he *does* know. It's hard for me to tell. Pasang knows only the general outline."

"What the hell are we talking about?" I managed to say.

"Why we have to climb onto the North Col tonight," said the Deacon.

"Tha's absurd," I slurred. "I'm too tired to climb into anything but a sleeping bag." We'd recovered five more eiderdown bags at the Camp III cache. They were lashed to the outsides of the rucksacks we'd stupidly left a quarter of a mile from here in deep snow, back at the base of the North Col.

"I also agree that we should climb to the North Col tonight, Mr. Perry," said Pasang. "Allow Lady Bromley-Montfort and Captain Deacon to explain."

She turned her tired face to our former infantry captain. "Do you want to explain, Richard?"

"I'm not sure I know enough," he said, and his voice sounded almost as tired as mine had. "I mean, I know the who and when and why, but I'm not certain about the what."

"But you admitted to knowing—and perhaps working for—our friend who writes a lot of cheques but who prefers gold," said Reggie.

The Deacon nodded wearily. "Knowing something about what he's up to, yes," he said. "I work for him—with him—only from time to time."

I said, "Would you two mind speaking in goddamned English?" Perhaps it came out a little sharper than I'd meant it to.

Reggie nodded. "My cousin Percival had the reputation, as I presume you have all heard, of being a wastrel, a disappointment to his family, a discredit to his country during the War—he never enlisted, never fought, and spent all of the War in Switzerland or other safe places, including, his mother was ashamed to admit, the peaceful parts of Austria. Cousin Percy seemed only one short step away from being an active traitor to Great Britain. And as a final touch, Percival was known both in England and on the Continent as being a debauched playboy. And a deviant. A homosexual, to use that new word."

There was nothing to say to that, so we all kept our mouths shut.

"All those appearances were false," said Reggie. "Artificial. Prepared. Deliberate."

I looked to the Deacon for an explanation—severe mountain lassitude with delusions for Reggie, perhaps—but his gray eyes were intent on her face.

"My cousin Percival was an intelligence agent before, during, and after the War," said Reggie. "First for His Majesty's Secret Service, then for British Naval Intelligence, and finally for... well, for a private network of agents run by someone very high up in our government."

"Percy was a fucking spy?" I said, too exhausted even to notice my language.

"Yes," said Reggie. "And young Kurt Meyer—who was *not* a mountain climber—was one of Percy's most deeply embedded and most valued Austrian contacts. Eight months before the two met up in the Tibetan village of Tingri, northeast of here, Meyer had been forced to flee Austria. He fled east—then further east—eventually into China and then south, to Tibet."

"This is a very long way to flee," Jean-Claude said.

"He had a pack of German monsters after him," said Reggie. "Tonight you've seen what those monsters can do."

"What did Meyer have—and give to Percy in Tingri—that the Germans need back so badly?" asked the Deacon. "That's the one part of the puzzle I don't have."

"Neither do I," said Reggie. "All I know is that our national futures—France's as well as Great Britain's, Jean-Claude—may depend upon it."

"It sounds like that leaves me and the United States out," I heard myself say. My voice sounded almost angry.

Reggie looked at me. "It does, Jake. Leave you out, I mean. I'm sorry you ever got involved, but I didn't know how to keep you from coming along with your English and French friends. Whatever the rest of us—or whoever joins me, that is—do next, I think you should curve around the glacier valley to the southeast and head for Serpo La into India. That is the safer and more direct of the two eastern passes. With a lot of luck and traveling light, you can be in Darjeeling in three weeks or so."

I opened my mouth to speak, but no words came out.

"The Germans will not pursue you, Jake," continued Reggie. "They have no interest in you. None whatsoever. They've come back here for the second straight year because they were unable to retrieve what Kurt Meyer had, what he gave to my cousin Percy, and because they think there's one chance in a hundred that the five of us may have found it. Or that they can find it themselves somewhere up on the mountain."

"They killed thirty Sherpas, thirty *men*," I say, blinking away tears of sheer fury and frustration, "to get back...what?...some goddamned blueprints for a dreadnought or plans for some more effective reciprocating airplane machine gun or some such goddamned nonsense?"

Reggie shook her head. "These Germans, however many there are of them—I'm convinced there were only seven of them last year, under the command of Bruno Sigl, and that they *did* see, or even make, Percival and Meyer fall, somewhere on this mountain. But for whatever reason, Sigl and whoever was with him weren't able to retrieve the item Meyer had been trying to get into British hands. Into my British agent *cousin's* hands. Just remember that *these* Germans don't represent the Weimar Republic, don't represent Germany. *Yet.* But they may someday...all of these monsters who follow that monster named Hitler...and whatever Meyer was trying to give to Percy was something that can hurt them. Hurt *him,* their leader. And that's all I care about."

I was too tired to follow that.

"All I know," I said, "is that if we climb up to the North Col again, we're trapped. Like rats. Even if there are only four or five Germans, they have guns—we don't. They have rifles. What's the effective distance of your 'scoped Lee-Enfield, Richard?"

"Effective range is somewhere above five hundred yards," said the Deacon. "Maximum range is somewhere around three thousand feet."

"The better part of a mile," I said.

"Yes," said the Deacon. "But not terribly accurate at that extreme range."

I ignored his footnote. "Accurate enough to pick us off the North Col or even the low parts of the North Ridge without their shooter even climbing *onto* the Col," I said.

The Deacon shrugged. "Probably. Depending upon wind and weather conditions."

"Well, the goddamned wind and weather conditions haven't exactly been friends to us so far," I cried.

No one responded.

Finally Jean-Claude said to Reggie, "I agree with Jake that it would be folly to surrender our lives for the sake of a machine gun or dreadnought design that other spies will certainly steal someday anyway. Besides, we're not currently at war with Germany. I have already given three brothers, two uncles, and five cousins to fighting *les boches,* Reggie.

You would have to assure me that whatever Herr Meyer stole from the Germans or Austrians is, first of all, unique, irreplaceable, and, second of all, truly something which the survival of my country as well as yours might hinge upon."

Reggie sighed deeply. It was the only time I ever saw her close to tears. "I can't be certain of the second thing, Jean-Claude. But I can guarantee that whatever it was that took the better part of a year for Meyer to try to hand off to Cousin Percy, it was *unique*. That much Percival himself assured me of before he headed off to his death here last year. It was not anything as banal as the plans for a new machine gun or bomb."

"So Percy admitted to you last year that he was a British spy," I said. I didn't know if it was a question or not.

Reggie smiled slightly. "I'd known that for years, Jake. Percy loved me. I've told you that we were more brother and sister than mere cousins. We'd played together as children, climbed in the Alps and the foothills of the Himalayas together as adults. He *had* to let me know that he was not a traitor to England...or even a decadent playboy, for that matter."

"But you don't even know," I pressed, "what Meyer had and carried with him across all of eastern Europe, the Middle East, and China...all the way into Tibet? Something so important that your cousin was ready to give his life for it, but you don't have a clue as to what it is?"

"No, only that it was very portable," said Reggie. "That's all Percy would let me know. He was supposed to have returned to Darjeeling by early July...*with* the thing, whatever it was. Sir John Henry Kerr, the acting governor of Bengal, and Sir Henry Rawlinson, currently the CIC and head of British Intelligence in India, both have been briefed by London—at least to the extent that Percival was trying to retrieve something of vital importance—and both are still awaiting word from me."

"I don't understand," I said dully. "Why would anyone choose the slopes of Mount Everest for such an exchange? That's nuts. There's no way off once you've gone up—if someone's waiting for you, I mean."

Reggie looked at me. "Percy and Meyer didn't choose Everest, Jake. They met up in Tingri Dzong. But Bruno Sigl and his thugs were close behind Meyer. In the end, Percy must have gone up the ladder that Mallory's expedition left behind—first onto the North Col, and then, according to Kami Chiring, much higher, perhaps even to the North

East Ridge. He must have prayed that the Germans couldn't climb as high, couldn't follow Meyer and him that far up the slopes—perhaps Percy thought that with the extensive caches of food that the Norton-Mallory Expedition had left behind on the mountain they could outwait the Germans below, or slip away in the imminent monsoon storms. Percy guessed wrong. Sigl must have brought some of Germany's best climbers with him...all political fanatics. And now they're back."

There was more silence, broken only by the ever-lessening sound of wind through the ice walls around us.

Finally the Deacon said to Reggie, "But you're willing to risk—even give up—your life to retrieve what your cousin Percy died to get."

"Yes."

"I'm going up the fixed ropes to the North Col with you tonight," the Deacon said flatly. "We'll keep climbing until we find Percy or until..." He stopped, but we all heard what came after the "until."

"I'm going as well," said Jean-Claude. "I hate the goddamned *boches*. I'd like nothing better than to plant a thumb in their eye."

Before I could say anything, Reggie said, "I'm serious about you slipping away over the Serpo La and heading straight for Darjeeling, Jake. As an American, you're neutral in all this."

"The hell we are!" I said. " 'Lafayette, we are here!' The Battle of Belleau Wood. The Battle of Cantigny. The Second Battle of the Marne. The Battle of Château-Thierry. The Meuse-Argonne. The...the..." I was so tired that I'd run out of American battles. "Tippecanoe and Tyler, too," I added irrelevantly. Well, it had sounded good in my buzzing head.

"I'm going with you guys," I said. "Just try to stop me."

No one said anything or patted me on the back. Perhaps we were all too tired.

"One thing," said Jean-Claude. "Do the rest of you think we have enough energy left to get up that thousand-foot snow wall and climb the rope ladder to the North Col, then cross the Col to Camp Four? Tonight?"

"We'll find out soon enough," said the Deacon.

Far below us and behind us, somewhere in the Trough forest of seracs and *penitentes* and 60-foot-high snow-shrouded ice pinnacles, came the echoing sound of three pistol shots. Then silence.

9.

⸻⸙⸻

A few years ago as I write this memoir in the winter of 1991–92, in this combination hotel-for-old-folks and assisted-living-home where I live here in Colorado, the manager—Mary Pfalzgraf, a wonderful woman—asked me to fill the Wednesday "guest speaker" role in the atrium by giving a little talk on mountain climbing. I did just that—gave a "little talk" (seven minutes by my watch)—to half a dozen other residents, mostly about night climbing in the Andes and Antarctica and about how beautiful the starry skies were in both places (with the *aurora australis* shimmering and dancing in curtains of light in the latter). There were only two questions from the tiny audience of my chronological peers: Howard "Herb" Herbert, my most faithful dominoes opponent, asked, "Where'd you lose those two fingers on your left hand, Jake?" (I had a hunch he'd wanted to ask that question for a long time but had been too polite to do so.) "Alaska," I told him truthfully. (I didn't go into the details of the nine days in a snow cave at 16,000 feet; nine days that had cost the lives of two of my fellow climbers.) Then Mrs. Haywood, rather far gone in Alzheimer's, I'm afraid, asked, "Can you climb mountains in your sleep? *While* you're sleeping, I mean?"

"Yes," I answered at once. I knew that because to this day I have no memory of the first forty-five minutes of our climb to the North Col that Wednesday morning in the wee hours of May 20, 1925. I was climbing in my sleep.

What woke me on the ice cliff climb to the North Col was suddenly poking my head and shoulders above the solid blanket of thick cloud. It felt like coming up and out of the sea into the open air, and it awakened me at once.

My God, it was beautiful. It was very late, so I was sure that the last fingernail crescent of waning moon had risen, but it was still hidden somewhere behind the looming North and North East ridges of Everest. The summit of our beloved/hated mountain and its omnipresent plume of spindrift, however, were beautifully backlit by intense starlight. Even when I'd gone out west in my Harvard climbing days, hundreds of miles from any city, I'd never seen stars this bright. Nor so many at once. Nor had they ever appeared this brilliant to me even from the depths of the Alps while bivouacking on a peak shielded from city lights or farm lanterns by countless other alpine peaks. This Himalayan sky was unprecedented. The Milky Way arched above the starlight-on-snow-lit summit of Everest like a solid highway bridging the night sky; there was no diminution of the number or brightness of stars near the horizons, merely an abrupt cutoff between thousands of stars and hundreds of star-lit snowfields and glaciers and summits.

The wind was gone. For the first time in days, the air—at least at this altitude of about 23,000 feet—was still. The nearby and distant peaks—Changtse, Cho Uyo, Makalu, Lhotse, Ama Dablam, Lho La, and ones I couldn't identify in my exhausted state—appeared close enough to reach out and pluck, like white-tipped coneflowers.

When we pulled ourselves off the swaying rope ladder and onto the narrow inset ice shelf of the North Col, I realized that the Deacon wasn't with us. Had he fallen off when I'd been climbing in my sleep? Had he been shot?

"He stayed below to tie loads on," J.C. explained.

"Tie loads on what?" I said.

"Onto the continuous rope attached to the pulleys attached to the bicycle," said Jean-Claude. "Remember? That's how we're going to get those dozen or more heavy loads from your foraging at Camp Three' up here to the North Col."

It came back to me as I forced myself to be more awake. When the Deacon had said he'd stay below and tie on loads until they were all ped-aled and cranked up, I'd thought it was nuts—any of the Krauts could hear the rope and pulley working, freeze him in the beam of a powerful searchlight or electric torch from Camp III, and easily shoot him with the rifles they had—but I hadn't said anything at the bottom of the 1,000-foot face to the North Col. I'd been too intent upon remembering how to attach my jumar clamp to the fixed ropes, how to release the cam when I had to slide J.C.'s device upward, and how to haul my already too-heavy pack up the rope ladder for the final 100 feet or so without tumbling backward into the shifting ice mist.

With our crampons and flashing ice chips kicked up by the crampons gleaming in the bright starlight, J.C., Reggie, Pasang, and I hurried along the slippery ledge to where Jean-Claude had secured his bicycle apparatus.

It was like a dream. Because of the weight of the oversized loads that the Deacon was tying onto the rope down in the roiling clouds below, J.C., Pasang, Reggie, and I took turns pedaling the pulley-bicycle. It was exhausting. Two of the others who weren't pedaling would signal the pedaling person to stop, lean out over the sheer drop or use their ice axes to hook onto the load, and pull it to the ice ledge, and the third person would untie the ungainly load from the continuous pulley rope and begin carrying or dragging it to the far end of the ledge.

This extreme effort went on for almost thirty minutes, and then there came four fast tugs on both ropes—the prearranged signal from the Deacon that all the loads had come up and he was cutting the rope from below and coming up himself—so we pulled the long pulley rope up, tied it onto one of the rucksack loads, made sure the rucksacks and other loads were secure over where we had to climb up off the ledge onto the North Col proper, and then we went back to the top of the rope ladder to wait.

After an endless wait, feeling the ladder and fixed ropes tugging and jiggling under our testing hands like a line with a big fish on it but never sure in the silence whether it was our friend or nine or ten Germans climbing toward us down there in the cloud, the Deacon emerged from the fog, climbed the last 30 feet or so to the ledge in the clear air, dumped the huge coil of fixed rope he'd brought up with him, and laboriously pulled himself up and over to where we were waiting with outstretched, ready-to-help arms.

"Shall we pull the ladder up behind you?" asked Reggie.

Too tired to speak for the moment, the Deacon shook his head. A moment later, and after we'd given him a brief snort of English air, he said, "Leave it in place. I brought a full-sized axe and two hatchets from Camp Three in one of those loads. When the Germans start climbing up that ladder in the morning, we'll wait...wait...wait until they're high enough on it, then cut it from here."

So that's why he'd brought up the fixed rope that we had rigged as a handhold along the length of the vertical section, but especially along-side the caver's rope ladder. Without that rope there'd be nothing to cling to if the ladder suddenly gave way.

"We'll have to post a guard here through the night," said Jean-Claude. "*Les boches* may start climbing the ladder at any time. Or perhaps they will fool us by chopping steps on the slope and ice wall."

"No," said the Deacon. He paused another minute to regulate his breathing and said, "I don't think they're coming tonight. It's been so cloudy down there for the past two days, I'm not even sure they *saw* the ladder and fixed ropes."

"But they will follow our footsteps to them," Pasang said.

The Deacon managed a tired nod. "True. But in the daylight, I think. And Sigl will send someone up the rope ladder to test it."

"You are sure it's Bruno Sigl down there, then?" said Reggie.

The Deacon shrugged. "Sigl or someone just like Sigl. It doesn't really matter. They'll be climbers and right-wing German political fanatics and I can only hope that their political fanaticism overwhelms their climber's common sense. But no guards for us tonight. We're going to haul as much of that gear as we can across the Col to Camp Four, get as warm as we can get, and sleep for as long as we can. It's a calculated risk—and there'll be hell to pay if the Germans *do* come up that ice cliff in the dark—but we all need the rest."

"But if Sigl and his killers do come up that rope ladder tonight...," I began. I was happy when the Deacon interrupted me; I really hated hearing my voice tremble the way it was.

The Deacon put his hand on my shoulder. "We're too tired already,

Jake. We've had almost no sleep for three days and nights at altitude. And sometime in the morning we'll all have to start climbing again, no matter what the weather's like. I say we sleep now and deal with the Germans in the morning, when they try to make it up here to the North Col."

No one said anything for a moment, but then, one by one, each of us nodded. "Reggie, Dr. Pasang," said the Deacon, "if you'd be so kind—drag one or two of those heavy loads across the Col top to Camp Four and please set out our sleeping bags there. We have extra bags in each load if you need them. The Unna cooker is in the load I chalk-marked Number One...we should get that out tonight and set it up in the vestibule of the tent, even if we wait till morning to use it. Pasang, perhaps you could coil and carry these hundreds of feet of rope from both the bicycle pulley and from the caver's ladder railing. Just set it outside one of the tents at Camp Four, along with whatever load you can drag there.

"Jake, Jean-Claude," he continued, "why don't you come with me over to the wonderful bicycle-pulley-lifting thing and we'll cut all the tie-downs and pull up all the anchors and stakes and lug that metal monstrosity over to this part of the ledge."

"Why, *Ree-shard?* We have already cut and coiled the long rope that worked from the pulley. Why bring the bicycle machine here?"

"Because we don't have any boiling oil handy," said the Deacon.

10.

*W*e slept relatively well, despite everyone's headaches and the return of my terrible coughing. My guess is that none of us dreamt of Germans machine-gunning our tent with their Schmeissers. We should have, probably, but I don't think any of us did. We were just too damned tired.

When I woke in the cold night, I would turn a valve, enjoy a little foot- and finger-warming oxygen, and drift back to sleep. The others were doing likewise, except for Pasang, who I believe slept straight through without any English air. I didn't truly awaken until almost seven a.m. according to the watch my father had given me.

Pasang and Reggie were heating coffee and a pot of something to eat on the Unna cooker just outside the tent vestibule. The day was sunny. The air was cold but still. The sky above the North and North East ridges was a heart-stopping blue.

"Where are J.C. and the Deacon?" I asked, alarmed.

"They went to stand guard near the top of the rope ladder around four thirty this morning," said Reggie. "Before it started getting light."

"I'll check in with them and then come back for coffee and breakfast," I said between coughs. I was busy strapping my crampons on.

"Oh, the Deacon asked me to tell you to wear your Finch duvet jacket on the outside of everything else," said Reggie. "If you must use the Shackleton anorak, he said to put it under the goose down jacket. Oh, and keep the goose down trousers I made for you on the outside as well, and, he said, keep your goose down hood up at all times."

I noticed for the first time that both Reggie and Dr. Pasang were dressed that way, hoods up and tied tight. "Why?" I said.

"The Deacon says that we're within range of the three rifles," answered Pasang. "Especially his own Lee-Enfield with the telescopic sight. The balloon fabric on the Finch jackets is a dull white—harder to see against the snow of the North Col and the first part of the North Ridge than our gray Shackleton jackets."

"Okay." We were dressing in winter camouflage now. I wondered what other new wonders this day would bring.

"Here," said Reggie. "Two thermoses of moderately hot coffee. You can share them with J.C. and Richard."

The thermoses in the large pockets of my down jacket, long ice axe in hand, mini-Very pistol in my free hand, I hurried across the North Col to the ice ledge, remembering to keep my head down most of the time. It felt foolish to waddle along that way, but the idea of being a sniper's target made my testicles want to crawl back up into my body.

J.C. and the Deacon weren't on the ice ledge but were lying prone against a wall of snow and ice on the North Col proper about 40 feet from the head of the ladder. I plopped down beside them and handed out the thermoses.

"This is very welcome, thank you, Jake," said the Deacon, accepting one thermos and setting it in the snow while his hand returned to steadying the large pair of binoculars. I'd forgotten to bring my own glasses from Camp IV. J.C. handed me his.

"They've been moving around since dawn," Jean-Claude said. "Burying the dead and scattering or burying the ashes of the tents."

"Burying the . . . ," I said and looked through the binoculars.

Down at the remnants of Camp III, eight men, their faces mostly hidden behind white scarves or handkerchiefs, all wearing white overparkas, were indeed dragging away the last bodies of our murdered Sherpas. Others were shoveling ashes and detritus from the previous night's destruction onto large flat tarps.

"I would give a thousand pounds to have my 'scoped Lee-Enfield back right now," whispered the Deacon.

"Why are they . . . ," I began.

"The Germans don't know if another British Everest expedition

might be coming next year or the year after that," said the Deacon, finally putting his glasses down and unscrewing the lid on his thermos.
Jean-Claude was already drinking his steaming coffee and had handed
me the cup to share with him. "But they don't want evidence of the
slaughters," continued the Deacon. "The Germans are usually very good
about covering such things up."

"Where are they burying them?" I whispered. I was trying to think of
the names of *all* our Sherpas.

"Probably in that deep crevasse at the edge of the moraine on the west
side, beyond the ice pinnacles there," said the Deacon. "This coffee tastes
good."

"So when they finish with burying and dispersing the…evidence," I
said, "they'll come up to get us?"

"Almost certainly," said the Deacon.

I craned my neck to look at the blue sky and clear, still air. The North
Face of Mount Everest loomed over us like some impossible stage prop.
"We've lost the advantage of the wind and clouds." I'd inadvertently said
what I was thinking.

"Yes, we have," said the Deacon. "But it's a beautiful day for a summit
attempt."

I wasn't sure whether he was joking. But I wasn't amused.

"They have both of the hunting rifles we had at Base Camp plus your
rifle," I said. "And you said that your modified Lee-Enfield is effective up
to five hundred and fifty yards, with a maximum range of more than a
thousand yards."

"Yes," said the Deacon.

"Well, this North Col is only a thousand-some feet above them," I
said angrily. "Everything up here is well within the thousand-yard maximum range of the rifle. And so will we be if we try to climb up the
North Ridge."

The Deacon nodded. "But they don't have a good angle on us, Jake.
I suspect that the German with my sniper's rifle is up on the glacier
below Camp Three right now—at the highest point on the glacier, actually—trying to get a clear shot. But the North Col is just high enough
that they can't see us up here—especially when we stay back away from
this edge. Not while they're anywhere close to being within firing range.

As long as we don't poke our heads up along this ridgeline, I don't think they'll try to take a shot."

"But aren't we all doing that right now?" I asked with a little too much excitement in my voice. "Poking our goddamned heads up like ducks in a shooting gallery, I mean! Won't they catch a sun glint on the lenses of the binoculars?"

The Deacon pointed east. "Not anytime soon, Jake. The sun's still climbing over the North East Ridge and the summit, all behind and to the right of us. In the evening, we'd have to be very careful about where and when to use the glasses. As for seeing our heads poking up... you may have noticed these little snow-and-ice tunnels that Jean-Claude and I have constructed. It restricts our width of vision but keeps us in the shadows here and more or less invisible to anyone not staring straight at us."

"You seem so sure of yourselves," I snapped.

"We're not," said J.C. "But I think the Deacon is right that the odds are in our favor in terms of being targets for their rifles—at least until we begin climbing up the snowfield on the North Ridge toward Camp Five."

"Why didn't we do that during the night if showing ourselves in the daylight is going to be so dangerous?" I demanded of the Deacon.

"Because," he said in soft, deadly tones, "we want to kill some Germans before we abandon the North Col."

I almost laughed at this. "How! By using the two rounds in your stolen Luger against eight or ten Germans? By firing our Very flares down at them as they come up the ladder that we've so conveniently left behind for them?"

"Not quite," said the Deacon.

"What are we going to do, then, 'to kill some Germans'?" I said. "Drop rocks on them?"

"You're getting closer to the plan there," said the Deacon.

I could only stare. Suddenly a thought made my stomach muscles clench. "While you're peering out your little snow-and-ice tunnels here, how do you know that the Krauts aren't chipping ice steps up the whole wall to the North Col a few hundred yards east of here?" The image was so clear I could almost see it.

"We would hear them chopping steps," said Jean-Claude. "Also, they have been very busy cleaning up the evidence of their crimes. Carrying and burying bodies, even with a crevasse handy, is hard work at twenty-one thousand–some feet. And they also have the slaughter at Base Camp to conceal, not to mention the wrecks of Camps One and Two. *Ree-shard* and I think it will take them all until sometime this afternoon to finish hiding the evidence of their crimes."

"But a sniper's still out there watching and waiting for us to show ourselves," I said.

"Yes," said the Deacon.

I looked him straight in the eye. "If you were that sniper, what would *you* have done? Where would *you* be now?"

The Deacon removed his pipe from his pocket and stuck it between his white teeth. He didn't light it. I'd never seen him actually smoke his pipe at real altitude.

"I would have started climbing the slope of Changtse in the middle of the night," he said calmly. "Find a concealed shooting point at or near the summit at twenty-four thousand eight hundred–some feet. Come first light, all of us here on the North Col would have been in his range and in his sights. My Lee-Enfield has an attached magazine of ten rounds. I would have picked off all of us without ever having to change clips."

I thought I might suddenly vomit. My head jerked upwards and my eyes scanned the high, snowy slopes of Changtse looming above us immediately to the west.

"How do you know the fucker's not there now, taking aim?" I asked.

"Because we were out here before four thirty this morning watching for lights ascending Changtse," Jean-Claude said. "There were none. And even Herr Hitler's German supermen cannot climb that treacherous slope in the dark."

"But since dawn...," I began.

"We have been watching," said J.C. "Nothing. We saw one of *les boches*—the tall man carrying *Ree-shard*'s rifle with the odd scope—disappear back into the *penitentes,* headed in the direction of the glacier path. The rest have been busy carrying off the bodies of our friends they killed and shoveling and sweeping up ashes and the remnants of our tents and crates."

I shook my head. I'd never been a soldier, so I didn't understand tactics, much less strategy. But I also had never felt as afraid as I did at that moment—not even during the most dangerous moves I'd made on mountains or ice. As if reading my thoughts—or expression—the Deacon set his hand on my shoulder again.

"We have a plan, Jake. I promise you. Remember, these are Germans. They're arrogant people. They're going to come at us straight-on sometime today—straight up the ladder we left for them, feeling safe in their near certainty that we don't have any weapons that can really hurt them—and then we're going to kill as many of them as we can. Only then will we begin our tactical withdrawal up the mountain."

I did laugh this time. Easy and loud enough probably to be heard down at Camp III, where men in white anoraks were dragging away the bodies of our friends. But it wasn't a hysterical laugh.

"What?" asked Jean-Claude.

I stifled the laughter but still had to grin. "Only my friend Richard Davis Deacon, current Earl of Watersbury whether he wants to be or not, could call *climbing to the summit of Mount Everest* a 'tactical withdrawal.'"

11.

*T*he Germans came for us around five o'clock that afternoon. They'd been chopping their way up the slope below the caver's ladder—their lack of 12-point crampons and of the fixed ropes we'd brought up with us slowing them down some for almost three hours before they reached the base of the ladder.

The Deacon still thought that their plan was to rush up the ladder, keeping us pinned down with rifle and automatic weapons fire as they came, boil out onto the North Col—our guess was that, with Karl Bachner dead and buried in his crevasse, there were no more than ten of the white-garbed Krauts—shoot us all, burn our camp and kick the ashes (and our corpses) into the nearest crevasse, and be back at their unseen camp in the ice pinnacles below our old Camp III before dark. By their dinnertime.

That, said the Deacon, was their plan.

The early part of their plan had gone like clockwork. They were out of our two-cartridge pistol range as six of them chopped their steps up the slope where we'd had our fixed ropes—the Deacon wasn't going to take his two measly shots at that range anyway—and before long all six of the white-garbed men below were clustered at the base of the rope ladder. We knew this because I'd been sent out to burrow spy holes through the snow ridge about twenty yards east of the ledge, and Jean-Claude had done the same about twenty yards west of the ledge. Now we both had good views east and west; at least no one was going to sneak up on us by carving steps somewhere else on the 1,000-foot slope to the North Col.

J.C. whistled, I saw the Deacon's white-hooded head pop up—behind a berm of snow at the edge of the precipice, out of sight of those below, even snipers in the ice pinnacles or on the glacier—and Jean-Claude held up both gloved hands, flashed six fingers, and then made the sign for climbing.

They were coming up, all right. Six of them. All armed, of course.

The five of us hadn't exactly been lazy this long day. Pasang and Reggie, working on the Deacon's instructions—or at least on the plan they and the Deacon had come up with that morning—had struck camp, packed essentials in our five rucksacks there at Camp IV, and then taken the heavy loads and one more load consisting of the main Whymper tent from the camp to find a suitable crevasse up on the Col. There they lowered the pack loads we'd dragged up the night before and the folded, tightly tied tent and its poles down into the darkness of the crevasse, covering over the anchoring stakes with kicks of snow. The cache could be found by someone hunting hard for it and following all of our boot prints on the North Col, but they had no reason to search—we'd left decoy gear and two of the Meade tents at the site of Camp IV for them to burn with their Teutonic efficiency—and we'd left a *lot* of boot prints atop the Col.

When I'd asked the Deacon about what Pasang and Reggie were doing and why, he'd said only, "We'll need food, gear, clothes, and cooking stuff if we come down this way after we find Percy's body."

If?? I'd thought with some inner urgency. *This way???* What other way off Everest was there?

I saved such questions for later.

At the present moment I was burying my face and body in the snow as the three stolen rifles and what sounded like one Schmeisser submachine pistol opened up on us. The Germans were unsure of precisely where we were, so their rounds slammed into the ice wall and snow berms all along a 60-yard front on either side of the point where the rope ladder ended at the ice ledge. Other bullets came whistling through the air overhead.

I found it astonishing that no one had ever told me—or that I'd never read—the simple fact that bullets flying close to you sound very much like bees humming by on a summer's day in some farmer's field of white wood beehives.

Being shot at for the first time in my life, even though none of the rounds were striking that close to where I hid behind the berm, created odd and interesting physical reactions: I had the tremendous urge to hide behind something or someone else, even behind myself; and my primary urge, which I began working on, was to burrow down into the snow and rock of the North Col until I was somewhere else completely.

This is what war feels like, I thought. *And this is what a coward does in wartime.*

I quit burrowing, forced myself to raise my head a bit, and watched.

J.C., the Deacon, and I had been busy all day as well: besides keeping an eye on the Germans below—and we'd handed that job over to Pasang and Reggie when they joined us in late morning—we'd been staying low and rolling the largest blocks of ice we could find to a place right behind the snow berm above the ice ledge where Mallory and the previous expeditions had pitched their Camp IV tents. And where our rope ladder now terminated on the ice ledge.

The night before, with clouds still filling the valley, the Deacon had taken quite a while to splice on another ten feet of his Miracle Rope to each of the staked ends of the caver's ladder, then pulled out the old stakes after pounding in new ones near the rear wall of the ledge. It had been incredibly hard work for one tired man, even disregarding the debilitating altitude; the Deacon had been the only one lifting, loading, and tying on the hugely heavy loads that we had been pedaling up on J.C.'s bicycle apparatus.

Now the six Germans climbing the rope were using their free hands to fire pistols—mostly Lugers, I could see through my peephole, but also a few other semiautomatic weapons I couldn't identify—up at the berms and ledge near the head of the ladder. They knew how precarious their position was, but with snipers covering them and with their own suppressing fire keeping anyone from getting to the top of the ladder, they must have felt fairly safe.

I thought of enemy knights clambering up siege ladders against a castle wall in the Middle Ages. The North Col was our castle, all right, but these Nazi Party Germans coming up the rope ladder were no damned knights. More like barbarian Huns.

Jean-Claude was using his hands to indicate to the Deacon, Reggie, and Pasang, where they crouched behind the berm directly above the ledge and ladder, how high the Germans were getting. Five fingers and a fist meant 50 feet. Six fingers and a fist . . . eight fingers and a fist.

We had set in place 115 feet of caving ladder. They were getting close to the top, firing at any imagined movement as they came. The snipers were directing their rifle fire at the berms near the top of the ladder ledge now. I had no idea where the Schmeisser's slugs were going, but the ripping sound of its near-constant firing made me almost sick with fear. I could hear the Deacon's former sniper rifle slowly firing from somewhere on the glacier further away.

I confess that I was terrified.

Not too terrified, however, to do what I had to do when the Deacon whistled twice. Jean-Claude and I crouched low, took a few steps back deeper onto the Col, and ran as quickly as we could to the place where Pasang and Reggie were waiting amidst the huge blocks of ice we'd rolled up to the berm above the ledge.

J.C. stopped just short of that berm to peer through a gopher spy hole he'd dug earlier. A pumped fist showed us that the Germans were still climbing and eight fingers showed us that they were within 20 feet of the top of the ladder.

Now the hard part for me—I really wasn't sure I could do it until after I did. I threw my body up and over the berm and rolled down onto the ice ledge, immediately half-rolling, half-crawling on my belly toward the back wall of the ledge.

Bullets slammed into that wall five or six feet above me, knocking painfully sharp ice chips into my face. More slugs struck the icy lip of the ledge in front of me. But the Deacon had been correct; even the sniper with the 'scoped Lee-Enfield couldn't get an angle on me here if I kept low. *Of course,* I thought, *I'll have to* leave *this fucking ledge sometime.*

But that was planned for as well.

"Come on," gasped the Deacon, shifting over behind Jean-Claude's giant heap of bolted metal load-lifter with its bicycle seat, handlebars, pulley, flanges, and long metal support post. "We only have seconds."

I nodded, and we both set our backs against the ice wall behind us as we planted our cramponed boots right where we'd practiced, coiled our legs tight, and pushed with all our might.

The massive bicycle pulley machine slid across the ice between the two guide furrows we'd dug with our ice axes. We'd even used four thermoses of our precious melted-snow water earlier to spill between those lines in the snow, creating an icy skidway.

The hundreds of pounds of bolt-assembled metal moved easily enough, and the Deacon actually stood at the rear section to steady the disappearing last support leg, risking getting shot in order to guide it down the ice wall. We shoved the mass of metal over the edge.

The Deacon dropped back down seconds before a fusillade of bullets slammed into the rear wall of our ledge and splatted into the snow berm above.

Men were screaming yards below us. The screams Dopplered away from us. The bullets kept coming, but fewer men were firing at us now.

J.C. held up three fingers. His beloved bicycle pulley device had taken three Germans off the ladder with it. It was one hell of a long fall from that ladder—not merely the vertical 100 feet of the ice face, but hundreds of feet of very steep slope below that. The screams of the falling Germans stopped, and the sudden silence seemed almost violent to me. But a quick flash of another three fingers meant that there were at least three more Germans climbing toward us. *Unless they're retreating down the ladder* was my sudden thought, which felt strangely like a prayer to me.

Jean-Claude pumped his fist from his peekaboo position.

The three other Germans were still coming up, obviously using both hands to climb now since the pistol fire from the direction of the ladder had fallen to nothing.

"Ankles," said the Deacon.

I dug my crampons into the ice of the ledge as deep as I was able and grabbed Richard Davis Deacon's ankles as hard as I could—and my hands and wrists were *very* strong from my years of rock climbing. Still, it had seemed easier when we'd practiced on the flat snow and ice further up on the Col as the Deacon propelled himself forward like some circus acrobat, the belly of his off-white Finch jacket sliding across the almost smooth ice slide we'd created for J.C.'s bicycle pulley.

I'd driven my ice axe as deep into the ice at the junction of the back wall and the ledge as I could, and my right arm was around it. I was still almost pulled forward and off the ledge, until my crampons found deeper grip and the muscles and ligaments of my right arm tried to tear free, but I stopped the Deacon's wild forward slide with the entire upper half of his body hanging horizontally out over nothing.

Taking his time, he aimed the black Luger, took another two or three seconds—I could imagine that first white German face, probably with blue eyes, turned up to the Deacon only 20 feet or so above him—and then the Luger fired. Rifle bullets were striking the ice wall near the Deacon now—the snipers obviously nervous about hitting their own men, two of them left on the ladder—but still the Deacon waited another few interminable, terrifying seconds before firing his second and last round down and inward along the vertical ice wall.

"Back!" he cried and I madly pulled his ankle, then his powerful calf muscles under the high wool stockings, then his thighs and rump, until he was back at the base of the wall with me.

"Both men fell," he gasped. Then, more loudly, "The snowballs!"

Each "snowball" was a block of ice that must have weighed at least thirty or forty pounds. We'd had a hell of a time through the long day's wait finding them and rolling them over to the "ammo dump" of ice blocks we'd built up just behind the berm.

The Deacon and I slowed each block's impact on the ledge as much as we could—we didn't mind if some of the ice broke off—and then we got behind each ice clump snowball and kicked it down our frozen sluiceway. Reggie and Pasang fed us another big chunk of ice every time we shouted, and we halted its slide, got behind it, aimed it, and kicked it out.

We had twelve such ice blocks in the ammo dump. We kicked them all over. The 900-and-some feet of steep slope beneath the point where the rope ladder started was very prone to avalanche.

Jean-Claude sprinted low to his peephole. The Schmeisser had stopped firing—the Deacon had said that their barrels heated up fast on full automatic—and only slow, deliberate rifle shots were spoiling the calm of the Himalayan late afternoon.

"Four more Germans down for good. One guy self-arrested and ran back to the rope and is climbing again," shouted Jean-Claude. "Moving fast. About halfway up. Closer now . . . two-thirds of the way up the ladder."

The Deacon nodded, reached for the fire axe he'd planted along the base of the rear wall of the ledge, counted to ten, and then, in two swift, sure movements, cut both ropes that now anchored the ladder.

The scream from below was very long and very satisfying.

"Now!" said the Deacon, and I ran for the west end of the ledge, leaping up into the low burrow we'd hollowed out there, rolling behind the berm even as shots rang out. A few seconds later the Deacon jumped into the low furrow we'd dug out at the east end.

Rendezvousing behind the tall berm with J.C., Pasang, and Reggie, the Deacon and I gestured to show that neither of us had been hit.

"I was watching," said Dr. Pasang. "Five men, including the one who fell with the ladder, are dead. One man was still writhing, but I'm all but sure that his back is broken. Others were injured, but the German with the Schmeisser and another German hurried out of the ice pinnacles to help them back to cover."

"If they started with the dozen we thought we saw last night," said the Deacon, "they're down to five now—counting out Bachner, whom Reggie removed from the game last night—and some of those five aren't feeling all that chipper right now."

"Do you think they'll give up and leave?" I asked, my heart pounding so loudly that I could barely hear the words I'd just spoken.

The Deacon looked at me as if I'd just broken wind.

Reggie answered. "They won't quit, Jake. They don't know if we've already found Percy and Meyer and recovered what they had, but they can't take the chance that we have. They could never return to Germany if they fail again...nor to Europe. Their own Nazi Party would have them killed. Their would-be Führer, from what Percival told me, is not a man who ever forgets or forgives. These top Nazi-German climbers will all be marked men if they fail."

"Jesus," I whispered. "What was Meyer handing off to your cousin, Reggie? Some sort of revolutionary bombsight? A piece of the True Cross?"

"I don't know what it was, Jake," she said. "But I do know that it is far more important to Bruno Sigl's political faction than any bombsight or the Holy Grail would be."

"*Les boches* will try to climb again," said Jean-Claude. "Climbing at several places along the face of the North Col, most probably. There may well be more than five of them left. They obviously came in force this year. The sniper will stay behind again, covering them, as they cut steps up the face. It is a very formidable rifle with a very formidable telescopic sight, *Ree-shard.*"

The Deacon grunted. I knew that he blamed himself for leaving the rifles at Advance Base Camp.

"Do you think they will come again soon, Mr. Deacon?" asked Pasang.

"I don't think so," said the Deacon. We'd been passing around a single oxygen tank with mask that we'd left here for just this recuperation time, and he took his turn getting a few deep breaths of English air before he spoke again. "Cutting steps on a virgin ice slope anywhere down there is going to take them hours—until well after sunset. And they'll still have to solve the last hundred feet or so of vertical ice. I'm not sure if they'd want to try this last vertical pitch of the climb several hours after dark."

"*Les boches* probably do not know that *Ree-shard* had only two cartridges in Herr Bachner's Luger," said Jean-Claude. "The gunfire probably surprised them, no?"

"All the more reason for them to climb at night," I said. I kept alternating hits on the English air tank with sips of water from one of the thermoses. After my first battle, modest as it was, I felt...strange. I hadn't known that after a battle a man could feel both elated and strangely depressed and deflated at the same time. But I was aware of my strongest reaction: I was just damned glad to be alive.

"But they'd have to use electric torches strung around their necks for the hard parts of that climb," said the Deacon. His voice was almost as husky as mine. "If I were still waiting with eight rounds left in the magazine of Karl Bachner's Luger, that would be bad news for eight of them."

"You're that good a pistol shot?" asked Reggie. "Shooting straight down into the darkness, at only a flickering chest lamp, while you're hanging out over the edge of the abyss in the cold?"

"Yes, I am," said the Deacon.

I saw a strange smile pass between them. Something was being said, or acknowledged, that I wasn't privy to. I felt a stab of jealousy and then mentally kicked myself in the ass.

"So are we sticking to the plan?" asked J.C.

"We are . . . unless anyone objects," said the Deacon.

No one objected.

"The rucksacks and extra gear for above are all ready, correct?"

"Correct," said Reggie.

"Then we'll get the loads and head for Camp Five now," said the Deacon.

I held my hand up like a student asking permission to go to the lavatory. "It's not dark yet. The German down there who's been firing your 'scoped Lee-Enfield has shown some talent. Won't he pick us off one by one when we get to the snowfield on the North Ridge and become visible to anyone out on the glacier?"

The Deacon looked at the summit and ridges of Everest blocking the sunset—the Yellow Band and highest boulders and the North Ridge glowing brightly, the rest of the mountain and all of our North Col now in shadow.

"It will be almost dark by the time we're on the North Ridge snow slopes," he said softly. "We won't be roped up. As we discussed this morning, we'll be moving erratically—different paces—zigzagging up the slopes until we get to the fixed ropes, using no lights, not even our headlamps."

"What about when we're on the fixed ropes?" I said. "We'll have to use the headlamps then—it will be too dark to climb and check our footing without them. Won't we still be in range of the German sniper on the glacier?"

"Extreme range, yes," said the Deacon. "But we're not going to use our headlamps when we're on the tough pitches where the fixed ropes are waiting, Jake. We're going to use starlight and body memory and J.C.'s jumars."

"Great," I said.

"It *will* be great, *mon ami*," said Jean-Claude. "Except for your constant cough, we all seem to feel well. We've acclimated—at least for this part of the climb. And climbing Mount Everest by starlight has to be the apogee of any climber's lifetime."

"So long as it isn't the *end* of that lifetime," I managed between coughs.

"I shall give you a little more of the anti-cough mixture, Mr. Perry," said Dr. Pasang. "But not too much. We don't want you getting sleepy and careless from the codeine. Luckily, I also have a pill that can help you stay awake."

"We all may need that pill before the night's over," said the Deacon.

"And we're climbing all the way to Camp Five in the dark?" I asked, feeling how tired I was from the day of constant coughing mixed with adrenaline rushes.

"No, Jake, my dear," said Reggie, taking my gloved hand in hers. "Remember? We'll pause to brew up and collapse the Big Tent at Camp Five, but we're going all the way to *Camp Six* before dawn."

Now I remembered the whole plan. *Holy shit and fuck me,* I almost said. But because there was a lady present and because I was a Harvard graduate and a gentleman—but mostly because it was 1925—I didn't say it aloud.

Leaning against one another for support, keeping our heads low, we slouched our way toward Camp IV and our waiting loads and an absolutely unprecedented climb.

12.

With the possible exception of my solo night climb of the Mount Erebus volcano in Antarctica some years later, in the 1930s, I've never had a more beautiful and enjoyable climb than that night's climb in May of 1925 up Everest's North Ridge from Camp IV at 23,000 feet to our Camp VI at 27,000 feet. It was perhaps the most perfect mixture I've ever experienced of the physical joy of climbing in a staggeringly beautiful starlit setting with the psychological joy of climbing with friends I loved.

Of course, later, I wondered if the combination of codeine and Benzedrine that Dr. Pasang had ladled into me had anything to do with the profoundly good feeling I was enjoying. I was dimly aware that my throat still felt as though I'd swallowed a jagged metal object about the size of my hand, but since the coughing had been alleviated to the point where I could use an oxygen mask again easily, that strange sensation was no longer so urgently bothersome.

We climbed unroped, spreading out during the initial snow-on-rock stretch of the ridge just above the North Col, then back in line—but still with our headlamps and electric torches dark—and using our jumars to clamp onto the many fixed ropes we'd set in place during all the steep parts of the tilted-slab sections of the climb.

Rather than taking turns leading, as a team would when breaking through deep snow, we took turns bringing up the rear, since the last person had the fatiguing job of pulling each length of fixed rope free from its eyeleted stakes, coiling it, and hauling it over his or her shoulder until the next length needed to be undone.

"Ah...," said Jean-Claude during one of our pauses to change anchor climber, "...I understand the need to...ah...deny our fixed ropes to *les boches* who will be climbing in pursuit...but will not the lack of any fixed rope make our own descent a tad difficult?"

"We'll discuss that when we take a five-minute break at Camp Five before pushing on," said the Deacon. As far as I could tell, he hadn't had his oxygen mask up or flow valve open during the entire climb so far. We were hauling so many oxygen rigs up with us, I didn't understand why he might be hoarding O_2 now.

We pushed on. None of us were using our bottled air now, although we had extra rigs and bottles cached at both Camps V and VI. We seemed, by silent agreement, to be saving it for...something.

Twice we heard the distant echo of a rifle shot from the valley far below, but neither time did I hear a ricochet on the rocks around us or that somewhat disturbing new sound of steel-jacketed bees buzzing past me. Even with the telescopic sight that the Deacon had thought-fully put on his Lee-Enfield for the Germans to use against us, finding dark-gray-suited human figures—we'd swapped our Finch duvets for our dun Shackleton jackets as an outer layer once again, along with our canvas wind trousers over the down leggings—against rock and dirty snow at night evidently was, as the Deacon had said, a near impossibil-ity from one vertical mile below. Hitting us with aimed rifle fire from that distance, the Deacon reassured us, was a less likely threat to us than lightning, being run over by a lorry, rockfall, or avalanche. (But since the last two were *real* threats to us, even at that moment, I might have done a little more worrying, had I not been in a state of pharmaceutical near bliss.)

We paused at Camp V for five minutes of the promised rest and high-flow O_2, but then spent another fifteen minutes or so there taking down Reggie's Big Tent and parceling out the staves and canvas and rain fly and ground cloth into our various rucksacks. There were more oxygen rigs there than we could carry, so we spent even *more* time laboriously hauling them fifty yards or so out onto the rock and scree field of the North Face, where we hid them behind a large triangular boulder. The somewhat distinctive shape of that boulder would be our only guide if we needed to find that English air on our way down—assuming any of us *came* down alive—since we could hardly mark the cache with our wands or flags for the Germans to find and use.

We also left most of the heavy, coiled fixed rope we'd retrieved there with the oxygen rigs. Each of us carried about 150 feet of coiled Miracle Rope over our shoulders or in our rucksack—even though we still had no plans to rope up during this part of the climb—and we just had to hope that this would be enough if a particularly difficult stretch presented itself.

We were all panting and gasping after we'd packed away all the parts of Reggie's Big Tent—and renewing our own rucksack-carried oxygen bottles after storing the extra and partially empty tanks on the North Face and traversing back to the North Ridge—when I finally asked the question I'd been waiting to ask. "What *about* the lack of fixed ropes coming down?" I asked the Deacon. "Are we going to retrieve them from the pyramid rock out there and from wherever we stash the next ones above and reset them on the way down? We'll probably be *very* tired."

"That's one answer," said the Deacon between hits from his own oxygen tank. He was *finally* using English air like all the rest of us except for Pasang. "*If* the Germans give up—or if we can kill them all somehow—and *if* we come back down this way."

"How else could we get back down?" asked Jean-Claude. "The North East Ridge back toward Lhakpa La is impossible, *Ree-shard*. It is a sheer knife ridge studded with cornices, arêtes, pinnacles, and thousand-foot drops. Descent to the Kangshung Glacier beyond the North Ridge is a ten-thousand-foot vertical impossibility. So what other ways down—besides falling—might you be considering?"

The Deacon was leaning on his big ice axe, his massive load looming over his head. He gave J.C. a wolf's grin. "I was considering a traverse," he said. Only the absence of any real wind this amazing night allowed us to talk using normal tones.

"A traverse," said Jean-Claude and looked out at the face, up at the summit, back to the face where the Grand Couloir gleamed in the starlight. "Not to Norton's Grand Couloir and down, I trust," he said. "It becomes a sheer drop a few hundred feet below here, but the avalanches would carry us away long before that. No traverse on or across the North Face can get us down, *Ree-shard*."

"True," said the Deacon. "But what about a traverse from the North Summit across to the South Summit and then down to the South Col, to what Mallory named the Western Cwm?"

There was a moment of silence at that suggestion, but I could see Reggie's teeth gleaming in the starlight. Between the Deacon and Lady Katherine Christina Regina Bromley-Montfort, it was suddenly as if we were being led up the tallest mountain in the world by two hungry wolves.

"That's...nuts," I said at last. "We have not a single clue as to what the ridge is like between the North Summit and the South Summit...or even from the First Step to the North Summit on this side, for that matter. Even if we were somehow to reach the highest summit of Everest and make that traverse to the South Summit, which I doubt is possible in itself, the descent from the South Summit to the South Col is probably doubly impossible. No one's ever *seen* that bit of ridge, much less attempted it...ascending *or* descending."

"This is true, my friends," Jean-Claude said solemnly.

"Let's talk about it more when we get to Camp Six," said the Deacon.

"I see little lights down where Camp Three used to be," said Reggie.

"*Les boches* are going to start chipping steps in the wall to the North Col in the dark and will climb towards dawn," said J.C.

I wanted to continue the conversation about this impossible traverse over the two summits of Everest, but there was no time for that. We hitched up our rucksacks, left the tumbled Meade tent and the torn-to-rags Meade tent where they lay in the snow, and began trudging up the steep ridge slope again. Luckily for all of us, the fixed ropes began again less than 200 feet above Camp V. With the Deacon falling back to last place to retrieve and coil ropes as we climbed, doing the really heavy work, the rest of us clamped our jumar devices onto the thick ropes and began sliding our way up, the entire line of us stopping every fourth step to gasp for more air.

We were all using what the Deacon had taught us as the "Mallory technique": take in as deep a breath as you can—even while knowing it's not enough in the thin pressure at this above-8,000-meter altitude—and use it for those four steps before stopping, panting, and repeating the process.

And so the five of us kept climbing toward the dawn.

13.

The single two-man Meade tent that Reggie had set up as our Camp VI was invisible during the climb and much further out on the North Face than I remembered, but Reggie led us right to it. There were some spare oxygen tanks and a small cache of food we'd left there before fanning out to look for bodies on the North Face that seemingly long-ago Monday, as well as our two sleeping bags from Sunday night. We were now hauling water, tea, coffee, and other tepid liquids with us after the boiling of snow we'd done at Camp V before departing the North Col.

"Looks very comfortable," the Deacon said as he stared at the tiny tent pitched atop one boulder at a 40-degree up-angle and almost absurdly wedged between two other large boulders. Much of this part of the climb on the North Ridge, not far below the Yellow Band, had been through rock gullies and mazes of larger boulders. But Reggie had decided to pitch our Camp VI four days ago—eternities ago—at this site hundreds of feet off the ridgeline. There hadn't been any near-flat places on the ridge, either, even if the high winds there had allowed us to consider it.

The pre-dawn indirect sunlight was slowly brightening the entire sky behind the North East Ridge—which was not so far above us now—and it wouldn't be long until direct sunlight struck Everest's summit just a mile or so west and some 2,000 feet above us.

We took our rucksacks off for the first time since Camp V and collapsed onto them, each of us taking care not to let either the pack or ourselves go tumbling down the steep-roof-slate slabs of the face. We were all very tired, and I felt both the codeine and Benzedrine wearing off. The coughing had returned with a vengeance.

Only J.C. was currently carrying his binoculars outside his many layers, so I took turns looking through his glasses for the men who wanted to kill us today. We scoped what we could see of the North Col and of the North Ridge up to the slight glimmer of collapsed but still visible green tent that was Camp V. I couldn't see any figures moving anywhere.

"Maybe they gave up and went home," I said between gut-wrenching coughs.

Reggie shook her head and pointed, her arm extended almost straight down. "They're just leaving Camp Four, Jake. I see five men."

"I also see five," said the Deacon. "One of them seems to be carrying a pack and my rifle slung over his shoulder. There's a chance that could be Sigl, unless he brought a more experienced sniper with him...which is a real possibility."

"*Merde,*" whispered Jean-Claude.

"I agree completely," I said. I realized that the Deacon was no longer training his glasses below, but had turned them and was studying something beyond the North Summit—the highest and true summit of Everest. "Looking for that mythical traverse?" I said, regretting my sarcasm as soon as I'd aired it.

"Yes," said the Deacon. "Ken Owings said that there's a very nasty step in the ridgeline between the two summits—he could see it from as far away as Thyangboche in the Khumbu Valley, where he lives. It's a damned rock step, like our supposedly unclimbable Second Step here on the North East Ridge above us, but Ken says that this rocky step between the summits is about forty to fifty feet high from the downhill side."

"That would be unclimbable at such an altitude, *Ree-shard,*" J.C. said.

"Perhaps," said the Deacon. "But we don't have to *climb* it, Jean-Claude. If we get past *this* summit, we'll be heading down. We just have to rappel *down* the damn step and then down-climb to the South Summit and lower."

No one said anything, but I suspect the other three were thinking what I was; I didn't have the energy to climb another single step, much less a mile of the North East Ridge and two major steps—the Second Step above and to the right of us supposedly the "impossible" one—much less the steep Summit Pyramid and actual corniced summit. It simply wasn't going to happen.

"Do we have to worry anytime soon about Sigl or whoever's carrying your rifle taking potshots at us?" I asked, if only to change the subject.

"I think the chap carrying my rifle will be careful about when and where he shoots at us," said the Deacon.

"That's reassuring," I said. "Why should he be?"

"Because he's looking for the same thing we are," said the Deacon.

"Escape from crazy Nazis?" I said.

The Deacon shook his head. "Whatever Meyer and Bromley had with them. I believe that Bruno Sigl made the mistake one year ago of shooting either Meyer or Bromley or both—I'm sorry, Reggie, but I do think that's the case—at a place where the bodies fell or avalanched beyond Sigl's ability to reach them."

"I agree," said Reggie. "That fits with what Kami Chiring saw last year from near Camp Three using the Germans' binoculars. He thought he saw three figures up on the North East Ridge...then, suddenly, only one. And he heard what could have been the echo of pistol shots."

"So that's where we search," said the Deacon. "Along the ridgeline. The North East Ridge—where few people save for Mallory and Irvine have ever gone."

"And, if you are correct in your theory, *mon ami*," said J.C., "Sigl and Reggie's cousin Percival and this young Meyer fellow."

"Yes," said the Deacon. "I don't think Sigl will make the same mistake twice—or allow his sniper to, if someone else is carrying my Lee-Enfield. If they'd shot us anywhere on the North Ridge or during this climbing traverse to Camp Six here, our bodies might easily have fallen—probably *would* have fallen—down one of the gullies toward the main Rongbuk Glacier or all the way down and over the North Face onto the East Rongbuk Glacier six thousand feet below. The chances of whatever they're looking for surviving such a fall in one piece, even if it's just a document, would be very small."

"What an encouraging thought," said J.C.

"So they'll be reluctant to shoot unless they know we won't fall far," continued the Deacon, undeterred. "So my suggestion is that we just keep outclimbing the bastards."

Reggie rubbed her pale forehead. I wondered if her head ached as abysmally as did mine. At least she didn't have my terrible cough.

"What do you mean, Richard?" she asked. "We've come pretty far. We're very tired."

"I mean we keep climbing until dark," said the Deacon, turning his goggles up toward the Yellow Band and North East Ridge above us. The wind was blowing spindrift along that ridge and out away from the two impossibly distant but strangely near-looking Steps and the Summit Pyramid. There was snow underfoot—or I should say "under-crampon"—everywhere now. We were moving into a different world. And one that tolerated almost no forms of life.

"We either climb or traverse around that First Step—we could even bypass it by traversing along that narrow ridgeline atop the Yellow Band—and then climb back up toward the ridge and get the best of that damned Second Step," continued the Deacon. "We stay just below the ridgeline on this side so we don't show ourselves in silhouette to the shooter below, then set up Reggie's Big Tent in the first-ever French-Anglo-American Camp Seven somewhere below the final Summit Pyramid."

"What does this achieve, *Ree-shard?* Does it not merely postpone the inevitable? I need not remind you that *les boches* are armed, and we have . . . Very pistols."

"First of all," says Reggie, speaking for the Deacon, who was out of breath, "getting to the North East Ridge *is* the best way to look for my cousin Percy and whatever Kurt Meyer spent months sneaking out of Europe. That's important. That's the real reason we're here."

"But the odds of actually finding them . . . ," I began.

"You found George Mallory," said Reggie.

I sighed. "In that huge *open* area down there. And I literally almost stumbled over him. I've been looking through my binoculars for ten minutes, but I can't even see his body from here. I know where *it* was."

I still felt bad about our not taking the time to bury Mallory.

"Well, there's always the chance that we shall stumble over Herr Meyer or my cousin," said Reggie. "At least if we climb to the North Ridge, we shall be walking where Kami Chiring last saw him. But camping above the Second Step, Richard . . . if the usual wind rises, I don't think even my domed tent could survive it. And it will be *very* cold up there so near to twenty-nine thousand feet."

"You're all forgetting something," I rasped between coughs.

"What, Jake?" said the Deacon.

"You and Norton compared the Second Step to the prow of a battleship," I managed to say before coughing again. "A hundred feet of near-vertical rock. No man alive—not even Mallory—could climb that. Not at that ungodly altitude. And the North Face below that Second Step looks too steep to traverse."

"You're wrong, Jake," said the Deacon. "There's one man alive who *can* do that vertical rock free climb of the Second Step."

I mentally scrambled to think of all the great European and American rock climbers who might be up to the challenge of free-climbing the Second Step at this debilitating altitude, but could think of no one.

"*You, Jake,*" said the Deacon. "You, my friend. Let's go."

He pulled the straps of his heavy rucksack on again. This time, I noticed, he clipped his oxygen face mask in place. All the rest of us did the same. The Deacon put the two heavy, full oxygen bottles we'd left cached there at Camp VI in his already overloaded backpack. Then he led the way up the boulder-strewn face toward the very steep rock gullies that would lead us up and through the Yellow Band and out into more such gullies and rock mazes before we could reach the windswept North East Ridge.

14.

This climb up the North Face through the Yellow Band and beyond toward the North East Ridge was the most demanding
and technical climbing we'd yet encountered on Everest. Despite the
much steeper incline, the more challenging terrain, and ever more terrifying exposure to the 8,000-foot drop, we still hadn't roped up. There
were numerous ways through the maze of overhanging rocks and snow
masses, most of them up steep snow gullies, and most of them leading to
dead ends with dangerously overhanging snow masses or blocking boulders. The Deacon had chosen the one he thought would have the best
chance of exiting onto the somewhat shallower slope that should open
out onto the ridgeline not too far east of that large outcropping on the
ridge called the First Step. I suppose we weren't roped together both out
of stupid habit after hours of parallel climbing and because we were concentrating on front-crampon-kicking our way up the steep gully, jabbing
our ice axes in ahead of us, leaning heavily on them, panting for breath
(we were using our bottled oxygen only intermittently, which added to
our mental dullness), and then kick-stepping our separate ways up another agonizing step or two. All this kicking led to clumps of falling
snow—theoretical precursors to real avalanches—that no one wanted to
follow directly below and behind. We were spread out with no one person really leading the climb, no prescribed order of climb, and no one
within grabbing distance of anyone else should anyone slip and start
sliding. But every time I looked, the Deacon was first, the highest, the
one breaking trail; then came Jean-Claude, then me, then Pasang, and

then—at least 15 feet lower than her Sherpa friend and following in his tracks—Lady Bromley-Montfort.

Reggie fell when we weren't quite two-thirds of the way up the steepest part of the snow gully.

I was leaning on my ice axe and looking almost straight down past my boots at the moment and I saw her slip. Her right cramponed boot came down on a rock that should have been the protruding point of a solid boulder beneath the snow—we'd used many such boulder tips as footholds already in this gully—but it wasn't. The loose rock rolled out from beneath her, Reggie fell heavily onto her side, the air going out of her with an "Ooomph," and she began sliding immediately.

To her credit she'd held on to her ice axe during the hard fall and then rolled onto her front, braced herself properly, and dug the broad adze edge in to begin her self-arrest. It was done with the sure, sudden grace of an accomplished climber.

But the damned 12-point crampons—so useful in our climbing the last few days—dug into the snow as she was sliding, the points digging deep, and flipped her over, the large ice axe flying out of her hands.

Now she was sliding down the gully headfirst toward the steep drop-offs and sharp rocks below. Pasang swung around at once and began loping in impossibly broad strides down the steep gully snow, but he had no chance of intercepting her. She was two-thirds of the way down the gully now and picking up speed toward a 100-foot drop-off that fell to the high point of the great catchment basin where I'd found Mallory's body far below. Beyond that point, it would all be terrible tumbling and smashing.

Then Lady Katherine Christina Regina Bromley-Montfort did an incredible thing.

Instead of grabbing helplessly at snow with her mittens or gloved fingers to slow her accelerating slide as most of us would do, she continued spinning down the ever-widening gully-chute but deftly reached back to her rucksack, which had somehow stayed on her as she plummeted toward the drop-off, and pulled the two short J.C.-designed ice hammers from where she'd had them strapped securely in webbing above the side water bottle pockets.

With almost no time left before she was launched out over the most vertical part of the North Face, Reggie made sure she'd looped the wrist straps of the hammers around her wrists, used the tip of one hammer to spin herself around so that she was head upwards, and then raised each arm and hammered the pick points deep in the snow. Three lightning-fast blows like that and she'd stopped spinning, but she was still sliding.

Two more deep thrusts, using the weight of her upper body to keep the points of the hammers buried so deep in the snow that her mittened hands weren't visible, she slowed to a stop just yards above the drop-off to the full North Face.

The Deacon and Pasang continued hopping and crampon-bouncing perilously back down the gulley, losing in minutes countless feet in alti-tude that it had taken us the better part of a painful hour to gain. They arrived at Reggie's side—she was still lying spread-eagled and facedown in the snow, her crampons raised—at almost the same instant. J.C. and I turned to join them, but the Deacon shouted at us to stay put—we'd lost enough time.

Within a minute, Reggie was sitting up—Pasang's cramponed boot giving her a footrest to keep her from sliding as she sat on the snow—and soon she was drinking hot tea from a thermos the Deacon had produced.

The wind was still so negligible that J.C. and I could hear everything Reggie said from almost 100 feet below our site on the near-vertical slope. "Stupid, stupid," she kept muttering. "Stupid!"

Pasang was looking her over—reaching beneath her outer layers to feel her arms, legs, and torso in ways that made me sorry that I wasn't a doctor—and called up to us that other than some bruises and contu-sions, Lady Bromley-Montfort seemed all right.

"We need to know about your ankles," the Deacon said in a worried tone. Often the impact of crampons flipping one over during a steep slide sprains or breaks ankles, or snaps the lower leg bones, as we'd seen so clearly with George Mallory's corpse—and he hadn't even been wearing crampons when he died. It had just been his heavy boots that had caused that compound fracture of the tibia we'd seen gleaming whitely.

With both men's help, Reggie stood, wobbled slightly, was steadied by Pasang's huge hand, and said, "They're sore—my ankles, I mean—but no real sprain. Nothing broken."

Pasang knelt in front of her right then and for a moment I thought he was praying; then I realized he was simply re-tightening the lady's crampon straps.

"Here's your ice axe back," said the Deacon, handing it to her.

Reggie frowned—I could see the side of her face from where I stood leaning on my axe 100 feet up-slope—and said, "This isn't my ice axe."

"It has to be," said the Deacon. "I found it where it bounced about twenty feet to the base of that gully to your right."

Reggie pointed. "There's my old axe up there, half buried there about halfway down the gully. I feel stupid for letting go of it. This is a new Schenk ice axe."

"You did not let go of your own ice axe, my lady," said Dr. Pasang. "It was ripped out of your hands. Had you tightened the wrist strap on *it*—as you did on the ice hammers—the wrenching torque certainly would have snapped your wrist."

"Yes," said Reggie in a distracted voice. "But whose axe is this? It looks brand-new, but the wood of the shaft is darker than mine. And it has three notches on it here about two-thirds of the way up the shaft."

"Three notches?" said the Deacon in an odd-sounding voice. He took the ice axe from her and studied it carefully. Then he removed his binoculars from his pack and began scanning the narrower gully to the right of the one in which J.C. and I were still standing. Every second I was not moving made me colder, especially my feet.

"There is something up there," said Pasang, pointing upward.

"Yes," said the Deacon. "A man. Or a body."

With the two tall men half-supporting Reggie for her first dozen cramponed steps or so, all three of them started climbing steadily—not back up the gully we'd almost climbed and in which J.C. and I waited, but toward the narrower, steeper one to our right. Someone or something was waiting up there for us.

15.

I was the first one to reach the man-in-the-other-gully because I
cheated a bit; rather than descend our gully and re-climb the
adjacent one, as Jean-Claude and the others were wisely doing, I used up
most of my dwindling energy in free-climbing the nine-foot-high ridge
of boulders separating our gully from the next one and dropping down
into the snow there, barely arresting myself with wildly waving arms and
a firmly and quickly sunk ice axe. But my idiotic and risky exertions got
me to the corpse minutes before the others arrived.

And corpse it was, I saw at once. And—even with my very limited
experience with dead bodies—it seemed a strange one.

The tall, muscular man looked as if he'd been sitting on a flat rock
just a few yards above where his body had come to rest after it had finally
tumbled over, still in a stiffened, seated position.

He was an English climber, there was no doubt of that. Like Mallory,
he had no oxygen tanks or frame on his back—only a wind-tattered
anorak over a Norfolk jacket and several visible layers of wool
sweaters—and there were the remnants of a leather motorcycle or flying
helmet strangely bunched up on the right side of his head, along with
tattered and flapping remnants of a large wool overcap. He wore no goggles, and his face was bare to the elements.

What made his posture seem so strange to me, I realized, was that he
was still frozen in a sitting-forward posture, his hands pressed together,
fingers clasped, either in the motion of praying or trying to keep his
hands warm. Those hands were pressed between his knees, which were so

tightly closed against one another that they seemed a single frozen mass.

I steeled myself to crouch and look closer at his face.

It had been a handsome face and probably very young, although at least a year's worth of Everest-altitude winds and sunlight had weathered it in odd ways. I could still see deep marks where a standard oxygen mask had been pressed down on the last day of his life near the bridge of his finely shaped nose and on both sides of what must have been a well-shaped mouth. It was disturbing to look at his mouth, actually, since either a final death scream or the tightening tendons associated with death had pulled it bizarrely open, shriveled lips pulled back and away from the white teeth, exposing a brown gum line.

His eyelids were closed—and the eyes themselves seemed deeply sunken, as if the eyeballs were missing—and frost and snow had settled in the occipital orbits. The right side of that once handsome young face appeared almost untouched except for odd, translucent strips of skin hanging from his cheeks, forehead, and chin. What I first took to be a wound from a fall, a split of flesh and skin on the left side of his face, was, I realized just before the others arrived, only an open gouge where goraks had been pecking at the frozen flesh to get at softer tissue below. This had exposed the poor man's left cheekbone, all of his teeth on the left side of his face, and ridges of brownish ligaments and muscle tissue. It was as if that side of the corpse's face was smiling broadly at me, and I confess that the effect disturbed me.

Half of his forehead and scalp had come free from the dislodged motorcycle helmet and wool cap, and the hair I saw there was short and so blond as to look white through my Crooke's glass goggles. I tugged the goggles up for a moment to look more closely and realized that the short, still-combed-back hair *was* white—but almost certainly because it had been bleached so by a year of exposure to the ferocious ultraviolet rays at this altitude. There was white stubble on the intact right side of his face, but some of the stubble was still blond along the shaded jawline of the damaged side.

I looked around for a rucksack or other detritus from a fall, but the only pack the corpse carried was a small canvas gas mask carryall slung around his neck in front, just as George Mallory's had been. Fighting down a sudden surge of nausea, I reattached my face mask to my leather motorcycle helmet, set the regulator valve to low flow, and gulped down some English air to get my brain cells working again.

I stepped back from the body just as my four climbing companions kicked their way up the last yards of the gully to stand beside me. There was a shared moment of silence, more to let our lungs fight for oxygen than out of any intentional respect for the dead man at our feet. That would come later...For now, I drank in the rich air set to the 15,000-foot level from my pressurized tank and blinked away black dots that had been briefly dancing in my narrowing cone of vision. That free climb over the ridge rocks, at above 28,000 feet, wasn't the smartest thing I'd done this endless week.

I tugged my mask down. "Is this your cousin Percival, Reggie?"

Reggie shot me a glance almost as if she was unsure I was being serious. Then she saw I was and shook her head. Her tumble on the slope had allowed a few strands of her beautiful blue-black hair to escape her fur-lined leather flying helmet. She had also just pushed up her heavy goggles, the better to inspect the corpse, I assumed, and her eyes were a more lovely ultramarine color than ever.

"This man looks to have been in his early twenties when he died," said Reggie. "My cousin Percy turned thirty-four last year. Also, Percy has—had—dark hair, longer than this, and a sort of thin black mustache the way Douglas Fairbanks wore it in *The Mark of Zorro*."

"Who is this, then?"

"Gentlemen," continued Reggie, her voice sad, "you are looking at the mortal remains of twenty-two-year-old Andrew Comyn 'Sandy' Irvine."

Jean-Claude crossed himself. It was the first time I'd seen him do that.

I tugged my mask down long enough to say, "I don't understand. I found Mallory seven or eight hundred feet lower...but there's a rope around Irvine here, too. Also snapped off fairly close to the body..." I stopped.

The Deacon looked around. "You're right, Jake," he said. There was still only the lightest of breezes here above 28,000 feet. "Mallory didn't fall from this height—down through the Yellow Band and across those poorly defined ridges and all those rocks—or his body would have been much more torn up."

"They were down-climbing separately, then?" asked Jean-Claude. The disapproval in his tone of voice was that of a veteran Chamonix Guide.

"I don't think so," said the Deacon. "I think the accident—the fall—happened quite a ways below here, below the Yellow Band and that ridgeline, somewhere in those rock gullies below. One of them fell first—and, hard as it is to believe, I think it was Mallory."

"Why?" I asked.

"Because of the injury to Irvine's knee," said Pasang, panting.

I hadn't noticed it. The fabric there just above the once light-colored but now filthy puttees was torn and caked with dried blood, the knee an exposed mass of gristle and smashed cartilage.

"What does that prove?" I asked before setting my mask back in place.

"It proves that Irvine had a small fall, Mallory a longer one," said the Deacon. "But notice that the three-eighths-inch climbing rope has been broken off only ten or so feet from Irvine's body—same as from Mallory's—so my guess is that it snapped over a sharp rock edge, but not before giving both men internal injuries."

"Which they died of?" asked Reggie.

"No," said Pasang. "Mr. Mallory died from the results of his fall and the freezing night temperatures. But I think, as we all saw, that he must have lost consciousness from the terrible head wound, if not from the agony of the broken leg, within minutes, if not seconds. Mr. Irvine here was, I believe, pulled off his perch, probably a belay stance on a boulder somewhere below here, broke his knee in the short fall—very, very painful, by the way, a broken knee is one of the most painful injuries the body can sustain. But, with the rope broken, and probably hearing the diminishing screams and rock sounds of Mr. Mallory's long fall, Mr. Irvine crawled some yards or even hundreds of feet uphill to this point before he sat in the darkness and froze to death."

"Why would he go *up* the hill?" asked Jean-Claude. "Their Camp Six was several hundred yards downhill and to the east."

"You remember that neither Mr. Mallory nor Mr. Irvine had a compass," Pasang said softly. "Mr. Mallory was leading the way down through the rock mazes below the Yellow Band when he fell—perhaps—but definitely pulling Mr. Irvine off his belay stance before the rope broke, causing Mr. Irvine's broken patella."

"Patella?" said J.C.

"Kneecap," said Pasang.

"But still," persisted Jean-Claude, "why would Irvine drag himself *up* the hill when Mallory had fallen *down* it?"

"Perhaps because there was a remaining band of sunset light up here near the ridge and Sandy was very, very cold and thought it might give him a few more minutes of warmth and life," Reggie suggested. "Anyway, here is his notebook."*

She'd taken it not from the gas mask carryall but from Irvine's Norfolk jacket breast pocket. We all crowded around. As we'd seen before, Sandy Irvine's spelling was atrocious—probably a case of dyslexia, I realized many, many years later—but here he'd used a dull pencil to abbreviate most of his words, and reading it was like deciphering a German code.

I tugged my mask down again. "What does this mean—*dsdkd 1st btl 3.48 m. in2 asnt aft V jt blw 1st st aft u fl fl 2.2l alwy?*"

Jean-Claude answered. He couldn't read Sandy Irvine's abbreviated scribble any better than the rest of us, but he was an expert on George Finch's, Sandy Irvine's, and his and his father's modified O_2 tanks. *"Discarded the first bottle—of oxygen—three hours and forty-eight minutes into the ascent after leaving Camp Five,"* translated J.C. But he wasn't done. *"Just below the First Step,"* he continued, *"after using the full flow of two-point-two liters all the way."*

"That would be right," said the Deacon, his voice almost hushed in respect. "If they'd gone on full flow all the way from Camp Five that morning, they would have discarded the first empty bottle somewhere just short of the First Step."

"How many bottles of air did they have?" asked Reggie.

The Deacon shrugged. "No one's sure. But from those notes I saw jotted on the margins of one of the old letters from Mallory's pocket, wrapped in the fancy handkerchief... my guess is at least five between them."

"My Lord," whispered Reggie. "With five tanks, and leaving just before or after sunrise, they could have reached the summit of Everest and had enough bottled air to get them at least down past the Second Step again."

"What do those last two entries say?" asked the Deacon.

"*M lft R in btfl pls. bf vry prd. acd cnt b hlpd/Msl rp sn. ne hts bt nt as much as bee4. m sbfc hts mr. nt. mny srrs. Btifl. Vry vry cld noiw. Gby M I lv u an F and H nd Au TD. Im sry.*"

The Deacon thought a minute then tried to snap his fingers through his thick mittens. "*Mallory left the photo of Ruth in a beautiful place. Both very proud. Accident couldn't be helped... Mallory slipped, rope snapped.*"

"What about this last part?" asked Pasang, peering at the note in the bright sunlight. He pointed to the "*ne hts bt nt as much as bee4. m sbfc hts mr. nt. mny srrs. Btifl. Vry vry cld noiw*" line.

"*Knee hurts, but not as much as before,*" translated Reggie, who was getting the hang of the dead man's shorthand. "*My...*" She paused at the "*sbfc.*"

"*Sun-burned face?*" suggested the Deacon.

Reggie nodded and sighed. "*My sun-burned face hurts more. Night. Many stars out. Beautiful. Very very cold now.*"

I didn't want to start crying, so I stared hard through my thick goggles at the dead man. There was no emotion on his face either.

"This part?" asked Jean-Claude, pointing to the last few jumbled jottings: "*Gby M I lv u an F and H nd Au TD. Im sry.*"

The Deacon and Reggie looked at one another, the Deacon nodded, and Reggie translated in a strained but steady voice. "*Good-bye, Mother. I love you and Father and Hugh*—that would be Sandy's older brother—*and...Aunt T.D.*" Reggie paused. "Aunt T.D., I'm all but certain. Christian name Christina. He mentioned her twice at that last dinner at the plantation. And then only...*I'm sorry.*"

"But it would have been just really dark, no moon, when they were trying to find their way down through these ledges and gullies," said Deacon, almost as if he were speaking to himself. "Thus the goggles in their packs and pockets."

"This is all...*merde.* Mere conjecture," said Jean-Claude.

"*Oui,* my friend," said the Deacon. "But Jake there may have found the proof that they made it to the summit."

"What's that?" I asked.

"Sandy Irvine's note that Mallory had left the photograph of his wife,

Ruth, in a beautiful place. And that they were both—Irvine and Mallory—very proud. It sounds like a modest summit claim to me."

"Or perhaps Mallory left Ruth's photograph at their highest point below the summit," said Reggie. "Their turnaround point...when they decided they had to retreat or really be trapped by darkness. The view from anywhere up above the Second Step would be beautiful."

"We'll never know," I said.

The Deacon looked at me. "Unless we try the two-summit traverse," he said. "And find Ruth's photo on the higher, North Summit up there."

No one spoke for a while after that. I realized that we were all standing with our hands folded, as if praying for Sandy Irvine. We were certainly giving him that moment of silent respect I mentioned earlier.

"I'm sorry that the damned ravens got at his face," I said suddenly.

"They did not on this side of his face," said Dr. Pasang. He pulled his two layers of mittens off and pointed a thinly gloved finger to the strange translucent strips hanging from the right side of poor Irvine's face. "This is peeling from a terrible sunburn when he was alive," said Pasang. "That—especially with the oxygen mask digging into his raw and sunburned flesh—must have been terribly painful in his last few days and hours of life."

"Irvine wouldn't have complained," Reggie said flatly.

The Deacon blinked. "I'd almost forgotten that you met him last year at your plantation near Darjeeling."

Reggie nodded. "He seemed to be a marvelous young man. I warmed to him much more than I did to George Mallory." She pointed toward his shoulder carryall and oversized Norfolk jacket pockets. "We should see what he's carrying."

"Please pardon us, Mr. Irvine," said the Deacon. And with that he opened the flap of the gas mask carryall and started removing things.

As with Mallory, there were personal things—tins of throat lozenges, some papers, the same strap-on bit of leather to attach his oxygen mask—but there was also a small but heavy little camera.

"I do believe that this is George Mallory's Kodak Vest Pocket camera," said the Deacon.

"It is," said Reggie. "He was showing it to Lady Lytton and Hermione's brother, Tony Knebworth, at my *bon voyage* dinner at Bromley plantation the night before they left last March—a year ago March."

"Let's all put our goggles back on," said the Deacon. "This snow's bright." He handed the Kodak Vest Pocket camera around saying only, "Please don't drop it."

The camera was small and black and not much larger than a tin of sardines. It would have slipped easily into one of either man's oversized shirt pockets, but for some reason Irvine had chosen to carry it in his canvas carryall instead. J.C., bolder than I with historical artifacts, unfolded the little camera by pulling out the bellows that was attached to hinged and folding metal X's. The mechanism opened easily, just as if it had not just suffered a summer monsoon and endless winter and hard spring at 28,000 feet on Mount Everest.

There was no viewfinder. To take a photograph, one held the expanded camera at chest level and peered down at a very, very small prism. The shutter release was one tiny lever. Mechanically, the Kodak Vest Pocket camera could not have been much simpler or more foolproof.

Still holding the camera to his chest, J.C. took a step back and uphill from all five of us—five including Sandy Irvine's corpse. "The image is upside down." Then he said, "Everyone say *fromage*."

The Deacon started to say "Don't, we—" but J.C. had already clicked the shutter.

"It works," said Jean-Claude. "The Kodak Company should be commended. Perhaps I shall write them an advertisement recommendation."

"How can you joke at a moment like this?" asked Reggie. Her voice was soft, but J.C. hung his head like a reprimanded child. None of us wanted to fall out of Lady Bromley-Montfort's favor.

"If there was an image on that frame of film," the Deacon said tiredly, "you may have just double-exposed it and ruined it."

"No," said Jean-Claude, pulling his goggles back in place. "I saw the little flange for advancing the film and advanced it before taking your group portrait. Fascinating that the mechanism hasn't frozen." He looked at the Deacon steadily. "If this is Mallory's camera, why did Monsieur Irvine have it in *his* bag? Or did each man carry a Kodak Vest Pocket camera?"

"According to Norton and John Noel," said the Deacon, "only George

Mallory had a Vest Pocket Kodak. Irvine was supposed to have taken a couple of cameras with him from Camp Four those last two days, including one of Noel's miniature cine cameras, but he doesn't have any others in his pockets or messenger bag."

The Deacon shook his head gloomily—the presence of Sandy Irvine's body seemed to have oppressed him deeply, even though he'd never met the man—but then he brightened and looked up, moving his goggled gaze from one of us to the next. "Remember what Pasang said way below? When one wants his portrait taken with a Kodak, what does one do?" He seemed happy, almost giddy.

"Hand it to someone else to take the photo!" Reggie answered quickly. (More quickly, I noticed, than *my* mind was working, even fortified as it was now by English air.)

"If they reached the summit," piped up J.C., "then Mallory would almost certainly have snapped a photo of Irvine, then handed the little camera to Irvine to take a snap of *him*. Irvine might have then put it in his own carryall. It makes sense."

"We have to keep this camera," said the Deacon.

"If we keep the camera," said Reggie, "then we must take this final note from Sandy Irvine as well, send it to his mother and family."

"We shall," said the Deacon. "But only if we *don't* find Cousin Percival and Meyer and their . . . whatever it is . . . and have to keep this expedition secret for a while. But you take the notebook, Lady Bromley-Montfort. If we survive the next few days and are allowed to talk about this expedition when it's over, then I—hell, *everyone*—will want to know if Mallory and Irvine reached the summit of Everest last year."

"Here, Jake," said the Deacon. "I'll keep Irvine's notebook. You carry the camera. I would bet anything that in it are the exposed negatives that will answer all our questions about whether Mallory and Irvine summited last year."

"Why me?" I said. For some reason the thought of carrying Mallory's camera around bothered me, as if it were a great weight.

"Because you have the smallest load and because I think you just may survive this climb," said the Deacon.

16.

*I*n truth, I never thought we'd make it to the North East Ridge
of Everest at 28,000 feet, but when I'd fantasized stepping onto
it anyway, I'd always imagined the three of us shaking hands solemnly or
slapping each other on the back fraternally or perhaps just staring out at
the view of the world from one of the highest places in the world.

As it turned out, we were all too exhausted to move when we actually
reached the ridge, and when we did finally move, it was for Jean-Claude
to stagger to a nearby rock, tug down his oxygen mask, and tidily vomit.
Pasang just stared out to the south as if something awaited him there.
When we'd rested and inhaled more English air set at the high 2.2-liter
flow, the Deacon, Reggie, and I used our binoculars to scan the lower slopes,
looking for the Germans who were working so hard to catch us and kill us.

"There they are," I said finally, pointing. "All five of them. Just climbing toward the exit cracks above the Yellow Band about three hundred
feet northwest of our Camp Six. They'll be up on our ridge in another
thirty minutes.

"See them?" I asked.

"*Oui.*"

I could actually make out that the climber in the lead—the strongest
climber of the five by the looks of his progress and the brevity of his
stops—was carrying a rifle slung over his chest. "Do you think that's
Bruno Sigl?" I asked the Deacon.

"How should I know, Jake?" snapped the Deacon. "They all have
white winter-combat anoraks with hoods on and are wearing some sort

545

of white scarf or face mask below the goggles. How could I identify Sigl from this distance?"

"But do you *think* it is?" I said.

"Yes," said the Deacon and lowered his glasses until they dangled from the thick leather strap. "He's their leader. He's their best climber. He's most intent on finding and killing us. And he climbs with a certain strange aggressiveness. Yes, I think it's him."

"I still do not understand something, *Ree-shard,* Madame Reggie," said Jean-Claude. He'd taken a little water from his bottle, rinsed his mouth out, and spit in the snow. "What could this Kurt Meyer—or your cousin Percival for that matter, Reggie—have taken from the German government that would make them so insane about retrieving it? After all, England and France are at peace with Germany... for now."

Reggie sighed. "It's not the current German government that Percy was assigned to... learn about," she said. "The Weimar Republic is weak and indecisive. It's that far-right-wing group of nationalist extremists that the Deacon's and my... mutual friend... asked Percival to get some damning information on."

"*Deutschland* is filled with far-left and far-right-wing nationalist groups," said J.C.

"Yes," said Reggie, "but only the Nazis, the group Bruno Sigl and his friends are part of, represent a great danger to Great Britain... and France... in the years and decades to come. At least according to our friend who writes so many cheques and who prefers gold."

"I'm sick and tired of you two always talking in this cute code," I said between terrible coughs. I was angry. "Spies—even those on our side—are supposed to work for governments, ministries, secret services, not for individuals who like gold. Just tell us who the hell you're talking about and how one man can send spies to Germany. We're risking our lives up here. We have a right to know who this British master of spies is."

"He sent British spies to Austria in this case," corrected Reggie. "And you may well meet this man someday yourself, Jake. Until then, we have to decide what to do. Those bast—those *Germans*—will be on the North East Ridge in another forty minutes or so, and unless we decide what to do quickly, we'll be in rifle range soon."

There was silence except for the wind howling. As calm as it had been down on the face and in the gullies, the wind was wild up here on the thin line of the North East Ridge. A moderate spume of spindrift was being flung our way from the summit less than 1,000 feet above us. Now we had to shout to be heard, and it made my aching, constricted, blocked throat hurt all the more for doing so. I decided to shut up and let the others sort things out. In truth, I didn't give a shit who this British spy boss was. The fact was, he'd gotten Bromley and Kurt Meyer killed, and now it looked likely that he'd finish us off as well.

A hundred or so feet below the ridgeline, Jean-Claude had patted me on the shoulder and said, "Jake, you're still carrying Mr. Irvine's ice axe."

I was. We'd decided it was best to leave Sandy Irvine's corpse where it lay, since certainly another British Everest expedition would be coming this way in a year, two years at most. If we buried him—and if our expedition had to remain a secret for whatever arcane reason—they'd never find him.

This was the Deacon's reasoning. But I'd absentmindedly carried Sandy Irvine's ice axe with the identifying three notches in the shaft almost to the ridgeline here on the east side of the First Step, and when J.C. reminded me, I set it carefully on a boulder, its metal tip pointing downhill to where the body lay out of sight in the gully, laid it where British climbers could find it next year or the year after.

How were we to know that another British expedition wouldn't attempt Everest until 1933 and would find the ice axe I'd left but not go downhill a couple of hundred feet to search for Irvine himself?

"We have to climb or get around the First Step," the Deacon was saying. "Put it between the Germans and ourselves. What do you think, Jake... you're our rock man. Climb it or traverse around the base? If we climb, do we try the large boulders or try to work the rocks on the left side of the ridge, closer to the Kangshung Face?"

I shook myself out of my reverie and took the few steps to the south lip of the ridge. We'd grown as accustomed as one can to climbing with a constant 8,000-foot exposure while clambering around on the North Face, but at least down there we'd had the *illusion* of a gradual slope before everything went vertical. But from the *south* edge of this disturbingly narrow North East Ridge, it was a straight vertical drop of more than 10,000 feet to the shark-toothed jumble of the Kangshung

Glacier below. Absolutely nothing between us and the glacier almost two miles below us but howling wind.

"Holy shit," I heard myself say as I peered over the south edge.

"I agree completely," said Jean-Claude. He was standing by my right shoulder. I didn't want him behind me right then, jostling me. I stepped back, looked up the North East Ridge at the rocky obstacle of the First Step, and considered it for a long moment of silence broken only by the rising wind. There was an ominous, whirling white cap of cirrus cloud forming over Everest's summit.

"If we were just free-climbing this First Step the way Mallory and Irvine probably did," I said, my voice sounding much more authoritative than I really felt, "I'd say stay to the left near the Kangshung Face. Easier climbing. More handholds. But we have good ropes and J.C.'s jumars. With the others able to use the jumars, I think it would be easier for one climber to shed his rucksack and oxygen, climb those tougher boulders to the right — up and over the top — get a good belay stance there, and fix ropes along the way for the rest to jumar up."

I was certain that the Deacon was going to ask me to do the climbing — I was their rock man after all, it was why they'd brought me along here to the top of the world — but what they didn't know was that a sharp-clawed lobster had taken up residence in my lower throat and upper breathing tract and was moving around from time to time. Every time it did, it blocked my breathing almost completely.

"I'll lead this pitch and lay the rope," the Deacon said at once. "We'll save Jake for the Second Step. That's where the *real* climbing will be called for."

I didn't argue. We'd moved to the base of the stacked boulders at the south side of the First Step and were laying out ropes, the Deacon had removed his rucksack and mittens, when suddenly I said, "Wait! What about looking for Bromley's body on this north side of the First Step? I thought that was the plan."

Reggie gripped my upper arm. "We did that already, Jake. We found Sandy Irvine instead. It would take hours, days, to search all of those gulleys — and you can see that he's not dangling from the south face of this ridge. Besides, I think Kami was right — whatever he saw...three figures and then just one...happened on this ridge *between* this First Step and the higher Second Step, near a boulder that looks like a mushroom. That's where we'll look now. *After* we get past this First Step."

"Besides, Herr Sigl and his friends are coming too quickly for us to tarry here longer," said the Deacon.

"But...," I began and had to stop to cough a minute.

Reggie touched my back. "Pasang," she called out to the silent Sherpa, "can you give our friend something for his terrible cough?"

"Not more codeine," said Dr. Pasang. "It would have too much of a soporific effect at this altitude. But I have an ancient Hindu cough remedy in my bag if you'd like to try that."

"All right," I said and held out my mitten as Pasang dug around in his rucksack and then in his small medical bag.

Pasang dropped a small box of Smith Brothers Cough Drops into my palm — the new menthol kind that had come out only two or three years earlier.

Reggie looked over her shoulder as she belayed and actually laughed, but I just opened the package and put three of the drops in my mouth.

"I'm ready to climb," said the Deacon, tying onto a rope and coiling more rope over his shoulder. "Who wants to belay?"

"I will," said Reggie and J.C. at the same time. Both passed the rope over their shoulders, and Jean-Claude tied it off around the thinnest vertical boulder. Both said "On belay!" at the same instant.

The Deacon shook his end of the belay rope loose, giving himself slack, looked at the ugly heap of steep boulders a moment, and started climbing in that gangly, electrified-spider form of his. His style wasn't pretty, but it certainly worked well on most rock. He played out the longer rope behind him as he climbed from handhold to toehold to precarious handhold, always moving upward with the spread-eagled speed that climbers used to stay attached to vertical rock if only through sheer fleeting friction.

I turned around and lifted my binoculars. Less than eight hundred yards behind us, the Germans moved onto the North East Ridge — up to our altitude, level with us. I watched as they paused a long moment to catch their breath, and then the tall leader with the rifle slung over his chest said something, gestured, and all five began slogging west toward us.

"Hurry!" I called up to the Deacon.

17.

*C*limbing the First Step, even with the use of the Deacon's fixed lines, was exhausting—*every* action was exhausting up there above 28,000 feet—but after we'd crossed over the top, we felt better about being out of the line of sight of the five German climbers who were following us. Then, just after we'd retrieved and coiled our fixed lines from the First Step, Reggie had to tug down her mask and go and spoil my newfound sense of relief.

"Of course," she said, "if Sigl really *did* confront Cousin Percy and Kurt Meyer here on this section of the North East Ridge, as Kami Chiring thought he saw him doing, then that means that Sigl has already climbed to this height. He probably holds the record—for anyone living, that is—for reaching a high point on Everest before this. He may know a faster way *around* this First Step."

"How high did Colonel Norton get in his climb up the Great Couloir?" asked Jean-Claude. "I thought it was about even with our ridge here...twenty-eight thousand feet."

"Norton turned around at twenty-eight thousand one hundred and twenty-six feet, his high point in the steep Couloir itself," said the Deacon. "Somervell reached twenty-eight thousand feet, below and behind Teddy Norton, just making the traverse across the North Face without climbing much in the Couloir."

"High-climb records won't count for much if Sigl and the other Germans really do know a faster way around this First Step," I gasped out over my mask.

The Deacon ignored me and pointed out over the steep, snow-blown, and rocky North Face. The Great Couloir looked like a vertical white scar on that dark face. "Norton and Somervell were out there, several hundred yards west of us and almost directly below the summit before they turned around. We'll beat Norton's record if we keep climbing along this ridge to the base of the Second Step…it's up around twenty-eight thousand two hundred and eighty feet."

"Just seven hundred feet below the summit," whispered Jean-Claude, his words almost lost under the rising wind that was making us lean toward the west, every loose rag or tag end of our clothing flapping like wash on the line in a mild hurricane.

"Seven hundred feet," agreed the Deacon. "But still quite a distance to our west and about three to five hours of ridge climbing from here. Come on. I see the Mushroom Rock, do you?"

We all peered into the wind and blowing snow—it hurt when it struck the few exposed parts of our faces. About halfway between this First Step and the much more imposing and terrifying huge Second Step was a low boulder that did indeed appear to be shaped like a mushroom.

"We can't stay on the ridgeline here!" shouted Jean-Claude. "Too narrow. Too corniced. Wind too high. Too exposed to the Germans' rifle fire if they get over or around this First Step."

The Deacon nodded and started the traverse by dropping down onto the North Face and trying to find footholds and a rough route westward. We were roped in two groups at this point—the Deacon, Reggie, and Pasang on the first rope. Jean-Claude and me on the second. Before we separated into two single-file groups for this tricky traverse, I shouted to Reggie, "What do we do to look for Lord Percival during this part?"

"Just try not to fall," she shouted back. "It looks—at least through my field glasses—as if there's a relatively flat spot there at Mushroom Rock. We'll pause there and look around. My guess is that if Percy and Meyer actually fell from the North East Ridge, it was from there."

And this is what we did—dropping down below the ridgeline and seeking out a traverse route there. The exposure along the crumbling rocks and bands of snow just yards north and below the razor-sharp ridgeline was terrifying—I could look straight down and see the tiniest specks that were the tents on the North Col some 5,000 feet lower, a full mile of empty air between them and me, although I couldn't tell if they were our tents or the Germans'. I *was* certain that if we fell roped together, we'd just keep bouncing and being torn apart until those bits and pieces of us showered down all across the East Rongbuk Glacier somewhere east of the old Camp III.

It didn't help our sense of too much exposure when three of the five of us ran out of air in our first oxygen tank and had to stop on uncertain footing in order to switch the valves over, get help pulling the empty tanks out of our rucksacks, and then get more help from the next person on the rope unhooking the fittings and tubes. Nor did it lessen my sense of insecurity on that slope when Reggie—quite deliberately—lobbed her silver metal tank as far out from the face as she could throw it underhand. It first struck some 200 feet below and kept clanking and bouncing its way on down the North Face long after we could no longer see it. The goddamned tank seemed to make falling noises for goddamned ever. I decided then that Lady Reggie Bromley-Montfort had somewhat of a sadistic streak in her.

J.C. and I tossed our tanks out as well, but it bothered me to watch mine keep falling and falling and falling, so I turned my face back into the snowy rock wall and set my leather-helmeted forehead against the cold rock. Jean-Claude and I helped each other make sure that our flow valves for the second of our three tanks were set at the lower flow rate of 1.5 liters per minute and that the regulator definitely was set to "On." I needed oxygen along this stretch; I didn't want to do *anything* stupid or to perform more clumsily than I absolutely had to. I was tempted to set the flow valve to 2.2 liters per minute, but I knew that I had to conserve what little English air was left.

What made this traverse so dangerous was the loose footing—the entire slope for 100 or 200 feet below the ridge on this north side was made up of small, downward-sloping, and wobbly slabs, a slippery mess of loose, sliding chips of stone, and entire gravel fields of what looked to be shale broken up by ages of extreme freeze and thaw. There were also apparently innocent patches of snow between boulders that were actually deep pits. "Tiger traps," Reggie called them, and I presumed she'd had some experience with shooting or trapping tigers in her decade in India. But I doubt if the noble members of the Raj actually trapped the tigers in snow pits. One could drop chest-deep into such snow-filled pits, and it would be hellishly energy-expending and dangerous for his climbing mates to try to get him (or her) out.

The Deacon avoided the snow pits, probing ahead of him always with his long ice axe, using the same axe to point out the pits or especially slippery parts to the rest of us. So far, no one had fallen in or fallen *off*.

And then we came to a dead end.

"Damnation," I heard the Deacon say softly from 40 feet in front of me. Like everything else up here, words were blown from west to east.

It wasn't exactly a boulder blocking our way, but rather a long, smooth extension of granite that ran from the razor ridge above to a point about 20 feet below our current traverse route. But I saw at once that there'd be no easy going under or over or around *this* obstacle. Above us, the mass of smooth rock turned into an airy arête—a high, brittle, serrated pinnacle that *was* the North Ridge for those few fatal yards. No one would be free-climbing *that* today. At least not by starting from this point on the North Face.

Our traverse line at this level below the ridge offered the best solution to solving this smooth-bulge problem, but as best solutions often go in mountain-climbing problems, this one stank to high heaven.

It was a blind step…a blind leap…the kind of move a climber has to make in the Alps, perhaps 20,000 feet lower than where we were at that moment, when he just pushes out around a smooth slab, hoping that the friction of his spread-eagled self against the steep rock will keep him from falling for the three or four seconds he needs to get his foot to the other side—a side still invisible because of the curve of the damned rock. So the climber just has to pray that there will be a foothold or fingerhold there on that other side. Sometimes there is. Too often—as the number of deaths of alpine climbers showed each year—there isn't.

Doing this kind of blind step in the Alps was dangerous, but many of the falls there were manageable if one's partner had a good, solid belay stance.

None of the five of us on this steep, slippery traverse slope had a belay stance worth a plugged nickel. All four others could be belaying the Deacon—or whichever one of us was stupid enough to try this blind step—and a fall would almost certainly mean that all five would be pulled off the rock of the North Face. There were a few stubby rock protrusions at our feet or above our heads, but none big enough and solid enough to provide a tie-off belay—and even with Deacon's Miracle Rope, the odds seemed overwhelming that the rope would snap with such a sharp belay point anyway.

"Okay," I called from the rear. "What next? We go back to the First Step to think about this awhile? Throw rocks at the Germans?"

"To hell with going back," called the Deacon.

He untied from the rope he shared with Reggie and Pasang, and then peeled out of his Shackleton jacket and Finch duvet, then put the gabardine Shackleton anorak back on. He stuffed the jacket and his two layers of mittens into his rucksack, which he removed and carefully handed to Reggie to prop between her body and the cliff wall. Then he looked down at his goose down trousers and stiff mountain boots and I knew he was considering removing his 12-point crampons. In the end, he chose to keep them on.

He then took the climbing rope back and tied it around his waist. I thought that perhaps only J.C. and I noticed that the knot he used was made to look like a simple overhand loop knot but was really a slipknot, certain to come undone from the Deacon without any tension or tug on the belayer if he fell. I understood and said nothing; Jean-Claude said nothing. Perhaps it was at that moment that I fully realized how brave a man Richard Davis Deacon really was.

Reggie cried, "No! Let us *try* to belay! *Please,* Richard!"

The Deacon didn't even look at her. "There's no belay stance anywhere along this line I took," he said, already staring at the smooth rock of the blind step he had to take. I could sense him going over his moves in his mind, mentally rehearsing what his body had to do physically in a few seconds.

"All right," he said and extended his right leg as far as it would go and hopped out onto the smooth stone of the abutment column.

He began to slide at once, and rather than follow the human instinct to claw for a handhold—of which there was none at all—the Deacon spread his palms, the wool of his gloves pressing hard against the stone, his anorak and belly and groin and balloon-fabric outer trousers pressing against the smooth rock face. He slowed, then almost stopped. The

Deacon was connected to the mountain now only by the slightest hint of surface friction. I knew from experience that it was not enough friction to keep him from sliding and falling.

And he *was* falling. His sickening downward slide toward the overhang slowed almost to a stop and then began—inexorably—again.

The Deacon didn't wait. Friction and speed were his only weapons, and of the two of them, speed was the more important. He scrabbled to his right as he slid, his body still spread-eagled, his palms and cheek and belly and thighs and crampon points pressing and scraping against rock, keeping himself from peeling off with all the pressure his tired body could exert, and when he'd slid to the far side of the arched seven-foot column, he pushed off the other side of the bulge just as if he were sure that there was a ledge or foothold or handhold waiting for him there.

Of course, he couldn't see that any of these things were there around the blind step of the rock column. It might be another no-holds smooth rock column for all he knew.

The Deacon disappeared, and there was no sound or visible motion for a long moment. But the rope hadn't played out, the lying knot he'd tied around himself to no purpose hadn't given way. Yet. Most important, there was no scream yet from a human body hurtling down through 8,000 feet of empty air.

I found myself wondering if the Deacon *would* scream when he fell.

Finally, the steady voice came from somewhere on the other side of the rock bulge—"Wonderful ledge over here. Perfect belay stance with tie-offs on the rock. And I see where we can easily climb up toward the Mushroom Rock."

We let out a collective breath, but no one said anything. Somewhere in the back of my weary mind was the question of all questions—*What about when we have to come back this way?* Normally a climber would use one or more fixed ropes in a situation like this; if one were an iron-mongering German climber, perhaps he would find the tiniest crack to drive in pitons for footholds.

But we couldn't rig a fixed rope here. It would only help those who were pursuing us. (And I confess to thinking—hoping—that perhaps one or more, or all, of the Germans would fall to their deaths on this terrible blind step.)

But no, if Reggie's Sherpa friend Kami Chiring was telling the truth, the great German alpinist Bruno Sigl had already solved this problem once.

"Let me do all the belaying," came the Deacon's voice from out of sight around the column. J.C. and I understood, and Reggie did as well, I was sure. It meant that only the Deacon had the stance and backup to hold if someone slipped, and we were to stay the hell away from any belay attempt.

Reggie's boots did slip, but she scrambled, the belay rope went tight from the Deacon's end, and he all but pulled her around the rock and out of sight onto the ledge with him. Pasang went across like a great, splayed spider. Jean-Claude did the blind step with pure, sure speed and rock-slapping friction. I managed, coughing even as I scuttled.

Then we were on a real ledge on the other side, together again, and I saw the path up through the overhanging rocks that the Deacon had shouted to us about.

"Think it's close enough to where the ridge widens out to Mushroom Rock?" asked Reggie.

"Yes," was the Deacon's only response. And then, all tied together for the first time—the Deacon using an actual, reliable figure-eight-on-a-bight knot when he tied in this time—we clambered upward toward the North East Ridge. One by one we kick-stepped our way up and then out onto the narrow ridgeline.

The sun was past the zenith. The wind was stronger and colder than before. The lenticular cap around the summit of Everest had become a large gray mass pressing down on the mountain at an angle; it reminded me of the jostled-sideways unraveling wool cap on Sandy Irvine's corpse.

We were too busy celebrating the wonderful flatness of the bit of wider ridge here at the odd mushroom-shaped rock. I knew that kind of wind- and tectonic-shaped top-heavy rock spur was actually called a bollard. More important to us than the stupid rock formation, after the miles of wildly tilted and slippery slabs and boulders, this snowy but relatively flat area on either side of the Mushroom Rock—roughly eight feet wide by about twelve feet long—seemed like a great, flat, safe football field to all of us.

"Perfect place for a camp," said the Deacon.

"You have to be kidding," I said between gasping coughs, removing my oxygen mask at every paroxysm. "We're above twenty-eight thousand feet here." It was true that our hearts were swollen, our muscles were failing, our kidneys, stomachs, and other internal organs were not doing their jobs properly, our blood was too thick and ready to spawn embolisms, our red blood cells were doing without the oxygen they needed, and our brains were oxygen starved and running like an automobile with its last few dregs of gasoline in the tank. We were metaphorical inches from hypothermia—which has a wider range of terrible symptoms than merely going to sleep and freezing to death, not the least of which would be intemperate belligerence and a need to rip our clothes off as we froze—and literal inches from a 9,000-foot drop to our south side and a 10,000-foot drop a few more feet away to the north side.

But for the moment, we were very happy. There were no armed Germans in sight yet, and we'd reached our temporary objective.

And maybe the Deacon was right. This would be one hell of a Camp VII. With the use of O_2 tanks, climbers could get a relatively good night's sleep here—especially in Reggie's solid, wind-proven Big Tent—get a *very* early start with Welsh miner headlamps glowing, and have only a two- or two-and-a-half-hour climb to the summit of the world.

Unless, of course, the winds came up during the night. Or the Germans shot us. Or we froze to death first.

It didn't matter. We all collapsed on a solid little snow platform on the north side of Mushroom Rock, adjusted our oxygen flow to "High" for a five-minute O_2 fix, and stared dully through our thick goggles. Only Reggie was active, and what she was doing made no sense to me at all.

At the north edge of this platform there was a tiny extrusion of rock protruding out into a snow cornice that had been building and accumulating there for years, if not decades. Even in our stupefied mental states, we all knew that this cornice was death—one step there and the weight of a man (or woman) would send one plummeting right through it and all the way down to the Kangshung Glacier on the south side of the ridge.

But Reggie was crawling on her belly toward that stone lip and treacherous snow cornice.

J.C. was the first to realize that we were about to lose our female climbing partner. He pulled down his mask and shouted, "Reggie, don't! What are you doing? Stop!"

She glanced back over her shoulder at us. She'd tugged up her goggles, but otherwise her face—or the few square inches around her eyes that I could see of her face—didn't look all that insane. Of course, hypothermia sufferers rarely do when they go into their death antics.

"See that bite taken out of the cornice?" she asked. Her voice did sound a little excited and breathless, but not necessarily irrational.

We looked and then we did see it—about six feet to the left of her rocky diving board to hell.

"So what?" I said. "Come back here, Reggie. Please. Just crawl back."

"Oh, shut up, Jake," she said over the wind whistle and low howl. She pointed to the "bite" she'd mentioned. There was about a five-foot-wide arc missing in the otherwise wind-formed and geometrically ruled snow-and-ice cornice.

"Lady Bromley-Montfort is saying that someone could have fallen through there," Pasang said in his not unpleasant Oxbridge singsong. "Perhaps a year ago."

"If someone had fallen a year ago," I said between heavy coughs, "that cornice would have rebuilt itself."

"Not necessarily," said the Deacon. "Go ahead, Reggie. Be careful."

She wiggled her way further out onto the tiny spur of rock—I certainly wouldn't have trusted my weight to that wee bit of stone overhanging such a fall—and then she pulled her binoculars from where she'd hung them against her back. Looking straight down, she slowly swept the glasses back and forth twice and then froze.

"There they are," she said.

"Who?" I cried. My first thought was that the Germans were sneaking up on us from the vertical south side of the ridgeline.

"Meyer and Cousin Percival," said Reggie, her voice flat.

"Certainly you can't see all the way down to the glacier with those field glasses," said Jean-Claude.

Reggie sighed, shook her head, and shouted over the rising wind. "They didn't fall that far and they're still roped together. The rope caught on a crag projecting out about a hundred feet below this ridge.

Meyer's body is hanging head down on the left side of the crag. Percy's body is hanging free, turning in the wind, head up, on the west side of the crag."

"How could Mallory clothesline rope stay intact in such a fall, against sharp rock, for a full year, at this altitude?" whispered Jean-Claude.

Reggie couldn't have heard him over the wind, but the Deacon did. "Who knows?" he said. Then, loud enough for all of us to hear—"What we have to do now is to figure out a way to get both of them up here before that old rope finally snaps."

I thought of the Germans with guns in hot pursuit . . . or perhaps "cold pursuit" would be a better term. Had they reached the First Step yet? The Blind Step rock on the traverse? No matter, they were behind us, and the Deacon had said that Bruno Sigl would never give up. And the Nazi had both a Luger and the Deacon's sniper rifle. And other armed fascists had been climbing with him.

I decided not to mention the Germans right then. Or to think about them.

"Uncoil the ropes," said the Deacon. "Reggie, stay where you are. We'll come to you. Somebody has to be lowered down to get ropes around each of the dead men."

"I'll do it," J.C. said at once. "I'm the lightest."

The Deacon nodded.

I thought, *Thank God it won't be me,* and then was immediately ashamed.

The Deacon and Pasang standing, J.C. and I crawling on all fours, we all moved toward Reggie and the north lip of the North East Ridge.

18.

*W*orking out the rope, knots, harness, carabiner, and belay logistics for attempting to recover the two dangling bodies was a tad complicated—at least for weary, oxygen-starved minds laboring to be minimally coherent above 28,000 feet.

First we anchored four ropes to the bollard of Mushroom Rock, whose stone "stem" looked solid enough to tie off several grand pianos with no strain. One of the ropes went to Reggie, who—at Pasang's and the Deacon's insistence—had to carabiner-clip her waist harness onto an anchored rope. But watching her lying on the spur of rock, her head and shoulders far out over the breathtaking drop, was still unnerving.

With the belay rope tied off on the bollard and two ice axes near the lip of the cornice keeping the ropes from cutting through the snow and ice at the edge—Pasang was holding two more ropes with the proper lariat loop and knots already tied in—the Deacon and I slowly belayed Jean-Claude over the edge of the long drop. Reggie was our eyes.

"All right...slowly...good...good...slowly...good...he's about fifteen feet above the spur and the bodies now...good...slow...stop... no a little more...there!"

I was glad I couldn't see my French friend dangling there next to that rotten-tooth rock spur almost ten stories below with the ancient frayed three-eighths-inch rope caught over it, the rotting cotton line holding two dead bodies slowly twisting in the incessant winds.

"He's gesturing that he wants to tie Percival on first," said Reggie. "He needs about six feet of slack and the second rope."

Pasang blithely walked right up to the edge of the rock spur next to Reggie and dropped the rope needed for tying onto the body. Then he calmly walked back and handed it to me. The plan was for the Deacon to continue belaying J.C., for me to pull up Bromley's body once J.C. cut him loose from the old rope, and for Pasang to pull up Meyer's corpse once it was secured. *If* it was ever secured.

But first Jean-Claude had to get the two extra ropes over the corpses' heads and shoulders and knotted and firmly secured under their arms.

"Jean-Claude has his feet on the crag and is leaning out almost horizontally to pull in Percy's body," reported Reggie.

Even just *hearing* that description made me a little queasy. We'd learned to trust the Deacon's Miracle Rope on this expedition—mostly in the heavy loads it had hauled up without snapping while we were using J.C.'s bicycle-pulley device—but no one's life had depended upon the rope in the way J.C.'s did now. All four of us mountaineers—including Reggie (but not Pasang, whose mountain skills seemed to come naturally)—had come of age in an era when ropes, like Mallory's and Irvine's, broke more often than not when any serious load or drop pressure was applied.

"Keep lowering...," said Reggie, talking to me now because I was to the Deacon's right and letting out the first 100-foot-long rope that Pasang had handed me, one with a pre-made lasso at its end. "All right, he's got it...another four or five feet of slack, please, Jake...all right he's trying to get the loop over Percy and under his arms...Percy's arms won't move."

"Rigor mortis?" I whispered to Pasang, who was standing nearby with the second long strand of rope.

"No, that was over a year ago," Pasang said softly so that Reggie wouldn't hear the words above the wind. "Lord Percival has just been frozen solid for a long time."

"Okay," I said, feeling very sorry I'd asked.

"He's got the loop over but is having trouble getting the slipknot pulled tight," said Reggie.

Out of the corner of my eye, I could see the Deacon's face covered with sweat. His belay rope to Jean-Claude was tied off to Mushroom Rock, but the Deacon was carrying all the weight over his shoulder and once around his waist. He'd taken all the layers off his hands except for the thin silk gloves that made up the bottom layer, and now I could see blood soaking through the silk.

I admit that I was nervous. The phrase "dead weight" takes on a terrible reality when one actually has to lift a dead person. Nothing on earth seems quite so...heavy.

"All right, Jake...he has Percy's body tied on...," said Reggie.

I started to pull on the rope but Reggie shouted "Stop!"

I'd forgotten that J.C. had to finish securing Meyer's corpse to the new rope belayed by Pasang and only *then* cut the old rope that had held both bodies hanging there for almost a full year. We'd lose more than the corpses if those four ropes got tangled or crossed, or snapped.

"Jean-Claude's feet came off the crag," reported Reggie. "He's swinging free, trying to get his boots back on the rock."

I closed my eyes and tried to imagine the feeling of swinging freely, on a single rope held by a single man, over a drop of that magnitude.

The Deacon grunted, more from the exertion of the belay, I realized, than in acknowledgment of Reggie's report. The tug from J.C.'s fall from the crag when I made him lose his footing with my premature pulling on Percy's rope had been fast, hard, and harsh against the Deacon's hands, shoulder, and middle.

"All right, his boots are touching rock again," reported Reggie.

Sweat dripped from the Deacon's stubbled chin. We'd all been off oxygen for quite a while now. Our rucksacks were stacked against the south side of Mushroom Rock.

Pasang had started lowering the third rope—the rope and lasso for Kurt Meyer—even before Reggie called him forward to do so. When 50 feet or so were played out, he ducked on all fours under my taut rope and then under the Deacon's line to J.C. so that he'd be to the far left of our line of three busy belayers.

"A little more...a little more...slowly now...," Reggie was reciting. "There, he has it. Give him another five feet or so of slack, Pasang."

Pasang calmly did so.

"Darn...," said Reggie. "He can't reach Meyer from his half-perch on the crag. He's going to have to swing out to grab him."

"Oh, Jesus," I whispered. Anything can and usually does go wrong when there are multiple ropes dangling in such a confined area.

"Do you need help?" I whispered to the Deacon, who was bracing his boot soles—he'd removed his crampons for this—hard against a little ridge of rock about five feet north of the Mushroom Rock.

He shook his head and beads of sweat flew west in the rising wind.

"He's swinging...he's swinging again...he missed," reported Reggie. "Now he's pushing off almost horizontally from the crag to try again."

"Jesus," I whispered again. I think it was a prayer this time. I realized that I'd come to trust the Deacon's Miracle Rope in most basic rappel and belay situations, but if the frayed old rope parted before Jean-Claude got the loop tight around Meyer's body—and if J.C. then tried to hold on to the corpse, as I was sure he would—the weight of the *two* men, one living and one dead, suddenly would be on the single line that the Deacon was belaying. Even though the end of that rope was tied off to the Mushroom Rock, I doubted if it could hold the doubled weight.

J.C.'s belay rope grew tauter than ever, the line cutting through the edge of the cornice and pressing down hard on our double-ice-axe setup. We'd run multiple lines from those axes to other anchors, and two back to the much-encircled Mushroom Rock bollard.

The Deacon grunted and held J.C.'s swinging weight. The silk of his gloved hands was dyed red now.

"Meyer's upside down," reported Reggie. "Jean-Claude is working to spin him around right-side up."

How can even the Deacon's Miracle Rope keep from snapping under this pressure? I thought again. Well, we'd see in the next minute or two. In the meantime, I kept a steady but not lifting pressure on the rope running down to Lord Percival Bromley, the man who could have been the sixth Marquess of Lexeter if he'd survived.

"He's got him!" cried Reggie. "He's tying the loop off under Meyer's arms. Now Jean-Claude's swinging back to the crag."

The Deacon grunted slightly. The blended rope was stretched so taut that it looked as if he was trying to land a giant marlin with only his bloody hands, arched back, and braced body.

"Jake, Pasang, get ready," called Reggie. "Jean-Claude is going to cut the old rope now. He has his penknife open."

I'd found a low boulder-ridge on which to brace my boots—I'd kept my crampons on since I didn't know if I'd have the dexterity to strap them on again—and now I leaned back, bracing myself for the pull and dead weight to come.

The rope grew taut…but there was very little pull and almost no sense of weight. Had goraks hollowed Bromley's corpse out the way they'd eaten into George Mallory's abdominal cavity through the poor corpse's exposed rectum? Jesus Christ, for Reggie's sake, I hoped that wasn't the case.

"Pull!" cried Reggie—needlessly, I thought, since both Pasang and I were pulling in our loads hand over hand. Only the Deacon remained on passive, strained belay. We'd decided before J.C. went over the cliff that we'd get the bodies up before pulling in our living friend—just to keep the various ropes free from tangling, for one reason; to keep J.C. and his belay line free of a free-falling corpse for another reason.

Bromley reached the cornice, and naturally his corpse hung up under the overhang of ice and snow.

"Give me a second," said Reggie and leaned most of her weight out on the rotten, treacherous, already once-broken cornice, fishing around with her extended ice axe the way a captain's mate would use a gaff to reach under a boat to bring in a big fish.

She hooked the rope. Percy's head and shoulders bobbed up into sight, and I pulled for everything I was worth.

"Get back on the rock!" growled the Deacon, and I realized he was saying it to Reggie. She did so, creeping backward in no great hurry.

Now Meyer's corpse, being pulled in by Pasang, came up onto the North East Ridge with no problem, the dead man's head and shoulders sliding up and through the crescent-shaped hole that he and Percival Bromley had broken through the cornice almost a year ago. I noticed—distantly, since all my sense impressions seemed to be coming from a great distance at that moment—that yards of the old, frayed rope, cleanly cut in the middle by Jean-Claude just minutes before, still dangled from each dead body.

When the bodies were secure, pulled as far up toward us and Mushroom Rock as we could get them while leaving some room for ourselves, Pasang and I dropped our belay ropes and joined the Deacon on his. Reggie stayed on the rock spur, her head and shoulders hanging further out than before. She signaled down to J.C. that we were ready to bring him up.

This, I knew, would be the real test of the Miracle Rope. I wished we'd had enough rope with us to pass two lines around Jean-Claude, but 200 feet of what we did have had been needed for the dead bodies.

Now we pulled—slowly, constantly, the three of us in perfect rhythm, watching the frail line snake over the doubled shafts of the anchored horizontal ice axes. Reggie was calling out the distance remaining after each pull.

"Forty feet...thirty...twenty-five...Jean-Claude's feet can't reach the cliff face, he's just hanging free..."

We knew that from the weight against our shoulders and hands. The Deacon was still bearing the brunt of that weight.

"Fifteen feet...ten...five...careful now!" Reggie quit calling distances, reached down, grabbed our friend's anorak, and helped pull J.C.'s shoulders into sight. The three of us on belay tugged again and he came up and over and onto his hands and knees and quickly crawled away from the cornice. Reggie had almost fallen forward when her burden popped up onto the ridge, but Pasang had shifted his large right hand to her anchor rope and pulled it hard, tugging her back onto the rock spur. She also crawled toward us on all fours. After we'd retrieved all of the ropes, undone knots, and coiled and safely stowed the ropes under Mushroom Rock, we crouched in a tight circle around both bodies.

"This is my cousin Percival," Reggie said just loud enough to be heard over the wind. She pulled off her mittens and gloves and set her bare hand against the worn wool and tattered Shackleton gabardine over his chest.

There was no smell of decay. The exposed portions of both bodies' faces and hands—and a bit of Meyer's chest under a rip in the fabric there—were bleached almost white by ultraviolet rays, as Mallory's back had been, and the skin of each man looked slightly mummified, and their eyes and cheeks had fallen in the way corpses' faces do, but the goraks hadn't been at them. I had no clue as to why not. There was a bullet wound visible in Meyer's upper left shoulder—it shouldn't have been an instantly fatal wound, the Deacon said—but although we rolled Bromley's body over carefully, we found no entrance or exit wounds on him.

"So the Germans didn't kill Lord Percival?" I said, my voice thick with fatigue, altitude, and emotion.

"They killed him, my friend," said Jean-Claude. "But not by shooting him. Rather, by shooting Herr Meyer and making Lord Percy either jump or be shot the same way."

"Put your gloves back on, Reggie," the Deacon said gently. I'd just watched him pull wool gloves over his now bloody silken ones.

"Lady Bromley-Montfort," said Pasang, "we shall search Lord Percival for you."

Reggie shook her head. "No. Pasang, will you please help me with Percy? Then analyze Meyer's bullet wound. The rest of you can look through Meyer's clothing."

"What are we hunting for?" asked Jean-Claude.

"I don't know exactly," said Reggie. "But it will be very portable. Meyer carried it for thousands of miles across Europe, the Middle East, and then Persia and China."

We treated the bodies with a slow gentleness, although they were far beyond feeling any insult or injury. Perhaps we were just following Reggie's tender-touch lead.

The first thing I noticed about Meyer, despite the weathering effects of hanging in midair off Mount Everest for a year, was that he looked very, very young.

"How old was this Austrian?" I asked no one in particular.

"Seventeen, I believe," said Reggie. She was absorbed with going through her cousin's pockets.

Neither Meyer nor Bromley had a rucksack on. We went through the many pockets of what was left of their outer anoraks, wool trousers, Norfolk jackets, and waistcoats. Meyer had multiple letters in German in his left jacket pocket—I couldn't even decipher the *Fraktur* handwriting on the envelopes—and his Austrian passport, stamped at a score of border crossings.

In Meyer's left jacket pocket was a large wad of pound notes.

"Good God," I said. "Are these real?"

The Deacon fanned through them. The clumps of bills were still banded, and the writing on those bands was still quite clear—NATIONAL PROVINCIAL BANK LTD. LONDON.

"This is a real bank, *Ree-shard?*"

"It had better be," said the Deacon. "I have what little money I have left stored there." He was counting the bills. "There's fifteen thousand pounds here."

"So your cousin Percy was paying for this information," J.C. said to Reggie.

She looked up from the pockets she was searching. "Probably. It's what he did with his sources willing to risk their lives and their families' lives to betray their Austrian or German masters. From the little Percy told me—usually after a fine dinner and much wine—espionage is mostly about paying unsavory characters."

"So," I said, pointing to the body of the dead young man we were still searching, "this Austrian was an unsavory character."

"I believe not," said Reggie, her words almost lost in the gusts of wind from the west. "Look at his passport again and you'll see why he probably did what he did, and risked everything to do it."

I looked at the Austrian passport and its description, but I could find nothing especially interesting. NAME: Kurt Abraham Meyer. BIRTH-DATE: 4 Oct. 1907. OCCUPATION: apprentice typesetter.

"Here," said the Deacon and pointed to the *Fraktur*-labeled category: RELIGION. Under it was written, in the perfect penmanship of some bureaucrat: HEBREW.

"He spied for your cousin because he was a Jew?" I asked Reggie, but she didn't respond.

Instead, she'd removed a thick, solid manila envelope from the Norfolk jacket breast pocket of her cousin's corpse. She was careful not to let the increasing wind gusts grab the envelope out of her hands, shielding it with her body.

Inside the larger envelope were five smaller ones. Each one seemed to hold the same number of photographs—seven. I couldn't exactly see what the photographs were because Reggie was still hunched over the package, but I was thinking that for £15,000 in cash, they'd damned well better be photostats of Count von Zeppelin's newest military airships.

"Ahhh," said Reggie, and the syllable combined a sense of the air being knocked out of her and the confrontation with some revelation. "Do you want to see what Percy and Meyer died for, gentlemen?"

All of us, except for Pasang, nodded. The doctor was busy cutting away waistcoat and shirt fabric on Meyer's corpse to inspect the bullet wound in his upper shoulder, just below the collarbone.

"Be careful," said Reggie. "There are five identical sets of these, but this set has the negatives. Don't let any of the pictures blow away." She handed one of the packets of photographs to the Deacon, who looked at all seven, nodded slowly, and carefully handed the packet to Jean-Claude.

J.C. made up for the Deacon's nonreaction by responding physically and vocally, his head snapping back as if he'd been confronted by a bad smell, his arms thrusting the photos further from him, and crying, *"Mon Dieu*, these are . . . this is . . . these are . . . *abominable."*

I strained to see the pictures over his shoulder but only could catch glimpses of white figures against a dark background.

"Abominable," J.C. rasped again, shaking his head. *"Completement abominable!"*

He turned his face away and handed me the photos. I had to clutch them tightly in both hands and lower my face toward them to see them in the wind. Then I remembered that my snow goggles were still in place and roughly shoved them up as I went through the seven black-and-white photographs.

Each photo was of a very pale, very thin man in his late twenties or early thirties having sex with what I counted as four different young men—no, with boys. The oldest boy having sex with this man must have been about thirteen. The youngest was no older than eight or nine. The photographs were very clear, the naked flesh very white against a background that was very dark save for the gray blur of tumbled sheets. The room looked to be a cheap European hotel room, perhaps Austrian, with heavy furniture and dark painted walls. The photographer must have used a flash or a long exposure, because shades were drawn on the one window visible in the snapshots. The sharpness of each photograph and the critical depth of field suggested a high-quality camera. Each print was about five by seven inches, and the negatives were in a paper sleeve at the bottom of the packet.

For only seven photographs, an incredible variety of deviancy was on display. I confess that my expression must have shown my shock as I looked through the pictures and then looked through again. Modesty should have made me look away after seeing the first print, but I *had* to see — it was the same compulsion I would feel in later years when passing a serious highway accident.

The adult male was a very thin and obviously poorly fed fellow, his ribs and hipbones rampant, some scabs visible; a man who probably looked bourgeois enough, with his hair parted on the left side as suggested in these photos and his severe, short, greased-back haircut carefully combed — but in the tumble and passion of these moments, that greasy hair stood out in wild tufts. The man had thin lips and a stern demeanor in the only photograph where his mouth was not hanging open either in the throes of passion or in the midst of some more explicit and disturbing sex act he was involved in.

In one photograph, the man was buggering the youngest boy while simultaneously sucking the small, stiff penis of the thirteen-year-old. In another photograph, a boy no older than ten was masturbating the adult male while the man played with the genitals of two of the younger boys as the fourth boy, the oldest, perhaps fouteen years old, stood naked and looked on with a dull, almost drugged expression.

The oldest boy's face was strangely familiar, and then it hit me with a shock — it was Kurt Meyer! And only four years or so younger than when he'd died here on Everest.

"Oh...God," I whispered.

One photograph was almost impossible to make out — a sprawl of five white, emaciated bodies on the tumbled sheets, connecting and pleasuring each other in so many disturbing ways that my innocent Protestant American mind couldn't quite take it in. The only face fully visible in that shot was of the adult — the older man. I stared at the face, trying to ignore all the couplings and gropings in the photograph, and realized I'd also seen him before. Once. In a photograph on a poster in a Munich beer hall. The face had been somewhat older, a little fuller, the man in the Nazi poster in his mid-thirties rather than the early thirties that these photos suggested, but the intensity of the dark gaze was the same, as was the ridiculous Charlie Chaplin mustache. At that moment, I couldn't remember his name.

I put the photos back in the envelope and looked up at Reggie, J.C., and the Deacon. "*This* is what your cousin died for?" I gasped out at Reggie. "These are what we've been fleeing for our lives about...these...*obscenities?*"

"It is abominable," Jean-Claude repeated softly, his gaze averted.

"Abominable?" I shouted. "It's goddamned *nuts!* I've never seen anything like this before and never want to again. But who cares if some
German does deviant things with street urchins? Who could give a
damn about any of these photographs!"

"The adult man using these children is not German," said Reggie.
"He's Austrian, although he lost his Austrian citizenship when he moved
to Germany a few years ago. And you know that he's the leader of
the *Nationalsozialistische Deutsche Arbeiterpartei*—a very dangerous group,
Jake."

"He's in jail!" I shouted. "The Deacon and I heard that last November
when we met Sigl in that damned beer hall in Munich!"

"He was released last December," said the Deacon. "While we were
buying boots and rope in London."

"I don't care if he's a socialist!" I shouted, standing and pacing around
the Mushroom Rock in my agitation. "Who cares about goddamned so-
cialists—we have thousands of them in New York, probably hundreds
in Boston where I live. Why would Lord Percival risk his life...*die?*" I
pointed at the corpse at my feet. I noticed the "Douglas Fairbanks mustache" now, as well as dark stubble on the dead man's cheeks and chin.
For a sickening moment that almost made me swoon, I remembered that
hair kept growing after a person died.

"...all this for nasty photos of a damned socialist?" I finished weakly.

"He's not a socialist, Jake," said Reggie. "He's a Nazi. *The* Nazi." She
was fumbling in her rucksack for something.

"Who cares?" I said again. "Even I know that there are a hundred
crackpot political factions in Weimar Germany. Even *I* know that, and
I can barely tell a Democrat from a Republican. Why should we climb
almost to the summit of Mount Everest...and have that climb ruined
by *this*...and suffer all we've suffered just to receive filthy photographs
of one sick pederast and his victims? And, for God's sake, you can see
that one of the victims—one of the kids in that room—was young Kurt
Meyer. The guy who sold your cousin Percy this package of trash!" In
my fury, I held the envelope up into the wind between two fingers and
said, "I'm throwing this crap away."

"Jake!" snapped Reggie.

I looked down at her. She had her 12-gauge flare pistol held steady in both hands and was aiming it directly at my gaping face.

"If you let those photos go," she said in flat tones, "I'll kill you with this, I swear to God I will. I love you, Jake. I love all of you. But give me the photos back or I'll shoot you in the face. You *know* I will. I did it with the German on the glacier."

In that instant and that second, I knew she was telling the truth—both about loving me, probably like a brother, alas (or like her dead cousin), and also about being ready to kill me in a second if I threw those photos away. Then I remembered the red flare burning through the gaping mouth of Karl Bachner and the liquid from his eyes running down his cheeks like melted wax.

I carefully handed the envelope of photos and negatives back to Reggie.

"What I'm curious about," the Deacon said in conversational tones, as if nothing had happened between Reggie and me, "is who took the photos. Not...Bromley?"

"No," said Reggie. Her voice suddenly sounded infinitely weary. "Although Percival had to frequent some of those...establishments and circles...in his guise as a dissolute pro-Austrian, pro-German British expat. It was Kurt Meyer who took those photographs. With a rather sophisticated little camera that had a time delay. Percy had given it to him for just this purpose."

All of us shifted our gaze to the body of the dead Austrian. He was so young. I noticed for the first time that a ginger-colored shadow under Meyer's nose was obviously a boy's attempt to grow a man's mustache.

"So Meyer was also a spy?" I said, not really expecting an answer.

"He was on the payroll of British intelligence," said Reggie. "And Kurt Meyer was also a Jew." She said it as if that explained everything.

For a moment I thought she was saying that, naturally, Jews were greedier than anybody else and would do anything for money—I'd known no Jews at Harvard or in my Boston social life, of course—but then I remembered that the Nazis weren't overly fond of Jews, even German or Austrian Jews. But this Hitler bastard had been in bed with a bunch of Jewish boys—everyone in the photos except the adult Nazi had been circumcised. Nothing made sense. Everything was just...*dirty*. I shook my head.

"Kurt Meyer was also one of the bravest men my cousin Percival ever worked with," she said. "And Percy had worked with hundreds of brave men, most of them doomed to terrible deaths by their courage."

I had nothing to say to that.

"Here it is," said Reggie, who'd continued looking through her dead cousin's pockets after setting down the Very pistol with which she'd threatened to kill me.

She pulled out a folded piece of green silk that I first thought to be a fancy handkerchief—rather like the one that had been on George Mallory's body—but, when unfolded by Reggie, turned out to be a three-foot-by-four-foot flag of a gryphon battling an eagle over a gold medieval-looking lance.

I'd last seen that flag—or a larger version of it—flying over the Bromley estate when we'd gone to visit Lady Bromley.

"Did your cousin seriously think that he and this...*boy*...might really summit Mount Everest?" asked the Deacon.

"Obviously their only choice was to keep climbing higher from their Nazi pursuers," said Reggie, still rather tart in tone. "With Mallory and Irvine's expedition's fixed ropes and camps still intact, it gave them a chance. But the Germans turned out to be better climbers. Still...Percy approached everything he did with more than one hundred percent effort, so perhaps he *could* have summited this mountain from Mallory and Irvine's highest camp had Sigl not caught up to them, although that hadn't been Percy's intention when he climbed away from the Germans." She put the folded flag away somewhere in her own layers of clothing. "Now I will climb it for him."

"No one's going to climb anything if we don't hurry," called Jean-Claude over the wind roar.

While we'd been busy looking at pornography, chatting, deciding whether to kill one another, and so forth, J.C. had taken his binoculars from his rucksack and walked over to the snowy, treacherous south edge of the North East Ridge, looking down and back the way we'd come.

"*Les boches* are just now solving the Blind Step problem," he called to us. "They will be here in thirty minutes or less, depending upon Herr Sigl's climbing skills. I suggest that we finish our business here and leave soon."

"Leave for where?" I said between terrible fits of coughing. I knew I had to get *down*, down to where the air was thick enough for me to breathe even with these shards of lobster shells and clacking claws in my throat.

The Deacon turned his head and looked to his right and up—and then up some more—at the looming and impossible Second Step less than a hundred meters away. Not that far above that impossible Second Step—or so it seemed—the summit of Mount Everest looked to be exhaling a twenty-mile-long howling tail of gale-driven spindrift.

19.

*T*he second half of the distance between the First and Second
Steps was as iffy and frightening as the first half.

A series of sharp and uneven upthrusts, slippery rocks, and snowy crests
make the ridgeline itself impracticable, so the Deacon—who was leading
on a rope that now included all of us—forged a trail in the snow about ten
feet below that windy ridge above the North Face and Great Couloir on
the East Rongbuk Glacier side. The exposure just kept getting more and
more absurd, and when the Deacon would take a new step and the snow
would slide inches or even feet under him before building up into an unstable platform just capable of stopping his slide, all of us held our breath.
Not one of the four of us had a belay stance worth a tinker's damn.

We didn't look behind us for the five Germans, but we could feel
them breathing down our cold necks. The last J.C. had seen with his
glasses while the rest of us were preparing Percy and Kurt Meyer for
"burial" was that the German lead climber—we still thought he was
Bruno Sigl—had managed to get himself around the Blind Step and was
fixing rope for his four climbing partners. Obviously Sigl was the strongest climber of the five Germans, and we were glad that the others were
slowing him down slightly.

But not enough.

Then Jean-Claude came back to the group and we took a moment over
the bodies of Meyer and Bromley.

Reggie said a brief prayer, and I was surprised to see the Deacon
saying the words right along with her. Years later, I looked up the Angli-

can burial service and prayers and realized that Reggie had done some thoughtful editing, but evidently the Deacon had repeated the words so often over dead comrades on the battlefield that he could keep up with her ellipses and edits. Anyway, it sounded right—although a tad too long, I thought, what with the Germans coming up the North Face behind us—when we sat there with the two bodies laid out on the short rock spur above the north edge of the cliff. Reggie had taken out her own gold and green silk handkerchief, smaller than the flag Percival had been carrying, with the Bromley coat of arms on it, and had knotted it around her cousin's face. Kurt Meyer's face was covered with a clean white handkerchief from the Deacon's pocket.

Reggie bowed her head—goggles still in place—and intoned:

I will lift up mine eyes unto the hills; from whence cometh my help. My help cometh even from the Lord, who hath made heaven and earth.

He will not suffer thy foot to be moved; and he that keepeth thee will not sleep.

Behold, he that keepeth the glory of this high mountain world shall neither slumber nor sleep.

The Lord himself is thy keeper; the Lord is thy defence upon thy right hand;

So that the sun shall not burn thee by day, neither the moon by night.

The Lord shall preserve thee from all evil; yea, it is even he that shall keep thy souls.

The Lord shall preserve thy going out, and thy coming in, from this time forth for evermore.

Thus unto Almighty God we commend the souls of our brothers here departed, our brothers of the rope and of high places—Percival Bromley and Kurt Meyer—and we commit their bodies to the ground and air and ice; in sure and certain hope of the Resurrection unto eternal life, through Percival's trust in his Saviour Jesus Christ and through Kurt Meyer's love of the Lord-God Jehovah, whose coming, in glorious majesty, shall judge the world when the earth and the sea and these high places shall give up their dead.

We brought nothing into this world, and it is certain we can carry nothing out. The Lord gave, and the Lord hath taken away; blessed be the name of the Lord. Amen.

"Amen," the rest of us said, and then Jean-Claude, Pasang, and I pushed at the booted feet of the two men until they slid over the edge of the rock spur and spun silently downward into shattered oblivion somewhere on the Kangshung Glacier almost two miles below. None of us watched the bodies fall. Immediately we set to repacking our rucksacks. I saw Reggie put her envelope of photos into some pocket in her inner jacket—we'd distributed copies before the ad hoc funeral—and now I slid mine down in a safe place against the back of my pack. Then we retrieved our ice axes and started the trudge toward the Second Step.

The sun had been warm when we'd sat a moment on the east side—the leeward side—of Mushroom Rock, but as soon as we got down off the ridgeline to the North Face again for the traverse, the rising wind blowing over miles of vertical snow and ice leached the warmth right out of us. We had to keep moving or freeze.

No one spoke until we came back up onto the ridgeline proper right at the base of the Second Step. The thing was terrifying to look at, even without the sure knowledge that trigger-happy Germans would soon be popping up behind us and within easy rifle range.

"If you get us up there, Jake...," the Deacon said when he'd tugged down his oxygen mask. "...No, I mean *when* you get us up there, the flat but boulder-strewn top of this Second Step will be a perfect defensive position for us, even for an army fitted out only with Very pistols."

I looked up at the steep snow slope rising to the impossible heap of boulders ending in a sheer rock face. *Tell the Deacon about the obstruction in your throat, your trouble breathing,* insisted the oxygenated part of my dying brain. *He'll take the responsibility and try to free-climb this fucking thing himself. Or let Jean-Claude do it. Hell, Reggie and Pasang are better rock climbers right now than you are, Jake Perry.*

I said, "Yeah, it'll be a veritable Alamo up there."

"What is this 'Alamo'?" asked J.C. He seemed far too cheery for the circumstances.

I was coughing again, so Reggie explained the history of the Alamo to him in three or four succinct sentences.

"It sounds like a glorious battle," said J.C. after Reggie had just sketched the outline of the fight without revealing its ending. "What was its outcome?"

I sighed. "The Mexicans overran the place and slaughtered all the defenders," I said between coughs. "Including my hero David Crockett and his pal Jim Bowie, the guy who invented the Bowie knife."

"Ahhh," said Jean-Claude and smiled. "Then thanks be to God that we shall be fighting mere Germans and not Mexicans."

I was in the process of taking off my Shackleton jacket, goose down layers, and all outer mittens down to my thinnest silk gloves.

We'd crampon-climbed together as high as we could up the snow slope to the base of the rocky Second Step proper. The rock cliff looked to be about 90 feet high, its great slab sides absolutely unclimbable, but there was a crack—"joint" was the better word—in the rock a bit to the left of its central mass, and at the base of that narrow crack and 90-foot wall, J.C., the Deacon, Reggie, and I were all busy scouting a climbing route. I'd shoved my Crooke's goggles up for a better view.

The problem—as life-and-death challenges are so cutely called in mountain-climbing circles—was just too damned hard to solve. Especially at this impossible altitude. And *especially* for a man with broken glass in his throat. This entire Second Step consisted of amalgams of rock that wore away much more slowly than the shale and other stone beneath it.

The first ten yards or so of the 90 feet of cliff would probably go, because there were various tumbled boulders, rock extrusions, and smaller cracks on the lower third of this six-mile-high impossibility. A groove between the largest of those boulders and the cliff face angling east from it might work, with perfect rock climbing and a serious expenditure of energy, but I'd have to step out and balance atop that damned boulder before attempting the second pitch of the three-section climb.

This first pitch between the boulders and the cliff face and then smack dab atop the boulders onto the steep snowfield would have been a challenging but fun afternoon's scramble in Wales near Pen-y-Pass. I couldn't imagine the amount of energy it was going to require at 28,246 feet.

But I kept looking—trying to figure the best route. If there *was* a "best route." Neither premier rock climber next to me, not Jean-Claude, not the Deacon, said a word to interrupt my thinking. In truth, probably neither of them had so workable a route either.

From somewhere atop that big boulder some 30 feet and change up the cliff, there would be a high, risky step onto a steep snow band or—more appropriately—steep cone of snow, on which I'd have to traverse steeply uphill and back to the central crack where the cliff here met the face at almost a right angle. God knows whether that cone-shaped snow patch would stay on the cliff or avalanche off with me on it. Then, if I made it back to a point higher on the central crack, I'd have to learn how to levitate like a Buddhist holy man to get to the base of the final and most impossible third of the climb.

The "crack" looked to be a fissure never wide enough for my body to wedge in sideways and in most places not much wider than the flat of my hand. Another crack, much smaller, ran in tree-shaped fracture lines upwards at odd, probably unusable angles from the snowy jump-off point.

This last, vertical pitch of the climb was the killer—almost certainly in the literal sense.

Those last 20 feet or so would be listed in the "Extremely Difficult" category in any country's or continent's method of rating climbs—what we today in the spring of 1991 as I write this would label a 5.9 or 5.10 climb—a pitch requiring not only great expertise but absolute commitment even to attempt. *Absolute commitment or a simple death wish.*

And that near-impossible difficulty rating was for sea-level climbing. How would it be rated here at more than 28,200 feet *above* sea level?

How could I say to the Deacon and Jean-Claude and Reggie and Pasang the simple sentence "I can't *do* this"? Not just because I was getting about a third the amount of air I should be getting through my frozen and clogged and pain-wracked throat and frozen upper respiratory system, but because I couldn't do the fucking last 20 feet of this sort of pitch problem on a summer day in Massachusetts if the face were ten feet off the ground with mattresses spread around beneath me, much less here, more than 8,000 vertical feet above the East Rongbuk Glacier.

No one could do it. At that moment I was certain that George Leigh Mallory couldn't have done it and *didn't* do it. I was certain that Mallory and Irvine must have taken one close-up look and turned around here at the Second Step. Whatever delay had made it necessary for them to scramble down through the rock ledges below the Yellow Band down there after sunset, I was absolutely sure at that moment that it had *not* included time they'd taken to climb and then later down-climb this Second Step.

It was impossible.

"How do you see it, *mon ami?*" Jean-Claude asked.

I coughed and cleared my throat. "Start at the top of the snow pyramid," I began, "about six to ten feet away from the face and big crack. Free-climb those boulders to that central boulder and up, chimney if I have to, and then take one goddamn big step onto that steep snowfield. Then try to traverse back to the central crack, use it and those fractures to get up to the vertical part, and then...well, I'll figure it out when I get to that point."

This sounds more solid and linear than it was delivered. I'd had to stop three times to cough, bending over for the last gut-ripping spasms.

"I agree on the route," said the Deacon. "But do you feel up to doing this, Jake? Your cough is terrible and getting worse by the minute. I'd be happy to give it a go."

I felt myself shaking my head. I'm not sure to this day whether I was saying *No, I bloody damned well* don't *feel like doing this impossible free climb and dying this way* or whether I was insisting that I give the climb our first shot.

My friends interpreted it the second way.

I was down to Norfolk jacket, wool trousers, and my thin silk gloves now. Everything else had been crammed and lashed down into my rucksack. Absurdly, I'd pulled my thick wool cap so low down over my leather motorcycle helmet that it covered the goggles I'd pushed up on my forehead. During this climb—this climb of all climbs—I *had* to be able to look down and see my feet. My oxygen mask and goggles restricted my vision and made me feel too removed from this cold, windy top of the world. So no rucksack or oxygen or gas mask carryall or ice axe was coming with me. There would be nothing on my back to pull me off balance. I was keeping the crampons on because I'd learned to trust climbing with them on rock, but nothing else to get between the rock and my *feel* for the rock; nothing, that is, other than my illness and exhaustion and almost debilitating fear.

"You know," I said almost conversationally to the Deacon and Reggie, my casualness broken only by my wheezing and coughing, "I did think of a way we might get out of all this with no more loss of life on either side."

Both the Deacon and Reggie cocked an eyebrow and both waited.

"Let me go out with a white flag when Sigl and his boys show up," I said between coughs, "and I'll give them the photographs—maybe even the negatives, too."

"*Comment?*" said Jean-Claude. He sounded shocked and disappointed.

"But we'd give them four of the envelopes and hide the fifth one somewhere here in these cracks and boulders," I hurried to say...as much as one *could* hurry with so little oxygen getting to one's aching lungs. "Keep one set for ourselves, you see."

"And you'd give the Germans the negatives?" asked Reggie. I couldn't interpret her expression.

I shrugged, which was easier to do with my outer layers off. But I was getting cold very quickly now.

"I know enough about photography to know that you can make a sort of new negative from actual prints...a 'dupe,' I think they call it," I said as if it were not a matter of great interest or import for me, just a passing thought. "That way, Sigl and his goons might consider their mission fulfilled and we'd be left alive with all seven of the photos to share with...well, with whoever your mystery man is, the fellow who loves checks and gold. There'd be no reason for the Germans to kill us if they get what they want...what they came for two years in a row."

The Deacon shook his head—sadly, I thought. "They'd kill us anyway, Jake. Even if they thought they had all the photographs, which they wouldn't risk in the first place. Remember, they've killed almost all of our Sherpas this week as well as murdering Lord Percival Bromley and an Austrian boy last year. They couldn't leave us alive to tell about all this."

"And *les boches* don't *need* a reason to kill people," said Jean-Claude. "It is their nature."

I nodded as if I'd worked all that out on my own. And I would have...eventually...at least the Deacon's part. My mind was still on the cracks, fissures, boulders, snowfields, and sheer face looming almost ten stories above me at the moment. And it didn't like being there.

"But our using those photos..." I felt I had to say this, even if they were my last words in this life. Now I looked at all four of my companions as I spoke. "Even if it was to win a war or help preserve a peace...and all that's just·conjecture right now...using *those* photographs, that kind of thing, to blackmail someone...it wouldn't...I mean, it couldn't be...*honorable.*"

Only the wind through the rocks and cliff wall spoke for a minute.

The Deacon said, "If Germans like Herr Sigl and his friends get in power, Jake, there will be another war. Count on it. And in the end, there's nothing honorable in war. *Nothing.* Trust me on this one truth. The only shreds of honor that can be salvaged when war looms is either avoiding the fight completely, which men smarter than you and me suggest that these *dirty, tawdry* photographs might possibly do, or—when the real fight comes—behaving the best one can, even while you're afraid every waking second, and while doing *everything* one can to keep one's men alive."

"You did that for four years, *Ree-shard,*" J.C. said. "Worked to keep your men alive. You're doing it now, here on the mountain."

Surprisingly, shockingly, the Deacon barked a laugh. "My dear friend," he said, touching Jean-Claude's shoulder. "My dear friends," he said, looking at each of us in turn. He pulled his goggles up to say this to us with his gray eyes visible, and I could see that the cold wind was already causing them to tear up. "My friends, I failed miserably at keeping men under my command alive. I couldn't even keep our thirty Sherpas alive during this peacetime expedition. They were under *my* command on the mountain. Most of them are dead. Dear Jesus, I couldn't even keep track of my own rifle, much less be smart enough to keep our Sherpa friends from being killed. If all the good men I killed or helped to *be* killed in the Great War were to come with us on this climb up Mount Everest, the line would extend from Darjeeling to the bloody summit."

He fell silent.

"Well," I said after too much of that wind and silence, "I'd better start climbing before I freeze up. This is a decent belay point, so I'll stay roped up until I get to the top left of that snowfield about forty-five feet up. It looks like one of you could come up and belay me—or at least spot me—from that point. We'll kick up a little platform of snow there for you if need be. But, no, it's a shitty belay point—if I fall from that face, I'd pull the belayer right off—so let me help get one of you and the fixed ropes that high, to that snowy point right at the base of the vertical last pitch, and then I'll free-climb it without tying on, just carrying the rope loose around me so someone else can give it a try if I peel off."

"I'll follow you up to that point when you find some belay points on the boulders," said the Deacon.

Jean-Claude was leaning over the edge of the North Face, studying our footprints and route with his field glasses. "The Germans are climbing toward Mushroom Rock," he said over the wind. "We shall have to climb quickly if we are to reach our Alamo in time."

20.

I didn't know a damned thing about Zen meditation, if that's
what the Deacon really had been doing when he sat cross-
legged and apparently lost in thought every morning before breakfast as
Reggie recently suggested, and I certainly hadn't had the time or interest
on this insane climb to ask him about it.

But I suspected then and I *know* now that mountain climbing—especially rock climbing under extreme, no-forgiveness-for-errors conditions—is a strange and beautiful equivalent to Zen. Everything empties
out of the climber's mind except the moves he's planning to make, the
holds he sees or senses or hopes for, the speed he'll need to move at in
order to stay attached to a steep or vertical face. One imagines—envi-
sions, rehearses, *feels*—the motions he's about to make, the stretches and
reaches he's ready to go for, the fingerholds or footholds he needs to find,
the life-saving friction he'll have to create where no friction should exist.

So, with the Deacon's belay rope tied on for only the first half of
this impossible climb, I began the scramble—first to the left toward
the off-width crack corner where the faces met at a sharp angle, the all-
important joint starting just below that meeting of sheer faces, a mere
fracture there but widening to become the 15- or 16-foot-high off-width
crack 45 feet higher up. That crack was filled with rocks and pebbles—a
joint—down low and appeared from below to be no factor whatsoever
in this first half of the climb.

That wasn't quite true, actually, for as I quickly traversed left toward
the south-facing wall near that joint, I moved into full shadow, and sud-

denly the air was painfully colder. Working near the useless joint would make me much colder—a *negative* factor. I had to move fast through these shaded parts, or later I'd be losing fingers, toes, feet, hands, and God knows what to the surgeon's scalpel.

I scrambled up the narrow groove near that meeting of cliff faces, then shifted right, my fingers finding holds that my eyes couldn't see, my crampon points balancing on cracks that were less than half an inch wide. Then a short vertical climb, my left hand jammed deeply and painfully in a vertical crack just below the cone of snow halfway up, feet scrambling to the left and then to the right before finding the faintest traction, then up again until I could balance and cough and pant on the four-inch-wide top of a tall, skinny boulder. Four inches was a boulevard up here...a Kansas prairie.

This was the "high step" up onto the snowfield I'd seen from below and had decided to worry about only when I got there.

Well, I was there. There was really nothing to wedge my crampons or hands against to get any lift for that four-foot or broader step up onto the steep, snow-covered, downward-tilting slab. (It was never level enough at any point to be called a ledge.)

Death in such rock climbing can come quickly when you pause to think things out. Sometimes you must trust to instinct, experience, and the brief advantage of adrenaline over rational thought.

Knowing now that the Deacon couldn't hold me if I fell during this giant step—*leap* was more like it—and seeing 8,000 feet of empty air under my boots and between my legs as I made the upward lunge—I was, for a fraction of an instant, sorry that I'd tied onto the belay rope even for this lower, "easier" part of the climb. I really, *really* didn't want to pull the Deacon with me when I slid over the edge to my death.

I landed on my belly on the slippery snow. The steep shelf had been exposed to sunlight for hours now, and parts of the snowfield were wet, slippery...my fingers clawed into loose snow and found no grip whatsoever. I began sliding on my belly backwards and to the right, toward the sheer drop-off.

Then the front-point crampons on my flailing boots found some traction in the six- to eight-inch-deep snow on this slab. My sliding slowed, then stopped. Moving in slow motion, the crampons on the front of my stiff boots the only real contact with the snow—much less the unreach-able rock beneath the snow—I managed to use the four steel points at the front of my crampons to push my body inch by inch up and to my left. Eventually, despite the steep slant and the absurd exposure, I stood, reaching for a higher rock to balance myself.

Then I walked to the far left—north—side of this cone-shaped snow shelf, found a corner there where I could kick together a tiny snow plat-form on which to stand, ran the rope once around the only rock belay I could find—a three-inch upward-slanting spur about the height of my nose but smaller than my nose—shook the rope loose, took up its slack, set it over my shoulder in the way I'd done a thousand times, and shouted "On belay!"

"Climbing!" shouted the Deacon and—sometimes using my taut rope to keep himself from catapulting off the face backward—he clam-bered up toward me in his George-Mallory-cum-electrified-spider mode.

Within minutes he was up with me. I knew I had to start mov-ing—we were in the shadow here, and I was freezing without my goose down outer layers or serious mittens and gloves, my body was already shaking (perhaps partially from the adrenaline as well as from the cold)—so I wedged myself up two or three feet along the off-width crack in the corner and let Richard Davis Deacon take my place on the marvelously level square foot of snow I'd piled up in the corner. (An off-width crack, in climber parlance, is one that's too wide for your hand or fist to find traction in, far too wide for a piton to be driven into—if you happen to be one of those iron-mongering Germans who even *use* pitons—but too *goddamned* narrow to wedge your entire body into. To most intents and purposes, other than tossing bottles or something into as a garbage pail, off-width cracks are useless.) Now my foot was in that crack, the pressure of the crampons on limestone and my two extended arms merely holding me a few feet higher than the top of the Deacon's head there in the angle where the two cliff faces met. It was an exhaust-ing position to hold at any altitude, and up here I knew I couldn't hold it for more than a minute.

"Keep the belay rope tied on," gasped the Deacon. His face was ashen from his climb, even with the help of my taut belay rope at times. I can't imagine what my face looked like, but at the moment I felt like Moses coming down from Mount Sinai with two horns of light emanating from his temples. Only I was going *up*—with luck—not *down*.

"No," I said. I held myself in place with my boot, my back, and one extended hand while I untied from my waist-rope harness, looped the belay rope twice over the cloth belt of my Norfolk jacket so it would stay with me as long as I was climbing but would pull loose the instant I peeled off the face, and started scrambling upward while I still had a trace of warmth and energy and will left anywhere in my shaking body.

21.

I knew the instant I started free-climbing the impossible Second Step that whether I lived another three minutes— including the time I'd still be conscious while falling a mile and a half—or lived another seventy years, this would be the climbing effort I would be most proud of.

I couldn't breathe well because of the ragged constriction in my throat, but to hell with that. I'd taken in one deep but unsatisfying gulp of the frigid open air here above 28,140 feet, and now I would complete this climb on that single gulp of oxygen. Or not.

Conventional wisdom and climbing experience suggested that I should try to stay to the far left of the 25-foot face, using the off-width crack for *something*.

To hell with that. Staying close to that off-width crack, I felt in my aching gut, meant death. I took a narrow branch of one of the smaller rising cracks to the right instead.

The largest of the vertical cracks on the right was all but filled with small, loose stones. Again—death to get one's boot or hand in there. Forget that as well.

Hand-jams and fingers on nonexistent holds—and speed, as much speed as I could muster—got me up the first two-thirds of the flat face. Looking down would have just made me laugh out loud—the curve of the earth had been visible since we'd reached the foot of the First Step; here on the Second Step, the tops of mountains 200 miles away were peering over the haze of that impossible curve, and the summit of every 8,000-meter peak in the Himalayas was *below* me now—so I just refrained from sightseeing and kept moving upward like a lizard on hot rock.

Only this rock wasn't hot; it was freezing with the deep cold of outer space. This damned slab faced mostly north and rarely got the sun's rays to warm it. My hands and every part of my body coming in contact with it, and I wanted *all* my body in contact with it, were absorbing that numbing cold faster than I could scramble.

I put my freezing hands where I somehow knew invisible fingerholds would be. The steel tips of my crampons shot sparks from limestone and granite.

I was nearing the top now—which was a fucking overhang, of course, and one unclimbable even in Wales on a summer day unless you had Prusik knots galore, a stout rope to hang from, and one of Jean-Claude's dog-name jumar doohickeys to cam-slide up and over it with—so I kept clawing my way upward, one crampon point finding a hold, then slip-sliding to my left toward that hitherto useless goddamned off-width crack.

Okay. Just because the crack was still too large up here for my hand or forearm to jam in, and still too narrow to hold my body, that didn't mean I couldn't jam my elbow into the crack with an angled arm lock, then, a fraction of a second later, cram my left foot and leg in below. That, I realized, was my plan.

Some plan.

There were no solid footholds or handholds anywhere near that crack, of course—God wasn't going to make it *that* easy—but friction and speed *are* God in such a free climb, and I prayed to, and used, both to get a few feet higher.

Lungs burning now, vision tunneling, ignoring the pain as the sharp rock of the crack ripped at my leg, I knee-barred a couple of yards more up toward the top of the Second Step and encountered...another overhang.

Once again I had to stop myself from laughing. It would have used up the last oxygen in my lungs, not that my lungs *had* any oxygen left in them.

The overhang petered out about six feet to my right, so I extended my right leg as far as I could, crampons scraping, until my boot found a ledge there that was about the width of a broken pencil. I shifted all my weight to it, couldn't find a hold for my sliding, questing right hand, and just used a friction grip against a slightly less than vertical part of the slab.

One more ledge, three feet higher, for my left boot, a few more seconds of teetering above absolutely nothing, and then I was up, the top half of my body over the lip of the overhang, my right hand finding ridges and rocks and holds galore. I was on top of the Second Step.

I pulled myself all the way up and rolled a few more inches away from the edge so that the 8,000-foot drop wasn't directly under my head and shoulders or feet or butt any longer.

I still couldn't get a breath, but I could stand, and I did so. Just a couple of feet beyond the cliff face of the Second Step up there was a nice four-foot-long-by-three-foot-wide limestone bench, with plenty of rock ripples, ridges, and even a few stunted bollards behind it for tying off belay ropes.

Thank you, God.

My breath rasping so painfully in and out of my sore throat that I thought I might scream, instead I called down—in a steady and calm voice, I was told later by Dr. Pasang—for everyone to start coming up as I belayed them. I'd brought 120 feet of Miracle Rope with me; with the tie-offs around the rock bench and bollards, I used 97 feet of it.

The Deacon took his time, trying to free-climb major parts of the route himself but saving himself by falling back on the tension of the rope two or three times. I didn't care and would never mention it to him. We weren't in a contest here.

Everyone else—except Jean-Claude—fully used the tension of the tied-off rope, belayed by two of us now, then three, then four, to make the impossible climb possible.

No one could resist looking around from the summit of the Second Step. There was a Third Step beyond this one, further up the North East Ridge and just before Everest's snowy Summit Pyramid, but that last step was a marshmallow compared to this crag. It was immediately obvious that we could traverse around it on the snowfield there if we didn't want to scramble up and over the boulders.

Beyond the Third Step—which it seemed we could throw a stone and hit—a snow slope led, first gradually and then very steeply, to the Summit Pyramid. That would be careful climbing, but nowhere near as technical as this Second Step.

And then there was only the snowy summit with its treacherous cornices, all perfectly visible in the crystal air and pure sunshine. A little raggedy remnant of the former lenticular cloud trailed westward from that summit, but it wasn't a change-of-weather-to-a-storm sort of lenticular. The wind here atop the Second Step was very strong, blowing, as always, from the northwest, but we leaned into it and screamed our joy aloud.

At least some of the others did.

I finally realized that I was not breathing at all. As my four friends took several steps further west atop the Second Step, I fell to my knees and then to all fours just beyond the limestone bench.

I couldn't breathe; I couldn't even cough. No air was moving in or out of my aching, battered lungs. The sharp lobster claw in my lower throat—feeling more like a jagged mass of cold metal now—was blocking all breathing. I was dying. I *knew* I was dying. My four friends were shouting and clapping each other on the back and looking up at the summit of Everest in the noon sunlight and I was dying, my vision already changing from dancing black spots to a quickly closing tunnel of blackness.

Dr. Pasang turned around and took three quick strides to my side. He went to one knee, and I was distantly—irrelevantly, with real death this close—aware of the other three also surrounding me now, the men looking down at me in confusion, Reggie kneeling next to me but obviously not knowing what to do. *It's true,* I thought and learned forever in that second. *We do all die completely alone, no matter who's nearby.*

"Help me prop him up," came Pasang's voice down an infinitely receding passage to sight and sound. I distantly felt someone's hands roughly hauling me up off the rock, steadying me on my knees.

It didn't matter. It had been a minute and a half or two minutes now when I could draw no breath, expel no breath. The broken thing in my throat was cutting my throat open from the inside. I was drowning. Had already drowned. But without even the false gift of water rather than air filling my lungs. I made a few final gagging sounds and tried to topple forward, but someone's hands still held my shoulders, insisting on making me die in a kneeling position. I was only vaguely sorry I was dying—I would have liked to have helped my four friends a little more.

But I got them up the Second Step. This was my last conscious thought.

Pasang's palm—I *believe* it was Pasang's broad hand—pressed so firmly against my chest that I was sure he was breaking ribs and my breastbone with the terrible pressure. It didn't matter.

At the same second, he slapped me so sharply on the back that my spine almost snapped.

In one mighty, bloody push—as if some terrible sharp-edged creature were being born through my throat and mouth—the obstruction came up and flew free.

Reggie finally allowed me to fall forward over the thing I'd coughed up—it looked like a bloody part of my spine, a crimson-covered super-trilobite that must have crawled down my throat while I slept at Camp V some nights earlier—but I didn't care what the monster was, I was nearly weeping with the joy of being able to breathe again. Breathe painfully, it was true, but breathe. Air moved in and out. The tunnel of vision blackout widened and went away. I squinted in the bright light until Reggie gently pulled my goggles back into place. I'd climbed the Second Step without the goggles on so I could see my feet, see everything, but I didn't want Colonel Norton's agony of snow blindness.

I'm going to live after all, I thought giddily. I retched a little, spat a lot, and spattered some more blood onto the spiny thing I'd coughed up onto the rock.

"What is it, Dr. Pasang?" asked Jean-Claude.

"It is...was...the mucous membrane surrounding his larynx," said Pasang.

"But it's as solid and spiky as a crab," said the Deacon.

"It's been frostbitten for days," said Dr. Pasang. "Frozen solid. Filling his throat and esophagus more and more as it expanded until it completely blocked his airway."

"Can he live without it?" asked the Deacon. To my ear, he sounded only mildly curious. I made a mental note to ask him about that later.

"Of course," said Pasang, smiling. "It will be painful breathing for some days for Mr. Perry, and we'll have to get him down to thicker air soon, but he should be fine."

It bothered me that they were talking about me as if I weren't even there; as if I'd died after all. With only a little help, I struggled to my feet. God Almighty, my friends' goggled faces and the amazing Summit Pyramid and deep, deep blue sky behind them and the white peaks and amazing curve of the earth beyond *that* were beautiful. I almost wept with joy.

"Do not move," said Bruno Sigl from just six or eight feet behind us. I glanced over my shoulder just long enough to see the black pistol aimed at us, the Luger held steady in his right hand and the Lee-Enfield rifle slung over his left shoulder. He stood atop the limestone bench where I'd tied off the climbing ropes, his legs apart, his body perfectly balanced, too far away for us to try rushing him, towering over us with the Luger held steady. Victorious.

"If anyone moves the slightest bit," said Sigl, "I will at once shoot all of you. I do not need any of you alive any longer. And thank you, Herr Perry, for the helpful fixed rope up this interesting Second Step."

he wind shoved at our backs. We stood now roughly in a line atop the rock of the Second Step, all facing Bruno Sigl, our hands raised as ordered.

The Deacon still has Bachner's Luger, was my frantic thought. And so he did. But he'd fired both shots and the pistol was empty now. Sigl's Luger, on the other hand, was almost certainly fully loaded. How many rounds had the Deacon said a Luger held in the box magazine in its pistol grip? Eight? Enough to shoot all of us, reload quickly, and apply any *coups de grâce* that were necessary.

We'd come a long, long way for this absurd and pathetic ending. And all because my choking fit distracted everyone from pulling up the 100-foot belay line that was still anchored to the limestone bench there atop the Second Step. My mind flitted like a crazed moth from one possible trick to another; none would work.

"Please tell me where the photographs are," said Sigl. "To save me the time and effort of searching your bodies and rucksacks."

"What photos?" asked Jean-Claude.

Sigl shot him. The report seemed very loud, despite the wind. J.C. dropped to the snowy rock. I could see blood flowing from his right side, but it didn't seem to be geysering . . . didn't seem to be arterial. But what did I know? Other than the Himalayan climber's hard-earned certainty that any serious injury or illness at this altitude meant death?

We all started toward the fallen J.C., but stopped at a wave of the

Luger, our hands going back up. Pasang said, "May I look at him and treat him, Herr Sigl? I am a doctor."

Sigl laughed. "No, you may not. You're an Indian nigger and your hands should never touch Aryan flesh ... even that of a dead Frenchman."

I ground my molars. But I did not move. I did not lunge for my rucksack eight feet away to dig for my pathetic, unloaded Very pistol. I did not lower my hands. Even if only for just a few more minutes, I found that I very much wanted to live.

"I watched through my field glasses while you took the photographs from the bodies," said the German. "Five envelopes. Do not insult my intelligence again."

"Herr Sigl," I rasped. "May I spit?"

"What?" He aimed the Luger at my face.

"Blood, Herr Sigl. I'm ill. May I spit this blood out of my mouth before it makes me sick?"

The German said nothing so I turned sideways, careful that the wind would not carry it toward Sigl or anyone else, and spat out a glob of blood that had been building up in my ravaged throat. "Thank you," I said to Sigl. *Thank you for not shooting me, sir.* Pathetic.

"That does not look good, Herr Perry," said Sigl with another laugh. "You might be suffering a pulmonary embolism." He waggled the pistol at us. "Everyone strip naked, please. Drop your clothes at your feet, then step away. Do nothing stupidly heroic or you all die now."

"I'll start," said Reggie, taking a single step forward. In a few seconds she had set down her rucksack—out of her easy reach—and had pulled off her anorak and Finch duvet and goose down trousers, holding them in place with her foot as the wind at her back blew hard on her. In another fifteen seconds, she was down to a wool blouse over what looked to be silken underwear. Sigl was watching her and chuckling, but he also never took his eyes off the rest of us, the Luger steady. If it had been Reggie's plan to distract Sigl to give the Deacon or me a chance to rush him, the plan wasn't working. The distance was still too great to cover without being shot. None of us was in front of another, blocking the German's shot, so Sigl had us all covered with that ugly pistol.

Reggie dropped her shirt, kept it from blowing away with a quick stab of her booted foot back onto the growing pile of garments. She pulled off the cotton and silk layers beneath that shirt. Now she was in wool knickerbockers from the waist down, and nude except for her brassiere on top. She reached around and undid the brassiere.

I felt like weeping. Delicate parts of Reggie would be frostbitten within minutes, more probably within seconds. Jean-Claude continued to writhe on the snowy rock, the blood continuing to spread.

"I'm sorry, Frau Bromley-Montfort," laughed Bruno Sigl, "but I've seen English women's tits before. *Sogar die Titten von englischen Mädchen!* And larger. But when you are naked, I will kill you last...perhaps leave you for my men to look at and play with while you are still alive." His face seemed to transform into something beastlike then and he snarled, *"Where are the photographs, you English cunt?"*

"In my rucksack," began Reggie. "I can get them if..."

Sigl started shaking his head.

Then Jean-Claude catapulted to his feet, not even holding his bloodied, wounded side, and rushed Sigl.

The German took half a step back and fired twice. Both slugs hit home somewhere in J.C.'s chest or gut. Jean-Claude kept staggering closer.

Sigl took two steps to his left, toward the South Face but still yards from the rotten snow cornice there, and fired twice more. The fourth 9-millimeter slug tore out through J.C.'s back, passing through the oxygen tank still in his rucksack and sending a hissing stream of English air up and out into the wind, enveloping both men in a hissing fog of ice crystals.

We all moved now, but it was Jean-Claude who had his arms around Sigl in a bear hug, forcing the larger man back one step, then two, then four...

"Nein, nein, nein!" screamed Sigl, hammering at Jean-Claude's head with the black steel of the Luger's grip. They both staggered another three steps back onto the snow at the cornice.

"Bâtard boche!" gasped Jean-Claude, coughing great amounts of blood all over the chest of Sigl's pristine white anorak. Even with five bullets through him and oxygen hissing white and freezing in the air around them, J.C. continued flailing away with his bloody right hand at Bruno Sigl's left side.

The cornice broke beneath them. They both dropped out of sight through the hole in the snow. Everyone but Reggie rushed as far to the south edge of the Second Step as we could. Sigl was screaming for a very long time, the scream Dopplering away from us as the two entangled men fell and tumbled over and over and then fell and then fell some more. No miracle crags to break their fall as one had with Percival and Meyer, and Sigl and J.C. weren't roped together anyway — just bound by the iron vise of Jean-Claude's one-armed bear hug. Eventually they were both lost to sight, dots and then less than dots disappearing against the background of the Kangshung Glacier 10,000 feet below.

I heard not a single scream from Jean-Claude. I believed then and choose to believe to this day that he was dead before he really knew he was falling, although falling through the cornice with Sigl had been his plan from the first.

The Deacon looked down, not at the drop but at the edge of the rock, and I saw the reason for J.C.'s flailing with his free hand.

He'd wrested the Deacon's Lee-Enfield rifle off Sigl's shoulder and dropped it behind them a second before they fell.

I picked it up. "The telescopic sight was broken on the rock," I said dully.

"That doesn't matter," said the Deacon and took the rifle from me. He snapped the trapezoidal metal magazine free from its place in front of the trigger guard and quickly emptied into his hand and counted the long, brass-bound cartridges. Then he quickly reloaded them into the magazine, using his thumb. I'd counted ten rounds. The lead nose of the bullets looked very heavy and very pointy.

Reggie was getting dressed again with Pasang's help. She was shaking uncontrollably with the cold and her lips were blue. Despite Bruno Sigl's sneering at her, she'd distracted him just enough for Jean-Claude to do what he did.

I crossed the top of the Second Step with the Deacon to the limestone bench at the top of the 90-foot drop. He went to one knee behind the bench, supporting his elbows and the rifle on the stone. I took a knee next to him and accepted the binoculars he'd just pulled from his rucksack.

"Be my spotter," said the Deacon.

"I don't know what that means, Richard."

"It means keep looking and tell me if I'm shooting low or high, too far left or too far right," he said. "If I miss, tell me in which direction I missed and how many yards left, right, up, or down. I'll correct according to your calls." His voice was so calm that we might have been discussing railway timetables in Paddington Station.

"Got you," I said and raised the heavy field glasses to my eyes.

The four other Germans were only halfway between Mushroom Rock and the Second Step. They must have taken a break on the east side of the bollard, somewhere out of the roaring wind, while Sigl—the fittest and best climber in the group—had gone on ahead without a rest.

Before Reggie and Pasang could come up to join us, the Deacon—using only the iron sights on the rifle, ignoring the off-kilter telescopic sight on the left—had taken a breath, held it, and fired his first round. The sound of the shot made me jump and deafened me for a moment.

The first German in the line on the ridge dropped backward as if someone had jerked his legs out from under him. Through the binoculars, I could see the crimson stain spreading across the chest of his white anorak and into the white snow.

"Down," I said. "Direct hit in the chest."

Two of the other three Germans turned to run, forgetting that they were roped together and still tethered to the man who'd just been shot. The bloody body of the dead German was dragged some yards east behind the running men. The Keystone Kops aspect of the scene might almost have seemed funny to me if absolutely everything else right then hadn't been so fucking sad.

Then two of the running Germans tripped and went down in a pile while the third man, still standing, whirled our way, took a pistol from his anorak pocket—I couldn't tell if it was a Luger or some other sort of gun—and began blazing away in our direction. I heard one distant bee buzz, but other than that, nothing came near us. The sound of his shots was almost lost in the wind.

The Deacon took another breath, held it, and shot that German in the face. I saw the explosion of blood, flesh, and skull fragments all too well through my wavering binoculars. The pistol fell out of his dead hand, and he dropped and lay on the snow and rock, his long legs still twitching from random nerve impulses. But through my binoculars, I could see the lumpy gray stream of his brains fanned out behind his leather-helmeted head.

"Dead," I said. "Head shot." I didn't know if such announcements were part of a spotter's job, but I'd have done anything right then to help the Deacon.

The other two men struggled to get to their feet. One was still look-ing toward us, his head cocked back to see us on the top of the Second Step; suddenly the German thrust both arms and hands in the air in the universal sign of surrender.

The Deacon shot him twice, both times in the chest above the heart. Watching through the glasses, I realized that my spread hand would have covered the tight cluster of the bloody death wounds on that man's chest.

The last man simply threw back his hood and tugged down his oxy-gen mask and balaclava—showing a bare face that looked very German and very young indeed, not even any chin stubble visible through my glasses—and appeared to be weeping while crouching on all fours. I wanted to say *He's not much older than a boy!*

I didn't say a word. *Kurt Meyer had not been much older than a boy.*

The Deacon shot him three times, once before the man in the white combat anorak tumbled over and twice more until he stopped wriggling.

Nothing and no one was moving on that part of the North East Ridge now, other than the occasional flap of torn fabric in the wind.

Reggie and Pasang stood behind us, looking down at the ridge. No one said anything. As if motivated by a single, shared thought, we all turned and took the few steps to the south, stopping well short of the collapsed cornice. The glacier so far below still seemed empty.

"Fuck," the Deacon said very softly.

"Yes," whispered Reggie.

We stepped back from the edge and moved around to sit on our ruck-sacks on the leeward side of the low bench—now littered with seven empty brass cartridges that the Deacon policed out of habit, picking them up and setting them in one of his outer pockets—and, the remain-ing four of us all hunkering lower from the wind, we started talking over what we were going to do next.

23.

*W*e huddled low on the east side of the bench rock at the top of the face in order to talk, but first we all indulged in five or eight minutes of English air, on full flow. It helped a little, and I didn't cough anything else up while inhaling or exhaling.

Finally we put down our masks and got down to business.

"I can't believe that Jean-Claude is gone," Reggie said. We leaned closer to hear her, but the high winds seemed to be moderating somewhat, as if Everest were allowing us a brief moment for remembrance of our friend.

But despite that lull in the wind, no one else said anything for a long minute or two. "It's decision time," said the Deacon.

I didn't understand. "What decision? A dozen Germans, including Sigl, are dead, including the one Reggie shot with her flare pistol and the ones who fell from the ladder on the North Col. There's nothing stopping us from going back down the mountain, back to what's left of Base Camp, and then getting the hell out of here. Back to Darjeeling." That was a long speech for a man with such a sore throat, and I was sorry my three friends had been forced to hear the rasp and scrape of it.

"I think Herr Sigl came in force this year," said the Deacon. "A dozen of them may be dead, but I'd be surprised if someone with Sigl's cunning didn't leave one or two on the glacier, in the Trough, or down by Base Camp. Just to make sure none of us get away."

"We have to get those photographs and negatives back to London," said Reggie. "That's our highest priority. That is what Jean-Claude and all our Sherpas died for, whether our Sherpa friends knew it or not."

The Deacon nodded and then nodded some more but then shook his head. Then he looked up, over the top of my head to the west, and said, "I want to climb the mountain. But I've never abandoned a fellow climber in need and I won't start now, Jake."

I was stunned at this. "If you want to keep climbing, I'm fit to come with you," I lied. It felt like the bloody trilobite I'd coughed up had eaten out my insides—the way the goraks had got at Mallory and hollowed him out.

"No, Mr. Perry, you are not fit to go with him," Pasang said quietly.

I blinked angrily at him. Who was *he* to deny me my life's dream?

A *doctor,* responded the oxygen-supplied remnant of my brain.

"The summit should be about two hours' climbing from here—maybe two and a half with slow going and breaking trail in deep snow on the Summit Pyramid," said the Deacon. "But we have oxygen for the entire round-trip."

"No, we don't," I rasped, confused again. "We've barely one full tank apiece."

"Jake, didn't you notice the tanks on Sigl and the other Germans we just shot?" said the Deacon. "They're *our rigs*—Jean-Claude's rigs. The Germans must have looted them from our reserve cache at Base Camp. They probably didn't use more than two full tanks each in their climb to the North East Ridge...that should leave at least eight extra tanks for us. Full tanks."

I understood then that we were in a unique position to try for the summit—a far stronger chance than Mallory and Irvine's on their last day. They'd had to climb all the way from Camp VI at 27,000 feet on two or three tanks each. And their carrying rigs were much heavier. We were already above the Second Step—two hours away from the summit and only about 800 vertical feet below it. And we had not only a surfeit of oxygen rigs but also Reggie's Big Tent, which we'd hauled up with us...something we could use if we were forced by sudden bad weather to bivouac up here. For every expedition before ours, a bivouac above 27,000 feet meant certain death. For our expedition, with Reggie's tent, our goose down clothing, and ample tanks of English air, it would be just another first. One of many for the Deacon-Bromley-Montfort-Pasang-Perry-Clairoux Expedition.

The thought of J.C.'s name and the memory of his joyous drive to climb this damned hill made tears freeze on my lashes.

"I want to go, too," I rasped. "We'll all go. Step onto the summit at the same time."

"No," said Pasang. "Mr. Perry—you must excuse me, sir—you didn't bleed too much when you coughed up the frozen mucous membrane to your larynx. But further climbing, more hours or even days at altitude, might cause a pulmonary embolism at the very least. Another night at this altitude would almost certainly be fatal."

"I'll risk it," I rasped. But already I felt the lethargy trying to pull me down onto the snowy rock.

"Can we make it to the summit and back by nightfall?" asked Reggie. "Or would we have to pitch my tent somewhere exposed, like at Mushroom Rock?"

The Deacon took a breath and shook his head. "I'm planning to go alone. And I'm not planning to return."

I tried to shout then but my throat hurt too much. I took a shot of English air instead.

"You plan to commit suicide up here just to climb this hill?" Reggie shouted. "You *are* a coward despite what Cousin Charles told me and despite all your shiny medals!"

The Deacon smiled.

What's funny? I remember thinking. I kept hearing and re-hearing the hiss that had flowed out of J.C.'s oxygen tank after the bullet had passed through both him and the metal bottle. It had sounded, even at the time, like the sound of Jean-Claude's soul being forced out of his body.

"If going to the summit and not coming down isn't suicide, what is it?" Reggie demanded of the Deacon. She looked about ready to punch him.

"You remember when Ken visited me in Sikkim...?" asked the Deacon.

"K. T. Owings!" I rasped. "What the hell does he have to do with anything?"

"Yes. Well, Ken has lived in Nepal on his own farm in the Khumbu

Valley just below the south approach to Everest ever since he decided to leave the world right after the Great War. He's still a poet; he just doesn't show anyone his work now. And he's still a climber, although no one hears about his climbs now."

"Are you saying," Reggie said testily, "that your chum Ken Owings has climbed Everest and will be waiting up there for you on the summit with an airship or something?"

The Deacon flashed a grin. "Nothing so dramatic, Reggie. But Ken has reconnoitered the approaches and cols and ridges to Everest from the other side—the south approach—and promised me that he and some Sherpa friends would leave path wands and crevasse ladders in place way down in the Khumbu Glacier Ice Fall. He says that may be the most dangerous part of the climb, and it's right near his Base Camp on the south side."

"There is no Base Camp on the south side," I croaked, my voice sounding like long fingernails being dragged down a blackboard.

"There is now, Jake," said the Deacon. "Ken has been climbing the last week and more—setting fixed rope—leaving tents on the South Col for me." He looked at Reggie. "For us."

"South Col," I repeated, wincing from the pain. I'd heard and thought "North Col" so many thousands of times in the last nine months that it hardly seemed possible that there was a South Col to Everest—or that it might ever be relevant to anything.

"Nepal's forbidden to foreigners," said Reggie. "You'll be imprisoned, Richard."

The Deacon shook his head a final time. "Owings has friends there. His farm in the Khumbu Valley employs about a hundred locals, and he's respected. He converted to Buddhism in nineteen nineteen—really converted, not like my meditate-in-the-morning, shoot-Germans-in-the-afternoon shallow sort of conversion—and many in Nepal consider him a holy man. He'll find a place for me."

Reggie looked at him for a very long silent moment. "Why do you want to go away from everything, Richard? Leave everything you know behind?"

When he finally spoke, the Deacon's voice was thick. "I feel—as you once put it so beautifully, Reggie—that the world is too much with me, and not necessarily in a Buddhist sense. The best part of me never came back from the Great War."

Reggie rubbed her cheek and then looked up at the white Summit Pyramid gleaming behind the Deacon's head. "I've been fulfilling my duty as a Bromley and as a proud Briton since I came to India when I was nine years old," she said. "I took over managing the tea plantation when I was fourteen and have run it ever since. Our income from that plantation keeps the House of Bromley in England going. When I was twenty-six, I married an old man I didn't love—to get an infusion of fresh funds to keep the plantation going. Lord Montfort died before I really got to know him...and he never made any effort to get to know me. I'm tired of doing my duty."

"What are you saying, Reggie?" I asked.

"I'm saying that I would love to set foot on the summit of Everest and wouldn't mind seeing forbidden Nepal for a few years, Jake."

"I will climb with you then, my lady," said Dr. Pasang.

She touched his arm. "No, my friend. This time you do not come with me. Jake needs to get down to Base Camp and Darjeeling. We need to get those photographs to the right people. I've never ordered you to do anything, my beloved Pasang, but I beg you to take Jake down and return to the plantation while I do this thing."

Pasang looked for a second as if he was going to argue, but in the end he only bowed his head. His dark eyes looked moist, but it might have been the wind that caused that.

"You know where I keep my will," Reggie was saying to him when I'd finished taking another snort of English air. "You know the combination to that safe. You'll find that I've left the plantation to you and your family, Pasang.

"There is a clause in the will," continued Reggie. "A codicil that stipulates that should I die or disappear, one-third of the plantation's profits shall continue to flow to Lady Bromley in Lincolnshire...until her death. Then all profits are yours to do with as you wish, my dear Pasang."

He nodded again, not lifting his eyes to hers.

"Wait," said the Deacon. "No one's going to attempt the summit this afternoon—much less try to traverse beyond to where Ken left fixed ropes and tents and supplies—unless we're absolutely sure that Jake can get down safely with only Pasang accompanying him."

"Wait a minute," I croaked. "We can spend the night in Reggie's Big Tent at Mushroom Rock and decide all this in the morning. I'll probably be fit as a fiddle by then. We can all go to the summit, and you can try that idiotic idea of traversing south to Nepal if you want—both of you! Pasang and I will come back down this way."

Pasang was shaking his head. There was a soft but final firmness in his voice. "No, Mr. Perry. I am very sorry. You must go down today." He turned to Reggie and the Deacon. "Mr. Perry can walk almost unassisted—I believe he will continue to be able to do that for a while, especially during a descent. When he no longer can, I shall carry him. When we are off the mountain and his breathing improves, I shall escort him down to Rongbuk Monastery and then make arrangements for us to return to Darjeeling."

"Hey!" I croak-coughed. "Don't I get a say in . . ."

Evidently I didn't.

We all stood. The wind had died down appreciably, but the lenticular hat was back on Everest's summit.

The Deacon pulled out his large Very military pistol and fired a flare high into the sky toward and beyond the summit. A white star-flare, the phosphorus burst much brighter than our regular mountaineering flares.

White, green, then red, I remembered K. T. Owings saying to the Deacon about ten thousand years earlier in Sikkim.

"I believe," said the Deacon, his voice a strange mixture of sadness and a weary sort of exaltation, "that I . . . that we"—he looked at Reggie, who nodded—"can reach this summit, traverse the steep crest line between the two summits, rappel down that Big Step Ken told me about, and get to the fixed ropes Owings and his Sherpas have set up on the southern approach ridge by . . . before . . . midnight. If we can't down-climb with our torches and headlamps, we'll bivouac in the Big Tent somewhere beyond the South Summit and leave the tent behind us when we continue our descent in the morning."

"That's nuts," I said. "The first ascent of Everest—that we know about—and you want to do a damned traverse down the southern way. Totally nuts."

The Deacon and Reggie only grinned at me. The world had gone insane.

"One favor," said the Deacon. "Keep all your belay rope and the extra coils—and J.C.'s coil there as well—but leave that hundred feet of rope going down the Second Step for us to pull up after you've descended. If we do have to turn back from the summits, we'll need it. All right?"

I nodded dumbly.

The Deacon took a folded piece of paper from some inside pocket and said, "Here's the name and address of the man in London to whom you have to deliver those photographs, Jake. Deliver them to him personally. No one else. For God's sake don't lose this."

I nodded again and put the folded paper in my buttonable wool shirt pocket beneath all my outer layers. I didn't unfold the paper or think to glance at the name, I was so shocked and depressed at realizing that I really was going to have to go down rather than up . . . and after I'd free-climbed the Second Step for them!

But mostly, I think, this sudden surge of deep depression came from my bottomless sense of loss at Jean-Claude's sudden death. The truth was just settling deep into my mind and soul that I'd never see my friend from Chamonix again, nor hear his laugh.

"Pasang," said Reggie, "if for whatever reason you rather than Jake needs to be the one to go to London to deliver your various copies of the photos, you know whom to see and where to go, do you not?"

"I do, my lady."

The Deacon offered his hand. I shook it, still not believing we were parting.

"Stay alive," I heard myself saying to him.

"I will," said the Deacon. "Remember, my destiny is to die on the North Wall of the Eiger . . . not on Everest. You feel better soon, Jake."

And then Lady Katherine Christina Regina Bromley-Montfort kissed me. On the lips. Hard. She stepped back next to the Deacon, and I had a last look at her beautiful, incomparable ultramarine eyes.

"Don't forget to pull your goggles back down," I said dully.

Then Pasang and I were jumaring down the rope we'd so conveniently left for Bruno Sigl to climb, then we were down on the snow at the base of the still-terrifying Second Step, and then I could see the Deacon hauling up the long rope, and then, in an eyeblink—he was gone. They were gone. Presumably hiking up the widening west end of the North East Ridge onto the snowfields that led to the Summit Pyramid and the summit.

And I was heading back down.

Walking single file along the knife-edge ridge toward the dead Germans lying in the snow, I started crying like a baby. Pasang patted my back and squeezed my shoulder. "It is the trauma of your choking," he said.

"No it isn't."

I hadn't heard the Deacon give orders or suggestions to Dr. Pasang, but as we came to each of the four dead Germans, he seemed to know exactly what to do. I confess that I only leaned on my ice axe, trying to breathe through my ragged, torn throat, and watched.

First, he searched each German, removing certain documents but mostly the pistols they carried. One of the dead men had a Schmeisser submachine gun tucked under his outer shell and another had the Deacon's Webley pistol, which Pasang handed to me. I tucked it into my duvet pocket under my Shackleton anorak. Pasang was also relieving each of the four dead men of their oxygen rigs before going through their carryalls or small rucksacks, pulling out anything we might need or that might be of intelligence importance and placing it in his own full bag. He filled one of the canvas carryalls and handed it to me.

"We shall wear the metal oxygen rigs from now on, Mr. Perry, and leave the heavier rucksacks behind," he said. "We will carry our other items in these shoulder bags."

My mind was so dull that it was hard to do the math, but I was pretty sure that three full oxygen tanks for each of us should get us down to Base Camp—or at least to the lower camps where we'd hidden some of Jean-Claude's new breathing rigs. I doubted if the Germans had found them all.

"You concur with the plan, Mr. Perry?"

I nodded, still unable to speak.

Before we set off—before Pasang even tugged up the heavy shoulder straps of his new O_2 rig and various kit bags—he took out a long, curved penknife, cut the ropes connecting each of the four dead men, and dragged the bodies one by one to the lip of the south side of the ridge and shoved them over the edge. I felt a strong emotion through the general numbness at the time, but I couldn't have said whether it was outrage at these four Germans despoiling the glacier below, where J.C.'s body must lie, or some raw, unholy joy that four of the Germans had paid for Sigl's crime.

The actual disposal of the bodies made sense to me only much later. All five of us had assumed in 1925 that there would be more English expeditions coming soon—perhaps as early as 1926. None of us could have guessed that the next expedition wouldn't be until 1933, and that—although they found Irvine's ice axe, they wouldn't think to climb down to where it pointed to find Irvine himself—the '33 expedition wouldn't even get beyond the First Step. The '38 expedition, a small one, would be England's last try at conquering Everest from the north.

But we didn't know that. Leaving a trail of dead Germans just beyond Mushroom Rock, especially Germans all shot by a British sniper rifle, might cause some sticky diplomatic cables between Berlin and Whitehall. And pushing the corpses off the North East Ridge onto the North Face wall wouldn't have been wise: we'd found Mallory's and Irvine's bodies on that face through sheer chance. It wouldn't be good for these Germans ever to be found.

As I watched Pasang dispose of the last of the German bodies, I did realize one important thing. The coughing up of that frozen... thing... from my throat, combined with the illness that frozen mucous membrane had given me for days now, had weakened me far more than I'd been willing to admit. Even to myself. Standing there on the ridge, watching Pasang do the work of tidying things up, I felt the last of the adrenaline-rush energy that had gotten me up the Second Step flow out of me like water down a drain.

Dr. Pasang was right. If I'd tried to push on to the summit—as much as I thought I needed to—or even spent one night camped at this altitude, I would have died. This truth came to me while I was standing on the North East Ridge so close to the summit, but ready now to head down, wanting only to survive and to do my duty for Reggie and the Deacon and Cousin Percy and Kurt Meyer—and in a way for our Sherpa friends who'd been killed. And for Jean-Claude. Especially for Jean-Claude.

Just get down, survive, and get those photographs to the British authorities who needed to have them.

When we got down off the ridgeline beyond the Mushroom Rock, I was certain that I didn't have the energy to do the Big Step around the embedded boulder on the North Face again. But I stood and watched as Pasang made it look easy—knowing where the ledges and handholds are on the other side makes a huge difference—and then he belayed me across with no problem, although I did slip at the end of my swing and Pasang had to lift me up to the ledge as if I were a bag of laundry.

I was too tired and battered to feel embarrassed. I kept glancing up toward the summit, and once I thought I saw two tiny dots moving next to each other at the top of the snowy Summit Pyramid, just below the summit itself.

But I was too tired at that moment to pull my field glasses out of my canvas bag and look through them. I've always wondered since then whether I could have made out Reggie and the Deacon, if it truly was them on that final, steep Summit Pyramid.

Clipping on fresh oxygen tanks the Germans had found cached at Base Camp or east of Camp V where we'd hidden them, Pasang and I continued descending into the sunny afternoon. He wasn't actually holding me up, but most of the time we walked together, and his arm was a steadying influence as I began to feel more and more woozy.

He guided me through the rest of that traverse along the ridge and then remembered precisely where to descend through the exit cracks onto the lower face and thus to our pathetic one-tent Camp VI, still standing (albeit still at the steep angle). The Germans evidently hadn't seen it on their way up. There was a bit of food left—some chocolate, a can of sardines, one thermos of water we hadn't taken up to the ridge with us—and we added all of it to our overflowing canvas carryalls.

It was at Camp VI, just before the clouds closed in and the snow began to fall again, that—while sitting on the boulder on the high side of the tent and bracing my elbows on my knees—I trained my field glasses on the summit of Mount Everest and, for the briefest few seconds before clouds shut off the view, saw something green and gold flapping there, right where the snowy peak of the steep pinnacle of the actual summit ridge should be.

Green and gold? The wind and weather were worsening up there, as they were down here at Camp VI at a mere 27,000 feet, but certainly the Deacon and Reggie wouldn't have pitched her Big Tent right on the summit. That would be suicide.

Unless they meant to commit suicide together there, perhaps curled up together under both their sleeping bags, arms around one another, to be found by the next expedition to reach the summit.

Had they been lovers throughout this trip? I found myself wondering dully and with a true ache in my heart and belly. Had they made some insane pact to die together on the summit?

Then I remembered that Reggie's Big Tent had no gold on it. It was the family crest flag of the Bromleys—gryphon and eagle battling for a golden lance or pike—that was green and gold. The silk flag that Percy had brought to the mountain and that Reggie had taken from the dead man's pocket.

Percival's and Reggie's flag at the summit!

But the flapping I'd seen for so few seconds had been almost a person's height off the snowy summit. How could they have...

Then I remembered. Reggie had taken Jean-Claude's ice axe when we all parted, lashing it onto the outside of her pack next to the two short ice hammers there.

I grinned and rasped out a description of what I'd just seen to Dr. Pasang. He borrowed the glasses to look up, but the clouds were thickening then, and I don't think he had a chance to see what I'd observed. That three-second glimpse of green and gold fabric flapping horizontally in the summit jet stream would stay with me for the rest of my life.

I was having some trouble breathing now, and when I'd pulled the straps of my metal-frame oxygen rig back on and set things back in their carryalls, I stood there next to that Camp VI boulder for a full moment, doubled over with rasping coughs. I realized that I'd coughed paint spatters of bright red blood onto the black boulder.

"Is this another frozen something in my throat?" I managed to rasp at Pasang when I'd finished my second spasm of coughing.

He had me open my mouth so that he could inspect it with the tiny light from one of Reggie's Welsh miner headlamps.

"No, Mr. Perry," he said at last. "No more obstructions. But what's left of the lining of your throat is so raw and swollen that it may completely shut off your upper air passages unless we get down low very soon."

"And then...I die?" I said. It was a sign of my fatigue that the answer to that question did not interest me more than it did.

"No, Mr. Perry. Should that happen, I will perform a simple tracheotomy...here." His gloved finger touched near the hollow of my throat. "We have plenty of spare glass tubes and rubber hoses from the oxygen kits," he added.

Will perform a simple tracheotomy—the import of that sentence struck me only later.

"What if that doesn't work, Dr. Pasang?" My rasping, pained voice sounded dangerously close to a whine.

"Then, to prevent your lung from collapsing, I make a small entrance hole here to reinflate your collapsed lung and to get you breathing again," he said, placing that gloved finger on the left side of my chest. "Again, the various bits of hosing and valves we have would work perfectly. The only problem will be sterilizing them with water boiling at such a low temperature up here."

I looked down at my chest: a hole there with a bit of rubber O_2-rig hosing sticking out for me to get air? Reinflating my collapsed lung?

I rucked the oxygen rig higher on my back, tightened the straps, readied the face mask, and said in the firmest voice I could muster, "I'm strong enough to go down."

24.

━━━◯◯◯━━━

racts of Mount Everest that take days—or even weeks—to ascend can often be descended, at least to the glacier camps, but
many times even to Base Camp, in a mere matter of hours: a long afternoon.

But that's with fixed ropes in place. We'd pulled up most of our miles
of fixed rope to deny the Germans an easy ascent. We'd also pulled out
route marker wands and flags that separated the proper path up...or
down...from dangerous dead ends in a vertical couloir snowfield ending
in a long drop to the Rongbuk or East Rongbuk Glacier.

Pasang seemed to know his way. The afternoon clouds were closing
around us in earnest now, and pellets of snow were lacerating the tiny exposed parts of my cheeks outside the oxygen face mask. I was on full
2.2-liter flow—Pasang didn't even seem to be using his oxygen most of the
time—but I simply couldn't get enough air down through my swollen-
shut throat. And every breath I did manage to swallow hurt like hell.

Certain odd things happened during these hours.

When we were at the site of our old Camp V—the Germans had
set the last remaining Whymper tent on fire for some reason—Pasang
parked me on a rock near the burned remnants, actually tying off my
climbing rope to the rock for a few minutes, as if I were a child or a
Tibetan pony to be kept in place, while he went to search for the extra
oxygen rigs and food stores that we'd hidden in the boulders to the east,
toward the North Ridge. Any that Sigl and his friends hadn't found and
appropriated, that is.

While I was sitting there, taking my oxygen mask off at regular intervals in desperate and doomed attempts to drag in more air and oxygen from the thin atmosphere, Jean-Claude came down the snowy slope and sat next to me on the boulder.

"I'm really happy to see you," I rasped.

"I'm happy to see you as well, Jake." He grinned at me and leaned forward to rest his chin on his mittened hands propped on the adze of his ice axe. He wore no oxygen rig, no oxygen mask. I figured that they must have come off during his fall to the glacier.

"Wait," I said, straining to think clearly. I knew that something wasn't logical here, but I couldn't quite put my finger on it for a moment or so. "How can you have your ice axe?" I said at last. "I saw Reggie carrying it on her rucksack as she and the Deacon headed for the summit."

Jean-Claude showed me the light wood shaft of the axe. There were three notches about two-thirds of the way toward the blade. "I borrowed Sandy Irvine's axe from where you left it on that rock," said J.C. "Sandy said he didn't mind."

I nodded. That made sense.

Finally I worked up the courage to say, "What's it like being dead, my friend?"

J.C. gave me that Gallic shrug I was so used to and grinned again. *"Être mort, c'est un peu comme être vivant, mais pas si lourd,"* he said softly.

"I don't understand. Can you interpret that for me, J.C.?"

"Sure," said Jean-Claude. He slammed the point of his ice axe deep in the snow again so that he could lean on it as he faced me. "It means..."

"Jake!" came a call from Pasang through the shifting snow flurries.

"I'm here!" I rasped as loudly as I could without screaming from the pain in my throat. "I'm here with Jean-Claude."

J.C. took his watch from his Finch duvet pocket. "I need to go down ahead and mark the routes for you and Pasang. I will talk to you later, my dear friend."

"Okay," I said.

Pasang came up out of the swirling snow cloud carrying two fresh oxygen tanks for us to swap out to and yet another canvas bag of edibles, water, and other supplies.

"I couldn't hear you well, Mr. Perry," he said. "What did you just shout?"

I smiled and shook my head. My throat hurt too much for me to repeat it. Pasang added the replacement tank to my rig, set the flow valve to high again, made sure that air was flowing, and helped me attach the leather strap of my oxygen mask to my leather motorcycle helmet.

"It's getting colder," he said. "We'll have to keep moving until we get to Camp Four on the North Col. Is it all right if I tie you in close on the rope... fifteen feet? I want to be able to see you—or hear you if you need help—even through the blowing snow."

"Sure," I said into the mask and valves, the syllable almost certainly unintelligible to Pasang. After he'd tied on the short rope, I stood, swayed, got my balance with the tall Sherpa's help, and started to head off down and to the left toward the steep North Face rather than the North Ridge. Pasang tapped me on the shoulder and held me back. "Perhaps I should lead for a while, Mr. Perry."

I shrugged, trying to make it as exquisitely Gallic as J.C.'s shrug had just been—but of course I couldn't. So I stood there stamping my cold feet until Pasang passed me on the rope, and then I began to plod along close behind him.

25.

*T*he North Ridge was still all downward-tilting slabs, usually under snow. I'd almost forgotten. If Reggie and the Deacon had done their traverse to the South Summit and down—rappelling down that big rock I was thinking of now as "K. T. Owings's Step" (and would, nearly thirty years later, smile at its being renamed "the Hillary Step")—the two of them would be descending on the upward-tilting friendlier slabs of the Southwest Ridge of Everest by now, moving down that rocky stairway toward the South Col and Western Cwm below that.

Or was that possible yet? They'd have had to make that traverse of the snow-corniced knife ridge between the summits—the one we'd been able to see from a few vantage points during our approach and climb. Was that even down-climbable, or was it the death trap that the cornice on the North East Ridge had been for Bromley and Kurt Meyer and Jean-Claude? No, not a trap for J.C., I thought. He'd known the fragile cornice was there and shoved Sigl onto it deliberately, knowing it couldn't bear the weight of two men, even if one of them was a small, light Frenchman.

But could the Deacon and Reggie be on the Southwest Ridge by now, down to where Owings had promised fixed ropes? I had a vague memory of seeing two more flares in the skies over Everest's summit before Pasang and I had reached our old Camp VI. Green and red. White, then green and red.

Owings had discussed that sequence. What was the message from the

Deacon to his old friend? Put the Bovril on the Primus, we're only hours out?

I doubted it. The Deacon had never liked Bovril.

Or perhaps the Deacon and Reggie had summited by now and done the smart thing: retreated back the way they'd come. Would they be at the single tent at Camp VI yet? No, wait, I dimly remembered that the Deacon had been carrying the heavy load of Reggie's Big Tent and Reggie had an Unna cooker. They could stop anywhere.

But had they? How late was it? How many hours had passed since Pasang and I had left the Second Step? . . . Camp VI? . . . Camp V? I fumbled under my layers for my watch but couldn't locate it. Had I loaned it to Jean-Claude when he'd visited me a while ago? I didn't think so.

It would be dark soon, the sun soon to be eclipsed by the summit of Lhotse. We'd come out of one layer of cloud into a cold but fairly clear afternoon. I could see two green tents far, far below on the North Col.

I looked to my right and noticed three odd-looking objects floating in the sky about 10 degrees above the angle of the North Ridge. Odd.

They vaguely resembled kites or balloons in shape but were much more organic. Obviously living beings. They floated rather the way jellyfish do, but always keeping parallel with the uncomprehending Pasang and me as we descended the ridge. All three were translucent, and I could see dim colors—red, yellow, blue, white—flowing through them almost like the pulsing blood in someone's veins. One of the floating objects had squarish stubs on each side, somewhat like vestigial wings. Another had an extension of its head part that looked a little like a bird's beak, though almost transparent. The third thing had a tourbillion of cascading light particles near its center, almost as if it hosted a brilliantly lighted interior snowstorm.

All three floating things were pulsating in rhythm with one another, but not, I clinically noticed, in rhythm to the beating of my own straining heart. As Pasang led me lower, never turning to his right to look at them, the three objects floating above the ridgeline—each transparent but oddly dark, especially when a cloud passed behind them—kept pace with us.

I looked away. They did not stay in my field of vision when I turned my head.

To see if my mind was being affected by illness or altitude, I looked at the peaks spread out seemingly at our feet and tested myself by recalling their names and altitudes—Changtse beyond the North Col at 24,878 feet, Khartaphu there on the other side of the pass to the Kharta Glacier at 23,894 feet, the shoulder and summit fields of Pumori to my extreme left, 23,507 feet, and to its right, abutting the Rongbuk Glacier, the summit of Lingtren at only 21,142 feet.

My mind and memory didn't seem to be malfunctioning.

I looked back to my right. The three organic objects still floated parallel to our path of descent, always staying at the same angle of degrees above the line of the North Ridge but shifting positions amongst themselves: now the one with the blunt bird's beak on the left, then the one with the square little penguin wings pulsating and floating to the left of the triad, and finally the one with the coruscating center of pulsing light taking the lead as they descended with us.

Souls? Could souls look like that? Is that what we really look like—after we shake off our bodies?

I reminded myself that I didn't believe in God, Heaven, Hell, or any sort of afterlife, not even the tidy Buddhist theory of reincarnation.

But three of them? What three souls would follow us into the darkness this evening?

Jean-Claude. Reggie. The Deacon.

I pulled my oxygen mask down so as not to screw up the valves and tried to speak, but succeeded only in choking out a cough...or perhaps a sob. It was loud enough to make Pasang, carefully picking his way down slabs ten feet ahead of me, stop and turn around.

Realizing that tears were freezing to my exposed cheeks, I could only point toward the three hovering objects. Pasang turned his head and looked. A few seconds later I followed his gaze.

Another wisp of snow cloud had moved in. The three organic floating things were gone. Although I'd seen other small clouds move in front of them and block my view before, they'd always been there after the cloud passed, but this time I was sure they would be gone for good. When the streamer of cloud passed, they were.

Whatever message those...creatures...had brought, they'd wanted to share it only with me.

I shook my head, signaling to Pasang that it was nothing and that I was okay, pulled my mask back into place, and we continued the long, dangerous slog downward.

There were three tents near the old site of Camp IV on the North Col—two of our green Whympers and a smaller, tan-colored German tent. All three were empty. Pasang thoroughly searched the German tent, coming out with only a few more documents, and then kicked it to shreds.

He untied from our common rope, gestured for me to sit on an empty packing crate while he went off to see if our hidden caches—gear we'd dangled down into one of the crevasses—was still there.

I went off oxygen for a while and just sat panting, every inhalation hurting my throat, every exhalation hurting it more, and tried to enjoy the heat from a Primus stove Pasang had lighted.

It was deep twilight when Pasang returned with two fresh oxygen tanks and some more food to put in the bubbling pot. All of the North Col and most of the North Ridge we'd come down were in deepening shadow now. Only the upper ridges, top fifth of the North Face, and actual summit of Everest continued to glow red and orange and white in the last, rich rays of the setting sun.

The snow plume from the summit was stretched out farther east than I'd ever seen it. The winds up there must be terrible—inhuman—fatal to any living thing.

They're both on the Southwest Ridge or already huddled together in their buttoned-together sleeping bags in Reggie's domed tent on the South Col, I told myself. But I didn't believe it. I imagined their bodies lying frozen and stiff as Mallory's and Irvine's somewhere up there on this side of the summit or on the terrible snow ridge beyond. Or hanging dead on their climbing rope the way Meyer and Percival had. Waiting for the goraks to find them.

I knew at that second that even if I survived this day, this retreat from the mountain, even if I ever climbed again someday, I would never, ever, under any circumstances, return to Mount Everest.

Our caver's ladder no longer dropped down the 100-foot vertical ice wall section of the 1,000-foot descent from the North Col, of course—we'd chopped away its support and dropped it and some climbing Germans so long ago—but the Germans had replaced it with some of their three-eighths-inch clothesline climbing rope attached to two new deadman anchors they'd sunk into the snow of the ice ledge at the lip of the Col.

Pasang and I took time to add a third deadman—we filled an empty rucksack from Camp IV with snow, buried it as deep as we could, and trampled the snow heavy on top of it—and I used a girth-hitch runner and one of the spare German carabiners to add our anchor to the two other deadman anchors.

But we still didn't trust the damned rope they'd left. Luckily we both carried 120-foot lengths of the Deacon's Miracle Rope we'd hauled from the Camp IV crevasse cache, and now we tied these to our rope waist harnesses with figure-eights-on-a-bight knots, and I then set the separate friction knots for rappelling. We no longer had any of Jean-Claude's clever jumars with us. I realized that I should have asked him for a couple when he'd paused to chat with me up at Camp V.

So now we had two dangling ropes, one of which we trusted, so we could rappel down the ice face at the same time. The last thing we did before rappelling was to retrieve our Welsh miner's headlamp rigs from the carryalls and fumble through the small batteries we'd brought until we found a few that would still work.

Then, with me leading for a change, we stepped backwards over the edge of the North Col and off Mount Everest proper in a quick belay to the remaining 900-foot snow slope below.

We discussed bivouacking for the night somewhere down past Camp III—we had a sleeping bag apiece—but both of us wanted to keep moving. Even at a night-hiking pace with our little headlamps showing the way through the glacier crevasses, we should be at Base Camp or beyond by dawn.

Pasang was leading on 30 feet of rope across the glacier as we'd just left the empty Camp III site when I fell through covering snow into a crevasse.

Pasang, hearing my shout, reacted immediately—as professionally as any professional climber who's ever climbed—slamming his ice axe deep in the firm snow at his feet and bracing himself for the belay, so I only fell about 15 feet. I'd kept my ice axe as well, and it was jammed against the opposing walls above me, giving me a solid handhold to cling to while I formed Prusik knots with my free hand for the climb up.

But then I made the mistake of looking down deeper into the crevasse with my headlamp beam.

Twenty feet lower than me were dead, blue faces, dozens of them, with dozens of open mouths and frozen, staring eyes. Dead arms and blue hands reached up toward my boots from their snow-covered dead bodies.

I screamed.

"What's wrong, Jake?" shouted Pasang. "Are you injured?"

"No, I'm okay," I gasped as loudly as I could through my swollen throat and damaged larynx. "Just pull me...pull..."

"You do not want to Prusik while I belay?"

"No...just pull me up...fast!"

Pasang did so, ignoring the fraying of the rope over the icy edge of the crevasse. He was very strong. I had my ice axe free and was chopping holds as I came up. Then I was out.

I crawled over to where Pasang stood, winded and gasping—he hadn't been using the oxygen rigs at all, reserving all the tanks for my use—as I described what I'd seen.

"Ahh," said Pasang. "We've accidentally stumbled upon the crevasse that Herr Sigl and his friends used for the mass grave of our Sherpa friends at Camp Three."

I started shaking and had trouble stopping. Pasang produced a blanket from one of his overstuffed carryall bags and laid it over my shoulders.

"Don't you want to...go see?" I asked.

"Is there a chance that any of them might be alive?" he asked. Our headlamp beams danced upon one another's chests in the dark.

I thought for a moment of the blue faces, frozen eyes, and frozen hands and bodies I'd seen piled down there. "No," I said.

"Then I do not want to see," said Dr. Pasang. "I believe I was some yards off the proper path. Would you care to lead for a while, Mr. Perry, the better to avoid more crevasses?"

"Sure," I said and, setting my oxygen mask back in place, took the lead on the rope. Most of our marking wands were gone, but Sigl's Germans had left readable boot prints where the original safe trail through the crevasses had been. I lowered my head to play the beam along ahead of me and concentrated on route finding and on forgetting everything else for a while. I knew that if I wandered off the true path, Jean-Claude would come back to set things right.

Camp II at 19,800 feet and Camp I at 17,800 feet were simply gone. Whatever the Germans had done with the remaining tents and caches, Pasang and I could find no trace with our headlamps. Because of our careful descent—and more due to my slow pace—it was approaching the false dawn now as we did the last mile or so from Camp I down to where Base Camp used to be at 16,500 feet. If there were a couple of Germans waiting for us down here as the Deacon had feared, our Welsh miner's lamps would be a dead giveaway in a literal sense, but Pasang and I found that—as exhausted as we both were—we couldn't stop until we got out of this damned valley.

Again and again I imagined Reggie and the Deacon alone, perhaps ill or injured, stuck far up there at Camp VI or Camp V—a different universe from this one in the glacier valley—stuck and ill or injured and awaiting rescue from Pasang and me.

There'd be no such rescue. I was having so much trouble breathing that I could barely stand and was staggering more than striding down the long moraine slope between looming *penitente* pinnacles and ice walls on either side. I couldn't have climbed back up to Camp II if my life depended on it, and that didn't even entail any glacier travel.

We came carefully out of the moraine ridges and pinnacles to where Base Camp had been. There was nothing left. All of the bodies had been removed, all the tents taken somewhere and most probably burned. It was as if the Deacon-Bromley Expedition had never been here at all.

The sky was getting lighter now—the black of night giving way to the slight gray glow of the predawn. Taking a wide half-circle around where the tents and *sangas* of Base Camp used to be, Pasang and I—still roped up for some reason—came out onto the gravel flats beyond the last of the moraine ridges. We clicked off our headlamps and put the leather rigs in the carryalls that we'd shifted to carrying on our backs, over the oxygen rigs. I had four of the heavy gas mask bags back there, bulging with everything from an Unna cooker we hadn't used to extra pots and pans we'd brought along.

"What now?" I whispered painfully. "Can I take off these last two oxygen tanks?"

"Not yet, Mr. Perry," Dr. Pasang whispered back. "You are still having great trouble breathing because of your inflamed and swollen throat. I really do not wish to do a tracheotomy unless I must."

"Amen to that." Even my whispers sounded ragged. "Which way, then? It's eleven miles to the Rongbuk Monastery and we can ask for help there, but I doubt very much if I can make it beyond the monastery to Chobuk or Shekar Dzong."

"Herr Sigl may have left friends at the monastery," observed Pasang.

"Oh, shit."

"Precisely," said Pasang. "But let us try to walk those last miles to the vicinity of the monastery and then, dressed in a pilgrim's cloak I've brought with me, I shall reconnoiter Rongbuk while you wait in the rocks at the base of the approach. If there are no Germans there, we shall place ourselves under the care and protection of the reincarnation of Padma Sambhava, Guru Rinpoche, the good Dzatrul Rinpoche, Holy Lama of the monastery."

"A man, a plan, a canal...," I rasped, not even amusing myself. "But first I think we should..."

I didn't hear the shots until after the bullets struck.

The first impact made Pasang's head snap forward in a mist of blood that covered my own face and lowered oxygen mask. An instant later I felt the second slug tear through my packs and O_2 rig and hit me high in the back, above and to the right of my left shoulder blade.

Pasang had already fallen forward, apparently lifeless, onto the sharp rocks beneath our crampons. Before I could open my mouth to shout, there was that impact against my upper back and I fell forward next to him, not even staying conscious long enough to break my fall with my forearm.

There was the pain in my back and throat and encroaching blackness; and then only the blackness.

26.

———— ∞∞ ————

I came partially conscious sometime later to the sound of two
men talking loudly. They were about ten feet uphill and up-
wind of us—the wind was roaring down the Rongbuk Glacier valley
with a renewed ferocity—and the two were speaking in German loudly
enough for me to make out the words over the wind.

Pasang was lying dead, also on his belly, so close that our faces were
only inches apart. He'd had no part in his black hair before, but now his
leather cap and woolen top cap had been knocked off and a terrible white
streak of what I assumed was exposed skull or brains ran down the top of
his scalp. His face was completely covered with blood. I started to raise
a hand from my side to touch him—to shake him to make sure he was
really dead—when Pasang whispered without moving his bloody lips,
"Don't move, Jake." The whisper was almost inaudible to me six inches
from him, so I was sure the two Germans arguing ten feet away against
the wind could not hear him.

"I'll translate," whispered Pasang.

"Your head . . . ," I whispered back.

"Scalp wounds always bleed dramatically," was his whispered response. "I will have a headache—if we survive—nothing more. They
did not search us. Let me translate, Jake, so we know when to reach under our outer jackets for our pistols."

I'd almost forgotten the Webley revolver tucked in a pocket in my
Finch duvet and the fully loaded Luger that Pasang had put in the pocket
of his goose down jacket.

Amazingly, I recognized the voices from Munich. The heavier, deeper voice belonged to that right-wing German radical's bodyguard...what was the bodyguard's name?...Ulrich Graf.

The other voice belonged to another man at the table that night—he'd said little but I recognized his near-lisp—Artur Wolzenbrecht.

Ulrich Graf was saying, almost whining, *"SS-Sturmbannführer Sigl...hat gesagt, dass ich sie aufhalten soll, und ich habe sie aufgehalten."*

In a burst of surreality, Pasang's bloody mask of a face, his eyes still closed and caked with pooled blood that all but concealed his moving lips, whispered a simultaneous translation. If I'd known that he spoke German, I'd forgotten it.

"SS-Sturmbannführer Sigl said to stop them, so I stopped them." It took me a second to realize that he was translating what Graf had said and another sickening second for me to realize that the "them" being stopped and shot was "us."

"Idiot!" barked Wolzenbrecht. *"Sturmbannführer Sigl hat gesagt, dass du sie aufhalten sollst, bevor sie das Tal verlassen können. Aber nicht, sie zu erschiessen."*

Pasang whispered the translation. *"Idiot! Sturmbannführer Sigl said to stop them before they left the valley. Not to shoot them!"*

Ulrich Graf's voice came down the wind to us in the tone of a stupid, sulking child. *"Na ja, mit meinen Schüssen habe ich sie doch angehalten, oder?"*

"Well, my shooting them stopped them, didn't it?" translated Pasang through blood-caked lips.

I heard Wolzenbrecht sigh. *"Sturmbannführer Sigl hat befohlen, sie zu verhören und sie dann nach Fotos zu durchsuchen. Aber keiner von ihnen sieht so aus, als ob wir sie noch verhören könnten."*

"Sturmbannführer Sigl ordered us to interrogate them, then search them for the photographs. But neither one looks alive enough to interrogate." This gave me a second's hope. But I'd fallen with my right hand under my body and that hand never stopped moving—millimeter by millimeter—first under my Shackleton anorak, and then to the right pocket of my Finch duvet, where the Webley revolver painfully pressed against my lower ribs.

"Was sollen wir jetzt machen?" said Graf. *"Warten, bis einer wieder zu sich kommt?"*

I caught a hint of movement from Pasang and realized that he was moving his hand to the Luger in his down jacket. His whispered translation was almost inaudible even to me—*"What shall we do, then? Wait for one of them to regain consciousness?"*

Wolzenbrecht's reply sounded to me like a rough imitation of a German shepherd gargling gravel. *"Nein, vergiss das Verhör. Töte sie erst, und dann durchsuchen wir sie. Aber mit Kopfschuss, nicht auf den Körper zielen."*

"No. Forget the interrogation," Pasang interpreted in a fast whisper. *"Kill them first, then we will search. But fire into their heads, not into their bodies."*

That convinced me to run the risk of pulling the Webley free of my jackets and lying on it. My finger found the trigger guard, then the trigger. My thumb found the hammer. I remembered the Deacon telling me that a revolver had no safety. I could see the slight motion as Pasang freed the Luger beneath him.

"Warum denn?" demanded Graf.

"Why?" whispered Pasang, and I realized that the semi-retarded bodyguard wasn't questioning why Dr. Pasang and I should be shot, only why we should be shot in the head and not the body.

"Damit wir keine Fotos beschädigen, falls sie welche bei sich haben, du Trottel," snapped Wolzenbrecht. *"Sturmbannführer Sigl kommt sicher bald aus den Bergen zurück. Stell die Schmeisser auf einen Schuss ein."*

Since their boots were already crunching in our direction before Pasang whispered his translation, I already had the gist of what Wolzenbrecht was saying.

"So that we don't damage the photographs if the pictures are hidden on their persons, shithead," whispered Pasang. *"Sturmbannführer Sigl should be coming down from the mountain very soon, so set your Schmeisser to single-fire and let's get it over with..."*

Schmeisser! That goddamned submachine gun! These Nazi fuckers were going to shoot us in the head just to avoid punching holes in the obscene photos each of us was carrying—me in my carryall, Pasang in a large pocket in his wool jacket. They were content to search our corpses after shooting us in the next few seconds. Time was up.

Pasang and I rolled in opposite directions in the same instant and came to our knees with our pistols raised.

What happened next is still not clear to me. There had been two Germans striding toward us, now there were blurs of gray motion all around them. Massive figures. Glimpses of gray fur in the swirling snow. *Hair everywhere.*

I saw Ulrich Graf's head flying through the air, suddenly removed from its body. I had time to see and hear Artur Wolzenbrecht scream shrilly as something looming very gray and very large in the snow flurries rose over him.

Then something hit me in the side of the head, I fired one shot from the Webley—hitting nothing, my aim knocked high—and only had time to see Pasang also falling forward from where he'd risen to his knees on the moraine rock, the Luger already dropped from his hand, his eyes closed again in that bloody face—before I went down face-first onto the stones and blackness again.

27.

—⊗⊗⊗—

I came to lying in a fresh-smelling silken tent, tied facedown onto many not-so-fresh-smelling silken pillows. My wrists were tied to stakes driven into the ground between an array of elaborate Persian rugs that covered most of the floor of the tent. My head hurt terribly. My upper back hurt quite specifically—I could feel where the German bullet had entered when Pasang and I were first shot. I moved my head to look in both directions—more rugs, tall tentpoles, more tent, more pillows, no Pasang. Maybe he was dead. Perhaps I was.

But I hurt too much to be dead. I noticed that I was shirtless in the cold—I'd accidentally dislodged blankets when I'd first stirred—but there was something bulky and sticky on my back. I wondered idly if the bullet was in my lung or spine or near my heart. My head hurt too much for me to work on that problem with the mental effort it deserved.

I heard something behind me and I swiveled my head quickly enough to send so much pain coursing through my skull that I almost fainted, but I did manage to see a very Asian-looking Tibetan, or perhaps Tibetan-looking Mongolian, step into the tent with a steaming bowl in his hands, see him notice that I was conscious, and then he beat a hasty retreat.

Bandits, I realized. I could only hope that it was the band that Lady Bromley-Montfort was friends with and had already bribed with pistols and chocolate. What was the name of that band's leader...??

Jimmy Khan. How can one forget that?

The little Asian-looking man in furs and still carrying the steaming bowl came back through the tall tent entrance with Pasang and the bandit Jimmy Khan walking next to him. Pasang had obviously bandaged his own head and also washed the blood from his face. He did not look dead any longer. I could see the end of the bullet furrow as a white scar raised against the dark skin of Pasang's left temple.

The bandit Jimmy Khan said something in Tibetan and Pasang translated. "Khan says, 'Good, you are alive again.'"

From our first encounter the month before, I remembered that Jimmy Khan spoke and understood some English. "Why am I staked out here, Pasang? Am I a prisoner?"

"No," said my tall Sherpa friend. "You were a bit delirious, Jake. I decided to remove the bullet from your back while you were unconscious, and the ropes were the only way to keep you from rolling over onto your dressings." He produced the curved penknife from a pocket and cut the twine binding my hands.

"I had a bullet in my back but I'm alive?" I said, head fuzzy and hurting.

"Mr. Ulrich Graf—he had his identification on his body—appears to have shot both of us," said Pasang. "The bullet that hit me just tore through scalp and left a groove in my skull. I was unconscious only a short while from that. The bullet that hit you high in the back passed—as far as I can tell—through both of your oxygen tanks, a steel fitting on your flow regulator, as well as through the Unna cooker and two of the cooking pots you were carrying in the gas mask bag slung over your back. Oh, and the slug also had to pass through the aluminum frame of the oxygen rig before it struck you. Most of its kinetic energy was spent by the time it reached your body, Jake. I removed it from beneath only about an inch of skin and a small layer of shoulder muscle."

I blinked at this. My back hurt but not as much as my head. I'd been shot! "How do you know that Graf was the one who shot us both?"

"I found the mashed-flat slug that grazed me at the base of the boulder we were standing near," said Pasang. "But it was the slug that I pulled from your back that settled the matter. Both were nine-millimeter Parabellum rounds... essentially you were struck by a pistol shot from long distance, otherwise you'd be dead."

"Artur Wolzenbrecht also had a Luger in his hand when he was coming toward us in that last second or two," I managed to say. *What did it matter which one of those Nazis shot us?* was what I was really thinking.

"He did," said Pasang and held up a shortened bit of lead. "Evidently they paint the points of the Schmeisser nine-millimeter rounds black. Both of ours had black tips. Graf's Luger carried that kind of ammunition."

I sat up on the cushions and swayed a bit with dizziness. "So what happened to Graf and Wolzenbrecht?" I asked. I tried to remember through the throbbing blur, but all I could recall was starting to raise the Webley, blurs of gray and dark masses moving in the swirling snow, screaming.

"That's a good question," said Pasang. There was some warning tone in his voice, but I was too preoccupied with pain to sort it out.

"If you can stand, Jake," said Pasang. "Let me help you outside so that you can see something before more vultures arrive."

"You explain," said Jimmy Khan to Pasang and patted me on the back right where the dressing covered my wound. I managed not to scream.

Over on the broad, flat boulder near where we'd been standing when we'd been shot from distant ambush—evidently the two Germans had been hidden behind a boulder only about twenty yards beyond the memorial pyramid of stones that had been raised last year for Mallory, Irvine, and the seven lost Sherpas in 1922—Ulrich Graf's and Artur Wolzenbrecht's decapitated heads were set on short stakes lined up very neatly next to one another. Their wide eyes—just beginning to glaze over thickly with the white caul of death—seemed to be staring at us in total surprise. Next to the heads were four severed arms complete with hands, two right arms to the left of Graf, two left arms to the right of Wolzenbrecht.

"Jesus Christ Almighty," I whispered to Pasang. Looking at Jimmy Khan standing and beaming a few yards away, I also whispered, "Khan and his boys really did a job on these poor devils."

Dr. Pasang looked at me without blinking. His voice seemed too loud when he spoke. "Mr. Khan explained to me that he and his fifty-five men arrived thirty minutes or so after whatever happened here. He and his men are very impressed with how four or five *yeti,* angered at the Germans' presence, took care of our enemies."

"That's ridiculous," I began. But then I finally sorted out the tone of warning in Pasang's voice and gaze and shut up. For some reason, the bandits wanted us to buy the story that *yetis,* rather than fur-covered barbarian bandits on horseback, had killed the Germans amidst all that swirling snow. I had no idea why they'd want us to believe that, but I was finally conscious enough to know to keep my mouth shut. These bandits had already knocked me on the head once.

The wind blowing down the long Trough from Everest whistled through the boulders and ruffled the short hair on the dead men's staked-out heads. The vultures were arriving in force now, and I looked away as they started their meal with the two men's eyes.

"How long have I been unconscious, Pasang?"

"About five hours."

I checked my still-ticking watch. (My father never chose anything cheap for a gift.) It was just after noon. Jimmy Khan and two of his lieutenants stepped closer, folded their arms, and grunted with satisfaction at the decapitated heads, four lopped-off arms, and strangely shriveled-looking dead hands. For the first time I noticed, about fifteen yards behind this large flat boulder, a tall pile of what could only be the two men's intestines. I could see no other evidence of their bodies.

"Metohkangmi," said Jimmy Khan, and his two lieutenants grumbled and nodded assent. *"Yeti."*

"All right," I said. I staggered away from the trophy stakes and heaps of body parts and found a small boulder to sit on. "Whatever you say, Mr. Jimmy Khan."

"I've found no bullet wounds in the skulls or other detached parts," said Dr. Pasang, as if that gave forensic support to the bandits' idiot *yeti* theory.

As Khan grinned, I gave Pasang a look that should have melted him but somehow didn't. Perhaps my melting powers were being interfered with by the tremendous headache that continued to throb.

"What next?" I asked.

"Well, Mr. Khan and his associates allowed me to raise the one tent so that I could cut the bullet out of you and let you rest a few hours," he said softly, "but they won't allow their camp to be set up anywhere near here. Evidently they feel that Guru Rinpoche, Dzatrul Rinpoche at

Rongbuk Monastery, will be displeased when he hears of the violence here today."

"I thought the Guru Rinpoche liked spreading stories of *yetis* being up here in the Rongbuk Valley," I said. "Remember the fairly new mural in the monastery? It helped keep his people and monks away from the hills here."

"Well, Mr. Khan and his friends insist that we start on the voyage back to the east right away—this afternoon. They have Mongolian ponies for both of us."

"We can't leave here," I said, shocked. "Reggie and the Deacon..."

"Will not be coming down...this way at least," said Pasang. "Of this I am certain. So we should go with Jimmy Khan and his friendly bandits, Jake. They've offered to lead us almost due east from here and then south again across the high Serpo La. That will take us straight down into India. And since we're traveling so lightly, and if the weather on the high pass holds, the entire trip back might be made in three weeks or less rather than five weeks the way we came in. Jimmy Khan and his band will ride with us and protect us the whole way to Darjeeling, providing a palanquin for you if your wound and headache begin acting up."

"He must be demanding something for all this friendly help," I said dully. "Even his old friend Reggie had to pay him so that we could pass through his band's territory."

"I offered to pay him one thousand pounds sterling when we're safe at Lady Bromley-Montfort's plantation."

"What?" I cried. "We don't have a thousand pounds to pay these bandits with! We don't have a hundred quid between the two of us."

"You forget, Mr. Perry," Pasang said sadly. "Lady Bromley-Montfort left the entire tea plantation in my hands—full ownership if she does not return, which I sincerely pray to our Savior that she does. And soon. Her only stipulation was that I pay one-third of the annual profits to Lady Bromley in Lincolnshire as long as the aunt lives. Suddenly—and I pray God, temporarily—I find myself awash in funds. At any rate, considering the importance Mr. Deacon and Lady Bromley-Montfort placed on what you're expected to deliver directly to London, I agreed that a thousand pounds was reasonable for Khan's protection and ponies on our voyage back. Khan's men rarely travel as far into India as the outskirts of

Darjeeling, so Mr. Khan *is* being generous. He will even leave two of his men to stay here near Base Camp for two weeks just in case our friends *do* come this way."

I had nothing to say to that.

I looked up toward Mount Everest—mostly hidden by snow clouds, wind blowing wildly from the North Ridge and North Col—and then back at the two Germans' staring heads on the boulder. The vultures were very busy now.

"If we're not going to wait here days or weeks in person to see if Reggie and the Deacon end up coming down this way," I said slowly, trying to think clearly, "then we might as well get headed toward Darjeeling sooner rather than later. Let's go see what shaggy ponies they've chosen for us."

28.

*L*ondon in mid-August on rare occasions can be sweltering, but there was a chill in the air that reminded me of our visit to the Royal Geographical Society ten months earlier. Of course, the leaves on the trees weren't changing in August, but there was some tinge in the air...smoke from coal and wood fires in the houses and buildings, I decided. I was wearing my second-best suit—three-piece, heavy wool, since my one bespoke suit had gone missing in my absence—and I hoped that the brief cold front would make the choice of apparel stand out a little less.

The building was brown with age and soot, its lobby quite imposing. Footsteps echoed on tile and marble. I told the first guard I encountered about my appointment with the Chancellor of the Exchequer, and he led me to a receptionist, who led me to a clerk, who led me to the important man's aide, who parked me on a tattered leather couch in a wallpapered waiting room for only a two- or three-minute wait before I was shown into the Chancellor's inner office.

Chancellor of the Exchequer. How very cute Reggie and the Deacon had been with their mildly coded talk about "our mutual friend who now likes to write cheques" and "our friend who really prefers gold." The latter phrase, I'd learned just by reading and asking questions during my long solo boat trip from India to England, referred to this Chancellor of the Exchequer's decision, under the Baldwin government, to return the British economy to the gold standard.

This had happened the previous May, while my friends and I were climbing Mount Everest, so I don't know if Reggie and the Deacon had heard of the actual return to the gold standard, but they'd obviously known this man's preference for an economy based on gold. I'd also read all about this return to the gold standard—and the continuing hubbub and disapproval of it and disapproval of the Chancellor of the Exchequer himself by many economists—during my boat trip to England.

The male secretary left us, and I was looking across a broad room with a rather worn carpet, a large desk and chair—currently empty of its occupant—and a very rotund man with his back to me. He stood silently looking out a sooty window as he smoked a cigar, his legs wide apart in almost a pugilist's stance and his pudgy hands clasped behind his back.

He turned a minute or so after his secretary or adjutant or whatever the hell he was announced me and looked me up and down, frowning a bit—perhaps at my wool suit—and said, "Perry, correct?"

"Yes, sir."

"Good of you to come, Mr. Perry." He waved me to an uncomfortable-looking chair while he took the large padded chair behind his desk.

I'd heard the name Winston Churchill during the months I'd stayed in London prior to the beginning of our expedition, but I didn't recall seeing photographs of him. I dimly remembered that there'd been a buzz about him in the press in 1924 when he rejoined the Conservative Party after having left the Conservatives to join the Liberal Party some years before. I remember the Deacon laughing at an edition of the *Times* as we were sorting gear in our London hotel room and quoting Churchill to Jean-Claude and me (on whom the humor was totally lost)—"Anyone can rat, but it takes a certain ingenuity to re-rat."

Evidently the re-ratting had worked: Churchill now had an elected seat in Epping as a Tory and this high position in Baldwin's Conservative government. The only other thing I'd learned about the position of Chancellor of the Exchequer was that it earned Churchill the honorific of "the right Honorable" and a rent-free home at No. 11 Downing Street, evidently right next to the Prime Minister's digs.

"You're an American, Mr. Perry?"

Had that been a question? "Yes, sir," I said.

I confess that if this man was the intelligence chief for whom Lord Percival Bromley died—and most likely former captain Richard Davis Deacon and Lady Katherine Christina Regina Bromley-Montfort as well—he certainly didn't fit the role of spymaster. He reminded me more of a big baby in a pinstripe suit and waistcoat, with a cigar in his mouth.

"You American fellows are putting me—and His Majesty's Government—in the most frightful position," he boomed from across the wide desk. He opened a box of cigars and shoved them across the expanse. "Cigar, Mr. Perry? Or a cigarette, perhaps?"

"No, thank you, sir." I had no idea what he was talking about with the "frightful position" line. Certainly it couldn't be in the pending handover of the envelope holding seven damning photographs and negatives that I had tucked in my oversized jacket pocket. I just wanted to get on with that exchange and to get the hell out of this office, and London.

"It's the war debt, man," said this Churchill person. "Great Britain owes you Yanks the rather preposterous sum of four billion, nine hundred thirty-three million, seven hundred one thousand, and six hundred forty-two pounds. The annual interest payment on that alone is more than thirty-five million pounds a year. And your President and Secretary of State and Treasury Secretary keep clamoring for payment on time. I ask you, Mr. Perry, how will that be possible until France pays His Majesty's Government more of what they owe us on *their* war debt? Heaven knows France is getting *its* reparation payments and share of German steel sales coming out of the Ruhr Valley, but the French are as slow to pay as a renter who puts all his monthly income on the lottery rather than give it to his landlord."

I nodded vaguely. My throat had improved sufficiently during my weeks in India and at sea that I could speak now with only a slight rasp rather than my former frog's croak, but I could think of nothing to say. All I knew was that the envelope with the photos seemed to be burning a hole into the upper-right part of my chest, and if this fat little man didn't shut up and quit blowing cigar smoke in my direction, I was going to leap across that too-broad desk and strangle the son of a bitch, American-British relations be damned.

"Well, not your fault, not your fault," said Chancellor of the Exchequer Churchill. "Do you have the items with you?"

I said, probably breaking fifty rules of spy craft, "Do you mean the photographs and negatives from Lord Percival, sir?"

"Yes, yes." He stubbed out the cigar and crossed his pudgy fingers over his chest.

I removed the envelope and set it as far across his desk as I could reach without standing up. To my shock, Churchill didn't even glance at the envelope before one of those pudgy hands swept it up and slipped it into a red briefcase propped next to his feet.

"Good, then," he said.

I took that as my dismissal and stood to leave.

"This is Friday," said Churchill, still sitting, not rising even to shake my hand before I left. And I knew what goddamned day it was. I'd made the appointment with his lackeys for this day.

"I believe we should chat about the circumstances surrounding the acquisition of these items," said Churchill. "Do you have anything on for tomorrow?"

On for tomorrow? What the hell was that supposed to mean? I'd never felt as alone and stranded as I had the last few days waiting here in London without the Deacon and Jean-Claude. These British people spoke a strange and cloudy language.

Churchill must have seen my vacant look, for he said, "For dinner, I mean."

"No, sir," I replied with a sinking feeling in my gut. I didn't want to socialize with this...*mere man*...who I was sure had gotten three of my dearest friends killed, as well as my friend's cousin.

"We shall plan on you dropping down to Chartwell sometime in the afternoon, then," he said as if it were already an agreed-upon thing. "Clemmie's not there this weekend, but we have a few very amusing dinner guests, and of course the children will be there. Come get a good meal, Mr. Perry, spend the night, and we shall talk more at length when we have some privacy.

"We do dress for dinner," continued the Chancellor of the Exchequer. I'd read somewhere that he was 50 years old, but between the roly-poly appearance, flushed fat-baby cheeks, and bouncy energy, he seemed much younger. "Did you happen to bring white tie, tails, that sort of thing with you to London?"

"No, sir," I said. I was already sick unto death of calling this Churchill nobody "sir." "Just this suit I'm wearing."

Churchill nodded judiciously, then pushed a lever on a contraption on his desk. The male secretary who'd seen me in appeared as if by magic. "Colonel Taylor," said Churchill, "could you run this chap around the corner to my tailor at Savile Row and have him expedite a proper suit of evening clothes as well as a summer and autumn suit or two and perhaps a pair of pyjamas and some shirts and proper ties...by tomorrow noon, please. And tell them the bill is to be paid by His Majesty's Treasury."

I didn't even know what to think of this, much less what to say—since all I wanted to say was *I don't need white tie and tails and I don't need your damned charity, either*—so I nodded at Churchill, who'd lighted a fresh cigar and was already perusing some papers even before I was out of the room.

"Wait," I said, stopping and turning. "One thing."

The round face with its cherubic little smile looked across the width of the room at me and waited.

"What and where is Chartwell?" I heard myself ask.

29.

*C*hartwell was Churchill's country place near Westerham in Kent, some twenty-five miles from London. I dropped by to pick up my new clothes at the tailor's at noon, tried them on, let the tailor pronounce them proper, stayed in one of the white shirts they'd chosen for me and in the tan linen suit they'd just made for me—the tailor chose a modest green and burgundy tie for it—and caught the 1:15 train with the help of a waiting car sent by the Ministry. (Which "Ministry" I had no idea.) Another such chauffeur-driven limousine picked me up at the Westerham station and drove me the few miles to Chartwell proper.

I'd expected another huge estate such as Lady Bromley's or the one I'd heard described that Richard Davis Deacon had given up after the War, but Chartwell looked more like a comfortable house in the country somewhere in Massachusetts. I was to learn much later that rather than its having been in the Churchill family for a dozen generations, Chartwell—a rather plain brick house made ugly by additions and bad landscaping in the 1800s—had been fairly recently purchased and more or less rebuilt by Churchill's workmen.

And by Churchill himself.

After I'd been shown to a room by a servant and had time to "freshen up" a bit, an older male servant came to the room and told me that Mr. Churchill would like to see me and asked if the time was convenient for me. I told him it was.

I expected to be led into a huge library, but instead the tall gray-haired servant who'd answered my query about his name only with

"Mason, sir" led me around to the side of the house where Winston Churchill, wearing a white fedora and a dark mortar-spattered coverall, was laying bricks.

"Ho, welcome, Mr. Perry," he cried, using a trowel to level off some mortar before laying another brick in place.

It was a long wall.

"I spend ten hours a day in my office in London, but this is my real work," continued Churchill. I'd already come to realize that the monologue was his favorite form of conversation. "This and writing histories. I took care to contact the bricklayers' union before I did my first wall. They made me an honorary member, but I still pay my dues. My real work this week has been two thousand words written and two hundred bricks laid."

He set the trowel down and, taking me suddenly by the elbow, led me around to the back of the house.

"The 'Cosy Pig,' I call it," said Churchill.

"Call what, sir?" I said.

"Why, the house, of course. Chartwell. And if you're Mr. Perry, then I am Mr. Churchill; no more 'sirs.'"

"All right," I said, just avoiding uttering the "sir."

We stopped on a patio amidst a low formal garden, but it wasn't the garden that the Chancellor of the Exchequer had brought me around the house to see. "This is why I bought the place three years ago," he said.

I knew he meant the view from this hilltop. It was then—and remains today—the single most beautiful and verdant view of a peacetime countryside I'd ever seen. There were distant forests of beech, chestnut, and oak, countless wide green meadows, and the longest, grassiest slopes I'd ever encountered.

"The Cosy Pig sits in its eighty acres of all this," said Churchill, "but it's this view of the combe and the larger Kentish Weald that convinced me to buy the place, although Clementine said it was—and would be in its rebuilding—too dear for me. For us. And I suppose it has been."

"It's beautiful," I said, realizing how inadequate the words were.

"Not as beautiful as Mount Everest, I would imagine," said the heavy-set little man. His bright eyes were watching me carefully.

"That's a different beauty, si—...Mr. Churchill," I said. "All rock, ice, harsh light, air. Almost everything, including the air, is so cold it cuts. There's no green there, usually, above Base Camp, not even a lichen. Nothing alive but the climbers and the rare raven. No trees, no leaves, no grass... almost nothing soft, Mr. Churchill. Just rock and ice and snow and sky. This is infinitely more... gentle. More... human."

Churchill had been listening carefully, and now he nodded. "I'd best be getting back to work. When I finish that wall for what will be the final terrace extension to Clementine's bedroom, I need to build another dam." He waved his short arm and chubby hand to the left. "I built those ponds as well. Have always enjoyed looking at water and things that like to live in water."

The ponds were beautiful and natural-looking. But this time I said nothing.

"Make yourself at home, as you Yanks like to say," said Churchill. "If you're hungry at all, tell Mason or Matthews; they'll have cook make up a sandwich for you. The liquor's in the drawing room, and there is some good whisky—Scotch, I believe you fellows call it on your side of the pond—in your suite. There are books in your room, but feel free to borrow from the library. If you can't reach the book, it's because you weren't meant to be able to. Anything else is fair game. We'll have sherry or whisky at six, dinner's at seven thirty—early tonight because one of our guests had his people bring a projector with a motion picture for us to see later. Or for the children to see, I should say. I think you'll find all our dinner guests amusing tonight, but three of them especially so. See you in a while, Mr. Perry."

The first guest I met was T. E. Lawrence—"Lawrence of Arabia," the American reporter Lowell Thomas had called him during and after the War—who was descending the stairs for drinks just when I was. Lawrence was wearing the full robes of a prince of Arabia, complete with a jewel-handled curved dagger tucked in his sash.

"Silly, I know," he said after we'd introduced ourselves and shaken hands, "but the children love it."

We were soon joined by an older man whom Churchill called "Prof." This was Professor F. A. Lindemann, and Lawrence later whispered to me that in 1916, when countless RAF pilots were dying because they were unable to get their flimsy paper and wood aircraft out of a flat spin, "Prof" Lindemann had worked out, using advanced mathematics, a maneuver which he announced would bring any aircraft out of even the worst tailspin. When the RAF establishment and the pilots said the maneuver wouldn't work—according to Lawrence, who was still wearing his rather effeminate white cotton headdress and headband as he told me all this—the professor had taught himself how to fly, taken up a SPAD while wearing no parachute, deliberately put the craft into the worst flat spin imaginable, and deftly pulled it out—using his mathematically concocted maneuver—with hundreds of feet to spare. Evidently the secret was in getting one's hands and feet off the controls; the aircraft, said Professor Lindemann, *wanted* to fly straight and level and would do so if the pilot left it alone. It was, he announced, all the correcting and over-correcting inputs to the controls that turned spins into death spins. And then, according to Lawrence, the "Prof" had taken up another, older bi-plane, set it into a terrible spin, and allowed it to recover yet again.

After that, T. E. Lawrence assured me, all RAF pilots were required to learn the Prof's maneuver.

During dinner that night—there were about a dozen people at the table, including the children: a sixteen-year-old daughter, Diana; a son, Randolph, who looked to be about fourteen; and an eleven-year-old girl named Sarah, as well as two cousins, a boy and a girl (whose names I forget) roughly the ages of Diana and Randolph—Churchill challenged Prof to "tell us in words of one syllable, and taking no longer than five minutes, what this quantum theory rubbish is all about."

While Churchill checked the watch from his waistcoat pocket, Professor Lindemann did so with twenty seconds to spare. Everyone at the table, including me, burst into applause. I'd actually understood it.

The other "special guest" for that night's dinner had taken me aback somewhat when I first saw him in the drawing room accepting a large glass of chilled champagne.

It was, I saw, Adolf Hitler. I'd been reminded of that name during my month of convalescing—in truth, merely waiting in hopes that the Deacon and Reggie would show up someday—with Dr. Pasang at the tea plantation. I'd read everything I could get, at the plantation and during the weeks on the boat coming back from India, about Herr Hitler.

And here Hitler was—for a moment I was filled with a terrible indecision (not *what* I should do, *had* to do, but *how* could I do it then and there?)—but then I noticed the wavy hair and pleasant expression, the slightly longer bone structure in the face, and realized it was only the fake mustache—which he removed after amusing the children but before dinner—that really caused the resemblance. This man, as Churchill introduced us, was Charles Chaplin, who although born in England was now a fellow U.S. resident.

This, then, was why we were dining earlier that evening and the children dining with us—Chaplin had brought his most recent release (along with a portable cinema projector) to show us his new movie after dinner, before it got too late for the children.

But as pleasant and smiling as Chaplin was, he irritated our host even before drinks were finished and we were shown into the long dining room. Chaplin, it seemed, was very serious about his politics, and was pressing Churchill on why the Chancellor of the Exchequer and the Baldwin government had insisted on going back onto the gold standard. "It will hurt your economy, you know," pressed Chaplin over drinks. "Most of all, it will hurt the poor people as the prices of everything will go up."

Churchill obviously hated being told he was wrong, much less confronted with such an argument in his own home, so he was in a full, silent sulk by the time we all found our places around the table.

But then Chaplin did an odd thing to break the ice. "Since I have to get back to London tonight and we may not have time to chat after I show our new movie to you, I'll give you a preview of it here at the dinner table," he said. He'd brought a print of his new four-reeler called *The Gold Rush,* which had premiered in the States in June but not yet reached England.

Chaplin took two forks and stabbed them into two dinner rolls. "My Little Tramp," said the actor, "is up in Alaska hunting for gold and trying to impress a young woman he's met. At least in his fantasy, he's with her and trying to impress her. And since he cannot speak, he communicates with her in this way instead."

And with that, the political, serious Charlie Chaplin disappeared and a smiling, lovable version of his Little Tramp character appeared, shoulders hunched over his forks and the dinner rolls as if the rolls were his feet, the forks dug into the rolls his legs, and he proceeded to do a little dance with the rolls and forks, humming the tune as he went, even doing high kicks and athletic "splits" with the forks and rolls, and finally ending it with a dinner-roll-and-forks curtsey and Little Tramp simper.

Everyone applauded again. The ice had been truly broken. Churchill, who'd laughed hardest of all, became his gregarious, host-like self again, all signs of his petulance fled.

There was one other odd moment to the otherwise witty and delightful dinner. At one point T. E. Lawrence leaned over the table toward Chaplin on the other side, the silk wings of Lawrence's headdress almost dipping into the sorbet, and he said to the movie star, "Chaplin, Chaplin. Is that Jewish? Are you a Jew, sir?"

Chaplin's smile never wavered. He raised his glass of white wine—we were having pheasant—in Lawrence's direction and said, "Alas, I did not have that honor at birth, Mr. Lawrence."

Later, when the children and guests were rushing into the long drawing room where chairs and the projector had been set up, I excused myself—saying I was tired, which I was—and shook hands with Chaplin, telling him that I hoped we might meet again someday. He returned the warm handshake and wished me the same.

Then I went up to my room and to sleep while gales of laughter floated up from the main floor for the next ninety minutes or so.

I was awakened—softly but insistently by .the servant named Mason—in what felt like the middle of the night. My father's watch said it was just before four a.m.

"If you do not mind the hour, sir," whispered Mason as he held a candle, "Mr. Churchill is in his study, just finishing his work, and would like to speak with you now."

I did mind. I minded not only the rudeness of the hour and being so summarily summoned to the Great Man's study at his whim, I minded *everything*. The previous evening's dinner and conversation had been interesting—meeting Charlie Chaplin had been an experience outside my realm of reality—but no amount of social niceties could make up for the anger and despair I still felt about what had happened on Mount

Everest and why my friends had been sent there. My heart was filled with darkness, and I was in no mood for any more witty chatter or social merrymaking. I resolved to ask the Minister of the Exchequer directly and bluntly why he thought he had the power to waste lives such as Percival Bromley's, Jean-Claude Clairoux's, Richard Davis Deacon's, Lady Bromley-Montfort's, or the lives of the fine Sherpas who'd died and the young Austrian Kurt Meyer, who—I wanted to track down T. E. Lawrence and shout in his face—*had* been a Jew. And one with more balls than any silk-dress-wearing English-Arab fop I'd ever met.

I must still have been frowning when I joined Churchill in his study. Despite my black mood, I had to acknowledge to myself that the top-floor room *was* impressive. Being shown in by Mason through a Tudor doorway decorated with what I later learned was called a molded architrave—Mason silently slipped away and equally silently closed the door behind him—I looked around and up. And up. The ceiling had obviously been removed and now revealed vaulting beams and rafters that looked to be as old and solid as England itself. The huge room had broad and faded carpets on the floor, but much of the center part of the space was empty. Built into the high wall were bookcases overflowing with volumes (and I'd already seen that the downstairs library would have been sufficient to serve the reading needs of any mid-sized city in the American Midwest). There were a few chairs scattered around and a couple of low writing desks, including one magnificently carved mahogany desk with a comfortable upholstered chair behind it, but Churchill was standing and writing at a high slanted desk made of old, unvarnished wood.

"A Disraeli desk," barked Churchill. "Our Victorian predecessors liked to work standing up." He touched the ink-stained slanted writing surface carefully, as if he were caressing it. "Not Disraeli's actual desk, of course. I had a local carpenter knock it up for me."

I stood there, feeling foolish in my robe and slippers. But I'd seen immediately that Mr. Churchill was in his robe and slippers: the robe a silken explosion of green, gold, and scarlet threads. His ill-fitting slippers made a sound—*hirff, hirff, hirff*—whenever he moved, as he did now to pour a sizable glass of whisky for each of us. I took the glass but did not drink.

Churchill noticed me glancing up again at the high rafters and old paintings on the wall.

"This happens to be the oldest part of Chartwell," rumbled Churchill. "It dates to ten eighty-six A.D., just twenty years after the Battle of Hastings. I do my writing in here. Did you know that I make my living as a writer? Mostly historical tomes. Usually I dictate to one secretary, who has to be good at her shorthand to keep up. Tonight, since I'm working on two volumes simultaneously, I've been dictating to two young ladies. I also had two of my male researchers here helping me. You must have just missed them all on the staircase."

I nodded but kept silent. We continued to stand facing each other. Churchill sipped his whisky. I ignored mine.

"You're angry, Mr. Perry," he said over the top of his whisky glass. His bright little eyes missed nothing but kept moving from side to side, as if staying wary that no one was sneaking up on him.

I gave him my best approximation of J.C.'s Gallic shrug.

Churchill smiled. "I don't blame you for being angry. But what are you angriest at, young man? The sordid nature of the photographs you delivered to me yesterday or the seeming waste of your friends' and others' lives in obtaining those nasty things?"

We moved toward two chairs set near the large mahogany writing desk—the desk's surface uncluttered and, to all appearances, unused by the writer whose books and manuscript pages were all stacked on the long, high Disraeli desk—but we didn't sit down.

"I'm wondering, *Mister* Churchill," I said, "exactly what makes a turncoat politician, someone who can't even decide which party he should be in—as long as he clings to power in one or the other—decide that *anyone* should die for *anything.*"

Churchill's head snapped back, and he seemed to see me for the first time. For a moment, the entire household was silent except for a clock chiming four somewhere three flights down. I don't think either Churchill or I blinked during that interval, much less spoke.

Finally the pudgy Chancellor of the Exchequer in his bold silken robe said, "Did you know, Mr. Perry, that my mother was American?"

"No," I said, allowing the flatness of my tone to express my total lack of interest in the fact.

"It may be the reason that I have always been rather interested in American politics as well as British politics, not to mention what passes for politics on the Continent. Would you like to know the major difference between politics in your country and in the United Kingdom, Mr. Perry?"

Not much, I thought, but stayed silent.

"I don't pretend to know who President Coolidge's cabinet advisors really are," said Churchill, just as if I were interested. "Perhaps at first he kept on some of Harding's people after your previous president's sudden death in California. But I guarantee, Mr. Perry, that after Mr. Coolidge's election on his own last year, defeating that weak Democrat Davis and that rather interesting Progressive chap, La Follette, Calvin Coolidge has not only become his own man but has, by now, fully surrounded himself with *his* own men. Does this make any sense to you, young man?"

"No," I said. I was thinking of J.C. grappling with Sturmbannführer Sigl and the air rushing out of Jean-Claude's perforated oxygen tanks as both men fell through the snow cornice into 10,000 feet of empty air. I was thinking of the last glimpse I had of Reggie's and the Deacon's faces before they turned west and started climbing the last of the North East Ridge onto the snowfield toward the Summit Pyramid.

"What I'm saying, Jake... may I call you Jake?"

I remained silent, just staring coldly at the heavy man with the babyish face.

"What I'm saying, Mr. Perry, is that American parties elect their presidents, but those presidents' advisors and cabinets change from election to election. President Coolidge even replaced a few of President Harding's lower choices after Harding's death... before Coolidge *was his own man.*"

"What are you trying to say?" I demanded.

"I'm saying that in England, things do not work that way, Mr. Perry. Different parties win and different prime ministers move in and out of power along with their parties but the same basic core of the political class—*politicians,* you would say—stay in power over the decades. I will be only fifty-one years old as of this coming November, and yet in my few decades of public life I have been President of the Board of Trade, Home Secretary, First Lord of the Admiralty... until the fiasco that was

Gallipoli... then in the army fighting at the Front for a bit, then back to the corridors of power as Minister of Munitions, Secretary of State for War, then Secretary of State for Air, and now Chancellor of the Exchequer."

I waited. Finally I took a drink of the Scotch whisky. It was strong and smooth. It did nothing to settle my nerves or lower my level of anger.

"A British politician such as myself needs to keep a network of friends—and even foes—tied to him, you see," continued Churchill, "even when we are out of power. And those of us who have run intelligence operations in the army or navy or ministries of state or war—or, in my case, all four—do not abandon those networks. Information is *power,* Mr. Perry, and the proper intelligence, however gathered, can mean the life or death of one's nation and empire."

"A very impressive résumé," I said, trying to make all four words of the sentence sound sarcastic. "But what does it have to do with a private citizen such as yourself ordering good men and women into harm's way to steal some... filthy photographs?"

Churchill sighed. "I agree that the entire affair—the entire intelligence effort—of obtaining such images from Herr Meyer was sordid, Mr. Perry. *Most* actual intelligence work is sordid. Yet at times it is the most sordid elements of life which make for the most effective weapons of war or peace."

I barked a laugh at this. "You're not going to convince me that a few photographs of that German... that mustachioed *clown* and madman... are going to make any difference to the future safety of England or any other country."

Churchill shrugged his shoulders. Such a motion for such a heavy man wearing such a fancy robe gave a sort of vague Oliver Hardy feel to the gesture. "Those photographs may make a great difference," said Churchill, and his voice changed. I sensed he was using his public voice on me—a goddamned *radio* voice. He reached for a book he'd been reading when I arrived and which he'd laid facedown to one side of a counter near the mahogany desk. "I have here an advance copy of the book that Herr Adolf Hitler spent his time in prison writing and months while you were in the Himalayas rewriting and copyediting and, in general, making perfect for his small but fanatical readership. Herr Hitler wanted to title this monstrous thing—and I assure you, it *is* monstrous, Mr. Perry—*Vierinhalb Jahre Kampf gegen Lüge, Dummheit und Feigheit,* roughly translated as 'Four and a Half Years of Struggle Against Lies, Stupidity, and Cowardice.' As one writer to another, Mr. Perry, I could have told Herr Hitler that his title would not sell books. Luckily—for Hitler—his German publisher shortened the title of the actual published book to *Mein Kampf,* 'My Struggle.'"

I waited for the punch line. There didn't seem to be one.

Churchill held the book toward me. "Take it, Mr. Perry. Read it. Feel free to keep it. It may be on sale in England and America in a few years. In Germany, it may be *required* reading in a few years. See what mad plans Herr Hitler and his Nazi"—Churchill pronounced it *Nah-zee*—"goons have for Germany, for Europe, for the Jews, and for the world."

"I don't read or speak German," I said coldly. I was holding the book in my free hand; I took another drink of the Scotch. Part of me wanted to thrust the volume back at him and just turn and walk out of the room, pack my bags, and get the hell out of this place even if I couldn't find a taxi out here in the country in the middle of the night. I'd walk.

But I hesitated instead, still holding the heavy Hitler volume in one hand and my whisky glass in the other.

"Anyway," I said, "even as a writer, you should know that books aren't important. People's *lives* are important."

Churchill's old slippers made their little *hirff-hirff* sound as he took a step closer. "Know this, then, before you leave, Mr. Perry. I knew and revered Richard Davis Deacon's father and knew Richard himself before, during, and after the War. *He* understood what I . . . what *we* . . . were doing. Richard Deacon had seen the price of unchecked aggression.

"Know this also," he continued, no bluster in the slow rumble of his somewhat singsong voice. "That I have known and loved young Reggie Bromley since she was nine years old. Her cousin Percy was not only loved and valued by me, but was the centerpiece of my Naval Intelligence network both during and after the Great War. He sacrificed much—including his reputation—for our nation, Mr. Perry. And now I weep, I actually and literally have wept, sir, that I cannot even let his valor and sacrifice be known . . . but such are the ways of intelligence services, Mr. Perry."

I set the empty whisky glass on the inlaid leather of the mahogany desk—what years later I would read had been Churchill's father's desk—but I did not set down the heavy book he'd given me. The larger part of my mind wanted to lash out at this fat little man, sting him with words the way my memories of my three friends were stinging my heart, but another part of me only wanted to get away from here and think about what Churchill had just said. Reject it in the end, I was sure, but think about it nonetheless.

"Do you wish to leave this morning—when it gets light, of course, and the morning trains start running—or stay at Chartwell for the rest of the weekend so that we can chat again?"

"Leave," I said. "I'll have my things packed and ready to go by eight a.m."

"I'll have a breakfast laid on for you by seven and my driver take you to the station at your convenience," said Churchill. "I'm afraid I shan't see you in the morning since I sleep rather late and then do much of my day's work in bed before rising for the day. Will you be in London for a while, Mr. Perry?"

"No. I'm leaving London and England as quickly as I can."

"Back to the Alps, perhaps?" said Churchill with that red-cheeked baby's smile.

"No," I said sharply. "Home. To America. Away from Europe."

"I wish you a safe trip, then, and I thank you for the extraordinary things you've done and for all you've sacrificed, along with our dear mutual friends," said Churchill and finally extended his hand.

I paused only a few seconds before shaking it. He had a surprisingly firm and even calloused grip, perhaps from all that bricklaying, pond digging, and dam building.

As the car flowed almost silently down the long lane carrying me away from Chartwell later that morning—away from, what had he called it? The "Cosy Pig"? God, the Brits could be insufferably cute—past the giant old oaks and elms, the laurels and cut-back rhododendrons, then past the final thick clusters of conifers near the entrance gate, all gleaming from dew in the morning light, I resisted the impulse to turn and look back.

30.

*I*n the second week of May in 1941 — with America still seven months away from Pearl Harbor and our entering the war that had been going on in Europe for the better part of two years — I was climbing in the Grand Tetons with an American physician-climber friend, Charlie, and his newlywed wife, Dorcas (our joint campsite at Jenny Lake was Charlie and Dorcas's honeymoon suite), when I read that Rudolf Hess, the so-called Deputy Führer and second most powerful man in Germany's new Third Reich after Hitler (and also the beetle-browed silent man who'd been at our dining table at the Bierhall in Munich, sitting next to SS Sturmbannführer Bruno Sigl), had stolen a German Air Force plane and flown to England, bailing out over Scotland.

The facts in the newspaper were sketchy and seemed to make no sense.

Hess's Messerschmitt Bf 110D had been specially rigged out with long-distance drop tanks, but he'd flown alone. Picked up by British radar and with Spitfires and other fighter aircraft vectored to intercept him, Hess had flown very low — evading the radar and eluding his pursuers — but had seemed to be flying an illogical course over Scotland: low over Kilmarnock, climbing up and over the Firth of Clyde, then banking inland again, ending up over Fenwick Moor. British interception radar — still top-secret apparatus at that point — then reported that the solo fighter had crashed somewhere south of Glasgow, but not before Rudolf Hess had parachuted from the plane, coming down in the village of Eaglesham, where he injured his ankle on landing.

Hess was taken into custody and thrown into some British prison and that's all we learned about his strange flight to England that spring of 1941.

After Pearl Harbor, my climber friend Charlie enlisted to become an Army Air Force doctor. Being 38 years old, and having no special skills other than lots of travel and some mountain climbing under my belt, I ended up being rejected by several branches of the service but finally accepted into a very ad hoc American intelligence group with the alphabet soup name of OSS—the Office of Strategic Services. There I was taught Greek and eventually parachuted onto Greek islands with names like Cephalonia, Thassos, Kos, Spetses, and—my favorite—Hydra. There my modest job was to help organize and arm the partisans and to create as much mischief for the German occupiers as we could.

I'm ashamed to say that "creating mischief" mostly consisted of laying ambushes for German generals or other high-level officers and assassinating them. I'm both ashamed and proud to say that I became rather good at that job.

So it was in the OSS during the war that I stumbled upon more information, still classified then (as it still is now), about Rudolf Hess's seemingly insane 1941 solo flight to England.

When he was first questioned by officers of the Royal Observer Corps in Giffnock after his capture near Eaglesham, Hess insisted that he had a "secret and vital message from the Führer, Adolf Hitler," but that he—Hess—would only speak to the Duke of Hamilton.

Hess was taken to the Maryhill Barracks in Glasgow, where he did indeed get a private audience with the Duke of Hamilton. Immediately after that conversation, the duke was flown by the RAF to Kidlington near Oxford, then driven to London, where he met secretly with Prime Minister Winston Churchill at Ditchley Park.

Remember that this was during the darkest days of the Battle of Britain. The British Army had been soundly defeated during its retreat to Dunkirk and was literally driven into the sea, leaving most of its heavy weapons and far too many dead Brits on the beaches behind it. With France totally defeated and occupied by early summer of 1940, Germany gathered more than 2,400 barges to bring German troops and panzer divisions across the Channel. The battle plan called for hundreds of thousands of German soldiers to invade England, with Fallschirm-jägern—paratroopers—landing near Brighton and Dover just hours before destroyer- and Luftwaffe-protected barges and specialized landing craft were to be launched from Boulogne to Eastbourne, Calais to Folke-stone, Cherbourg to Lyme Regis, Le Havre to Ventnor and Brighton, and Dunkirk and Ostend to Ramsgate.

But, it was whispered, Winston Churchill had sent some private ul-timatum to Adolf Hitler that spring through the former King Edward VIII, who had abdicated so that he could marry the American divorcée Mrs. Simpson. By 1940 the ex-king was being called the Duke of Wind-sor, and he and the ever-sulking duchess lived in the Bahamas—and I knew through the OSS that English intelligence services and Churchill's government so distrusted the couple's pro-Nazi tendencies that they hadn't allowed them to stay in France or Spain right before the war broke out. It was understood by all intelligence agencies (including our various American agencies) that, even stowed away in the Bahamas, the Duke of Windsor and his circle of friends and official retinue were lousy with German intelligence agents from half a dozen Nazi services and depart-ments.

The rumor I heard in 1943—on the island of Thesprotia, where we were busy targeting Italian, Bulgarian, and German officers for assas-sination, as well as rubbing out the Cham Albanians and the Greek National Socialist Party (the Elliniko Ethniko Sosialistiko Komma), who were aiding and abetting the occupiers—was that Churchill had sent evidence to Hitler, via the Dupes of Windsor in the Bahamas, that His Majesty's Government had some very incriminating and embarrassing photographs of young Adolf, but were willing to refrain from publish-ing them to the world in exchange for the Führer's simply calling off the imminent and otherwise inevitable invasion of England.

According to my OSS link—who'd just finished a tour in London, Cuba, and the Bahamas, and who knew everyone involved in this elabo-rate operation (including, he said, the American writer Ernest Heming-way in Cuba, who, while playing spy himself, had stumbled upon some of the negotiations and was under close scrutiny by the FBI, OSS, and U.S. Naval Intelligence)—Hitler had been so panicked by this threat that he'd secretly dispatched his Deputy Führer and ultimate lackey, Rudolf Hess, to England on this secret and definitely one-way trip. Hitler's offer, reported my OSS control officer, was simple: no publication of the photos (whatever they might contain), no invasion of England.

No one was sure exactly how Churchill's acceptance of those terms was transmitted to Berlin—not through the Duke or Duchess of Windsor in the Bahamas this time, was all my friend and OSS boss knew—but transmitted it was. Late that summer, *Unternehmen Seelöwe,* Operation Sea Lion—with all of Hitler's elaborate and fully ramped-up plans and logistics and new weapons for the invasion of England by sea and air—was canceled. The official explanation from His Majesty's Government was that the Germans had backed down after Hermann Göring's Luftwaffe had failed to crush the British air defenses, even though German air superiority over the Channel was very close to being established and destruction of RAF aerodromes was almost complete when Hitler gave the stand-down order. Thus the Battle of Britain in the air, and not the existence of seven incriminating photographs from 1921 along with seven negatives delivered from Austria by way of China, Tibet, and India, has always been given the credit for saving England from German invasion.

In the cave in the mountains of my little Greek island in 1943, I smiled and I wept a little and I lifted my cup of Basbayannis Plomari Ouzo—an anise-flavored drink that I usually despised—in honor of thirty brave Sherpas, a certain brave and very young Austrian Jew named Kurt Meyer, Lord Percival Bromley, Lady Katherine Christina Regina Bromley-Montfort, Dr. Sushant Rabindranath Pasang, Richard Davis Deacon, and Jean-Claude Clairoux, four of whom had been the best friends I had ever had or ever *would* have.

EPILOGUE

April 1992 Note to Dan Simmons: I'm still enough of a reader to know that an "epilogue," especially one with the quaint "ue" at the end, went out of style in novels around the same time that spats went out of men's sartorial style. But, still, I wanted to mention a few things that really weren't part of my story from 1925, so I'll use this clumsy "Epilogue" to share these short additions with you and trust you—should you ever read this far into my endless stack of notebooks—to exclude them if you ever share my story with anyone and find the epilogue cloying or irrelevant. Or both.

After my return to America in the autumn of 1925, it took me a few years before I even thought about resuming any real mountain climbing. When I did finally climb again, I tended to stick to the Colorado Rockies—there was a reclamation job there in the mountains west of Colorado Springs where I worked for two years—where the highest peaks are in the 14,000-foot range, and then in the Grand Tetons, which may be the most beautiful string of sharp peaks in America. I met Charlie and his wife there in Jackson Hole long before Jackson Hole became a destination for the rich and famous. All three of us shared a love of skiing.

When I did start climbing outside the States again in the late 1920s, it tended to be in the South American Andes. There were many peaks there that no one had even attempted yet. I would work my way to whichever country I wanted to climb in by serving as an able seaman on a freighter or on some rich man's yacht, and that background helped me get the job I mentioned to you in person when you and I met—the job in the mid-1930s, when I spent my two years in Antarctica with Admiral Byrd.

But it was in 1929, roughly four years to the last days I'd spent on Mount Everest with my departed friends, when I received a postcard from Nepal.

First, I should mention that after 1928 it became increasingly difficult to get a permit to enter Tibet or make an attempt on Everest, and the first British expedition after Mallory and Irvine's in 1924 was Hugh Ruttledge's in 1933. They climbed high enough to find Sandy Irvine's ice axe where I'd left it on a boulder before and below the First Step, but they hadn't seen it as an arrow pointing downhill to Sandy Irvine's body as I'd hoped they would. Or perhaps by then the long flow of loose rock where we had left Irvine's corpse—frozen hands still folded together between his locked, frozen knees—had slid much further down, or even off, the mountain.

Anyway, the fourth British Everest expedition under Hugh Ruttledge's leadership in 1933 didn't reach even the altitude Teddy Norton had in 1924. Nor did Eric Shipton's 1935 expedition, which followed Ruttledge's route, although they did find and photograph more *yeti* tracks. Many of the same climbers, including Eric Shipton and Bill Tilman, returned to Everest again in '36 and '38, with the 1936 attempt being a simple "alpine style" attempt of the sort that the Deacon had planned for us in 1925, but Shipton and Tilman and their men were kept low by bad weather.

The Dalai Lama did not officially ban outsiders from Tibet until a horoscope he had cast in 1947 informed him that his country would be threatened by foreigners. He closed Tibet to all foreigners until 1950, turning it into the "Forbidden Kingdom" that Nepal had been for us in the 1920s, but this did not stop the Chinese from planning their aggressions: aggressions that would end up with five *million* murdered Tibetans and more than thirty thousand holy Buddhist shrines and monasteries—including our Rongbuk Monastery—deliberately destroyed by the

Chinese, the Buddhist priests and nuns (or at least the ones who didn't flee to India in time) hunted down like wild animals by the Chinese Army.

But at the same time that Tibet was shutting down to foreign climbers, Nepal was opening up.

It was in October 1929—the week after the stock market crashed—that I received my postcard from Nepal; the small card had the exotic, never seen by most Brits or Americans Nepalese stamps on it, but overlaid with both Indian and British stamps, since it had been forwarded to me by officials in New Delhi and by the Royal Geographical Society in London, and on the back was a brief handwritten message:

Jake—

Hope you are well. The farm here in the Khumbu Valley is quite productive and we're both very happy. Little Charles and Ruth-Anne send you their love.

Your friends forever

There were no names under that closing. Farm in the Khumbu Valley? The only Westerner I'd ever known of who had succeeded in living and farming in Nepal was K. T. Owings, but he had barely noticed my existence during his visit to our Sikkim camp in 1925, and certainly wouldn't have closed a greeting with "Your friends [plural] forever."

Who else, then, but the Deacon and Reggie? If "little Charles and Ruth-Anne" were children born to my two friends since they'd disappeared on the mountain in late May of 1925, I could understand their naming the boy Charles; it had been the name of Reggie's cousin, Percy's older brother so terribly wounded in the Great War and the Deacon's childhood friend—but Ruth-Anne? It took me some digging in old London records years later to find that Charles Davis Deacon had had a younger sister, Ruth-Anne, who had died a month after her birth in 1899.

So I choose to believe to this day that Reggie and the Deacon married—or at least stayed together—and elected to live separate from the world in Nepal through the rest of the 1920s, '30s, and '40s. But would the Deacon really have sat out the second war with Germany? Perhaps he felt he'd served enough.

I had various real jobs, but my climbing—especially with my friend Charlie—included an Alaskan expedition (along with another Harvard alumnus, Brad Washburn) to Mount Crillon in 1933, and another to Alaska's Mount Foraker in 1934. It was during a third expedition to Alaska in the late 1940s that I spent nine days pinned down with four other men in a tiny snow cave at 17,900 feet. Two of the men died of hypothermia; I was lucky—losing only the last two fingers on my left hand to frostbite.

My first—almost reluctant—return to the Himalayas after my time with Byrd's people in' Antarctica was a reconnaissance of Nanda Devi, a beautiful mountain with a surrounding sanctuary protected by almost impenetrable cliffs, an amazing experience that I shared with my friend Charlie, Bill Tilman, Ad Carter, and other friends in 1936. In 1938 I also took a whack at K2—at 28,251 feet the second-highest peak in the world and, in my opinion, a far more dangerous one than Everest—along with some Harvard Mountain Club alums. (I believe I've mentioned that the club hadn't quite come into existence when I was at school there.) No one summited that year.

I've also mentioned my work with the OSS during World War II and shan't bore you with more details of that, other than to say that I used some classified channels to hunt for any mention of Reggie and Richard Davis Deacon—or even of Lord Percival Bromley and Kurt Meyer and Bruno Sigl—but nothing new came to light.

In 1953, at the advanced and decrepit age of 51 years, I accompanied my friend Charlie on my last Himalayan adventure—acting as support climber on their second attempt on K2. No one reached the summit that year either—K2 is an even harsher mistress than Everest and holds her secrets dear—but I did have the unique opportunity to watch one man, Peter Schoening, belay four of his fellow climbers (including my friend Dr. Charlie) who'd slipped and fallen on a fatally steep ice slope. To my knowledge, a four-man-belay save at such an altitude has never been done before or since.

Unfortunately, one of the men with us—Art Gilkey—had been injured on the descent, and during our group's attempt to get Gilkey off the mountain, the other members of what Charlie later called his "Brotherhood of the Rope" had securely tied Gilkey off—wrapped in his sleeping bag—on a steep slope while we crossed a dangerous spot by chopping steps, when either an unheard avalanche or Gilkey himself (for unknown reasons) slipped the secure anchors we'd left him tied to, and he slid to his death.

I've mentioned before that such falls in the mountains are not antiseptic—they almost invariably leave behind a trail of blood, torn flesh, ripped clothing, rent limbs, brain matter, and more—and Charlie never really recovered from our down-climbing for hours past the blood and torn remains of his close friend. Years later, Charlie would have severe bouts of depression and hallucinations of the highway ahead of his car filling with blood, almost certainly a result of what doctors are calling, now in the implausible future of 1992, "post-traumatic stress disorder."

After that second K2 adventure and Art Gilkey's death, I was done with the Himalayas forever.

But I've neglected the most important event during those decades. Some epilogue writer I am.

In 1948 I was in Berlin as part of an OSS Nazi officials debriefing mission and was reading a German newspaper—I'd picked up the language during the war—when I came upon an article that made me put down my beer and stare for several minutes.

Four crack German climbers had been trying a midwinter climb of the Eiger following Heinrich Harrer's first successful route up the Eigerwand—the ferocious and climber-devouring North Face of the Eiger—when they came across the frozen body of a solo climber at the top of the so-called Spider, above that white web of deadly vertical snowfields and just below the Exit Cracks that lead to the final summit ridge of the 13,022-foot killer mountain.

The climber—who appeared to be far too old to be attempting the Eigerwand, a man in his mid- or late 50s at least—had obviously been stopped in the last pitches of his climb by a terrible storm that had swept across the North Face, trapped the man in his solo bivouac on a six-inch-wide ledge where he couldn't climb or descend because of the weather, and frozen him to death. The man had no ID, wallet, or other forms of identification on him, and no one in the nearby village or the

Kleine Scheidegg Hotel in the valley at the base of the Eiger's North Face remembered seeing him pass through. The article also said that the German climbers reported there had been a slight smile on the frozen middle-aged climber's face.

Richard Davis Deacon would have been 59 in the winter of 1948—an insane age to attempt any serious mountain face, much less while climbing solo, much *less* the Eigerwand. Although the body was never identified (or even seen again, since an avalanche had carried it away before the next summit attempt reached that height again in the late summer of that year), and the German climbers had no camera with them when they found the body, I can clearly imagine the Deacon's face. I can even imagine his thoughts as the storm stopped his climb so very close to the summit as hypothermia began to set in. He would not have blamed the mountain.

He had always said that his destiny was to die on the North Face of the Eiger.

Whether this solo attempt by the Deacon—if it was the Deacon (no evidence other than my inner certainty says it was)—was something that happened after Reggie died or returned to India, or whether she was waiting for him to return to Nepal from the mountain, I can't be certain. I can't imagine her allowing him to attempt the Eigerwand solo, in winter, so soon after the war in Europe, but then neither can I imagine the Deacon being stopped if he'd set his mind to do something. The Germans had reported that the man had graying hair but that his frozen body looked to be in tip-top athletic shape—the body of a serious climber.

Finally, I kept in touch with Dr. Pasang for decades after we parted in 1925 and went to see him twice in India, once in 1931 and again in the summer of 1948. I made the second trip largely to show him the newspaper article about the solo climber who had died on the Eigerwand that winter.

Pasang was one of the richest non-maharajas in all of India, and he used his wealth well. Lady Bromley died in 1935, and the full wealth from the former Bromley Darjeeling tea plantations came to Pasang and his family—he had seven children, all of whom were successful later in life and three of whom, including a daughter, served in India's parliament. Pasang passed much of his wealth along to the Indian people, endowing hospitals, hospices, clinics, scholarships, and grants for young Indian students with dreams of becoming doctors. The Lady Bromley-Montfort Research Hospital—specializing in treating and finding new ways to treat war wounds such as those from the land mine explosions in the Third World that have crippled so many children—is famous and thriving to this day.

Pasang died in 1973. His name and legacy are still revered not just in Darjeeling but across India.

Our correspondence over the decades was intermittent but rich with memory and emotion, and I've left word that our letters are to be sent to you, Dan, along with these notebooks and the Kodak Vest Pocket camera.

Ah, yes, the camera. *George Mallory's camera.* I brought two important things back from the 1925 Everest trip—the Deacon's Webley revolver, which I used in the Greek isles and elsewhere during World War II, and Mallory's little Vest Pocket Kodak that we found on Sandy Irvine's body above 27,000 feet on that May day in 1925.

I never developed the film in the camera—indeed, never removed the film from the camera—but years ago, in 1975, I believe, I was talking to a researcher from the Kodak Company who was doing some basic climbing with me in the mountains around Aspen, Colorado, and I asked him if film from such a camera left in the Himalayas ("at a high altitude" was my only other description) might still be developed... might still have images on it.

"Almost certainly," said the expert. "Especially if it spent a good part of that time in the cold, dry air of the Himalayas." Then he squinted at me almost slyly and said, "I bet you're talking about the Kodak Vest Pocket camera that George Mallory had when he disappeared and which has never been found, aren't you? I know even though you don't talk about it that you once went to the Himalayas—K2, wasn't it? You're wondering if that camera *were* ever found, whether we could recover prints of Mallory and Irvine on the summit... come on, Jake, fess up. You were thinking of that camera, weren't you?"

Sheepishly, I confessed that I had been. I didn't mention that it was in my small apartment in Aspen just a mile or two from where we were scrambling at the time.

So I bequeath George Mallory's Vest Pocket camera to you, Dan Simmons, with apologies for not letting it remain in the film-healthier conditions below zero at nearly 28,000 feet. I admit that I'm curious what the photographs will show, but not curious enough to develop them while I'm alive. I have my own opinions about whether Mallory and Irvine made it to the summit or not, just as I have my opinion on whether the Deacon and Lady Bromley-Montfort summited one year after Mallory and Irvine attempted it. I always hate to confound quite solid opinions with mere facts.

I apologize for the length of this endless manuscript—all these dozens of scribbled-in notebooks for you to strain your eyes reading—but I've found in the last six or eight months that a death sentence, by cancer or any other means, tends to focus one's mind wonderfully on who and what have been important in one's life and what has been dross. I've been blessed with many experiences and with knowing many people—some of the experiences were terribly painful at the time, since they entailed losing the people, but none were ever dross.

The three men and one woman I've written about in these scrawled pages *were* important, as were the brave Sherpas whose names I remember to this day.

I confess that I hurt too much to write any more of this amateurishly sentimental "epilogue" letter to you, so I'll close now with these simple words—

Your friend,
Jacob (Jake) Perry
April 28, 1992

*E*ven before finishing Jake Perry's last handwritten notebook last year, I put in a shamefully desperate call to Mr. Richard A. Durbage (Jr.) in Lutherville-Timonium, Maryland—the son of the lady to whom the package with the notebooks and camera had mistakenly been mailed almost twenty years earlier in 1992.

Mr. Durbage Jr. was very pleasant and tried to be helpful on the phone, although I sensed that I was taking him away from something important on TV—a football game, I thought I heard in the background. Did Mr. Durbage Jr. know of such a camera in the package accidentally mailed to his mother, Lydia, Jake Perry's grandniece? I asked, my voice almost shaking. It should have been with the notebooks. It had also been meant for me, I added, hearing the possessive—almost obsessive—tone in my own voice. I didn't tell the gentleman in Maryland that the camera mailed to his mother almost certainly would tell the world whether Mallory and Irvine made it to the summit of Mount Everest in June of 1924.

Mr. Durbage Jr. did remember the camera lying in that box in the basement with Mr. Perry's scribbled notebooks—it was an old thing, he said, like some sort of camera from the 1800s—but he was sure he no longer had it. He'd moved from that house just that year, 2011, and his daughter and son-in-law had pitched away a lot of junk in preparation for his move to "a smaller place." But mostly Mr. Durbage Jr. was almost certain that his mother, Lydia Durbage, had sold that old camera at one of her weekly garage sales, perhaps shortly after she'd received the junk from Mr. Perry, probably back in the early 1990s. He distinctly remembered that there'd been a heavy old pistol in the box as well—not loaded, thank God—and his mother had personally taken it to the Lutherville-Timonium police department for them to get rid of the horrid thing.

But, yes, now that Mr. Durbage Jr. thought back on it, the more sure he was that his mother had sold the ancient camera at a yard sale, probably that same summer of 1992, when the package had arrived from the nursing home in Colorado. He had no idea who'd bought it during her yard sale, though he thought he remembered that she said she'd gotten two dollars for the old thing. Could he be of any other help?

"No," I said. "Thank you." And I hung up.

A little bit of research on the dates of the Alaska, Nanda Devi, and K2 climbs quickly showed me that Jake's climbing friend, the doctor he called "Charlie," must have been Dr. Charles Houston, a famous American mountaineer, eleven years younger than Jake Perry, who had died in September of 2009. Houston had been one of the four fallen men held onto the slopes of K2 by the now legendary belay hold by Pete Schoening in 1953. This belay is beautifully described in Houston's now classic 1954 book about that expedition, *K2, the Savage Mountain,* co-written by Houston's expedition partner Robert H. Bates.

Most of Houston's books written and published solo were scholarly medical works on the effects of hypoxia—high altitude—on the human body and brain.

Although I'm fairly good at getting information from the government through the Freedom of Information Act (much of the information I culled about Ernest Hemingway's wartime Cuban exploits as a spy for my novel *The Crook Factory* had been classified until I liberated it through FOI requests), in the past year I haven't been able to turn up a single page of redacted official reporting about Jake Perry's years in the OSS during and just after World War II. I have no doubt, however, as hard as it is for me to imagine that old gentleman as an assassin, that he was where he said he was and had done what he said he did.

Finally, late this autumn of 2012, as I was working on typing and annotating Jake's many notebooks for this oversized MS—possibly for publication, although few publishers would touch a book (by an amateur, no less) of this size, and I'm not even sure I can get my own literary agent to read it all—I decided to drive over to Delta to see Jake's grave.

Jacob Perry had asked to be buried not at the cemetery in Delta but in a smaller, out-of-the-way cemetery some forty-eight miles down Highway 50 and 550 at the little Colorado town of Ridgway in Ouray County, population 924 people in the 2010 census. When I arrived there at this remote hilltop cemetery on a cold, clear, blue-sky Colorado late-autumn day, I realized why he'd chosen the place.

Visible from the cemetery that day was Mount Sneffels and the entire Sneffels Range of high peaks, Mears Peak looming up white against the blue sky, and behind the last few dulled aspen leaves still clinging, the dramatic San Juan Mountains, Uncompahgre Peak and the entire Uncompahgre Wilderness visible to the west, Owl Creek Pass Road with its dolomite vertical slabs and ridges not far away, Teakettle Mountain with its frighteningly sheer north face, dramatic Chimney Rock visible along with various white-topped "fourteeners" in addition to Uncompahgre and Mount Sneffels—Mount Wilson, El Diente, Mount Eolus, Windom Peak, Sunlight Peak, Redcloud Peak...Incredible.

I'm not a religious man, but I'd brought a bottle of the Macallan twenty-five-year-old single-malt Scotch and two small glasses that day. I filled both glasses, left one on the small headstone that said only JACOB WILLIAM PERRY April 2, 1902–May 28, 1992, and lifted the other.

Long ago, just for the hell of it, I'd memorized the English translation of some of Virgil's lines from his *Eclogues*. Now, holding my Scotch glass high toward the San Juan Mountain peaks catching the last slanting rays of the fall day's sunlight beyond little Ridgway, I recited some of those lines as best I could remember them—

"As long as rivers shall run down to the sea, or shadows touch the mountain slopes, or stars gaze in the vault of heaven, so long shall your honor, your name, your praise endure."

And I drank my fine whisky in one swallow, left the bottle and the other glass on the headstone, turned my car north and east, and drove back out and away from the snow-topped high peaks toward home.

THE END

Colorado
May 2011–September 2012